Praise for *Haze*

"*Haze* is the first book by L. E. Modesitt, Jr., that I've ever read. . . . Exceptional."   —*SF Site*

"Modesitt has proved before he can write good action adventure, and *Haze* will certainly satisfy his fans. It also has a bit more political science than usual, but that is seamlessly woven into the story."

—*Booklist*

"This psychological SF thriller by the prolific author of the multivolume Recluce fantasy series incorporates carefully delineated characters with believable far-future scenarios. Modesitt's fans as well as readers of hard SF should appreciate this story of imminent interstellar war."

—*Library Journal*

Praise for *The Hammer of Darkness*

"Prolific author Modesitt has created a fully developed world with minimal words, focusing on the 'ordinary' man as hero."   —*Library Journal*

TOR BOOKS BY L. E. MODESITT, JR.

HAZE

[AND]

THE HAMMER of DARKNESS

L. E. Modesitt, Jr.

A TOM DOHERTY ASSOCIATES BOOK
NEW YORK

This is a work of fiction. All of the characters, organizations, and events portrayed in these novels are either products of the author's imagination or are used fictitiously.

HAZE AND THE HAMMER OF DARKNESS

Haze copyright © 2009 by L. E. Modesitt, Jr.

The Hammer of Darkness copyright © 1985 by L. E. Modesitt, Jr.

All rights reserved.

A Tor Book
Published by Tom Doherty Associates, LLC
175 Fifth Avenue
New York, NY 10010

www.tor-forge.com

Tor® is a registered trademark of Tom Doherty Associates, LLC.

ISBN 978-0-7653-8948-0

Our books may be purchased in bulk for promotional, educational, or business use. Please contact your local bookseller or the Macmillan Corporate and Premium Sales Department at 1-800-221-7945, extension 5442, or by e-mail at MacmillanSpecialMarkets@macmillan.com.

First Edition: July 2016

Printed in the United States of America

0 9 8 7 6 5 4 3 2 1

CONTENTS

HAZE

For Hildegarde and her mistress

Some call the planet Haze
for its gray shield of sky;
But Doubt of other ways
Is what refutes the lie.

1

The man in the drab pale blue Federation shipsuit sat inside the oblong cubicle just large enough for the chair and hood that provided direct sensory-reinforced information—useful for everything from maintenance data to in-depth intelligence briefings. After thirty standard minutes, he removed the hood, rose to his feet, pushed back the screen as he stepped out onto the dark blue of the third deck. The bulkheads were an eye-resting blue, close to the shade of his shipsuit, and devoid of any decoration or projections. That was true of all bulkheads on the *WuDing,* and of all Federation deep-space vessels. He eyed the three datastations for a moment, now all empty, then shook his head.

He stood 193 centimeters and massed 104.4 kilograms, and under the ship's single grav, mass and weight matched. His hair was nondescript brown. His eyes were silver gray.

He frowned for a moment, still trying to ignore the residual odor of burning hair that remained trapped in his nostrils. The odor was a side effect of the suspension cradles in which he and much of the *WuDing*'s crew had spent the transit out from Fronera, and it would pass. It certainly had on his missions to Khriastos and Marduk. He just wished the odor had already departed. He remained motionless, trying to organize the mass of information he had been mentally force-fed.

ITEM: The planet was too close to the K7 orange-tinted sun to be habitable under normal conditions, although the system was older by at least a billion years than the Sol system.

ITEM: The planet had a mass of 1.07 T-norm, with an upper atmosphere that suggested optimal habitability.

ITEM: The planet itself was impenetrable to all forms of Federation scanning and detection technology.

ITEM: The planet presented an image of featureless silver gray haze to normal human vision and remained equally featureless to all forms of observation technology.

ITEM: It had no moons or objects of significant individual mass in orbit.

ITEM: Identical objects massing approximately .11 kilograms orbited the planet in at least three differing levels. The number of such objects in each orbital sphere could not be quantified, but estimates suggested more than two million per sphere.

ITEM: The planet radiated nothing along any known spectrum. No electromagnetic radiation, no gravitonic waves, no nothing . . . except a certain amount of evenly dispersed heat and radiation consisting of energy reflected from the planet's sun.

ITEM: He had to find out what lay below that silver gray haze.

He nodded slowly, then stretched. He disliked info-feed briefings. He always had. He turned and began to walk toward the *WuDing*'s Operations Control. His shipboots were silent on the plastiform deck.

Major Roget, to OpCon.

Stet. On my way.

There was no response. The colonel disliked unnecessary communications, particularly on the shipnet, and particularly when he had to deal with an FSA agent transferred into his command at the rank of major. The other four FSA agents accompanying Roget were lieutenants and captains, though he'd known none of them before boarding the *WuDing*.

An Ops monitor tech, also in a pale blue shipsuit, hurried in Roget's direction. As she neared him, her eyes took in his collar insignia, and she averted her eyes, just enough to display the proper respect.

Roget inclined his head fractionally in response and continued to the first ladder, which he ascended. Two levels up, he headed aft.

The hatch to Colonel Tian's office irised open at Roget's approach and closed behind him. Roget took two steps into a space four times the size of the briefing cubicle and halted. The office held two chairs. The colonel sat in one.

"Sir," offered Roget.

"Please be seated, Major." The colonel gestured for Roget to take the other chair. The thin operations console was folded flush against the aft bulkhead. Hard-connected systems worked far better in battle than broadband links, although no Federation warship had been in a pitched space battle in centuries.

Roget sat down and waited.

The colonel steepled his fingers, his eyes looking not at Roget, but through the major. He was a good half a head shorter than Roget, but slender, almost willowy despite his age, and his black eyes were youthfully ancient. Finally, he spoke. "According to the report forwarded by FSA, you are most capable, Major, especially when acting alone. Your accomplishments on Marduk and on system station Khriastos appear particularly noteworthy." Tian paused. "Independent action, in particular, may be needed on this assignment, and that is why the FIS requested assistance from FSA."

"Yes, sir."

"What do you think lies behind that haze-shield, Major?"

"An alien culture. Probably Thomist, but that would be speculation, sir."

"You consider the Thomists as aliens?" The colonel's tone suggested raised eyebrows, but his face remained serene.

"Alien to the goals and aims of the Federation, certainly."

"How would you define alien?"

"Not aligned and unfathomable," replied Roget easily. He'd reported to more than enough hard-eyed and unnamed FSA colonels over the years that an FIS colonel was hardly anything to worry about.

"Unfathomable?"

"Theoretically intellectually understandable, but not emotionally comprehensible."

The colonel offered the slightest nod. "Analytics calculate the probability at 73 percent for the likelihood of a Thomist world."

Again, Roget waited. Even for a Federation Interstellar Service security officer, the colonel was being casual, if not blasé, about the discovery of a human splinter culture or an alien world. Unlike Roget, he had to have known of the world long before Roget's briefing.

"Do you have any questions?"

"How long have we known about this world?" Roget asked the question because it was expected, not because he anticipated a meaningful answer.

"If it's Thomist, we've known about the possibility for quite a time."

"How long might that be, sir?"

"Long enough. We're not absolutely certain it is a Thomist world. That's your task. You will, of course, wear a pressure suit until you confirm that the world is not environmentally hostile, and your dropboat is configured with some additional survival features to deal with that eventuality, although the scientists believe such is unlikely."

The colonel's response confirmed Roget's feelings. The senior officer wasn't about to answer the questions Roget would have liked to ask, and the ones he would answer had already been addressed by the console briefing. The issue of a hostile environment had also been touched upon and dismissed, as if the colonel knew far more than he was revealing.

"Any other questions?"

"No, sir."

"Your outward complacency exemplifies your inner arrogance, Major."

"Yes, sir."

"Inscrutability behind an emotional facade. The heritage of failed Noram supremacy." Tian's short laugh was humorless.

"As opposed to inscrutability behind inscrutability, sir?"

"There is a difference between inscrutability and deception, Major. It's called honesty, I believe."

"Yes, sir."

"If you're successful, Major, you'll doubtless end up in a position similar to mine, if within the Federation Security Agency."

That was a large "if," Roget knew. So did the colonel.

The senior officer looked at Roget. "You won't like the entry."

"You don't expect most of us to survive it." Roget's silver gray eyes never left the colonel's face.

"We do hope you will. We'd rather not lose the investment, and we'd like some confirmation of what lies beneath that haze. The dropboat and your suit are designed to handle everything engineering could anticipate."

That didn't reassure Roget. The Thomists had left the Federation with enough high tech that they'd only been

rediscovered—if the planet called Haze was indeed theirs—
by accident more than a millennium later. But if what lay
beneath that silvery shifting shield happened to be nonhuman
alien, then matters would either be far better . . . or far, far,
worse.

He wasn't certain whether he would rather face the
Thomists or nonhuman aliens.

"That is all, Major." The colonel's smile was cool. He did
not stand.

"Yes, sir." Roget stood, smiled politely, turned, and walked
from the small office.

He couldn't help but wonder what surprises this mission
held. In one way or another, every mission had provided
something he hadn't anticipated, and often had revealed matters that even the FSA had not expected. Not that he had
ever revealed all of those.

2

27 GUANYU 6744 F. E.

Roget and Kuang sat on the balcony. The only hint of the
snoopblock was the slightest wavering in the night air, an almost invisible curtain that extended upward from the pewter-
like circular railing. The multicolored towers of Taiyuan rose
around them, glittering and gleaming with lines of day-stored
and night-released light. The air was warm, but not uncom-
fortably so, and held a fragrance Roget could not identify,
doubtless one specified by Kuang and released from the railing and dispersed as a side effect by the snoopblock.

"Beautiful, is it not?" asked Kuang, setting down his near-
empty glass on the table between them.

"It should be. It's the heart of world culture and the capital of the Federation." Roget offered a polite smile.

"It's been a capital before. Capitals come and go. They've done so here for more than sixty-five centuries." Kuang's voice was matter-of-fact above the whine of some form of ground transport, muted by the snoopblock, that rose from the street some eleven levels below. A mock lightning bolt flashed across the top of a tower bordering the river.

"Taiyuan has lasted longer than any other . . . and in greater glory."

"So has its intrigue."

"If there are people, there's intrigue," Roget said, taking a last sip of the amber brew. He would have preferred a true lager, but Kuang had once mentioned that a preference for western lager was a sign of less than discriminating taste, and Kuang was the senior officer-agent in the team. He'd also report on Roget's performance, and that would determine whether Roget would remain a team member . . . or head his own team or be given an independent assignment. Either of the latter options was preferable to reporting to Kuang . . . or anyone else, Roget felt.

"True, and, like most people, the intriguers never learn."

"I wonder," mused Roget, setting his beaker on the table. "Is it that the intriguers never learn, or is it that the ones we catch are the ones that never learn?"

"You're suggesting something." Kuang offered a thin smile. "You often do."

"We never catch anyone involved in the Federation government, but we all know that there's intrigue there. We seldom catch anyone in the upper levels of the multilateral corporations, and we all know that they're not always pure."

"Purity doesn't have much to do with legality," said Kuang. "We aren't given a choice. Our job is to uphold the law, not to monitor personal ethics."

"That's right. How could it be otherwise?" asked Roget. "But the most skillful intriguers know how to operate within the law, and they do. Then there are the misguided idealists like the ones we're pursuing. They believe the laws are corrupt. Because of that, they never learned how the laws operate. They couldn't use them if they tried."

"They're not idealists. For all their rhetoric about the lack of freedom in commerce, and their protestations that they're only trying to restore full freedoms, they're antisocial thugs. Full freedom is another word for chaos and mob rule. You should remember that." Kuang's voice was calm.

Roget managed another polite smile at the veiled reference to the fall of old America, a reference that Kuang managed to make more than infrequently.

"It's time to go." Kuang stood. "You have the datacard?"

Roget rose as well, nodding.

"Make sure you get them to say that you'll be paid."

"I can do that." Roget followed the senior agent from the balcony through the living area to the front door, then out into the corridor. The dull polished metallic composite of the corridor wall reflected but vague image of his dark blue singlesuit and light gray vest—the standard garb for a midlevel datager or multilateral proffie.

The two FSA agents walked without speaking to the center of the tower, waiting for a descending lift car. Two passed, presumably full of residents, before a third, half-filled, stopped. No one in the car spoke as the lift continued downward. Once they stepped out of the lift at the concourse level of the residence tower, Kuang headed north. Roget continued straight ahead, toward the Chiacun Tube station. At close to ten, the evening was still young, and people streamed to and from the underground transport. Most were couples, but some of the groups were either of young men or, more frequently, of young women.

Roget held an open-link, but neither Kuang nor Kapeli pulsed him. As the most junior member of the team, Kapeli was tasked with the routine tailing of the targets, but he'd have contacted Roget if anything looked out of the ordinary, and that meant that Sulynn's group had headed to the rendezvous.

When Roget reached the Chiacun station, he swiped a dayproxy Cred-ID past the scanner at the entrance, then headed down the moving ramp. Once he was on the concourse level, he joined the queue for the southbound riverside express. According to his internal monitors, the wait was nine minutes and twenty-one seconds.

Once the tube train doors opened, Roget moved with the crowd into the nearest car. He took a position with his back to the silvered train wall, just to one side of the doors, his hands apparently loosely folded over each other as he surveyed the others nearby, taking in the pretty dark-haired schoolgirl with her parents, the three female clericals chatting amiably, the off-duty space-forcer with the eyes that seemed veiled, and the groups of datagers who had clearly just left work.

Twelve minutes—and roughly seventeen klicks later—Roget stepped from the train at the Shengli station, brushing through others, his internal monitors registering so many energy sources that they might as well have been useless. Amid the crowds, energy weapons were unlikely, knives or muffled projectiles far more probable. Keeping with the fast-moving crowds, he walked swiftly up the moving ramp and then out into the chill evening air. He strode across the Plaza that opened onto the River Fen.

Not more than fifteen meters into the crowded Plaza, from his right, he sensed the quick movement. He turned, his hand stiffened, and struck, hardly moving his upper body, as his movement fractured a lower arm. Then he slammed his boot heel down on the top of the would-be lifter's foot. "So very sorry." His Mandarin was impeccably polite as the youth half-crumpled, half-cringed away. While Stenglish was the official Federation language, Roget had found that in some circumstances Mandarin was preferable.

The others in the crowd parted just slightly, hardly altering their paths or changing their verbal or commnet conversations. Another youth turned and hurried away from his wounded partner.

Stupid, thought Roget. The vidcams would note it, and the patrollers would have both members of the lifter team in custody in moments. While the patrollers could stop him, legally, that was highly unlikely. They had more than enough to do than to detain someone who'd acted to prevent being assaulted or robbed.

On the far side of the Plaza, Roget turned north on the promenade that overlooked the River Fen. His destination was the LeClub Henois, some three tower-blocks from the Plaza. Strains of plaintive and perfectly repitched kaluriolk—*perfectly boring,* thought Roget—drifted through a night lit with piped sunlight split into monobeams that played across the walkways as if at random.

Once he passed the first tower, the crowds thinned. Even so, he had to step aside to avoid a commlinked-couple, their eyes blank, who walked automatically southward toward the Plaza.

Two youths ran down the walkway, dodging pedestrians as they exchanged long passes of virtie dirigibles that morphed into miniature spacecraft far sleeker than the real vessels.

At the door to LeClub Henois, Roget again flashed the proxy, triggering the reservation code. The broad-shouldered Sinese doorman barely nodded in acknowledging his presence, despite the fact that a good third of the proffies in the capital were Euro. A whisper projected in Stenglish to Roget's ears announced, "The corner table to the northwest."

Roget turned to his right and continued. LeClub Henois was furnished in fifty-first century—or twenty-fifth century by the western Gregorian calendar—Vietnamese decor, which was, in turn, an offshoot of earlier French colonial. Roget doubted that many knew or cared about that, not after more than a millennium of Federation one-worldism. Those who might care, in the still radioactive and glassy ruins of TransIslamia or in the scattered eco-isolates of Afrique, were in no position either to object or to do anything about it.

Few people looked directly at him as he wound his way through the tables toward the northwest corner. From below the low stage, under the shifting multi-images, some of which were real, and most of which were not, a small combo played, and scents and sounds wafted across the club. Roget winced as bitter lime clashed with pepper cinnamon and -oversweet bergamot, amplified by three wavering and atonal chord lines playing through each other.

As he neared the corner table with the two couples—and the two vacant chairs—he glanced around casually. He didn't see Sulynn, and that wasn't good. Yet he hadn't heard anything from Kapeli.

Roget slipped into the chair across from Huilam. "Very lively place."

"It will do," replied Huilam. "It's not authentic in the slightest, but any orbit in a flux. It is amusing, in a degrading sort of way."

"Degrading?" Roget raised his eyebrows. "Isn't imitation the sincerest and noblest form of flattery?"

"Good imitation is, but that is infrequent. The Sinese merely absorb, without true regard for the subtleties of other cultures, while demanding full respect for all the meaningless subtleties in their own."

"That's been true of all dominant cultures in history," Roget replied.

"Except for your own. When the old Americans had power, there was no subtlety at all. That was refreshing at first, until the world realized that the lack of fine distinctions reflected a corresponding lack of depth and an innate contempt for true culture."

"That's what history says, but it's always written by the winner. Look at Ramses the Great."

"Ah, yes. Part of the longest-lived imperial culture in

history, the most stable, and the one with almost no technical and scientific advancement from beginning to end. Your American ancestors redeemed themselves for a time by their scientific advances, many of which they stole but made available to the world. Then, conformity and that contempt for true education stifled even their science. That always happens in empires."

"Even the ancient Sinese fell prey to that," Roget pointed out.

"But of course. One expects that of empires, without exception. That is why they should not last forever." Huilam's lips twisted into a momentary sardonic smile. "You have the entertainment card?"

The "entertainment card" meant the specs and keys to certain proprietary economic accounts in the Federation Bank of Taiyuan. Theoretically, use of that information, as planned by Huilam and Sulynn, would cripple banking functions, if not disable them permanently, until the entire system's architecture was restructured and reformulated. It would also allow them short-term access to billions of yuan to fund their "revolution."

Roget slipped the thin leather folder onto the table, making certain it was in plain sight of whatever monitors Kuang had arranged. "Both hard-copy and molecular-key. You should be able to enjoy yourselves immensely and most profitably with the subjects appearing there. They're absolutely without cover. Quite amazing." Roget smiled, not quite lewdly. "I expected to see Sulynn here."

"You just missed her," said Pryncia, from beside Huilam. "I'm most certain she'll catch up with you."

"She had something to tell you," added Moriena from across the table.

Huilam nodded, half-smiling.

"Payment?" asked Roget.

"You'll be paid, just as agreed. We have the proxy-drop." Huilam lifted his goblet and sipped, as if to dismiss Roget.

"Within the day," Roget emphasized.

"Of course."

Roget stood. "If you need any more special entertainment, you know how to reach me." He did not move, letting his greater height emphasize the point.

"That we do," Huilam nodded. "We will be in touch."

"Until then." Roget inclined his head, then turned and began to wind his way back through the tables. Once he left the LeClub, he'd have to be most careful. Leaving a drop was one of the most dangerous parts of any operation, and especially of this one, he feared. But what choice did he really have? What real choices had he ever had?

The doorman didn't even look in his direction as Roget stepped back out into the moderate warmth of the late summer evening . . . and under the shifting lights of the promenade. He'd taken less than ten steps, deftly avoiding close contact with anyone, still mulling over Huilam's point about how empires stifled scientific advances, when he heard a voice.

"Keir!"

Roget recognized Sulynn's voice. Should he ignore her? He'd completed his immediate part of the operation. That would be the safest, but it would also make her more suspicious, and the rest of the team could use more time to round up all the terrvert group.

He turned slowly to his right, as if trying to locate the caller.

Sulynn stood alone, a good ten meters away, between one group of young women and another of two couples, her black hair up in a stylish twist.

As a young man hurried past leaving the space between them open, Sulynn offered an embarrassed smile, then shrugged.

Roget saw the glint in her left hand too late.

Blackness slammed into him.

3

Roget scanned the controls one last time, then nodded, before triggering the link.

DropCon, this is three. Checklist complete and green.

Stet, three. Estimate one seven to release.

Even through the link, Roget could sense the warmth of Major Zhou. Too bad more of the Federation officers weren't like the scoutship's pilot. She was also far and away the best pilot on the *WuDing,* certainly better than he was, he had to admit.

DropCon, two here. All green.

DropCon, four here. Green.

DropCon, five here. Green and good.

Waiting, his dropboat in the exterior cradle, Roget nodded as Fierano reported, the last of the five survey operatives, and the only woman. All he could do was wait. The dropboat's systems wouldn't kick in until it was clear of the scoutship.

One five to drop one.

Roget swallowed. All he could do was wait . . . and review the drop procedures. He tried not to think about his options *after* he completed his survey evaluation of Haze—*if* he completed it. If the landing boat survived the transit of all the objects in the three orbital shells, he could take off and attempt to reach low orbit where a scoutship could retrieve him. Or he could program the boat to climb as far as it could, far enough into or beyond the haze to burst-send his report. Or he could commandeer local transport, assuming any such existed. None of the options were optimal. But, after his last two missions, his situation had been anything but ideal. Not because he had failed, but because he had been expected to fail, and had managed at least limited success. The FSA had been forced to take over governing Khriastos station because of the degree of corruption when all the colonel had really wanted was the removal of Station Administrator Sala-Chung.

Roget took a long slow breath. In a fashion, all of his independent assignments had ended that way. Was it because the FSA hadn't wanted success? Or because they'd only defined success in limited terms.

Roget forced his mind back to the drop.

Dropboats, stand by.

Standing by.

Another five minutes passed. Then the scoutship shivered once. Another five minutes passed before the second shiver. Then another interval passed, not quite five minutes.

Drop three, stand by . . . ten, nine, eight . . .

With the linked *one!,* Roget was pressed back in the half-cocoon for a moment before weightlessness took over. He swallowed to keep the bile in his stomach, rather than let it creep into his throat, then used his implants to link with the dropboat—now fully powered.

The farscanners showed no ships above the planet—except for the scoutship returning to the *WuDing* and the five dropboats, spaced far enough apart and with enough difference in course, velocity, and trajectory so that they would not land all that close to each other.

Roget gave the steering jets a quick squirt to orient the dropboat to the planned courseline.

"You won't like the entry." The colonel's words went through Roget's thoughts as he waited for the dropboat to encounter the outer orbital shell. Theoretically, the first shell shouldn't be too bad, because the scoutship had dropped all the boats on trajectories that would ensure they entered the shell at a velocity only slightly slower than that of the outer level of orbiting objects—whatever they were.

After that, it was up to the operative and the dropboat's nav systems and shields . . . and luck.

The farscreens showed nothing but the other dropboats . . . and the grayish haze. Was that haze something totally alien, perhaps even alive? Or was it a form of technology that comprised the planetary defense system? And what lay below it? Were the readings correct in assuming a breathable atmosphere, or was the whole operation a way to remove him and the other FSA agents?

It couldn't be the last. Cold as they could be, even the upper-level Federation Mandarins wouldn't have sent a battlecruiser and its escorts across the stars and dispatched five operatives and dropboats to their death to remove one operative whose attitude had been less than exemplary. Nor would they have forced the FIS and FSA into a semicooperative joint effort.

Colonel Tian's nonanswers suggested much more was at stake, and that the Federation regarded the Thomists as far more than an historical curiosity.

Roget continued to watch the closure with the planet below looming ever closer. All he could do was wait until the outer fringes of the atmosphere began to impact the shields. The screens and systems still registered nothing in any energy spectrum except some reflected light and emissions from the boats.

Then . . . what could only be called noise appeared, concentrated in the orbital layers, creating three levels of smokelike spheres. That was how his implants registered the data.

The dropboat neared the outermost sphere, the one whose shardlike components appeared to orbit from polar south to north, unnatural and implausible as it was. As the dropboat entered that outermost layer, angled to go with the apparent flow, the outside temperature sensors went blank.

The dropboat seemed to skid sideways, then drop, slewing sideways to the courseline.

Roget *knew* that couldn't happen, but the instruments

confirmed what he felt, and the system pulsed the port steering jets. When nothing happened, Roget overrode the controls and then fired them full for an instant. Sluggishly, the dropboat returned to courseline and orientation.

The dropboat shivered, and a chorus of impacts, like metallic hail, reverberated through the craft. Cabin pressure began to fall, and Roget closed his helmet, letting the direct suit feed take over.

The EDI flared. Drop one was gone.

More impacts battered Drop three, and Roget eased the nose down, adding thrust. He'd pay later, but there was too much of a velocity differential between the dropboat and the orbital shards or whatever they were.

The intensity of the hammering decreased. But even inside his sealed suit, Roget could feel the heat building in the dropboat.

The hammering vanished, and the screens showed that the dropboat was below the outer orbital layer. They showed nothing except Drop three and the two layers, one below and one above.

The nav system, as programmed, increased the thrust and began a course correction to bring the dropboat onto a courseline at right angles to the previous heading. Roget watched intently, ready to override again if the dropboat did not complete the heading and orientation change before it entered the second orbital shell.

Heading, course, orientation, and the smokelike shell all came together at once.

This time the hammering was louder. Was that because there was some atmosphere or because the dropboat and its shields were being punished more? Roget couldn't tell. He was just glad when they dropped below the second level. By then he was sweating heavily inside the pressure suit, and he hoped that he didn't fog the inside of his helmet.

The third level was worse. By the time the dropboat was clear, the shields had failed, and the craft had no atmospheric integrity. The automatics had dropped offline, inoperative, and Roget was piloting on manual. The dropboat shuddered and shivered.

Roget eased the dropboat's nose up fractionally to kill off more speed and decrease the rate of descent. That might bleed off some of the excess heat that was close to cooking him, even within his suit, and the dropboat's remaining functional systems.

His entry and descent had to have registered on every planetary tracking system. Yet the screens showed no aircraft, no missiles, and no energy concentrations. Roget concentrated on maintaining control of the systems and holding as much altitude as possible, especially given the ocean directly below. The waters were silver green. He thought the screens had shown small islands, but he was still too high and too fast to try a landing there. Besides, getting off an island might be more than a little difficult, given the failing state of the dropboat.

Before long, the screens registered a mountainous coastline ahead. In moments the dropboat was approaching a coastal range and passing through twenty thousand meters in a gradual descent. Less than five minutes later, the dropboat had descended to twelve thousand meters and was passing over the tallest of the peaks, less than three thousand meters below.

Roget's scans showed that the mountains were the center of a peninsula. To the east water stretched as far as the screens could show. He immediately banked to the north, paralleling the lower hills because of the short distance between where the hills ended and the ocean began.

With that sharp a turn, the dropboat's glide ratio began to approximate that of a flying brick hurtling downward toward the forested slopes below. Roget hurried through the landing checklist while scanning the terrain ahead, finally settling on a long brushy area some three klicks ahead.

When the radalt alerted him at five hundred meters AGL,

he eased into a partial flare, using the dropboat's lifting body form to trade off speed to kill his rate-of-descent—but not enough to stall.

Less than a hundred meters above ground, the dropboat shivered with a sudden crosswind. Roget corrected, angling the nose to the wind and easing the nose up just a trace.

The power levels were at less than 7 percent when the dropboat's tail touched the ground. Roget let the nose drop slowly, and the boat skidded and bounced across the uneven ground. It came to a stop less than a hundred meters from the tall evergreens to the north.

The farscreens were fading. They showed no one and no large animals anywhere nearby. Given the sonics that had preceded the dropboat, that didn't exactly surprise Roget. The diagnostics did tell him that the atmosphere composition was T-norm, or close enough that it made little difference. He doubted that the dropboat would be useful for much of anything after the descent and rough landing. Still, he went through the standard shutdown checklist before he unstrapped his bruised and sore figure from the pilot's couch and eased himself out through the narrow lock hatches, one after the other. Once he was clear of the still-warm hull, he cracked his helmet. He could smell evergreens and charred vegetation. For all that, there were no fires around the craft. That suggested that the area wasn't all that dry.

For several moments, Roget stood beside the dropboat. All his implants and systems checked, despite the rough entry. There was one problem. They registered nothing beyond himself and the fading residual energies within the dropboat.

No emissions. No signals. Nothing. Was there no intelligent life on the planet? Or had all his implants failed, despite the internal telltales that indicated they were functioning? That couldn't be. He was getting indications from the dropboat.

He shrugged.

One way or another, he had a mission to complete. He

needed to retrieve his gear from the sealed locker and get on with it—preferably before any locals showed up. If there were any.

After a last set of scans of the area around the dropboat, Roget moved quickly, stripping off his pressure suit and helmet, then retrieving his gear and the modest backpack to contain it, and finally locking the boat. If the locks were forced, certain key parts of the controls would melt down. Since the screens and shields had been tried to their limits on the descent, the boat didn't have enough power to carry Roget more than a few klicks, let alone return to orbit.

He checked his equipment a last time, then paused, taking a deep breath. The air was heavy and damp and carried a faint scent, somewhere between a sultry perfume and the clean dankness of a virgin forest. He had a feeling that the sea-level atmospheric pressure was higher than T-norm, possibly as much as 10 percent. The oxygen content was a bit higher, and that might offset the slightly higher gravity.

Finally, he strode into the forest, heading north. There certainly hadn't been any signs of technology or habitation farther south on the peninsula. He decided against powering up the camouflage capacity engineered into his singlesuit. That burned power, and he saw no reason to drain his limited supply, especially since the background melding capability was only useful for optical detection. Even had he used the camo feature, the last thing he wanted was to be caught in the open. The tall pines, while spaced in a way that suggested a natural and mature landscape, provided enough cover that an attack from something like aircraft or even an advanced flitter would be difficult. If there happened to be a local culture with nanotech capabilities, they wouldn't need anything that crude to deal with him.

That was what he hoped.

4

⊚

Wearing a dark gray proffie singlesuit, like any number of young professionals, Roget sat in the reception area, a space with shimmering dark gray walls and green accents. The chairs and the couch were a muted dark green. The piped sunlight added a note of cheer to the semicircular chamber that could have been one in any multilateral's headquarters. It wasn't. It was one of a number of similar reception areas in the Federation Security Agency's Taiyuan headquarters.

Roget did not read nor did he access any of the entertainment nets. Instead, he amused himself by tracking the energy flows everywhere, although he couldn't discern the purpose of most, except for those designed to locate explosives, metals, and other potentially lethal objects. Some were doubtless merely routine dataflows. A polite-looking young man sat at a console, occasionally glancing indifferently in Roget's general direction. Behind the receptionist/guard and the console, three wide corridors fanned out into the north half of the tower.

Roget had been waiting for sixteen and a half minutes when a tall Sinese with silver gray at his temples emerged from the left-hand corridor and walked past the receptionist. Another seven minutes passed before the receptionist looked up.

"Agent Roget . . . the colonel will see you now. Take the left-most corridor to the second door, also on the left. Just open the door and enter."

Roget stood. "Thank you." He walked past the reception desk, noting that there were no open screens behind it. The reception agent was direct-linked, another simple security procedure. If anything happened to him, hidden gates would doubtless seal the corridors.

When he reached the door, he touched the entry screen. The door slid into its recess, and Roget stepped into the office. He stopped and offered a slight bow. The door closed silently behind him.

"Agent-Captain Keir Roget, do come in." The man behind the desk console did not stand. To his right was a wide window that offered a sweeping view of the silvered side of another tower. "Please be seated."

"Yes, sir." Roget bowed, then took the seat across the desk from the Agent-Colonel, whose name he did not know . . . and might never, not unless he encountered the man in another setting, and that was unlikely in a capital city of ten million plus, surrounded by satellite cities that each held millions.

A long silence followed as the colonel scrutinized Roget.

"Your last assignment left you in some physical difficulty," observed the colonel.

Two weeks in the medunit hadn't been easy, but there was no point in saying so. Roget waited.

"The other members of your team were successful in apprehending the terrvert group. All but two. One was killed in the operation. Because the weapon used on you was tracked to Huilam, they all will face capital assault charges."

Capital assault meant intelligence reduction and locality restriction—usually to an isolated marginal community. It also suggested that there wasn't enough evidence to prove more than conspiracy to commit cyberterr.

"And the other?" asked Roget.

"The other is still at large, but not for long."

"Sulynn?" asked Roget.

The slightest hint of a frown appeared above the colonel's black eyebrows. "You have something not in your report that would shed light on that?"

Roget wasn't about to comment on the most obvious

point—that Sulynn had left the weapon solely in order to implicate Huilam. "No, sir. She was the smartest and most wary. That's all. If anyone might have escaped, she would have been the one. There was a caution in my reports about her." For all the colonel's assurances, Roget doubted that security would soon locate her . . . or that her identity had ever been Sulynn. He had his doubts that she'd ever even been a cyberterrorist.

What he didn't understand was how they'd managed to miss her, when she'd been the one who'd nerved him—unless she'd disabled Kuang or Kapeli. Even with his internal backups and contingent blocks against neural cascades, Roget almost hadn't made it. That was what the Security doctor had told him. But . . . if she'd been a plant, why had she almost killed him? Or had she either used too much power or too little? He withheld a wry smile. That was something else he doubted he'd ever know.

"Just so." A pause signified that the comments on Roget's previous assignment were at an end. "You are being given a single-agent assignment in St. George in Noram District 32. The local community is primarily Saint. . . ."

Saint? It took a moment for Roget to place the locality and the culture. The Saints were a religious community that had been founded by an old American prophet and, against all logic, had survived the Wars of Confederation. He should have known that. His sister lived only a district away, but then, they'd been raised in the American southeast, and she'd moved there after the southern climatic disasters had forced her and Wallace to relocate.

". . . Your cover will be that of an E&W Monitor. No additional technical training will be necessary. The previous agent died of heat exposure after a fall. While it is unlikely his death was natural, he was merely a data-agent. You're aware of the possible dangers, and you should be able to handle the situation. It should be far less stressful than the assignment you just completed, and it should allow the additional time for your nerves to heal before you return to more . . . strenuous duty."

Another not-so-subtle reminder of his failure to exercise adequate caution in dealing with Sulynn, Roget thought. Yet . . . if she had been a plant . . . He pushed the thought away. He couldn't do anything about the past. He'd just have to be even more careful in the future.

"Your briefings will begin at eight hundred tomorrow morning. Kuyrien has the details, including your cover and travel schedule."

"Yes, sir." In short, he was supposed to conclude that he'd been a good boy, and he was getting an easy and relatively straightforward investigation as a reward. He didn't believe it. Officer-agents never got easy assignments, especially non-Sinese officer-agents who were neither junior nor senior.

"That is all, Agent-Captain."

Roget rose. He'd never understood the reason for the short and summary assignment process, since what the colonel had conveyed didn't require any personal contact, unless it was to remind him that he had flesh-and-blood superiors— even if their names were never disclosed. Or to remind him that all agents lived on sufferance of one sort or another. He inclined his head politely, then turned and left the office.

5

16 MARIS 1811 P. D.

On the first day, Roget walked a good fifteen klicks before the daylight died away into a deep twilight that was not quite night. With the higher humidity, he'd had to put the all-weather jacket in his pack. Even so, he'd sweated a lot, and he'd had to stop and refill his water bottle several times. His treatment tabs would likely run out far sooner than he'd anticipated. With only the silver gray haze overhead, he had been able to make out only in a general fashion where the sun was. For some time before twilight, the western half of the sky appeared slightly brighter, but that might have been his imagination. The twilight had lasted longer, and that hadn't been just what he believed.

He'd seen tracks of animals that might have been deer or elk, or something similar, and paw prints of what could have been any type of large canine or nonhoofed mammal. All were quadrupeds. The leaves and needles of the trees were similar enough to those on earth, if a far darker green that verged on black, that the trees had to be Terran-derived, or some form of parallel evolution too alike to be coincidental. Those facts alone tended to confirm the colonel's suggestion of a Thomist world, but the ecology looked far too settled to have been established in a mere thousand years. There was also the fact that, while the colonel had paid lip service to the possibility of a hostile environment, the entire mission had been set up on the tacit assumption that Haze wasn't environmentally hostile.

He'd keep that in mind, but he just didn't know enough, not yet.

In setting up his camp, he decided on the hammock, although it took him some time to find a tree with branches high enough to be well above ground predators, low enough for him to be able to reach the branches, and strong enough to bear his weight. Although the not-quite-perfumed air was pleasant, there was something about it, the slightest of subscents, that nagged at him, and he didn't sleep that well. He also thought he heard movements, but whenever he woke, he saw nothing in the dimness that was as bright as a starlit night.

After Roget woke under a gradually brightening light, he surveyed the area around him from within the hammock. He could hear various sounds, from insects to bird calls, but he did not see any larger creatures. Again, his implants revealed no broadcast signals or power.

He struggled out of his hammock and then climbed along the stronger and wider branch closest to his head until he could swing down to the ground. Underneath where he had swung in his hammock were large paw prints. While he was carrying a sidearm, and a limited shot stunner, he was just as glad not to have had to use either.

Breakfast was not immediate because he needed water for the small self-heating ration-pak, and he did not find a stream for several klicks. After treating the water in the bottle he carried, he started the ration-pak, then refilled the bottle before he ate. Once finished with his mostly tasteless meal, he began to walk northward at a quick but comfortable pace.

He'd traveled less than an hour before the first butterfly fluttered down from the overhanging branches, swooping by his face so closely that its wings actually brushed his cheek. Its wings were a brilliant blue with swirls of gold. Then, there were two, and three, and then a handful, all swirling around his face and neck, and all with similar wing markings.

He half jumped at a needlelike jab on the back of his neck, then swatted at the swarm, which retreated. He spent the next klick waving off the butterflies, until they finally lost interest. He hadn't expected biting butterflies, but they were definitely a reminder that Haze was not just another exact earth-type world.

Sometime before midmorning he finally found a trail. He'd actually been paralleling it for more than a standard hour without knowing it, but it was higher on the slope by almost a klick. He caught sight of it from a large clearing stretching both uphill and down—a burned out area that had likely been the target of a lightning strike several years back, judging from the regrowth. Hiking uphill wasn't that bad, although his legs ached some by the time he reached the trail, not much more than packed earth stretching north and south under the predominantly evergreen canopy. The trail was of an even width, though, with a covering of wood mulch, and that suggested both continual use and maintenance.

As he hiked north, he studied the trail. In several places, he could make out relatively recent boot prints. They seemed no different from those left by any other human. In one place, the entire print was clear in the dried mud. Regular studded tread, the kind that was most likely produced by at least a midtech culture. So . . . where were the people? Could they have all been evacuated? How? There had been no sign of any broadcast comm. Or was he walking the trail at a time equivalent to midweek, when few were out and about?

As he kept walking and watching, he tried to review what he'd learned about the Thomists. Initially, they had been a loose movement scattered throughout the Federation in its early years. Their slogan or watchwords were simply, "Doubt it." Their initial political activities had revolved around providing factual information that cast doubt on the statements and policies of politicians, administrators, multilaterals, and others in positions of authority and trust. Later statements and papers suggested scientific skepticism as well. A number had been detained or sequestered in the second War of Confederation, but a larger number had obtained an early jumpship and had begun to ferry followers and equipment out of the Sol system. After a cat-and-mouse game lasting several objective centuries, the jumpship had been intercepted by a Federation flotilla and destroyed when it refused to surrender. The High Command had never been fully convinced that there was but a single renegade ship, but the ships of the Federation Interstellar Service, which patrolled all of the systems that held Federation worlds—not that there were any other kind, to date—had never found any trace of any other worlds that had ever been inhabited by intelligent life—until Haze.

So why were the colonel and the High Command convinced that Haze held Thomists, as opposed to some other unknown splinter group that might have fled during the disruptions that had surrounded the establishment and consolidation of the Federation? Roget didn't know, but the boot print, the empty trail, and the lack of power and broadcast emissions all left him with a most uneasy feeling.

He kept walking and watching . . . and shooing away the carnivorous, or at least biting, butterflies.

By what he felt was late afternoon, he had the definite sense that the planet had a quicker rotation than T-norm. From his implants and senses, he had a general sense that the local "day" was around twenty-one or twenty-two stans, but without a sun directly in the sky, it might be several days before he could pin it down exactly. The other matter was that of clouds. He'd seen a few, although they were thin, almost stratuslike. Was that because the planet didn't have spots of more localized heat created by the direct rays of the sun?

Another standard hour passed, according to his own internal clock, which was clearly out of synch with the rotational pattern of Haze. Ahead of him, on the downhill side of the trail, he saw something. Something unnatural.

He froze, then stepped sideways and into the widely spaced trees.

Step by step, Roget moved over the carpet of pine needles, a sign that there were no earthworms in all likelihood, passing from tree to tree, taking time and care. After he had covered the first fifty meters, he could make out the stone building set into the hillside so artfully that it was almost invisible. Even the slates of the roof had been cut irregularly and were of differing shades of gray and black.

When he finally got within twenty meters of the building, he was largely convinced that no one was there. The brown shutters on the two windows flanking the east-facing door were fastened shut. The gray brown door was closed.

Roget sensed no one, heard no one. He moved closer, edging along the side of the small building. In the clay in front of the door, there was one set of boot prints that seemed to

match the one he had seen earlier, and they showed someone leaving. A paw print over part of the boot imprint suggested that it wasn't that recent.

With the stunner in one hand, Roget pressed down on the
smooth, dull gray metal door lever. To his surprise, it de-
pressed under the pressure of his hand, and the door opened
inward.

There was no one inside. A wooden table that might have
been oak stood in front of the shuttered window on the south
side of the single room. Four armless wooden chairs were set
around the table. In the middle of the west wall was a stone
hearth. Behind it was a stone wall. A radiant heat pipe ran
up one side of the wall, across the top, and down the other.
In the middle of the hearth was a small iron stove with two
heating elements. Roget suspected all were light powered,
with some sort of concentrator. On each side of the hearth
were built-in double bunks, one over the other, simple wooden
shelflike spaces.

The roof slates were clearly more than they appeared to
be. That, or the heating elements were geothermal in nature.
He eased into the building, leaving the door open. Was he
under observation? If he happened to be, that observation
was all passive, because he could sense no energy flows.

There was a small metal plate set at eye level in the stone
wall on the right side. The plate was of the same pewter-
like gray metal as the door lever. Protruding from the plate
were two studs and a dial, also metal. Roget stepped forward and pressed the left stud, then the right one. Within
moments he could feel warmth flowing from the dark gray
heat pipe—made out of some sort of composite, he judged.
He turned the dial to the left, and the heat flow increased.
Immediately, he turned it all the way to the right, and the heat
flow died away. The building was warm enough. Then he
stepped back and in front of what he had taken to be the stove.
On the thin angled surface between the stove top and the front
were three inset dials but only two elements. He looked

down at the front and shook his head. A sliding panel provided the entry to an oven of some sort.

In the end, after all his prodding and investigating, Roget could detect nothing except what he had observed. What he saw disturbed him a great deal. The cabin was simple, but it had heat and a power source for cooking. But there was no source of artificial light. It was spotless, as if it were scarcely used, yet there was no sign of recent construction. The exterior looked to be years old, and it was situated on a trail that had been traveled regularly, if infrequently, for years.

Roget was tired. The last two days had been long—very long. He decided to spend the night in the building. The back of the door did have a sturdy metal bolt that could be slid into place to lock the building. While the cabin might be a trap, that didn't make sense. But then, he had the feeling that not much about Haze was likely to make sense. He did know that anyone who could build such a structure wouldn't have much more trouble running him down in the forest than cornering him in the building.

That, too, was disturbing.

Still, after he'd eaten and was ready to go to bed on one of the bunk shelves, he locked the door and wedged a chair behind it. He hoped he'd be able to get some sleep.

6

12 LIANYU 6744 F. E.

Roget wore the white singlesuit of an energy and water monitor, if without insignia. He sat alone on the aisle in the second double seat on the left in the electrotram that ran down the center of the boulevard, flanked on each side by lightly traveled lanes. Back in the glory days of the United States of America, St. George had once been a small city. Now it was just a large town, an old, old town that had baked in the sun of Noram District 32 for the millennium and more since the founding of the Federation.

Almost all the neat stone dwellings were roofed with solar arrays designed to resemble ancient ceramic tiles, and most had shaded rear courtyards. Beyond the town limits, red rocks and sand and dry mountains stretched in every direction, with a towering bluff on the immediate west end of the town proper and a ridge along the north side of the town, with a gap in it to the northeast, a gap blasted out in the old days that had allowed expansion to the northeast. Coming in by the single maglev line that ended on the northeast end of St. George, Roget had noted the track of the old highway where it deviated from the maglev route, and he'd wondered why the maglev hadn't been extended through that gap. It hadn't, though.

As the tram neared 200 East and the stop there, Roget glanced to the south, taking in the shimmering white of the ancient Temple. Close as it was to a thousand years old, it was still a replica. The original had been destroyed in the first War of Confederation, but once it was clear that the violent hostilities were over, the local Saints had rebuilt it faithfully, although it had taken some thirty years because times had been so difficult. But then, they'd rebuilt their original temple at Nauvoo twice.

They'd also cleared the ground so that a hundred-yard-wide greenbelt ran the nine blocks between the boulevard and the Temple. Similar greenbelts ran from the Temple to the south, east, and west. The ground cover was desert green, good at retaining water, but off-limits to pedestrians or anything else weight-bearing. The Saints didn't seem to mind, and there hadn't been many tourists since the Federation had imposed regional energy curbs and geometrical incremental pricing nearly a millennium before. Not that there had been that many once the Virgin River dam had been completed and blocked the old overland route through the gorge to Mesquite. Only scholars in clean-suits visited the still-radioactive ruins of Las Vegas or the giant concrete ruins of the Hoover Dam. Other scholars visited the Saint Genealogy Center on the south side of the Temple. The Saints had an interest in all aspects of genealogy that bordered on obsession.

Peaceful as it looked to Roget, and notwithstanding the colonel's assurances, he had his doubts. The previous Federation Security agent—acting as a nature photographer—had died in an "accident" while hiking. The accident had been a loose boulder that had knocked him unconscious in the midday summer heat. His body and equipment had been found three days later, and his death had been reported as heat dehydration. One agent-captain Keir Roget had been assigned to investigate. Roget didn't think it would be the almost-vacation the colonel had promised after Roget's efforts against the Taiyuan economic terrorists. Not that he could do anything about it, but he still wondered exactly what had happened to Sulynn and who she really was.

His cover in St. George was as a regional E&W water monitor. The man holding the position—an actual monitor—had been promoted and transferred to Colorado Springs. Roget was listed on the payroll and everywhere else as a temporary replacement.

The only information Roget had was a list of four names: Brendan B. Smith, Mitchell Leavitt, William Dane, and Bensen Sorensen. He'd run searches on all four. Smith managed the local data/print center that specialized in Saint-oriented religious and entertainment material. Leavitt was a collateralizer. Dane was the assistant manager of the Deseret First Bank's local branch. Sorensen operated a guest-house complex for Saint pilgrims and the infrequent tourists.

When the tram halted at the 200 East station at a quarter to eight, Roget exited by the front door, along with the other men, and one couple. Only a handful of unaccompanied women left by the rear doors. The station platform was of hardened and polished native Navaho sandstone. So were the columns supporting the roof that held the photovoltaic arrays. Of necessity, such systems topped all public structures in southern Noram that did not have historic significance.

He stepped from the shade of the platform onto the stone sidewalk that stretched northward toward the Red Hills Bluff and the Federation Services Station. A bronze plaque on a sandstone pedestal offered a local map. Prominent on it were the Temple and the summer home of the second Saint prophet, the one who had laid the groundwork for the Saint faith to become a world power before the wars of consolidation and federation.

Just beyond the station was a small shop. A woman had just unlocked the door and was raising the blinds. Her blond hair was French-braided, like that of most married women, at least those older than twenty-five whom Roget had seen over the past day in St. George.

The window featured mannequins displaying female attire, mainly below the knee dresses in subdued shades with brilliant flashthreads. There was one feminine singlesuit set in the corner, as if as an afterthought. Except for the shimmer of those threads, the dresses would not have been out of place in ancient Deseret or the state of Utah that had followed that short-lived Mormon dominance of the Noram southwest.

Ahead on Roget's left was a small café. "JOHN D. LEE HOUSE" proclaimed the modest sign above the windows that were already darkening in response to the intensifying sunlight. Most of the tables were taken by men. He only saw one couple—both white-haired.

He glanced westward across 200 East at another restaurant—Lupe's. There, two Sudams with their darker skins emerged from the doorway and hurried toward the tram. They wore the darker blue denims of manual workers.

Another man walked toward the café from a battered electrocoupe parked at the curb behind a small lorry. A shaggy brown dog was tied in the open bed of the lorry, and it was already panting. Roget frowned, but he couldn't do anything. The dog wasn't being overtly abused, and it wasn't running free, something not allowed in environmentally fragile areas like St. George.

Roget took his time walking the four long blocks uphill to the Federation Services Station on the north side of where 200 East ended at Red Hills Boulevard. Already the temperature was over thirty. Even on fall days such as the one he was beginning, the afternoon temperature was often above forty-five degrees. He didn't want to think about how hot it would be in the height of summer.

The vent-weave of his singlesuit kept him from getting too hot. He was still sweating when he stepped into the cooler air of the FSS entry hall. There, a single guard sat behind a gray synthstone-fronted stone desk. Roget's implants sensed the energy fields around the man and around the screening gate beside the guard position.

Before Roget reached the gate, the scanners picked up his imbedded ID. Many had tried to counterfeit Federation IDs. A very few had succeeded. The rest had vanished.

"Good morning, sir," offered the guard. "What can we do for you?"

"I'm Keir Roget. Reporting for work as an E&W monitor."

"Last door on the left at the end, sir."

"Thank you." Roget stepped through the gate without any alarms being triggered and walked down the long corridor.

At the end he opened the door on the left and stepped through it. He closed it behind himself. The man who rose from the wide console filled with datascreens had silvering black hair and an oval face. His skin was an olive tan that minimized the blackness of his eyes. He smiled but did not speak.

"Keir Roget, sir. Are you head monitor Sung?"

"Elrik Sung, and we're not all that formal here, Keir. St. George is smaller than it looks, and formality wears thin when you're a minority. Those of us who are Feds or multis are a very small minority."

That was something Roget had been briefed on, in far more depth than a standard monitor would have received. So he nodded again. "Is fraternization a problem?"

"Yours. Not theirs. Everyone will smile and be quite polite and friendly, and you'll be fortunate to have been invited to two Saint houses in the course of a year. Both of those, if they happen, will be to determine whether they think they can convert you." Sung motioned. "Over here. Let's get your ID into the system."

Roget stepped toward the chief monitor.

Sung lifted a tube scanner, then turned to the console. "Enter. Personnel. Code follows." He straightened, gesturing to the wall display with the shifting views of St. George and the various data-drops. "There. Now the guards won't question you every time you come in. Here's the main console, not that you'll spend all that much time here after today and tomorrow. It's like every other one you've seen. The system analyzes what it finds and offers a set of prioritized options. Then it sends you out to verify what's happening. You never inform or confront the offender. If asked, you just say that you're checking systems. I'm certain your training has emphasized that, but I want to reemphasize it. You just confirm and document the situation and enter the report. If it's a criminal offense, the local security patrollers will deal with it. If it's merely a civil offense, the power board will issue the requisite compensatory levy. Our job is strictly to verify and certify any excessive use of energy or any escape of water beyond the minimums. I'm not sending you out on verification immediately. They're a little old-fashioned here. I'd prefer that you have at least a basic familiarity with the local geography and usage patterns first. Also, it won't hurt if you're seen around town for a few days."

Roget nodded. He'd almost said, "Yes, sir." Instead, he asked, "You want me to take the console and learn what I can?"

"That's right." Sung pointed to a pair of narrow built-in desks with small screens and two drawers inset into the wall. "When you're not on the main console or out on verification, the one on the left is yours."

"Thank you."

"Go ahead and take the main console. You'll get better visuals there."

Roget slipped into the thermacool seat. Following Sung's indoctrination protocol was fine with him. The more quickly he learned about St. George the better. He glanced up. "Is there any area or sector where I should start or where I need to be wary?"

"The Temple complex has a 10 percent variance under the religious leeway provisions. That includes the Tabernacle. Also, there's a history of faint geothermal activity to the east of Middleton Ridge. You won't notice that, if at all, except on cool winter nights."

"They haven't tapped it?"

"According to the old surveys, there's not enough volume for consistent power, and it's right along the fault line. No one here has the yuan to do that kind of speculative exploration and development, and no one elsewhere has any reason to fund such a low-yield project."

Roget nodded once more.

"I'll leave you to get yourself familiarized, and I'll check back in a bit. I need to attend the weekly supervisors' meeting." Sung stepped through the side door into what had to be his private office, then returned almost immediately and departed.

Roget linked to the system through his implants, using only those standard for an energy and water monitor. He had no idea who had betrayed the previous agent, or what systems had been compromised. He did know that any new Federation employee in St. George would be scrutinized closely.

In less than half an hour, he had a solid overview and understanding of both energy and water usage patterns, along with daily and current comps. The inputs came from hundreds of thousands of minute sensors across and within St. George, all integrated and tabulated by the systems beneath the FSS building. Energy and water use defined a culture, from those who were a part of it to those who wanted to change it or overthrow it. Even with a stable planetary population of three billion, there weren't enough resources for the kind of profligate squandering that had marked the last days of the Saint-dominated Noram Confederation.

The Sino-Fed mandarins had learned the lessons of history. Let the market system allocate resources, and make sure everyone has the minimum for bare comfort, but ensure that excessive uses or waste required extraordinarily high recompense. Equally important was the understanding that whoever controlled energy, communications, and water controlled society. Food could always be found, made, or stolen, and the same was true of weapons. Industrious and inventive humans could turn anything into a weapon.

The Federation understood that most people just wanted to live their lives, to work at what they could, enjoy what they could, and live without fear or insecurity. Anyone could follow any belief system or religion he or she wanted—but only where those beliefs did not conflict with the rights and health of others or contradict Federation law.

For those who didn't want to follow the laws, FSA had very simple rules. Concentrate on the top, and eliminate those few who ignored or flaunted Federation law. Keep the eliminations to an absolute minimum and do it without publicity or notice. Relocate and reeducate all others involved, especially the flunkies of the lawbreakers, wherever possible, and send them to locales and situations where they had to work to follow the rules. If that didn't convince them, implant location monitors and nerve-blocks that did.

Roget began to manipulate the board to learn all the local coordinates and match them to the scanned images and maps. He wondered whether the dead agent had been killed by some Saint underground or because he'd uncovered commercial corruption.

Roget would find out.

In time. He was in no hurry, not with intermittent residual nerve soreness.

7

17 MARIS 1811 P. D.

Roget woke early and uneasily, sore from lying on the hard bunk shelf, barely cushioned by his jacket. For a moment, he had no idea where he might be because the cabin was pitch black. He eased halfway off the bunk shelf where he sat and pulled on his boots, then sealed them. He walked to the door, unbolted it, and opened it a crack, listening intently, and letting his internal systems scan the area.

He could sense no energy radiation of any sort, and he heard nothing except insects—or their equivalents. He opened the door more widely. It was before what passed for dawn, but the sky still held a hint of amber radiance, and to the east he could see a faint brightening. With a nod, he turned back, leaving the door open for light. For breakfast, he drank the last from his water bottle and chewed field rations. He had enough for another three days at full diet, but he had the definite feeling he wouldn't go undetected for anywhere near that long. He supposed he could, if he headed out into the wild, but that wasn't what he'd been sent down to do. He couldn't really assess the culture without getting into it—and that meant he had to meet the locals . . . and risk internment or incarceration.

He stretched enough to loosen tight muscles. After that, he left the cabin as he had found it, the small amount of trash he had created tucked into his pack. He covered close to two klicks before the sky brightened fully and amber light filtered down through the dark-needled pines and onto the needle-covered ground and the trail. Twice he glimpsed something that looked to be fast and yet rodentlike. It wasn't a rabbit but resembled a miniature kangaroo, except with shorter legs and tail. He also saw more of the large pawprints in places beside the trail. One set looked to belong to a creature larger than a wolf. Possibly much larger. He checked his sidearm and stunner. He didn't see or sense anything like squirrels or ground rodents, but he did see a few small holes that looked like possible burrows. He also caught sight of a number of large raptor-looking birds from a distance and got a close look at a flock of tiny gray and brown birds that could have been ground-feeding bushtits.

About an hour after what might have corresponded to dawn, he walked over a low rise in the trail and saw what looked to be a small pile of blue and gold leaves a meter or so to the right of the path—scores of the butterflies, their wings moving slowly. Did they sleep or gather in piles?

He stepped toward the pile. The butterflies rose in a cloud that split into lines and then vanished into the overhanging branches. Roget looked down and swallowed. Lying on the carpet of evergreen needles were the remains of a ratlike or squirrel-like animal. What little fur remained was shiny, but mostly all that was left were bones. Were the butterflies carnivorous or scavengers, or both? He couldn't help but wonder what else lay in and around him in the trees. The heavily scented air didn't seem quite so much perfumed as holding a hint of sickly-sweet decay.

By late midmorning he had covered close to ten klicks along the trail. He'd seen no aliens or people, but he had found a small fountain. It was simple enough, just a spout in the middle of a circular stone basin forty centimeters across from which water flowed over a lower section of the rim into a stone drainage sluice that fed a stream perhaps half a meter wide. The stream looked clear, although it was hemmed in by low brush and grass.

A small splash downhill caught Roget's attention. He watched the area for several moments but couldn't tell what had made it—a fish, an amphibian, or an oversized arthropod. He filled his water bottle from the fountain and returned to the trail.

Less than an hour later, passing through a small clearing, Roget glanced uphill. He thought he saw another trail, just below the top of the ridge line. That might give him a better view. In any case, higher was probably better.

He started uphill through the trees. It was pleasant walking on the needle carpet, and the trees were far enough apart. There was also very little brushy undergrowth—only in places where there was a break in the evergreen canopy.

The distance uphill was farther than he'd thought, and after a time he paused to catch his breath. He judged he was still half a klick below where he thought the trail might be.

"Hello, there!" The voice came from higher on the slopes.

Roget froze. He couldn't see anyone through the pines, widely spaced as they were.

"Did you have difficulty coming through the shields?" came the second inquiry. "Your descent was steeper than optimal."

Then he smiled wryly. The words were in Federation English, and well-pronounced, with a feminine tone. That implied continued observation of the Federation and considerable technology. If whoever she represented had detected his dropboat coming down, there wasn't much point in trying to evade her. Not obviously. He didn't want to walk right up to her . . . if the caller were even female . . . or human. But he didn't see any realistic alternative. While he couldn't sense any broadcast emissions, that didn't mean that she didn't have reinforcements. Or that she or it or they were friendly. On the other hand, it didn't mean they were unfriendly. Her words did suggest that there was little use in activating the singlesuit background blending camouflage.

"Some," he called back.

"I'll meet you up ahead at the rest stop. When you get to the trail, turn to your right. It's about half a klick ahead on the trail."

Should he take the caller's word? He could attempt to escape, but they'd found him in the middle of a forest, and not even on a trail—and they knew standard, including measurements. Thomists? That was looking to be the most probable conclusion, but anything was still possible.

He continued making his way uphill. He came to the trail after less than a hundred meters, although he hadn't been able to see it until he was almost upon it. Again, it was a manicured and wood-fragment-mulched walkway. Roget stopped, then looked north and south. He saw no one. He turned north, walking at a deliberate pace.

The rest stop was little more than two benches on the uphill side of the trail, with another stone fountain on the downhill side. A woman wearing a long-sleeved green shirt, gray trousers, and gray hiking boots sat on the bench nearest Roget. There was no one else in sight except the two of them.

She stood as he approached. She was a good thirty centimeters shorter than Roget, and muscular, but neither slender nor stocky. Her hair was white blond, and her face was oval with deep gray eyes, wide cheekbones, and a jaw that was just short of being square. Her skin was either lightly tanned or that shade naturally. With the planet's shields, how could he tell?

He stopped a meter short of her but did not speak. He saw no obvious weapons.

"I'm Lyvia. I'll be your guide to Dubiety."

"That's what you call the world?"

"Officially and unofficially. What does the Federation call it?"

"Haze."

"You haven't told me your name. Or the cover name you've adopted. Either will do." Lyvia smiled.

Her expression was fractionally warmer than polite, and slightly amused, Roget noted. "Keir. Keir Roget."

"We have a hike ahead of us, Keir. It's a good twelve klicks to the trailhead station. I'll explain a few matters along the way, and you can ply me with questions. Some I'll answer. Some will have to wait, and some you'll be able to answer yourself in time."

"All your responses will be Delphic, I'm certain."

"Only if you take them that way. We try to be factual. Oh, and I'd ask that you be careful with the weapons and those powerpacks built into your suit. Matters could become difficult if you hurt anyone." She turned and began to walk.

Roget had to take three quick long steps to catch up with her. The trail was wide enough for two to walk comfortably side-by-side. As he matched her pace, he couldn't help but think that she'd shown no surprise meeting him, and no fear and no hesitation in turning her back to him. It hadn't been a bluff. Nor had it been naiveté. Haze—or Dubiety—knew where he'd come from and had been prepared to meet him within a day and a half of his landing in what appeared to have been a relatively remote area . . . or at least an area removed from easy transport access. That raised the question of how much more the Federation knew than he'd been told. It also suggested just how expendable he was.

"This is one of the Thomist worlds, I take it?" he finally said.

"Thomists settled Dubiety. You should be able to tell that once you've seen more."

"What sort of commnet do you use?"

"There's a full planetary net."

"You don't care much for the standard broadcast spectrum. Why not?"

"Broadcomm has definite physical and physiological effects. We've avoided those."

"Such as?"

"Both implants and hand-held devices have adverse impacts on brain physiology. That's especially true for certain genetic profiles. Overall, the economics don't work out, either."

What did brain physiology have to do with economics? Roget was getting the feeling that all her answers might hold the same sort of non sequiturs. "Would you mind explaining that?"

"Any answer I give," replied Lyvia, "would be either simplistic or wrong. It's not my field."

"It might give me an idea, at least," said Roget mildly.

"That's exactly the problem in too many high-tech societies, even in some that are not so high-tech. Simplistic and wrong ideas lead to simplistic and wrong public opinion and wrong-headed public policies. That retards progress far more than is gained by so-called open dialogue by those who don't understand. Generalizations breed misunderstandings, and misunderstandings lead to greater problems in maintaining an orderly society."

"But most people don't want long and technical answers to simple questions."

"That's their problem."

"How do you keep people from giving those simplistic answers?" asked Roget.

"Personally, in conversation, and privately, they can say what they want. Anything meant for public communication falls under the libel and slander laws." She laughed. "That's what keeps most litigators in business."

"They can get damages if someone says or writes something factually inaccurate?"

"Exactly. One of the factors in governing the award is the number of people to whom the inaccuracy was conveyed."

Roget was both intrigued and appalled. "What about the use of accurate facts or figures to misrepresent?"

"If it's by a public figure, either a representative of an organization or elected official, and it's bad enough, it's a criminal offense."

"How can anyone determine that?"

"The test has to do with relevant information withheld or omitted."

"In a noncriminal case, what if they can't pay?"

"We have a great number of public service positions, both for criminal and civil offenders. We've found that well-compensated litigators, solicitors, business directors and managers, and elected officials have a great aversion to maintaining trails such as this one or handling sanitary duties in the subtrans system or working land reclamation and enhancement . . . or any other number of equally necessary and not always tasteful tasks."

Roget kept a pleasant expression on his face and asked, "You mentioned elected officials. What's the governmental structure?"

"Nothing too unfamiliar to you, I'm certain. Representative democratically elected lower House of Tribunes. The upper chamber—that's the House of Denial—consists of those with specific areas of expertise. They're elected from nominees from various occupations and subjected to denial by the House of Tribunes."

"Do you have political parties?"

That brought another laugh, one more rueful. "Oh, yes. At the moment there are seven."

"Proportional voting of some sort?"

"It's not quite that simple. I'll have to get you a copy of the constitution."

For roughly three hours, Roget asked question after question. The answers provided by Lyvia were as satisfactory as her first replies. That is, they answered almost none of his real questions. Dubiety was sounding more and more like a fascist state run by environmentally-oriented lunatics. Yet, he reminded himself, lunatics didn't create orbital shields that could shred dropboats and keep the Federation at bay.

As the trail came to the top of a low rise, the trees ended abruptly. Lyvia gestured at the low circular grassy depression ahead. "There's the trailhead station."

A columned portico with a domed roof some fifteen meters across stood in the center of the grassy swale. Trails radiated from the circular stone walk that bordered the structure. All the stone was of a pale gray that was probably almost white but looked faintly rosy in the amber light that filtered through the orbital shields.

As they walked nearer, Roget could see two ramps under the low domed roof, each slanting into the ground—one on each side of the portico. A couple wearing hiking gear emerged from the ramp opposite the one immediately in front of Lyvia and Roget. Neither hiker so much as looked in Roget's direction.

"This way," Lyvia said pleasantly.

The mouth of the tunnel holding the ramp was encircled by a deep green band. On each side, waist-high, protruded four black squares, each some ten centimeters on a side. Lyvia raised a black tube and pointed it at one of the squares.

"Paying the fare?" asked Roget.

"Paying yours. Mine is deducted automatically."

The tunnel beyond the entry formed an oval with a flat base, roughly three meters wide, and the top of the ceiling was about four meters above the ramp. The flooring looked to be a deep green composite that offered a certain amount of give, combined with enough roughness to provide easy traction. The walls were a deep greenish gray, except for the two curved lighting strips some thirty centimeters wide set three quarters of the way up from the ramp surface. The light from the strips was slightly whiter than the amber that filtered through the atmospheric shields.

As he walked down the curving and sloping ramp, Roget asked, "You don't have any aircraft, flitters, that sort of thing?"

"We don't use them. They're energy intensive and excessively hard on the environment. They also create unrealistic expectations."

"Don't use them? That's an interesting way of putting it."

She smiled. "It's accurate. You'll see."

"Unrealistic expectations?" asked Roget.

"I'll explain once we're on the subtrans."

Roget started to protest in exasperation, then just smiled politely.

The ramp descended in a semicircle, then straightened for the last few meters before emerging onto a simple concourse that stretched some twenty meters to Roget's right. The walls of the concourse curved slightly, suggesting that they were but a fraction of a larger arc. A series of four archways punctuated the straight wall facing Roget. A half-transparent, half-translucent light green substance filled each archway.

Lyvia walked briskly to the third archway, halting there. "It shouldn't be long now. Not too long anyway."

Two older men stood talking several meters away, right before the last archway. While Roget thought he heard some familiar words, clearly language on Dubiety had diverged from the Federation standard. Yet Lyvia spoke Federation standard perfectly.

"If you listen closely for a while, you'll begin to understand," she said. "It's more a matter of cadence and localisms."

Roget hoped so. He could feel a gentle but persistent breeze, and he glanced to his right, taking in the slots in the end wall of the concourse. Even straining his senses, he could detect no sounds of machinery.

"About expectations?" he asked.

"Later, after we're on the subtrans," she repeated.

Roget decided not to push her. A good fifteen standard minutes passed before the translucent green doors slid back to reveal the interior of the subtrans. Again, Roget had been unable to detect the approach of the underground conveyance.

Lyvia stepped through the archway, and Roget followed her. The subtrans's interior was simple enough, two individual seats on each side of a center aisle, set in groups of four, two seats facing two others. The flooring and walls flowed into the graceful seats, a deep green, with a brownish amber "trim." There were no windows, just a featureless wall.

Lyvia took a wall seat and gestured for Roget to take the seat across from her. He eased his small pack off his back, then settled into the seat, expecting it to be excessively firm, if not hard, since it looked to be the same material as the walls and flooring. Surprisingly, the seat was yielding and comfortable. His pack went between his legs.

The platform door closed, leaving a wall as blank as the one facing it.

"That's a great deal of wasted space." Roget pointed to the open area between the doors.

"That's where large packs, luggage, and sometimes freight get placed. There are concealed and recessed tie-downs."

The acceleration of the subtrans was gentle but continued for a time.

"Air travel? Expectations?" pressed Roget.

"Oh . . . that. Letting people travel by air creates a whole host of expectations. One expectation is the feeling that they ought to be able to go when they wish and exactly where they want. After all, there's nothing like a maglev tunnel or the obvious limitations of one train at a time to reinforce the idea that not all things are possible. The expectations are even higher for those with resources and power, especially if the society allows them private aircraft of some sort. They believe their time is more valuable; they're more important.

That reinforces the feeling that anything can be bought, regardless of the cost to others."

"That sounds like old-style socialism, even communism."

Lyvia shook her head. "We're very capitalistic, extremely so. We just price things at their total value. We don't allow people to buy privileges at the cost of other people's health or future, or life expectancy. Those are real costs. Most so-called market systems don't include them." She smiled. "At least, they haven't in the past. We don't always either, but we keep trying."

Roget didn't believe a word. "What about other expectations?"

"There's the expectation that immediate travel at comparatively low costs is a right, rather than a costly privilege. There's also the expectation that personal freedom of movement is a right, regardless of what it costs others."

Roget decided that he was getting nowhere. "Where are we headed?"

"To Skeptos, of course. It's the capital. Isn't that where you wanted to go? To find out our weaknesses?" Lyvia smiled warmly.

8

17 LIANYU 6744 F. E.

By the time Roget arrived at the FSS on Friday, his first four days on the job had given him a very good understanding of the routine of an E&W monitor in St. George. Immediately after reporting each morning, he went over the status reports and reviewed all the anomalies reported by the system. Then he'd set up a preliminary prioritization of the anomalies, with recommended observation points. He'd offer those to Sung. Once the head monitor had approved his plan for the day, Roget was free to head out with his portable official E&W monitor. The monitor held all the data for the day. That way, no one could hack or razor transmissions because there weren't any, and it kept down unnecessary energy usage.

Unless there happened to be an urgent surge in excess energy or water usage, Roget was free to arrange his observations to minimize his travel time. Since he was limited to public transport and his feet, he'd learned after the third day to be most careful in planning his route. Even so, his feet had ached by Wednesday evening, and Thursday night hadn't been that much better.

He actually was in the office on Friday before Sung. The anomaly list was short—four shops; two residences in the historical district—probably poor insulation or equipment that needed maintenance; and an increase in ambient temperature in the Virgin River that couldn't be accounted for by weather or solar radiation intensity.

The river had to come first because there was no telling how long that anomaly might last. He also might have to take several readings over the course of the day. He'd just finished his proposed priority listing when Sung appeared and settled himself before the main console.

"The list is up," Roget said.

"Good." After a moment, Sung turned in his swivel. "You've got the Virgin first. That's right. But you need to move your first observation farther north, out east beyond the Green Springs tram terminal." Sung called up a map on the console and motioned for Roget to join him.

Roget did.

A red triangle appeared—a good klick to the east of the station. "There," announced Sung. "Don't forget to check to make sure nothing's coming down the Mill Creek wash, either. A reading there will determine whether it's natural, or whether it's coming from a source in town."

Roget thought about the long walk ahead.

"Oh . . . you can sign out a bicycle if you don't want to walk it." Sung grinned.

"I don't believe you mentioned that."

"Supply keeps one for us, down on the lower level. They fold and fit in the carriers at the rear of the tram cars."

"Thank you. I could use it today."

Sung smiled. "I thought you might. You'll need three locations on the river and three different intervals at least an hour apart."

Roget had planned on that. He just nodded. "I'd better get going."

Sung returned his attention to the console, and Roget finished loading the data into his duty monitor. Then he left the office and took the ramp at the end of the corridor down to the lower level. He had to walk the entire length of the corridor on the lower level to reach the supply office—a small cubicle with a door behind it, presumably to a storeroom.

The supply clerk was a black-eyed and black-haired woman. She looked up with a cautious smile. "Yes?"

"Keir Roget. I'm the new E&W monitor."

"Caron Fueng."

"Monitor Sung said that there might be a bike I can sign out?"

"There is." The clerk smiled. "Sung must like you."

"Oh?"

"He didn't tell Merytt about the bike for close to a month. I'll get it for you."

Roget laughed. But as he waited for Fueng to return with the bike, he wondered if the head monitor suspected what he really was.

The bike that Fueng wheeled out was the compact type with wide balloon tires. Not the speediest on paved surfaces, but much better on trails and lanes or unpaved surfaces.

"Just a thumbprint, please." She gestured to the authenticator on the corner of her desk. "I checked the tires. They're fine."

Roget thumbed the authenticator panel. "Thank you."

"If you don't bring it back before five, you'll have to keep it in your office. You can't take it home." She shrugged. "That doesn't matter to me, but accounting doesn't like it. Rules." She shook her head.

"I appreciate the warning. I should have it back by then." He offered a smile as he took the bike from her.

He wheeled it up the front ramp and managed to get it through the security gate and the front doors without banging anything. Once outside the FSS, he rode down to the tram station. The morning was already warm and clear, more like late summer than late fall or early winter. Then, he doubted that there was really any season besides summer in St. George.

His ID implant allowed him entrance to the platform and train—but only during working hours. The carrier in the rear of the second car was empty, and the bicycle did fold—if not as easily as Sung had suggested. He sat down in the seat next to the carrier.

A young man scurried onto the tram just before the doors closed. He wore the white short-sleeved shirt and dark trousers that all the Saint youths affected. As soon as his eyes took in the white monitor's singlesuit, he looked away and slipped into a seat two rows forward from the one where Roget sat.

Three rows forward on the other side sat two white-haired women. After the tram left the platform, they began—or resumed—their conversation.

". . . still think it's a shame the way the Federation limits missions . . ."

". . . say it's to reduce energy spent on travel . . . don't want us converting people . . ."

". . . Jared's oldest is in Espagne . . . says it's hotter than here . . . and almost as dry . . ."

"What do they have him doing?"

". . . building a new stake center there . . . they can't offer their testament, except in church or on the premises . . . just show faith by example . . ."

"So much for freedom of speech . . ."

Roget wanted to snort. He didn't. Why did so many people think that freedom of speech meant the ability to harangue other people when they didn't want to be bothered? True believers had the idea that once someone understood what they were saying, the listeners would be converted. Understanding didn't mean accepting, and that was why, under the Federation's freedom of speech provisions, people could harangue all they wanted, but it had to be on their own property, or in their own dwellings, or with the consent of the property owner. Public thoroughfares or property were to be free of any form of solicitation, ideological or commercial, and soliciting others in their dwellings or on their property, without their permission, was also forbidden.

". . . how can anyone learn the Way if no one can tell them?"

". . . time will come . . . the Prophet says . . . after the great tribulations . . ."

". . . not too soon, if you ask me . . . had enough tribulations . . ."

"How is Jared?"

"Doing mission duty this year . . . Wasatch reclamation team . . ."

By the time the electrotram came to a halt at the Green Springs platform, the northeastern terminus of the system, and across from the maglev terminus, Roget was the only one in the car. He lifted the bike out of the carrier and carried it onto the platform, just before a large group of young women entered on the other side of the car. All of them looked to be fresh-faced and far younger than he was—and yet all had the braided hair of married Saint women.

Were they all headed to the Tabernacle or the Temple? For what?

He smiled faintly and snapped the bike together. Then he wheeled it down the ramp from the platform to the street, where he swung onto it and began to pedal eastward along Green Drive South, past white stucco dwellings larger than any he'd seen nearer the center of town. Like the others, though, they had walled rear courtyards. Only a handful of small electrocoupes passed him, all headed westward.

Roget stopped where Green Drive South ended at Riverside Parkway West—on the west side of the Virgin River. It scarcely deserved to be called a river. While the reddish clay, sandbars, and low vegetation of the riverbed varied from a good fifty to a hundred meters wide, the water itself was less than three meters wide, and certainly less than a meter in depth in most places. It was the largest watercourse between the Colorado River and Reno. No wonder the old American republic had left the place to the Saints.

For several moments, Roget looked at the thin line of water that effectively bordered the east and southeast of St. George. Generally, building was limited to the ground inside the borders of the Virgin River and the Santa Clara wash, which had once been a stream of some sort. Then he leaned the bike against the low sandstone wall that marked the edge of the protected area of the riverbed and studied the ground.

Several minutes passed before he determined the approach to the water that would disturb the vegetation the least. He walked north almost forty meters. There he walked along a line of mostly buried black lava, and then picked his way from rocky point to rocky point until he stood on a flat boulder that overlooked the water. He flicked out the microfilament probe and let the stream flow over and around it until the monitoring unit flashed. Then he stored the data and retracted the probe.

After carefully retracing his steps back to where he had left the bike, he looked back out over the river. He certainly hadn't seen any sign of gross thermal or other pollution, but the master systems would compare the water temperatures and composition to the river's environmental profile, once he returned and linked the monitor to the system. He continued to study the riverbed for several minutes longer, but nothing changed, and there was no one nearby. To the north he thought he'd seen a heron, or some sort of crane, but he wasn't certain.

Roget took the bike and rode southward down Riverside Parkway West. He didn't want to go through the process of riding back to the tram station, folding the bike, going two stations, then unfolding the bike, and riding back out east and south again. It wasn't that hot yet.

The parkway wound more than he'd realized. He rode close to five klicks before he reached the second monitoring point, just east of where River Road ended at the parkway. Reaching the water was easier there because there was a nature overlook.

Just as he had finished his monitoring and was walking back to his bicycle, a group of youngsters appeared. They were escorted by a young woman—a teacher, Roget thought.

"Good morning," he said politely.

"Good morning," she replied with a smile.

After he had passed the group, behind him, he heard the teacher.

"Who was that, class?"

There were various answers, all politely framed, before the woman's voice replied, "He's an environmental monitor. You can tell by the white uniform and the monitoring unit at his belt. He was checking the river. That's to make sure everything is as it should be. . . ."

Roget mounted the bike and rode farther westward on the parkway and then continued south until he reached the point where the dry Santa Clara wash joined the river—

close to another six klicks. There he repeated the monitoring process.

After he finished, he took a long swallow from the water bottle at his waist and looked out to the south. It was still hard to believe that the blistered expanse of red clay and sand, dotted with scattered cacti and occasional tufts of some sort of desert grass, had once held thousands of dwellings and other structures. Or that hundreds of thousands of Saints—as many people as some main Federation locials— had populated the area. That had been before the wars and the Reconstruction, of course. St. George hadn't been funded for reconstruction by the Federation. All the work done in the area had been by Saint volunteers, and the Federation had only grudgingly accepted the environmental results, and only because the outcome had been to keep the Saints, who had been a quiet but destabilizing factor in the fall of the American republic, somewhat more isolated. That wasn't exactly what the briefing materials had said, but Roget had read between the lines.

He replaced the water bottle, then checked the monitor for the map and coordinates of the other sites he needed to check and verify. Three of the shops were north and slightly west of him along Bluff Street, in the area reserved for commerce. He was getting hot, and he decided to ride the bike to the south station and let the tram carry him north to the station closest to the southern-most shop on his list.

The station turned out to be only a quarter klick or so from the river, but he found himself sharing the rear car with fifteen youngsters—all about ten—being chaperoned by two large and jovial-looking young men. Yet none of the seventeen said a word during the time Roget was on the tram. He was almost relieved when he carted his bike off at the platform on the corner of Main and 600 South.

From there he rode the bike three blocks west to Bluff Street and found himself right beside his destination. Ken's Cleaners was a small shop set at the south end of the block.

The stucco finish was a pale bluish white, rather than plain white, and the door was set on the southwest corner of the building, looking out on the street corner, rather than in the middle of the building facing Bluff Street. Through the tinted thermal-conversion windows, Roget could only see the untended counter. He leaned the bike against the side of the building and then walked back eastward alongside it, flicking on the atmospheric sampler and tabbing the results so they'd be linked properly. Then, halfway back along the side of the building, he extended the microfilament used for air sampling and flicked it as high as he could, swinging it over the top of the low structure. He walked to the rear of the building and repeated the process.

Then he paused. He could hear a low mechanical rumbling, almost a groaning, coming from inside the back of the cleaners. Some sort of mechanical problem, he thought. He could feel the excess heat from the building. That much heat meant excess energy use or poor insulation or malfunctioning equipment or some combination of those factors. Those weren't his problems, for either his overt or covert job.

As he turned, he saw two older men standing in the thin band of shade cast by the building across the side street from him. Both wore white shirts—but long-sleeved—and dark trousers. He smiled politely, then turned and began to walk back toward Bluff Street.

". . . hecky-darn monitor . . . snooping round . . . worse than the DTs, if you ask me . . . tell by the all white . . . not really proper . . ."

". . . ChinoFeds ought to have more to do than bother small businesses . . ."

". . . bother everyone now and again . . . why they're ChinoFeds . . ."

ChinoFeds? Roget thought that epithet had vanished a millennium ago, and his ancestry certainly had no Sinese in it. Even the apparently meticulous genealogy records kept on virtually all Noram citizens would have proved that. The briefings had mentioned rumors that the Saints had even kept tissue samples of prominent deceased Saints, but those had never been confirmed. And St. George certainly didn't look like a technology center, but more like it had been frozen in time a millennium ago.

Roget kept a pleasant expression on his face. What so many people refused to accept was that, when thousands of small businesses in thousands of towns and cities all exceeded the limits, the results on the environment could be significant. That attitude had been the principal cause of the deterioration of the old United States. Everyone had thought that they could question any authority and that they could do what they wanted because what they did didn't matter. In the end it had, and by then it had been too late.

He completed his readings and returned to the bike. He pedaled north in the bike lane for another three blocks, where he stopped in front of the next commercial establishment on the list—Santiorna's. The shop looked to cater to Saint women. While the fabrics on the mannequins were flashy enough, the cut of the garments, and especially the lengths of the skirts, were conservative. The other fact was that there were actual garments displayed, rather than holographic images. Was that because of the Saint culture . . . or because of the cost of power?

Roget knew that power costs were far higher in rural areas and in smaller towns and cities. The higher costs of power, indeed of living, were designed to reflect the true impact of development on the environment as well as to discourage movement from the metroplexes and contained locals. Location pricing and transportation costs of certain energy-intensive goods effectively limited their use away from the metroplexes and locals. By implementing that pricing and adding geometric pricing for incremental energy usage, as well as a few other regulatory and pricing devices, the Federation had minimized population migration. In effect, the more desirable the location, the higher the cost of living there and the fewer personal amenities effectively allowed, except at exorbitant costs. Federation citizens could have personal luxuries or the luxury of open space, but not both.

He set the bicycle in the corner stand and then walked toward the shop, checking the monitor. Unlike Ken's Cleaners, Santiorna's displayed no possible causes of excessive energy usage, even when he made his way to the end of the block and walked up the alley. He could sense eyes on him as he did so, but no one actually appeared. When he returned to Bluff Street and the front of the buildings, he saw two young women walking south toward him. When they saw the white monitor's uniform, they immediately stepped inside what looked to be a craft shop.

At that moment, Roget took another look at the business between the craft shop and the apparel outlet. DeseretData read the sign, with a design next to the name that incorporated two interlocked Ds. Why was the name familiar?

He nodded as he recalled. DeseretData was Brendan B. Smith's establishment. Just on an off chance that Smith might have something to do with the anomaly attributed to Santiorna's, Roget took out the monitor and tabbed in an entry for DeseretData. Then he scanned the front of the shop and used the air sampling microfilament. After that, he walked back around to the alley and took readings there.

He walked back to his bike, then paused as several small lorries drove silently by, followed by a brilliant yellow coupe that whined almost imperceptibly. He followed the coupe for all of a block, even as it pulled away from him, before he realized that he was getting hungry.

The iron grilles and pseudo-aged stucco of the Frontier Fort caught his eye. He angled the bike off the street, dismounted, and walked it through the drawn-back iron gates into the shaded courtyard. There was a rack that could hold four bikes. One other bike was locked in place. Roget set the bike there and walked to the door and then inside the restaurant. Inside was notably cooler, but not chill. The hum of conversation filled the space. Close to half of the twenty or so tables were taken. That surprised Roget because he'd heard no sound when he'd been out in the courtyard.

Good insulation, he decided.

The hostess was a smiling, slim, but weathered and older woman, dressed in an old American-style pioneer ankle-length black skirt and a high-necked cream lace blouse. "Just you, sir?"

Roget nodded.

"This way."

He followed her to a small table near the north wall. She handed him a printed menu. He hadn't ever seen one of those.

"We're out of the lamb, but there's a venison stew for the same price. Jessica will take your order."

Roget decided to try the stew and ordered it and a pale lager, almost absently, when the round-faced and blond Jessica arrived. Then, while he waited for the venison, he intensified his implants and listened to various conversations taking place.

". . . monitor . . . what's he doing here?"

". . . don't know . . . don't care . . ."

". . . this one's a young fellow . . . liked the other one . . ."

Roget wasn't all that young, but to the weathered older man, he probably looked that way.

"That's because you never saw him."

". . . young Joseph wants a Temple wedding . . ."

". . . problem with that?"

". . . Dad doesn't have a recommend . . ."

". . . his fault . . . think blessings come free . . ."

The venison wasn't bad, especially with the new potatoes, but for all his listening, Roget couldn't say that he'd picked up a hint of anything. He hadn't expected to, but one could always hope.

After he left the Frontier Fort, feeling refreshed and cooler, Roget pedaled to the nearest tram station, where he wheeled the bike onto the first car, folded it, and stowed it. Then he rode the tram to the town center station, where he changed to the east-west tram and let it take him back out to the Green Springs station.

The next two hours consisted of repeating his first round of monitoring of the Virgin River. Then he took the tram back to the town center station. From there he rode the bicycle north and uphill, crossing St. George Boulevard, turning two blocks west, and finally coming to a stop outside the first residence unit. It was actually a guesthouse called the Seven Wives Inn. To Roget, the name sounded more like an opera, something like *Bluebeard's Waiting Room,* a classic Grainger chamber work dating back to before the fall of the west, and one of the few still performed, perhaps because it had a certain atonality that appealed to the Sinese.

Unlike the stucco-walled stone or block dwellings that dominated St. George, the inn—or at least the original on which the now-ancient replica was based—had high gables and a sharply pitched roof with reddish-yellow brick walls . . . and more wood than Roget had seen anywhere else in St. George—even more than the replica of the house of the Great Prophet—set less than a hundred meters away at an angle across the old wide street. The Great Prophet's house had tall trees. That suggested that the Saint church organization had obtained waivers for the water necessary to keep them alive.

Roget set the bike carefully against the white picket fence and took out the monitoring unit. He finished the first scan and began the air monitoring.

A young man hurried out of the inn and toward Roget. "We just discovered a whole power network in the upper level. My wife turned it on inadvertently yesterday."

"One of the old cooling units?"

"Yes, sir. I turned it off this morning."

Roget nodded. "I'll still have to take readings. That's my job."

The man winced visibly. "I understand." Then he turned and walked slowly back into the inn.

As he completed his monitoring, Roget heard raised voices from inside the inn. That didn't surprise him either. Neither did several yaps from a dog, but they were too sharp to have come from a dachshund.

The second residence unit was a small dwelling up behind the historic opera house, not that far from the Seven Wives Inn. No one was there, and Roget completed the readings.

Before he headed to the remaining commercial sites, he decided to make a slight detour. According to what he'd discovered so far, the inn owned by Bensen Sorensen was only a block away. In less than five minutes he had come to a stop outside the white picket fence of The Right Place. He tabbed in another entry and ran through the scanning and sampling. No one even looked out from the windows.

Then he pedaled downhill to the boulevard and eastward to the Deseret First Bank building and the row of shops to the south of it. The shop there that was on the list was vacant, but that didn't excuse the owner. Roget finished the readings. Then he had to pedal another block to where he monitored OldThings—an antique shop and antiquarian bookshop.

When he finished, Roget rode slowly back to the central tram station. There he waited for a good fifteen minutes before catching the eastbound tram. Once more, he wheeled the bike into the second car and folded and stowed it, and tried to cool off as he sat there for the journey back out to the Green Springs station—again.

He thought that several of the women in the front of the car might have been among those he'd seen leaving Green Springs when he'd first traveled there that morning. They didn't look as hot and as tired as he felt, and he still had another three sets of readings to take and ten klicks on the bike.

When he'd left the FSS that morning, Roget hadn't thought that the day would be that long. By the time he finished the last river readings and took the tram back to the town center station and then rode uphill to the FSS, it was approaching five. He wheeled the bike down to the supply office and got there at five before the hour.

"You cut it close," offered Caron Fueng.

"Long day."

"You look like it."

"That good?"

Fueng just smiled.

It was after five when Roget returned to the office. Sung was gone, and the system was locked down. After unlocking it and keying his codes in, Roget took out the thin fiber cable and linked the monitor and the system. Then he waited while the analytics processed the data.

The first set of Virgin River readings showed a lower reading than the initial anomaly, but the second reading showed a thermal spike above ambient, while the third was lower than the second but clearly higher than the first. The system could not identify any probable cause, except "natural conditions, probably intermittent geothermal infusion." Some help that was, but if it happened to be natural, that wasn't something a monitor could do anything about.

Ken's Cleaners was definitely using excessive energy and emitting excessive heat, and a citation would go out, with a copy to the enforcement arm of the local patroller, once it was approved by Sung. The Seven Wives Inn's readings were normal. A single spike might only result in a warning, if that, in addition to a slight energy surcharge. The other residence was running a slight overage, and Sung would have to decide how to handle that.

The results from The Right Place were also intriguing. They showed that the inn wasn't exceeding any limits. In fact, the readings seemed low compared to the Seven Wives Inn and even the single small residence. Then, that just might mean that Sorensen hadn't had any recent tourists or pilgrims. On the other hand, the inn's exterior walls were of native sandstone, and thick stone and modern insulation might be a factor.

OldThings was borderline, but the vacant shop was running well above its limits.

The first unexpected reading came from those taken at Santiorna's. They showed nothing out of the ordinary. But . . . the monitoring information from DeseretData showed marked excessive energy radiation, but the system did not indicate any excessive energy usage.

Roget frowned. That seemed more than a little strange.

He shrugged and locked the system down again. He closed down the office. Then he stepped out into the corridor and ID-locked the door. He'd taken less than ten steps toward the front of the building when a figure backed out of a doorway and almost into him.

"Excuse me," he said politely, stepping aside.

"Oh . . ." The woman turned. She held a large box in her arms. Her eyes were wide, blue, and innocent, and her shoulder-length blond hair was unbound. Rather, it was held in place by a dark blue headband. "I'm sorry. I didn't think anyone was still around." She offered an embarrassed half-smile. "I'm Marni. Marni Sorensen."

"Keir Roget. E&W."

"You're the new field monitor, aren't you?"

"The same. And you?" Roget smiled politely, offering but a trace of warmth.

"I'm the junior fiscal compliance auditor."

"Quite a title. What does it really mean?"

"It means I ask the system if everyone is staying within their projected budget, and most of the time everyone is."

"No offense," Roget said with a laugh, "but how could they not?"

She grinned. "I didn't say that well, I guess. No one can spend more than their budget, but what if a section obligates

80 percent of its resources in the first 20 percent of the accounting period?"

"I see what you mean. But the system . . . ?"

"The system would flag anything that obvious, but what if it's 7 percent over a time period when it should be 5? Is that a trend or just the result of capital equipment replacement?"

Roget nodded.

"It's nice to see a new face, but if you would excuse me? I'm running a bit late."

"Go." Roget grinned sympathetically. "Don't let me keep you."

With an apologetic smile, she turned and walked quickly down the corridor.

Roget knew one thing. She wasn't running late. What he didn't know was whether that was just a polite way to excuse herself from a non-Saint or whether she had some other reason for brushing him off.

He took his time walking from the FSS building down to the town center tram station where he caught an eastbound and took it out to the station at 800 East. From there it was a five-block walk south to the apartment, a relatively new structure with twenty-one units that had been rebuilt on the site of a defunct university, located as many had once been on the basis of local politics and concealed vote pandering. Roget didn't care for the desert landscaping of the space around the central bloc of units, much as he appreciated its necessity. His unit was at the south end on the ground level, and that made it the hottest one. For that reason, among many, he definitely wanted to complete his assignment before full summer descended upon St. George.

He thumbed the scanner plate, then opened the door, his implants alert to possible intruders or energy concentrations. Although he sensed neither, he entered cautiously, glancing around the living room and the nook kitchen through the archway at one end. Then he checked the bedroom and attached fresher/shower.

Only then did he use the antisnooper to scan himself for spyware. The device didn't discover any. He took out his compact personal monitor and used the publink to run a check on Marni Sorensen. Most subs and mals didn't have the equipment or the software to decrypt Fed burstlinks.

He was somewhat surprised to find out that she had a doctorate in biology. He had also suspected she might be related distantly to Bensen Sorensen, not surprising when something like three hundred of the ten thousand–odd residents of St. George happened to be Sorensens. Saints had a proclivity for Scandinavian names—Jensen, Bensen, Swensen, Hansen, and more than a few others.

He was wrong. She was Bensen Sorensen's much younger sister. *That* was interesting, and disconcerting. Even so, there wasn't much he could do. Not yet. His instructions were clear enough. He was not to begin anything invasive out of his line of work for at least two weeks, nor to do anything that might call undue attention to himself.

He snorted at the last. Just being an outsider in St. George called undue attention on himself.

He checked for spyware again, but his antisnoop insisted he and the apartment were clean.

After showering, he changed into clean underwear and a white shirt and dark slacks. Then he walked up to St. George Boulevard and toward a restaurant he'd noted earlier—the Caravansary. Although the sun had dropped behind the bluff to the west of town, the air remained warm.

No one was waiting when he entered the Caravansary, and a solid-looking woman of indeterminate age merely nodded and gestured for him to follow her. As he did, Roget could see that, like most of the eating establishments in St. George, it was modest in size. There were no more than twenty tables set in a single L-shaped room. The lighting was muted and amber, imparting a sandy glow to the white plaster walls, on which were mounted, at irregular intervals, odd pieces of tack and other items meant to suggest desert, ranging from a faded and battered maroon fez to half of what must have been a camel saddle.

"The menu is on the table. Thereza will be with you shortly, sir."

"Thank you."

Roget settled into the chair that allowed him the wider view of the patrons and who might be coming or going. A small slate was set in a holder on the polished wooden table with pseudo rattan legs. On the slate were chalked the night's entrees: Lamb Marrakesh, Chicken Arabic, Mixed Kebabs, Rice Sansouci, and Brigand Lamb. None of the names meant anything to Roget.

"Sir?" Thereza was twentyish, blond, and offered an infectious smile at odds with the severe flowing brown dress and its wrist-length sleeves. "I'm Thereza, and I'll be your server. Everything on tonight's menu is available."

"Is there anything else available?"

Thereza looked at him. "You're new here, aren't you?"

"Does it show that much?" Roget grinned.

"Not that much. Most people who come here are regulars, except in full winter, when we get a few tourists and pilgrims. Most of them stay closer to the Temple. You're the only new face I've seen in weeks."

"There must be more newcomers than that."

"Not many. You have to have a job, or money, or family to relocate here."

"And it helps if you're a Saint?"

"Not to get a job. The Feds watch that. But most who aren't Saints leave sooner or later. Usually sooner."

Those who couldn't leave, Roget had been briefed, often ended up in rehab for substance excess . . . or as suicides. Outsiders had a high rate of depression in St. George.

"I could get you some sliced lamb with rice and gravy. That's not on the menu."

"Of the items on the menu, which is the best?"

"There's no best. They're all good. The Marrakesh is very spicy. The kabobs are tender but subtle . . ."

That translated to bland, Roget suspected.

". . . the Arabic is sweet, sour, and mildly spicy. The Sansouci is hot, and filled with diced lamb and vegetables, and the Brigand Lamb is my favorite."

"I'll try that."

"It comes with brown rice and sauce."

"Sauce on the side, please."

"That you'll have."

"Red wine?"

"The Davian or the Banff are both good."

Roget had never had the second. "I'll have the Banff."

Once Thereza had left, Roget turned up his implants to see what he could hear.

". . . haven't seen him before . . ."

"He has to be new. She spent too much time with him . . . flirts with all the handsome ones . . ."

". . . can you blame her . . . after all that last year?"

Roget wondered exactly what the speakers were talking about, but that couple returned to their food. He kept listening.

". . . council's going to petition the Federation regional administrator to release 100 hectares from the land bank . . ."

"The Feds won't do it . . . say we have more than enough land for the population . . ."

"Of course they do, but they're using the amount of land to limit in-migration. That policy keeps families from gathering . . ."

"Unless they're born here . . ."

"Half the fellows end up leaving . . . can't get decent jobs here, and the Feds won't hire many locals . . . heard the E&W monitor's job went to an outsider . . . pay's good, but you think any of our boys'd be considered? Be the same thing when Sung retires . . ."

In the end, Roget found the food acceptable, Thereza diverting, and the conversations he overheard uninformative, except in confirming what he had learned in his briefings before he had left Helena.

The evening was almost cool as Roget walked slowly back to his apartment. He wasn't certain that he looked forward to the weekend.

9

17 MARIS 1811 P. D.

Roget studied Lyvia Rholyn. While sitting, she was only ten centimeters shorter than he was. She had short legs and a long torso that resulted in a frame of slightly above average height. For earth, anyway. He hadn't seen more than a handful of people so far on Haze . . . or Dubiety, he reminded himself. Her shoulders were slightly broader than the Federation norm, as well. Her hair was straight and light brown, remarkable only for the silky fineness that became obvious when she turned her head suddenly, and possibly one of the reasons why the woman cut it short, barely long enough to reach the middle of her neck. She also seemed unbothered by the high humidity or by his study of her.

"Where are we headed, specifically?" he finally asked, blotting his forehead.

"Eventually to the MEC—the Ministry of Education and Culture. That will be tomorrow. Immediately, I'm taking you to a guesthouse near the main square in Skeptos. I assume you'd like to clean up, get a good meal, and a good night's sleep. After you clean up, I thought we could take a short walk to dinner, depending on your preference in cuisine.

That would give you a feel for the city. Compared to Federation cities, I'm certain Skeptos is quite modest."

"You're not afraid I'll vanish?" He raised his eyebrows.

"You can try if you want. Your shipsuit isn't that outlandish, and you don't look that different from anyone here, although you're a trace taller than most men. But you have no link into anything, and the only way you can get food or anything else would be by some form of criminal activity. We don't use currency or coins. We do punish criminals, especially those who use weapons or threaten with them."

"More public service?"

"Some of it can be back-breaking hard labor. Since criminals have proved untrustworthy, they're also limited either personally or by locale."

"Prison camps?"

"Restricted hamlets is far more accurate."

Roget had doubts about the accuracy of that description. "So I should behave? Or else?"

"You can do as you wish. We're quite willing to provide you with much of the information you were dropped to obtain. At the proper time, you'll even be able to return to your ship with it."

Roget doubted that as well, even more strongly, but she was right about the necessity of his playing along. For the moment. "Tell me more about Dubiety."

"Not until you've seen more."

"You've said that before."

"Verbal descriptions of places you haven't seen create the possibility of false and lasting preconceptions. In your case especially, we'd prefer not to create anything like that."

"Is everyone here a philosopher?"

"Hardly. Just those who are good at what they do."

Shortly, the subtrans slowed, coming to a stop. According to Roget's internals, they'd been traveling just over six minutes. Lyvia did not move.

"Where are we?"

"Avespoir. It's where the peninsula joins the mainland."

"How far from here to Skeptos?"

She frowned, as if mentally calculating. "A little over four hundred klicks."

Roget resigned himself to a good hour or more on the subtrans, perhaps several, then shifted his weight on the seat as three men entered the car. The tallest man wore shimmering dark blue trousers that were too loose to be tights, and far narrower than anything Roget had ever seen, despite the knife-edge front creases. His shirt was long-sleeved, pale blue, and equally tight-fitting with broad pointed collars that spread over a looser white vest.

The man in the middle wore something akin to a standard Federation singlesuit, but the fabric changed from a deep black toward vermilion as Roget watched. So did the man's boots. The third man wore a collarless, black tight shirt under a tailored burgundy jacket, fastened closed by a set of silver links, rather than by buttons. His high-heeled platform shoes were silver.

The three took the set of four seats behind Roget and continued talking animatedly. He listened intently. For several minutes, he understood nothing except a few stray words. Then more words made sense, including a phrase that sounded like "range of plasma-bounded energy opacity."

The subtrans decelerated for a minute before halting. The doors opened, and the three men left the subtrans, but two women got on. Both wore singlesuits of the kind that shifted color, except the lower legs of the taller woman's also turned transparent. The two talked so quickly that Roget understood not a single word. At the next stop, no one got off, but a rush of people boarded. Nine or ten, Roget thought.

Lyvia moved to sit beside Roget, and an older couple took the seat across from them. Both were fit and trim, and their skin was firm, their hair color apparently a natural brown for the man and an equally natural sandy-blond for the woman. Their age was obvious only in the fineness of their features and in the experience in their eyes. Both wore singlesuits, his silvered brown, and hers a silvered blue.

The couple exchanged several words, then addressed Roget and Lyvia.

"A very long trip and hike," Lyvia replied.

That was what Roget thought she said. He just nodded and smiled politely.

A few minutes later, the subtrans slowed, then stopped. The doors opened, and Lyvia stood. So did Roget. He lifted his pack and slung it over one shoulder, then followed Lyvia from the subtrans onto a larger concourse close to a hundred meters in length and toward one of two tunnels leading further upward. Lyvia was moving to the left tunnel, and Roget stayed close behind her.

A slender man in a black jacket and trousers glanced hard at Roget as the agent hurried to stay with Lyvia.

Roget checked the time. The trip from Avespoir to Skeptos had taken twenty minutes, but nine minutes had been for stops. Add another six minutes for acceleration and deceleration, although those were estimates, and the subtrans had covered the four hundred klicks in the equivalent of roughly fourteen minutes—figuring three additional minutes for speed changes. Something was wrong with his figures or the numbers Lyvia had provided. Seventeen hundred klicks an hour? Underground?

Roget drew abreast of his guide just before they started up the tunnel ramp, a good ten meters wide. "Four hundred klicks from Avespoir to Skeptos?"

"It's more like four hundred fifteen, actually."

"And a klick here is still a thousand meters?"

"So far as I know, it's never been anything else."

She could have been lying. Roget doubted it, and that had serious implications. Then, he had no illusions. He was supposed to reach those conclusions.

After some twenty meters, the tunnel joined another one, close to filled with men and women heading upward. Despite the number of people leaving the subtrans station, no one crowded anyone else. Still, Roget could sense the man in black not all that far behind him.

The air was markedly cooler than it had been in the tunnel when they emerged, and did not hold the semiperfumed scent of the forest . . . but it was still humid.

"This is the central square of Skeptos," Lyvia said, stepping to one side of the walkway and stopping to offer a sweeping gesture that took in the open space, as well as the buildings surrounding it, although none looked to be more than thirty meters tall.

Roget let his eyes range over the square, merely an expanse of deep green grass surrounded by four stone walks twenty meters wide. They stood close to one corner, the southwestern one, he judged, hoping he wasn't too disoriented by the lack of a distinct sky and no sun for direction. A single stone monument rose from the center, a round column some thirty-three meters high. Atop the column was a sphere of shifting silver gray haze. Narrower walkways led from each corner of the square to the circular raised stone platform around the column.

"The column?" he asked. "Some sort of memorial?"

"A representation of Dubiety."

Roget glanced around the square again. Beyond the perimeter walks were low buildings on all sides, low especially in comparison to those of Taiyuan, between which were the stone pedestrian ways that radiated from the corners of the square and from the middle of each side of the square. There was no provision for vehicular traffic or for airlifters of any sort.

"We need to get you settled. This way." Lyvia turned south and strode quickly along the wide walk, past what looked to be an eating establishment on the right.

"A restaurant?" asked Roget.

"Dorinique. It's very fashionable now. It's also good . . . and expensive."

"The more expensive restaurants and other establishments are the ones closer to the square, then?"

"Or to other subtrans stations. Not always, but usually."

"Isn't there any transport that's more . . . local?"

"Local transit is below the regional subtrans. Those were the people coming from the other tunnels."

Local transit was lower than the regional links? That definitely seemed odd to Roget, but he didn't ask, not yet.

They passed several other restaurants and a boutique that looked to cater to women. Overhead, the silver gray of the sky began to dim, just a touch, although there were no clouds below the haze. Roget noted that from outside of the shops on the street level there were no exterior indications of what might be housed in the upper levels of the buildings, but then, that was true in Federation cities as well.

The next shop caught his eye. "Finessa? A man's boutique?"

"Why not? In most species, the males are the ones who strive the most to display." Lyvia smiled. "Be careful with preconceptions here. My cousin Khevan—my mother's cousin, really—is the marketing manager for the twenty-odd shops of the group. He's also a former cliff ranger."

"Cliff ranger?"

"They deal with poachers and collectors in the mountain wilds. Very stressful and physical occupation."

"I got the impression you didn't have that sort of unruliness."

"All societies do. How one handles it is a fair measure of a civilization." Lyvia kept walking.

Roget's feet were getting sore, but he said nothing.

Six very long blocks later, Lyvia stopped before a two-story structure some thirty meters wide. The stone archway framing the door was trapezoidal. "This is the guesthouse. You might want to fix it in your mind." She turned and pushed open the door.

Roget followed her into a small antechamber. The door on

the far side was closed. A single eye-level keypad was mounted on the wall. Above the keypad was a screen. She took the small tube attached to her belt and pointed it at the screen.

For a moment Roget sensed the faintest of energy emissions or emission reflections.

"The keypad is for the use of residents who are not linked or are unable to access services. You're one of them. The code is written down in your rooms."

The door hummed, then slid into a recess, revealing a small reception area where several chairs were grouped around a low table. The chairs were wooden armchairs but looked to have deep blue permanent cushioned seats similar to the yielding composite of the seats on the subtrans. All of the chairs were empty, and the top of the polished wooden table was bare as well.

"Are you coming?" asked Lyvia.

Roget responded by stepping through the door, which closed behind him. Except for the fleeting emissions involving the door screen, Roget had sensed no others, and still didn't, even inside the guesthouse.

Beyond the reception area was an open but railed circular ramp leading upward.

"You're on the second level." Lyvia started up.

Roget once more followed.

Halfway down the bare corridor off the ramp, illuminated by an amber light from the ceiling strips, similar to the sunlight filtering through the orbital shield arrays, she halted before the second door, again using the belt-linked tube to open it.

She stepped into a room some eight meters by four, with a window looking westward at another building. The view was clear, but Roget had observed the heavy tinting on the outside of all the windows they had passed and had no doubts he'd only see the tint from outside if he looked up from the wide walkway below. The chamber was sparsely furnished with a single couch flanked by two armchairs, all three pieces set around a low wooden table. On the left wall, less than a meter from the window that stretched almost from wall to wall, was a wooden desk set against the wall, with a chair of matching wood.

Lyvia walked to the desk, then turned. "There's a sitting room, a bed chamber and fresher, and a small kitchen with a standard replicator. Directions for the replicator and other systems and the code for your rooms and the guesthouse itself are here." She pointed to two sheets of paper on the desk. "The holojector controls are in the left desk drawer and the comm unit is in the right."

"Just like that?"

"I'm certain you can figure them out, and you'll learn more of what you came to find." She paused. "Oh . . . there are two singlesuits that should fit you in the bedroom closet."

"Should fit me?"

"They'll be close enough." She smiled. "You have internals for time. I'll meet you down in the reception area in forty minutes, and we'll go to dinner."

"Hours are the same here?"

"The hours are the same length, but there are only twenty-two." She walked back to the door, which opened for her, and left Roget standing in the middle of the sitting room as the door closed behind her.

He walked toward the door. It didn't open. He headed back to the desk and picked up the single sheet with the word "Codes" at the top. There was a single alphanumeric line: RogetW976A. Roget looked at it for a long moment. She'd never been out of his sight, and he'd never sensed any emissions or transmissions.

He took a deep breath of the heavy air. He smelled more of himself than anything else. Lyvia was definitely right. He needed a shower or the equivalent . . . and a good meal, preferably not from the replicator. He also needed to read all the directions.

But first he went to the keypad by the door and punched in the code.

The door opened. He nodded, stepping back into his temporary quarters and letting it close.

10

Roget slept late on Saturday. For him, late was eight, even in St. George.

After he roused himself and finally made his way to the kitchen side of the main room, he checked the menu on the replicator. Nothing looked all that appetizing, but he selected hot tea and eggs romanov, which fell within his caloric and energy budget. They turned out to be a very poor replication of the original concept, but he forced himself to eat most of them before sliding the remnants into the recycler. He wouldn't have them again, not from a cheap replicator with a limited ingredient basis.

Then he washed up and donned another white shirt and a fresh pair of dark slacks, since the heat limited anything to one wearing before cleaning, at least for him, and then headed out for a day of ostensible errands. He walked up 800 East to St. George Boulevard to catch the tram.

An older couple was already standing on the platform when Roget got there. The man was tanned and had brilliant white hair. The woman's hair was blond, as appeared to be the case with most Saint women. Roget couldn't help but wonder why the older men affected such silver white hair when standard hair treatments allowed people to retain their natural color throughout their lifetime at minimal cost.

"Good morning," he offered pleasantly.

"Morning," replied the man. "Must be new in town."

"Relatively," Roget admitted. "I'm Keir Roget."

"Mason Bradshaw . . . my wife, Leitha."

Leitha inclined her head politely.

"Pleasant weather we're having right now," said the man. "Enjoy it while you can." He turned as the tram pulled up to the platform, then stepped forward into the tram car once the doors slid open.

Leitha scuttled after him, every movement an apology.

Roget followed but took a seat farther back in the car.

Two young men hurried in after him and sat midway between him and the couple, but on the opposite side from Roget. For the short trip to the center station, none of the other four said more than a few words.

Once the tram came to a stop, Roget waited until the others exited, then took his time leaving. He paused at the top of the ramp leading down from the platform, looking southward at the single St. George branch of the Deseret First Bank, located on the southeast corner of Main and St. George Boulevard, just south across the boulevard from the electrotram central station platform. Like most financial institutions, DFB was global in scope. Unlike most that had originated out of the WestEuro culture, its clientele was largely based on sectarian affiliation or—in a place like St. George—local residence. Roget walked down the ramp, taking in the building, a two-story Navaho sandstone structure that, like much in St. George, was a replica of an earlier historic edifice, except for the solar panels. William Dane's office was there, but Roget doubted Dane would be in on a Saturday. Even so, given the screen-based banking services, no customer ever saw bank officers except by appointment. Roget didn't have a plausible reason for requesting one. Not yet, and his superiors would be less than pleased at any immediate obvious outreach.

Roget's first "errand" was to stop by the art gallery in

History Square. In some places, local art galleries revealed more about a place than weeks of talking to locals might. In others, they were merely commercial outlets. He waited at the boulevard for several electrocoupes and a lorry to pass before he crossed, then turned west and crossed Main Street in turn, grateful for the single patch of clouds that momentarily blocked the bright desert sun.

The redstone-walled gallery was on the northeast corner, and the door and windows were trimmed in a deep green. The sign on the dark-tinted front window read Glen-David's. Roget opened the door and stepped inside, finding it comparatively cooler than most other shops. For a moment, he wondered why. Then it struck him. Certain establishments, like art galleries and medical facilities, had higher energy limits before geometric pricing kicked in.

"Good morning, sir." A silver-haired and slight man stepped forward. He smiled politely, but not warmly. "Are you looking for anything special?"

"No. I haven't been here before. Someone at work suggested I should." Roget returned the smile.

"You should indeed. We do have images or prints of most of what's on display. We can size them for whatever space needs you have."

"I'll keep that in mind."

"Just let me know if you need anything, sir."

Roget nodded politely, then turned his attention to the various works.

The art displayed was in a wide variety of media—hololight images, multishifts, pastels, watercolors, oils, and even a charcoal portrait. Most if not all of the subject matter was definitely local or Saint-derived. *The Flight of Nephi* was a multishift, an imposition/transformation of images flowing from that of a boy in ancient Israel to a man amid the jungles of Central America. *The Destruction of the Temple* was an angular and stark oil rendition of the Salt Lake Temple in the brilliant blue light of a focused nucleonic disrupter beam just at the moment before it turned to ashes and dust. That temple had never been rebuilt, not with the crater, now an extension of the Great Salt Lake, where much of the center city had been. *The Long Walk* was a pastel that depicted people in old American pioneer garb pushing carts along a trail flanked with prairie grass and bushes. Roget didn't doubt its general accuracy, even if he didn't know the historical context. One seemed slightly out of place, a portrait of a younger man in some sort of flight gear with a hazy combat aircraft that Roget did not recognize in the background. The card beside it read, "Original Not for Sale, images available." The portrait was good technically, but not outstanding. There was no indication who it depicted.

Then, there were the landscapes—Kolob Canyon, the Patriarchs, the Gorge—and the portraits. Some of the names were familiar, but most were not.

A handful were terrible. Most were good. Some were better than that. Few of them appealed to Roget, and only one was good enough for him to consider buying even as an image. He wouldn't ever have considered it, had someone described it to him. It was simply an oil of a small black dachshund sitting on the cushion of a blue velvet sofa. On one side was a knitted afghan of maroon and cream, disarrayed almost as if the dachshund had been sleeping under it and had just darted from it. The sun poured across her—the dog had to be female, although there were no obvious clues—from an unseen side window, and she looked expectantly out of the canvas, as if her master or mistress had just entered the room. Yet the skill—or love—of the artist was such that the dachshund was alive. She almost leapt out of the ancient canvas.

"The sunshine dog," Roget murmured, in spite of himself. He turned away and took several steps. Then he stopped and returned to study the painting again. He couldn't say why, but just looking at the image made him feel better.

After several moments, he shook his head and walked

toward the front of the gallery where the proprietor sat behind a small console. "How much for an image of the sunshine dachshund?" Neither the original nor prints would do. Not as often as he would be shifted around.

For a moment, the proprietor frowned, as if he didn't understand why Roget would want the portrait of a small dog. "Full density image is 117 yuan, with tax."

"That's fine. I'll take it with me." Roget held his CredID before the scanner, then tendered his datacard. "Do you know the dog's name?"

"I'd guess it was Hildegarde. That's what she said the title was—Hildegarde in the Sunlight."

"Thank you." Roget thumbed the scanner to authenticate the charges, then took back the datacard. "It's a good painting."

"It's not that expensive. You could have the original for six hundred."

Roget shook his head. He wished he could, but he could take the image with him, and he couldn't take the original, and he'd end up having to give it away, and no one he knew would see what he saw.

After watching the proprietor load the image into his personal flash monitor, he smiled and left Glen-David's. Once outside in the warm sunlight, he walked uphill a block and turned west, stopping after about a hundred meters outside the picket fence surrounding the summer home of the Saints' great second Prophet and Revelator. It was closed, but he read the brass plate on the pedestal outside the gate. When he finished, he tried not to frown. According to the plate, the dwelling was the actual original and not a replica, as he had thought. When the first War of Confederation loomed, a dedicated group of Saints disassembled the dwelling and stored it in a hermetically sealed cave in the mountains to the northwest of St. George. When it was finally reconstructed, a nanitic covering was applied to the wood to prevent further deterioration.

Roget had his doubts about the explanation on the plate, for many reasons, but it wouldn't be wise to voice them. He turned and walked eastward in the direction of The Right Place. A slender blond woman was sweeping the sandstone slabs that constituted the walkway from the gate in the picket fence. Her back was to him as she swept around a redstone sculpture of a heavyset bearded man who wore a frontier-style coat. Roget assessed the sculpture as moderately good, but not outstanding.

The woman faced the front porch with its deep overhanging eaves and the low sandstone wall on each side of the stone steps up to the porch. Somehow, she looked familiar.

As he walked nearer, he recognized Marni Sorensen. There was no reason she shouldn't be sweeping the walk to the guesthouse of her brother, but it bothered him.

The front door opened. Another blonde stood there. "Marni! It's Tyler."

Marni did not look in Roget's direction, but hurried inside, barely stopping to lean the broom against the stone pillar on the left side at the top of the porch steps. The door closed with a *thunk* clearly audible to Roget.

Were energy/comm costs so high that the locals didn't even use direct personal links? Or were they privacy obsessed the way the survies were? Or was beautiful Marni part of the reason why he was in St. George?

While he took his time, Roget kept walking, past The Right Place and then downhill and back toward Main Street and the electrotram station. He waited in the shade, his eyes straying to the white of the old Temple and the western edge of the Genealogy Center, most of which had to be underground, until he could take the tram west to Bluff Street. From the station there he made his way south until he arrived at DeseretData, the only EES the directory listed in St. George. That was doubtless correct. Most people got their entertainment through direct-links, but there were always a few specialty and local shops for the material that didn't have enough of a customer base to pay net access charges or for material that didn't meet Federation standards, either technically or in terms of its content. Not that all that much content was banned, mainly prurient material aimed at underage children and direct or indirect religious or secular incitements to armed revolt, but there were always a few individuals who seemed to want to press the limits, no matter how loose they might be.

Even in fall, the day was warm, and Roget was glad to step inside the shop, although it wasn't that much cooler.

"Are you looking for anything in particular?" asked the fresh-faced young man seated on a high-backed stool behind the short and narrow counter just beside the door.

"Do you have sloads about the history of the area?"

"If you take the end screen and key in 'color country,' that will show most of what we have that's not on the FedNet."

"Thank you." Roget walked to the end wall console and flat screen and entered the keywords. He expected perhaps twenty sloads, all of them short. There were close to a thousand, some dating back three hundred years, another reminder that he was dealing with a culture that not only respected its history, but wallowed in it. On top of that, few of the sloads were short. It took him over an hour to select ten that he hoped would prove helpful—not about the history, which he knew, but about the slants and views of the local institutions that had scripted and produced them.

When he walked back to the front counter, it took a minute for the young man to look up from the screen in front of him. "Oh . . . yes?"

"You related to Brendan?"

"No, sir. Not really. Brother Smith is a friend of my parents. Did you find anything?"

"I left ten of them on the queue."

"Let me run the charges." After a moment, the clerk nodded. "If you want all ten sloads, it will be three hundred."

"I'll take them." Roget let the scanner take the CredID

codes, then added his thumbprint before handing over his flash monitor.

The clerk inserted it in the loader, then handed it back. "There you go, sir."

"Thank you."

On his way back from DeseretData, Roget stopped by the supply store—Smith's—where he picked up a replicator supply pak. He chose the full-range version, expensive as it was. The apartment replicator needed all the assistance it could get. He also picked up a few local apricots . . . three—at ten yuan each.

By the time he returned to his apartment, he had already decided which sload he'd scan first—*From Deseret to Federation District*. It purported to be a history of the area, produced almost a century ago. The production company was Deseret Documentary. The others were more recent, and all had been done in the local district by Saints.

Then he'd have to see exactly what steps he'd take next.

11

17 MARIS 1811 P. D.

Roget did enjoy the shower, although he hurried through it, and some of the toiletries supplied were not what he would have picked. As Lyvia had indicated, there were indeed two singlesuits, one in tasteful deep gray and one in dark green, as well as two pairs of underwear and socks as well, plus what looked to be short pajamas. Although his systems could detect no overt snoops built into the clothing, he had no doubts that they contained nano-level locators, and probably a great deal more.

More of concern was that the singlesuits fit so well that they seemed tailored to him personally. How could they have been? He hadn't detected any radiation or any active energy fields around him. Nor had he detected any direct comm links from Lyvia, and he hadn't been around any Dubietans except in the last five hours or so. All the little details of those hours were providing him with a picture whose outline he didn't like at all, and he'd scarcely begun to look at Skeptos and Dubiety.

He even half-wondered if Lyvia were some sort of private operator who'd picked him up on her own. After a moment, he dismissed that . . . mostly. She spoke Federation, and no one else seemed to. She'd known where his dropboat had landed, even something about his angle of descent through the orbital shields, and she'd addressed him immediately in Federation. If she could muster those kinds of resources as an individual . . . he had even bigger problems than he'd thought. And so did the Federation.

He left his temporary quarters with five minutes to spare, walking down the utilitarian upper hallway wearing the deep gray singlesuit and carrying inside it the small stunner. Besides the stunner, his boots were the only item of his own that he wore, but he hadn't cared for the almost slipperlike slip-ons that had been left in the closet of the bedroom. When he started down the circular ramp to the reception area, he saw that Lyvia had also changed. She wore a rich green and feminine one-piece suit, with a dark gray vest and dress boots that matched his singlesuit.

She waited until he reached the bottom of the ramp before speaking. "You like solid footware, I see."

"I always have."

"I can understand that. You look good in a dressy singlesuit." Both her mouth and her gray eyes smiled.

"Thank you. So do you." Roget inclined his head. "How do the locators in the singlesuit work?"

"I have no idea," she replied, "except that they're passive. No one but me knows where you are right now."

"That could change in a moment."

"It could. That's up to you." She paused. "What are you in the mood to have for dinner?"

"Something good, not excessively spicy, nor so subtle as to be boringly bland, and preferably something that you'd also enjoy. In short, I'm in your hands . . . as I've been all day." Roget kept his voice light and ironic.

Lyvia laughed. "You do have a sense of humor." She turned. "We'll go expensive."

Roget followed her out through the antechamber and into an evening under a sky that remained ever so faintly amber. Already he missed seeing stars in the heavens.

"I've confirmed reservations at Dorinique."

"That was on the central square, wasn't it?"

"Yes. We'll have a window table. That way you can watch the square."

Watching Lyvia was likely to be more interesting and practical, but there was no point in saying so. Roget slipped to her left and matched her steps, much less hurried than earlier.

The walkways were slightly more crowded than before, but Roget saw more couples, and their pace seemed more leisurely. The air was slightly cooler and comfortably humid, but barely so.

"Things are slower in the evening."

"They should be, don't you think?"

Roget hadn't thought about that. Taiyuan was far faster, Fort Greeley far more utilitarian and worn down, and St. George and Colorado Springs far slower, but Skeptos was a planetary capital. "Are there continental or regional capitals on Dubiety?"

"There are regional administrative centers, but we're not a republic with regional governments. That's an inefficiency that's no longer necessary."

No longer necessary?

There was something about the way the walkways and buildings were lit, but they had walked almost a full block before Roget realized exactly what it was. The light from the buildings or the almost invisible arching street lights didn't scatter. Nor did the pavement reflect it in the slightest. Yet the walkways were well-illuminated in a fashion that afforded no shadows for lurkers or those up to little good.

As they continued walking, Roget could hear a violin playing, cheerfully, rather than sounding lonely. He glanced toward the center of the square where a young woman stood on the low stone platform below the monument. He didn't see any form of amplifier or projector. "Buskers, yet?"

"No. Musicians apply for the privilege, and they're paid. If enough citizens register approval, they get a bonus. Sometimes it's considerable."

"What if people don't approve?"

"No one is allowed to play who isn't technically proficient."

"That sounds rather . . . restrictive," suggested Roget.

"We don't cater to unrestricted public taste. That panders to the lowest common denominator, and the more it's catered to, the lower it goes."

"Elitism, yet. What about popularity?"

"That's fine, but only when it's based on excellence."

"Great elitism, then," Roget said lightly.

"There's a great deal to be said for elitism, so long as it's only a barrier to incompetence and not to ability."

"An interesting way of putting it."

"What other way is there to put it?" Lyvia turned toward the door, which opened from both sides.

They walked inside, and the door closed.

A woman in a singlesuit with angled alternating stripes of white and black stood waiting. She wore a white sleeveless vest.

"Rholyn, two," Lyvia said.

"By the window, yes?"

Roget had to strain to make out even those simple words.

"Please. This is my friend's first trip to Skeptos."

"This way." The hostess turned and walked around a head-high partition. Behind it was a row of tables for two set against the window.

As Roget followed, his eyes and ears were caught by the four musicians playing on a small circular stage in the middle of the restaurant. He recognized the large keyboard instrument as an ancient acoustical piano—except it clearly wasn't ancient—while a tall woman played some sort of reed instrument. The two others played strings, a violin and a cello, he thought.

Roget took the seat facing the door, from where he could observe the comings and goings of patrons, once they stepped past the partition, and both the square and the restaurant. His eyes drifted back to the instrumentalists.

"You look surprised," observed Lyvia.

"Acoustical instruments? With all your technology?"

"Technology is a focused application. It doesn't do particularly well with the best forms of music, especially in dealing with overtones, because they're not always consistent, and they're not meant to be."

Rather than reply, Roget studied the table. The cloth covering it was pale green, but looked to be synthetic, as was the upholstery on the comfortable and supportive chairs. The cutlery, while curved slightly in a fashion he had not seen, was recognizably human. Each setting had a darker green cloth napkin, and a crystal tumbler and a matching goblet. To the left of the setting was a single shimmering sheet with writing on it—a menu.

The muted sounds of conversation and the continuing music seemed familiar, and yet unfamiliar, because Roget still understood few words and did not recognize any of the music. He was thankful that it was melodic and not driving.

Lyvia said nothing.

"You said that I was a friend," Roget finally spoke. "I'm glad you think of me in friendly terms."

"You haven't proved otherwise. I hope you don't."

"Courtesy as a conversion tool?"

"You're suggesting that Dubiety is an enemy of the Federation. Why? Have we done anything to harm you or the Federation? Besides leave the Federation behind more than a thousand years ago?"

Gently spoken as her words were, they brought Roget up sharply. "Are you? An enemy?"

"Have we sought you out? Attacked you? Sent agents down from warships to spy on your planets?"

"I wouldn't know," admitted Roget.

"We haven't, but I can't prove a negative." She smiled and picked up the menu. "We should order."

"Are you paying for this?"

"I'll be reimbursed. Have what you like. I imagine it's been some time since you had a truly fine dinner."

"That's true enough." He couldn't even remember when that might have been. He picked up the menu. He squinted, trying to decipher the words before he realized, belatedly, that the words were printed in old American script. While some of the spellings were unfamiliar, he could make out most of the fare descriptions. The entire menu was simple, listing four appetizers, three salads, two soups, and five entrees.

A young man appeared tableside, wearing the same type of striped singlesuit as the hostess had. "What would you like to drink?"

Roget actually understood the antique clipped words.

"I'll have an Espoiran red," Lyvia said.

"A pale lager, if you have it," Roget offered.

"Lager? Oh . . . pilsner. We have Cooran or Sanduk."

"The lighter one."

"Cooran." The server inclined his head. "Thank you." Then he was on his way toward the rear.

"You'll pick up the word patterns before long," said Lyvia.

"How did you learn Federation Stenglish?"

"I studied it, of course. It's broadcast all over the Galaxy."

Roget saw the server returning with a tray on which were a goblet and a chilled glass that looked like a cross between a tumbler and an overlarge champagne flute.

"Here you are, sera and ser."

"Thank you," replied Roget.

"Might I take your order?"

Roget ordered the Chicken Emorai, whatever that was, and a green salad with patacio nuts and a crumbled cheese. He thought Lyvia ordered some sort of beef in pastry.

Lyvia lifted her goblet. "To your enjoyment of dinner."

Roget inclined his head. "And to yours."

Her goblet held a pinkish vintage. Roget looked at it questioningly. "Red?"

"It tastes red, but there are some side effects of the shields, and we don't do artificial colorants in anything edible."

"How do the orbital shields work?"

"They deflect some solar radiation, transmit the majority, and reradiate the remainder. I don't know the physics behind their operation."

"Why are they there?"

"Dubiety is really too close to the sun. It was more like Venus until the terraforming."

"Ice asteroid and comet bombardment?"

"Among other techniques."

"Such as?" pressed Roget.

"High atmospheric bioengineering, nanitic heat dispersion . . . I don't know all of them."

"Why not just seek out a planet in a habitable zone?"

"At the time, that wasn't feasible."

"Why not?"

"There were traceability issues."

"From the Federation?"

"Who else?" She smiled wryly.

"We still found you."

"Much, much later, and that makes a difference."

"What sort of difference?"

A smile was the only answer he got.

"How long have the orbital shields been there?"

"Exactly . . ." she shrugged. "Today's date is 17 Maris 1811 P. D. That's 1,811 years since the first landing. The basic terraforming took something like two-thousand real-time years before that."

"Two thousand years before the landing eighteen hundred years ago, when you left the Federation less than two thousand years ago?"

"Give or take a hundred years."

Roget laughed. "That's quite a story."

"Time isn't what you think it is," Lyvia said mildly, stopping to take a sip of the pinkish wine.

There were two possibilities. Lyvia was lying. Or she was telling the truth. Roget didn't like either one. He didn't have any sense that she was lying. In fact, she seemed to be almost taunting him with the truth, but that could be because her lies were so outrageous. If she did happen to be telling the truth . . . then the Thomists possessed technology that posed an incredible threat to the Federation. But that raised yet another question—why hadn't they used it?

No human culture had ever failed to use superior force against a former enemy, if only as a coercive tool. But did the Dubietan technology provide enough of an edge against the obviously numerically greater Federation? When did numbers outweigh technology . . . or vice versa?

The entire restaurant seemed to swirl around Roget for a moment, but he knew that was just his own mind trying to deal with the surreality of the situation in which he found himself. He'd been dropped onto an unknown planet beneath a series of shields that were technically impossible, and he was having dinner in a fine restaurant, and he'd just been told that the culture had been founded some four thousand years before by refugees who had left the Federation barely less than two thousand years before.

The other possibility was that he was unconscious, and some alien intelligence was playing with his mind to such a degree that he just thought he was having dinner. That didn't make him feel any better because he was fully aware of the tastes, the smells, and the sounds. While Lyvia Rholyn was attractive to the eye and had a nice figure, she wasn't exactly his type. Any alien intelligence that could simulate all that and orbit a shield system in three layers was potentially deadly.

But . . . if it were that deadly . . . why bother to play with his mind at all?

He took a swallow of the Cooran.

The server reappeared with his salad and a thick cream-like soup for Lyvia.

Roget glanced out the window toward the square. A couple was walking toward them, and the woman had a leash in her hand. On the end of the leash was a small dog. Roget smiled. "That's the first dog I've seen."

"We had one when I was growing up."

Roget watched as the dog—seemingly a long-haired red dachshund, not short-haired and black and tan like Hildegarde or Muffin—made his way past Dorinique, almost strutting as he did. "Are pets less common?"

"Less common than what or where?" Lyvia raised her eyebrows.

Roget shrugged. "That's the only one I've seen." He took a bite of the salad, with a dark greenery that didn't taste that unfamiliar, for all its deep coloration. The nut fragments were good, but not a taste he recalled, and the cheese crumbles were similar to, but more tangy than, a blue cheese or gorgonzola.

Lyvia took several spoonfuls of her soup before replying. "They're expensive to license, and having one without a license can be a criminal offense."

"For a pet?"

"Animal companions require care, attention, and feeding. They can't speak for themselves, and that requires protection."

"I suppose you protect the wild animals as well."

"From people."

"What about food animals?"

"We don't have any, except for some chickens. All nonreplicated meat is tissue-cloned. It's less wasteful that way, and it's easier to balance the ecology."

"Oh . . ." The Federation had simply made natural meat horribly expensive. Most restaurants used high-level replicated protein.

"It also tastes better if it's cloned and grown properly, and uses less energy than replicator technology."

"I wouldn't think that energy was a problem for you."

For just an instant, a hint of surprise appeared in Lyvia's gray eyes. "Energy supply isn't the problem. Excessive use is. It disrupts the ecology and the climate. Any form of energy use creates heat somewhere along the line. Enough usage . . ." She shrugged.

Abruptly, Roget understood. "Dubiety's closeness to the sun."

"Exactly."

There was something there . . . but Roget couldn't quite grasp what it might be.

"How is your salad?"

"Quite good. Is it vat grown, too?"

"I wouldn't know. Some is free grown, and some is hydroponic. There are many mixed systems on Dubiety."

"As well as on other Thomist worlds?"

"You are persistent, you know?"

"That's what I'm here for."

"Leave those kinds of questions for tomorrow . . . if you can."

In the end, while he enjoyed the food and the company, he learned little more during the rest of dinner, except about the general geography and layout of Skeptos.

By the time Roget finished a small lemon tart, he was doing his best to stifle yawns and look attentive. Lyvia paid for the meal and ushered him back to the guesthouse.

Once inside, she stopped at the reception area. "I'll pick you up for breakfast here at seven o'clock local. In case you oversleep, I'll have the comm buzz you a half hour before. After you eat, we'll head over to the MEC. You can bring the stunner you're carrying if it will make you feel better."

"You don't miss much."

"The idea is not to miss anything, Keir."

Roget smiled. That he understood, but he was so tired that he'd definitely missed more than he should have. "I'll see you in the morning."

She nodded, then turned and left.

Roget started up the ramp. Although he heard a door close on the second level, by the time he was at the top, the corridor was empty. He thought he could detect a faint fragrance, but that might have been his imagination. He paused. As he thought about it, Lyvia hadn't worn any noticeable fragrance or perfume, but he'd caught whiffs of scent from other women he'd passed. So it wasn't his sense of smell.

When he stopped outside his quarters, he had to think for a moment to recall his code before entering it. The door opened and he stepped inside, letting it close behind him. He studied the living area. Nothing looked any different. He walked into the bedchamber. The closet door was open. While they'd eaten, Roget's pale blue singlesuit and underclothes had been cleaned and hung in the closet, or folded and put on the open shelves on the right side, the one nearest the fresher. They also now held locators. Of that, he had no doubts.

He used his implants to trigger the camouflage, and the suit blended with the back of the closet. The power readings registered full. He deactivated the camouflage.

After shaking his head, not sure he understood what all that meant, he stood there for a long moment. There wasn't any doubt that the Federation had set him up, somehow, but for what? How could they not have known a high-tech society existed beneath the Haze? Was he just a probe to get a reaction? Or an excuse—when he didn't return—for military action against Dubiety?

All he could do was play along and see what developed. He walked back to the living area and the corner desk, retrieving the holojector controls and then picking up the sheet of directions. He had to puzzle out the letters, but those were mostly understandable, based on old American, and that wasn't all that different from Federation Stenglish.

So far as he could tell, the system offered access to something like a hundred fixed program screens, plus an ordering option that he couldn't use because he didn't have a line of credit or system access or whatever. He began to experiment but finally lowered the controls in frustration.

For the most part, the characters in any of the dramas or comedies, or whatever they were, talked too fast for him to follow what they said. The news presentations were somewhat better, but he lacked most of the local referents for what he did understand to make much sense. One "popular" science program dealt with astronomy—and was far more clear . . . but told him little. At first. Except that several of the images were of the skies as they would have been seen from Dubiety—and they were crystal clear. Were they a virtual creation, or did their technology allow them to see in or around or through the orbital shields?

The holo projection was crisper than anything he'd seen, even in Taiyuan. Yet his implants registered nothing. Could

Lyvia have somehow disabled them? On an impulse, he walked into the projected image, and his detectors registered immediately. When he stepped out of the image, he could sense nothing.

How did they do it?

He collapsed the image and just sat down in the desk chair. Maybe if he got some sleep, things would make more sense in the morning. Maybe . . .

12

23 LIANYU 6744 F. E.

Roget's second week at the FSS continued just like the first had ended, except that the anomalies he investigated were all different—with one exception. The FSS system kept flagging the Virgin River anomaly. Roget had run a profile on the river readings going back a hundred years, and the thermal spike was well out of normal ranges. He'd taken more samples, and by Wednesday night he had located the general area of infusion as being close to where a dry rocky wash—Middleton wash—met the Virgin River.

According to the maps and history, the area to the north of Middleton wash had once been an intensely commercial shopping area. It had been partly slagged in the wars, then reclaimed and returned to something resembling the original topography, with several permitted low-impact exceptions. After more than a millennium, even in the desert climate, there were no overt signs of its ancient past. The wash itself had been dry on Wednesday. Roget still wondered if something buried beneath all that stone had come to life, if the natural geothermal systems had created a subterranean pathway down the wash, or if some other factor were involved. He couldn't help but wonder if it had anything to do with the death of his predecessor—whose body had been found on the other side of the Virgin River from the wash on the way to one of the cinder cones left from a prehistoric volcanic area.

Then, that could be coincidence, much as Roget didn't like to believe in or accept coincidences.

Thursday morning, Roget had his listing and schedule waiting for Sung.

The head monitor settled at the main screen, then spent almost ten minutes scanning various subscreens before turning his attention to Roget's proposed monitoring schedule. He finally turned. "Middleton wash? There's nothing there."

"There's nothing we can see, but that's where the thermal spike enters the river. I'd like to pin this down so that we can either find a human cause or identify it as natural with hard proof. I'm spending a lot of time checking that anomaly, and I don't want to still be doing it come summer."

Sung laughed. "All that exercise is good for you."

"It probably is. I just don't want it to be a waste of time."

"There's always something." The head monitor shook his head. "Go ahead. It can't hurt, and you're not swamped now."

"Thank you." Roget rose from his small console, turned, eased the bicycle away from the wall, and wheeled it toward the door. He'd given up on trying to check it in and out of supply and had signed it out for a month, leaving it in the corner of the office overnight.

The corridor outside was empty, although he half expected to run into Marni Sorensen, as he had several times over the last week. But then, that had usually been in the late afternoon when he'd just returned to the FSS building at the end of a long day, and they had never exchanged more than quick pleasantries.

Once past the building security gates and outside, he rode down to the main tram station where he waited a good fifteen minutes before the next tram arrived. After taking the tram out so far as the Red Hills station, the last stop before the final Green Springs station, Roget carried the bicycle from the tram and then unfolded it on the platform. He was the only one who got off. That was scarcely surprising since there were only a few houses on the east side of Red Cliffs Drive, and they were tiny and shabby, with the stucco more pink, from the years of bombardment by red sand, than white.

As was usual, the sky was clear, and the sun beat down on Roget as he pedaled less than a hundred meters northeast of the station. Once there, he discovered a narrow walking or biking trail running along the north side of the wash. He rode only a few meters down the trail before he dismounted and laid the bicycle at the side, then slowly clambered down over and between sandstone boulders and chunks of black lava. While he knew there were extensive lava beds in the area, the lava looked out of place along the wash, weathered as it appeared.

When he reached the bottom he surveyed the area, but all he saw was rock and red sand. He scuffed the sand with his boot heel, digging a small depression. He struck rock after some ten centimeters, and all the sand was dry. He walked downhill for another ten or fifteen meters and tried again, with the same result.

Climbing back uphill left him even hotter and sweatier, even with the cool-weave fabric of the white monitor's uniform. Before he raised the bike to resume riding, he blotted his forehead, then studied the north side of the wash. The red stone and sand looked as desolate as anywhere around and outside St. George proper.

After taking a swallow from his water bottle, he pedaled slowly and carefully down the trail for half a klick until he came to a side path leading uphill. He stopped. Less than fifty meters uphill on the winding path was a waist-high stone wall and an iron gate. Roget left the bicycle beside the trail and hiked up the path. As he neared the gate, he could see a long and low sandstone building farther uphill. The south-facing wall that extended from each side of the gate was of finished and polished black lava, so smooth that it looked like onyx, but the edges between the polished front and the mortar were rough and lavalike.

An iron sign on the gate read: DELBERT PARSENS, SCULPTOR. On the top of the posts on each side of the gate were figures sculpted out of hard red sandstone. On the left was a woman in a long flowing dress with an antique apron and wide collars, cradling an infant. On the right was a man in a waistcoat and trousers with his sleeves rolled up. The sculptures were so similar to the one on the stone pedestal outside The Right Place that Roget knew the same sculptor had to have done all three. Presumably, that was Parsens.

He opened the gate and stepped through the wall, then closed it behind him. He followed the path uphill. Even before he reached the building, Roget could hear the sound of a hammer and chisel echoing through the warm morning air. The path circled eastward around the low structure whose eaves were barely above Roget's head. The lower level looked to have been quarried out of the solid stone. At the east end of the building, at the top of three stone steps, he came to a doorway. A wooden sign in a niche cut out of the redstone wall to the left of the door announced: STUDIO OPEN. PLEASE COME IN.

Roget lifted the small sign and turned it over. The reverse read: STUDIO CLOSED. He replaced the sign as it had been. Then he looked to the north side of the building. A narrow road angled back toward Red Cliffs Drive.

The door squeaked as Roget pushed it open, but the sounds of hammer and chisel did not slow or stop. Once inside, he stood on a wide landing. In front of him was a ramp down to the long studio. A wiry blond man, stripped to the waist, looked up from the block of redstone, then lowered the hammer and chisel and waited.

Roget walked down the ramp.

"Do you want to commission something, or are you just looking?"

"Looking, I'm afraid. I didn't know your studio was even here."

"Even most folks in St. George don't know that, and my great uncle built it close to a hundred years ago." The clean-shaven sculptor's voice was soft. His blue eyes did not quite meet Roget's.

"I saw one of your statues somewhere . . . near the Prophet's house. At least, it looked like the ones on the gateposts."

"You must have seen the one outside The Right Place."

"You took this over from your great uncle?"

"His daughter Felicia. Been working here for twenty years or so since then."

"Where do you get the stone? Isn't it hard to come by?" Roget knew only a few quarries were permitted anywhere.

"I can cut stone on the east end of the property, and there's another quarry toward Silver Reef. Neither's the best, but I've got a limited permit here, and the Silver Reef quarry is one of the few permitted outside the protected and pro-scribed areas. I don't need many huge blanks. Most of the large blocks I do are for repairs and replacements, and those don't come along all that often these days. Once in a while I do a large sculpture, but mostly folks want smaller pieces."

"You do a fair number of . . . religious works." That was a calculated guess on Roget's part. "Are those mainly for local people?"

"Not necessarily local, but Saint-inspired," admitted Parsens.

"You were fortunate to be able to inherit this. I take it that you've made some improvements." Roget gestured at the heavily tinted windows on the south side of the studio.

"I've made some, but those windows were already here. Felicia was the one who really made the improvements." Parsens paused. "Could I interest you in one of the smaller pieces?" He gestured toward a glass-fronted case on the west end of the studio.

"You could interest me," Roget said, "but monitors get transferred a lot, and we don't get that big a weight allowance in moving. I tend to pick up projection print art. I did want to see your work, though." He nodded toward the roughed-out form beside the sculptor. "Might I ask?"

"It's a replica of an old work—John D. Lee. He was a rather controversial Saint during the founding period. Not sure I would have chosen it, but," Parsens shrugged, "when it's a good commission, you do your best."

Roget could sense a certain unease, but not whether that was because of the subject of the commission or for other reasons. He didn't want to press. "I won't keep you, but I appreciate your time." He nodded, then turned and headed back up the stone ramp to the door.

As he walked back around to the path down to the wash trail, he studied the building closely. Although it wasn't obvious, there was a lower level, not under the studio, but under the western side. Yet it would have made more sense to have the lower level on the east where, with just a little work, obtaining natural light would have been easier.

Roget returned to the trail and his bicycle where he mounted and pedaled down along the wash, investigating the bottom at four other locations. All he found was dry sand and drier hard red sandstone. When he reached the Virgin River and the parkway, he took two measurements—one upstream of where Middleton wash joined the river, and one fifty meters downstream.

Then he went on to his other monitoring assignments. Again, he didn't get back to the FSS until after five. He wheeled the bike through the security gate and down the corridor to the office. He had to unlock the office and set the bicycle in a corner before he could unlock the system and upload his readings for the day.

The residential and commercial monitoring results were

the usual mixture of false positives, probable mechanical failures, and carelessness. The thermal spike from the reading taken just downstream of Middleton wash was the most pronounced of any of the river readings taken over the past two weeks. The system offered a 64 percent probability that a geothermal plume of heated water was entering from beneath the stream bed, with a likely temperature of some thirty degrees, well above the river's twenty-degree norm.

A low-grade geothermal plume made perfect sense, since St. George was in fact situated in a geothermal basin. What bothered Roget was the lack of water anywhere else in the wash, and the fact that the plume appeared in midstream. Usually nature wasn't that tidy.

There wasn't anything that he could do about it, not yet. He'd talk it over with Sung in the morning. Even so, he had the feeling that Parsens had something to do with the situation. He finished up, including copying the data back to his own flash storage, then locked down the system.

A minute or so before quarter to six, he stepped out into the corridor . . . just in time to encounter Marni Sorensen again. The encounters couldn't have been coincidental.

"Good afternoon, Marni," said Roget.

"You did remember my name." Her smile was disarming.

"How could I forget when we keep meeting this way?"

"Oh . . . and do you have another way in mind?"

"We could try lunch some day . . . like tomorrow."

"You're never here."

"That's because I have no reason to be. If you give me a reason, I certainly will." He paused. "Lunch tomorrow?"

"I could do that."

"I'll meet you here."

She smiled. "I'll see you then, Keir." She stepped back into the office from which she had come. The door closed.

Roget nodded, then walked down the corridor to the security gate. She'd wanted him to initiate something. The question was why, and he was afraid he knew, even if he couldn't prove it.

After he reached the apartment, he used his other personal monitor to run a search on Delbert Parsens. The results showed nothing out of the ordinary. That was what Roget had expected.

Then, to take his mind off Parsens and Marni, he transferred a copy of *Hildegarde in the Sunlight* to the image projector. It took almost a quarter hour before he decided on the right location and dimensions. He opted for a life-size image of Hildegarde. He knew it was an illusion, but the sunlight from the image seemed to spill into the apartment, and Hildegarde was better company than most as he ate his replicated dinner.

13

18 MARIS 1811 P. D.

Breakfast was in a small bistro around the corner from the guesthouse. Roget didn't see the name anywhere, and it wasn't on the menu. He wore the gray singlesuit, again with his heavy boots. He had French toast, strips of crispy bacon, orange slices, and a flavorful hot tea that any Sinese would have envied. Lyvia gave him a range of information about what was located where in Skeptos and little else. She wore a pale cranberry singlesuit with a deep gray sleeveless vest, one without the flashing light-threads, Roget noted. The faintest hint of a light fragrance drifted about her, but the scent was so light and fleeting that he'd never have noticed had he not been trying to detect it.

When they stepped out of the bistro, Roget was aware

that the amber light filtering through the orbital shields seemed noticeably brighter than it had on previous days. "Variable star? Or variable shield translucency, for seasonal purposes?"

"Some of both," replied Lyvia.

"Did the original settlers know that?"

"They built the shield system with that in mind, I understand."

That was so like most of her answers, never quite complete or directly responding to his inquiries. Was that his problem in framing questions, her avoiding the thrust of his inquiries, or a little of both?

"We're headed back toward the central square. MEC is north of there," Lyvia said. "Just a few blocks."

As they walked northward, Roget could see a steady flow of pedestrians fanning out from the central square ahead of them. All sorts of differing clothes styles were present, from ancient ankle length skirts and long-sleeved blouses for women to shorts and formfitting shirts that left very little to the imagination. The same range was present on men, although Roget didn't see any togas or Mandarin-style robes, and more men seemed to opt for singlesuits, although the variety of colors and cuts, not to mention the light-threads, was considerable.

From the southwest corner of the square, Lyvia walked briskly past Dorinique.

"I see they're not open," said Roget.

"Just from noon to midnight. That's always bothered my cousin Clarya. She works nights, and she doesn't like starting out with a heavy meal. With her schedule, most days that's her only option if she wants to eat there. Besides, she says, who wants to spoil such exquisite—and expensive— fare with the thought of work to follow?"

Roget laughed. He could understand that.

When they reached the northwest corner of the square, Lyvia turned eastward until she reached the midpoint of the square. There she gestured to her left at the wide walkway north.

Roget had to take three quick steps to catch her, but she did not say more until they reached the end of the block.

"The building on the right holds the Ministry of Transportation, and the one on the left is the Ministry of Finance."

"Is your space force under transportation?" asked Roget.

"Your question makes assumptions that I can't really address."

"Can't or won't?"

"Does it really matter?"

"Not really," Roget admitted, keeping his voice cheerful, although he couldn't help but feel frustrated. He was in the middle of the capital city of a planet, and for all the time he'd spent with Lyvia, he felt he didn't know all that much more than he had a day earlier. That wasn't entirely true, but it was definitely the way he felt.

As they neared the next corner where the walkways intersected, Lyvia said, "The one on the left is the Ministry of Education and Culture."

The structure was a full five stories, a story above the others around it. "What other ministries are in buildings that tall?" asked Roget.

"The Ministry of Science has about as much space, and so does the Ministry of Environment."

"How many ministries are there?"

"That's it. We don't need any more. Some people think that five is five too many. Probably most do, but that's just my opinion." Lyvia headed for the main entrance on the south side, pushed open the glass door, and walked into the entry hall. There were no guards—just a series of shimmering consoles as tall as a person, each set a good yard from the adjoining one. She stopped before the one on the right end.

"Lyvia Rholyn and Keir Roget. We have an appointment at eight thirty."

"Please enter your confirmation code."

Roget didn't see Lyvia do anything, but the console replied, "Please take ramp three to the third level. The door there will respond to your code. No other door will."

Roget accompanied Lyvia as she walked past the console toward the wall that held five doorways, each with a silver number above the stone square stone arch that held a shining steel door. The door slid open as they approached, then closed behind them. Illuminated as it was by amber piped light, the wide ramp with its gentle circular turns allowed them to ascend side by side.

At the third level, beside the door was a screen and keypad. Again, while Lyvia seemed to do nothing, and Roget's internals detected no energy flows, the door clicked, and she pushed it open. The two stepped out into a small reception area where several chairs were arranged in a semicircle that faced the wide window overlooking the east side of the building. The doors on both the south and north sides of the chamber were closed.

After a moment, Lyvia took one of the chairs in the middle and sat down. "It shouldn't be long."

Roget took the chair to her left. He grinned. "Even you organized Thomists make people wait."

"Not any longer than necessary." The words were in accented but clear Federation Stenglish. A tall sandy-haired woman stood in the now-open doorway on the south side of the chamber. She wore a silvery green singlesuit with a dark green vest.

Roget stood. So did Lyvia.

"Agents Rholyn and Roget, this way, if you would."

Roget followed the two women along the corridor that slanted toward the middle of the building, past one closed door to the second door on the left, already open. The space held little more than a small circular wooden table, around which were four wooden armchairs. The window overlooked the north walkway from the central square.

The older woman closed the door and took the seat on the south side of the table.

Lyvia and Roget settled into the chairs facing her.

The woman looked directly at Roget. "I'm Selyni Hillis, and I'll be interviewing you for the Ministry of Education and Culture. This interview will be recorded."

"Interviewing? Education and Culture?" asked Roget.

"Why not an interrogation for a Ministry of Defense or War or a Dubietan Ministry of Security? Is that what you mean?" Hillis's laugh was surprisingly low and rough, yet not harsh. "Interview sounds so much better. Besides, interrogation implies either criminal behavior or a wartime situation, and to date, you've committed no crimes on Dubiety, and we're certainly not aware of a state of war. Should we be?"

"I'm not aware of any hostile action either undertaken or planned by the Federation," Roget replied.

"You'll pardon me if I don't find your words terribly reassuring," replied Hillis. "Your awareness is most likely ignorance. Not only does the Federation's left hand not know what the right is doing, but adjoining fingers are unaware of each other's actions."

"I can't help that. I only know what I know."

"What sort of ship dropped you?"

Roget shrugged. "A Federation ship."

Hillis shook her head. "You're not a green agent. You're probably an agent-captain or an agent-major. You know the class ship. So do we."

"Then you tell me," suggested Roget.

"A Federation light battlecruiser of the history class, most probably the *WuDing, MengTian,* or *DeGaulle.*"

Much as he had expected some accuracy, the identification of three cruisers of the same class brought Roget up sharply. Her response concerned Roget more than if Hillis had identified the *WuDing* directly. "Why do you even need to interview me? You know more about Federation naval vessels than I do, and you obviously trained Lyvia to deal with Federation scouts long before I even knew Dubiety existed."

"That may be, but what happens to you depends on you. That is, of course, true of all individuals in all situations." Hillis cleared her throat, gently. "When we learned that the Federation had located us, it seemed prudent to train a few individuals who would be able to make the first contact, as necessary."

"I only knew that Dubiety had been discovered just before I was dropped. You had to have known for years. How long have you known?"

"Two centuries or so."

Two centuries? "That seems unlikely as well as improbable. You knew the Federation had discovered you, and all you did was train people for contact?"

Hillis smiled. "I don't believe I ever said or intimated that."

"So you have a fleet hidden somewhere, ready to smash any Federation forces?"

"Such a fleet would be a terrible waste of energy and resources. We avoid that. We'd prefer just to be left alone. We're hoping you'll be as helpful as you can in assuring that outcome. It would certainly be best for all concerned."

"Why should I?"

"Look at it this way, Agent Roget. We knew that the Federation would attempt to insert an agent through the haze before finalizing its options. They operate according to well-laid plans, and they have for a millennium. We knew those agents would be predominantly male. Federation agents always are."

Roget frowned but did not speak.

"The Federation is a stable patriarchal culture. Techno-reinforced stability doesn't allow much change. It's the high-tech equivalent of the ancient water empires." Another smile followed.

"That suggests that the Federation has known about Dubiety for a time as well."

"That is highly likely, but I wouldn't claim to know what information is available to the Federation."

"You knew how the Federation would approach Dubiety."

"That was scarcely difficult. The Federation is predictable. We predicted five dropboats, and five were released. You can take my word for that or not."

Roget stiffened inside. "What about the other scouts?"

"We tracked five dropboats. One other made it through the shields. He's in Aithan. His landing site was somewhat more remote than yours. Sometime tomorrow morning, local time, he'll be interviewed, just as you are now."

"And I have your word for this? I can expect that, sometime tomorrow, I'll be told that he's told you everything, and that there's no reason for me to withhold anything."

"That would certainly be your expectation. The conventional reasoning—and the Federation is nothing but conventional and oh-so-logical—is that we have no reason to keep you alive once you're no longer a source of information. Therefore, the less you tell us, the longer you have to live. If . . . if we were conventional, that might well be true."

"I'm glad to hear that you recognize that." Roget didn't bother to keep the irony out of his voice.

Abruptly, Hillis stood. "That's all for today. Lyvia will show you more of Skeptos and give you some more information on Dubiety."

Lyvia rose from the table, and after a moment so did Roget.

"So soon?" Almost before the words were out, Roget wished he hadn't said them.

"There's no point in continuing until you see more." Hillis nodded to Lyvia. "You can leave as you came in. Take him to the second level map room and then down to the new exhibit. Your codes will grant you both access."

Lyvia nodded.

Hillis smiled, then turned and left.

"What is her position?" asked Roget.

"Director of External Affairs."

"And what do those duties entail?"

"External Affairs. We need to go to the map room." Lyvia stepped away from the table and headed back up the corridor toward the reception area.

Roget could sense both displeasure and exasperation . . . and perhaps resignation. The thought of resignation bothered him.

From the reception area they descended one level. After passing through another door, another reception area, and then into a corridor that appeared identical to the one on the third level, they walked almost to the end, passing two men and a woman in singlesuits. All three nodded politely but did not address either Lyvia or Roget.

The map room appeared to be little more than a blank-walled, semicircular conference room with a table set forward of the flat rear wall and four chairs behind it. On the table was a small console roughly forty centimeters by twenty. Lyvia settled herself behind the console and touched it. The room darkened, and a map appeared on the circular wall.

Roget turned and began to study the map.

"This is the southern hemisphere, centered on the continent of Socrates," began Lyvia. "The area highlighted in the brighter golden light is the capital district . . . Skeptos in the center . . . to the left you can see the Machiavelli Peninsula." A point of light appeared. "That's about where you landed your dropboat and where I met you . . . there's Avespoir. . . . The next map is a topographic view of Socrates . . . next is Thula . . . northern hemisphere and farther to the west than Socrates . . . and to the east along the equator is the continent of Verite . . ."

"It's rather small."

"So is the truth."

Roget glanced sideways at Lyvia.

"Great illusions are always spun out of the smallest grains of truth," she said. "All empires and bureaucracies know that."

Roget continued to study the maps. From the planetary gravity—so close to T-norm as not to be that easily distinguishable, except at the end of a long day—and the maps, it appeared that Dubiety had slightly more land area than most Federation water-worlds and that it was older, with less tectonic activity and lower mountains and shallower seas.

After the maps came a series of real-time images of cities and towns. At least Lyvia assured him that they were real-time current images.

". . . Petra . . . in the hills of Cammora . . . Aknotan, overlooking Lake Theban . . . Solipsis . . . Zweifein . . . that's where Northern University is . . ."

Finally, the lighting came up, and the curved front wall blanked. Lyvia stood. "Now for the exhibit area."

"I can hardly wait." Roget's tone was ironic. "What exhibit are we going to view?"

"I'd rather not say."

"Whatever it is, you clearly want a reaction."

"Of course. We're providing you with information. It's only fair that you provide some for us."

"I'd be delighted."

Lyvia ignored his words and stepped from the map room and back out into the corridor.

Once more Roget accompanied Lyvia to the ramp, where they headed down, all the way to the level below the ground floor, although the ramp looked to descend two more levels below the one where they walked off. There was no reception area beyond the ramp door, just an antechamber with two corridors branching from it. Lyvia went right. They only walked ten meters before they reached another door, which opened as they approached.

Roget managed to keep abreast of Lyvia, even as he caught sight of his dropboat, or a remarkable reproduction. It sat on a low black dais in the middle of a large chamber.

Roget glanced around. He saw no obvious bay doors large enough to afford the dropboat passage. He also saw a simple placard in a stand before the dented and battered nose. He walked toward it and read:

Federation Dropboat [Model 3B, developed circa 6699 F. E. (1760 P. D.)] Used for dropping agents or couriers onto planetary surfaces in unfriendly locales or those without orbital elevators or normal orbital-attaining conveyances.

He turned to Lyvia. "How did you get it in here?"

"There are doors in the south wall, and the freight lifts are beyond that." She pointed her belt-tube, and the wall split and recessed on both sides, leaving a blackness beyond.

Roget thought he could see two large tunnel mouths, both semicircles wide enough to encompass the dropboat, before the wall resealed itself, leaving a seamless expanse. After a moment, he walked up onto the dais and stood next to the access hatch. He rapped on the hatch. The boat was solid, not a holo image as he had hoped. He touched it and used his internals to pulse the craft.

ID response accepted. Interrogative instructions?

"It's as you left it," Lyvia said from where she stood by the placard. "We did depower a few items. We preferred that you not try anything suicidal. The self-destruct and control locks are inoperative."

Roget looked over the dropboat. It wasn't huge, but it still massed more than ten tonnes. The Thomists had located it, transported it something like two thousand klicks, if not more, in less than a local day, and casually deposited it in an "exhibit" area under the Ministry of Education and Culture. Even if they had used air transport, that suggested, again, more than met the eye. Were his very perceptions being altered?

Why would any perception alteration even be necessary? Any human or alien culture that could do that would have no problem infiltrating and destroying the Federation from within. Or, at the very least, destroying all information on Haze/Dubiety within the Federation archives.

Finally, he stepped away from the dropboat. He smiled politely at Lyvia. "Where do we go from here?"

"I thought you might like to see the subtrans control center."

Roget stepped off the dais. "Lead on."

14

24 LIANYU 6744 F. E.

On Friday, Roget spent the morning walking around the center of St. George doing spot monitoring, something he was supposed to do at random at least twice a week. This was the first time he'd managed it since he'd begun the job.

Just before noon, he walked up past the tram station, checking the time. He was earlier than he'd thought. Instead of waiting around the monitoring office until he went to meet Marni, and getting trapped by Sung, or fielding the chief monitor's questions, he crossed the boulevard and then Main Street to get to the east side of History Square. Glen-David's was open, and he stepped inside.

"Good day, sir," said a young woman.

"And to you." Roget didn't see the older proprietor.

"Can I help you with anything?"

"No, thank you." Roget smiled and moved toward the

paintings and the few multis hung on the north wall. He kept looking, but the dachshund painting wasn't there. Finally, he walked back to the young woman. "There was an oil of a dachshund . . ."

"Oh . . . that." The woman looked embarrassed. "That was a terrible mistake. Someone bought an image, and Father almost sold him the original. They didn't realize . . ."

"An old master? Held in the family, and the heirs didn't realize it?" asked Roget.

"Not a master, but very valuable. The appraisal came back at over a hundred thousand yuan."

"It was a good painting." Roget grinned. "I bought the image."

"You're fortunate. It's never been made public. It dates back to before the wars."

"It's that old?"

"It was nanocoated less than a century after it was painted, Father thinks." She cleared her throat. "The owners would appreciate it if you held the image privately."

That suggested the painting was worth more than the appraisal, possibly far more, but Roget hadn't bought the image for gain, nor would he have bought the original for that reason. Because the image wouldn't ever have that much value, he did wonder why they wanted it held privately . . . unless ownership of the painting was in doubt. That wasn't his problem, and he certainly had no way of pursuing it, nor any interest in doing so. He just liked the image. "That shouldn't be a problem. I bought it for myself."

"Thank you, sir."

Roget couldn't help but smile as he left. He'd had better taste than he'd known.

He reached the door to the accounting office at one minute before noon.

Marni Sorensen stepped outside before he could open the door. She wore a long pale blue skirt and a deeper blue, short-sleeved, round-collared shirt. "You are punctual."

Roget inclined his head. "When I have a reason. You're a very good reason."

"You're also gallant."

"Shouldn't all men be? Shouldn't all women be charming?"

"The first perhaps. The second . . . I'll reserve my options there." She laughed.

"We do need to eat. Where would you recommend?" asked Roget.

"Have you been to the Lee House?"

Roget recalled seeing it, but it had looked less than promising. "No. I tried Lupe's, but my mouth burned all afternoon. I've been to the Caravansary and the Frontier Fort."

"They're small-town attempts at city cuisine. Do you want to try the Lee House? It's not far, and the food is better than the ambiance."

Ambiance? An unusual word for a small-town girl, except she was more than that. "I'll take your word for it." Roget smiled.

They walked side by side down the corridor, through the security gate, and out into an almost comfortable midday. High hazy clouds muted the desert sun as they started down 200 East.

"How was your morning?" asked Roget.

"The same as every other morning. Check yesterday's entries. Run projections against expenditures. Cross-check problem areas." Marni shrugged.

"You make it sound so fascinating." Roget kept the irony in his words light.

"I'm not interested in fascinating. Neither is the regional comptroller. Fascinating would mean some sort of budgeting disaster. What about your morning?"

"The monitoring equivalent of yours. Check the anomaly list. Work out the schedule. Then go out and do the random spot-monitoring so that I can have lunch with someone before I go out and take more readings in the afternoon to check the possible anomalies. Most of the anomalies will be either one-time ambient spikes or the results of mechanical failures that people haven't yet noticed, and they'll be upset when they discover the costs of deferring maintenance or overworking underengineered equipment."

"That's because equipment and energy are so expensive here. People try to get by on as little as possible."

"They could add soltaic cells."

She raised her eyebrows. "They're expensive. What good is all this sunshine if you can't afford soltaic panels? Most of the smaller businesses are stretched thin as it is. The panels are just too expensive, and they have to be replaced."

"Not that often."

"Any replacement is too often in a small town, and parts are sometimes as expensive as the original panel."

"That's because of the environmental costs of manufacture," Roget pointed out.

"Then why are the panels cheaper in Fort Greeley, Helena, or Colorado Springs? Or even in Topeka?"

"Transportation costs, I imagine."

She laughed. "You have an answer for everything."

The answer that Roget hadn't given, and that Marni hadn't voiced, was that the Federation made living in smaller and environmentally fragile communities almost prohibitively expensive, as well as uncomfortable. That was an understandable reaction to the excesses that had preceded the Wars of Confederation.

When they reached the John D. Lee House, Roget opened the door and held it for Marni before following her inside. The café was as unprepossessing as Roget recalled. An old battered wooden door with tinted windows so old that they were barely translucent was framed by two far wider windows that functioned better as mirrors. The entire café was no more than eight meters wide, with two lines of tables alternating with booths running back some ten meters. In a small open space in front of the door was a dark wooden stand. Both tables and booths were bare dark wood—or synthwood—covered with a hard transparent finish that revealed all the abuses the wood had taken over the years. Almost half the tables were taken, mostly by men, but there were several mixed groups, and even one table with three women.

"We just sit at any table that's vacant and set," Marni murmured, leading the way to the left and to a narrow wooden booth that could barely accommodate two, one on each side.

Roget gestured for her to take the front seat. That would allow him to watch whoever came in . . . or left.

Once he was seated, he looked around the booth, then saw the two menus—film-covered paper with a simple listing. He handed one to Marni.

"Thank you, kind sir." She barely glanced at it before saying, "I think I know what I want."

"You've been here often."

"There isn't that much choice in St. George, and it is close to work and not too expensive. I don't come that often."

Roget smiled, then studied the menu, finally deciding on Southwestern chicken with Mex-rice.

An older woman in a long skirt and a short-sleeved gray blouse appeared. Her gray eyes were as washed-out as the blouse. "What'll you be having, Marni dear?"

"The Dutch-oven beef and potatoes. Lots of sauce. Water."

"You, sir?"

"Southwestern chicken and the Wasatch lager."

"Be right out." The woman stepped away, neither rushing nor dawdling toward the serving window at the back of the café.

After a moment, Marni said, "I sometimes have the chicken. It's not bad for a change."

Roget looked across the shiny but battered wood booth table at Marni. "You seem rather overqualified to be a finance clerk."

"It's about the best a university biology grad can get in

St. George. You might notice that jobs aren't exactly plentiful here. I thought about trying to become a monitor, but I wasn't that interested in the kind of science you need to know."

"The kind of science? That's an odd way of putting it." Even as he said that, Roget wondered why she hadn't mentioned her advanced degrees.

"The kind of science that is as much environmental propaganda as science."

"The Federation does have a certain bias against excessive consumption."

"Only in Noram and Sudam . . . and Europe, what of it that's still livable. I've seen the holos and the figures for the Sinese sector. They aren't stinting in Taiyuan or Peiping or . . . lots of places."

Roget didn't point out that losers didn't often get to be choosers. "They're always looking for finance types. You could go there."

She shook her head. "My family's here. Besides, it wouldn't be the same." She paused. "Have you been there?"

"For training courses." That was understating matters, but true. "It's not bad. Different. Expensive on a monitor's pay. Very expensive."

"I don't see how you could stand it, having to spend so much, and especially being so close to so many people . . ." She shuddered.

"There's more privacy than you'd think. Most people just aren't interested in others. We'd like to think so, because we want to believe we matter to others."

"That's why I like it here. People share so much, and they do care."

"You're fortunate." Roget glanced around the café. "Who was John D. Lee?"

"He was an early pioneer."

"I never heard of him." Not before Del Parsens had mentioned Lee, anyway.

"That's not surprising. He was tried for murder after he led a troop against early U.S. government infiltrators posing as settlers passing through. He was executed because he was Brigham Young's adopted son, and the U.S. feds wanted to make an example out of him when they couldn't get to the Prophet."

"Oh." While he didn't know the history of the area in that kind of depth, Roget had some doubts. "An early Saint martyr."

"Of sorts."

At that moment, the serving woman returned with two plates, setting one before each of them and then returning with two glasses, one filled with water without ice and one empty and with an amber container. "There you go."

The lager was cold; the glass was cool, but not chilled. Roget poured the pale amber liquid into it but did not drink, waiting for Marni to sip her water or take a bite of her food.

She sipped the water first, then began to cut the beef, covered with a reddish-brown sauce. "I wonder if grass-fed meat tasted that different."

Roget shrugged. "Supposedly, high-end replicated beef is no different." He cut a thin slice of the chicken and then ate it, finding it moist and tangy.

"How would we know? There are only the control herds anymore."

"Maybe that's why I prefer chicken. It makes more sense to grow it than replicate it."

"How do you like it here?"

"It's better than the Fort," he said.

She nodded emphatically. "The Caravansary isn't bad, but you pay less here. You might try Vhasila's some time, too."

"What kind of food do they serve?"

"Old Mediterranean."

Roget took a swallow of the lager, then concentrated on his meal. He enjoyed the rice even more than the chicken and did not speak for a time. The lager was surprisingly good. He'd have to remember the brand, except it would doubtless be prohibitively expensive outside the region.

As he finished the last bits of rice and chicken, at the *clank* of crockery clashing, Roget glanced toward the rear of the café. There, a heavyset young man was clearing dishes from a table.

"Ernest isn't always as coordinated as he should be," observed Marni.

"Do you know everyone in town?"

"Most people do, after a while."

"Where else would be a good place to eat?"

She frowned, thinking, before replying, "I told you about Vhasila's, and the Desert Grille is good if you don't want another replicated breakfast."

The busboy stumbled, and the dish tub he carried jolted into Roget's shoulder.

"Sir . . . I'm sorry . . ."

Roget blinked. For a moment everything went black.

Then he was sitting at the table, as if nothing had happened.

"Keir . . . are you all right?" Marni's voice was urgent. "You looked so strange for a moment."

"I'm so sorry, sir," repeated Ernest.

"I'm fine," Roget said. He wasn't sure he was. His internal monitors indicated that he'd lost a full minute of consciousness, but there were no recognized toxins in his system. Not yet. He'd known Marni wasn't trustworthy, but he hadn't expected her to attack or do whatever in a public restaurant in the middle of the day. Still, he seemed to be all right. So far. Did he accuse her? He almost smiled. Of what? Even as a security agent he had to have *some* proof.

He took another swallow of the lager.

"You looked dizzy there for a moment," Marni said, guilelessly.

"I was. It could be that I got dehydrated."

"That can happen. Every so often, visitors wander out into the hills and die because they don't bring enough water."

"I'll remember that," he said dryly. Then he finished the last swallow of the lager. "I suppose we need to return to our various routines."

"That might be best. Adabelle will be getting nervous."

"Your superior?"

"She's been here forever. You hang on to good jobs here." Marni nodded toward the front of the café. "We pay at the stand."

Roget rose, checking his internal monitors again. Nothing. As he followed Marni toward the front of the café, their server hurried to the wooden stand.

"For both," Roget told the woman who had served them, "and 15 percent."

"Yes, sir."

Roget extended his CredID, checked the total appearing on the small screen, then thumbed the scanner.

Once they were outside, walking north on 200 East, Marni said, "You didn't have to pay, but thank you."

"You're welcome." Roget smiled. Paying for being attacked was something that hadn't happened before. He had the feeling it might not be the last time, assuming he survived. He was getting worried. Why didn't his system show whatever they'd done to him? What had they done? They couldn't have brain scanned him, not in a minute and without equipment.

"How long have you been working at the FSS?" he asked.

"Eight years."

"Do you think you'll stay?"

"With what else is available here, where else would I go?"

Roget nodded, although he sensed a certain falsity behind her words.

"What about you?"

"They don't like monitors to stay in one place too long."

Nor security agents. "We're not supposed to get too close to too many people, and it's hard not to in places like St. George. In the cities . . ." He shrugged, noting a faint twinge in his upper right arm. Should he go to the local med-centre? He almost shook his head. His internals were better than the local diagnostics. They'd find nothing.

Neither spoke as they crossed St. George Boulevard.

When they finally reached the FSS building and the door to the accounting office, he stopped and smiled. "You're a very surprising woman."

"Any woman can be," she demurred.

"We'll have to have lunch again. It will be my choice."

"It's always the man's choice in the end," she replied lightly.

"That's what all women say."

"What else could we say?" She paused, then added, "I need to get back to work." She slipped into the accounting office.

Roget returned to the monitoring office, sitting down at his own console. He checked his internals again. So far, so good, but there was always the possibility of something delayed, and he needed to take care of that. He created a brief report on his personal monitor, including Marni Sorensen and the restaurant incident, then encrypted and burst sent it to his controller.

He hoped nothing would happen, but if it did . . . someone needed to know, and a report before something like a poisoning was a form of proof he hoped the Federation didn't need to follow up on. Then he stood and reclaimed the bicycle.

"Where are you off to now?" asked Sung.

"Another river reading. Then I'll check on the repair shop over on South Bluff."

"You're wasting your time on the river. It's got to be geothermal."

"I'm taking full water chem readings this time. That should tell me. Then I can compare them to the geothermal composition. If they come close to matching, you'll be right." He wheeled the bike out of the office and down the corridor.

From the FSS building he rode down to the tram station, where he folded the bike, boarded the tram, and rode out to the Red Cliffs station. Then he rode to the Middleton wash path and down it to the parkway, where he got off the bike and walked down to the river.

Roget took out the monitor, then flicked the sampler fiberline across the water, letting it sink and ride some before reeling it in.

After making sure that he had the data, he walked downstream to where there was a narrow footbridge over the river. He crossed and walked back upstream, but stopped short of a point opposite where he'd taken the first sample. He repeated the process, then reeled in the line and slipped the monitor back into its belt case.

He almost reached the bridge when a wave of dizziness washed over him. He staggered to the bridge and grasped the railing, steadying himself.

Then the blackness rose, blotting out everything.

15

18 MARIS 1811 P. D.

Once they left the Ministry of Education and Culture, Lyvia walked straight toward the central square of Skeptos, striding past the building she had said housed the Ministry of Transportation.

"We're not going there?" asked Roget. "Isn't that the Transport Ministry?"

"No. That's just offices and the few administrators necessary to keep track of matters. You won't see anything useful there. We're going to the central subtrans center for all of Socrates. I would assume that you're interested in the technology and operation of our transport system."

"You assume correctly." As the amber outside light flickered slightly, Roget glanced skyward, but there were no clouds and no aircraft visible beneath the omnipresent gray haze, not that he expected aircraft any longer. "Do all towns and cities have access to subtrans?"

"Towns, cities, and villages. Either to a local system or a regional system, depending on a number of factors."

"Such as?"

"Distance and imputed total costs, for starters."

"What if the costs will always be prohibitive?"

"Then . . . there's no town, unless it's a protected recreational area like the Machiavelli Peninsula. The costs there are paid by taxes levied as a benefit on all inhabitants."

"Just like that?"

"No. The House of Tribunes had to approve it, as did the House of Denial."

"With a House of Denial, I'm surprised anything gets funded."

"Many things don't, but the worthwhile ones do, sooner or later. We don't exempt politicians from the libel, slander, and misrepresentation laws. In fact, the penalties are higher for them."

"And people run for office?" Roget's words came out sardonically.

"A different kind of people."

Were people really that different? Again, Roget had his doubts.

When they reached the walkway that ran along the northern edge of the square, Lyvia turned eastward. At the next corner she turned south. Before long, the two were descending the ramp down to the subtrans concourses.

Roget wondered where they were headed, because the tunnel was clearly leading down to the subtrans concourses, and he didn't see any other tunnels, and he didn't recall seeing any on the way into Skeptos. He assumed that there must be an entrance to wherever they were headed somewhere off the concourses. Instead, Lyvia walked to the side of the tunnel just short of the point where the larger tunnel for the local access joined the regional tunnel. There, she came to a halt. The section of one of the curved side panels where she stood looked slightly different to Roget, although he could have sworn it hadn't a moment before. As he approached, an oval area glowed, then slid aside.

"Come on," said Lyvia.

Roget stepped through the doorway with her, noting that almost no one looked in their direction. The metal sections closed, leaving them within a niche no more than three meters by two. After a moment, the back of the niche, also metallic composite, opened.

A muscular blocky man stood in the short arched tunnel, waiting for them, but how he had known when exactly to expect them, Roget didn't know, except that it had to be something Lyvia had done, even though he had sensed absolutely no communications and no energy flows.

The stocky man wore a singlesuit of royal blue, without a vest, and his dark hair was less than a centimeter long. "Welcome to the subtrans operations center, Agents Rholyn and Roget. I'm Tee Tayler. Please follow me." Although his words were heavily accented, Roget could understand them.

Less than thirty meters along the tunnel, Tayler turned through an archway on the left and led them into a chamber some ten meters wide and five deep. The only other person in the space was a woman seated behind a console set some three meters back from the wall—on which was displayed a floor-to-ceiling projected image.

Their escort gestured to the wall screen. "This provides an overview of the Socrates continental system, as well as the deep-tubes to Thula and to Patagonn."

Deep-tubes? Roget stepped closer. The map represented the continent. From what he could tell, there were three separate systems. The red lines represented local subtransit; the blue ones regional links; and the dark green ones the deep-tubes under the oceans. He mentally calculated. Assuming the map was to scale, Socrates was over nine thousand klicks from east to west at its greatest distance, and a good four from south to north.

"How much of the southern peninsula is ice-covered?"

"None of it," replied Lyvia. "Because of the shields, we get more even heat and light diffusion, and Dubiety's axial tilt is only about seven degrees."

"I know it's not transit, but . . . ocean stagnation?"

"We're closer to the sun, and the oceans are shallower," said Lyvia. "That provides more solar tidal movement than one might otherwise expect."

"But not enough for life to evolve originally."

"Life evolves everywhere that there's water or something that fulfills that function. It may or may not be large or intelligent . . . or it may be surprising." She pointed to the wallscreen. "Questions?"

Roget turned to the blocky man. "You have to be maintaining a vacuum in the tube tunnels." There was no other way that the subtrans could reach the velocities that Roget had calculated without a buildup of air that would stall or halt a high-speed tube train.

"Precisely. There is a slight leakage when the car doors open at each station, but we use that to cushion the stops."

"How?" asked Roget. "The tunnels look to be open."

"We create partial deceleration shields as the subtrans nears a station. They're an adaptation of space shields. After all, we're in a vacuum in both places. The stray atmosphere

builds up against the shield, and we use the decel pressure
to force the air through filters as a boost to the ventilation in
the stations."

"What's the propulsion system?"

"Oh . . . it's just a grav-twist system set into a maglev,
shield-contained, bottle effect."

"How do you manage to work that in a planetary gravity
well?"

"That's why we have a completely integrated system,"
said Tayler. "It's actually locked into the planetary mass
distribution."

Roget didn't see how that was possible, but then his physics background was fairly basic. Once more he was faced
with the fact that the Thomists were doing something that
the Federation either couldn't or hadn't. Whether they were
doing it in the way they claimed or otherwise didn't make
much difference from a practical point of view. They had
subsurface transport as swift as most planetary air travel,
and if one considered other factors, probably as fast, if not
faster, in point-to-point passenger and freight delivery as any
powered orbital or suborbital craft could manage. As deep
as the tunnels were, they would be difficult to block or destroy with any normal weapons.

"What's the system capacity?"

"We can transit up to six cars in a given subtrans train.
That's based on the size of the concourses, not on the system itself. We could easily run trains with twelve cars in an
emergency, but it would take two stops at each destination
to get the passengers or cargo out. Each local car will hold
forty-two seated passengers with room for another twenty-
eight without freight or crowding. So . . . say 350 a train. The
regional and deep-tube cars are configured for thirty-two
passengers, and two cars on each run are usually reserved
for freight, except on holidays when we may only run one
freighter. We also run six-car freight runs on off-times, and
the system is designed so that we can run them to special

freight concourses. Those are the green triangles on the system map."

"No separate freight system, then?"

"What would be the purpose? To waste resources?" asked Tayler, not quite scornfully.

"Are all the lines dual tube?"

"Yes." Tayler gestured to the system overview. "Also . . . you can see that every major city or large town can be reached from at least two other points on the system through redundant lines."

"That's quite an engineering feat." And a substantial resource commitment, noted Roget.

"It makes sense," Lyvia pointed out. "We don't worry about weather. The ecological effects are minimal, especially compared to the alternatives, and the materials used are impervious to just about anything. That doesn't count the shielding effect of the ground itself, and that's considerable, given the depth of the lines."

Lyvia was just confirming that the transit system could operate unhampered even under full-scale attack.

Abruptly, Tayler turned and walked toward the woman at the console.

Roget listened, although he couldn't catch every word of the low-voiced conversation in what seemed to be, he now recognized, a clipped and faster version of old American.

". . . car three on Principia alpha . . . field strength fluctuations . . . decel . . ."

". . . personnel at Matera . . . empty . . . run as a fiver . . . have Falcon station bring up a replacement . . ."

The woman nodded and Tayler returned. "Equipment replacement. Do you have any other questions?"

"What's the empty weight of a car?"

"Passenger cars are . . . roughly fifteen tonnes. A full freight car is three times that in length and weight. There are special cars that can carry three times the mass of a standard freighter."

"What's the mass the freight cars can carry . . ."

"How long is a car's service life . . ."

"What's the materials composition . . ."

Roget fired off as many questions as he could think of, and for close to a standard hour Tayler answered most of them.

Finally, Roget shrugged. "I think you've addressed everything I can think of."

Tayler smiled. "It's fair to say that I haven't had to recall so much in years. I'm surprised I remembered so much."

"Thank you." Roget inclined his head.

"I'll escort you out."

Despite Tayler's words, Lyvia and Roget walked back along the tunnel, followed by Tayler.

Once they were back in the subtrans tunnel, Lyvia turned to Roget. "Are you ready for something to eat?"

"That would be good." He wasn't particularly hungry, and that might have been because his system was anything but used to a twenty-two-hour day. He did want a chance to sit down and talk. "You pick the place."

Less than fifteen minutes later, they were seated in a small establishment off a walkway running north and south two blocks east of the central square. The decor inside Lucasan wasn't anything that Roget had ever seen. On the wall opposite their table were two crossed sabers, but their blades were not metal but shafts of light, one bluish white and one a sullen red. Occasionally, a burst of static issued from one saber or the other. Set on a pedestal between their table and the next was a cylinder set at a slight angle on tracked wheels with a domed top, its metallic finish in silver and blue.

Roget glanced toward the sabers.

"Nostalgia for a time that never was in a galaxy far, far away." Lyvia laughed softly. "At least we're honest about our nostalgia."

Roget didn't pretend to understand and picked up a menu, looking over the short list of unfamiliar names. At least written Dubietan was far easier to puzzle through than the spoken version.

"What do you suggest?" he finally asked.

"The Crepes Jedi are good. So is the Filet Leia."

In the end, Roget settled on Veal Mos Eisley, which seemed to have an interesting conglomeration of spices, and an amber Yoda Lager.

A server arrived, wearing an ancient and severe black and gray uniform of a type Roget had never seen, took their order, and returned almost immediately with their drinks.

Lyvia took a sip of something vaguely ruby in shade, before asking, "Why do you think you were chosen for this mission?"

Roget knew her words weren't as casual as their tone suggested. "I could guess, but I couldn't say that I really knew."

"It might be wise to guess." The faint and almost sad smile indicated her words were a suggestion and not a threat.

"I've had a fairly wide range of experience, both on- and off-planet, and in- and outsystem." He couldn't help but think about the hack/razor job required in his assignment on Khriastos station, which had amounted to being a cyber thief reinserting data deleted from the station's archives so that the Federation Finance Monitors could find it.

"What else?"

"What are you suggesting?" countered Roget.

"What is the cultural background of the average Federation Security Agent?"

"Our backgrounds vary." Even as he spoke, Roget saw where she was pointing him. "You're suggesting that . . . FSA Operations knew Dubiety had an AmerAnglo cultural foundation."

"Don't they send you where you'll fit in?"

"Or where we'll fit a role." Roget thought back to his mission in Taiyuan, where only an AmerAnglo would be considered "degraded" enough to deal in grayware. So degraded that no one had any problems with Sulynn's trying to kill him once she'd gotten what she wanted. Had that all been a setup for her next assignment? Roget wouldn't have been surprised.

"Ethnic stereotyping. A pity it hasn't gone away."

"You don't have to worry about that. From what I can see, everyone here is AmerAnglo descended."

"Not really. Everyone's light skinned, but that was a necessity. Otherwise, the genetics vary widely."

"The shields? Vitamin D?"

"Precisely."

The server returned with Roget's Veal Mos Eisley and Lyvia's Crepes Jedi, each accompanied by a small side salad of mixed greens, except that the greens—again—were almost blackish green. He took a small bite, but he didn't notice any great difference in taste from the "greener" salads he'd had on earth.

As they ate, Roget listened to the conversations around them. He was beginning to be able to catch words and phrases, but the total meaning of most exchanges eluded him.

"You'll pick it up." Lyvia finished the last sip of her drink. "What else would you like to see this afternoon?"

"What about the local spaceport . . . or orbital shuttle system?"

Lyvia smiled. "We can't. We don't have anything like that."

He didn't believe that, but there was no point in protesting. "All right. What about a manufacturing facility? Or a composite formulation mill? Surely you don't replicate everything, not as concerned as you all seem to be about the environmental costs."

After a moment, Lyvia nodded. "We can manage that. Both, in fact. We'll start with the composite facility." She paused. "Are you done? Or would you like dessert?"

"I'm fine." Roget glanced around.

"I've already paid."

"Direct link?"

"Yes." Lyvia stood.

Roget did as well. "How do you manage that?"

"You mean, without stray radiation that your implants can detect? It's a very tight beam, a form of coherence that classical physicists said was impossible. Our scientists have been very good at doubting pronouncements of impossibility."

"Your whole society is impossible," he said with a laugh as they walked out of Lucasan.

"Magic is impossible, too, but an old Anglo scientist—I think he was a scientist, but maybe he was a writer—said that any sufficiently advanced science is indistinguishable from magic."

"How does this coherence work?" When Lyvia didn't answer and continued walking westward toward the central square, he added, "I know. It's not your field, and you don't intend to give me a simplistic and misleading reply."

"Exactly."

"I could use a few simplistic but misleading answers."

"You only think you could."

"Where are we going now?"

"We'll take the local subtrans south three stops to Coventral."

After they reached the southeast corner of the square, Roget was surprised at how long it took them to get down to the local concourse. Unlike the regional concourse, the local concourse was shaped like an L, with the north-south section a good fifteen meters below the east-west section and joined by another tunnel ramp. As far as appointments went, both sections of the local concourse looked almost the same in layout as did the regional one. When they stopped before an archway, waiting for a train, he asked, "Why are the local concourses so deep?"

"They all aren't, but it makes a certain sense here in Skeptos. That's because we get more regional travelers, and if they have luggage, it's easier for them. Also, it puts the local concourses on the same absolute level."

The concourse door opened, and Lyvia waited for a man and two women to leave before stepping through the archway. The local subtrans train had cars that looked to be the same dimensions as the regional subtrans, but the seats, if made of the same material, were slightly smaller and definitely closer together.

Since the car wasn't crowded, Roget sat across from Lyvia. "What about the agent on the other side of the world?"

"I haven't heard anything. I wouldn't. Not for a while. I'm assigned to you."

"What have you learned from me?"

"You're comparatively perceptive and well-integrated with your internal monitors and sensors." Lyvia's voice was low, barely carrying to Roget. "You represent a dangerous but passively aggressive culture that is looking for an excuse that will allow itself to justify an attack against Dubiety on almost any grounds. You're not entirely in sympathy with your own culture's objectives, and you were sent on this mission because your superiors feel that you need to understand the danger we represent and because if you don't return, the difficulty posed by the combination of your abilities and attitude will be resolved. If you do return, they will find some way to discredit or retire you. Or they might promote you to a comfortable but meaningless and powerless position."

"You're so encouraging."

"You asked." Lyvia glanced toward the doors as the train came to a stop.

One woman who had been sitting at the end of the car left. No one entered.

Neither Lyvia nor Roget spoke again until the train made the third stop.

"This is where we leave," said Lyvia.

Roget followed her out onto a nearly empty concourse and

then up a tunnel ramp. About fifty meters up the ramp, the tunnel split, with a maroon tunnel curving to the left away from the standard gray and green tunnel. Lyvia took the maroon tunnel, and Roget kept pace with her. None of the half-dozen other passengers followed them.

"There aren't any signs or indications," Roget said.

"Haven't you noticed? We don't use them, except for places like restaurants in public spaces."

Roget hadn't, but as he thought about it, he realized that he hadn't seen any, except for the restaurants around the main square of Skeptos, and not even all of those had borne signs.

"Anyone who's linked to the commnet can find out where they want to go," Lyvia continued. "Posting signage is another waste of resources."

"I suppose everyone is linked."

"All except very young children and those few who have proven untrustworthy."

"And foreign agents."

"You're presumed untrustworthy. I don't think that's an unfair presumption, do you?" She smiled as she spoke.

"No. I can't dispute that."

After a less than ninety degree turn, the tunnel straightened, stretching ahead for what looked to be a good quarter klick.

"Do you people walk everywhere that the subtrans doesn't go?"

"Yes, except for people who are temporarily disabled. They can use individual powerchairs."

Before long, Roget saw an archway on the right side of the tunnel. As they walked nearer, a couple appeared and walked toward them at a good clip. They smiled and nodded as they passed. Roget returned the smile. "Are we taking the archway?"

"Yes. That's the entrance to CPInd."

Beyond the archway, outlined in maroon, was a narrower

corridor that ended after twenty-odd meters at a shimmering metal composite door. Lyvia pointed her belt-tube. After a moment, the door split into two halves, each retracting into the wall. As soon as they were inside the squarish and empty chamber, the doors closed behind them.

Before Roget could say more, a door to his left opened, and a tall woman in a flowing red skirt and a skin-tight, black, short-sleeved top stepped through.

The angular woman studied Roget, then turned to Lyvia and spoke. "There isn't that much to see. The constitutors are sealed processors."

That was what Roget thought she said.

"He'll get an idea." Lyvia turned to him. "Did you understand her?"

"Something about not seeing much because the units are sealed?"

"Good. I told you it wouldn't take long."

Something about her tone bothered Roget, but he couldn't have said why.

They followed their guide down another ramp and out into a massive enclosed space, one large enough to hold several attack corvettes, Roget suspected. The constitutors, if that happened to be what they were, were shaped like rough half cylinders with annular rings set at unequal intervals, and with various large protuberances in other places. Each rose a good twenty meters above the floor and looked to be fifteen meters wide and a good hundred meters long. There were five, set side by side, with ten meters between each. At the far end of the chamber at the output end of each cylinder was a maglev freight car, one end opened and swung up. Two men guided the sheets of composite into the car.

Roget walked slowly along the side of the constitutor. Again, he could sense no energy emissions. Nor did he feel any heat radiating from the enormous machine.

Lyvia said nothing as he came to a stop near the end and watched the loading process.

Large as the chamber seemed at first sight, Roget realized that it was but a fraction the size of the works he'd seen outside Parachute years earlier—and far cleaner. The output rate was far greater as well.

Finally, he turned. "How do you do it?"

"It's standard molecular reassembly. Each unit handles a different type."

"You have, what, three of these for the planet?"

"Five actually, but one is always on standby."

Roget glanced back at the loading area as a freight maglev glided away, only to be replaced by another.

"Have you seen enough? There's not much else to see."

"How many people work here?"

Lyvia looked to the angular woman.

"Sixty-seven. Most are loaders."

"Why do you need human loaders?"

"They work better, and they're more flexible. Also, composite is hard on scanning perceptors."

"Why?"

The woman just shrugged.

Roget asked more questions, but most of the answers he got were either meaningless or consisted of shrugs.

"We need to go," Lyvia finally said. She turned to the woman. "Thank you."

"My pleasure and interest."

Once they were outside CPInd, Lyvia stepped through the maroon archway and turned right.

"We're not headed back toward the subtrans."

"No. We're going to take a private tube to MultOp."

"Is it subsurface as well?"

"Of course. When you insist that everything is underground and below much of the water table, it becomes easier to assure that there aren't any harmful emissions. We also insist on unified ventilation systems."

"So that the supervisors and owners breathe what everyone else does?"

"It works better that way."

"They could just move their administrative functions else-where."

"They could, but there's a heavy surtax on nonintegrated facilities, and that makes it hard to compete and stay in business."

"Do you people charge for everything you don't like?"

"No. Just those things that would otherwise harm people and the environment."

"What if people pay to pollute?"

"Some have. They haven't stayed in business long. They lost customers and employees because they had to pay more in production costs and because they had to pay the employees who stayed even more to keep them. Some people don't like buying from polluters, especially when their goods cost more."

The next archway from the maroon tunnel was on the left, and it was a bluish gray. After taking a short ramp and a left turn, Roget and Lyvia found themselves in a small concourse. The doors to a car that might hold twenty people were open. Once they stepped inside the private subtrans, the doors closed. Several minutes later, they opened onto a slightly larger blue gray concourse.

Roget stepped out alongside Lyvia. "What do they make here?"

"Everything. We don't operate along the old models. Basically, any manufacturer can fabricate anything once they receive the specs. Designers create prototypes or new versions, and all those are available on a royalty basis to any assembler."

"How does the assembler know if the specs work?"

"There aren't many single designers. They're businesses that have a number of designers and engineers. Designing is just part of what they do. They have the responsibility for product design and specifications . . . and the legal liability for them."

"So the designer really takes the place of the old multi-lateral, at least in terms of name identification or make or brand? And legal responsibility?"

Lyvia nodded.

The tour of MultOp was about as useful as the previous tour. Roget saw machines that essentially sprayed matter into predetermined shapes and colors . . . and functions. The finished products were covered in a thin biofoam and shipped.

As he watched the last stages of loading and shipping, a thought occurred to him, something that he should have picked up earlier. "How does all this get delivered? People can't cart dining tables or anything else large home on the subtrans."

"There are freightways under the walkways in all towns and cities. Intelligent lorries take goods to the various buildings, or to common points in those places that allow individual dwellings. You can rent a delivery vehicle as needed, and some manufacturers or designers include local transport rental in the price." She rubbed her forehead. "You look hungry. I know I am. I'll answer any more questions you have about the day while we're eating. There's no place that's all that good out here. Do you mind if we head back to Skeptos?"

"No. How far south are we?"

"Twenty-one klicks."

Neither spoke except in pleasantries and short comments on the way back to Skeptos, but Roget did keep listening to the others on the regular subtrans train, which was far more crowded than it had been earlier. He was definitely understanding more, just enough to be even more frustrated.

Lyvia picked another restaurant within four blocks of the central square, except to the northeast. Classica was the almost invisible name on the tinted glass. Unlike Dorinique, it was small, and the decor was spare, with white plaster–finished walls and pale blue tile flooring. The table linens were a blue so deep that it was almost black.

Roget sank into the chair across from Lyvia. He was more than happy to order another lager, along with a chicken and broccoli feta pie and a Mediterranean salad. His eyes were burning slightly, but he didn't know whether that was some allergic reaction or just because he'd been straining to see and pick up anything that he could.

Once the lager arrived, he took several swallows before speaking. "What's the point of all this?"

"All what?"

"You show me around Skeptos. You give me a general idea of how your society works, but no details and no real information. If you intend to let me report back to the Federation, no one will believe me because I can only provide generality after generality and my own unsupported observations and calculations. If you don't intend to let me return, why bother? I'll either be dead, or I'll have plenty of time to learn."

"In time, and that will not be that long, we will provide you with proof. Proof that even senior security officers should find convincing."

Two salads appeared. Roget took a bite, discovering that the brownish olives not only had pits, but were strong and salty. Still, the tangy bite of the salad was refreshing.

"What's the nature of that proof?"

"We'll send you off with a certain amount of documentation."

"You know the dropboat is in no shape to lift off, and that would be so even if Dubiety didn't have orbital shields."

"That has also been considered." Lyvia didn't look up from her salad. "You will return."

The certainty in her voice wasn't totally reassuring.

As soon as they finished their salads, the server took the plates away and presented their entrées.

Roget had no trouble eating every bite of the creamy chicken and broccoli sandwiched between baked phyllo sheets. As he waited for Lyvia to finish her skewers and rice, he ventured another inquiry. "I've just assumed . . . but do you have traditional marriages here?"

Lyvia frowned. "We have marriages and civil contracts and people who live together without either, and people who live alone. Some relationships are what you'd call traditional, and some aren't. We don't apply any stigma or prohibition to same-sex unions, if that's what you mean. All couples are treated the same. We do apply certain restrictions on those situations where more than two adults are involved in a relationship. History has shown such multiple unions do have a tendency not to carry their own weight in society."

"Restrictions? Such as?"

"If someone in that kind of relationship decides to have a child, someone has to post an educational and support bond."

"If they don't . . ."

"They can terminate the pregnancy, or they can be relocated into a situation where they can both work and have the child."

"Even you can't make everything work through economics."

"No . . . but mostly personal economics work. Some people always require the force of the state to behave and not to take criminal advantage of others."

"What about you?"

"What about me?" replied Lydia with an amused smile.

"Are you in some sort of . . . arrangement?"

"I have a partner. She and I have a daughter."

That explained more than a few things, Roget thought, including Lyvia's ease in maintaining a professional relationship and the very light fragrance that she used.

"Most arrangements here are still heterosexual," she went on. "That's the way human genes usually operate." Lyvia stood, stifling a yawn. "I'd like to get home to see Aylicia."

"Then you should." Roget slipped from his chair.

They walked toward the front of Classica, and along the way Lyvia paid the bill with her belt-tube.

Once outside, Roget asked, "What about tomorrow?"

"I'll have to see what we can work out. I'll meet you for breakfast, the same as today."

Lyvia said little as she walked with him back to his guesthouse, and while Roget knew he should be finding out more, he discovered that he was too tired to press the issue. When he did reach his quarters, his feet ached, as did his shoulders. The shoulder pain had to be from the tension he'd only been peripherally aware of—at least, that was what he hoped.

But how could he not be tense when it was getting clearer and clearer that both the Federation and Dubiety were trying to use him? How could Dubiety be so aware of the Federation without the converse being true? Unless . . . Dubiety was more advanced than he'd even thought. Yet, if that were so, then the casual attitude of the colonel made no sense, unless he happened to be so arrogant that he and the Federation could not believe any splinter human culture might have surpassed Federation technology.

Roget could see permutations upon permutations.

Finally, he downloaded a duplicate of *Hildegarde in the Sunlight* to the quarters' system, amazed that the system actually accepted his flash memory, then adjusted the projection to the wall opposite the sofa. The dachshund he'd seen through the window the night before had reminded him. He sat down and looked at the familiar image of Hildegarde on the blue velvet sofa. He smiled.

"You've been in a lot of places, little girl," he murmured. "I'm not certain that you haven't learned more than I have. Especially here."

Hildegarde just continued to look at him expectantly, and that was fine with Roget as he leaned back and closed his eyes, trying to let his thoughts clear.

16

Roget stood in the high-roofed chamber. He glanced around but didn't recognize it . . . and yet, in some way, he did. There were small dark wooden desks arranged in a tiered semicircle. Most of the desks were occupied, primarily by men. A considerable proportion of those in the chamber were white haired. The ceiling was high and domed, and there were murals painted on the lower levels of the dome, just above the gallery where only a few people sat, looking down.

Why couldn't he make out the subjects of the murals? The light wasn't as bright as it could have been, but his eyesight was better than that. He squinted. It didn't help.

"A point of order has been raised against the motion to consider the amendment." The words boomed from somewhere, amplified.

Roget glanced toward the front of the dais opposite the middle of the tiered desk. A heavyset man with jowls sat at the single desk. He was the one who had spoken. Above and behind him on the wall was a large seal that featured an eagle. One claw held stylized thunderbolts. The other held some sort of branch.

"The amendment is germane. Under the rules, any amendment that references a specific clause in the bill . . ."

Roget's eyes flicked around the chamber. For some reason, he felt light-headed, and he put out a hand to steady himself on the nearest desk.

"Are you all right, Senator?" The young man who asked the question wore a dark jacket with a silver emblem in the lapel.

Something about the coat nagged at Roget. He couldn't say why. "I'm fine."

"Yes, sir." The young man moved away, as if relieved.

His feet seemed to turn him, and Roget found himself walking out of the chamber along an aisle between the evenly spaced desks. None of those at the desks looked up at him as he passed. Two women made a point of looking away.

He walked through an empty reception chamber or anteroom and then out a long colonnaded hall into another area where arched steel door frames were flanked by men in unfamiliar dark blue uniforms. He took the narrow exit space and made his way outside the building, where he stood between two massive marble columns at the top of a wide set of marble steps. Beyond the columns where he stood stretched others, holding up a long marble pediment above him. Below him stretched wide marble steps that descended and descended, finally ending at a wide concrete sidewalk.

People walked up and down the steps. Only a few looked in his direction, and they looked quickly away.

The sky overhead was dirty, covered in a haze of gray and brown. For all the haze, an orangish sun poured out heat. Sweat oozed from all over his body. After several moments, Roget walked down the marble steps. The stone felt gritty under his shoe soles, and the sun beat down on his uncovered head.

"Senator . . ." A young woman hurried toward him. She held a thin and angular microphone that she thrust at him. "Can you tell us the progress on the debate on the agreement proposed by Beijing?"

"Progress?" Roget laughed. "What progress? They want to take us over. We don't want to be taken over, but we don't want to pay the cost of independence . . . or of an effective military. Everyone wants someone else to pay, but now that you've taxed the upper middle class out of existence and driven the rich offshore, who's left to pay? You people have crucified anyone brave enough to explain that. There's no one left in there who has enough nerve to tell their constituents that . . . or to tell you." He pushed the microphone away and resumed walking down the marble steps.

Behind him there were murmurs.

". . . say he's lost it . . . coherent only some of the time . . ."

". . . why they keep electing him . . ."

". . . blaming us . . ."

Roget walked to the base of the steps and turned left on the sidewalk beside the empty asphalt drive and toward the low white buildings to the north beyond the trees at the end of the short expanse of green. Why couldn't they see it? Why was the obvious so impossible for them to understand? He felt so tired.

He reached inside his jacket for his phone. Except he wasn't wearing a jacket, and the phone had vanished. He needed to call . . .

Who was it that he needed to call? He couldn't remember. Why couldn't he remember?

Where was his jacket? He had been wearing a jacket. He couldn't go out into the chamber and speak on the floor without it. Where was it? He looked around. How could he have been so stupid as to have forgotten his jacket?

A blinding pain shot through his chest, and he staggered. His eyes watered. A moment of blackness washed over him . . . and passed.

When he could see again, the white marble buildings that had been less than a hundred yards before him swirled and melted into oddly shaped red stone. Some were only a few meters taller than he was. The green grass and trees had vanished, and he was walking on red sandy soil.

He stopped and glanced down at his chest. He was clad in a one-piece coverall of shimmering white. So white . . .

An institution? Had the administration had him committed? Carted off because he'd said too much? Or had they used national security as an excuse?

Roget blotted his forehead. How had it gotten so hot? He tried to swallow, then moisten his lips. They were dry and cracked.

He shook his head. It felt like it was splitting, and everything wavered around him. Where was he?

Something brushed his hip. He looked down at the white cylinder attached to his belt.

It was . . . he grasped for a name.

What was it?

His monitor! That was what it was. With that recognition, he looked around again, then reached down and grasped it. His eyes burned, and his fingers were clumsy, but he finally managed to get his position. He was nearly at the foot of Shinob, a good klick east of the Mill Creek wash and the Virgin River.

How had he gotten out here?

Dehydration. That must have been it. How could he have been so stupid? He reached for the small water bottle at his belt on the left side. It was full. He drained it.

After several moments, his head seemed to clear, and he turned back west. He kept his steps measured as he followed the old and dusty trail back toward the Virgin River. He still didn't understand how he had gotten on the east side of the river. He'd only been at the bridge itself. At least he hadn't fallen in. He could have drowned, even in the shallow water, but his boots and his singlesuit showed no sign of dampness.

And what about the delusions about being called "Senator"? Or the marble buildings and the hazy sky? He knew he'd never been anywhere like that. He'd never seen buildings like those, nor had he seen a sky that polluted.

He knew about dehydration, but there had been nothing about delusions. Nothing at all.

He kept walking. No one was about to come after him any time soon, even in the comparatively mild midday heat of winter. He was just glad that he wouldn't be in St. George in full summer.

He hoped he wouldn't be.

He tried not to think about the dehydration delusion as he walked on. While it had seemed so real, it had been a delusion, hadn't it?

Or . . . his thoughts were still foggy . . . Something had happened. What? In a dingy café . . . that was it!

The Lee House. The lunch with Marni and the momentary blackout when the busboy had hit him with the tub of dishes, but what they had done must have been what gave him the delusion. He finally accessed his internal monitors, but they indicated no toxins, only borderline dehydration, and how had he gotten here?

Slowly, he recalled. He'd been taking a water chem reading . . .

He shook his head. He needed to get back to the bicycle and back to the FSS building, and he needed to drink more, as soon as he could. Dehydration . . . that had to be it. Didn't it?

17

19 MARIS 1811 P. D.

Roget woke earlier than he would have liked on Saturday, while it was still dark, or as dark as it ever seemed to get on Dubiety. He did have another thought, something he should have considered far earlier. Before he even dressed, this time wearing his own blue singlesuit, he walked into the main room of his quarters and began to search the holojector menu. If it accessed entertainment and other real-time material, there was always the possibility that it offered more.

After close to fifteen minutes, he located something called "Inquiries" and pulsed it.

"State your inquiry, please." The words seemed projected into his ears and nowhere else.

"Orbital shield system, functions and construction. Respond in Federation Stenglish." All the system could do was refuse to answer.

"Stenglish not an option." But the holojector did create an image of Dubiety, shown as a schematic cross-section of the planet. The molten core was somewhat smaller than Roget expected, and the planetary magnetic field depiction showed six poles, rather than two, and none of the three sets had anywhere close to the same orientation, nor did they correspond even approximately to geographic poles. The maximum field strength of each set was also at differing distances from the planetary surface. The fields generated by each looked to be more tightly focused than "normal" planetary mag-fields.

Roget grinned, if momentarily, until he realized that he could have discovered the inquiry aspect of the holojector/commnet earlier.

He did have to ask the system to repeat the explanation three times before he thought he had a general understanding of how the shields worked. Supposedly, each shield level was linked to a specific magnetic field, and the fields generated some sort of current or secondary field that created the orbital motion of the shield components.

When Roget couldn't get any more information on how the fields were structured or maintained or precisely how the orbital motion was accomplished, he tried another tack.

"Internal construction of each individual orbital unit?"

"Please restate your inquiry."

Between his nonexistent Dubietan old American and his use of simple words, it took close to a dozen attempts before the system projected another schematic. Each piece looked like a miniature modified lifting body, but that didn't make any sense because there was no atmosphere to speak of, not for aerodynamic purposes, at the orbital levels of even the lowest shield. The diagram showed a thin outer skin with what looked to be some sort of miniature devices along the inside of the rounded edges, but the system did not provide dimensions or details on the internal devices.

"No simplistic explanations on public comm? And that's not simplistic?" muttered Roget.

Next he made an inquiry on the subtrans. There was more detail there, including technical material on the placement of the magfield generators, but Roget was left with the definite sense that certain critical details were missing—such as how the Dubietans could generate enough power to power an entire transit network with trains moving at the speeds he'd calculated.

That led to an inquiry on planetary power generation. The system informed him that local power grids were generally supplied by fusion units, since fossil fuels, solar surface radiation, tidal, and geothermal technologies were all impractical. Planetary power was supplied by other means.

Planetary power? To what did that refer?

The only answer he got to that question and all sort of variations was that the information was unavailable due to the complexity involved.

"It's only complex when they don't want anyone to know the details," he murmured, not caring that his words were doubtless being transmitted and studied. After a moment, he realized something else. He couldn't have gotten as much comparable information off any Federation net.

He pushed those thoughts aside and inquired about communications specifics. The holojector showed him schematics on how all dwellings were linked by a form of fiber optics, but he couldn't get a description or much of anything on how they managed to transmit all kinds of radiation and energy without scatter.

Finally, after other even less fruitful searches, he put aside the holojector controls, cleaned up, and dressed. It was just after what passed for dawn when he left his quarters and walked along the upper hall and down the ramp to the reception area, looking for a door or some access to a lower level.

He found it in a niche beyond the ramp. It even opened as he neared, revealing a wide straight ramp headed down. At the base of the ramp, some eight meters below the ground floor, was a spacious open area and another wide corridor headed back in the direction of the front of the guesthouse.

He followed the corridor to another door, this one with a screen and keypad, which opened to his code. Beyond was another large antechamber, and to his left was what looked to be another code-accessed door. Roget ignored that for the moment and walked forward toward what he hoped was the door to the freightway. It opened as he approached.

Deciding on caution, he stood in the middle of the open door and studied the space beyond. It was simply an underground tunnel that looked to be the width of the walkway above. As he watched, a small lorry glided by silently, followed by another coming in the opposite direction and on the opposite side. Both had drivers, or loaders, or someone, sitting in the cab.

After a time, Roget stepped back into the large room—a receiving chamber, perhaps—and walked over to the screen and keypad on the side wall. Then he shrugged, stepped forward, and tapped in his guesthouse code.

A single off-key note chimed, followed by, "You have no deliveries in storage, Agent Roget. If you are expecting anything, please try later."

Roget nodded. While he hadn't actually observed the storage area, he had seen the freightways, and the response to his inquiry strongly suggested the truth of Lyvia's descriptions. He had to use his code on the other screen to reenter the guesthouse. Then he made his way up to the reception area.

He waited less than ten minutes before Lyvia arrived.

"Good morning." He stood as he spoke.

"You're cheerful this morning."

"Would it do me any good if I weren't?"

"Probably not." There was no humor in her response. Instead, Lyvia extended a small tube with a belt link. "Here. There is a limited credit authorization on this. You'll have to tell anywhere you use it that you'll need to input your code manually. It's the same code as the one you've been given for the guesthouse facilities. Using the tube without a link is not common, but it's frequent enough that no one is surprised."

"The poor?"

"No. It's usually for people who don't want their identities known, or those whose assets are encumbered by litigation, or those who have had ID difficulties."

"You actually have those sorts of problems? I thought you'd solved everything through economics and regulations."

"Sarcasm doesn't become anyone, Keir, you especially."

He inclined his head. "If my attempts at levity have offended you, I apologize. I am having a great deal of difficulty in obtaining any meaningful information."

"I'm not at my best before breakfast," Lyvia replied.

"What about using this on the subtrans?" Roget held up the tube.

"There's enough there for you to travel freely on the local system, and that's the one area where you can just point it at the black recorders and you don't need a code authorization."

"I mean no offense, but how much is there on the tube? I don't want to order meals or goods I—or your government—can't pay for." Roget used the clip to affix the tube to the waistband of the singlesuit.

"For now, there's a thousand dollars. The average meal at Dorinique is fifty, at a bistro perhaps fifteen to twenty. Local subtrans for you is a flat four dollars per entry."

"Why me?"

"The system adjusts for those who are linked. Those who aren't linked pay the average."

That made sense to Roget. "Why now?"

"It is Saturday, you know? And tomorrow is Sunday. More important, the Ministry wants you to explore Skeptos on your own. Security services don't listen to agents who are only on guided visits. I can't imagine those in the Federation are any different. Now . . . you can take me to breakfast."

"Where?"

"I thought we might try Veronique's." Lyvia turned and headed for the door to the outside walkway.

Roget found himself hurrying after her—again.

Veronique's was a small café four blocks west of the guest-house and two south. Roget noted that Lyvia had picked where they ate so that he'd walked in every direction around the central square.

Once they were seated, Roget barely had time to look around the rear room with its plaster walls and pseudo-uncovered bricks that suggested an ancient French farm-house, when the server arrived, smiling. Roget ordered something called eggs bernaise with tea. Lyvia asked for the breakfast crepes.

Once the server delivered the beverages, Lyvia took a long sip of her coffee, then looked at Roget. "I had some hard-copy maps printed for you because you can't link to the system and ask for directions. I'll give them to you after we finish. Just remember not to litter or try to force your way where you're not granted access. Since you're not linked to the commnet, you won't hear warnings or instructions."

"Is there anyplace I shouldn't go?" He took a sip of the tea.

"Anywhere that you're not granted access. Don't assume that's because we're keeping you from such places. They just may be private dwellings or places where the owners don't allow any strangers."

Roget nodded but wondered just how much access he would actually have.

The server returned and set a platter before him. The eggs bernaise turned out to be a pair of poached eggs, each set on top a half muffin, a slice of ham, another of a sharp cheese, then topped with a piquant sauce with tarragon.

Roget looked to Lyvia. "How much is real?"

"The eggs probably are, and the cheese started with replicated milk products, but the process after that was old style. The ham is high-level replicated."

"That's a lot of power going into replication," he observed.

"Less than the total would be for a fully agricultural society. Besides, the planetary ecology wouldn't take the strain of that much so-called natural farming. There are still areas that aren't much more than barren rock and sand, especially in Thula and Westria, and to a lesser degree in Verite."

Partly replicated or not, the dish was tasty, and Roget didn't leave any scraps. Neither did Lyvia.

"Are you finished?" she asked.

"Yes."

"Good. I promised Aylicia I wouldn't be too long." She rose from the table and slid a long envelope from the hidden thigh pocket of her singlesuit. "Here are the maps I promised. They're fairly high resolution."

Roget stood quickly and took the extended envelope. "Thank you."

"You need to pay," Lyvia reminded him.

"Gratuities?"

"They're very optional. Nothing for standard service. Ten percent for exceptional service."

"Five percent today?"

"Generous, but not out of line." A faint smile crossed her lips and vanished.

Roget walked toward the podium/payment station and the hostess standing there. "I'll need to enter my code manually."

"Of course, sir." She stepped away from the podium. "The total is on the screen here. Just use the pad on the side."

The transaction process was as simple as Lyvia had indicated it would be.

As they walked out of Veronique's, Lyvia glanced at Roget. "I'll meet you in the lobby of the Ministry of Education and Culture at ten on Monday morning. Director Hillis thought another interview and a briefing might be useful. Enjoy your weekend."

With those words she hurried away, leaving Roget standing on the walkway.

He had to admit that had a Thomist landed anywhere on earth, he or she wouldn't haven't been given funds, maps, and access, and allowed to explore, not at least without some form of escort. Still, the Dubietans could certainly keep track of him.

He looked over the maps, then shrugged and folded them back into the envelope, slipping it into a thigh pocket. He might as well wander at first. He turned and began walking. He covered another four long blocks westward past a mixture of small shops, bistros, and unmarked buildings, before he came to an expanse of green that he judged to be a klick square. Evergreens of a type he'd never seen before, with long soft blackish-green needles, marked the perimeter of the park, if that was indeed what it was. All of them ranged in height from four meters to six at most. He walked through the pewter-colored metallic archway between the evergreens. Ahead, the path split.

Roget took the left branch, leading toward a circular grassy field where children, ten or eleven years old, he thought, were playing a game of some sort on what looked to be a circular grassy field. They carried short lengths of a metal shaft ending in an oval mesh frame. There was a single post in the middle of the field, and four narrow open cones branched from the post at a height of five meters.

Half the players wore silver jerseys, and half wore a shimmering purple. Both teams contained girls and boys, it seemed, and the object of the game appeared to be to use the mesh-sticks to fling a yellow ball into one of the cones on the post.

Roget followed the path up a slight slope to where several benches were located. Grass sloped down to the field some thirty meters away. A few handfuls of adults, both men and women, stood around the edge of the field, but the benches were empty. Roget seated himself and began to watch the players. After a time, some aspects of the game became clearer. Narrow strips of the grass had been colored to show four circles. The first circle was red and ran around the post some three meters out. No player crossed that line, nor the other red line, the farthest one, some thirty meters out. The other lines were a brilliant yellow, at ten meters, and a brilliant blue at twenty.

A whistle shrilled as one player smacked another's arm with his stick. Immediately, the smacker left the game and stood in a yellow box just outside the perimeter.

"Are any of them yours?"

Roget frowned momentarily—not at the friendly tone, but because he had understood the words and because they had definitely not been in Stenglish. He turned to the older man, wearing old-style black trousers and a black shirt with a shimmering gray vest, who stood at the end of the bench and smiled. "No. Just watching."

"They're worth watching."

Roget nodded. He didn't want to say much, aware as he was that, while his understanding was better, his speech certainly remained alien.

"To be young again, and carefree." The man shook his head, then walked eastward in the general direction of the central square.

After the man left, Roget stood, then continued to follow the path as it wound toward a set of gardens bounded by a rough wall of black stone, behind which were more of the dark evergreens. As he followed the path through the opening in the wall, he could see that most of the plants were not the green of earth, but either a paler green or of a green so dark that it was almost black, like much of the lettuce in the salads he'd had on Dubiety. Less than a third of the plants were flowering. The blooms were, again, either on the pale side or very dark. One striking flower was a purple black trumpet with gold-fringed blossom ends. He'd never seen anything like it before.

He bent forward and sniffed. The fragrance was lilylike, if not exactly, with a hint of gardenia. Then he straightened and continued through the garden. He walked another thirty meters along the garden path when he saw a pale-leafed plant that was wilted and desiccated, either dying or dead. For some reason, the dying plant struck him, but he kept walking. Another thought struck him. He hadn't seen any butterflies. He turned back to the garden.

Deliberately, he inspected the first flowering plant at the end of the garden. It had a variation on traditional earth flowering plants—stamen, pistil, and pollen. So did the second. The third had tiny blue flowers, but as he studied it, he heard the faintest whirring, and an insect—more like a tiny hummingbird—appeared, flitting from flower to flower.

Roget resumed his walk.

Beyond the garden on the southwest side of the path, he neared another game of the same sort, but the players were clearly older, and there were more adults ringing the field or pitch or whatever it was called.

A path ran around the park, just inside the evergreen hedge. Roget hadn't noticed it before, but what called it to his attention were two women running in long easy strides. Both wore but minimal clothing—skin-tight, low-cut briefs and minimal breast bands—and none of the men standing around the game even turned their heads.

Roget was definitely distracted, enough so that he walked right into one of the benches, cracking his upper shin on the seat. He winced, then bent and rubbed the spot gently.

After a moment, he straightened and continued walking.

By the end of the day, as he walked back toward the guesthouse, he had covered close to twenty klicks of walkways through and around the center of Skeptos. He'd eaten a meal hardly passable at a tiny café without a name, and a slightly better one at a place called Calderones, where the servers all had their hair tinted purple. He hadn't asked about it, not trusting his command of old American.

He had seen a section of the city where there were individual dwellings, but, elegant as they appeared from without, they were comparatively modest in size, the largest being but two stories and encompassing perhaps six hundred square meters at most. He'd also seen small multiple dwellings that, while not decrepit, verged on shabbiness, or what passed for it on Dubiety, and where teenage males lounged on the corners.

He'd walked through three other parks and entered a natatorium with a gallery, where some sort of competition was taking place involving boys and girls of all ages. What he had not seen was anything that looked like an industrial or production facility. He had passed buildings and grounds that looked to be schools, although he did not see anyone there, except a few children playing, with an adult or two nearby.

When he trudged up the guesthouse ramp, well after dark, he was exhausted. Once he entered his quarters, he resolved that he would use the subtrans on Sunday to widen his explorations. Even so, as he sank into the sofa in the main chamber, he almost didn't want to consider the implications of what he had seen. During the entire day, he had neither heard nor seen any form of aircraft. Nor had he encountered anyone or anything who looked like a police officer or a patroller, or an E&W monitor. He had seen people of all ages, and even those with significant variations in their physical features, although none were extremely dark skinned, possibly because lighter skin was a biological necessity under the orbital shields, and . . . most important, he had understood almost every word he had heard spoken.

He couldn't help but wonder if the Thomists were doing

something to his perceptions . . . or if his entire thought processes were being manipulated by some alien intelligence.

Yet his feet ached, and the place where he'd cracked his shin was definitely sore and probably bruised. His internals matched what he had sensed and felt, and even his physical condition. He had tasted food, some of it barely palatable. He had smelled the flowers, heard children playing, and seen all manner of buildings and dwellings.

Either way, he reflected . . . he was in trouble.

18

Once he'd returned to the FSS on Friday afternoon, Roget had explained his early return because of a bout of dehydration. Sung had given him a lecture and let it go at that. Roget had thought about sending another encrypted linkburst report to his controller, then decided against it. He didn't want either dehydration or delusions on his record. He had kept monitoring his internals, but once he'd increased his fluid levels, they continued to indicate he was normal.

Even so, on Saturday morning, Roget slept until close to ten. When he finally woke, he realized just how exhausted he'd been the night before. When he was alert enough to check, he found that his internal monitors indicated that he was in good shape. But then, they hadn't given him any warning on the dehydration/delusion induced by whatever charming Marni and her compatriot had done. His shoulder wasn't sore, but he thought he could see the faintest hint of a circular patch of redness in his upper arm. That would fit with some sort of nanojector, but why were there no other signs? And what had Marni had in mind? She wasn't the type to do something without a purpose.

After eating a leisurely, if not particularly appetizing, replicated breakfast, cleaning up, and dressing, Roget carried a case from the bedroom out to the main area. There he laid out the gear he had available on the table that doubled as desk and eating space. When he finished, he glanced toward the projection to his right. He couldn't help smiling at the little black dachshund with the tannish brown patches over her eyes. "You are something, Hildegarde."

He knew that the dachshund was only an image, but who else could he talk to in St. George? Besides, she did remind him of Muffin.

"You made a lot of people happy, I'd bet, little dog."

Hildegarde didn't answer, but Roget imagined that she bounced a little and wagged her tail as he turned from the image to the gear on the table. He finally decided on the wrist dart gun, a waist-pak that contained various tools designed for circumventing security systems and locks, and, just for emergencies, a small explosive and incendiary device. He had been in St. George for two weeks. That meant he no longer was restricted to mere observation, and he was getting tired of being a target.

Once he arranged the gear, he went back to the bedroom closet and ran a check on the nightsuit, a dark gray, long-sleeved singlesuit. When activated, the special threads and sensors created the image of whatever was behind the suit— from all angles. If Roget slipped the hood over his head and face, even in bright light, he merged with the background, and in darkness, he was close to invisible.

The next step was to use his personal monitor to access certain information and dig out what he could about his putative targets for the evenings ahead. That would take more than a little time.

By the time twilight had begun to creep eastward from the western bluffs across the town, Roget had discovered quite a bit more to put with what he'd already discovered. The women's clothing shop Santiorna's was owned by Julienna Young, the sister of one Brendan B. Smith. While interlocking family ownerships were not uncommon in smaller towns, when energy anomalies occurred involving two properties side by side and when one of those properties was owned by someone already flagged by a Federation agent—a dead agent—Roget thought that was carrying coincidence a bit too far.

In addition, William Dane, Bensen Sorensen, and Brendan Smith had all been classmates at Deseret University, and Smith's father had been a director of Deseret First Bank at the time Dane had been transferred from the Elko branch of the bank to St. George . . . and the elder Smith still was a director, from what Roget could determine. The only one who seemed to have no direct links to the other three on the initial listing Roget had received was Mitchell Leavitt—except that financial dealings usually touched everyone in a town as small as St. George. Leavitt, the collateralizer, had held a second deed of trust on the property owned by one Delbert Parsens, and Parsens had done the sculpture outside The Right Place, Bensen Sorensen's guesthouse. The deed of trust had been released three years earlier for one thousand yuan and "other considerations of value."

Was that too tenuous a connection? Was it just another example of small-town financial incest, so to speak? Or a lead to something larger? One way or another, Roget needed to find out, and that would take some on-site investigating, beginning with DeseretData.

He donned the nightsuit, along with matching dark gray boots, but left the fine mesh hood tucked inside the collar. Then he looked toward Hildegarde. "I'll see you later, little dog."

Wearing the unactivated nightsuit that looked like a casual gray singlesuit, remarkable only for its plainness, Roget left his apartment and walked up 800 East to the tram station. He and two youths, who barely looked in his direction, were the only ones to board the westbound tram. At the main station, Roget transferred to a southbound car, which he took to the 300 South platform. That left him a three-block walk to Bluff Street.

The evening was slightly cooler, and he could hear the occasional buzz of insects. He only saw one older couple on the other side of the street, and they had waved and then continued onward.

A block short of Bluff, when he could see no one nearby and in the shadow of an ancient mulberry tree, he activated the nightsuit and eased the hood over his head. Then he walked the last block to the corner where Santiorna's was located. The shop was dark, and Roget's detector showed no energy emissions at all. Next door, to the north of the clothing boutique, DeseretData had closed, but the lights were still on inside.

Roget walked back along the side of the boutique, but his equipment and monitors detected nothing. Then he slipped up the alley to the rear of DeseretData. Even there, his detector showed no energy emissions whatsoever. Roget moved to the building's energy monitoring box and focused the detector there. Only a slight energy flow was apparent, and there should have been more. Roget glanced down at the alley surface, lightly covered with the red sand that was everywhere. Something caught his eye. He turned, but it was only a cat skulking away. He looked back at the alley surface again.

There was something . . .

He bent down and brushed the sand away. Under the thin layer of sandy grit in the alley were old bricks. Roget looked closer. The bricks were indeed old, but their spacing was perfect, and old bricks in alleys didn't stay perfect for very long. In fact, the bricks along the entire rear of DeseretData had been replaced recently, probably within the last year or so, out to a good two meters from the rear wall.

Roget brought the energy detector to bear on the bricks. Beneath them was the faintest hint of energy flows. As he sensed, rather than heard, voices, he straightened and stepped farther into the shadows.

The rear door opened, and the young man who had answered Roget's questions when he had bought the infosloads stepped out, then looked back into the shop. "You sure you don't need any help, sir?"

"No. I won't be long," came a voice from inside.

"Nine on Monday, sir?"

"A few minutes before. Don't be late."

"No, sir."

Once the young man closed the door and hurried down the alley toward the cross street, Roget stepped back and studied the thick roofing tiles, noting the lines of mortar at each corner of the rear roof. Even for St. George, the tiles were thick, thicker than necessary even for solar tiles. . . . He nodded. They were industrial solar tiles, soltaic cells designed to produce and store electric power. While there was no direct prohibition of their use, tiles like those were extremely expensive, far too costly for a small EES in St. George. Yet, from what he'd discovered earlier, DeseretData was drawing a full quota of power from the grid, and it shouldn't have needed that much with the soltaic array set up on the shop roof.

He walked back along the alley. From what he could determine, Santiorna's also had soltaic tiles across its entire roof. By clambering up on top of a sealed recycling bin, Roget managed to trace the almost hidden connectors that linked the roof grid of the boutique to that of DeseretData. Again, that wasn't proof of anything—except that someone was using a great deal more power than was being registered or monitored. In itself, that certainly wasn't illegal.

He eased himself back down to the alley.

A faint click and then a flash of light that vanished alerted Roget, who flattened himself against the rear wall of Santiorna's. A tall blond man—presumably Brendan B. Smith himself—stepped out of the rear door, locking it, and then sending an energy pulse upward toward the eaves. Immediately, a low-level ambient motion and mass detector field cloaked the two buildings. Roget backed away quickly, slipping to the far side of the alley.

Smith frowned and looked down at a device in his hand. He glanced around, then stepped back several paces from the rear door. Then he nodded, slipped the system controller into a belt holder, and began to walk down the alley.

Roget remained motionless until Smith was well out of sight. He hadn't expected that DeseretData would have such a sophisticated system. Why would a mere EES local outlet need it . . . unless it was more than just an EES? Then he moved silently toward the rear door, stopping well short of the detection field. He took out his monitor and called up the field diagnostic functions.

Even with his equipment, it took Roget almost half an hour before he managed to create a diverter field, and another fifteen minutes to bypass the rear lock circuits. Then he had to pick the mechanical lock as well. The more he had to do, the more convinced he was that whatever Brendan Smith was doing was something Smith didn't want anyone to know about, particularly the Federation.

Once Roget was inside, he slipped on a pair of flat night goggles, and the narrow backroom of the shop turned shades of pale green. He began to search for a doorway or some access to a lower level, although neither was apparent. Eventually, he found a sliding panel at the side of what looked to be a closet. Behind it was a wooden circular staircase down to a basement. Roget took it, if carefully.

The lower level contained three microfabrication units—ancient but effective molecular fabricators. Their presence definitely explained the power requirements of the building. Roget moved to the first, but the fabrication bay was empty, as were those of the second and third machines. A short workbench was set against the south wall, and several objects had been laid out there.

Roget bent down to see them more clearly, then swallowed. While not fully assembled, the pieces definitely looked like an old-style pistol, except for the barrel, which was a dark solid material flanked by two thin metal rods, each of which terminated a fraction of a centimeter short of the end of the solid barrel. The grip had not been fitted, but inside the frame were the mounting and leads for a quick discharge capacitor. Roget was standing over a device that looked suspiciously like an antique narrow-beam nerve shredder.

There was something about the basement walls. They were all dark and metallic. Although he couldn't tell for sure, he thought they were covered with lead sheets nanocoated with something to keep the lead from getting into the air. The last thing he noted was the heavy vault door set in the east wall of the basement. He wasn't about to try to open that, not with the equipment he carried, but he was more than willing to bet that behind the heavy vault door lay an armory of some sort.

He made his way back up the circular staircase, then closed the sliding panel.

His internal sensors registered the change in energy fields. Someone had deactivated the outside security system. While he thought he'd bypassed all the alarms, there was always the possibility of another system, a totally passive one.

Roget slipped to the rear wall and then dropped into a squat, facing the door. He waited. After almost five minutes, the door opened.

Nerve-shredder blasts swept the back room even before the man stepped inside, and Roget flattened himself against the floor and rear wall. Despite his position, one bolt slashed Roget's right leg. Sheer agony slammed up his leg and spinal column, and it took all his concentration to keep still and wait for the man—Smith—to step fully through the rear door.

Roget fired a dart.

Smith looked blankly at the narrow penetrator protruding from his chest, then tried to grab for it, but his fingers slipped away as his body began to convulse. The nerve shredder dropped from his other hand.

Roget inched forward toward the paralyzed man, trying to get an impression of who or what, if anyone, remained outside. Just short of the still half-open door, he began to pick up signs of two other men, also with nerve shredders, standing outside, well back from the rear entrance. One wore goggles—heat/motion detectors.

There was no way for Roget to cross the open distance without getting hit by the shredders, especially with one leg burning and numb. He eased awkwardly into a standing position and opened the waist-pak. Out came the explosive device. Step by step, he made his way back to the closet and the sliding panel, which he eased open before he tossed the device down into the basement.

Then he hurried—as quickly as he could—out of the back room and into the front room, circling so that he would not be in the line of fire from the two men outside. He waited . . . and waited, keeping low so that he could not be silhouetted against the growing glow from the fire that was beginning to reach up the wooden staircase into the back room.

He slowly moved until he was positioned beside the front door, one hand on the heavy stool that sat beside the processing console.

Behind and around him the entire building shuddered, and the floor shivered, buckling upward in the back room. More flames began to lick upward in the rearward section of the building. He could sense one of the men behind the building rushing toward the rear door, hopefully to reclaim Smith.

All sorts of nanomists began to flood the premises, along with water from an old-style fire sprinkler system, but the oils and chemicals in the supply bins of the microfabbing equipment in the basement had begun to feed the flames, and with some of them supplying oxygen, the fire continued to grow.

Because the heat was getting oppressive, even as low as he was to the floor, Roget finally slammed the stool through the glass of the door. The rush of air offered a moment of respite before the fire intensified. Roget took a deep breath, then began to clamber through the lower part of the front door where the glass had been. A handful of people had gathered on the far side of Bluff Street, but Roget judged that his nightsuit would blur him enough against the shifting light created by the fire that his exit from the building would not be that noticeable.

The toe of his boot on his injured leg caught on the metal rim of the door, and he had to use his free hand to help lever his barely responsive leg high enough to free his foot. Even so, if anyone saw his figure, no one yelled or said anything as he limped slowly and painfully up Bluff Street. Behind him the sound of klaxons and sirens rose, and fire lorries and local patrollers converged on the burning building that held DeseretData.

It took Roget almost an hour to reach his apartment, by foot and slowly, because he didn't want any record on the tram system of where he'd been. From there, he immediately burst-sent a message to his controller, explaining the probable armory behind and beneath the smoldering ruins of Deseret-Data, as well as the microfabbing equipment and nerve shredders, and an explanation that the discharges from the devices used by the three men had apparently set the fire. He wasn't about to report that he had, and neither the colonel nor his controller would have wanted that in a report.

Within minutes, a response arrived. Roget read over it, his eyes picking out the key phrases.

. . . incendiary results unfortunate but understandable . . . will alert local authorities and request
complete inventory of weapons discovered . . . federal inspector will arrive within hours to cordon
area . . . remain in current status . . . do not contact
inspector . . . As necessary . . . authorization to use all
force required against those involved . . .

That might be, but Roget was in no shape to use force
against anyone, or do much more, for the moment and for at
least several hours, until the worst of the nerve pain in his
leg subsided.

He also wasn't in the least happy with the wording that
suggested the fire was unfortunate. Without it, he'd most
likely be dead or captured by the locals as an intruder, and
the FSA certainly wouldn't have been happy about that—
except that he'd have been disavowed, with no records remaining to show his affiliation, and he'd have ended up
relocated and brain-damped, if not worse.

19

21 MARIS 1811 P. D.

Monday morning, Roget was awake early. Sunday had been
a more detailed repeat of Saturday, except that he'd used the
subtrans to visit the areas around five other local stations.
While the geography varied somewhat, and the architecture
more than a little, the similarities were overwhelming. He
saw no sign of industrial facilities anywhere on the surface,
but he'd found more than a few tunnels from the subtrans
ramps that led to archways that didn't open to him. There

were parks and schools and shopping districts—and no wheeled surface transport, except for two powered chairs used by individuals who looked to have acute leg problems. He'd sweated through the humidity and observed happy people, sad people, laughing and crying children, and not a single individual in what looked to be a uniform. There were few overt signs of old age, but that was to be expected in an advanced society. There were also somewhat fewer children than he would have expected, which suggested a comparatively stable population—something rare in a society without apparent overt control measures. While he'd worn his camouflage-equipped blue shipsuit both Saturday and Sunday, there had been no place and no reason to use it, but he'd felt more comfortable having its capabilities.

When he finished breakfast Monday at the nameless bistro where he and Lyvia had eaten on Saturday, he took his time walking to the square and then north to the Ministry of Education and Culture. He was early enough that he saw a constant flow of men and women in roughly equal proportions leaving the central square—but not nearly so many as he would have expected in a capital city.

Surprisingly to him, there was a chill and brisk wind, as if fall or even winter were on the way. How could that be, given the redistribution of solar radiation by the orbital shields and the minimal axial tilt of the planet?

Lyvia was waiting inside the Ministry of Education and Culture. She wore a deep blue singlesuit with a short cream vest. "You look better in the green than the blue or gray."

"The gray and blue both need cleaning. I'm not used to the humidity here. Is everywhere on Dubiety as damp as Skeptos or the Machiavelli Peninsula?"

"The general humidity level depends on the altitude. People who have trouble with it often move to the Anasazi Plateau in the west of Thula. The altitude there is around two thousand meters. Some people think that Chaco is a charming town, with all the native stone. Andoya isn't bad either.

They're both quiet, though. Very quiet compared to Skeptos or even Avespoir."

"It's colder today," Roget observed.

"That's not surprising. We're headed into fall."

"But the shields . . . ?"

"Dubiety's orbit is elliptical enough that the change in total radiation makes a difference. We don't have hemispherical seasonal differences but planetwide seasons. It's fall everywhere at the same time. Oh, there are local variations, usually because of altitude and proximity to the oceans, and when it does get colder in the mountains, we have stronger winds." She gestured toward the doors that led to the ramps. "Shall we go? I imagine Director Hillis is waiting."

The fact that she spoke in old American reminded Roget, and he asked, "What sort of technology have you aimed at me so that I've been able to understand people better? I assume it's been in my sleep."

Lyvia nodded. "It's easier that way."

"What is it?"

"A linguistics booster. You only needed a little help. Stenglish differs from old American more in cadence and pronunciation than in terms of basic vocabulary."

"How does it work?"

"I have no idea, except that similar technology has been around for a long while, even in the Federation. Or it used to be." Without waiting for a reply, she turned and headed for the ramp doors.

The implication of her last five words bothered Roget, but he took three quick steps and caught up with her. He didn't say anything until she paused at the third level before the door opened.

"What about the other scout?"

"I have no idea. Director Hillis could tell you." Lyvia stepped through the door, turned to her left, and headed through the reception area, past a young-faced man who looked up abruptly as the two agents swept past him.

If Hillis would tell, thought Roget, and if what she said could be trusted . . .

Selyni Hillis stood waiting by the door to the very same conference room where Roget had first met her. "Please come in. We need to cover some matters quickly."

Roget and Lyvia had barely stepped into the conference room when Hillis closed the door and pointed to a bound volume set beside a blue case that was roughly five centimeters thick and eight centimeters on a side. Both rested in the middle of the conference table. "The Federation places a great emphasis on hard evidence. These briefing packets contain information printed on nearly-indestructible film sheets that can be washed and sterilized. In addition, the case contains the same information, as well as a great deal more, in link-insets compatible with Federation systems, including the portable versions that can be operated independently of ship systems."

"They won't let anything like that onto a Federation ship," Roget pointed out.

"We're aware of that. That's why the information is set out in multiple formats. It can be read from the dropboat, run through whatever filters you think necessary, and transmitted from there. If someone is particularly suspicious, it can be read aloud and transcribed, or scanned with your own equipment and retransmitted."

"Is the technique for language implantation in there?" Roget gestured toward the case and bound volume.

Selyni Hillis smiled. "We're not about to spend time reinventing what the Federation has lost or buried."

"Then what will you offer them?"

"Why don't you read the material and see? That's why it's here." Hillis took the chair closest to the door.

Roget took the chair that put his back to the window, sat down, and reached for the bound volume. He opened it. The first inside page was blank. The second was a table of contents.

The first chapter heading read "Planetary Radiation Shields." Roget flipped to the first page of that section and read a page, then a second. He couldn't say that he understood everything, or even that it was technically correct, but it purported to contain the theory and specifications for designing a shield like the ones around Dubiety.

He looked up. "Assuming this is correct and not technical double-talk, why would you give this to the Federation?"

"It's not double-talk, and we do have our reasons."

Roget went back to the table of contents. The second heading read "Pseudo-Event-Horizon T-D Transposition." He tried to read that section, but all he could glean from it was that it purported to be another form of interstellar jump drive. The next section dealt with a form of anomalous composite with radiation-damping properties. The next section was a proof of some sort that he could make no sense of at all, except for the title, "Trans-Temporal Entropic Reversal."

He looked up. "If I understand any of this, you're offering technology, or technological insights that the Federation doesn't have."

"Or has and has chosen not to employ. We're not exactly privy to what the High Council or the FSA has decided."

"I don't see the linguistic technology here, but you'll give them technology they don't have?"

"That's an interesting choice of words, Agent Roget. Let's just say that in the interests of friendship and a willingness to avoid conflict, we'll offer potentially useful technology." Hillis smiled.

"What's to keep a Federation fleet from just showing up and taking whatever they want?" he countered.

"We would hope that the Federation would read and consider our offerings first. That's why we'll be sending you back with the material. Our technical staff has been working on your dropboat over the weekend, and they believe they'll have both boats ready to launch for your return by Thursday, Friday at the latest."

"Exactly how am I supposed to get through your orbital screens?" asked Roget.

"We do have ways, but that is one matter that we'll keep to ourselves for now. I trust you do understand that."

If there actually happened to be such a way, he could see why they wouldn't be interested in revealing it. He was more worried that he was just being set up for what amounted to a suicide launch. But . . . if that were the case . . . again, why the elaborate charade? And if it weren't a charade . . .

"Why don't you just defy the Federation?"

"We believe in offering first," replied Hillis. "In technological societies, all conflicts cost more than they recover, even for the winner."

"Historically, that hasn't seemed to matter."

Hillis shrugged. "We hope that the Federation has learned something from that history. We have."

"You seem to think that—"

"What we think is irrelevant to what the Federation will do. What the Federation thinks is what matters. Your job as an agent is to provide information. Your job as a human being is to provide insight and persuasion. Also, we'd like you to return to the *WuDing* in one piece. We'd prefer not to give the Federation any unnecessary excuses for stupid actions."

"I'm just one agent." Roget paused. "I'd be interested to know how the other scout is faring."

"He isn't as adaptable as you. He attempted to attack a number of people. He's been restrained until he can be returned to the *WuDing*—or whatever Federation ship will handle your recovery."

"You're sending us both back? How thoughtful." Roget knew he shouldn't have been so sarcastic, but it was a measure of his frustration—and something else he couldn't immediately identify.

"You don't want to return to your beloved Federation?" Hillis's words matched Roget's almost perfectly in the degree of sarcasm. She turned to Lyvia. "He should see Manor Farm Cottages. Today might be best."

For just a moment, distaste flitted across Lyvia's eyes. At least Roget suspected it was distaste. Whether Lyvia found another escort duty distasteful or whether she found going to Manor Farm Cottages unpleasant, he didn't know, but either was possible.

"Might I ask what these cottages are for?"

"You'll understand when you see them. If you have questions after you do, Lyvia will certainly be able to answer them. We'll meet again tomorrow sometime." Hillis turned to Lyvia. "You know where to reach me."

"Yes, Director."

"That will be all for now." Hillis stood. "Good day."

As he rose, Roget's first thought was that he still didn't understand the almost disjointed interview/interrogation system the Thomists were employing. Was it merely to get him into a room where they could upset or confuse him and then use technology to pull thoughts and information out of his mind? But why would they go to all the trouble of putting together an information package and then design it so that its contents could be received without any Trojan horses? Or did the very words themselves constitute something like that? And then there had been the words about not giving the Federation any excuse for stupid actions. Had that really been the point of sending agent scouts in the first place? Certainly, the FSA had done that before, as Roget well knew . . . personally.

"We can go," Lyvia said quietly.

Roget followed her out along the corridor and down the ramp to the main level. Then she headed through the building foyer for the walkway leading to the central square. Her steps were long and deliberate. Once they were outside, Roget drew alongside her. He got the definite impression that she was less than pleased with the assignment the director had ordered.

"How long will this take?"

"Several hours, at the least."

"Where are we headed?"

"The regional subtrans in the square." Her words were cool and clipped.

Roget decided not to say more, not for the moment. In fact, he said nothing at all until they were seated side by side in a half-filled car on the regional subtrans line heading northward out of Skeptos.

"How many stops before we get off?"

"It's the second stop."

Roget sat quietly through the first stop and rose when Lyvia did at the second. From his internals, he calculated that the travel time had been approximately eleven minutes. When they stepped out onto the underground concourse, they were the only ones. Lyvia marched toward the ramp, and Roget matched her step for step.

"We're close to three hundred klicks from Skeptos," he ventured.

"There's a reason for that. The cottages are purposely isolated, except by subtrans. You'll see why."

"You people never explain anything before the fact," Roget observed.

"That's not true. We explain whatever we can. Some things have to be experienced or observed for the explanation to make sense, and trying to explain them before the fact just creates false impressions and preconceptions."

Roget couldn't help but wonder if overwhelming people with experiences that they were unprepared for did exactly the same thing but saw no reason for voicing the point, not given Lyvia's attitude.

When they emerged from the subtrans tunnel and ramp, Roget noted that there was but a single walkway leading due north out of a low circular grassy vale, totally without trees. At least Roget thought the walkway led north, but without a visible sun and with his questions about just how precise his

internal monitors were, his directional senses were as likely
to be assumptions as totally accurate. Beyond the grassy depression were trees in all directions, as if the subtrans station had been set in the midst of a vast forest.

"Can you tell me why the cottages are located in such an
isolated locale?"

"For safety purposes," replied Lyvia. "You'll see."

"How far do we have to walk?"

"It's four klicks to the outskirts of the cottages."

The forest held more deciduous trees than had the one on
the peninsula, and the air was even more humid. The underlying scents mixed a richness with dampness, but without
the hint of sweetness that had bothered Roget. "There aren't
any butterflies here."

"No. Their absence makes balancing the ecology more
difficult, but it's necessary."

"Is that because it's not that deep . . . literally?"

"There is an indigenous subsurface microbial ecology, but
it never evolved beyond that, and it's not hostile. Not any
more hostile than any bacterial or microbial ecology anyway,
and there are some interesting things going on there. It's
more a problem of balancing with people in a way that makes
sense practically and economically. We've opted away from
truffles, for example. If they eventually develop, that's fine,
but introducing that kind of gourmet and economic temptation is just asking for trouble."

Roget kept asking about the ecology as they walked, because that was an area where Lyvia was willing to talk, and
information, any information, was better than no information. Besides, he could deduce some things from what she
did say.

The forest ended abruptly, as if a line had been drawn, and
a good klick ahead, Roget saw a series of low dwellings—
cottages, in fact. Somewhere in the distance, the forest resumed, but the cleared area that held the cottages looked to
be a rough oval about three klicks across. The cottage walls

looked to be of local stone, and the roofs of something resembling slate, although Roget wouldn't have been surprised if it had been some form of composite.

"There are the Manor Farm Cottages, and there's the security station." Lyvia pointed.

Ahead on the right side of the path stood a single dwelling, separated from those farther north by a good hundred meters of open grassy ground.

"That's the first security establishment you've pointed out."

"It's been the only one to point out," she replied.

As they neared the security cottage, a muscular man wearing a short-sleeved yellow singlesuit stepped out of the dwelling and stood on the front stoop, waiting for them.

"How many security agents are there here?"

"I'd imagine just a few, either a couple or a pair of partners. They're really here to deal with outsiders or illnesses or accidents."

"Agent Rholyn, you're expected. I'm Mattias Singh." The black-haired man smiled, then turned to Roget. "What you see in and around the cottages may be disturbing. Please keep in mind that no one there can physically touch anyone else without suffering. It would be for the best if you did not touch them either."

Roget nodded.

"Take your time, and see what you need to see, Agent Rholyn."

"Thank you." Lyvia's voice was pleasant but cool.

Less than fifty meters past the cottage, Roget's internals registered a low-level energy field of some sort. Even without his monitors, he could sense something, a low sound that raised the hair on the back of his neck, but it passed after he'd taken another dozen steps.

Off to his left, a gray-bearded man wearing brown trousers and little else ran across the grass away from the cottages, then collapsed in a heap. Roget stopped and watched. The gray-beard rolled over, then crawled back toward the cottages before slowly standing. Then he again ran away from the cottages, as if trying to escape, before he crumpled onto the grass once more.

Roget turned to Lyvia.

"There's a subsonic fence around the cottage area. Didn't you sense it? All of those restrained here experience agonizing pain if they even approach it. Sometimes some of them will crawl halfway in and become so paralyzed with pain that they can't move. That's one of the things that Mattias or his partner have to watch for."

"Can't anyone else . . ." Roget broke off his question. The immobilizing nature of the pain and the fact that none of the inmates could touch another supplied him with the answer to his uncompleted inquiry.

As Roget and Lyvia neared the first line of cottages, a woman wearing antique hoop skirts with her hair piled into a conical shape that looked like the tip of an ancient artillery shell waddled toward them. "I dare say that you be visitors, and unwelcome you are. Please cease and desist, and depart henceforth."

"We'll depart soon enough." Roget didn't want to walk over her, but she was blocking the middle of the walkway, and he took another step.

She scuttled back. "Begone, evil one."

On the side porch of the next cottage, a painfully thin woman sat rocking on a makeshift rocker. Her eyes were fixed on the porch railing, even as she rocked herself methodically.

Roget blinked. A man hurried toward them, wearing a Federation shipsuit.

"You're not one of them, are you? I can see the difference. We're all prisoners here. Can you tell the Federation about us? Please! Anyone who's different they lock up here, and they say we're maladjusted, but we're not. I've been here years and years. I just want to go home. Please. I don't belong here. I really don't."

Roget couldn't help but stop, but when he looked more closely at the shipsuit, he could see that it was well-sewn but poorly designed, and with insignia and devices he'd never seen and that mixed officer and enlisted emblems.

"You have to tell them. You have to get help."

Roget looked at Lyvia.

She smiled sadly.

"You're no Fed! You're one of them. You're just trying to trick us . . ." Tears ran from the corners of the man's eyes, and he turned away.

Roget moved on.

"Come to the circus . . . come to the play, for all the world's a play, and the play's the thing . . ." Those words came from a thin-faced man who sat on a stool before a small table at the west side of the walkway, under an open window to a cottage. His fingers flicked out oversized cards onto the polished but battered wood surface. "I can call up Madame Sosotris for you, or even Tiresias . . . for you, sir, are the hanged man. You may not know it, but, that, you are . . . and you will return to your people, an alien people who clutch alien gods . . ."

Roget repressed a shiver. Mad as the man clearly was, Roget might well end up a hanged man, figuratively, of course, if dead all the same.

A woman of indeterminate age sat on the ground, leaning back against the wall of the next cottage, her feet splayed across dirt that might once have been a flower bed. She just giggled, then giggled again.

An odor of rancidness and outright filth crept more tightly around Roget the deeper he and Lyvia walked into the cottages.

"Doesn't anyone take care of them?" he asked in a low voice.

"Why? They've chosen not to be taken care of. We keep the replicators full and the houses functional. They can go to the clinic if they choose, or not, as they please. None of them is of exceptionally poor intelligence. All of them have chosen to remain here, and they did so while their minds were stabilized. We used to do stabilization once every five years and ask again, but the results were the same."

Everywhere Roget looked was madness, from glittering bright eyes to dull or vacant ones. What the inhabitants of Manor Farm Cottages wore ranged from almost any kind of clothing Roget had ever seen to nothing at all. Those who wore nothing tended to be painfully thin.

Abruptly, Lyvia turned to Roget. "You've seen enough. We need to head back to Skeptos. I'd like to pick up Aylicia before it's too late."

"That's fine with me." It certainly was, because it hadn't been Roget's idea to visit the cottages. Besides, both the sights and odors were beginning to get to him.

Lyvia turned. "We can go back this way. It's the other main walkway. That way, you can see a different view of more of the same." Her voice remained cool.

Roget frowned as he neared another cottage. The stones of the walls glistened. The windows sparkled, and the trim was even painted. An angular man was scrubbing the stones of the north wall of the small dwelling vigorously. He didn't look up or sideways as Lyvia and Roget walked by. Roget had the feeling that his scrubbing was what had polished the stones. He wondered how many years it had taken.

In an open grassy area to his left, Roget turned to watch a gray-haired woman running, holding a string with a small kite attached. Even at full speed, the woman could barely keep the little kite airborne.

Roget said nothing more. He just kept watching and walking until he and Lyvia were on the path away from the cottages and had passed the subsonic barrier.

"Now you've seen the Manor Farm Cottages."

"How can anyone do that? How can you?"

"It's their choice."

"That's no choice," snapped Roget.

"No . . . they have a choice. They can ask for personality modification or guided re-memory emphasis. All of them have rejected that. They claim that they wouldn't be themselves."

"Isn't that true?"

"Absolutely," Lyvia agreed. "But the people that they are as themselves make choices that impact violently and adversely on others, occasionally fatally, and individual freedom must always stop well short of other people's persons."

"So you'd turn them into automatons . . ."—he struggled for the word—". . . zombies, the living dead."

"They're very much alive. Not particularly sane, but definitely alive. Medicating or adjusting them might turn them into zombies, though."

"And you can't do anything better than this? There has to be a better way."

"Sometimes there isn't. There are limits to what one can do to the human brain," Lyvia replied. "Are you running around screaming that we're evil monsters who won't share our technology? Even if you feel that way?"

"Of course not."

"Exactly. Even you choose to behave civilly in a situation where you feel under threat. If they choose to live in what amounts to an animal farm . . . that's their choice," Lyvia replied. "We don't feel obligated, beyond the basic necessities, to coddle those who are unwilling to make decisions that allow them to function in society. We don't believe that we should have to spend huge amounts of resources keeping people who won't act responsibly comfortable and in better situations than those who work. Unlike some societies, we require accountability and real choices."

"What sort of choice is that?" He gestured back toward the cottages.

"It's a real choice."

"Why don't you just . . . adjust them?"

"Without their consent? And then where would it stop?" asked Lyvia. "Once you give governments the power to adjust people and their perceptions, you're on the road to empire and ruin. Throughout history, societies have forced unfree choices on people. We don't force the choices; we just insist on the consequences of those choices falling on the choosers—except when it's clear that there isn't the mental capacity to choose. There are very few people to whom that applies, and they're handled far more gently and warmly."

"What about the lack of emotional capacity?"

She gestured back toward Manor Farm. "They end up in cottages like these and they remain there for life . . . or until they decide they want to change."

"That's . . . cruel."

"Is it? All choices involve change," she said patiently. "These people wish to hurt others in one way or another, either by refusing to take responsibility for their actions or taking emotional or physical pleasure in inflicting abuse. That's not acceptable."

"What about those who seek adventure, the thrill of danger? Do you imprison their minds as well?"

Lyvia smiled. "No. Just as there is always another dynasty, so to speak, there are always frontiers, and we let them seek such—just not on Dubiety."

"What do you mean by 'another dynasty'?"

"Isn't it obvious? In stable empires, the rulers change. If matters get too bad, another family or group usurps power, and matters go on mostly as before. Societies that have frontiers tend to be more stable in the center because the adventure-and-danger seekers gravitate toward the frontiers, as do the antisocial or the less advantaged."

"How many of your well-adjusted citizens know about places . . . like these?"

"Every last one of them over the age of eighteen. It's called the Omelas requirement. I don't know the origin of the term, but it means that they have to see that, while all choices are possible, they all have repercussions, and that even in the best of societies, the greatest cruelty is freedom of choice. A society that eliminates all misery eliminates true choice and freedom."

"The great freedom to be miserable." Roget didn't hide the sarcasm.

"Without it, there is no joy." After a moment, she gestured behind them. "Do you think I really wanted to bring you here? That I enjoyed this?"

Roget was silent.

20

26 LIANYU 6744 F. E.

Roget did get some sleep on Saturday night and early Sunday morning, but he still woke with a headache—and a very sore leg. He could move his leg, and that would have to do. A very hot shower helped get rid of the headache and eased the soreness in his leg somewhat. As he hurried through a marginally palatable and fully replicated breakfast, he considered what he needed to do . . . and what the Saint dissidents might do—although he had no doubt that they thought they were patriots or idealists or true believers, something along those lines.

One possibility was that none of the conspirators would do anything and, if questioned, claim that Smith had been operating on his own. The other was that they'd attempt to remove any additional evidence located elsewhere. Roget was betting on the second, and that was another reason why he was up early on Sunday.

He sponged and wiped off the nightsuit as well as he could, then donned it. He did not power it up. That would come later. While it wouldn't be as effective in daylight, its background matching provided excellent camouflage during the day, especially inside and when he wasn't moving, and that might come in useful. Then he reloaded the wrist-dart, still with just paralyzing darts rather than the lethal variety, and gathered his equipment together. Within ten minutes he was out of the apartment, walking up 800 East to the tram station, where he waited ten minutes before he took the next eastbound. He was one of three people in the entire car, and the other two were Sudam men who seemed to be dozing.

Once he left the Red Cliffs station, and he was the only one who got off there, he walked to the path down Middleton wash, through the gate to Delbert Parsens's studio, and up the path and around to the east side of the building. The sign in the outside niche read STUDIO CLOSED. That didn't surprise Roget. He'd discovered that most Saint establishments were closed on Sunday, as they had been traditionally for centuries, if not longer.

He stepped into the shadows of the entrance at the top of the stone steps and powered up the nightsuit, then eased the mesh hood over his face. Roget could sense the energies of the building's security system, but it was on standby, suggesting that people were inside, for all that the studio area looked empty. The door was locked, but only manually, and it took but a few moments with his picks before Roget was inside. He locked the door behind himself, replaced the picks in his waist-pak, and moved slowly down the long gradual ramp from the entrance into the main studio, keeping close to the walls and display cases to his right.

No one was in the studio. Roget glanced at the block of redstone Parsens had been working earlier but didn't see that the sculptor had made that much progress on the John D. Lee statue. He continued through the studio and up a short and narrow ramp to the older section of the building. The staircase to the lower level wasn't concealed at all, but lay behind a partly open door off the old main foyer of the building. Roget could sense energies below, as well as hear the murmur of voices that grew louder as he eased down the steps. At the bottom was a small foyer and an open door to the right. The room there was empty, but was set up as a small lecture hall or classroom.

From where were the voices coming?

Then he realized that the mirror at the rear of the lower foyer wasn't anything of the sort, but a reflective holo screen. He started to ease his head through the screen near the edge, fighting the disorientation, and found himself looking at a closet. To his right was a side panel, barely ajar. He stepped into the closet, then peered through the narrow opening in the sliding side panel.

Beyond it was a long chamber, and along one side were piping and what looked to be antique heat concentrators and generators. Beyond them was an array of more modern and large flash capacitors. As Roget had suspected, a small geothermal power plant lay under the studio, most probably the source of the thermal discharge to the Virgin River.

Roget couldn't see that much beyond the three men who sat around an old table, except that there was a solid wooden wall on the west end of the chamber. That didn't mean there wasn't another hidden doorway or passage, not the way the Saint conspirators seemed to favor them. After a moment he recognized two of the three—Parsens and Sorensen. The third looked like the single image of William Dane he'd been able to find.

Roget listened.

". . . tried the antidotes with Brendan, but by the time we could get to him he was already gone . . ."

Antidotes? Roget had made sure that his wrist-dart had only used paralytic darts, not combat darts that immediately shocked the nervous system into a fatal shutdown. Had Smith had allergies? But if he had, why had the others been prepared with an antidote . . . unless they were waiting for a security raid?

"Mitchell . . . he said he'd be here later. Something came up in his ward . . ."

"Something always comes up in his ward, especially if there's anything possibly inconvenient to do . . . or decide . . . unless he knows someone else will do it . . ."

"ChinoFed has to be the new E&W monitor . . . no one else new in town . . ."

". . . early thirties and a temp appointment . . . says FSA to me . . ."

". . . could be a deep agent they activated . . ."

". . . wouldn't have two of them here. They don't think we're that big a problem . . ."

"No . . . just think that the only good Danite is a dead Danite . . ."

Danites? It took a moment before Roget recalled the religious terrorist organization that had been agitating for local regional rule, based on "cultural differences."

"They'll see."

"They might see too soon. They got Brendan, and Tyler says that there's a Federation inspector at DeseretData already with a military escort. They've found the armory."

"Not everything was there."

"Enough, and enough for proof."

"Only against Brendan."

". . . won't stop them . . ."

"Do we move everything out of here?"

"Where do we move it? And why? Except for some personal weapons . . ."

"The FSA can claim anything they find is illegal. You know that . . ."

"Too bad Marni's stuff doesn't always work . . ."

". . . converts some . . ."

Converts some? Chemical conversion? There was no way that could work. In any case, Roget didn't dare wait too long, and he'd heard enough. He lifted his arm and fired the first dart, then the second. Both Sorensen and Parsens were convulsing before Dane leapt to his feet and whirled toward the panel door, his hand reaching for the nerve shredder on the table.

It took Roget two darts to get a clean shot, but Dane struggled, then collapsed.

Roget pushed aside the panel and hurried toward the fallen men. All three were twitching, and Sorensen began to gasp.

Antidotes? Roget searched Sorensen quickly but couldn't find anything resembling an inhaler, a syringe, or an injector. He moved to Dane, but found nothing there. Parsens had an injector of some sort, and Roget immediately pressed it against Sorensen's bare neck.

Slowly, the gasping stopped—except both other men had begun to wheeze. Abruptly, Parsens shuddered and stopped breathing. Then, so did Dane.

Roget stood, slowly.

Had all of them been death-sensitized to Federation paralytics? Why? So they couldn't reveal the extent of the conspiracy or the underground—the Danites? He turned toward the west wall . . . too late.

"I wouldn't move if I were you."

Roget finished turning, slowly, to face the speaker, standing before an open door on the west end of the underground room. The one side of the door matched the paneling, one reason why Roget hadn't noticed it.

Marni Sorensen stood there, wearing motion-detecting goggles, with a nerve shredder trained on him. "Stay right there, Keir. You may be in a camosuit, but there's no one else quite so tall as you in town."

"I wouldn't think of moving. But I do have a question for you before you shred me. What was that business with the false memory?"

"It wasn't false. It's just a chunk of memory. Not yours, but one picked to give you a chance to understand. To learn what's really important in life. At worse, it would disorient you. We would have preferred that you understood. Live converts are far better than dead FSA infiltrators."

The whole idea of memories inserted into his brain chilled Roget, but he couldn't dwell on that. Not at the moment. "Whatever it was, it killed an innocent photographer . . ." That was a guess on Roget's part.

"He had the same chance you did. To understand—"

"And become an unwilling convert?" Another guess on Roget's part.

"It doesn't work that way. It just opens you to understand. He was another Federation spy who couldn't understand . . ."

"He was just an observer."

"*Just* an observer? Like you're just an E&W monitor." Her laugh was short and harsh. "It really is too bad you won't get to relive the rest of the memories. You might understand, then, you traitor . . ."

"Traitor to what . . . ?"

"I couldn't expect you to be loyal to Deseret, but you could have been loyal to the United States . . ."

"There hasn't been a United States in more than a thousand years," Roget protested.

"That's right. That's because of cowardly traitors like you, knuckling under to the Sinese to keep yourselves comfortable . . ."

"What's back in the other room, besides more geothermal power units?"

"It doesn't matter." She lifted the barrel of the nerve shredder fractionally, so that it pointed directly at his chest.

Roget stretched his arms slightly, bringing them forward just slightly. "What's the point? You've already killed one Federation agent, and you're about to kill another. For what? You don't have the funds or the resources to take on the Federation. Your hidden armory is already under Federation control."

"You don't understand, do you? Faith and knowledge will

always triumph. It takes both. The United States thought will and skill and knowledge was enough. It wasn't. The Republic of Faith and the Islamists thought faith was sufficient. It wasn't."

"Marni . . ." Roget said quietly. "No one else is coming. The Danites will lose. You won't get rescued."

"Neither will you. The Federation's weakness is that it doesn't ever send enough operatives to handle situations. You're more expendable than I am." Marni Sorensen smiled coolly as she kept the nerve shredder pointed at his midsection.

Roget almost felt sorry for her . . . and her ignorance. "That's its strength as well." He stretched, swinging his arms together and locking his fingers.

The dart took her in the eye, and she stood there, shivering, trying to press the stud on the shredder before it slipped from her fingers and *clunked* dully on the crimson carpet.

". . . you still have to live with the memories . . . understand . . . you will . . ." She shuddered, then collapsed into a heap, twitching.

Roget hurried toward her, then bent down and rifled through her singlesuit, searching for an injector that might hold an antidote. There wasn't one. He rushed through the open hidden doorway to the room from which she had come—and halted. The south side of the long chamber was filled with equipment, including more microfabbers and other devices he didn't immediately recognize, but the north side was bright and spotless . . . and looked like a small but equipment-intensive laboratory of some sort. Roget hurried through the laboratory, opening drawers, cabinets, and cases, but amid all the equipment, while he saw a case of unused and unopened injectors, he didn't see, or couldn't find, anything that resembled a loaded injector.

By the time he returned, empty-handed, Marni was dead.

Roget looked down at her still form, then shook his head. He checked Bensen Sorensen, but the innkeeper and

Danite was still breathing. Roget used a pair of restraints on Sorensen's hands and feet, although the dart wasn't likely to wear off before the Federation inspector appeared.

Then he walked upstairs and out to the studio, where he used the comm system and his personal monitor to burst-send an urgent report.

The reply was immediate:

Inspector and team on the way. Vacate and do not break cover.

Roget slipped his monitor back into its case, then moved toward the door. Marni had been the only one who'd actually seen him, if in the nightsuit, but his cover was still broken, no matter what his controller said. Still, he wasn't about to argue. Not where he was.

He hurried back out through the sliding panel, leaving it open, and up the stairs, and then to the studio and up the ramp.

Likely as not, more than a few members of the Saint Quorum and Presidency would end up vanishing over the weeks and months ahead. Then again, they might not, but they weren't his problem. Despite what had just happened, he wasn't an eliminator . . . unless he was threatened. He was just the one who uncovered the problems and started the resolution.

He told himself that again as he opened the door at the east end of Parsens's studio, then stepped outside, leaving it unlocked this time.

He took three steps out into the full morning sunlight before a wave—or a cloud—of dizziness brought him to a halt, the red rocks and stones to the east of him swirling like solid red clouds.

He staggered backward, then sat down on the bottom step, just before the blackness rose up and drowned him.

21

That Monday night, Roget sat on the sofa in his guesthouse quarters, sipping what amounted to barely drinkable formulated lager. He looked at the projection of Hildegarde. The cheerful little dachshund helped lighten his mood . . . a little.

"All you have to worry about is being loved and fed, little dog . . ."

Hildegarde continued to look expectantly out from the projection.

"That's the thing about dogs. You're always happy to see the ones you love, no matter what, and that's definitely not true of people." Roget knew that Muffin, his childhood companion, had been that way, but he'd been too young to fully appreciate her faithfulness and affection until long after she died. Was Hildegarde a way of reminding him? Quite possibly, but even from the projection, he could tell that Hildegarde was different from Muffin. There was a hint of seriousness, determination . . .

He laughed. Much as he enjoyed the projection, he was also projecting what he felt. As his soft laugh died away in the lowered lights, he turned his thoughts from dogs to his own situation.

He still hadn't learned what the colonel really wanted, even if he would never directly request it—and that was a military assessment of Dubiety. Not that Roget hadn't tried to find out more, but the entire Dubietan society made discovering and accurately assessing industrial, technological, and military capabilities difficult. He would have wagered that his estimations were accurate, but estimations didn't matter to the FSA, not when the Mandarins wanted hard facts and evidence, as bureaucracies always did. His lack of such hard information would, of course, provide a perfect rationale for instituting military action against Dubiety, and that was most likely what the Federation wanted. What empire wanted rivals that might surpass it?

The danger was that such rivals might already have surpassed it and that the Federation would refuse to see it. Like Midas of Lydia, for whom the oracles foretold the fall of a great empire, except it was his own.

Roget shook his head, thinking back over the day.

Once he and Lyvia had returned to Skeptos, she had taken her leave, right at the central square, and he had roamed through the city, heading more into the eastern sections, where he had found differing architectural styles, and a whole section that might have been lifted, if modernized, out of ancient Crete—at least as the archeological renderings he'd seen had depicted the ancient Minoan civilization.

Along the way, he had also discovered an opera house, featuring *The Wonder Age,* a work he'd never heard of, not surprisingly, and an art museum, with a wide range of work, all of it seemingly good, if not great. He'd gravitated to the paintings, especially nautical scenes, and to one deep-space painting, depicting a huge ovoid craft, partly eclipsed by an asteroid, with a small grayish silvery sphere in the distant background. The color of the sphere was wrong for it to be Dubiety, as viewed from farther out in the solar system, unless the artist had taken liberties, which certainly wasn't unlikely, but Roget hadn't gotten that feeling.

While it was difficult to determine the absolute size of the featureless ovoid spacecraft, a comparison to the detailed features of the asteroid suggested that the ovoid was far larger than any Federation battlecruiser and perhaps even as large as a small nickel-iron asteroid. Was it a planoforming craft? But if it happened to be, where had it been built, and where were the facilities for constructing it? And where was it now? The other aspect was the gallery in which the painting appeared. Everything else there was completely verifiably factual, scenes on Dubiety. There was even a scene of a cottage similar to those at Manor Farm Cottages, where a half-clad old woman sat in partial shade looking at a chessboard, while a bearded man wearing a formal jacket over a tattered singlesuit looked blankly beyond her from the other side of a table holding half-eaten food.

He had not seen anything like *Hildegarde in the Sunshine,* and that had pleased him, he had to admit.

He and Lyvia were scheduled to meet again with Selyni Hillis on Tuesday morning. Roget couldn't say that he was looking forward to it, although he couldn't have said why. Certainly he'd been treated with courtesy and given the freedom to go wherever he wanted—within certain limits. The problem was that he'd found little direct evidence of Dubiety's technical or military capabilities within those limits. There were more than a few indirect indicators, such as the engineering and speed of the regional subtrans trains, the quiet sophistication of the planetary economic system and its ability to function as a social control, the capability of the Dubietans to focus energy so tightly that virtually no stray radiation escaped anywhere—not to mention the orbital shields of the planet itself.

What these all signified—if his interpretations were correct—didn't bode all that well for his mission, the Federation, and Roget himself. But . . . they weren't proof either, and Roget had learned that the Federation tended to value hard proof, even proof that led to the wrong conclusions over accurate intuitive speculation—and that was without considering the hidden, or not-so-hidden, agendas.

Dubiety certainly wasn't all that it seemed. The carnivorous butterflies had been one indication, and the Manor Farm Cottages were another, both horrifying in more than one respect. The whole issue of choice nagged at him. The Dubietans seemed to have adopted an almost hands-off attitude—or one of minimal care—for those in their society who refused or who were unable to live by their society's standards. Yet . . . all societies needed some way to deal with sociopaths and worse. And he couldn't argue, not strongly anyway, against the idea that the antisocial and irresponsible shouldn't live comfortably on the efforts of others or against the premise that meddling with people's minds against their will was unacceptable. But they conditioned the inhabitants of the cottages against touching others, and that was certainly meddling.

The odors had bothered him, as well, and he definitely wasn't sure about the validity of the Omelas idea that the freedom of choice always created some misery. But then, didn't every society create misery? Wasn't the question only what kind of misery? And for whom?

The Federation didn't have cottages like those at Manor Farm, but it also didn't tolerate those who didn't accept the rules—and many of those dissenters died, and the rest certainly didn't end up with the best of lives, especially with the way the Federation conditioned them. With what Roget had seen during his years with the FSA, he'd never been sure that the Federation had had many better options for social control, given the range of human nature, passions, and beliefs. Yet the Dubietans had seemingly found a way to handle those without patrollers visible everywhere, but was that just because beneath their velvet-gloved surface lay an even more effective iron fist or an even more silent version of the FSA?

Or had they found a way to use technology and economics less disruptively?

He shook his head. He felt as though his thoughts were spinning in circles.

Finally, he looked back to the projected image. "After all

these years, I still wonder about your mistress, Hildegarde. She must have been quite someone for you to look for her so expectantly . . ."

Hildegarde didn't answer. She never had, but that didn't matter. Roget still smiled.

22

26 LIANYU 6744 F. E.

"Did I hear the mermaids singing each to each, as if I dared to wear white flannel trousers and walk upon the beach?"

"Not until human voices wake you," replied a warm and slightly husky voice.

"What?" Roget blinked. He sat at a table set with glittering silver cutlery. Crystal water and wine goblets stood just beyond the three knives and the gold and black rimmed white bone china before him. The wine in the goblet was dark red, or looked to be in dim light, and the table linens were brilliant white. The light was soft, from a single candle in a crystal holder.

Across from him at the table for two a woman smiled. Her mahogany red hair barely touched the collar of the pale green blouse that complemented the darker green jacket. She wore earrings, Roget realized, and her ears were pierced, something he'd not seen in years. There was the faintest trace of a warm smile on lips that were neither too full nor too thin.

"Your mind is wandering again," the woman said. "You misquote the old poets when you're someplace else in your thoughts. What political chicanery or legislative legerdemain are you concocting now?"

Roget wanted to protest that he had nothing of the sort in mind. Instead, he replied, "Merely an amendment to allow for greater local religious autonomy for the states."

"Merely?"

"So long as everyone's rights are protected, why should those who believe in nothing be allowed to dictate what those who believe differently can say in public places? Freedom of speech should work two ways, shouldn't it?"

"For all your parliamentary and political expertise, Joseph, I'd like to believe that you're still that young missionary trying to convert the faithless and provide a testimony for those who believe in the irrationality of reason rather than in the irrationality of God."

Joseph? Roget knew he wasn't Joseph, but the words still came out of his mouth. "You, Susannah? You'd *like* to believe?" He smiled warmly. "You of all people know who I am. You always have."

"The nonbelievers won't support it. You know that."

"I do know that."

"Then it's a gesture, a mere political move to solidify your support among the Believers."

"Is that really so bad? They need someone behind whom they can unite."

"They're already behind you. Who else do they have?"

"If I don't remind them, now and again, they lose total faith in the political system."

"You're more worried that they'll lose faith in you, I think." The woman smiled sadly, then took a sip from her wine goblet. "Isn't it late for gestures?"

Roget knew she was almost as old as he was, yet there was a beauty, and a melancholy behind the bright and yet deep green eyes. "If we're being frank . . . yes. But gestures are all I have left. The Believers want a return to a strong and Christian nation, but they'll sacrifice strength to hold off the atheist onslaught on religious expression. The atheists want neither a strong faith nor a strong nation, but one where commerce is king and where anything and everything has a price . . . and where the price for national economic and military strength is too high." He shrugged. "I've said that for years, and I've fought for rebuilding our military, especially the Navy. You know I have. What has it accomplished? Until the Democrats retook the House and Senate, I managed to stave off the worst. Now . . ." He let the silence speak.

"I would have liked things to have worked out differently," she said.

"You know how I feel about you."

"I know what you say."

"Then I'll do a riff on old Tom . . . if we became lovers in more than spirit, that love would die, because where we would be would be what we are not . . ."

Her laugh was short, and both warm and bitter at the same time. "You've been charming enough that I've even accepted the modern equivalent of courtly love for all these years, all because you can be so poetic, you old raven."

"Ah, yes . . . the raven ascending flames the air, for there are no doves in Hell . . . or in Washington where all are consumed by flame or fire."

"Or fire," she added. "Why is it, as you once said, that the end of all exploring is to find one's self where one began?"

"I only repeated what old Tom said more than a century ago."

"Oh . . . yes . . . the most erudite war hero, the noble Senator Joseph Tanner, who is adept with both his words and those of others."

"These days, dear lady, words are all that I have left, and sometimes, precious few of them. Occasionally, they suffice to gain me the votes to plug a hole or two in the dike of our foundering republic."

"Oh . . . Joseph . . . why . . . why did it come to this?"

"What else could we have done? How else should I have presumed."

"That is not what I meant, at all." The words of her reply were coolly ironic.

"I know that, too." Roget reached for the wine goblet, taking it and then raising it. "To you, dear one. I have so enjoyed these dinners. They're one of the few pleasures I have left."

As he saw the pain in the woman's eyes, Roget thought he should say something, anything, any small word of comfort. But he was mute. He struggled again to force the smallest word of warmth.

With that struggle, the blackness swirled around him, and phrases, strange phrases, rushed through his thoughts.

". . . to lead you to an overwhelming question . . ."

". . . the art of preparing a face to meet other faces . . ."

". . . not a hero, nor meant to be . . ."

". . . the knowledge, the wisdom, and the faith we have lost in gaining information . . ."

". . . continue the fight against darkness in air and fire, in words and deeds . . ."

A cold chill froze Roget's forehead, and he opened his eyes. He lay on the sofa in his own apartment in St. George, looking up at a junior security monitor. A cold compress rested across his forehead.

"He's awake, Inspector Hwang, sir."

An inspector? Roget slowly struggled into a sitting position, awkwardly catching the compress.

A solid black-haired man in the uniform of a Federal inspector walked toward Roget. "Don't try to get up, Agent-Captain Roget."

"Yes, sir."

The inspector pulled one of the straight-backed chairs from the table and turned it to face Roget. He sat down. "You were found unconscious by the door to that sculptor's studio. How did that happen?" Hwang's voice was calm, neither sympathetic nor critical.

"I couldn't say, sir, except that it might be an aftereffect

of whatever the Danites injected me with in the restaurant
on Friday."

"You let that happen?"

"Yes, sir. As I reported on Friday, I didn't expect the
entire restaurant staff to be Danite sympathizers. I hadn't
done anything except my cover duties as an E&W monitor,
but they apparently knew who I was from the beginning."

"We've discovered that," Hwang said dryly. "Why were
the three in the studio dead?"

"They all had some sort of suicide implant as a reaction
to paralytic darts. They carried antidotes, but they'd tried to
use them last night on Smith—he was the one who died in
the EES shop—and I could only find one injector, and that
was the one I used on Sorensen."

The inspector nodded. "He suffered considerable brain
trauma. We may not get much from him either. He'll end up
in a low-function security colony."

Roget had the feeling that he'd botched just about everything.

"You smoked out this cell, and that's what single agents
are supposed to do. You even saved us the trouble of dealing with most of them."

"I overheard them saying that there are more, all over old
Deseret."

"There always have been. There probably always will be.
True Believers never understand the need for secular ratio-
nality. That's one of the reasons why there's a Federation
Security Agency." Hwang paused. "Your cover is gone, and
you've got medical problems. We'll send you to Cheyenne
for rehab and recovery. Don't worry about anything but re-
covering."

"Yes, sir."

"I've sent for a lorry to take you and your personal effects
out to the local airfield for air-evac. It should be here before
long. There will be two guards outside until you leave."

"Thank you, sir."

Hwang nodded, then rose.

After the inspector and the junior monitor left, Roget couldn't help but wonder how he could not worry. The memory sequence had been so real . . . so very real.

Joseph Tanner—had Tanner been real? That was certainly something Roget could research. But then, what if the senator had been real? What did that mean? How had Marni ever captured those memories? Would Roget ever be able to escape the memory flashbacks? But then, there had been something about memory selection . . . but how?

There were so many questions he'd not had a chance to think through . . . so many.

He swallowed, sitting on the couch, not knowing when his transport might arrive. His eyes flicked to the projection of Hildegarde, still looking up expectantly. Just looking at the small black-and-tan dachshund helped, even if Roget couldn't have said why.

23

22 MARIS 1811 p. d.

Nine in the morning, local Skeptos time on Tuesday, found Roget and Lyvia seated around the same conference table where they had been the day before, with Roget again facing Director Hillis.

"How was your visit to Manor Farm cottages?" asked Hillis.

"Instructive and depressing," replied Roget.

"Why did you find it depressing?"

"How could one not?" countered Roget. "With all those dysfunctional individuals whom you've left with no hope?"

"They are provided with comfortable quarters, ample food, medical attention if they'll only seek it out, clean clothing if they choose to wear it, full incoming communications, not to mention considerable freedom to move about. What else, exactly, would you suggest that would not result in harm to other innocents?"

"What about curing them?"

"We cure those where, first, it is possible, and second, where they wish it. Those in the cottages have chronic conditions where any treatment would impair their intelligence."

There was no argument to the conditions stated by Hillis, not one with which Roget would have been comfortable or could support logically.

"You, Agent Roget, are afflicted with the old American illusion that insists, when you are faced with a difficult set of choices, all of which result in unpleasant outcomes, that there must be a better way. It's always useful to explore the possibilities, and even to give them a trial, but it's also bullheaded stupidity to insist that there must be a better way if you and other intelligent individuals cannot find such a way."

"How do you know there isn't a better way?"

"From what you've seen of Dubiety, if we'd discovered one, don't you think we'd have tried it? Do you really think that any one of us likes the cottages?"

Roget had seen Lyvia's reactions, and he had to admit that Hillis's words also sounded truthful. Somehow, that also bothered him, but more than a few things about Dubiety concerned him, and every day there seemed to be something else. "So when will you reveal to me your awesome military prowess so that I can report to my superiors that the Federation should leave you well enough alone?"

"Even if we showed you a battle fleet twice the size of any Federation fleet, they would not take your word for it. We will be allowing you to return with documentation and descriptions of technology the Federation does not have, and I will wager that it will be dismissed as irrelevant, insignificant, or a complete fabrication."

"So what's the point of allowing me to return?"

"I think we've already shown you that," replied the director, "if you will just think about it. I won't spell it out, because your superiors would then believe that you will have parroted our words." She rose and looked to Lyvia. "Perhaps a tour of the capitol building would help."

"Yes, Director." Lyvia stood, almost wearily.

Roget stood and inclined his head politely.

Selyni Hillis nodded. "Tomorrow at nine thirty." Then she left the conference room.

Roget waited for Lyvia to lead the way to wherever the capitol was, although from his recollections of the maps Lyvia had provided, he thought it was north of the central square as much as a klick, if not farther.

Lyvia said nothing until they were outside the ministry building. Then she stopped and fastened her jacket against the chill wind before she spoke. "The capitol is about ten blocks north. We can walk back to the square . . ."

"I'd just as soon walk if that's all right with you," he replied. "If it's not too cold."

"I'd prefer walking." Lyvia started out.

Roget matched her quick steps.

After two blocks, he had to admit that he was happy to have his jacket, which had vanished from his pack and then reappeared in his guesthouse closet when the gray singlesuit had been returned and cleaned. He wondered what had been added that had taken the extra time.

"The capitol isn't exactly in the center of Skeptos," he finally said.

"There's no reason for it to be. It has its own local subtrans station under the plaza."

"Was it planned that way?"

"It was."

"How many tribunes are there?"

"Two hundred and one, and the representation is by population in geographically cohesive districts. We don't allow gerrymandering."

"And those in the House of Denial? What are they called?"

"Popularly, they're the deniers. Technically, each has the title of reviewer. There are usually around fifty, but the number can vary. The limits are no less than forty and no more than fifty-nine. No reviewer can serve more than five years without remaining out of office for the same time."

Roget didn't pretend to understand how the Dubietans made a system like theirs work, but, from what he'd seen, it seemed to . . . at least for them.

Two blocks north of the Ministry of Education and Culture, the officelike buildings gave way to structures much more like the guesthouse where Roget was lodged, but sections of the ground level right off the walkways were given over to various shops. One featured a range of athletic gear, and he saw a display of the basket-sticks, similar to lacrosse sticks, that he'd observed in the games in the parks over the weekend.

Then, after they walked past a two-level apartment-style dwelling, there were no more buildings immediately before them.

"There's the capitol and the square," announced Lyvia, stopping and gesturing at the green-tinged marble structure set on a low rise in the middle of grass, knee-high hedges, and gardens. The square looked to be half a klick on a side, with the capitol a low two-story structure some hundred meters across the front and half that in depth. The only adornment was a low silvery dome in the middle, topped by the silvery hazy sphere that represented Dubiety. Three sets of pale green marble steps rose from a wide but narrow plaza. "The center steps are to the Judiciary, the ones to the left are to the House of Tribunes, and those to the right are to the House of Denial."

Roget saw only a handful of people on the plaza below the building, and all those were in the center, below the steps to the Judiciary, several of whom emerged from circular stone kiosks that doubtless were where the tunnels emerged from the subtrans.

Lyvia led the way toward the plaza, following a wide but winding stone path through the gardens that generally angled in the direction of the House of Tribunes. Most of the flowers had wilted or dried up, and those that had not looked as if they would not last all that long. The amber light that filtered through the orbital shields seemed less intense as well.

"How much colder does it get?" he asked.

"It stays close to freezing for around six weeks in winter, but you'll be gone before that happens. Then we'll be into spring, and that is long and chill but not freezing."

Roget hoped that meant he'd be on his way back to the *WuDing,* rather than permanently gone.

The west end of the Plaza was empty except for them, as were the green-tinted marble steps leading up to the simple arch that was slightly trapezoidal. The south facade of the capitol had no columns, no ornate decorations, just sheet walls of marble, interspersed with long narrow windows. At the top of the steps was a set of greenish translucent doors that opened as they approached. Inside was a foyer stretching a mere ten meters on each side of the doors and extending back six meters or so. On the north side of the foyer were two sets of double doors, wooden doors, rather than the translucent automatic ones.

Roget glanced around, but he saw no one in the foyer.

"This way." Lyvia walked toward the right-hand doorway. The old-style wooden door actually had brass handles. She pulled on the handle, and the door swung toward her. Inside the chamber, the lights flashed on. She left the door open until Roget took it when she walked inside.

As he released the door, letting it swing closed, Roget followed her into the chamber, a half-amphitheater with true wooden desks set on tiered daises, all facing a raised podium. Behind the podium was a holo projection—a starscape of some sort. Roget moistened his lips as he studied it. He couldn't be absolutely certain, but the image appeared to have been captured from orbit above Dubiety facing out-system. It was a true image, not exaggerated, because there was only one disk, and that was tiny, most probably the nearer of the three outer gas giants.

Most government assemblies featured flags, or seals, or symbols designed to create a sense of unity and/or patriotism. The only decoration in the House of Delegates was a vast projected hologram of the endless universe. Otherwise, all the walls were bare.

"Is that the only hologram projected?" he asked.

"There are three others, but they're all starscapes. Each is from a different quadrant of Dubiety's orbit. They change seasonally."

"This is the winter one, then?"

Lyvia nodded.

Roget continued to survey the chamber before finally speaking. "This whole part of the building's empty."

"Both ends are," replied Lyvia. "Neither House is in session. The Judiciary operates year-round."

"What about staff?"

"The Tribunes don't have official staff. Each has a small office on the upper or lower levels. It's just large enough for them."

"Are any of them around?"

"I couldn't say for certain, but I'd judge not. Anyone who has a problem with existing law or wants to propose legislation can comlink those problems or suggestions to their representative. That doesn't require that they be here."

"No one wants to meet face-to-face?"

"They very well might, but it's frowned upon, and in certain cases cause for dismissal from office."

"What?" Roget had trouble believing that. Dismissal for meeting with citizens and constituents? And she had called the Dubietan government representative?

"The right to personal representation is highly overrated, not to mention one of the greatest contributors to corruption in governments that are theoretically democratic and/or representative."

"If you wouldn't mind explaining that point . . ."

"You don't see why?" Lyvia's voice was tart.

"No. I don't. How can someone possibly represent a group or a district or whatever without being able to meet with them?"

"First, anyone who is eligible for election has to have lived in the same area with those they represent for at least ten years, and no one can be elected to the House of Tribunes who is less than forty-five. We don't much care for representatives who haven't been successful in something else first. Second, anyone can petition them and send them concerns. They just can't do it face-to-face."

"And image-to-image is different?"

"All images are recorded. Permanently."

Roget began to see where the explanation was headed. "Subject to recall?"

"Subject to examination by the House of Denial and by any concerned citizen."

"But some people don't present themselves well when it's not in person. They need to have physical feedback."

"For what? To play on the emotions of the representative? To influence by other than the merits of their position? To override careful judgment with an upwelling of sincerity?" The scorn in her voice was biting. "Or worse, to offer or suggest indirect favoritism? Or an out-and-out bribe?"

"How do people know what their constituents are thinking? Do they have to rely on polls or surveys?"

"Polls and surveys are prohibited."

That was another shock to Roget. "And you think you allow freedom of expression?"

"Anyone can say anything that's truthful to anyone through any commnet and in any public venue. You might remember that. They just can't contact others on an organized basis and ask what those others think. That also applies to debates and discussions in any governmental forum."

"That doesn't sound exactly like representative government."

"It's very representative, Keir. It's a systematized way of avoiding political mob rule where government bases its actions on what people think they want rather than on the best judgment of the representative."

"What about businesses? Can they survey the public to see what people want to buy? Or is that prohibited as well?"

"No. They have to offer the best they can and learn from their experiences. We try to reward leadership, not followship. We're not interested in following the lemminglike path that doomed the old United States and most of the Euroderived so-called democracies." Lyvia paused, then asked, "Have you seen enough here?"

With only an empty chamber before him, Roget had. He nodded.

Lyvia led the way back out and then around the front foyer and toward the rear of the building before turning to her right into a wide corridor leading toward the middle of the capitol.

Roget looked down the corridor, presumably to the Judiciary. "Are we going to see the justices?"

"We can walk down there and see what's in progress. Visitors aren't allowed in the chambers, but whatever is happening in the chamber is projected out into the main foyer. The same is true of the House of Tribunes and the House of Denial."

"Aren't you concerned that someone might present a false record of the proceedings or the debates?"

"With seven political parties and a very enthusiastic crop of attorneys who would love to seize the assets of anyone who did that? It's rather unlikely. Also," she added, "distortion or falsification of records of government proceedings is one of the few offenses that can merit a death sentence."

"But not murder?"

"Corruption of government kills and abuses everyone, and it's always for personal or professional gain, not for social improvement. In any case, we have very few murders," Lyvia said dryly. "Murder and child abuse are among the few offenses that result in a sentence of permanent alterations to brain functioning."

"And some of those in Manor Farm Cottages are there for that reason?"

"Possibly. There are some who cannot function in society after such treatment." Lydia resumed walking toward the Judiciary chamber.

Roget studied the corridor that seemed vaguely familiar, totally unfamiliar as it was, walking several meters before a wash of blackness swept over him. He took an unsteady step, then blinked. When he opened his eyes, the corridor was different.

Fluted columns lined both sides, and it was narrower, and the ceiling lower. The floor was a mixture of a reddish stone and one of grayish white, both highly polished. He stood in the middle of a group of people, all very young. Beside him was a tall and willowy brunette girl.

"Another explanation," she murmured, her eyes flicking to the front of the group where a fresh-faced guide had stopped.

"This corridor is known as Statuary Hall. That is because of all the sculptures that have been placed here over the years. . . ."

Roget/Tanner took in the guide's words as his eyes drifted from statue to statue. He recognized one or two, but most were unfamiliar, although he probably would recognize their names from American history.

"Joe . . ." whispered the youth to Roget's right, "Cari said you got your call. When do you leave?"

"In May just after the end of the semester."

"Where are you going?"

Roget—or Tanner—didn't want to answer that question. He just smiled. "Wherever they send me."

"You must know . . ."

Roget/Tanner shrugged. "It doesn't matter." Except it did. That he did know. He'd hoped for a mission somewhere in the Far East, but he was going to Peru. His parents had said that the country was like southern Utah, with red hills and mountains, but the Andes were far more imposing than places like the Wasatch Range or even Brian Head or Cedar Breaks. He'd wanted to improve his Mandarin, but it appeared that he'd just have to learn Spanish as well.

"This way," announced the guide, as the tour resumed.

"You could be a senator someday, Joseph," suggested the brunette in a low voice.

"I'm more interested in being a pilot, Cari."

"I suppose I could get used to being married to a pilot."

Roget/Tanner managed not to gape. He and Cari had dated, but he'd never tried anything serious, and he certainly hadn't proposed. How could he, with a mission coming up, three more years of college, and, if he were fortunate, flight training after that?

"You'll be more than a pilot. I know that."

"You know more than I do." His eyes drifted to the small rotunda ahead.

He could feel dizziness creeping up over him . . .

Roget found himself sitting on a stone bench. To his right and across the foyer was a holo showing a justice in a gray robe behind a judicial podium, looking down at a woman in a formal singlesuit and black jacket.

". . . did the defendant ever provide you with any evidence about the accuracy of the assertion in the prospectus . . ."

"Keir?" Lyvia's voice was strained.

That surprised him. "Yes. I'm . . . here." He'd almost said that he was back.

"You walked down the corridor as if no one were around you, and you were saying things about being a pilot."

"Flashbacks," he admitted. He wasn't about to admit that they weren't his flashbacks, not exactly. "It happens sometimes."

"And they sent you to Dubiety?"

"FSA doesn't know."

"Or they don't care."

That was certainly possible. "I couldn't say."

"Are you all right?"

"I'm fine. They don't happen often, sometimes not for years."

"When you're under stress, I'd imagine," Lyvia probed.

"Not even that, necessarily."

She nodded, not in agreement, but as if she had heard what he had said.

What was it about the Dubietan capitol? Or was it just that it *was* a capitol, and the first time he'd seen it?

"We should get you something to eat. A low blood sugar doesn't help."

"That might be good." He was hungry. He was also worried. He hadn't had a memory flashback in years, not since deep-space small-craft training, as he recalled. Dreams, yes, but not daytime flashbacks.

24

28 LIANYU 6744 F. E.

By the time Roget was escorted out of the unmarked Federation flitter at the FAF base outside Cheyenne, it was late on Sunday afternoon, and the two Air Force senior rankers were most insistent that he check into the medical facility immediately. Roget did . . . and then spent an uneventful evening and a restless night. On Monday he was ushered from medical test to medical test. None of the results were conveyed to him, and he had a quiet dinner in the officers' dining room. He slept somewhat better on Monday night, but not enough better that he didn't have vaguely uneasy dreams that he could not remember when he woke.

At nine thirty on Tuesday, two FSA guards appeared and "requested" that he accompany them in an unmarked electrocar to the base security building. He did, and at almost precisely ten hundred he was escorted into a large office that held a large, plain, and impressive desk without a visible console, and three chairs set before the desk. The walls were plain, doubtless to enable projections. Sitting behind the desk was a silver-haired Sinese in a colonel's uniform.

"Agent-Captain . . . please sit down." The colonel's voice was pleasant, almost musical. "You've had a rather trying month, it appears."

"I'm fine, sir."

The colonel smiled politely. "That's what the results of your medical tests show. You've recovered completely from the injuries of your previous assignment. Outside of a few abrasions and bruises, your body shows no signs of further abuse." The colonel paused. "According to the medical staff, there is no apparent physical reason why you should have been found unconscious outside the sculptor's studio, but the readings from your internals and the medical personnel present confirm that your consciousness had indeed been affected."

In short, Roget thought, the doctors had confirmed that he hadn't been faking, and they were all worried.

"Do you have any thoughts about this, Agent-Captain?"

Roget's internals could sense the various energy flows around the room, and he had no doubts that every bit of interrogation and surveillance technology known to the FSA was trained on him. "Yes, sir. I do."

"Please proceed to offer those thoughts."

"As I reported earlier, I was injected with an unknown substance by the Sorensen woman. Shortly thereafter, I suffered extreme dehydration and disorientation. I would surmise that the efforts involved in resolving the situation in St. George triggered a follow-up episode. Since I have experienced no additional symptoms, and since the medical tests, from what you suggested, sir, apparently indicated no remaining unknown substances in my system, it would appear to me that it's unlikely that there will be future occurrences."

The colonel nodded. "Your report suggested that this Danite terrorist organization might pose a regional threat to the Federation. I would be interested in why you think so—beyond the reasons you stated in your reports."

"I don't know that I have reasons beyond what I reported, sir. The terrorists seemed almost contemptuous of the Federation, as if we had no idea what we were up against. The fact that I could be assaulted with relatively sophisticated medical techniques openly in a public restaurant also suggests a wide degree of at least tacit public support."

The colonel's laugh was soft, short, and scornful. "The Agency has been aware of the Danites for many years. They meet and plot and think we know nothing, and so long as they do nothing, we allow them to have their secrets. When they do something, as they did in St. George, we act, as you did, and for a number of years thereafter they decide that meetings and muttered words in hidden rooms amount to rebellion. Then they attempt to act, and once more fail. It is predictable. It has been so for centuries."

"The Sorensen woman was a Federation employee," ventured Roget.

"All her communications were monitored. We thought they might use her as a lure. Did they not do just that?"

"I was aware that she had ulterior motives from the first, sir, as my reports indicated."

"As you should have been and were and as has been the

case for generations. They seem to think that we see nothing and hear nothing when everything is seen and heard." The colonel paused. "You reported on the geothermal power units, but your report was less detailed on the chamber adjoining the one where you observed the terrorists. Can you elaborate on your report?"

"I hurried through it. I was trying to find an injector that might have held an antidote. It looked like a combination of a small manufacturing operation and a laboratory. The facility under DeseretData was used to fabricate nerve shredders, but I couldn't determine what the equipment beneath the sculptor's building was used for. The lab looked more like a very professional medical facility. As I reported, Marni Sorensen had told me she had a background in biology." He didn't mention her doctorate because he wanted to see how the colonel responded or avoided dealing with that fact. "When I reported in, I was told to vacate immediately. So I didn't go back and make a more thorough investigation."

"Her background didn't deal with biological terrorism, and she would have known any number of agents that might have disrupted your system without registering on your internals. She would not have needed a laboratory so elaborate for that. It would appear that either someone else had to have been involved or that she had some other project of value to the Danites. Would you have any idea who or what those might be, Agent Roget?"

"No, sir. None of those I investigated had that kind of background, not that I could determine."

"A pity. We will find them. We always do." The colonel paused. "After consulting with the medical staff, we have decided that you will be granted three weeks' convalescent leave. You will report back here for medical tests three weeks from Thursday. If those tests indicate that you are fully recovered, you'll be posted to your new assignment. If not, but it appears that you will recover, you will be temporarily assigned to analysis."

"Yes, sir."

"That will be all, Agent-Captain. You are free to leave the base at your convenience. If you choose to spend any or all of your leave here, you may request a room in the officers' quarters. If you wish to spend time elsewhere, you're authorized to receive the government travel rates at any lodging establishment, but the cost is your responsibility."

Roget stood. "Thank you, sir."

"Thank you. You managed to keep a messy situation relatively quiet. All the people of St. George know is that a fire brought an inspector and several people vanished. That's enough to keep them looking over their shoulders." The colonel looked down at the desk.

Roget inclined his head politely, then left the office, closing the door quietly.

The only person outside was the colonel's assistant, an older woman who said politely, "Good day, Agent-Captain."

As he walked from the security building to wait for a shuttle outside, he considered his options. Three weeks' convalescent leave. He frowned. His sister lived in the Fort Greeley complex that had grown up after the reduction of Denver, and that wasn't all that far from Cheyenne on the maglev. He'd have to see if he could visit there for a few days, not that he'd impose on her for a bed, but he hadn't seen her in several years, not since she and Wallace had moved to Fort Greeley because he'd been posted away from Noram and couldn't justify the expense of transoceanic travel. He wouldn't stay that long because he didn't want to spend too much of his pay on lodging.

First, though, he wanted to do some research after he checked out of the medical center.

He had to wait almost a quarter hour for the shuttle, and it was another quarter hour before he was back at the base medical facility. By the time he collected his few personal items and authorized the various bureaucratic acknowledgments and releases, another hour elapsed.

Finally, some two hours later, he was settled into a small room in the officers' quarters, using his monitor to access the commnet. His first inquiry was for Joseph Tanner.

The response was close to immediate. While there were almost a hundred entries, none of the living Tanners, or those who had died in the last century, fit his criteria. When he eliminated them, just three remained, and only one fit his criteria. It was comparatively short.

> Joseph Jared Tanner, Senator, United States of America 2039–2127 A.D., reputedly a former naval military pilot who was known as an opponent of "excessive" social programs and a staunch opponent of global federation . . . instrumental in the temporary resurgence of U.S. military forces before the Wars of Confederation . . .

That was it. Roget still smiled. Joseph Tanner had been real. His smile faded when he thought about how few Joseph Tanners remained in the records once they died. Fame—even remembrance—was indeed fleeting.

His next inquiry was on Marni Sorensen. Interestingly enough, there was but a single entry matching her name.

> Marni Carpenter Sorensen, (3162 F. E.–) B.S., M.S., Deseret University, Ph.D., University of California–Davis. Coauthor, "RNA, 'Junk' Matter, and Memory Retention," *Noram Medical Journal* . . .

Following her name was a listing of articles and publications, but the last was dated some five years earlier. Given the delays caused by peer review and editorial matters, that suggested she had stopped researching and publishing when she'd returned to St. George. He frowned. She'd stopped publishing, but not researching. He also wouldn't have been surprised to learn that she'd contacted some of Tanner's descendants. Had she also obtained the basis of what she had used on him from Tanner descendants? Or from Saint genealogical tissue samples? He would have bet on one of those and given odds. But he wasn't about to say anything, because he'd either end up out of the FSA and being a medical guinea pig somewhere . . . or worse.

Was that why the major had dismissed Marni so cavalierly? While it might have been because he couldn't believe a woman was that brilliant, or because he hadn't been told the full extent of what had been going on in the laboratory, it was far more likely that the FSA didn't want it known, even among agents, exactly what she had been doing.

And that suggested . . . ? Did the FSA already have the ability to extract and process memories for reimplantation? Were they already using it? Perhaps in the low-function relocation communities?

Roget repressed a shudder. There wasn't much he could do about it if the Agency were doing that, but it was definitely something he needed to keep in mind. Even so, one way or the other, he had no doubts that Marni had been the source of his "flashback memories," although he doubted that he'd ever know for certain whether her research had resulted in an implantation of genetic-based memories or "merely" gene-based suggestions of memories that his own brain had reprocessed into coherence.

He could see why the Saints were interested in her work, though, especially if it rendered people more susceptible to being supportive of the Saints . . . or even made them likely to convert. He could also see, scientifically important as that research might be, why neither the Federation nor the Saints would want to make it public. He certainly was in no position to inquire more directly than he had. Even so, he'd likely face more questions about his inquiries. But he'd had to know. And now that he knew . . . there wasn't a thing he could do about it.

25

Roget had gone back to the capitol for an hour on Tuesday by himself after he and Lyvia had eaten lunch. Once there, he had watched and listened to the Judiciary proceedings, but he didn't see anything out of the ordinary. The case itself dealt with the issue of misrepresenting a product, as depicted on a fictional drama. The plaintiff contended that, regardless of whether the drama represented a series of fictional events, the defendant had used the setting of the drama to overrepresent the product's capabilities, with the active collusion and support of the designing firm, and that was an actionable event under the law, and the designing firm that had supplied the product was liable for damages.

Roget was shaking his head, figuratively, when he left the Judiciary, because the case wasn't something that he would even have considered. Yet it made perfect sense under the system Lyvia had described, and again, that bothered him.

Later that afternoon, he visited a series of art galleries on the south side of Skeptos, but while he saw all types of art— except art forms such as multis that required continuous energy output—he didn't see any other depictions of spacecraft, or any kind of aircraft. He did see depictions of sailing craft and something that looked like a human-powered submersible, as well as several scenes of mountain or highland villages with snow. One was even captioned *Winter in Chaco.*

He ate alone but decided on Dorinique, although he had to walk around the square several times before they could seat him. He only saw one dog, if from a distance, but it wasn't even a dachshund.

On Wednesday morning he was in the lobby of the MEC building by quarter past nine, and he waited for a good ten minutes before Lyvia appeared. They walked up to the third level and to the conference room with little more conversation than polite necessities.

Director Hillis walked in and came right to the point.

"Agent Roget, your dropboat will be ready for launch tomorrow. After breakfast Agent Rholyn will escort you to the . . . transport facility. You're expected there at eleven hundred—noon local. That will require your leaving Skeptos at about nine."

"What about the documentation?"

"It's already aboard the dropboat. You'll have time to check it after you reach the facility."

"The other agent?"

"He's already there. Given his mental state, it's questionable as to whether he'll be of much use to the Federation, but removal from Dubiety and the strain it created within him might allow personal restabilization. It will also make it slightly more difficult for the Federation to use his absence as a provocation."

With three other agents perishing in the attempt to land, would one make a difference? And why would Dubiety create that much strain on an agent? "Was he exposed to anything markedly different from what I was?"

"No. In fact, he saw far less before he became totally unstable and uncontrollable. That is understandable, however, since his background is Sinese."

"Did you apply greater distortion to his perceptions?"

"We have not attempted to distort either your perceptions or his," replied Hillis calmly. "What would be the point? It's against our beliefs, and once you return to Federation jurisdiction, any such meddling would be apparent."

"It's not likely that they'll believe me, you know?"

"That depends on you, doesn't it?"

"And on them and on whatever you send back with me," Roget added.

"The documentation will be there, as will other evidence if you choose to take it."

"You're being awfully casual about all this. You're the first splinter culture the Federation has encountered."

"The first of which you're aware." A wry smile appeared. "I also wouldn't say that we're casual. Weren't you met with someone prepared to talk to you? Haven't we attempted to show you how Dubiety operates? No . . . we're anything but casual. 'Resigned' might be a better term. Hopeful, but resigned. The Federation is rather set in its ways."

"Are you suggesting that they've hidden or destroyed other cultures?"

"I'm not suggesting anything. Remember, we're Thomists. I'm certain you know the origin of the name."

Roget did—a takeoff on the idea of Doubting Thomas.

"We well may be the first splinter culture the Federation has encountered. We may not be. We can't speak for that which is beyond what we know. Neither can you. Not accurately."

"I stand corrected." He kept his voice wry.

"I have two last observations for you to keep in mind."

Roget waited.

"First, the longer a culture or society exists without external pressures or conflicts and the more successful it is in maintaining its institutions unchanged, the more likely the slightest pressure, even the pressure of knowledge, is likely to result in unplanned change. Second, the speed of technological development is directly proportional to the true effectiveness of education and markets and to the amount of resources behind the discovery and dissemination of knowledge, as well as being inversely retarded by the degree of governmental control and regulation." The Director turned her eyes to Lyvia. "It occurs to me that Agent Roget has not seen any background on the planoforming of Dubiety. The Natural History Museum."

Lyvia nodded.

Hillis stood, smiling. "I won't see you again before you lift off to return to the *WuDing*. I do wish you the best. Whether you believe us or not, you, as an individual, are welcome here."

"Even if the Federation takes over?"

"One way or another, that is unlikely."

"One way or another?"

"We didn't leave the Federation to have it chase us down and incorporate us again. The Federation didn't look for us for centuries without a very definite agenda."

"You're suggesting . . ." Roget didn't want to voice the actual words.

"No. I've told you. We're opposed to war, but we will do what's necessary. We'd prefer an agreement in which both sides respect the other's systems and agree not to meddle."

"Just how do you expect to make that work?"

"We'll see how the Federation acts first. Remember, we've done nothing aggressive." She paused. "I don't know that it would help, but you might suggest they inquire into the events of 6556 F. E., and the disappearance of Federation Exploratory Force Three. Or possibly that your High Command review any stellar maps that might exist of this area in the year 4245 F. E. It might reveal something, Major, if they're wise enough to understand what they see."

Roget stiffened slightly. He'd never mentioned his rank, or rank-equivalent.

"Now . . . I think you really should see the museum." Selyni Hillis inclined her head, then slipped from the conference room.

"Keir . . ." Lyvia's voice was calm but surprisingly gentle.

Roget accompanied her out of the conference room, down the ramps, and through the lobby.

Outside, the wind had picked up, and with the ever-present humidity, the day was definitely chill and raw.

"Is the museum the only thing on the day's schedule?" Roget finally asked as they walked southward toward the main square.

"That's it," replied Lyvia. "After that, you can wander as you like. I'll meet you tomorrow at quarter to eight for breakfast. Bring your pack and anything you'd like to take with you back to the *WuDing*."

"I haven't exactly gathered souvenirs," Roget said. "By the way, exactly where is this museum?"

"Some six blocks straight south from the main square."

"Natural history? I didn't think Dubiety had that much *natural* history."

"Isn't whether you call history natural or unnatural merely a matter of viewpoint?" replied Lyvia. "Whatever your perspective, I think you'll find the museum of some interest."

Roget thought about asking why, then dismissed the idea, knowing what her answer would be. "Is there anything else you think I should see? After the museum?"

"If you haven't done so, you ought to sit in public places and just watch the people."

Roget almost laughed. He'd done a great deal of that already, even though he knew that the colonel couldn't have cared less about what Roget observed about the conduct of everyday life on Dubiety. Instead, he just smiled politely and kept walking.

Before long they were past the central square and then, after passing a line of clothing shops, Roget could see what could only be the museum. It was anything but imposing— merely a squarish two-story stone-walled structure that looked somewhat older than the buildings flanking it. The door toward which Lyvia and Roget walked was trapezoidal. Roget had the feeling that the trapezoidal doorways were more likely to be used on older buildings, but he decided against stating that observation. The milky-green door split, and both sides slid open as the two neared. Immediately inside the doors, which closed behind them, was a modest foyer, four meters by five, with a hallway to the right and another to the left.

"To the right," said Lyvia. "That's where we'll begin. There are a series of short time-lapse visuals with explanations."

Roget followed her to the first exhibit—a projection into a niche, which immediately displayed an image once they stopped. The image was of a planet with a thick swirling atmosphere. Roget watched and listened . . .

". . . Dubiety . . . as initially discovered . . . Venerian in general composition, but with a solidifying core more terrestrial, if smaller . . . planoforming began almost four thousand years ago with upper atmospheric bioseeding . . ."

Purplish dots appeared on the swirling atmosphere.

". . . less than a hundred years later, the process of bombarding Dubiety with ice comets commenced . . ."

Roget watched the initial time-lapse illustration, then followed Lyvia to the second niche.

". . . concurrent with midlevel atmospheric biotransformations, core reenergization was commenced using a variant on the trans-temporal entropic reversal process. Several transfer ships and crews were lost initially because of unforeseen temporal schisms . . ."

Temporal schisms and entropic reversal? Was the museum just a setup for him?

Three exhibits later, when he walked around the next corner, he saw a line of young people walking out through a set of double doors within the building. He looked to Lyvia.

"That's the theater. The museum runs a consolidated program and seminar for students."

"Do they have to know the physics for trans-temporal entropic reversal?"

"No. Just the basic application principles. The physics is beyond most scientists."

"Why are you giving it to the Federation?"

"We're not giving the applications—just the theory. They'll have to develop the applications themselves. That's if they have the insight and the will. Let's move to the next presentation . . ."

Roget was more than a little discouraged when he left the museum almost two hours later. The various presentations and explanations had made it very clear that the Dubietans—or a far larger Thomist culture—most likely had developed something suspiciously close to time travel, or time and distance travel. From what he could tell, it was practical only for the transfer of large masses and entailed massive quantities of energy, which they generated from a process he understood not at all, but which required conditions of most considerable pressure and heat—such as a planetary core.

Exactly how was he going to explain that? Or prove it? Or even provide some examples by which the Federation could investigate the possibility? Was any of it true? Or had he been guided through a total deception?

The other thing that nagged at him was that perhaps the Dubietans had even more applications than he'd been shown.

What he'd observed was disturbing enough. He'd measured travel times and distances. He'd experienced full sensory perceptions. So . . . those facts tended to suggest that either the Dubietans had the ability to replicate totally all sensory and intellectual inputs or the technology that they claimed or exhibited was in fact real. Neither possibility cheered Roget in the slightest.

In the damp and misty air outside the museum, Lyvia looked to Roget. "You look rather down, Keir."

"That's a fair assessment. In my position, you would be as well. Exactly how can I prove what I've seen and can't explain?"

"Believe me. We'll be able to help greatly with proof. Whether the Federation will accept the implications is another question." Lyvia smiled brightly. "I'll see you in the morning." With that, she turned and walked away.

Roget walked slowly back to the central square. While the wind had subsided to a slight breeze, the misty air was still raw and chill. Even so, he settled himself on one of the benches next to the walkway, just trying—again—to make sense out of the day.

From somewhere near in the square came the sound of a stringed instrument. He turned his head. Standing on the raised stone dais around the central monument was a woman with silver gray hair, playing an overlarge violin—no, a viola.

Roget began to listen more closely.

Finally, after almost an hour, the violist stopped and began to place her instrument in its case. Roget rose, somewhat stiffly, and walked toward the violist. She closed the case and lifted it, then paused as she saw him approach.

"I wanted to thank you," he said. "That's all I can do."

She inclined her head. "You are most welcome."

"You play elsewhere?"

"I'm second chair in the Skeptos Orchestra."

"And you like to play here?"

"Some of the members of the orchestra apply to play in the square." A mischievous smile followed her words. "Some think it's beneath them. I like to play in both venues."

"Why here?"

"You get to reach out to people as individuals. Half the people who attend concerts do it for other reasons. Here, anyone who stops to listen really wants to hear what you play."

"I can see that."

She frowned. "You're not from around here. Patagonn? Or the unsettled part of Thula?"

"Farther than that." Roget smiled. "Why did you decide to become a musician?"

"Why does anyone decide anything? Because it was what I wanted to do. I kept at it because I had the talent. I might have kept at it, even without the talent, but then, I wouldn't be playing here, would I?" She smiled politely. "If you would excuse me . . ."

Roget stepped back. "Of course. But . . . thank you."

"You're welcome." She walked along the walk to the northeast.

Roget watched her for a moment, then turned slowly in the direction of the guesthouse.

26

6 DONGYU 6744 F. E.

Roget arrived at the maglev station in Cheyenne at seven fifteen Thursday night. Even using a priority transportation code, he hadn't been able to get a seat on the maglev until the Thursday night train leaving at eight ten. While Meira had assured him that there wouldn't be any problem in his stopping by their apartment once he arrived in Fort Greeley, Roget still worried about arriving so late.

His codes were good for a window seat against a rear bulkhead at the back of the coach, but it was under a vent, and the faint mixed odor of ozone and hot oil was annoying. So was the additional odor of synthcheese and overcooked chips, but what regional public transport in Noram didn't smell of stinky cheese and chips? The stiff old polycloth of the seat crackled every time Roget shifted his weight, and the older Sudam woman who had the aisle seat frowned at every crackle, as if somehow Roget were deliberately trying to keep her awake.

Two seats farther forward sat two young Sudams in the rear-facing seats. Roget could tell they were looking him over, and he intensified his hearing.

". . . leave him alone . . ."

". . . big, but he doesn't look so tough . . ."

". . . Marshan caught the readouts . . . priority codes for that seat . . . traveling alone . . . means combat specialist or security agent . . ."

". . . so what?"

". . . guys like that . . . break you in pieces . . ."

The two Sudams turned their eyes toward a pair of hard-faced women, then looked away.

The hour on the maglev seemed far longer by the time Roget swung his small bag out of the overhead when the train stopped at Central Station in Fort Greeley. Given what he'd heard from the two seated across from him, he waited until most passengers were off the train before stepping out onto the platform and then making his way toward the tunnel leading to the electrotram station.

The vaulted waiting hall that served all the platforms was dimly lit, but Roget suspected it would have been dim in midday and even on that handful of days when the wind blew enough so that the sun shone unhampered by the miasma created by too many people at too high an altitude for too many centuries, even with relatively clean power sources.

"Personal soltaic cells, cheaper here than anywhere!" called out a thin, scraggly-bearded youth.

"Commcards . . . less than ten yuan a minute . . ."

"The best in personal servicing . . ."

Roget sidestepped a would-be lifter, then unbalanced him, leaving him to totter into a muscular man in the desert camouflage of a merc's uniform, who slammed the unfortunate to the composite tile. There was always a market for mercs in the chaos of Afrique where Federation control was limited to destroying large concentrations of anything, but primarily of soldiers or weapons.

Roget kept moving, his senses and internals alert to anything moving toward him, but he reached the eastbound tram platform without incident. According to the directions Meira had sent him, all he had to do was take the local tram east for three stops and then walk south along 100 Fourth for three blocks to the Willis-D'Almeida.

As large as Fort Greeley was—a good three million–plus people, close to 90 percent of those in the Federation District that encompassed all of old Colorado and half of old Wyoming—the trams ran frequently. Roget waited less than five minutes but kept an agent's scan going the whole time.

Even at close to nine thirty at night, once he was on the tram, he had to stand, but he did manage to slip into a corner where it would be difficult for lifters. Ten minutes later, he stepped out onto another platform, this one older and synthbrick-walled, a style that had graced midlevel condo areas a century before. Two older women, not gray-haired but excessively careful in their steps, left the tram by the same door as Roget, as did a couple with two children, a boy and a girl who looked to be twins, one of the few exceptions to taxation surcharges on families with more than one child.

Once he walked down the steps and onto the well-lighted walkway, flanking 100 Fourth on the west side, Roget was careful to stay in the center. A couple walked swiftly past him, each carrying a half-staff, one of the more popular self-defense weapons allowed by the Federation. Each capped end held an immobilizing jolt, and the staff was sturdy enough to inflict major structural damage to an immobilized or stunned assailant. Neither the man nor the woman gave Roget more than a passing glance.

The first block south of the tram station held a market complex, but it had already closed, and Roget could see cleaning personnel inside. Three young men paced around one of the entrances, glancing toward it now and again but not toward the walkway or the passing pedestrians. Roget's sister's condo was in the block ahead, on the third level, opposite the recreation area and park. Despite the late fall chill, Roget could see several volleyball games in progress and a soccer game on the main field. He shook his head. He'd never been that enthused about team sports.

The fifth-story Willis-D'Almeida was neat from the outside, and seemingly well maintained, but from the off-tan shade of the synthbrick facade, it probably dated back more than a century. All the security lights were functioning, although several flickered as Roget climbed the outside steps to the third level and then made his way along the wide balcony to the front door of unit thirty-three. There he pressed the buzzer.

Brighter lights flared around him, and his internals caught the energy from the low-grade scanner even before he noticed the faint hum of the unit.

The door opened.

"Keir!" Meira stepped back. "You're here. Come on in."

Roget stepped inside, and his sister quickly closed and locked the door, reactivating the security system as she did.

"Where's Wallace?" asked Roget, setting his bag down beside the door.

"He's on the night shift. The pay's better, and he's here when Neomi gets home from school. Let me get Neomi. It's really past her bedtime, but she wanted to see her uncle. She's talked about your coming ever since you let me know."

As Meira headed for Neomi's bedroom, Roget glanced around the main room, a space a good six meters by four, but with a couch and two worn brownish tan armchairs at one end and a table with four chairs at the other. He could see a narrow kitchen beyond the table. The short hallway taken by Meira at the other end of the main room led to two small bedrooms and a fresher. While the condo's living area was larger than the room he had in officers' quarters in Cheyenne, it certainly wasn't much larger than the apartment he'd had in his brief stay in St. George, and Meira had to share the space with Wallace and Neomi.

Meira returned, holding the hand of a dark-haired and gray-eyed girl who looked up at Roget sleepily.

"Uncle Keir?"

"That's me." Roget squatted so that his face was almost level with Neomi's. "It's been a while since I last saw you."

"A long time." Neomi yawned.

Roget straightened.

Meira led Neomi over to the couch, where she seated her daughter and then settled beside her. Roget took the nearer armchair. It squeaked as he sat down.

"How was your trip?"

"The maglev was like always . . . crowded and stinky, but Cheyenne's close enough that it took less than an hour."

"Where are you headed next?"

Roget shrugged. "They don't tell me until I report for my briefing after I get off leave."

"Can you say where you've been?"

"Let's just say it was hot and dry."

"That describes about half the world these days," she replied.

"And everyone speaks Stenglish."

"Everyone? That might limit it to a third of the world."

"It was definitely in a dry third of the world." Roget laughed softly. It was better not to reveal anything if he didn't have to.

"Do you use an assumed name?"

"I haven't had to so far. I'm just listed in all the databases as a Federation Information Specialist, along with the thousands of others. Most of them are Federation Information Specialists. I can do that job." *And quite a few others as well.*

"Is there anything you can tell us?"

Roget laughed. "Where's your holojector?"

Meira pointed to a square cube on the small end table beside her. "There."

Roget copied the image of Hildegarde to Meira's system, frowning as he could feel and sense the heat. The holojector was probably on its last legs, but it did project Hildegarde's image out from the blank section of the wall reserved for just that.

"Don't tell me you managed to get a dog?"

"No. That's an image of a painting. You can see how good it is. I was walking through a gallery, and I saw it. The actual painting was for sale for something like seven hundred yuan. If I had a normal job I would have bought it, but I liked it enough to buy an image. When I visited the gallery later, the painting was gone. It had been put up for sale by heirs before they realized its value and its antiquity. It was worth over twenty thousand." Roget deliberately low-balled the value, knowing what Meira's reaction would be.

"You should have bought it." Meira's voice was cool. "At the least, you could have sold it back. The fools."

"Pretty doggy," said Neomi.

"Couldn't you have bought it?"

"I knew it was good, but not that good," Roget replied. "If I had, I'd have bought it and worked out something."

"It is a good painting," said Meira. "You've always had a fondness for dachshunds. I hated the way Muffin followed you."

"She was a good dog," Roget said.

"She was friendly to everyone, but she loved you."

"She liked everyone." Roget didn't mention that it might have been because he'd been the one to play with her and let her sleep at the foot of his narrow bed. "Anyway, I thought it was interesting that I ran across such a valuable painting, and it was a dachshund." He collapsed the holo image.

"That's all you can tell me?"

Roget nodded. "It's a requirement and better that way."

"You always kept everything to yourself," Meira continued, almost as if Roget had not said that he couldn't say more. "I sometimes think that Muffin was the only one you talked to."

"That could be. Father was always using anything I said against me. Mother . . ." Roget shrugged.

"You're still rebelling against them, even after what happened . . ." Meira's eyes brightened.

"No. I gave that up years ago, even before that." Roget didn't want to get into recriminations. It certainly hadn't been his fault that they'd been killed in the great southern hurricane of 6741 that had destroyed what had been left of Baton Rouge. The Federation hadn't been about to spend billions of yuan on land being eaten away by the sea, especially not in Noram. "But I have thought about childish rebellion, Meira."

"Oh?"

"We react, one way or another, to the circumstances that existed when we were growing up, but so did our parents, and those in their generation. Usually, at the time when we were children, they couldn't do much, but as they got older they did their best to change things."

"My, aren't you being generous now?"

"When people try to change things, it can be bad or good," Roget pointed out. "All I'm saying is that they did the best they knew how."

"With the Federation restrictions, no one can do much, not unless you've got billions, and words are cheap." Her words held an edge. "You must be doing well after all these years."

"I'm still the same rank. I get a bit more pay for seniority."

"Doesn't it bother you that the Sinese get preference, no matter what they say?"

"I can only do the best I can do. What about you? How are things here?"

"I did get a half-time position with the local health outreach organization. They can always use trained nurses or medics. They say I can go full-time once Neomi is in school all day. She goes to the children's center here in the afternoon, but . . . going all day would cost more than I could make. Since Wallace is the night maintenance director at the university, we have staff family privileges, and that does help." She shook her head. "We lost so much in the hurricane . . . we'll probably never recover it all. Coming here was all we could do. What real choice did we have?"

Neomi yawned.

"I do need to put her to bed."

Roget stood. "You probably need sleep as well. I thought maybe I could take you all out to dinner tomorrow."

"That would be nice . . . and appreciated. If you could make it early, sixish, Wallace could enjoy it without rushing off."

"If you'd like to pick a place . . . ?"

"CindeeLee's!" burst in Neomi.

"We can talk about it later." A wry expression crossed Meira's face. "Oh . . . I forgot to tell you. You can stay with us . . ."

"No, there's no need to inconvenience you. I have a room at the Palais, and the Federation's paying for it." That wasn't true, but he didn't want Meira to feel guilty. She had enough problems as it was.

"We had a dinner there once, a banquet, actually," said Meira. "We couldn't have afforded it if we hadn't been guests."

The Palais was far from the most expensive hotel in Fort Greeley. Roget knew that. "I'll call you, and you need to put my niece to bed."

"It might be better, this late . . . You can get an electro-cab at the kiosk on the main level."

And safer, thought Roget, although neither of them uttered that thought. "Thank you."

He walked to the door of the condo, picking up his bag from where he had left it by the door. Then he turned and smiled. "It's good to see you."

"You, too, Keir."

The balcony walkway was deserted as he made his way to the central stairs and down to the main level to the kiosk. There was actually a cab waiting.

As he sat in the rear seat on the way to the Palais, he reflected, yet again, on the possible reasons why he and Meira had never been all that close. Had it been that she resented him and the extra costs their parents had borne to have a second child? Or just that they were so different? The health outreach job was so like his sister—trying to care for everyone. Roget had the feeling that, no matter how hard you tried, there were some people beyond help.

Societies had to have rules, too, and rules that applied to everyone. He couldn't help but think about Marni and her collaborators. They'd wanted a Saint-ruled world—or at least their corner of it ruled by Saint principles. But that was what had led to the Wars of Confederation and the iron crackdown that had followed. When every group's principles were different, and every group was willing to fight to the death for those principles, you couldn't have a civilization. You could only have warfare, rebellion, and chaos.

If he had to be honest with himself, Roget didn't agree 100 percent with all the Federation laws and policies, but . . . what was the alternative? As Meira had asked, what choices did any of them have?

Still . . . Meira had looked so tired. At least he could offer dinner and slip some credits into her account on the pretense that they were to be used for Neomi. They would be, but that would free some money for Meira. He hoped.

27

24 MARIS 1811 P. D.

After an early breakfast at yet another unnamed bistro, Roget and Lyvia walked four blocks to the central square, where they made their way down to the regional subtrans concourse. Roget had donned his original pale blue shipsuit, although he wore the outer jacket over it, but with the variety of attire in Skeptos, he certainly wasn't wearing anything nearly as outlandish as some of those they passed on the ramp heading down to the concourse.

As they stood waiting in front of the leftmost green translucent door of the eastbound side of the concourse, Roget asked, "How many stops?"

"Just two."

"How long?"

"Forty standard minutes or so."

That meant a trip of around eight hundred klicks. From what Roget recalled, that would have put them in the middle of flatlands between two mountain ranges and north of a large inland lake. There was a city near there, but he couldn't recall the name and didn't want to dig the maps Lyvia had given him out of his pack.

The subtrans doors opened, and Roget carried his pack into the train. There were few enough passengers that Lyvia sat across from him, and he put his pack in the seat adjoining his. The doors closed.

"Are you nervous?" she asked.

"Not about the subtrans. Later . . . wouldn't you be?" he countered.

"I thought Federation pilots had nerves of steel, or composite or something," she said with a smile.

"They might. I'm an agent first, and a pilot second."

"That's what the Director thought."

"What else does she think?"

"That would only be speculation on my part."

"I'm certain that some things aren't speculation."

"You're fond of dogs, and you've never had a deep relationship with anyone. You don't quite fit the Federation mold. That's why you're both useful and not totally trusted . . ."

Roget realized that Lyvia was speaking in old American, and he was having no trouble at all following her.

"It's also why you're still sane and the other agent isn't."

"Dubiety isn't *that* strange."

Lyvia laughed.

After a moment, so did Roget.

Superficially, he realized, the differences weren't that great, but beneath that superficial similarity was a huge gap. "Did the other agent slowly lose it, the more he saw?"

"I never saw any reports."

The way she said the words suggested to Roget that she thought so.

Before long, the subtrans glided to a stop. Three people from the back of the car got off. A man wearing an orange vest over a brilliant flame-green singlesuit towed a wheeled case that rumbled slightly. No one entered their car, and the doors closed.

"That was Knossos. We'll be getting off at Rhodes."

"Are all the towns and cities in Socrates named after something Greek?"

"No, but a disproportionate number are."

"The original skeptics?"

"Probably not. Just the first with enough power and confidence to write their doubts down. Even so, there were enough conformists in ancient Greece that they ended up forcing Socrates to suicide."

Roget wondered if there might be a village or town called Hemlock, but didn't ask. He still could help thinking about the last words the director had offered . . . about events two and twenty-five centuries earlier. They'd been almost tossed off, as if they were absolute and yet as if whatever the Federation found would be disregarded.

When they disembarked at Rhodes, so did some twenty young men and women, mostly from other cars. Only a handful of men and women were waiting to board.

"Just wait a moment," Lyvia said.

Roget slung his pack over his shoulder and stood there.

Only when the concourse appeared empty did Lyvia turn and walk to the end away from the ramp leading up to the surface. At the end of the concourse, as they neared, a section of the wall slid open, revealing a narrow ramp. The hidden doorway closed silently behind them.

The ramp led straight down for a good hundred meters, then ended in a small foyer. On the right side was a single set of translucent doors of the same type used in the subtrans concourses, except that these were a dull yet deep red—the first of that color Roget had seen. This time Lyvia used her belt-tube and the doors opened, revealing a much smaller conveyance, almost a large capsule with but four seats, two on each side facing each other. All four seats were a deep green without trim.

Lyvia gestured and Roget stepped inside, taking a seat and putting his pack on the one beside him. Lyvia settled across from him, and the doors closed.

Roget studied the capsule, deciding from the lack of wear and its compactness that it was not used heavily. He could sense that they were descending. Descending? To reach a launch site that would send his dropboat into space?

Roget shrugged. That made about as much sense as anything had on Dubiety.

When the tube capsule came to a halt and the narrow door slid open, he asked, "How deep are we?"

"Deep enough."

From what his internal sensors registered with the change in air pressure, Roget guessed that they had dropped a good klick, if not more, but that estimation was rough, not an exact calculation because he didn't know all the variables. He followed Lyvia out into a small foyer whose metallic walls glistened like brushed pewter. Opposite the doors to the tube capsule was a metal framed archway.

The archway door split open. Each side of the door was almost a meter thick, and he walked swiftly through after Lyvia. Two guards—stationed behind energy screens—watched as Lyvia and Roget stepped through the heavy metal and composite doors. For the first time, Roget did sense energy emissions and scanning. Another closed archway stood behind and between the pair of guards.

"This is where I leave you." She smiled. Warmly, Roget realized. "Good luck."

"Thank you." Roget unclipped the belt-tube. "I suppose I should give this back to you."

"You can take it with you," Lyvia said. "It's another piece of evidence." She smiled. "Besides, if you ever do come back, you can still use the credits."

Roget shook his head. "They'll want the evidence."

"It doesn't matter. The credits are registered in your name."

"If I don't come back, give them to Aylicia, if you can."

"Thank you." She turned and walked back through the still-open archway from the tube capsule. It closed.

"Major . . ." offered one of the guards. "The technicians are waiting."

Roget looked back toward the second archway, now open. After a moment, he said, "Thank you," and stepped through the archway.

On the other side waited a man in a white singlesuit, standing in another featureless and high-ceilinged foyer. "Major Roget, this way."

Roget nodded and followed the other along the wide corridor. In a way, he felt more comfortable—wherever he was—because the installation had the definite feel of a military operation.

The technician turned into the second doorway on the left, the first one that was open. A series of wide lockers lined one wall, and a bench was set back from them. An open archway led into another chamber, which looked to hold freshers and toilets or the equivalent.

At the end of the bench was a frame holding a suit similar to the pressure suit Roget had worn on his descent through the orbital shields. The suit was a lighter shade of blue than his had been, almost white. He set his bag down on the end of the bench.

The technician pointed. "That's a deep-space pressure suit. Yours was too degraded, and we didn't bother trying to figure out how to repair it. We modified the neck-ring so that it is compatible with the standard Federation helmet. That was for comm compatibility. We checked the seal against your helmet, and it's perfect. Your helmet is in the dropboat." He pointed to a flat bag on the end of the bench nearest the suit. "There's an emergency suit there with a quick-seal hood, in case you can't get to a full suit. You might consider taking it. Of course, it's only got about an hour of oxygen, but that's usually enough for us to get to people in our operations."

"Thank you." Roget didn't know what else to say.

Roget studied the emergency pressure suit, then paused as he noted the red triangle on the waistband of the suit. "What's this?" He pointed.

"That's an emergency beacon. Press and hold for several seconds. Not that I expect you'd want pickup from us." The technician laughed. "I'll be outside when you're ready, and I'll escort you to the . . . launch chamber."

Within moments, Roget was alone. Launch chamber? Possibly klicks below ground? And he was standing in a locker room that held a good twenty lockers. He reached forward to the nearest locker. It was locked, unsurprisingly.

Finally, he took off his jacket and folded it, setting it on the bench. Then he began to don the replacement pressure suit—far easier to get into than the one he had used before, yet he had the feeling it might well be more durable. The seals literally melded into a seamless fabric.

Once he had the suit on, he bent to retrieve his own pack. Then he paused as he saw the flat package on the bench. The tech's observations were as close to an absolute recommendation as he'd gotten. He picked up the pack and felt it, then scanned it. A Trojan horse?

He shook his head. Why would they bother? They could have turned the entire dropboat into that. Besides, it was another piece of evidence. Finally, he slipped the flat package into his pack, rearranging items so that the pressure suit was on the bottom and his jacket was on the top. Then he closed the pack, slung it over one shoulder, and headed out of the locker room.

The tech was waiting in the corridor.

"This way, Major."

Roget walked beside the tech toward the end of the corridor and another metal girded archway with a closed set of doors. "Is this the only launch center?"

"It's best that I don't answer that, Major."

"Can you tell me what entity operates it? It seems . . . military."

"When you deal with massive force, any organization needs discipline. In that respect, we're no different."

Roget couldn't argue with that, but before he could frame another question they reached the archway, and the doors opened. He and the tech stepped into a huge domed and circular composite-lined chamber more than two hundred meters across. The apex of the dome was at least two hundred meters above.

A dropboat rested in a massive cradle in the middle of the chamber. The floor was polished and perfectly level, but the cradle was centered in a circle of amber composite so large that the cradle and boat looked almost lost, yet the gray area outside the circle was far larger. Protruding slightly from the mouth of a tunnel to Roget's right was a second cradle with another Federation dropboat.

"You'll be in the first boat, Major. The second boat is slaved to yours. Don't make any course or power corrections until Drop four is in formation on you. The slave relay won't work until it's in position. But any power or course changes you make will be copied precisely by Drop four. Someone will probably have to do a maglock or a tow on it once you get close to whatever ship they want you to rendezvous with."

"The other agent?"

"He's . . . very erratic. We're going to keep you two apart because he's stable for the moment. We just want to get you both back in one piece." The tech walked directly toward the cradle. "His comm is also blocked, except for the links to our control, but he won't know it until after launch."

"And mine?"

"Yours is open all the way. You'll see."

Roget certainly hoped so.

As they neared the cradle and the dropboat, Roget saw a portable ladder set at the side, arching over the cradle and leading to the dropboat's hatch. The tech stopped at the bottom. "Once you're inside we'll roll the ladder back. Except for the cradle and the boat, the space inside the circle has to be absolutely clear. Do you have any last questions?"

"How long will the launch take?"

"Less than ten minutes once you've finished your checklist and are ready. After you finish your checklist, control will contact you, and we'll orient the cradle. Make certain you're fully restrained."

"I can do that." Roget smiled.

"Best of luck, Major."

"Thank you." Roget climbed the ladder, carrying his pack. The hull was a different color in several places although the metal or composite the Dubietans had used melded into the original exterior seamlessly, except for the difference in shading. The hatch was open, and he had no trouble entering the dropboat. He could tell immediately that extensive repairs had been undertaken internally, not because of patches or oil or dirt, but because the entire interior looked almost new. Shaking his head, he stowed his pack in the tiny bunk cubicle behind the pilot's couch and then inspected the interior.

Once he finished his interior inspection and settled

himself before the controls, Roget donned his pressure helmet, linked to the craft's systems, then went through the predrop checklist, hoping that it would cover what was needed for whatever kind of launch the Dubietans used.

He went through the checklist twice. If he could trust the linkage and the reports, all systems were green, and all power reserves were at one hundred. He ran another set of diagnostics, but the secondaries confirmed the primary reports. He knew he hated trusting in what he didn't understand, but, yet again, he had to put his trust in the Thomists. *Do you really have any choice?*

He didn't, but it seemed, in retrospect, that he'd had few enough in his life.

Dropboat three, this is Magna Launch Control, communications check. The words were crystal clear. They were also in old American.

Control, this is three. Loud and clear.

Interrogative restrained and ready to launch.

Restrained and ready to launch, Magna Control.

Stand by for cradle orientation.

Standing by.

No sound penetrated the dropboat, but Roget could feel the cradle and the boat moving smoothly and then coming to a stop, nose up, perhaps thirty degrees.

Cradle orientation complete and verified. Stand by for launch.

Ready for launch this time, Control. Roget pushed out of his mind the impossibility of a planetary launch from deep underground and waited.

Good luck, Major.

Roget had no idea what to expect, but what happened next was totally unanticipated—blackness through which he could see nothing while he felt pressure, barely two gees, if that, followed by a lifting of the blackness, weightlessness, and by readings on all of his instruments showing that he was in space.

He didn't have time to think about the impossibility of what had just happened.

Where was he? Roget scanned the screens. Dubiety/Haze was well insystem from him, and he could discern a good thirty Federation ships directly in front of him on his present courseline and solar inclination. Thirty? There had only been five when he'd been dropped nine days before. Only nine days? In some respects, it felt far longer.

He ran another set of checks, but all his systems were green, and he was on an interception course for the center of the Federation formation. Even his closing speed was within the parameters that would allow phase deceleration. His power was still just below 100 percent.

He checked for the other dropboat, but Drop four was nowhere around.

"They have to move the cradle," he murmured, forcing himself to wait . . . and wait.

Then, his screens blinked, and abruptly, he could see Drop four at his one seventy at a range of three klicks. Inside the pressure suit, he shivered. The Dubietans had launch-projected two dropboats something like a million klicks and set them within three klicks of each other?

"Frig . . ." he murmured. He cleared his throat, then transmitted, *WD-Con, this is Drop three, returning. Estimate CPA in one five. Drop four is incapacitated and slaved to three. Four will need maglock or tow.*

Drop three, say again.

Roget repeated his transmission.

Stet, Drop three. Stand by for further instructions.

Roget continued on course toward the Federation fleet, noting that he had been launched directly at the *WuDing*. He didn't know of any Federation system that could have achieved that kind of accuracy—let alone have launched a dropboat through a chunk of the planetary mantle. Clearly, they could have literally launched a torp or explosives to materialize inside any of the Federation ships. They hadn't.

That raised again the question of exactly what the Thomists had in mind. From what he'd seen, the Federation didn't have any technology that matched the best of what he'd seen on Dubiety. He'd questioned more than a few times whether he'd seen what he'd thought he'd seen, but now that he was returning—assuming he wasn't imagining that as well—it was appearing more and more likely that he had indeed seen what he recalled.

Drop three, maintain course. Zee one will rendezvous. I say again. Maintain course. Zee one will manage link and dock.

Stet. Maintaining course this time. Will await instructions from Zee one.

Within two standard minutes, the EDI screen indicated a ship accelerating away from the fleet on an intercept course. The parameters indicated that the ship was an attack corvette.

Roget smiled. No one wanted his dropboat anywhere close to the main body of the fleet. That suggested the colonel hadn't expected anyone to return . . . or perhaps not the manner of his return.

Another minute passed, then another.

Drop three, this is ZeeControl. Interrogative power for decel.

ZeeCon, power adequate for phased decel. He had to assume that the same would be true for Drop four.

Three, request ID this time.

Roget pulsed the transponder. The return link identified the oncoming ship as the *ZengYi*, one of the newer attack corvettes.

Several minutes more passed.

Three, maneuver to link. Maneuver to link. Leave your lock closed for examination and possible decontamination.

ZeeCon, Drop three. Understand maneuver to link. Will leave lock sealed for decon.

That's affirmative, three.

As he maneuvered the dropboat toward the *ZengYi*, Roget realized he did have more significant proofs than he'd thought. First . . . the Dubietans had literally hurled or transposed his dropboat from somewhere beneath the planetary surface . . . and literally dumped him right in front of the Federation ships. He also had a different pressure suit, not to mention the documentation sent by the Dubietans and the repairs to the dropboat. He even had city and local maps printed on local paper or the equivalent that should reveal something.

Yet Director Hillis and the others had seemed to think that no amount of proof would suffice to deter the Federation from attacking or attempting to annex Dubiety in some form.

Roget feared that they might be right, but he'd have to see.

28

21 DONGYU 6744 F. E.

In the end, Roget only spent three days in Fort Greeley, and another two at the Estes Park nature reserve, expensive as it was, before he returned to the Federation base in Cheyenne. As he'd anticipated, Meira had protested his giving her credits but did eventually accept them for Neomi. As he'd also expected, Wallace was polite and reserved, as he always had been to Roget.

The remaining nine days of his leave were long, but he really didn't want to spend credits like water on hotels and resorts. So he read, rested, and tried not to think too deeply about his last mission—and the possibility of more memory flashes—and what might await him on his next assignment.

He also spent more than a little time talking to Hildegarde, but only to the image on his flash and only when he was somewhere alone, away from Federation buildings, and not likely to be snooped. He had no doubts that all officers' rooms were fully monitored.

Finally, after another full day of tests at the FAF medical center, he was back at the FSA building at Cheyenne base, sitting across from the same unnamed colonel who had debriefed him after the St. George mission.

"Agent-Captain Roget, you're in good shape, according to medical. There don't seem to be any lasting physiological effects from the events of your last assignment."

"Yes, sir." Roget still worried about the false memories. The first he'd ascribed to dehydration. And then, especially after Marni's dying words, the second memory-flash had hit hard. Still, he hadn't had another episode, and he sincerely hoped he wouldn't have. For all their probing, doctors hadn't found any sign of anything wrong with him, thankfully. That didn't mean everything was resolved. Roget just knew he'd have to cope . . . somehow.

The colonel smiled.

Roget distrusted the expression, even as he returned the smile.

"You did some research immediately after you were debriefed. Some rather interesting research. Tell me about it, Agent-Captain."

"Yes, sir. I was curious. One of the Danites muttered something about a Joseph Tanner. I'd never heard the name, and I wondered what he'd meant."

"You didn't put that in your report."

"I should have, but I didn't remember that until later. At the time, I was much more concerned about trying to find a way to keep them alive so that they could be questioned. After that, as you may recall, the dehydration left me a bit disoriented. All I could find about Tanner was a historical reference." That was certainly true, although the colonel obviously knew what Roget had found, but Roget wasn't about to make that point. "Do you think he might have been one of the founders of the Danites, sir?"

"That's rather unlikely. The Danites date back to the original Deseret, before it was conquered by the old Americans."

"I didn't realize that, sir." Roget tried to sound properly chastened, hoping that would divert the senior officer.

The colonel looked coolly at Roget. Roget returned the look calmly, but without challenge.

"And the woman?"

"I was thinking she might have some connection with Tanner, in some way. She didn't, not from what I could determine. I do wonder why a biologist would walk away from a university position."

"Cults can do peculiar things to people, especially to women."

Roget nodded. "I did see that in St. George."

The colonel waited a moment before speaking. "It's a most unpleasant aspect of those who don't understand the benefits of the Federation."

Another warning, thought Roget.

"In view of your situation," continued the colonel, "your next assignment is particularly appropriate. We're going to send you outsystem. This has advantages and disadvantages for you. One advantage is that you've been approved for promotion to major. Another is that the assignment will broaden your experience base. The disadvantage is that you'll spend six months to a year in intensive training learning to fly various small orbital craft. Since you're already a trained atmospheric pilot, it shouldn't be too difficult a transition, and flight status also includes incentive pay. Another disadvantage is that there is often some time dilation, particularly in fleet-related assignments. You have no close family, and you work better alone. That combination makes you an ideal candidate for several assignments once you finish your additional training."

Roget felt a chill deep inside. Outsystem attachment to the Federation Interstellar Service was where FSA sent expendable agents. "I wouldn't know, sir, but it sounds interesting."

"I'm certain you'll enjoy these assignments far more than you would in spending years in data analysis as a permanent captain, Agent-Major Roget." The colonel smiled politely.

Data analysis wasn't a choice; it was a veiled death sentence, if not by disappearance when everyone had forgotten him, then by sheer boredom, or by bankruptcy and/or extreme poverty by being forced to live in the Taiyuan area on a captain's stipend.

"When do I start . . . and where, sir?"

"I thought you'd like the opportunity, Major. You'll leave on Saturday for Xichang. There you will undergo a three-week indoctrination into FIS customs and procedures and be fitted for equipment. Certain internals will also have to be reconfigured for space applications. Then you'll be sent to Ceres station. That's where the IS trains its small-craft pilots. You'll also be brought up to speed on deep-space station systems and datanets, as well as a few other technical applications."

If the FSA wanted to spend that many yuan on providing him with such intensive additional training, Roget reflected, it was likely that future missions might be highly risky but not necessarily suicidal. The FSA mandarins still had to justify their expenditures to the Council.

Besides, what realistic choices did he have?

29

⊚

While Roget had waited inside the dropboat, his outer hull
had been tested, inspected, prodded, and probed with every
device known to the Federation—or so it had seemed. Then
they had started in probing within, still from outside the
dropboat, accessing all data and scanning the interior of his
craft. An exterior physical inspection of the dropboat hull
and systems followed. Hours later, he had been allowed into
the corvette's loading lock, where he'd been scanned, remotely, along with all of his gear, and all of the documentation he had brought back. Then he'd had to strip and be
inspected once more. He'd been allowed to dress in his shipsuit, but the Dubietan pressure suit and his helmet remained
behind.

Once he'd been cleared onboard the corvette, he'd been
immediately escorted into the small squarish comm room
off the corvette's tiny ops bay, where he had been left by
himself. The consoles were all locked and on remote, and
so quiet was the space that he could hear his own breathing.
He could also smell his own sweat, not from fear, but from
the heat and the time waiting in a pressure suit. A large water bottle sat in a holder on the right side of the console bay.
Roget took a long swallow, then sat waiting, knowing that
all manner of scanners and the like were trained on him. His
eyes dropped to his pack, still holding the emergency
shipsuit in its packet. The maps had been removed, but not
his personal items and clothing. While the pack had been
scanned, no one had removed the shipsuit. Was it transparent

to Federation scanners? Or had the techs merely considered it as a shipsuit?

Abruptly, the image of Colonel Tian appeared, sitting behind his console on the *WuDing*. "Greetings, Major. Welcome back. You appear to have weathered your landing and the time on Haze."

"Yes, sir."

"Tell me what happened. Begin just before your dropboat reached the orbital shield. Please take your time. No detail is unimportant."

Roget had doubts about that, but replied, "Yes, sir. The orientation imparted by my initial course allowed insertion in the same orbital pattern as the upper orbital shield, but I had to increase my relative speed considerably . . ." From there, Roget continued through his rocky descent and landing and his time on Dubiety. He had to stop more than a few times for water, and he was hoarse and raspy when he finally finished his summary.

Colonel Tian gave a last nod but did not say anything immediately.

Roget understood. The colonel was getting the interpretation of all the data obtained from observing Roget.

Finally, the colonel did speak. "Your physiological workup indicates that you have been in a gravity well that matches that observed of Haze. Since there has been no indication of any mass large enough to generate artificial gravity anywhere else near here, it does appear likely that you have indeed been on the planetary surface. Likewise, you have been physically active, and your hair samples and tissue analyses indicate exposure to a T-type world, but one with a similar but differing ecology." The colonel paused. "Those results suggest that you were physically present and active on Haze, since replicating those results otherwise would require an extremely advanced technology at variance with what we have observed. Also, the sample distribution supports your presence on-planet."

The fact that the colonel continued to use "Haze" in speaking of Dubiety suggested his own doubts about Roget's account, but Roget merely replied dispassionately, "My own observations suggested that counterfeiting my experiences would have been difficult."

"But not necessarily impossible."

"Anything is possible to a sufficiently advanced technology, sir."

"To their technology?"

"I don't believe that they went to that extreme, sir, but there are certain aspects of their technology that appear unique, as I have mentioned."

"Which do you think are most unique?"

"The high-speed subtrans system is one, both its operating speed and its extent, especially the deep tubes between continents. Their ability to communicate without any stray radiation is another. The ability to create multiple artificial magnetic poles with enough power and variance to use to control the levels of orbital shields is a third."

"The first two are mere adaptations of existing Federation technology. Why do you find them so unique, Major?"

"The amount of additional resources and effort required to construct them suggests that there well may be other reasons for their use and existence."

"And what might those be, do you think?"

"I have no idea, sir. But the Dubietans I met seemed very pragmatic."

"It seems less than pragmatic to return any agents, especially one in a disoriented state."

"I doubt they do anything without a reason, sir."

"Nor do I, Major. Why do you think they returned you?"

"To show good will. To demonstrate that they could." *To warn you.* "To suggest they have advanced technology."

"That is certainly what they would wish you—and us—to believe. If they have such, why not use it in a way that leaves no doubt?"

"They claim that they do not wish to be the ones to offer any hostile action against the Federation or any action that might be perceived as hostile."

"A most convenient excuse not to show their supposed advanced technology."

"Sir . . . it would seem to me that the course line and velocity with which my dropboat was returned suggests an advanced technology. So do the orbital shields. So do the repairs to the dropboats."

"Comparable technology, Major, not advanced technology."

"Begging your pardon, sir, but I've not seen any Federation technology that is comparable to that."

"Begging your pardon, Major, how would you know?" The colonel's tone was flat.

Roget decided to offer another approach. "The Dubietans also stated that no amount of proof would convince the Federation if it were not disposed to be convinced."

"Did they say that in so many words, Major?"

"They were somewhat more blunt. They sent the technology documentation. They rebuilt the dropboat, and they returned me, and they suggested that the Federation would find none of that convincing." Roget could see that the Dubietans had read the colonel correctly.

Colonel Tian's image looked blandly at Roget. "The diagnostics on the dropboat and the tracking of your return course indicate that you didn't lift off from Haze at all."

Roget repressed a sigh. "In fact, I did. Rather the Dubietans launched me—"

"Exactly how did they launch you?"

"From a rather elaborate cradle in the middle of their launch complex, as I indicated."

"Are you still convinced this launch complex was underground? Are you certain that wasn't another illusion?"

Roget let the illusion reference pass. He'd never said anything was an illusion. "I traveled there by their tube system.

My internals indicated we descended quite a bit to get there. I would think that the dropboat recorders would have provided details."

"Nothing shows on the datacorders between the time of your landing and the time, within a few nanoseconds, when your dropboat appeared on the farscreens and EDIs of various Federation vessels."

That meant the dropboat had recorded his landing. "Then we have a record of the planetary parameters."

"If they can be trusted," replied Tian.

"They match what I've reported and what your analyses already show."

"And how do you know that?"

"Because, sir, you would have told me if they had not, and you would have dismissed all that I have reported far sooner. I would also guess that there is no evidence at all of tampering with the recording systems of either dropboat."

The faintest hint of a frown appeared on the colonel's face but vanished immediately. "Oh . . . and what might that indicate?"

"That they have a very advanced technology. If they did not tamper with the data, then what I have said bears that out, and if they did, and we cannot detect it, then they also have advanced technology."

"You are rather adamant about that, Major."

"I know what I saw, sir. I also know what I brought back and how I returned to the *ZengYi*. Has anyone had a chance to study the documentation the Dubietans sent?"

"We don't have a science team here, Major. The engineers are looking over what's been scanned to us. We're not about to datalink."

The Federation had known about Dubiety . . . and they hadn't dispatched a single scientist with the *WuDing*? "Supposedly, the data can be read on an independent system."

"That may be, Major, but the *ZengYi* doesn't have that

kind of equipment, and I'm not about to risk anything like that onboard a capital ship."

Roget could understand that, but he didn't understand why a portable console couldn't be transferred to the corvette . . . unless the colonel wasn't all that interested in the data.

Another series of questions followed, in which the colonel repeated and rephrased earlier inquiries. Then came yet another set of rephrasings.

Roget kept his answers shorter and more factual the second and third times he replied to the variations on the same questions, especially since the colonel clearly wasn't interested in knowing what Roget thought, only what he could prove.

Finally, Tian cleared his throat. "For the present you will remain on board the *ZengYi*. I would caution you not to speak to anyone else about the specifics of your mission. I trust you understand, Major."

"Yes, sir." *You don't want anyone to know what might be down there, especially if you're going to try to destroy it.*

The colonel's image vanished.

Within moments, the hatch to the tiny comm room opened, and a Federation lieutenant stood there. "Major . . . we're a bit cramped, but there's a spare bunk in the exec's stateroom . . . if you'd like to rest."

Roget rose, picking up the pack at his feet. "I would, thank you. It's been a long day." But not nearly so long as those ahead of him, he feared.

The executive officer's stateroom was all of ten meters down the main upper deck passageway. There, Roget stretched out on the narrow upper bunk but did not really sleep, lying there in a worried doze. He was more than glad to sit up when the hatch opened, but he barely remembered to keep his head down before he almost rammed it into the overhead.

"Major, Jess Uhuru," offered the dark-skinned Federation captain. "I'm the exec here. I just wanted to let you know that the wardroom is open. We didn't know what sort of schedule you've been on."

"Thank you." Roget swung his feet over the side of the bunk and then dropped to the deck. "I'm sorry to intrude on your space, Captain."

"We're happy to be able to accommodate you, sir. It's not often that anyone gets to see an FSA officer who's survived a hostile planet."

"It wasn't that hard once I landed. Their orbital shields are rough, but they're not hostile down there." *Not yet.* Roget paused. "What about the pilot of the other dropboat?"

Uhuru shook his head. "He's sedated and restrained in sickbay. He started raving about all of us just being tools of the creatures down below." After a moment, he asked, "Are they really alien down there?"

"They appear quite human, but they have a very different way of looking at things." That was accurate enough. "It can be very upsetting." Roget followed the exec out into the narrow passageway.

"Here comes the commander, sir." Uhuru stepped back.

A squarish major appeared in the passageway. He smiled broadly. "Major, Kiang Khuo. We're glad to see you made it back."

"Thank you. I'm sorry about being parked here."

"That's not a problem. We can handle an additional officer or two. Beyond that . . . let's just say that it gets cozier than anyone would like." The *ZengYi*'s commander gestured toward the open hatch to the wardroom mess, less than five meters aft from where he stood.

Roget made his way along the passage and into the officers' wardroom, compact like everything else aboard a corvette, a space some five meters long and slightly less than four wide, with narrow chairs that barely fit the four officers already seated. He took the seat to the right of the commander, who seated himself at the head of the table. Uhuru sat across from Roget.

Khuo served himself from the platter in front of him, then nodded to Roget. "Replicated sesame stuff, but at least the galley was overhauled just before we broke orbit. Last deployment . . . we won't go into that." He shook his head.

Roget took a moderate helping of the sauced meat, then of the sticky rice. "Did you come out with the *WuDing,* or were you with the follow-up fleet?"

"We were here from the beginning. We were the escort on the scoutships that did the drops. Have to say it was something watching all of you. One minute you were on the screens, and the next the gray haze swallowed you all— except the last dropboat. Poor bastard. He just exploded when he hit the gray." Khuo looked to Roget. "Was there a trick to it?"

"I just checked the relative motion. We didn't drop fast enough." Roget shrugged. "Had to goose the dropboat to keep from getting run down."

"Run down?"

"Oh . . . the shields are millions of chunks of grayish stuff all orbiting at pretty high speed."

"What kind of chunks?" asked a young lieutenant at the end of the table.

"That's all I can say about it right now," Roget replied.

"Major . . . you seem to have the Security types concerned," offered Uhuru.

"They're often concerned," Roget replied. "That's their job."

"We couldn't pick up any track of your dropboat," said the exec. "Then you were on the screens. Did the Thomists— they are Thomists, aren't they—somehow shield you?"

"So far as I know, they didn't. They repaired the dropboat and launched me back on a return course." While Tian had told Roget to say nothing, the officers of the *ZengYi* had already observed more than he'd said.

"How did you get so close without any trace?" pressed the young lieutenant.

"I don't know how they accomplished that," Roget replied. "But—"

"Lieutenant . . ." Commander Khuo's voice was quiet but firm.

"They're still analyzing the data and the materials I brought back," Roget said. "They might offer some answers. Until they do, I suspect, I'm likely to be your guest."

"How did you end up in outsystem security?" asked the commander, clearly signaling a change in wardroom conversation.

"FSA decided I was the type of agent who worked better alone and on challenging projects," Roget replied.

"I think that might equate to resourceful and expendable," suggested the commander.

Roget had long since come to that conclusion, but he just smiled. "We do what we can."

"That's all any of us can."

"What do you think will happen . . . with Haze?" asked the exec.

"What the fleet marshal—or anyone—least expects," Roget replied. "I don't know what that will be, but the Dubietans are surprising in their predictability."

"Surprising in their predictability?" The commander raised his eyebrows.

"What they do is extremely predictable in hindsight, but unexpected in its applications. That's all I can say." And more than the colonel would have wished, even if Roget hadn't revealed anything directly. He took a sip of the tea.

It wasn't bad, but it tasted flat, especially compared to the food on Dubiety.

30

Three pilots with fresh deep-space, small-craft certifications sat in the low gravity of the Belt Control operations office opposite a senior Federation Interstellar Service major. The major was speaking. Roget was one of the pilots listening intently.

"All three of you have excelled in your training. That is to be expected. Also expected, before you are dispatched to your next duty station, you have a proficiency flight. Call it a postgraduate assignment." The senior major looked over the three pilots. "The other name for it is 'the squirrel run.'"

Roget had heard of the squirrel runs through certain sections of the belt. Despite the best efforts of the Federation Interstellar Service, independent operators, often piratical, still tended to pop up—or be discovered or rediscovered among the smaller bodies scattered through the Asteroid Belt, or the Oort Cloud, or the Kuiper Belt. Most of these tended to die off, literally, because they'd escaped the Federation's outsystem control with too little equipment, but there were some who persisted . . . and some who raided outsystem mining outposts for hard-to-get technology or supplies when their own failed or were exhausted. The unofficial Federation policy was to leave well enough alone unless the belt colony appeared to be prosperous and growing, or unless the unapproved colonists had turned to piracy.

Not so benign neglect, thought Roget.

Lieutenant Castaneda exchanged looks with Lieutenant Braun, but neither spoke.

"Is this a pirate colony, sir, or an unapproved one?" asked Roget.

"Does it matter, Major? Orders are orders."

"Yes, sir. It does matter. A pirate colony is more likely to have amassed various arms and armament systems. An established and unapproved colony will be heavily dug in and fortified but is likely to have older weapons systems."

The senior major nodded. "It is older and unapproved *and* a pirate colony. You will carry a full range of armament. You are not to attempt any rescues, regardless of possible distress calls, because this colony has used that ruse to capture vessels and savage others for their equipment and supplies."

"Yes, sir." Roget appreciated that information. He would have wagered it wasn't laid out that bluntly in the official briefing materials.

"Major Roget will be the flight leader. Briefing consoles five, seven, and nine are reserved for you and will respond only to your IDs. You have two hours before you're to report to the attack boat locks. That is all."

The three stood.

"Best of luck, gentlemen."

Once the three were outside the ops section in the main wide corridor beneath the surface of Ceres, Lieutenant Castaneda glanced at Lieutenant Braun. Then both looked to Roget.

"Squirrel run, sir?"

"Think of tree rodents. They're hard to find in a forest. They duck in and out of things, and when they have a ship, they can circle around an asteroid or a chunk of rock as fast as you can, just like a squirrel around a trunk. They can dig in deep, so deep that all you can do is seal the entrance, and if they survive, they'll just dig out somewhere else. That's unless you take in really massive weapons and fragment the rock that holds the whole colony—and then FIS gets hell because you've scattered all sorts of missiles across the system that will have to be tracked to make sure that they don't impact other installations."

"What's the point, then, sir?"

"To keep the squirrel population down and wary," replied Roget dryly. "And to give all new pilots a solid idea of their limitations." He walked with long and low strides along the blue-walled corridor that led to the ready room—and the briefing consoles.

The two lieutenants followed.

A good standard hour later, Roget was fully suited and standing in the surface lock, ready to enter the needleboat he'd been assigned. He pulsed his ID and authorization code to the lock receptor, and the bar on the lock plate turned green. Then he twisted the wheel through three full turns—all locks on the station that could open to vacuum had manual wheels—before again pressing the plate. The lock opened, revealing the closed outer lock of the combat needleboat.

Roget pulsed his authorization codes and the outer lock door of the needleboat opened.

Once he'd closed the outer station lock door and then stepped into the needleboat, sealing it behind him, Roget began his preflight in the cramped needleboat lock. A good fifteen minutes later, he settled into the pilot's couch, where he linked to the boat's systems. His preflight check had revealed that the needleboat was one of the newer ones, and fully armed—not one of the worn and tired craft usually assigned to student pilots. The tiny single cabin area was also clean and the replicator fully stocked for a full four weeks, although the mission was scheduled to last slightly less than two weeks.

He took his time with the full system checks. Finally, he pulsed the others.

Digger two, Digger three, this is Digger one. Interrogative status.

One, two here, status green. Ready to launch.

Digger one, three is ready to launch.

Roget nodded, then pulsed, *BeltCon, this is Digger one. Digger flight ready for departure and launch.*

Digger flight, this is BeltCon. Cleared to linear this time. Quadrant Orange is your departure lane.

BeltCon, Digger lead, understand cleared to linear. Orange Quadrant. Digger flight delocking this time. Roget switched to tactical. *Digger flight, delock this time. Form on me.*

Digger lead, Digger two, stet.

Digger three here, stet.

Roget released the maglocks on both sides of the needle-boat and used a burst of steering jets to ease it up from the docking cradle and toward the intake chute for the orange quadrant linear accelerator.

Orange Control, Digger one, approaching intake.

One . . . cleared to enter and take position.

Roget checked his suit and all the connectors, then the system integrity indicators before he used the steering jets to ease the needleboat over the accelerator's magnetic cradle.

Orange Control, Digger one, in position this time.

Stet, One . . . stand by for lock-in.

Standing by.

Roget felt the needleboat drop, and a dull *clunk* echoed through the hull, a sound that Roget felt as much as he heard as he checked his suit once more.

Outbound velocity wasn't limited by the linear accelerator's capabilities, but by the design limits of the needleboats—and their pilots—as well as the need to decelerate at the destination, particularly if the destination didn't have a mag-grav attenuator net. No pirate colony had that. But because the force of the linear accelerator could stress the needle-boats and possibly cause a pressure loss, all pilots were fully suited for launch.

Digger one, locked in cradle. Interrogative ready for launch.

Roget ran a last set of checks. *Orange Control, Digger one, ready for launch.*

A wall of blackness pressed Roget back into the pilot's couch, an inexorable pressure that seemed to last forever before releasing him to the light gravity of the needleboat, set internally at one-third T-norm. Most of the training boats didn't have internal gravitics, but gravitic control systems were required for any flight lasting more than four standard hours, and most training hops were far shorter than that.

He checked the EDI as the accelerator launched Digger two and then Digger three.

Digger flight, close on me.

Digger lead, two here, closing this time.

Lead, three here, closing.

Digger flight, understand closure. Run systems checks this time.

Once Roget verified the integrity and pressure of the needleboat, and his outbound course, Roget removed his helmet, slipping it into the overhead rack where he could reach it immediately if the boat lost pressure.

Now all he had to do was endure six days of boredom before he and the others reached their target.

31

25 MARIS 1811 P. D.

Another day passed with more medical tests and screenings before Roget was transported to the *WuDing*. Once there, he was subjected to even more tests, and his pack was thoroughly screened as well, although no one actually opened it. Roget didn't bother to point out that shortcoming. After all the tests, he was escorted to the stateroom he'd occupied once he'd been revived on the way inbound to Dubiety. He was told to wait there.

Since he had left the dropboat, Roget had not been allowed near any screens or instruments that would have updated him on what the Federation fleet was doing. Even so, he had no doubts that they were preparing for some sort of strike against Dubiety. He also had no doubt that such a strike would be catastrophic—and not for the Dubietans. Of course, he couldn't *prove* that, not to the colonel's satisfaction and probably not to his own.

He didn't even look inside his pack, since he was certainly under observation, nor did he call up the flash image of Hildegarde.

Three hours later, two ship marines arrived and escorted him forward to see Colonel Tian.

Once Roget stood inside the small space off the operations bay, the colonel looked up from where he sat behind the folded-down console and motioned to the other chair. "Good afternoon, Major."

Roget's internals confirmed that it was late afternoon Federation baseline time, but how good the day was happened to be another question. "Good afternoon, sir."

"You're one of the two who were able to return. Or allowed to return." Tian's voice was as emotionless as ever. "According to what you said the Thomists told you, only one other dropboat made it through the haze. Do you believe them?"

"My dropboat was badly damaged," Roget pointed out. "The commanding officer of the *ZengYi* confirmed that dropboat five disintegrated immediately upon reaching the outer orbital shell. It's almost a certainty that the other two suffered great damage and were destroyed in the middle layers. I don't see that the Dubietans would have anything to gain by lying about their fate."

"You trust these . . . aliens too much, Major. I would have expected better from you."

"I don't trust them at all, sir, except where I can verify for myself what may have happened."

"You dismiss rather lightly that your perceptions may have been . . . affected."

"I did think, sir, and I continue to think about whether everything I saw or felt had been mentally induced." Roget smiled, ironically. "The more that has occurred, the less I think that is likely."

"That is a most interesting conclusion. Would you care to explain why you think it so unlikely?"

"Any society that could launch a dropboat with the velocity and accuracy with which I was returned, not to mention the ability to repair the dropboat and create the material for the pressure suit I wore, as well as create the orbital shields, would have little difficulty in dealing with the ships you've gathered. Therefore, what exactly would be the point of going to all the trouble of inducing all that detail, especially with the depth of sensation. If they do not have the technology that I have seen and whose results our ships have documented, then they have the ability to change the perceptions of all of us, as well as affect our instrumentation. Therefore, they either have the ability to do that or they have the advanced technology. In either case, attacking or angering them is unwise."

"Oh? You were planetside some nine days, and you know their psychology and strategies so intimately?"

"I'm not talking about psychology, sir, but about technical capabilities." Roget paused, just briefly. "Have you had a chance to go over what I brought back?"

"I've gone over your reports and the materials you brought back. All of them are quite unbelievable."

"That may be, sir. It's also what happened." Roget kept his voice level.

"No. It is what you believe happened. Whether what you

believe is what actually occurred is another question. Have you considered that?"

"Yes, sir." Roget laughed softly. "I considered it almost every day, if not every hour." *Why doesn't he want to understand?*

"And you don't think your thoughts were manipulated?"

"Everyone's thoughts are influenced by what they observe, or what they think they observe, sir. While I was planetside, I was fully aware of the complete range of human senses and sensations. Also, the Dubietans were not hesitant to suggest that they believed that they were essentially going through the motions in letting me see what I did and in sending back the materials that they did. You've tested me every way you can. Didn't the tests show I was planetside?"

"Isotope analysis of your hair indicates you were somewhere earthlike, yet very different. There were too few contaminants for you to be on a human-industrialized world capable of the kind of technology that could create orbital shields and high-speed launching facilities."

"Sir, given their emphasis on environmental costs, such a world wouldn't have a high level of contaminants."

"No human civilization has yet managed that degree of environmental control. Just how likely is it that an isolated world could do so?"

Roget had the strong feeling that Dubiety wasn't that isolated, but, again, all he had to go on was inference from what Hillis and Lyvia had said, and Tian wasn't about to take inference as proof. Not when he wouldn't take what proof there was and logic. "And the devices? How do you explain them if they don't have a high-technology capability?"

"Interesting, but hardly convincing. One projects a modulated form of energy that doesn't scatter."

"They apply that everywhere. There's not even light-scatter from streetlights, and my internals wouldn't pick up anything."

"Oh? There are other possibilities."

"What? Such as the fact that I was somehow mind-controlled from the moment of touchdown? That they're totally alien and planetbound because of other factors? That they fed everything I thought I experienced into me? I thought of those. If that's so, then they're no danger. At most, all the Federation would have to do would be to avoid Dubiety."

"That is not a possibility."

"All they're suggesting is that they be left alone."

"That is not possible," repeated Tian.

"Why not, if I might ask, sir?"

"You may ask. I will even tell you." The colonel leaned back ever so slightly in his chair. "Some three thousand years ago on earth, there was an ocean admiral named Zheng He. This admiral commanded the largest fleet in history. In terms of numbers of vessels, it may have been the largest ever. It dominated earth's oceans for three decades, until a rebel uprising led to the creation of a new emperor—Hongwu. Hongwu burned the great fleet and turned China away from the world. Why did he do this? Because the fleet only explored and destroyed. It never provided any significant gain to China, and the harsh conditions of the time only led to the conclusion that the fleet was useless and a drain on the people. That is the first lesson."

Roget waited.

"The second lesson concerns the relationship between the ancient United States and the Tojoite Japanese Empire. Japan had closed itself off to the world, much as China had. But when the emperor was forced to open Japan to American traders at cannon point, the Japanese embarked on nearly a century of frantic industrialization and modernization. In the end, they attacked and destroyed much of China and invaded and occupied all the American lands west of the Hawaiian Islands. For years the entire world was at war. In the end, the Tojoites lost, but the devastation blighted the world for more than a century and led to the eventual fall of old America. That is the second lesson."

By his choice of those examples, Colonel Tian was obviously suggesting that the Federation Interstellar Service was to be used for far more than mere exploration and that any isolated world posed a potential threat that the Federation could not ignore.

"There are other examples from history, sir," suggested Roget.

"They are not from our history and are therefore less applicable." The colonel's eyes hardened. "What else did you learn about their technology, if anything?"

"I detailed all that I could determine, sir, and brought back all that I could."

"You provided little of technical value, Major."

"I supplied you with maps, with a detailed description of the structure of their industry and transport systems, as well as how their communications are structured."

"*You* provided not one word about how this technology operates."

"I brought back a small transmitter, the technical material that documents how the orbital shields work, how some other transport systems may be possible . . ."

"I had the chief engineer study the material. He says that's all technical gobbledygook. There's no way that it could work as you say it can. Nor can the so-called transmitter."

Roget realized, abruptly, that there had been not one word about the language implantation technology. In his report, he had definitely mentioned what Director Hillis said about that being a technology that the Federation already developed. Yet the colonel had avoided asking about it. Because it had been suppressed and was being used covertly by the FSA and other security types? For more than language training? He wouldn't get an answer if he asked. Either Tian didn't know or wouldn't say. But he could try another approach. "Sir . . . how old is this solar system?"

The colonel frowned.

"According to my original briefing materials, it's

considerably older than the Sol system, yet Dubiety has a molten core, a core supposedly reenergized by their technology. If you can measure the planetary magnetic fields, you'll find three sets of magnetic axes—all offset to each other. Those fields have something to do with the structure and operation of the three levels of orbital shields. To me, sir, that suggests that their technology is anything but gobbledygook."

The colonel frowned. "We've already established that the magnetic field is odd, but many planets have different or off-angled fields."

"Three separate fields, sir? I doubt that."

"Doubts are not facts, Major."

"Sir . . . I am an agent, not a scientist or a theoretical physicist. I was never allowed more than limited access to their commnet, nor to any written material that might explain how they have accomplished what they have, except for what I brought back. Even so, I am a trained observer, and what I saw suggests great caution in dealing with the Dubietans."

"Tell me." The colonel's voice was soft. "What do you think that they have accomplished?"

"They have built a subsurface transport system that is faster and more reliable than any planetary air or surface or subsurface transport system in the Federation, and far more effectively designed and operated than any system we have. They have created a layered orbital shield system that selectively admits solar radiation, keeps the planet from being observed by any form of energy, and would probably destroy most vessels trying to land on the surface. They have developed a tight-beam directional broadcast technology that radiates virtually no stray radiation yet allows all citizens commnet access. They have structured their society in a way that makes most continuing or habitual criminal activity extremely difficult, if not impossible. They can launch a drop-boat at high velocity and with greater accuracy than any current Federation technology, and they can do so unobserved. Finally, they have some way of observing the Federation, and they have been doing so for centuries."

"Yet they allowed you to depart?"

"They helped me. The dropboat was badly damaged on the descent. You can tell that from the repairs. They wanted me to return. Why else would they go to all that trouble?"

"The techs have examined the dropboat. They can discern repairs, but no spy gear and no explosives or weapons."

"I assume they brought it into the engineering bays and totally disassembled it," said Roget mildly.

"That was unnecessary and unwise. All necessary inspection could be carried out with the craft on tether."

Since the dropboat wasn't exactly a great military threat, given its minuscule size compared to the *WuDing* and the armament and shields of the battlecruiser, Tian had to be more concerned about possible nano-snoops.

"And what is the nature of the repairs?" asked Roget.

"They're comparable to Federation standards."

Roget suspected the repairs were far better, and that the colonel wasn't about to admit that.

"Is there anything else, Major?"

"One thing, sir. Dubietan Director Hillis suggested that you make an inquiry into the events of 6556 F. E. and the disappearance of Federation Exploratory Force Three. She also suggested that High Command review any stellar maps that might exist of this area in the year 4245 F. E."

"That's almost a thousand years before the Federation was even space faring."

"Send a ship twenty-five hundred light years away and record what it sees," suggested Roget.

"We scarcely have time or resources for such."

But you and the Federation have enough to start a conflict that will cost far more. "It wouldn't take that long."

"I'm sure they suggested that. It would buy time."

"They didn't suggest anything except looking at maps."

"I'm certain you believe that, Major." The colonel offered a cold smile. "That would be in their interests."

"That may be, sir, but there are unresolved observations about Dubiety. I would suggest looking into those dates before taking any action."

"We look into everything, Major. We look at the facts, especially."

Only selectively. But wasn't that an all-too-human trait?

"You may go, Major. For the time being, I strongly suggest you confine yourself to the wardroom, the exercise spaces, and your quarters."

"Yes, sir." Roget wanted to shake his head, but there wasn't even much point in that. Instead, he inclined his head politely and rose. The colonel had made up his mind—or it had been made up for him before the *WuDing* had set out for the Dubiety system.

32

23 LAYU 6746 F. E.

After five days alone in the needleboat, the last thirty-odd hours on decel, Roget was restless but worried about what sort of reception might await them at the target destination. He hadn't gotten all that much sleep, either. Despite the vast distances between asteroids and the other ancient debris in the Belt, the needle's speed and course had resulted in the detector's alerting him a good twenty times, usually just after he'd dozed off. By the time he'd made course changes and regrouped the flight, he was awake, and getting back to sleep was difficult.

He considered the situation. According to the briefing ma-

terials, the pirates had raided the mining storage and consolidation outpost off Themis just after a solar slow-boat had
arrived. They'd discovered and disabled almost all of the
tracking devices in the cargo—except several of a newer design. Using those, the FIS had tracked the pirates to the pair
of asteroids that was Roget's destination—less than an hour
away. Given the raid, the FIS had decided that the pirate colony had been far too disruptive, but not enough to warrant
fleet action, given the costs. Also, a needleboat flight had far
more chance of making an initial attack unnoticed.

For a while yet, there was nothing Roget could do except
wait.

He used his belt flash to project the image of Hildegarde
just out from the side bulkhead, so close that he could
have reached out and touched her—had she actually been
there. The little black dachshund with the tan oval patches
above her eyes gazed at him, as expectantly as ever. Just
looking at the projected image of the ancient oil painting
seemed to relax Roget, far more than viewing one of the
scores of holodramas stored in the needleboat's entertainment
files. Even the incongruity of seeing Hildegarde sitting on
an ancient blue velvet sofa and a hand-knitted maroon and
cream afghan, with the entire scene framed by plasticoated
metal bulkheads, didn't bother him.

"It doesn't bother you either, does it, little girl?" he murmured.

Hildegarde just kept looking at him, expectantly.

Roget left Hildegarde perched on her sofa in midair above
his right shoulder as he checked the needle's course and the
data assimilation on the target.

Although the two asteroids revolved around each other,
the tracking signalers and the energy indications made it
clear that the target was the larger body—an irregular chunk
of rock shaped roughly like an elongated potato some eight
klicks long and three in diameter at the thickest part, one
bulbous end. The needleboat instruments confirmed the

briefing materials—that the target asteroid was half-nickel and half solid, stony basaltic material, the larger bulbous end being the metallic part. From the stray energy emanations picked up by his instruments, Roget pegged the "colony" as being located in the middle of what loosely might be termed the larger bulbous polar area.

The EDI showed only diffuse energy, barely above ambient. That wasn't surprising. While a pirate colony that had survived for any length of time had to have several fusactors, they would be placed where virtually all heat and energy would be used and trapped within the nickel-iron core of the asteroid.

Another twenty minutes passed before Roget collapsed the holo image, returning Hildegarde to her electronic kennel, so to speak, and squared himself before the controls. He donned his helmet, although he hoped that he wouldn't end up with integrity damage after the mission. A week's return in a suit would be sheer hell.

Like any FIS flight, the three needles would attack from widely divergent approach angles because pirate colonies were always energy limited, and a split approach required them to fragment their defenses or to ignore one or more of the attackers.

Digger flight, Digger one. Commence separation this time.

Digger one, two here, stet.

Digger three, stet.

The basic strategy Roget intended to employ was the reverse of the squirrel defense. Because the pirates/unauthorized colonists had to be dug in fairly deeply, the needleboats could appear, fire torps, and cross any area covered by defensive systems quickly enough that it would be difficult to track and acquire the attackers. The downside of the strategy was that the number of such passes was limited because the asteroid was too small for the needles to establish tight orbits and all passes had to be fully powered.

Roget's first pass would target a source of energy emanations—generally comm equipment or the colony's scanners. With luck, that would limit the pirates' ability to focus on the FIS needles.

Digger one will lead. Commencing run this time.

Stet.

The two other needles would follow his pass, but not from the same approach angle. Digger two would slip past the companion asteroid, while three would come in from an approximate reverse of Roget's pass. Roget doubted that the pirates had the equipment or the power to maintain a full sky scan. Most didn't . . . but there were always exceptions to everything, and unexpected exceptions could cause casualties.

The asteroid swelled in the screen projections before Roget.

Power at fifteen. Target lock-on, confirmed the needle's targeting system.

Fire one. Retarget to target two.

Roget waited just an instant before the system confirmed its lock on a pile of rock that held a ghostly rectangular shape—most probably a concealed launch or recovery tube and lock.

Fire two.

The screens indicated torp one's impact on target—and the pirate energy emanations died away.

An energy flash alerted Roget, but even before he or his systems could react, a pirate torp was halfway toward the needle. Within instants, it had fragmented into a cone of smaller missiles. Roget increased power, but he could see that the edge of the missile cone would impact his shields.

At the last possible moment, he diverted all available power into the needle's shields.

Even so, the small ship shuddered as the hail of solid-iron missiles pummeled its shields. Iron at even moderate speed was hard on shields. The pirates had one great advantage—lots of iron—and one disadvantage—a lack of power with which to propel it at more than a single incoming craft at a time.

Digger two, three . . . be advised target launching mass driver torps with iron missile cone.

Stet, Digger lead.

The needleboat's tracking system had flagged the source of the launch—another tube hidden almost a klick from the now-incapacitated comm array—and he relayed it to Digger two and three. Before his system had a chance to determine the location of the scanner arrays that the pirates had to be using to target the Federation needle boats, Roget was beyond the curved section of the asteroid where he'd begun his attack.

The backside showed no energy sources, and no torps rose from the basaltic surface.

Roget shifted his course and eased the needle behind the companion asteroid before readying the third and fourth torps and moving into position behind the third needleboat.

Digger three, will tail-chase you.

Stet.

Roget hung back slightly as Digger three angled toward the pirate installation, instructing the targeting system to search for the energy burst of the mass driver that was flinging the crude torps at them.

Target located, the system noted.

Fire three.

Digger lead, two here. Shields amber.

Two, break off attack. Stand off this time.

Stet.

Good, thought Roget. There was no point for two to risk getting turned into scattered mass and energy. Not yet, anyway.

A flare of energy spurted from the asteroid's surface.

Digger three, note last impact. Mass driver shaft. Target that impact on next pass.

Stet, Digger lead.

Roget fired his fourth torp at the mass driver shaft, but he was far enough past the target area that the asteroid's bulk blocked his detectors. He'd have to wait for the next pass to see how much damage they'd been able to inflict.

He swung the needle into another powered turn, one that would bring him back over the area of the installations, but at almost ninety degrees to his last pass. No sense in being predictable. The pirates might have something else waiting.

Digger lead, impact on target. Impact on target.

Stet. Coming in for last pass this time.

Once he was clear of the bulge of the asteroid, Roget zeroed in on the target display. Digger three's torps, following his, had opened a small crater in the uneven surface. Roget could see a roughly circular tube at one end of the crater. One advantage of attacking a low-gravity installation was that the debris tended to get blown clear, rather than just piling up in the crater.

The moment he had lock-on, he fired a single torp.

The torp ran true, vanishing into the circular opening. Then a wide semicircle of the basaltic surface buckled. Dust spurted everywhere, as did stone fragments.

Roget cleared the area well before stone fragments flew outward across what had been his flight path.

Digger flight, stand clear of target area this time.

Three, standing clear.

Two, clear.

Roget slowed his needle and swung into a turn that would carry him back over the target area. He expected dust to be hanging over the area because the asteroid was so small that its gravity was minuscule. Instead, the scanners revealed scattered areas of dust and other clear areas where dust plumes were already klicks out from the surface. For a moment, he didn't understand why. Then he swallowed. The last torp had done enough damage that the integrity of much, if not most, of the subsurface installation had been breached, and the release of the internal atmosphere had created those lanes of clearer space, even if the distinction between clarity and dust was so slight that only the scanners could pick it up.

The surface was far more uneven than before, but that and three small craters were the only outward indications of the destruction created by the three needleboats.

Record and document, Roget ordered the system.

Recording.

Roget checked the scanners and all the instruments, but outside of fast-fading residual heat, there was no sign of life below, and certainly no energy emissions.

Digger flight, report status.

Digger lead, two here, shields amber, all other systems green. Four torps remaining.

Digger lead, three, all systems green, no torps.

That was to be expected, since Roget had pulled two off the attack when his shields had gone amber.

Once the system announced, *Documentation complete,* Roget called up the nav system, then eased the needle away from the pair of asteroids.

Digger three, take station on my quarter. Digger two, close up and trail our shields.

Two closing up this time.

Roget nodded. That positioning would at least minimize the strain on two's shields for the long return flight to Ceres station. There was always the chance of debris of various sorts, perhaps even debris that they had recently created, or debris that dated back billions of years. Either way, impacting it without shields, or with damaged shields, was not something good for a needleboat—or its pilot.

Recommended return course set. Please approve, requested the system.

Roget checked, then cross-checked it. *Digger flight, sending return course this time.*

Digger two, stet.

Digger three, stet.

Digger flight, turn to return course this time.

Stet. Both other pilots responded as one.

Commence return course, Roget ordered the system.

Only when the needleboat was on the return course did Roget lean back in the pilot's couch and remove his helmet.

Had some of those in the colony survived? Roget had no way of knowing, and no ability to verify whether there were survivors or not. Even if there were survivors, life would be grim and most likely short—even if they had another functioning fusactor shielded deep within the asteroid. Power was vital but not necessarily sufficient, especially on a basalt-nickel-iron rock without much in the way of ice.

Why had the pirate colonists attacked the slow-boat at Themis? If they hadn't, Roget doubted that Belt Control would have sent out a three-needleboat flight for a two-week-plus mission, not with the equipment and costs involved.

Yet, he reminded himself, how else could those on the asteroid have gotten equipment? No one would sell it to them. What other choice had they had, except to surrender and beg for mercy? Mercy, in a relocation camp after marooning and leaving the slow-boat crew to die?

Earth hadn't been big enough, in the end, for many conflicting cultures and views. Would the same prove true of the solar system? Or the galaxy? Or did the problem lie in the Federation's views? That didn't necessarily follow, either, since there had been rebels and outcasts long before the Federation, and even old America had been founded by rebels.

Was there an answer?

Roget looked to the controls, not really seeing the readouts before him.

33

Roget lay stretched out on his bunk, his eyes open, wearing the same coverall he'd worn on his descent to Dubiety, with its still mostly undischarged capacitors. While he'd been waiting for the inevitable, he'd thought about projecting Hildegarde into the narrow space between the bunk and the bulkhead flanking the hatch, but he'd decided against it. His internals were operating normally, if not even better than usual, aboard the *WuDing,* and he could easily sense all the snooping and scanning gear focused on him. If the colonel had a record of him viewing—or talking to—the image of a centuries-old painting of a dachshund, that would be grounds enough for immediate confinement in the brig as mentally unstable . . . and that would make what he had to do even more difficult.

His eyes flicked toward the stateroom hatch—little more than a composite door, as were most quarters' hatches, for all the imported nautical terminology and the remote electronic lock that had not yet been activated. He smiled, faintly, and went back to waiting.

Less than twenty minutes later, the annunciators blared.

"All hands to battle stations. All hands to battle stations."

All hands to battle stations.

Almost simultaneously, the stateroom door locked itself.

Roget had expected both. Certainly, Colonel Tian would wish him contained while the *WuDing* led the attack against Dubiety.

With his first moves, Roget slipped the heavy, flat bag that held the Dubietan emergency pressure suit out of his pack

and up inside his nightsuit coverall. Then he powered up the
concealment features of the nightsuit and pulled the hood
over his head. Moving to the stateroom door, he slipped two
tools from the flat container inside his waistband. In less than
a minute, he was out in the passageway, empty because it
was in officers' country. He closed and locked the door behind him, deliberately but swiftly, and stowed the small
tools.

Could he get to one of the airlocks aft of midships before
the *WuDing* provoked the Dubietans into action? That was
likely, since the *WuDing* and the Federation fleet didn't have
the advantage of the Dubietan technology.

Moving quickly, he headed aft toward the first ladder. At
the top of the ladder he flattened himself against the wall.
Two ship's marines rushed up the ladder and past him in the
direction of his former stateroom, proving the usefulness of
the camouflage suit against the pale blue of the bulkheads.

He swung down two levels of the ladder and headed out-
board, moving to one of the maintenance ways that he didn't
think was snooped as thoroughly as all the main passage-
ways were. He made it down almost to the outer ring, where
the maintenance way ended, before he sensed another pair
of marines. He eased open the maintenance hatch, just a
crack, but the marines were not yet in sight. So he swung
the hatch inward, then used the heavy hinges as an aid to
wiggle upward and to wedge himself into the narrow overhead, hoping he didn't have to wait too long. The camosuit
blended into the dark blue.

Roget waited, easing out one of the narrow picks from his
waistband.

In less than a handful of minutes, he heard voices.

"Sensors say he's here somewhere."

*To your right somewhere . . . hard to get readings down
there.*

"There's an open maintenance hatch."

Check behind it.

One of the marines stood before the hatch, looking down it, a heavy shocker in hand.

Roget flicked the pick as far back up the maintenance way as he could.

Clink.

"He's got to be up there by that niche." The first marine charged through the hatch and toward the sound.

The second stepped inside the hatch and halted.

That made it all too clear that the marines hadn't been in any kind of real combat or fight for all too long. Roget struck, coming down with his left boot squarely into the marine's eye and nose at an angle that slammed the hapless man into the solid bulkhead. The marine did not move, although Roget sensed rather than saw that, because he kept moving, swinging himself out through the hatch, then flattening himself against the main passageway bulkhead, on the side opposite the hatch hinges.

"Carteon!" The second marine whirled, then moved quickly back down the maintenance way. As he peered through the hatch, Roget moved, yanking him forward so that his boots caught on the hatch lip, then dropping him. In another quick movement, he had the marine's shocker. He used it on both marines, then grabbed the unused weapon from the first marine.

Holding the shocker in one hand, Roget sprinted to the next ladder aft and swung down. He stopped halfway down, moving slowly so that the camosuit would not blur. Less than ten meters away was the hatch that was the entrance to the midships maintenance bay. Also less than ten meters away stood two crewmen in combat space armor, but without helmets, guarding the hatch that led to the maintenance area and the lower midships locks. Both men held heavy-duty shockers.

Roget eased forward a step at a time, keeping the shocker on the side away from the guards and hoping the camosuit was blending the weapon into the blueness of the bulkheads.

He didn't have that much time, not before more marines with heat-imaging units reached him, but he needed to get closer to use the weapon.

"You see something?" murmured one guard. "Down there a ways?"

"All I see is blue and more blue."

In the moment that both crewmen were not looking directly at Roget, he took two steps and froze. He was almost close enough. Almost.

"Spray the—"

Roget darted forward and fired.

"—passageway!"

The second crewman got off a shot, and Roget's right arm erupted in flaming agony. His entire body shivered, almost uncontrollably. Both crewmen were down, but Roget could hear more marines thundering down the ladders.

He pressed the hatch-access stud. The big hatch began to open. The maintenance area beyond the hatch went dark, as did the passageway behind him where the fallen guards lay. Roget jumped through the hatch just before it closed in response to the power cutoff.

He staggered against the nearest bulkhead, and at the impact his arm flared into more agony. Going to nightsight didn't help Roget because he wasn't in low-light conditions, but in no light.

The colonel hadn't cut power to the area to blind Roget, but to disable any equipment he thought that Roget might try to use. The power loss also meant Roget would have to find the emergency personnel lock in the dark and operate it manually.

Roget smiled. If . . . if he could remember the location, the power cut might be to his advantage because without power there were no snoops . . . and the emergency locks were designed to be opened manually—especially for times when there was no ship's power.

He forced himself to concentrate, despite the lines of

nerve flame running up and down his right arm, then began to move toward the aft side of the maintenance bay. While it felt as though it took hours to find the emergency lock, it was less than a minute according to his internal systems.

Although the lock wheel turned easily, it took several minutes before he was able to rotate it enough times left-handed to open the inner-lock door. He swung the heavy door toward himself, wincing momentarily as the emergency-lock lighting struck his dark-adjusted eyes. Once he was inside the lock itself, he had to repeat the process to close the inner door. He couldn't vent the lock chamber without the inner door being closed, and without venting, there was no way he could swing the outer door into the chamber even after he'd rotated the wheel to the open position.

At that moment, power returned to the area, and that meant the marines would be after him in moments. As he'd recalled, there was a broomstick racked beside the outer door. There was also a soft emergency pressure suit with an equally soft helmet—a poopysuit. He checked the broomstick propellant, then winced. Less than 20 percent. Not much margin for error. He pulled on the poopysuit, except for the helmet. Poopysuits usually held less than an hour of oxygen, if that, but the indicator showed forty minutes, and that should suffice.

While he'd thought to vent the lock last, he changed his mind, donned the helmet and sealed, then twisted the lock vent open immediately. That way the marines wouldn't be able to open the inner-lock door. Then he went to work turning the outer-lock wheel—again left-handed and even more clumsily in the heavy suit gauntlets.

Once he had the lock open, he grabbed the broomstick in his left hand and eased out into vacuum, forcing his almost-numb right hand to hold to the recessed grab-bar outside the lock.

With the disorientation of weightlessness, several moments passed before he finally located the tether—aft of the largest maintenance lock. His dropboat was still linked to the tether, and fortunately, not all that far from the rear of the large maintenance lock.

Abruptly, the tether separated from the dropboat, and a quick blast of gas from the tether pushed the dropboat outward. The colonel definitely didn't want Roget getting to the dropboat.

Roget straddled the broomstick and aimed it and himself at the dropboat's lock, giving both gas jets a solid jolt and hoping that his aim was good. If he missed, he was as good as dead . . . and not immediately. He hadn't planned to be in vacuum for more than a few minutes in the poopysuit. The emergency suits didn't have much insulation, and if he missed the boat, whether he'd asphyxiate or freeze first would be the only question left to ponder, and probably not for that long, because he couldn't reach the distress alarm in the Dubietan emergency suit without breathing vacuum.

He pulsed the broomstick's left gas jet just momentarily, correcting his course more to the right. After a moment, he could see that he was closing on the empty dropboat. He forced himself not to use the jets more. If he came in too hard, the absorber wouldn't handle the jolt, and the mag-grip wouldn't hold.

Another minute passed, and he was within ten meters of the dropboat. He glanced to his left. So far, he and the dropboat had only slid back fifty meters along the *WuDing*'s hull, and separated less than twenty. That was good because that left him too close to the battlecruiser for the colonel to deploy weapons against him or the dropboat.

The mag-grip on the end of the broomstick hit one of the patches repaired by the Dubietans. While the recoil absorber took up most of the shock, the mag-grip began to slide sideways.

"Shit!" muttered Roget. Just his luck they'd used a non-metallic composite.

The mag-grip skidded along the dropboat's hull, but finally

grabbed onto the metallic composite above and aft of the lock. Roget inched his way up the broomstick until he managed to grab the recessed handle next to the lock access panel. Holding on with his injured hand was painful, but he needed the other hand to manipulate the lock controls, while keeping his legs wrapped around the broomstick.

Once he had the outer lock open, he shifted grips, then eased himself and the broomstick partly inside. Eventually he managed to get everything into the lock and close it behind him. His entire body was shaking.

When the lock was pressured, he stripped off the poopy-suit, awkwardly opened the inner lock hatch, and tossed the emergency suit into the tiny bunk cubicle behind the control couch, before scrambling into position enough to power up the controls. Then he pulled the Dubietan emergency suit from under his coverall and out of its film wrapper. There were instructions—very brief and clear. He followed them in donning the suit up to the point of activation. That had to wait.

Next he strapped himself into the couch and checked the systems.

Power levels were as he'd left them—roughly 40 percent. That *might* get him close to Dubiety, but he wasn't about to try it yet. He'd ride along with the course vector and velocity already imparted by the *WuDing*. He was gambling on the fact that, so long as he did nothing detectable, the colonel would not be able to persuade the *WuDing*'s commander to use the drives for more separation in order to turn weapons on the dropboat.

Three minutes passed, then four. Suddenly the *WuDing*'s shields contracted, leaving the dropboat outside them, then expanded, pushing the dropboat away from the battlecruiser and effectively adding a ninety-degree vector to the battlecruiser's—and the small craft's—previous course. Roget swallowed but still did not activate the drives, just letting the dropboat angle away from the *WuDing* on a course that was inclined downward and at about 280 degrees relative to the battlecruiser's course toward Dubiety.

The slight downward velocity would soon carry the dropboat below the Federation formation. Despite the chill in the dropboat, so much so that his breath was steam, Roget was sweating. The hardest part of any operation, especially this one, was sitting tight and waiting.

He scanned the EDI. The Federation fleet was moving at a steady but almost stately pace toward Dubiety, one designed to save power for the weapons that whatever marshal was commanding would soon be unleashing against Dubiety.

Soon? He ran a quick calculation and came up with almost a standard hour before the fleet would be in position to bring everything to bear. Where would he and drop three be in an hour?

He ran another set of calculations. The results were as he feared. If he did nothing, he'd be too far below Dubiety. He reset the parameters and tried again.

If . . . if he could get away with a thirty-second max angled drive blast in the next few minutes, he'd stay within what he *thought* would be the Dubietan operational envelope, but still far enough from the fleet by the time he was in range of the Dubietan technology to avoid being an easy target for any of the Federation ships. Being in that Dubietan envelope would make him vulnerable to whatever the Thomists might do, but he hoped what he planned would resolve that difficulty.

Thoughts, guesses, and hopes. That's all you've got left. He pushed that thought away. He'd have had less than that if he'd remained aboard the *WuDing. No doubt about that at all. None.*

Once again he waited, letting the seconds tick away until the last possible moment before triggering the corrective drive blasts. His eyes flicked to the EDI, wondering if any of the Federation ships would waste a torp on him.

No one fired.

He'd hoped for that, basing his judgment on three things. First, he wasn't on a direct course to Dubiety. Second, the colonel might well believe that if the Federation succeeded, they could let him drift forever or capture him at leisure. And third, the dropboat had no weapons of any sort and posed little direct threat to any Federation ship.

When the dropboat's drive cut out, Roget checked his course and the EDI again. No torps, and he was headed into the edge of the envelope he'd calculated. Once more, all he could do was wait.

As the minutes ticked away, he kept checking the readouts, but nothing changed except that the fleet—and dropboat three—edged closer and closer to the silver grayish sphere that was Dubiety.

After twenty minutes, the EDI signaled a disturbance, but not from Dubiety. Rather the instruments were suggesting a large energy source coming from outsystem. More Federation ships? Was that the reason for the stately progress of the Federation fleet? Waiting for reinforcements to join up? All that for a single planet?

Because the dropboat's EDI was anything but specific for that distance, Roget kept studying his instruments and worrying. It was almost ten minutes later before his EDI— far less accurate than detectors in the capital ships—gathered enough information. Roget just looked at what appeared on the screen before him. What his instruments registered was not possible.

A single vessel sped insystem, and that ship had to embody more than a hundred times the mass and energy of the largest battlecruiser ever built by the Federation. Roget's eyes flicked from the outsystem screen to the insystem screen, but he saw no change in the speed or course of the Federation vessels.

At that moment, Roget remembered the painting in the museum in Skeptos—an oil painting depicting a ship the size of an asteroid. Was that what his EDI was picking up? Was it real? Or some sort of electronic illusion? But how could the Thomists counterfeit the impression of all that energy?

From the lack of response from the Federation ships, clearly the marshal in command of the attack force believed the vessel showing on the EDI screens was an illusion or a decoy. Roget's guts tightened, telling him they didn't believe it was an illusion of any sort.

He still wasn't within the Dubietan operating sphere. His lips twisted. For all he knew, he might be, but he was assuming that sphere only extended as far as they had been able to launch the dropship. Besides, even the rearmost of the Federation ships was far enough from the dropship that a torp launched at Roget had no certainty of hitting—or inflicting damage.

Roget kept waiting, his attention split between the two screens, watching as the massive Thomist vessel neared. Then he swallowed again because energy flared against what had to be the shields of the Thomist ship. The EDI energy levels indicated that whatever had been in the way of the Thomist dreadnought had not been something insignificant, perhaps even a small asteroid. Whatever it had been, it was gone as if it had never been, with no apparent effect on the monster craft.

The Thomist vessel was still well away from Roget and his dropboat when the EDI registered something like an energy cocoon encircling the largest of the trailing Federation warships. The *ZengYi,* Roget thought, a large attack corvette, the one that had met him. One moment, the energy cocoon and the *ZengYi* were there. The next, they were not.

Roget winced. The crew of the corvette hadn't deserved that. They'd just been following orders, and they hadn't even fired a weapon.

But they would have. Roget knew that, but he still wished it hadn't been the *ZengYi.*

The Federation fleet still did nothing. Not that the marshal could have, because the monster Thomist ship was well out of torp range.

Then something flared from the *WuDing* toward the silver haze of Dubiety—a planet-scouring missile with a modified light-drive. Moments after launch, the missile vanished.

Roget activated the dropboat's drive, pouring full power into propulsion and adjusting his course. He couldn't wait any longer. He had to get as close to Dubiety as possible. The marshal and the Federation vessels weren't about to worry about him and his tiny dropboat. Not with what they faced.

His attention went back to the two EDI screens.

Another energy cocoon formed around a cruiser—the *DeGaulle*. This time the ship's commander applied full power. Roget could tell that from the rapid rise in energy intensity. But nothing happened. The ship did not accelerate, and the energy cocoon only brightened—until both the *DeGaulle* and the cocoon vanished from the EDI.

Two more of the energy cocoons followed, enveloping two corvettes and disappearing them as well.

Roget glanced at the upper corner of the EDI. An energy glow had begun to surround Dubiety itself. Things like that weren't supposed to happen, but, unlike the colonel, Roget wasn't about to argue with what appeared to be reality. As he watched another cocoon of energy encircle another Federation ship, this time most likely the *Shihuangdi,* Roget unstrapped himself from the pilot's couch and scrambled the scant few meters aft to the airlock, where he opened the inner hatch and hurried into the chamber.

Did he want to do what he felt was his only chance?

No. But watching the Federation fleet vanish, ship by ship, was like . . . *Like the last twist of the knife?*

Absently, as he closed the inner airlock door and then pulled the hood of the Dubietan emergency pressure suit over his head and sealed it, he wondered from where that thought had come. He pushed that question away and vented the lock chamber, then let the automatics open the outer lock.

As the hatch opened, he grasped the broomstick and then kicked himself and it out into the vacuum. Nothing seemed to move, not the points of light that were planets, nor the small disk that was Dubiety. He glanced down at the ship, then up and beyond. His eyes picked out a small greenish white disk—the Thomist ship.

He slowly straddled the broomstick and pointed it at Dubiety, not that it would carry him any fraction of the distance toward the hazy planet, and flicked on the gas jets. With what the Thomists were doing to the Federation fleet, the farther he got from the dropboat, the better.

Only after eleven minutes, when the jets gave out, did he press the large distress stud on the front of the emergency pressure suit.

As a certain chill began to creep over him, another set of words whispered through his thoughts.

. . . consign him to the darkness that lies beyond all darkness, to the blackness so deep that it has no shade, for out of the void came he, and into it will the return be . . .

34

29 LAYU 6746 F. E.

The inbound trip back toward Ceres station had been long and boring, but that was the way space travel was. All interplanetary or insystem travel seemed longer because suspension cradles weren't often used and because more than a few FIS missions were single-pilot.

Roget checked the distance again. Another two hours remained until Digger flight reached the accelerator's grav net and they could begin the exterior-assisted decel. Without the magnetograv decel, they would have had to spend another two to three days for decel on the return leg, and he'd been cooped up in the needle far too long as it was. Like the accelerator, the decel net was harder on the needles. It also required a mass base, such as a moon or a large asteroid, and the environmental purists claimed that the continued use of the system had significantly changed Ceres's orbit. Roget had no idea whether the claims were true, but he didn't see that it would matter much one way or another. Ceres was big enough that the changes wouldn't go unnoticed and far enough away from anything but other asteroids that it shouldn't make that much difference.

As he sat and waited out the last hour or so of the mission, Roget couldn't help but think about the pirate colonists. Had they wanted to stay outside the Federation so much that they were willing to risk everything? How could anyone take such risks?

He almost laughed. The squirrel run had been almost as much of a risk. A little larger pirate torp or a slight variation in course, and Castaneda might not now be with them. The same could have been true of himself, he acknowledged. Any mission against comparable weapons was dangerous, and even missions against militarily inferior opponents carried risk.

Was the Federation that unbearable? There was no point in thinking about that, not when he didn't have any real alternatives.

Before him, the board shimmered, then somehow changed. In front of him, where the farscreens and displays had been, was a wraparound canopy, and on the lower section were projected displays. Roget/Tanner blinked, but the clear, wraparound canopy did not change. The clarity didn't help much, not in the darkness outside the aircraft.

His eyes kept a continual scan across the heads-up display and on the destination, the ultratanker *Deep Resource,* bound for Long Beach. While the tanker held something like six million barrels, even with all the green fuel sources that the United States had developed, that still amounted to just one day's oil imports—and that was with thirty dollar a gallon gasoline and power rationing.

A short burst of static was followed by a transmission. "Blackbolt lead, do not engage unless attacked. I say again. Do not engage unless attacked."

"Bolt Control," Roget/Tanner replied, "understand negative on engagement unless attacked."

There was no response, and Roget did not key another transmission. His eyes were on the RRD display, which showed two ships—high-speed SEVs from their speed— closing from the west on the big tanker. If Ops hadn't wanted him to keep the SEVs from diverting or sinking the tanker, why was he leading a flight out some four hundred miles east of Luzon in the middle of the night?

Because they want you to stop the interception with plausible deniability. Roget understood that all too well. He also understood that, at the moment, the good old USA needed every tanker it could get, at least until the Colorado shale projects were fully up and running.

He checked the RRD again.

Roget/Tanner had "official" orders not to attack the Chinese SEVs, but that didn't mean he couldn't warn them off in a way that would allow the tanker to continue onward toward its destination. Behind the night-visor, he moistened his lips. Then he linked to the fire-control computer.

After a moment, he nodded. It just might work.

"Bolt two, Bolt three, Bolt lead going down for flyby and recon. Hold position." He eased the stick forward and the AF-76 Raven screamed downward through the thin cloud layer. He leveled off at two thousand, headed directly toward the nearer SEV.

He switched to the CF, the common ship frequency. "Unidentified vessels, you are nearing hazardous waters. Approaching the *Deep Resource* may endanger your ship. I say again. You are nearing hazardous waters. Approaching the *Deep Resource* may endanger your ship."

"Unidentified aircraft, you are within Federation airspace. Bear off."

Roget snorted. The ChinoFeds claimed almost all the airspace in Westpac beyond Midway and Johnston Atoll, even if they didn't usually aggressively patrol more than three hundred miles eastward from their various "protectorates." Australia had fallen, as much a victim to global warming and drought as to the ChinoFeds, and so far Japan had held out, alone, but with a century of falling birthrates and economic difficulties, how much longer the Japanese could remain independent was yet another question.

"Blackbolt lead, two scrammers inbound. ETA in five."

That was all Roget needed—hostiles with greater speed.

"Bolt two and Bolt three, hostiles inbound. Stand by to take all measures for self-defense." What that really meant was to use the advanced standard hand missiles against the scrammers at the slightest provocation.

Roget adjusted the target setting. *Just a patch of water*, he told himself. *Just a patch of water.*

Target destination has no identified target. Confirm launch, requested Roget's targeting system.

Roget flicked his thumb over the glowing green stud on the stick and pressed down firmly.

As soon as the first missile was away, Roget turned the Raven slightly south, not that he needed it, and checked the second SEV.

Target destination has no identified target. Confirm launch, repeated the targeting system.

Roget pressed the green light a second time. Confirmation wasn't needed when the system had a target lock-on, but

Roget couldn't do that. Not in this situation. The software and satellite systems would confirm that he had not fired at either SEV. Not that the ChinoFeds or the cowards in Washington would be happy, but Roget had just followed orders to warn off the Chinese vessels.

He watched the RRD as the first missile plowed into the water just in front of the high-speed surface effect ship, leaving a temporary crater in the water, just enough to allow the heavily armed vessel to plunge forward, losing its air cushion and steerage, not to mention its engines, as it nosed into the water and waves surged over the bow, all the way up to the bridge.

Roget grinned momentarily, waiting for the second missile impact.

The effect was the same for the second SES.

Bolt lead, Bolt two. Scrammers in range.

Bolt two, Bolt three. Defense permitted this time. I say again. Defense permitted this time.

He watched the RRD as four standard hand missiles flew from the other two Ravens toward the incoming scrammers. Neither CF aircraft clearly expected the navy pilots to launch first, because in moments debris was sifting downward.

Roget eased the stick back, edging power up, and the Raven rose through the cloud layer.

Bolt flight, form on me.

Roger.

Roger, Bolt lead.

Both SEVs were dead in the water, disabled if not sinking, and the skies were clear except for the three navy birds headed back to the all-too-old and tired *Reagan*. And the *Deep Resource* was on course for Long Beach and a fuel-starved United States of America.

Blackbolt lead, interrogative status? The transmission was faint, but clear.

Like everything that the navy has, thought Roget. *Two*

*unknown vessels apparently suffering mechanical damage.
Resource vessel on course. No other aircraft in sight.* Let
Ops sort that one out.

Understand no other aircraft in sight.

That's affirmative this time.

Report approach.

Bolt Control, will report approach.

Roget/Tanner checked the RRD, but the skies remained
clear—for the moment and the mission.

Once more darkness swirled and one kind of blackness
replaced another, and the night-visor vanished, replaced by
the screens before Roget.

Roget shook his head. While he'd had short memory flashbacks during his training, they had been brief, almost momentary. This one had seemed far longer. Why? Because
Tanner had been an atmospheric combat pilot?

In what little information he'd discovered about Tanner,
there had been nothing about his attacking Federation
aircraft . . . and Roget certainly hadn't read anything about
the Federation's efforts to sink or divert oil tankers to energy starve the old American republic. All the histories just
mentioned that excessive reliance on offshore energy
sources had been a factor in the fall of old America.

Again, he reminded himself, he'd just have to cope. Telling anyone would cost him everything.

. . . interrogative status . . . The partial and garbled
transmission brought Roget up short. He and the other two
needleboats had to have been crossing some sort of systemic
energy flux or dead zone.

*BeltCon, Digger lead, returning this time. Estimate one
five to approach perimeter.*

*Digger lead, understand one five to approach. Interrog-
ative comm status.*

*BeltCon, comm is green. Transit of dead area. Comm is
green.*

Digger lead, report approach.

He could report his flight's approach. That he could do, even as he pondered how the ancient Americans had handled the unauthorized destruction of two aircraft and the disabling, if not the sinking, of two Chinese Federation warships.

Not for the first time, he also wondered again just how Marni Sorensen had managed to select the "memories" of an ancient hero that would resonate with him. Or had she injected him with snippets of memory from Tanner that his own mind had interpreted and expanded? How much really was Tanner and how much came from him? And did those memories make him part Tanner? Would he ever know?

35

27 MARIS 1811 P. D.

Darkness and cold swirled around Roget, and sounds he could not hear clashed and merged into a symphony he had not composed, a life he had not led, a path he had not followed . . . and yet had. From the darkness, he emerged into an even more immediate coldness.

Where Roget stood was chill, mainly because a torrent of cold air poured down on him from somewhere, cooling the sweat in his short silver white hair. He blinked as the lights around him intensified. All around him people were talking, generally in low and intense tones, and he found himself nodding to something he had not heard.

A slender young man in a navy blue blazer and a white shirt dashed up and stopped short of Roget. "Sir . . . St. George is coming in . . . coming in big. That should do it."

Do what? Roget did not even try to verbalize the question, belatedly realizing he was remembering yet another bit of Tanner's past.

"Joe! You can talk to them all now. It's about time . . ." came another voice from behind Roget/Tanner.

"Past time . . . they've been waiting hours," said someone else.

". . . didn't go off and leave people, like some . . . waiting here with everyone else . . . why he'll win . . ."

". . . indeed, now, there will be time to wonder if I dare . . ." Roget's words were to a tall and slender brunette woman, standing beside him. "After all this, Cari . . ."

She smiled sympathetically and warmly and said, "Go ahead. This is what you wanted, Joe . . . it's your moment."

"It's yours, too. I wouldn't be here without you," he replied. "April isn't the cruelest month. November is."

"You'd be here, dear, even if I weren't. Nothing could have stopped you."

"It wouldn't have meant much without you."

"You'd have found someone. You're too good to be alone."

He started to reply, but behind him a chant rose, swelling like thunder, or the cymbals of an unseen orchestra.

"Go! Go! Go! . . . Go . . . for . . . Joe! Go! Go! Go! We want Joe!"

Roget/Tanner glanced over his shoulder toward the crowd.

"You'd better talk to them before they shout down the roof," suggested Cari.

"No, Mrs. Tanner . . . he needs someone to do a proper intro." Mike Penndrake stepped up to the couple. "He just can't walk out there. They expect someone to tell them how special he is and how special they are."

Penndrake's sweaty square face looked more greasy than exercised, Tanner thought, but he nodded. "Make it short, Mike."

"As short as I can." Penndrake offered a wide smile, the kind that was all too common among political operatives,

Tanner/Roget had come to learn. Then he turned and stepped up to the podium and the small microphone, which he picked up. He tapped it several times, and the crowd's murmurs and the chanting died away.

"Welcome to Tanner election headquarters, such as it is."

Laughs rippled across the crowd.

"In just a moment, you'll all be hearing from the man you all supported, the man you came to see. I'd just like to remind you, not that you need any reminding, that from the day he was born, all through school, this man has lived an exemplary life. At a time when patriotism was often equated with stupidity and treason, he put his life and his career on the line. He stood off an entire ChinoFed force to assure fuel supplies for America. He was wounded three times in the Westpac War, and each time, he came back and flew again. If we'd had more men like Joe Tanner, all the Pacific would still be an American ocean, and Japan would be our ally and not a ChinoFed fiefdom." Penndrake paused, just for an instant. "Now . . . for the good news. We just got the results from St. George . . . and Joe Tanner is the new senator from the great state of Utah! I give you Joe Tanner, a genuine war hero who knows the cost of war and the price of peace . . . a man for the times ahead."

With a broad smile Penndrake stepped back and gestured toward Tanner/Roget.

The gymnasium erupted once more in cheers and whistles.

Roget/Tanner turned from Cari and stepped forward to stand behind the battered wooden podium. He smiled and looked back to his left where Cari stood, her face thinner than it had once been, but still holding the quiet supporting enthusiasm that she'd always offered.

As Tanner waited for the cheering to die down, smiling warmly, he surveyed those in the crowd, many of them older and graying, others looking scarcely old enough to be adults, trying to let everyone know that they were welcome. His eyes dropped slightly to the group standing on the floor just below the stage and podium. The stylish redhead stood there, looking up at him, her deep green eyes bright.

Susannah appeared far younger than when Roget/Tanner had last encountered her . . . or remembered her.

Tanner smiled directly at her, then raised his head and cleared his throat. "I can't tell you how much everything that all of you have done means to me. A year ago, no one gave us a thought, and without all of you, every last one of you, we wouldn't have had a chance. I don't want to kid any of you, nor mislead you. This is a great victory, but it's only the first battle in a long fight to reclaim our heritage. For too long, those in power in Washington have strangled our industry and technology with meaningless regulations that neither improved our economy nor our environment. They squandered billions on weapons technology that did not work and refused to fund what did. They exported jobs while watering down education so that all too many of our children struggled to compete in a global economy. They bailed out multinational financial corporations while bankrupting average citizens . . ." Tanner/Roget held up a hand for silence. "I've said all this before, and you listened, and you acted, and you all gathered behind us . . . and that's what this great country of ours needs more than ever—the will and effort of determined people like you who make real and meaningful change possible. Thank you! Thank you, each and every one of you . . ."

Tanner/Roget lowered his head for a moment, then raised his eyes and looked out at the crowd cheering in the antique gymnasium . . .

Streamers fluttered from the high ceiling, and lights strobed and flashed . . . and the sounds all died away into a deep silence.

A different kind of chill encased Roget, one that did not let him move hands or feet, or even his eyes.

"You'll be all right."

Roget heard the words, and the voice was familiar, but he couldn't identify the speaker before another kind of blackness, warmer, more comforting, swept over him.

36

29 MARIS 1811 P. D.

Roget opened his eyes, wondering if he could even move. He was lying flat on his back. He blinked. That was good. Then his eyes took in the overhead, a pale green. He started to take a deep breath, then stopped. His chest and lungs hurt. So did his legs, and his head ached and throbbed. He closed his eyes. That didn't help with the headache. So he opened them and studied the ceiling again. At least it wasn't blue. At least he wasn't in a Federation sickbay or brig.

Slowly, he turned his head.

He lay on a bed in a small room. Beside the bed he could see a bedside table and a chair. The room had no windows, and the door was the translucent green type he'd seen only on Dubiety. An acrid smell hovered around him. It took him a moment to realize that he—his sweat—was the source of the odor.

Since he doubted that the scene he beheld was any form of an afterlife, someone had rescued him, and his rescuers were presumably the Dubietans. He could only hope that he didn't end up in some place like Manor Farms, although that would be better than what had awaited him with the Federation. About that he had absolutely no doubts, not with the way the colonel had treated him at the end.

But why did everything hurt?

The door split, and the two translucent green sides slid back. Selyni Hillis stepped through it. Roget struggled into a sitting position in the bed, trying not to wince as he did, and trying to ignore the intensification of the headache. He closed his eyes again. That didn't help any more than it had the first time, and he forced himself to look at the director.

Hillis dropped into the chair. "Pardon me, but it's been a very long several days."

Roget managed the slightest nod. More than that and he had the feeling his head would fall off. He knew it wouldn't, but it felt that way.

"Where am I?" he asked, his voice raspy.

"In the med-center of the translation complex."

"Translation complex?" blurted Roget.

"What you thought was a launch complex, where we sent you and the other dropboat back to the *WuDing*."

"Oh . . . thank you for rescuing me."

"You're welcome." She offered a wry smile. "It took a while to get to you, and the recovery was rough on you. We will extract some payment for that."

Roget waited. He didn't want to ask. But Hillis didn't volunteer more. He finally asked, "What did you have in mind? For repayment?"

"Nothing physically that onerous. We'd just like your detailed memoirs and observations about the Federation. You can write or record them over several years, but it would be best to start while your memories are fresh."

"And?"

"That's just for the rescue. You'll still have to find an occupation. We'll talk about that later."

"What happened?"

"You must have seen, didn't you? The dropboat was functioning enough to split from the *WuDing*. I'm surprised that they let you depart."

"They didn't have that in mind," Roget admitted. "It took a little effort, and some luck."

"That part of your memoirs will be very popular, I'm certain."

"You'd . . . make them public?"

"That's the general idea. Anything the government says, even on Dubiety, especially on Dubiety, is regarded with a certain skepticism. You might even get a bit of continuing income from them."

"You didn't tell me what happened," Roget reminded her.

"What did you observe?" she countered.

"The Federation ships vanished. The huge dreadnought—it was your ship, wasn't it?—it destroyed them one by one."

Hillis shook her head. "We didn't destroy any of them."

"Then what did you do? I saw them vanish. It was your ship, wasn't it?" Roget asked again.

"One of ours."

"It wrapped energy around the Federation ships, and they disappeared."

"They did. We didn't destroy them. We translated them to the far side of the Galaxy. They might end up close to each other. They might not. Some might end up in a solar corona somewhere, or in the gravitational hold of a gas giant, although the odds are very much against that. We don't have that fine a control over those kind of distances. They'll just have to do what they can wherever they end up. Some of them might survive to build colonies . . . if they decide to create instead of trying to dominate."

Hillis could have been lying to him, but Roget didn't think so. There was a factual weariness behind her words.

"Won't the Federation just send another fleet?"

"They could. It wouldn't be very bright. This is the third one in two centuries. You should have gathered that from what we told you."

"But . . . why do they keep doing it?"

"Conditioned reflex. They've absorbed everything—they think—by waiting and patiently trying again. It will be another century, assuming the Federation lasts that long, before they can amass enough resources to replace the ships they lost."

Roget understood that. The Federation Mandarins couldn't afford to let it be known that a mere Thomist colony had wiped out an entire fleet in moments without suffering any losses. That would have undermined the Federation far too much because its order was supported by the illusion of absolute knowledge, power, and control.

"You don't think the Federation will last that long?"

Hillis shrugged. "It's hard to say. They lost a tremendous resource investment when they lost those thirty-three ships, and that's a significant drain that will fall mostly on earth. Sooner or later, some seemingly smaller event like that will trigger its fall." She paused, then added, "On the other hand, we did them a favor because they generally place potential troublemakers in the exploratory fleets, carefully spread around, or in fleets like the one that tried to attack. Some of the junior officers are those who think too deeply. That's how dynasties and empires survive, by keeping the able, the discontented, and the ambitious at a distance. The problem on old earth has always been that those on the frontiers turned back on the center."

Roget thought about his own earlier "squirrel run." "They don't allow rebels and troublemakers on earth or anywhere in the solar system."

"The Federation will take longer to fall, and it will fall farther," predicted Hillis. "Civilization as such might not even survive."

"But you send your own troublemakers out."

"We don't try to destroy them. We give them ships and resources. It solves their problems, and it solves ours. It's also a very good way of ensuring the survival of the human race, although there are some philosophers who question the eth-

icality of such survival, and of foisting off such aggressive-
ness on the rest of the galaxy."

"Has anyone found other intelligence?"

"We've found ruins and data, nothing more. It's a very big
galaxy, and civilizations don't last all that long in the galactic perspective."

"That dreadnought . . . did that come . . . ?"

"Some of the ideas behind it, but the Ryleni never left their
home system." Hillis paused, then said, "Now . . . I have a
question for you. Why did you cast yourself into space?
Couldn't you see that we were removing the Federation ships
one at a time? You didn't need to do that." A smile hovered
in Director Selyni Hillis's eyes, but not on her lips.

Roget had asked himself that before he had stepped out
of the dropboat's airlock. "Because I had faith that you could
pick me up, and because I wanted you to know that I was
choosing to leave the Federation behind. I wasn't certain that
you'd know that without some sort of . . . grand gesture. I
didn't know how else to make that clear, and I thought you
were destroying the Federation ships. Call it a statement of
intent, backed by skepticism and worry."

"Skepticism and worry . . ." A soft laugh followed the
words. "You're a Thomist at heart, I think." She shook her
head. "You did make your intent clear. So clear that you also
caused some difficulty and consternation." She paused for a
moment. "That was quite literally a leap of faith."

"I'm not that kind of Believer."

"We knew that. Still . . . there is a time for proof and a
time for belief—not in the supernatural, but in what one
knows exists, even if he cannot fully explain it." Hillis
smiled. "Faith in accomplishments and faith in others is far
more solid than faith in gods who have never passed the test
of proof of their existence."

"How could one ever really know?" Roget asked dryly,
stifling a cough he knew would hurt.

"One cannot ever definitively prove that a god or a being

does not exist. That is not possible, but time has proven that, if such a being exists, he or she or it does not interfere in our lives for either good or evil. That should be sufficient for any thinking being."

"For some it is not."

"I said 'any thinking being.'"

Roget smiled wryly at the correction before asking, "Where's Lyvia?"

"In Skeptos."

"Did she really dislike me that much?" He felt so tired, and all he'd done was to ask a few questions.

"No."

"She just didn't like me that much. Is that it?"

"Let us just say that you impressed her enough that she did her duty."

Roget nodded, holding back and swallowing a yawn. He had questions, so many questions, and he asked the next one that came to mind. "Some of that data in the information package . . . it might have gotten back to the Federation. Doesn't that worry you?"

"We hoped it would. That was one of the reasons for sending it back to the *WuDing* with you."

"Was the information false?"

"Oh, no. It was all absolutely accurate and technically correct."

"You wanted the Federation to have it? Why?"

"Think about it." Hillis smiled. "If you can't figure it out by the time you leave Skeptos, I'll tell you. But I don't think I'll need to."

Leave Skeptos? "I don't want to end up in something like the Manor Farm Cottages or whatever else . . ."

Hillis shook her head. "You're too well adjusted for that. If you want to, we can train you for a position as a balance coordinator. You have all the necessary background knowledge. Before all that long, there will be a vacancy in Andoya.

That's in Thula, and it's a pleasant place. It's a bit cooler there than Skeptos, but I imagine you'd prefer it that way."

Roget wasn't about to commit, not without knowing more. He stifled another yawn. "What's a balance coordinator?"

"The coordinators work to balance the environmental, energy, radiation, and other impacts in a region. By now, you should know how important that is for us."

"Because the shields insulate both ways?"

"Exactly." Director Hillis rose from the chair. "You need some more sleep. You're barely able to stay awake. It's not that often that someone recovers from near anoxia and close to terminal frostbite."

Had he been that close to death?

"Not quite," replied Hillis, clearly reading his face, "but it will make a great story when enough time has passed. We'll talk about what training you'll need when you feel better, assuming you're agreeable."

Roget eased himself back down onto the bed, then turned toward Hillis, who had almost reached the door.

"Hildegarde . . . my flash . . . the image?"

"The extreme cold destroyed the storage in your belt flash monitor. But we saved all the images you called up at the guesthouse in Skeptos, and they're waiting for you." Another smile crossed her face. "You won't need her for all that long, except as a reminder. Now . . . get some sleep."

They did have the image of Hildegarde. They did.

He closed his eyes.

EPILOGUE

Roget couldn't help but smile as he strode toward the nature walk on the west end of the hill beyond the conapt complex where he'd settled temporarily. He was learning the business of being a balance coordinator from the woman who had held the position for nearly two decades, a very hands-on proposition, and he found that he was enjoying it. He also enjoyed Andoya.

The worst of the frosts had lifted, as Lyvia had predicted months earlier, and the cool, but not-too-cool, spring in the highlands of Thula was definitely to his liking.

As he passed through the two stone pillars marking the beginning of the walk, he heard a sound he hadn't in years— a certain deep bark. Just one bark.

At that sound, Roget turned. He couldn't help but smile as he saw the black and tan dachshund leading her owner toward the pillars that marked the start of the nature walk circling through the low hills. Standing there, he waited until the dachshund and her owner neared before speaking.

"She's beautiful." Roget thought he'd spoken correctly. He squatted to get a better look at the dachshund, then extended his hand, letting the dog sniff it. After a moment, he stroked her head gently. "You are special, aren't you?"

The dachshund wagged her tail, and the woman laughed.

Roget stroked the dachshund once more before straightening. The dog's owner was, he realized, most attractive with mahogany red hair cut longer than most Dubietan women. It even brushed the collar of her pale green blouse. She wore a darker green scarf as well, both shades of green set off by her piercing green eyes. Yet she was older, perhaps even close to his own age.

"I'm sorry," he apologized. "It's just . . ."

"Do you have a dachsie?"

Roget shook his head. "Not now. I have . . ." He shook his head again. "It would be hard to explain."

"You're that Federation agent, aren't you? Or you were." Her voice was amused.

"I'm afraid I was. I didn't mean to bother you. It's just that . . ."

"Freya likes you. She's more careful with most strangers. She only barked once."

"Oh . . . I should introduce myself, other than as a former Federation agent. I'm Keir Roget. I'm training as a balance coordinator here." He wondered if her name might be Susannah, but that would have been too much of a coincidence.

"Emmelyn Shannon." Her eyes met his.

Roget wondered what she saw.

"Emmelyn . . . I like that." Abruptly, he laughed, embarrassed. "I'm sorry. It's not my place to approve or disapprove. I'm so sorry."

Her laugh was soft, amused but not cutting.

"Might I walk with you and Freya?"

"With Freya and me, I think. You didn't even look at me. You saw her first."

Roget laughed again, in relief. "I did. She reminds me of another dachshund who meant a great deal to me. She still does. Her name was Hildegarde."

"A very proper name for a dachshund."

"So is Freya." Roget glanced down.

Freya looked up expectantly, with almost the same

expression that the ancient artist had captured in the portrait of Hildegarde.

"She does like you." Emmelyn laughed softly again, a sound somehow familiar.

"I hope so." Roget squatted and stroked Freya's head and neck again, enjoying the feel of her smooth coat under his fingers. Finally, he stood.

He smiled at Emmelyn. "You don't mind, do you?"

"I'd only have minded if you'd ignored her." She flicked the lead gently, and Freya set out down the bark-mulched path, confident that the two would follow.

As he walked beside Emmelyn, Roget glanced sideways. Emmelyn had to be special. With a dachshund like Freya, how could it be otherwise?

THE
HAMMER _of_
DARKNESS

To my parents,
for the gift of words and the love of reading

part one

THE PLANET *of*
ETERNAL LIGHT

i

▼

In toward Galactic Center, the myth implies, there is a star so hot it is a mere dot in the sky of that planet where the God of Darkness and the Lady of Light live. Just as this sun has only one planet, so is there only one God, the God of Darkness.

In fact, stars that hot, FO or hotter, don't have planets. And if they did, the star wouldn't last long enough to allow planetary development of a terrestrial environment.

Even if such a god existed and if he could build a planet from scratch, why would he be humanoid or interested in humanity?

> —*Lectures on Pan-Humanoid Myths*
> Prester Smythe Kinsel
> University of New Augusta
> 1211 A.O.E.

ii

▼

The young woman sits on the edge of the ornate bed where she is being watched.

"Everyone watches the Duke's daughter," she says in a low voice. Even the Duke's security force. More since the accident, she suspects. She cannot remember much of what she knows she should know.

The Duchess was solicitous, and her father the Duke growled. Yet he cares.

She frowns and leans forward, letting her long black hair flood over the shoulders of her pale blue travel suit.

Why should her memories be so cloudy? She can remember everything since she returned so clearly, but the people around her, the rooms, they all have a clarity that the past does not have.

Yet she belongs. The well-thumbed holobook in her father's study shows images of her growing up, standing at her father's knee, holding his hand.

Perhaps her studies at the Institute will help. Perhaps time will remove the awkwardness of relearning her past. Perhaps . . .

"Back into the fishbulb," she says out loud, crossing the room that would have held five of the single sleeping room she had occupied at Lady Persis'.

Somehow, the long row of garments hanging in the wardrobing room does not surprise her, although she has not remembered them. She walks through the wardrobe to the tiles and direct light of the bath.

Neither does she remember its luxury.

Half shrugging, she catches sight of herself in one of the full-length mirrors.

"Disheveled," she observes, looking at her hair. Something is right about it, for the first time in a long while, and something is not, nagging feelings she cannot place.

She squints until her eyes close. She opens them again. Her reflection awaits her.

iii

▼

"I don't understand, Martin. You're not registered . . ."

Not registered . . . a Query on your name . . . blocked even from the Duke's code . . .

Kryn's words are clipped, and even without the underlying concern he can sense, Martin knows of her unrest from the shortened speech.

The courtyard, the one where they always meet, is chill, as chill as the weather controls ever allow on the Planet of the Prince Regent of the Empire of Man. The little winds shuffle the small needles from the miniature cone-pines back and forth along the interior walls. No shadows, for the overcast is heavy enough to block the winter sun, and the climatizers have not succeeded in dispersing the clouds.

Kryn shivers, and the blue-clad guard involuntarily steps forward out of the corner, then back into the columns.

Always the guards, Martin reflects, *always the trappings of power.*

His eyes flicker over the communit bracelet that links her into the Regency data system, the blue leather overtunic that costs more than his total tuition, the sunpearls on her ring fingers.

He clears his throat.

"It's not that simple, Kryn." Not simple at all. He cannot register for further grad study, not with the Query stamped against his name.

No reason is given, and the junior registrar with whom he'd managed to get a face-to-face appointment had not known anything . . . nothing except a few vague thought fragments unvoiced to Martin.

. . . has to be dangerous . . . deadly . . . not even Darin will meet him . . . why me? . . . Darin's ex-Marine . . . afraid of a student . . . why me?

"The real reason?" Martin had pressed.

"Imperial Security, Citizen Martel. That is all the University is told." Her smooth dark brow and open thoughts had revealed nothing else, even when he had probed deeply. And no one wanted to talk to him.

That had been it. Someone, somehow, had fed the results of the damned paracomm tests to Imperial Security, and he was out of grad school and on his way to the mines or the Marines . . . the only employment open to someone who was Queried.

"Why not?" snaps Kryn, her cold words bringing him back from his thoughts into the chill of the Commannex courtyard.

"Because I can't get a job, any job, on Karnak. With no credits, I can't free-lance. If I could, no one could hire my services. So it's either off Karnak, or the Marines and off Karnak shortly. That's the choice."

"There has to be another one." Her voice is matter-of-fact. So are her feelings, Martin can tell, and she is as calm as her mother, the Iron Duchess, in telling a subject he is mistaken. Kryn will be Duchess, or more, Martin knows.

"If you could be so kind, Lady Kryn Kirsten, as to suggest another alternative for your obedient subject, Martin Martel, I would be most deeply obliged. Particularly since my student status will be terminated rather shortly."

"How soon?"

"Tomorrow . . . today . . . perhaps three days. The term is over, and the minimum guarantees of the Regency toward a Free Scholar have been met."

He looks down at the flat white of the marble pavement, then lifts his eyes to watch the dust devil in the far corner scatter a small heap of cone needles.

The sunlight floods abruptly into the courtyard.

"The climatizers succeed again," the ex-Scholar remarks, "bringing light into darkness, except for a few of us."

"Martin!"

He realizes that she wants to stamp her foot but refrains because the action would be unladylike.

He chuckles, and the low sound eddies through the columns. The guard in the shadows, now that there are shadows with the full winter sunlight beaming down, edges forward.

"What will you do?" Her question comes almost as a dismissal, an acceptance.

"I don't look forward to spending five years in the ore mines . . . and I don't have the heroic build of the successful Imperial Marine. So I'm somewhat limited."

"You aren't answering the question."

"I know. You don't want to hear the answer."

"You could leave the Empire . . ."

"I could. If I had the creds for passage. But no one can hire me to pay my way, except an outsider, and outsiders aren't allowed to downport here. And I don't have passage to the orbitport."

"I could help."

"I've already made arrangements."

"You didn't!"

"The Brotherhood is looking for comm specialists, so . . ."

"But"—her voice sharpens—"that's treason."

"Not unless the Regent changes the law."

He ought to. Brotherhood is nothing but trouble.

"Perhaps he will," Martin supplies the follow-on to her thought. "But they do pay, and will clear me from Imperial space, if necessary."

"Why?"

"Because, Lady Kryn Kirsten," Martin answers the

question she meant, "I came off the dole, and I will not spend five years at slave labor in the *hope* that a black mark will be lifted from my name."

"May be Da—, the Duke, I mean, could take care of that."

Martin refrains from trying to read her thoughts.

"I doubt that even the Duke could remove the Prince Regent's Query. And why would he? For a penniless scholar who's attracted to the very daughter he's planning to marry into the Royal Family?"

"Martin Martel! That's totally uncalled for." *How did he know? Never said . . . paracomm?*

"Realistic," he says in a clipped tone, trying to allay her suspicions. "Duke of Kirsten holds the most powerful House on Karnak next to the Regent. What else?"

So obvious, so obvious even to poor sweet Martin.

He cannot keep the wince from his face.

"Martin . . . what, how do you know?" *He reads thoughts, I know he does. How long? What does he really know?*

"Nothing that the gossip tabs haven't already spread. Nothing every student in the Commannex hasn't speculated."

Sweat, dampness, runs down Martin's back, with the perception that the guard is drawing his stunner, edging the setting beyond the stun range toward lethal.

Martin concentrates on the energy flows in the stunner, puzzling how to divert them, to distract Kryn from her iron-cold purpose, to just leave without raising any more fear and suspicion.

Aware of his sleeve wiping perspiration off his forehead, strange itself in the courtyard chill, he stammers.

"Nothing . . . nothing more to be said, Lady Kryn, time to depart . . . fulfill my contract to the Brotherhood . . . and then if you hear of a newsie named Martel on a far planet . . . think about corel."

No . . . no! Treason? Corel. Romance and flowers to the last. But a Duchess is as a Duchess does.

Her hands touch the stud on her wide belt, the stud that

screams "emergency" to the guard. The tight-faced man in blue aims the stunner.

Zinnnng! The strum of the weapon fills the courtyard.

"I wish you hadn't, Kryn. Wish you hadn't," mumbles Martin, knowing that he has bent the focus of the beam around him, knowing that such is impossible.

The guard knows it also, looks stupidly down at the stunner, then raises it again, only to find that the blackclad student has disappeared, and that tears stream down the cheeks of the Lady Kryn Kirsten.

Along the courtyard wall, behind the black marble bench, lit by the slanting ray of the afternoon sun, the dust devil restacks the pile of cone needles.

iv

▼

AURORE

No shadows has the noon; no darkness has the night,
And no man wears a shade in that eternal light.

The night has not a star; the sky has not a sun,
Nor is there dusk nor dawn to which a man can run.

No breakers crash at night, nor fall on sand unlit.
No lightning flares the dark where coming years
    might fit.

No dawn will break like thunder; no eve will crash
    like surf.
No shadows seep from tombs to mark its golden turf.

And if that's so, then why does darkness stalk the sky,
And only one god cast a shade to those who die,
And only one god cast a shade for those who die?

V

▼

The overhead is pale yellow. The color is the first thing he notices. That, and that he is on his back, stretched out on a railed bed of some sort.

The second observation is that he wears a loose yellow robe, nothing more, that is hitched up close to his knees.

There is no pillow, no sheeting, just a yielding surface on which he lies. He lifts his head, which aches with the pain he associates with stunners. Kryn's guard had missed, but not Boreas.

"You'd think you'd learn, Martin," he mutters.

You'd think you'd learn, Martel.

He scans the room. No one else is present. The portal is shut. A single red light on the panel next to the portal is lit. The unlit light, he presumes, is green.

The railing lowers with the touch of a lever, and Martin swings his legs over the edge and eases himself into a sitting position. Rubbing his forehead with his left hand, he continues the survey of his quarters.

"Wonder if I'm being monitored."

Wonder if I'm being monitored.

Besides the bed, there are two chairs, a low table rising out of the flooring between them, a higher bedside table, an opaqued window screen, and a closet. The sliding doors of the wardrobe/closet are half open, and Martin can see that his few belongings have been laid out on the shelves or hung up. The travelbag is folded flat on the top shelf.

He shakes his head, winces at the additional pain the movement generates, and studies the room silently.

No speakers, no inconsistencies in the walls that could conceal something.

As he lowers himself to the floor the room wavers in front of his eyes.

"Not again!" He recalls the paratest that led to his confinement, that test which seems so distant, even though just days past.

Not again! The echo pounds into his skull.

Slow step by slow step, he covers the meter or so from his bed to the wardrobe, putting each foot down carefully, unsure of his perceptions and his footing. By the time he puts out a hand to lean on the wall edge of the wardrobe, he is dripping sweat.

He shivers.

The robe, which had felt almost silky when he awoke, grits against his skin like sandpaper. Martin fingers the cuff, but the material still feels smooth to his fingertips.

He shivers again, but ignores the chill to concentrate on the personal belongings laid out on the chest-level recessed wardrobe shelf.

Two items leap to his eye. The first is the solidio cube of Kryn, which glows with a new inner light.

The second is the Regent's Scholar belt clasp. Before, it had been a dull maroon. Now it glowers at him with a crimson malevolence.

One hand against the wall, still propping himself up, the former scholar and present fugitive/prisoner checks the garments. The robes provided by the Brotherhood have all been replaced with simple pale yellow tunics and trousers, three sets, and two new pairs of soft brown formboots lie on the floor.

After wiping his forehead with the back of his cuff, still looking silky and feeling gritty, he checks through the underclothes and folded personal items.

Most are missing . . . anything that might have linked him to the Brotherhood or to his time as a Regent's Scholar.

"But why leave the clasp?"

But why leave the clasp?

. . . leave the clasp . . .

. . . leave the clasp . . .

The room twists upside down, then right-side up, then up-side down.

Martin closes his eyes. The brochure he'd been studying before Boreas had stunned him had mentioned disorientation. But this wasn't disorientation. It verges on torture.

He opens his right eye. The room is right-side up. He opens his left eye, and the room jumps to the left and stays in the same place, all at once, so that Martin sees doubled images.

He concentrates on fixing the images into one, just that, keeping his visions of things firmly in place. The images merge.

The sweat streams from his forehead again.

Suddenly the floor looms in front of his face, and pain like fire screams from his nose. And darkness . . .

The overhead is still pale yellow, and his head still aches. So do his nose and a spot on his forearm.

Again he is flat on his back on that same pallet, in the same hospital, if that is what it is.

"Flame!" he mutters without moving his head.

Flame!

He closes his eyes and tries to think.

He must be on Aurore. So why is it so painful? Aurore is a vacation spot, a wonderful place to visit, where sensuality has its special delights and where some people gain extra powers. So why is one Martin Martel having such difficulty?

Too aware! The idea flashes into his thoughts. For whatever reason, his body is more sensitive to the environment.

Eyes still closed, he begins to let his thoughts, his perceptions, check out his body, starting with his toes, trying somehow to dampen the ultrasensitivity, to dull that edge, to convince himself that such perceptions should be voluntary, not involuntary.

He can feel the sweat again pour down his forehead,

scented with fear, fear that he will not be able to regain control of his own body.

Others do it, he thinks, suppressing the urge to talk aloud.

The headache and the soreness in his nose and neck retreat. Martin opens his eyes. The room is a shade darker now, and yet the light levels from the walls have not changed, he realizes.

He lifts his head slowly, turns on his side, and fingers the rail release. After a time, he again sits up, legs dangling over the edge of the bed, heels touching the cold metal of the lowered rail.

He wills his vision to lighten the room. Nothing happens.

He relaxes the iron control on his perceptions.

The room wavers; his back itches; the soreness across the bridge of his nose throbs; the light intensifies.

Martin clamps down on his control.

Not a matter of will, but of control. Of perception.

He experiments, trying to isolate one sense after another, until the room begins to waver. He lies down, lets himself drift into a sweating sleep.

He dreams. Knows he dreams.

He is on a narrow path, except there are no edges, no walls, and the path arcs through golden skies. In front of him is Kryn. Her golden eyes are cold, and her mouth is tight-lipped.

Martin does not care, and yet he does. He takes a step toward Kryn, and another one. With each step he takes, she is farther away, though she has not moved.

Soon he is running toward her, and she dwindles into the distance. . . .

He sleeps and, presently, dreams. Again.

Martin watches a mountain spire, covered with ice, which thrusts up from a floor of fleece-white clouds. A part of his mind insists that he watches a meteorological impossibility, but he watches.

In the thin air above the peak, from nowhere appears a black cloud, modeled after the Minotaur. Across from the bull-cloud stands a god, male, heroic, clad in sandals and a short tunic. His crown is made of sunbeams, and it hurts Martin's eyes to look at his perfect face.

Between the two arrives another, a full-bearded barbarian who carries a gray stone hammer, red-haired, bulky, fur cape flowing back over his shoulders. He sports leg greaves and a breastplate, both of bronze.

Above the peak hovers another figure, which is present, but not. Martin strains to see, and after a time penetrates the ghostly details. She is slender, golden-haired, golden-eyed, and glitters. Beyond these details he cannot see, and his attention is distracted by the appearance of another god, also ghostly.

Where the goddess is golden, the latecomer is black-shadowed.

Unwanted, as well, because the three older golds strike. The barbarian throws his hammer; the sun-god Apollo casts a light spear; and the bull-god sends forth a black mist of menace.

Precog? questions someone, somewhere.

Perhaps.

Martin loses his dream, drops into darkness . . .

. . . and wakes screaming!

The scream dies as he moves his head, discovers he is on his side, holding the railing of the bed. Discovers his fingers are sore. He releases his grasp, and knows he should be surprised. He is not.

The metal is crushed, with eight finger impressions and two thumb holes clearly visible.

Martin scrambles to his knees, ignoring the wavering effect, to study his handiwork. He grabs the railing in a new place, farther toward the foot of the bed, squeezes with all the force he can muster.

His palms and fingers protest, but the metal does not yield. He lets go. Tears well up, sorrow and frustration.

"Mad, I'm mad. Crazier than Faroh."

Mad, I'm mad, mad, mad. Crazier, crazier, than, than, Faroh, Faroh.

He closes his eyes, presses balled fists against them to shut out the double echo, and the incredible flare of light that accompanies it.

"You'll get used to it," a calm voice comments.

Martin hops around on his knees, feels awkward, embarrassed, and almost pitches over the side of the bed as the nausea strikes him in the pit of his stomach.

The glare dies with the closing of the portal.

The speaker looks like the sun-god of his dreams, with short and curly blond hair, even features, cleft chin, piercing green eyes, heroic body structure, wide shoulders and narrow waist, under a gold tunic and trousers.

Martin nods for the man to continue.

"You're going to have more trouble than the others. There are two reasons for that. The first is that you're an untrained, full-range esper, and fully masked. The second is that you have, shall we say, a certain potential."

The golden man clears his throat, and even that sounds oddly musical, matching the light baritone of his clear voice.

"During the times ahead, for a while you'll know you're going mad, Martel. At times you will be. You have a great deal to learn. A great deal."

The speech bothers Martin, but he cannot pin down why.

"Who are you?"

Who are you?

Martin winces.

"You can either sync your thoughts to your speech or put a damper on them to eliminate the echo. The resonance makes any long conversations impossible, not to mention the headaches, until you get your thoughts under control. That's a function of the field. It tends to amplify stray thoughts and reflect them. Really only a nuisance, but without controls you could upset the norms and the tourists pretty strongly."

Norms? Dampers? Field? And what about the glare from outside?

He settles on the simplest question, trying to block his own thoughts at the same time.

"Is it that bright outside all the time?"

"No. It isn't bright at all. Normally the intensity is about that of early morning on Karnak. Bright, but nothing to worry about."

"But . . . when you came in?"

The golden man smiles. "It only seems bright to you. You don't see me at all. You're perceiving paranormally, and any light hurts your eyes. Except for the solidio cube, the belt clasp, and the port light, your room is totally dark. We've even screened out the glittermotes."

Martin gulps.

"I'll put it another way. Off Aurore, you have to make a conscious effort to use esp. Here, you have to make a conscious effort not to. As I mentioned a moment ago, when you really weren't paying attention, you are a full-range esper, one of a double handful in the entire Empire. That's fortunate in ways I'll not explain, and unfortunate in others. Unfortunate because the Empire would want you dead off Aurore, and because your adjustment to Aurore will be difficult at best, assuming you do make it."

The golden man is lying. Martin cannot explain which statement is wrong, decides to let it go, and tries to keep his doubts about the man buried.

"You're doubtful, Martel?"

"Why do you keep calling me Martel?"

"Because that's your real identification. Subconsciously you think of yourself as Martel, and not as Martin. I would advise you to cut some of the confusion short and go with Martel. That's an easy problem to solve."

When the other makes no move to leave, with the silence drawing out, Martin/Martel clears his throat.

"Call me Apollo. I'm here because I can't resist danger,

however removed, and because someday you might decide to help me."

Not exactly the most helpful answer, reflects Martin/Martel, but it rings true.

"What sort of help?"

"I'd rather not say. You'll find out."

Another true statement, according to Martel's internal lie detector.

There are too many fragments. Norms, glittermotes, strength he doesn't have, but has. Seeing in total darkness . . .

He closes his eyes but wills himself to see. The room does not change, is still visible through closed eyelids.

As he realizes he can see behind the half-closed doors of the wardrobe, he begins to itemize the small personal trinkets.

He stops, half bemused, half frightened, when he realizes that Apollo has gone and that the portal had not opened.

The ceiling begins to glow, shedding a real light.

"Flame. Just beginning to tell the difference."

Just make it habit. The thought comes from far away. Apollo?

A low note chimes, and the green light above the portal illuminates. Martel braces himself for the glare, but with his eyes slit, the increase is bearable.

A thin older woman carries a small tray into the room. The mental static that surrounds her announces that she has some sort of shield or screen.

She does not look at him.

"Good morning. Is it morning?"

Her face narrows. The frown, her black hair, and her thin eyebrows all combine to form a disapproving look. Martel studies her, decides she is younger than he thought.

"It's morning. How do you feel?"

Despite the mental screen, Martel can sense her puzzlement.

"Confused," he admits. "How long have I been here? Asleep?"

"Two standard months. Not always asleep."

She puts down the tray and steps back, eyes taking in the bent metal railing.

"What do you mean, not always asleep?"

She backs farther away.

"That's something the doctors need to discuss with you. I will see what can be done. You're not scheduled yet."

Martel frowns to himself. Not scheduled? Scheduled for what? Two months? From a stunner? Has he been here ever since Boreas stunned him?

She drops a folder on the low table and scuttles for the portal.

"If you read that, it will give the right perspective." She darts out. The door irises shut, and the amber light replaces the green, but the ceiling glow remains.

Apollo had said that using paranorm powers was easy.

Martel reaches for the folder with his thoughts and is still surprised when it floats up from the table into his hands.

The folder is not what he expected. Rather than a general brief, it is an excerpt from a technical article: "Dealing with Fullphase, Full Awakening of Paranormals in an Ultrastimulatory Environment," selections from the full and uncompleted works of one Sevir Corwin, S.B., P.D., M.D., S.P.N.P., etc.

There is one introductory paragraph that catches Martel.

Inasmuch as Dr. Corwin did not live to complete his work, and could not be consulted on the selections, the editor has attempted to include those portions most likely to help clinical personnel working in high-risk situations.

Martel studies the folder. Cheap reproduction, right from an ordinary copy unit. More questions.

He reads the entire folder. Twice, despite the odd turn of technical phrases, while he eats the fruit and the protein bar and the flat pastry that the aide has brought.

Phrases ring in his thoughts.

Ultrastimulatory environments can be dangerous for newly aroused paranorms . . . transition under sedation . . . subconscious realization . . . LR_{50} for intervenors during I.P., . . . de facto ban on paranorm transfer to ultrastim (read Aurore) . . .

He leans back on the pallet, closes his eyes, tries to list what he knows, tries to get it in some sequence, something that makes sense.

Item: He is considered paranorm.

Item: Paranorms arriving on Aurore are dangerous as flame, to themselves and to those around them.

Item: Boreas has stunned him en route, under Brotherhood orders.

Item: The Brotherhood definitely wants him on Aurore.

Item: For two months he has been out of his mind.

Item: While dreaming, he had literally crushed a heavy steel railing.

Item: Apollo isn't afraid of Martel.

Item: The woman is.

Item: He is getting sleepy.

Item:

His last thought on the listing is *Don't you ever learn, Martel?*

Again, the dreams . . . but more confused, this time, these times.

He is floating above the same ice peak, but no one is around him, and there are no clouds, but the upper levels of the mountain are still in shadow.

He turns to move closer to the peak, but from his left a golden thunderbolt blasts in front of him. On his right, a dark thundercloud materializes.

He contemplates the needlepeak, waiting . . .

. . . and finds himself sitting at a table, across from a golden-eyed and golden-haired woman. She is speaking, but he cannot understand the words; though each is a word he knows, her sentences form a pattern and a puzzle he cannot assemble, and as he wrestles with each word the next catches him by surprise.

Finally he nods, and looks past her over the railing toward the golden sands that slope down to the sea. He touches the beaker by his left hand. Jasolite. A jasolite beaker. Jasolite, jasolite . . .

. . . LIGHT! . . .

. . . and he is strapped down on a cold metal table, under the pinpoint of a telescope. The telescope is gathering star-light, and that light is coming out of the pinpoint needle just above his forehead.

He twists, but the heavy straps and metal bands do not bend.

The light coming from the instrument burns his skin, and he wrenches his left hand free, then his right, and cups them under the enormous telescope to catch the torrent of light. But his hands overflow, and the burning light cascades over his palms and blisters his forehead.

Finally he throws the light back into the telescope, which melts, collapsing away from him.

Then he curls up on the metal table, and sleeps . . .

. . . and wakes in a lounge chair. For a long time, he is not certain if he is awake. A woman is stretched in the chair next to him, but he cannot turn his head. Perhaps he does not want to.

He is near the sea. The salt tells him so, and the slow crashes of the breakers do not confuse him, not the way the words the unseen woman speaks do.

She speaks slowly, and the words are in order, he knows. But some he hears twice, and some he loses because of those he hears twice.

". . . you, you, understand, stand, sedated, sedated . . . if, if . . . remember, remember . . . dream . . . dream . . ."

The strain of pursuing the words presses him back into the lounge, and he lets himself float on the vibrations of the incoming breakers.

". . . god, god, you, you . . . forget, get . . ."

The urgency of her tone chains him, whips across his cheeks like a blizzard wind, and he drowns in the sounds, drifting into a darkness.

Thoughts boom like drums in the darkness, out of the black.

This one troubles me.

As well he should.

That upstart?

Boom! Boom-boom! Each letter of each verbal thought brands his brain, and he screams, and screams . . .

He wakes.

The clarity of his surroundings announces that he does not dream, and may not be drugged.

Although his eyes focus on the pale yellow overhead, someone waits. Another woman. He knows without looking.

Instead of sitting up and reacting, he remains motionless, thinking. Deciding if he can sort out what he has dreamed from what he experienced under the sedation. Deciding that sorting can wait, and filing the memories in a corner of his mind for more scrutiny.

His thoughts scan the room.

The woman wears a mental screen. Both a laser and a full-range stunner are focused on him from the ceiling, and the thickness of the walls argues for a prison rather than a hospital. Idly Martel lets his perceptions change a few circuits in the laser and stunner to remove their immediate threat.

Then he stretches, slowly, and begins to sit up.

The woman is red-haired, and radiates friendliness.

Martel notes that she has appeared in his dreams, and files the note. He senses that her friendliness is genuine, and lets himself smile.

"I'm Rathe Firien, and I'd like to welcome you formally to Aurore. I suspect you know you've already been here for some time."

"Delighted," responds Martel, with a twitch of his mouth preventing a full smile. "How long?"

"Five standard months."

"Wonderful."

He puts his feet over the edge of the bed, lets them dangle, lets his mind range through the room again. The room is not the same one, but built like a Marine bunker, meter-thick plate behind the walls, and ferroplast behind that.

He shakes his head.

"Something the matter?" She is concerned.

"No. Just a little amazed. Do you go to this extent for all paranorms?"

She hesitates.

"Special instructions, huh? From the Brotherhood?"

"Brotherhood?" Confusion there.

"Apollo?" he pursues.

Fear, but validation.

He decides to change the subject.

"What's next on the agenda?"

"For you?"

Martel nods.

"I suppose you could get dressed . . ." She grins.

"I meant . . . in general terms."

"Once you're dressed"—and she grins again, and Martel cannot resist smiling back—"we'll get you out of here. Then we'll go over the things you need to do to get settled in."

Martel wraps the one-piece robe around him as he realizes that it has started to fall open, then relaxes. Obviously, the woman knows all about him. He shakes his head.

"Does it always take this long?"

"What?"

"Getting adjusted, or whatever this process is called."

"For a paranorm it varies."

So many questions . . . He gives up, and decides to work on one thing at a time. He stands up, feeling fit, stretches, and sees Rathe's mouth in an O, suppressing a laugh. He suspects he has grown somehow, until he discovers he is floating a good ten centimeters off the floor, and lets himself down.

"Sorry. Not used to this."

"I'll meet you outside. The fresher's next to the wardrobe. Touch the plates next to the portals to open them."

She leaves.

Martel discovers that he does want a shower. After cleaning up, he pulls on one of the yellow tunic/trouser outfits and a pair of the formboots.

He doesn't like the yellow. When he can, he will have to replace the clothes selected for him.

Wonder of wonders, the outer portal opens at his touch, and Rathe Firien is waiting.

vi

▼

Outside the portal is a balcony, and from it Martel can see a town spreading down a gentle incline toward the silver/green/gold expanse that has to be the ocean.

He still must squint against the unaccustomed strength of the light, indirect and unfocused as it is.

A light breeze ruffles his hair, and he notes that it is neither warm nor cool, but bears a faint scent of pine.

He is conscious of Rathe Firien, who has stepped back as he moves to take hold of the black iron railing.

The roofs of Sybernal are white. Some sparkle; some merely are white.

A wide dark swath of trees halfway between him and the sea breaks the intermittent pattern of roofs and foliage.

Must be some sort of park.

. . . some sort of park . . .

He shakes his head, trying to remember to hang on to his control.

"Is something wrong?" asks the woman.

"No." He pauses. "The dark stretch there?" He points.

"That's the Greenbelt. It surrounds the coastal highway where it cuts through Sybernal."

" 'Coastal,' and not on the coast?"

"It is, except in Sybernal. You can walk the Petrified Boardwalk there. You'll see."

Martel supposes he will.

He studies the grounds beneath the balcony. The grass is nearly emerald-colored and short. Roughly half the trees are deciduous, which seems wrong.

Why?

He knows it is "wrong," but also knows he is not thinking clearly enough yet to pose the question correctly, much less answer it.

The streets are little more than paved lanes, suitable for walking and for the electrobikes he sees under a covered porch at the far end of the building.

The square paved space in the middle of the lawn, he assumes, is a flitter pad, which would make sense for a hospital, or whatever institution he is confined in.

"What's next?" he asks.

"I've called a flitter."

"For what?"

"So you can leave."

"Just like that?"

"Do you want to stay?" She favors him with a half-smile, one that reminds him of the friendliness she radiates.

"I can't say that I do, but that's not the question. Don't I have to check out? Or see someone? Or sign something?"

"That's been taken care of. You're ready to leave."

Taken care of. Right. You've been taken care of. And how!

What's next? A quiet little trip to another secluded hide-away?

"Just a flaming instant! Just what other little tricks do you all have planned? If I'd been hospitalized, or institutional-ized, anywhere for this long, I couldn't possibly be let go the minute I woke up and the first pretty nurse to come along said, 'You. All right. You can leave now.'" He takes a deep breath.

Rathe Firien just waits for him to continue. Her smile is even more amused.

"Here I am, drugged, doped, and dreaming for months on end, and now—snap, bang, yes, sir, Mr. Martel, time to check out and get on with your business. Of course, we haven't told you where you are, why you've been here, how long you've been here, and where we want to take you. But let's get going!

"Now! Just what the flame is going on in this place? And what's the sudden hurry?"

He completes the last word with a slam on the iron bal-cony railing. The twinge that rips up his left arm reminds him that he is awake and that iron bars do not bend at his touch.

He looks down at his wrist, uncovered and pale, and at the yellow cuff of the tunic. Both are too light.

The woman stands just beyond his reach, waiting for him to insist on an answer.

"I won't," he whispers, understanding that his refusal only hurts himself.

. . . won't, won't, won't . . .

The day is still, and the breeze has died. The pine scent is gone, replaced with a heavier smell of flowers and freshly turned earth. A single bird chirp breaks the silence.

Swallowing, he finally looks up. "Would you care to ex-plain?"

"If you'll listen."

Martel nods.

"First, you're on Aurore. You know that. Nowhere else is like Aurore, and you don't seem to understand that. You're leaving because your mind is ready to cope with Aurore. With your background, the sooner you leave here the better. Besides, when He says you can go, you can go. I don't question Him, and neither should you.

"It may be months before you understand why, but please take my word for it now. If you don't agree, you can always ask your questions later." She purses her lips, licks the upper one with the pink tip of her tongue, and goes on.

"For the time being, please remember that you are *totally* responsible for the results of your actions. If you keep that in mind, you won't do too badly."

"*Totally* responsible for the results of my own actions?"

"There are a few exceptions, but, yes, that's a fair statement. This isn't the time or the place to get into that discussion. Wait until you've had some time."

He senses bitterness behind her statement and refrains from pushing that line of questioning.

"So what comes next? Where are we going, and why?"

"On a quick aerial tour of Sybernal, to help you get your bearings, and then for something to eat. After that, I'll help you look into lodgings, though that's scarcely a problem."

Scarcely a problem? Then what is? He keeps the questions to himself and looks toward the flitter pad in reaction to the *flup/swish, flup/swish* of a descending flitter.

Rathe Firien is already at the end of the balcony and headed down the wide stairs toward the lawn and the waiting aircraft.

Martel misses seeing the incoming pilot, if there is one, because when he arrives, breathing heavily, Rathe is at the controls.

"Whew! Out of shape."

"You'll recover, I'm sure," she observes with a twist of her lips.

By now the flitter is airborne, and she begins her travel-ogue.

"Sybernal is laid out like a half-circle around the bay, although it's really more of a gentle arc in the straight coastline than a true bay. Most of the beaches are straight, and those that do curve are generally perfect arcs. You can see the Greenbelt from here. That's the coast highway running through the middle."

Martel follows the direction of her free hand. As far as he can see, the so-called coastal highway, which rejoined the coastline south of Sybernal, has very little traffic on it.

"Not much travel."

"Natives and norms don't travel that far or that much. The touries use flitters. This one belongs to Him. For special use. Now, on the beach side of the Greenbelt, that's where the plush houses and the better restaurants are. This side is the trade district, and closer to us is where most norms and natives live."

The flitter's nose swings northward.

"There are a few large estates in the higher hills north of Sybernal. You can see the white there . . . and there? The owners keep to themselves. For all I know, some may be gods or demigods."

"Doesn't anyone know?" asks Martel, aware that his voice carries a waspish note. "Doesn't the government keep track?"

"Private property is private property, and trespassing is strictly forbidden."

Martel frowns. Rathe Firien's response doesn't exactly qualify as a direct answer.

"I'm not sure I understand," he finally says, pulling at his chin.

"Let's just say that the right to privacy from one's fellows is fully respected here. Generally, even the gods leave you alone. So long as you don't hurt anyone else."

"But—"

"I'll explain later. Right now you're getting a quick tour, remember?"

Martel can sense her amusement, as well as an underlying sense of fear. He reflects, and decides that the feeling is not just fear. As the flitter cabin swirls around him he breaks off the mental stretching and concentrates on regaining his equilibrium.

Aurore is going to take some getting used to, Martel.

"Wouldn't gods have palaces on mountaintops?" The question sounds stupid even as he asks it, and he shakes his head.

The pilot lets the question pass, and swings the flitter back toward the town.

Martel studies the terrain beneath.

In the distance to the southwest of Sybernal, a flash of light, brilliant red, catches his eye. He strains to make out the regular and angular shapes nearly on the horizon, shapes that seem familiar. His memory dredges up the map he had studied and supplies him with the answer—the shuttleport, one of only two on all Aurore. The flash has to have been an in-beacon call.

A single highway, no bigger than the thin strip called the coastal highway, arrows away from the city-town of Sybernal toward the port. Martel cannot spot any traffic at all on the roadway to the shuttleport, and only a few dwellings lining it.

The homes beneath the flitter cluster closer together the nearer to the center of Sybernal they are, Martel notes, although even those most closely packed have individual lawns and foliage surrounding them.

For all the whiteness of the roofs, for all the emerald green of the grass, the gold-green sparkle of the sea, and the darker green of the trees, something is missing. Martel cannot decide what it is, but there is a subdued drabness about Sybernal as seen from the air, a certain lack of color.

"There's the CastCenter, where you'll be working once you get fully adjusted."

"What?" Martel has not been following her gesture.

"Over to the right. The circular building on the low hill with the roof grids? That's the CastCenter."

Martel picks out the structure, notes its position, slightly to the northwest of what would be the center of Sybernal if one were that clearly defined. If his estimate of distances is correct, he could probably walk the distance from the farthest point in Sybernal to work in less than a stan.

Sybernal is not exactly the largest of cities, not a booming metropolis, particularly after Karnak. But his briefings had indicated that Sybernal is by far the largest city on Aurore.

He shakes his head again. He has questions, too many questions.

"Not looking forward to work?" asks Rathe, apparently misinterpreting his headshake.

"It's not that. It's just that I've got more than a little adjusting to do."

He turns away from her and stares out through the bubbled canopy toward the south. Is it his imagination, or is there a snowcapped peak just over the horizon? He can feel that there ought to be just such a mountain, but is there?

The land that stretches away from Sybernal toward the south lies in gently rolling hills, composed of roughly equal sections of cultivated fields, forest, and golden grass meadows.

The emerald lawns of Sybernal are at odds with the golden field grass.

Another contradiction, unless the city grass is an import.

The air is clear, cloudless, yet the high golden haze, uniform from horizon to zenith, conveys an impression of mistiness. Martel knows that impression is false by the clarity of landmarks, such as the hills to the north, and the sharpness of the thin highways angling into the distances.

They are nearly over the coastline now, and only faint traces of whitecaps streak the ocean. The breakers streaming into the beaches are sternly narrow.

"We're going to land near the South Pier and have something to eat. I'll answer some of those questions you had, and then we'll look into housing for you."

"Oh . . . fine."

Fine, right, Martel? Not much in the way of formality here, is there?

She eases the stick forward, and the flitter responds, dipping toward the pier.

vii

▼

"Before we really get started . . . the first and most important point is to defer to the gods."

Martel sets the jasolite beaker down on the transparent tabletop.

"Let's have that again. About the gods."

About the gods.

He rubs his forehead at the mental echo. Any lapse of control has immediate results.

"You're tired."

He hears the concern in her voice and senses the compassion. He hates it, hates being pitied. He hated being understood when Kryn had felt sorry for him, and he hates it now.

"Not tired. Careless. Go on. Why must one be so careful with the gods?" He picks up the beaker and takes another sip of the liqueur that warms his throat on the way down and seems to dull the ache in his head. Springfire, Rathe had called it.

A stray glittermote, a shining black rather than the usual gold, settles on his shoulder, flickers twice, and vanishes.

"You know about the gods, Martel. The ones like Apollo

who can kill with a gesture, manipulate your feelings with a song, throw thunderbolts if they feel like it . . ."

Martel looks away from her freckled face and east toward the incoming surf. According to his scattered knowledge, Aurore shouldn't have tides as substantial as it does.

"Apollo can't do all that," he mutters, not caring totally, but knowing that what he says is true.

"No, probably not all that, but each god can do at least one thing out of the ordinary, and by that I mean beyond the normal range of esping. Now, technically speaking"— she stops to purse her thin lips before continuing—"there are distinctions between potentials, demigods, gods, and Elder Gods. For a newcomer, even as esper, all god types are dangerous."

Martel doesn't believe it, half doesn't care. But Rathe is so earnest, and he is expected to ask. He does.

"Why?"

"They all can tap the field, and that's an energy source not open to nongods, not even to you."

According to his chrono, it is approaching local midnight, but the light level has not varied. While the tables on the balcony are only half occupied, those who are there keep their own schedules. Martel has observed three breakfasts, several midday meals, and after-dinner liqueurs delivered by servitors since he and Rathe had been seated so much earlier.

"Does everyone keep their own schedule?"

"You weren't listening?"

Another black glittermote settles on the pale gold collar stripe of Martel's tunic.

"I am, and I was. So many things to ask."

"All right." She sighs. "Yes. Everyone keeps his or her own schedule. How could it be otherwise? It's always day. Some stick to an arbitrary day/night schedule. Some follow standard Imperial. Others take naps around the clock. Gods never sleep."

"Gods, gods, gods. All I seem to hear is about gods."

She sets her expression. "And it's all you will hear until you show some signs of understanding who they are and what they can do."

She is serious. Martel can tell.

He spreads his hands in surrender. "So tell me about the gods."

"If I only could . . ." she starts.

Martel opens his mouth.

"No. Don't interrupt. Please. I'm not used to espers. Why you were assigned to me—Don't look into my thoughts . . . just listen."

He nods, seething at the idea that he would indiscriminately rummage through anyone's mind, wondering if he can, really can, at the same time.

Rathe sips her own liqueur, looks out at the breakers, and begins to talk, the words falling in a rush.

"Everyone says that Aurore is the home of the gods, and lets it go at that. Everyone thinks it's nice we don't have big government or much crime. Or that assassins can't even get off a shuttle here. Or Imperial spies or agents. I guess it is. But no one mentions the other side of the cred. We don't have a choice. The gods do. We don't."

"What do you mean?"

She goes on as if he has not spoken.

"We don't have any police, you may have noticed. No courts. No written laws."

Martel has not noticed. The brochures and infopaks he had read hadn't mentioned this aspect of Aurore.

"We have gods," Rathe Firien pushes on, "and they punish criminals. Rather, the demigods do. If the demigods exceed their rights, they get punished. By the gods. Simple, Right?"

"If you say so. But who judges the gods?"

"Other gods, all of them, or so I've been told. But that really doesn't concern you."

"What does?"

Rathe does not answer. Just shakes her head. Her short, fine hair fluffs out momentarily. With the light behind her, she seems to wear a crown, an image incongruous with the warmth and approachability she radiates.

The warmth is why she has the job she does.

Martel cannot think of anything to say, and the silence stretches out. As Rathe purses her lips prior to speaking an answer strikes Martel.

"Severe punishment?" he asks.

"Not necessarily severe, but certain. Unavoidable. Just."

"You didn't mention merciful."

"Mercy isn't the question. Justice is."

"But how?"

"The punishment fits the crime. Common thieves lose their right hand."

"That's punishment?" asks Martel, thinking about bionics and full-clone grafts.

"It is when the nerves refuse to take a graft. Ever."

"Oh . . . oh." Martel understands. Anyone who can alter the nerve structure to such a degree, the chromosome patterns, has powers beyond the normal.

"What about the more severe crimes?"

"Most don't get committed. They screen all incomers. People who have committed minor crimes get blessed. Very few criminal types escape. That leaves crimes of passion, and even a lot of those are headed off. Gods can sense trouble, when they choose to."

"Total conditioning."

"Not exactly. Just if you're antisocial or antigod. And it's not really conditioning. An absolute prohibition locked into your soul. Or a compulsion. A pyromaniac can't touch matches. He couldn't even light a signal fire to save a life. A man with a violent temper can't raise his voice or lift a hand in anger . . . even to stop a beating or a theft."

Martel shudders. Imperial justice is bad enough. But an absolute justice? He shudders again.

"It isn't bad. Really, it isn't. It works. You won't get cheated. You won't get mugged. Very civilized."

If it's so civilized, dear Rathe, why do you sound so bitter? He holds the thought to himself.

"And everyone has a job, and is happy to have one." She paused, then added, "Except mothers of small children."

"You will work, and you will be happy. Is that it?"

"Not exactly. If you want to work without a blessing, you'll never draw attention. If you don't want to work, and don't cause problems and can pay your service taxes, that's fine, too. You can't expect to live off society."

Martel squeezes his lips together. Somehow, Aurore doesn't sound quite so ideal, quite the paradise he'd imagined. All this was just the first lesson.

He drains the last of the Springfire.

"What about the second lesson?"

"You've already heard it. Two rules. Defer to the gods. Don't hurt anyone. That will cover most things. That and paying for what you use. That's it."

"That's it?"

"Does there have to be anything else?"

He thinks, looks out at the too-regular breakers, then back at the red-haired woman.

"I suppose not. What if you hurt someone accidentally?"

"If it's unforeseen and unintended, nothing. If you are careless, you'll be judged and punished."

Why do you know so much, Rathe? Why so much sadness beneath the friendly surface?

She pushes a small infopak across the table to him. Against the transparency of the surface it hangs in midair, along with the two beakers.

Martel ignores a faint bead of sweat on the woman's upper lip. The sea breeze has stopped momentarily.

"Possible lodgings. Available singles. You can choose house, conapt, or room."

"What would you suggest?"

"For you, I'd think a small house, as far away from others as possible. Until you have your mental defenses built."

"How could I pay for it?"

"No problem. The owner or seller knows you'll pay, and you're already on salary at the CastCenter."

Martel hadn't understood that section of his contract when it had been presented . . . why the pay had started when he arrived on Aurore, rather than when he started work. It made more sense now. But he felt guilty about the back pay, if there was any.

"Back pay?" he ventured.

"That's a crossover. Paid for your treatment."

It figured. He pushed the infopak back at Rathe. "Pick out some very small houses for us to look at."

"I'll suggest several."

Rathe pointed out two in the hills behind Sybernal, and one south of the town/city.

Martel didn't even leave the flitter for an inside view of the first two.

In the end, he settled on the hillside guesthouse with the view of the sea. He liked the idea that by walking fifty meters up the hillside he could look down the other side at a sheltered bay.

The landlady, a gray-haired woman of indeterminate age, Mrs. Alderson, offered no objection to Martel's immediate occupancy, and even supplied linens . . . for a deferred payment.

Rathe Firien pointed out the slight differences in the appliances, then sat on the bed as he unpacked his single bag.

"Don't know why I bother," Martel mutters as he hangs up the gold-and-white tunics and trousers that have been furnished for him.

"The colors, you mean?"

"Um-hmmm. Not mine."

"Yours is black."

"How did you know?"

"You said so."

"When?"

"When you were under treatment."

"What else did I say?"

"Who's Kryn?"

"The girl I loved. The one I thought I loved."

"She love you?"

"No." Martel folds the collapsible savagely, jams it to the back of the high shelf at the back of the built-in wardrobe. "Don't ask me!" he growls, afraid Rathe will ask more.

Don't ask me! Don't ask me! He cannot block the thoughts.

"I'd like to help." Her voice is low.

. . . have to help . . . The thought fragment is clear.

Martel turns toward Rathe, watches as she unbuttons her blouse, watches as she shrugs out of the tight trousers and stands, breasts firm, nipples erect, arms half outstretched, almost pleading.

. . . please . . . have to . . . gods are just . . . be merciful . . .

Her eyes do not meet his, and he wants to turn away, to bury himself in the memory of Kryn, in cool blue, even she who held a hot stunner. Instead, he lets his thoughts enfold the red-haired woman, who knows him while he scarcely knows her, lets his mind fall around hers, trying to understand.

As he takes a step toward her the pictures flood him, first one at a time, then in a tidal wave.

A red-haired young woman, a girl, swimming with a friend, sunning themselves on a deserted beach with even waves, the friend of a young man. Blond, handsome. An insistent young man, with insistent hands, hands knowing of her desires and her resistance, trying to trigger the former and brush by the latter. Kissing, leading to touching, and her breaking away, out into the water, half laughing, half crying, half wanting, and half turning away. The man's reluctant acceptance.

More pictures, blurring.

Another scene, high above the sea, on a ledge over white cliffs, secluded. More kissing, more touching, and again the girl breaks away. This time the man grabs for her, tries to force her back into his arms. She half turns, falls. He falls onto her, breathing hard, and she kicks at him. His feet go out from under him, skitter on the white gravel, and he loses his balance, bounces, and falls. Falls out over the hard rocks and down, down onto the jagged edges and foam hundreds of meters below . . . his scream . . . her tears . . . barely started before the thunderbolt, the god appearing, sunhair so brilliant his features obscured . . . his judgment . . . seared into her thoughts . . .

Martel tries to break out of Rathe's thoughts, tries not to, all at the same time, understanding at first/second hand what she alluded to in mere words.

Let the punishment fit the crime. Because she led on one who wanted her, who loved her in his own way, killed him, even accidentally, she had to pay, and pay, and pay, by easing the hurts of those who are lost, the Martels and who knew how many others, forever and ever and ever . . . world without end.

He stands there, his body nearly next to hers, but not touching her naked skin, with his own tears and hers streaming down his cheeks, shaking, wanting to touch her, wanting her to hold him, and unable to bring about either. He touches her hands, finally takes them in his, holds her, and she presses against him, gently, undemandingly, and their cheeks touch, their tears meet.

After a time he cannot measure, he lays her upon the low bed and holds her more tightly. Lips brush, and more, and they fold and enfold each other.

After the instants, after the quiet, in the silence that is no longer empty, sleep finds them, finds her.

In the day-lit time that seems like night, she tries to pull away, but asleep and awake all at once he will not let her go, strokes her short red-silk hair, touches her thoughts, touches the line of judgment within her soul and finds he cannot remove it, finds he can add something, a small something, restore a small sense of pride, and does. Holds her through the day that is morning.

And sleeps.

When he wakes, she is there, dressed, sitting at the foot of the bed.

"Leaving?"

She nods. Touches her fingertips to her lips, then to his forehead. She stands and leaves without a sound, having given, having received.

Martel wants to cry, cannot, will not, and feels the shadow within him grow.

After instants that feel like hours, he rolls over, stares at the open doorway.

More time passes before he sits on the edge of the bed, head down and resting in his palms.

Should he have let her walk out?

Martel stands and surveys the room, the empty shelves, the wardrobe where three outfits hang, the window that opens on the grassy hillside with its scattered pines and a single quince.

> *Tell me now, and if you can,*
> *What is human, what is man?*

The lines of the old song seem singularly appropriate, though he knows not why.

He pulls on trousers, tunic, boots.

The portal, which is really an old-fashioned doorway, beckons, and Martel follows it.

On his right, as he goes out of his bedroom, is an even more expansive window that frames the hillside running down toward the coast road and the sea beyond. To the left is a set of louvered panels that screen off the small kitchen. Straight ahead are a settee, a low table, and two stretched-fabric chairs. Behind the arrangement of furniture is a dining area with another, higher table and four chairs.

Walking around one of the fabric chairs, Martel stops in front of the window.

"A long day . . ."

A long day . . .

He rubs his forehead. The control is not automatic yet, not on this, his first day of return to the land of the living. From five months of drugged existence to a friendly face, a warm person, who greets you in the most intimate way possible, and then feels she must walk out?

Rathe Firien, Kryn or no Kryn, memories or not, will be part of his life. For now, for who knows how long. And who knows how long for anything?

Martel holds two images up in his mind, compares.

Kryn: long dark hair, light complexion, high-breasted, slender, blue girl. Mind and thoughts like a knife ready to cut. Fragile and strong as plasteel, uncertain, yet ambitious and ready and willing to stab for hers. Cold, and passionate.

Set the record straight, Martel. You think she's passionate. He makes the mental correction with a half-smile.

Rathe: short red hair, narrow-waisted and full-breasted, friendly, open, and vulnerable. Strong . . . he didn't know, but her mind said she was. Ambitious—no. How could anyone be ambitious with a compulsion like that laid across her soul? Passionate . . . yes, with reservations.

He shakes his head.

Are the gods really gods? Or men and women with larger-than-life powers playing god over a planet that wasn't really a planet? Playing with Martels and Rathes of Aurore, like toys in an endless game?

Does he, Martel, really want to find out? And risk the outcome for himself, for Rathe, for Kryn?

Does he have any choice?

And what about Kryn? Is she real or an inflated memory? Will she be part of the future? And Rathe? How long? How?

He turns from the window.

viii

▼

Reason would indicate that death either represents no state or a changed state, nothingness or somethingness, if you will.

Humanoid cultures, almost universally, represent death as a dark and grasping figure, which does not follow logically. Is there something about the source of this representation of which we are unaware?

—*The Dark Side*
Sidney Derline

ix

▼

A glittermote lands on his left arm, the one sprawled out on the sand next to his head.

Without looking up, he knows it is black. The black ones feel different, more attuned to him than the normal white or gold motes that seem to be everywhere.

He leaves his head on the sand, eyes closed, lets the diffused warmth soak into his bare back. For whatever reason, he can get a light tan at any time of day or night. Logically, whether or not the field diffused light, the tanning effect should have been limited to the technical "day." As with many things on Aurore, though, logic is wrong.

Martel corrects himself: Apparently sound logic is wrong.

Crunching sounds, footsteps, intrude.

He lifts his head, rolls over and into a sitting position.

A tall man, blocky, black-haired and dark-skinned, dripping ocean, walks from the foam at the water's edge straight up the beach toward him.

The black glittermote stays perched on Martel's arm. A second mote appears next to the first.

Martel half smiles . . . the first time he had seen two together. Black ones, that is.

So you're the one.

Martel blocks the thoughts and answers, "The one what?"

"If you want to handle it this way, it's your choice." The stranger stares at Martel, the sharpness of his study disconcerting.

Martel stands and wishes he hadn't, as the other towers a full two heads taller.

"Black glittermotes? Never seen any before. Must be something new, not that there hasn't been time for that."

Martel gathers his defenses, mental and physical. Will some sort of assault follow the verbal onslaught?

"Who are you?"

"Just a curious bit player. You can call me Gil Nash, if you want. It's close enough."

To what? thinks Martel, simultaneously blocking it from the other while drawing energy from somewhere, somehow.

A small cloud of black glittermotes appears from nowhere, circles Martel, and a handful array themselves across his shoulders, their feather touch electric.

"Don't draw any conclusions!" counters the tall man, backing up several steps. "I'm just watching."

Martel shakes his head to clear his sight from the momentary disorientation, focuses on the other's face as a stabilizer, finds himself reaching, evading the other man's sievelike screens, and picking up fragments, mostly images.

A tall ice-pointed peak . . . Apollo the sun-god . . . oceans and brass chains with links to dwarf a man . . . a sword that flames when drawn . . . a dark cloud that is a bull and a man and a god . . .

Martel retreats from Nash's thoughts, finds he can see the energy of the man, his ties to the field. Those are what the lines of energy have to be.

Nash retreats another step, far enough down the sloping beach that he and Martel are almost at equal eye level.

"Take your time, Martel. You have forever, and they don't."

"What about you?"

"Another century of causing tidal waves won't hurt, and that's what I'll get."

"What? And who are 'they'?"

"It's a long story. But since the thunderbolts haven't hit yet, how about a drink?"

Martel shrugs.

None of what the crazy giant says makes sense, but maybe it would. What seems logical isn't. So what isn't might be.

"My place is up the hill. All I've got is some local beer and Springfire." He turns and digs his toes into the sand as he starts upward, mentally reaching out and letting the towel sweep itself off the sand and over his arm.

"I'll take the beer. Springfire's the last thing I need at the moment." Nash does not comment on the acrobatics of the towel, as if they were only expected.

Either an esper or familiar with them, reflects Martel, letting his extended perceptions track the bigger man as he follows Martel out of the sand and onto the grassy hillside.

The two chairs and table on the covered deck wait for them, as well as a beaker of Springfire and a frosted mug of beer.

Martel gestures to one chair and seats himself in the other, the one closer to the door into the cottage. The nearly dry Nash, wearing only what seems a metallic loincloth, sinks into the chair, which bends, but does not give. Martel revises his estimate of the man's weight and strength up another notch.

The other downs nearly a full liter in one gulp.

"Not the best, but damned fine after all that salt water."

"Could you explain?" asks Martel. "None of this makes any sense. Black glittermotes, bit players, thunderbolts, chains, and drinking salt water."

"Young one, when you've been around as long as me, you take things for granted. It all seems so simple. Some things I won't tell you, because you won't believe them, and my telling will make it even harder. That'd hurt me. So I won't tell. Some things you're about to learn and half believe, and those I will tell you. And some things you won't understand."

Martel waits, but the tall man, who physically does not appear more than a handful of years older than Martel, drains the rest of the mug. Martel refills it without leaving his chair. He does not like using so much esping, but has the feeling that the stranger might disappear if he takes his eyes off him.

"I might, too"—the man grins—"but not quite yet. It's like this. First, the glittermotes. They're simple. They congregate around those who can or do tap the field. But in . . . say a long while . . . I've never seen black. Only gold and white. Not even . . . anyhow, that's the glittermotes.

"Bit players, demigods, bystanders, all the same. Strong enough to endure, but not to influence the game. Once in a while, we can point things out to the new ones. That's you. My chains rattled free before they were supposed to, and I won't say how, on the condition I have a beer and a chat with you. No illusions about that. I'll be back throwing waves shortly."

Martel listens, trying to accept the information, to take what is offered and sort it out later. In the back of his mind, he senses a change in the weather, a storm brewing over the hills to the west.

"You're educated. Talk about the chains of the sea. I've something to do with that. If you're in the chains of the sea, you drink salt water, and that doesn't do much for your thirst. Now ask why I don't try harder to get free of my chains. I do, every once in a while, for an adventure or two. But I don't stand up well against the storm-gods or their thunderbolts, and they don't stand up well to the Elder Gods, which says where I stand in the grander scheme of things. You're different, or will be, once you get the hang of it. You've got some of them stirred up. Can't see why exactly . . . seem too peaceful to me."

Martel stands, the blackness boiling out of him like night, the glittermotes clinging to him like a shadow cloak.

Explain! His command strikes the other like a whip.

Young god . . . and the older gods fear you. You are not ready to face them . . . by their own laws they cannot strike you down . . . but will tempt you to your own destruction . . . or to attack them all . . .

The perpetual day turns sudden dark, brooding smoke-yellow dusk, with the swiftness of a razor knife slicing day into night, and the thunder rolls in from the west and down the hillside like a war wagon to shake the cottage. The windows chatter with each quick drumroll.

Gil Nash freezes whiter than the white roads to Aurore, whiter than the white roofs of Sybernal, whiter than the snows of winter and the sands of Sahara.

Nash's eyes dart toward the clouds.

Martel throws a mental shell around himself, trying to gather all the energy he can, but as he draws he feels the golden bolt descending from the clouds in a blaze.

"Mr. Martel . . . Mr. Martel . . ."

Coldness, wetness . . . water across his face.

"What . . ."

He opens his eyes. He is sprawled on the deck on his back, looking up at the circular charred hole in the roof, and at the gray face of Mrs. Alderson.

He checks himself over, lets his unsteady perceptions review his body. The report is sound. No overt injuries. He sits up, concentrating on keeping everything in focus.

The chair where Nash has been sitting is a heap of ashes.

The one where Martel sat is untouched. There is no sign of the demigod who called himself Nash, nor any remains.

"Thought there weren't any thunderstorms on Aurore, Mrs. Alderson." He sits up.

"There aren't, 'less the gods are involved. You be messing with what you oughtn't, young man?"

Probably, thinks Martel.

"Don't think so, but the fellow I met at the beach may have been."

Martel stands up, uses the back of his hand to wipe the water off his forehead.

The table lies on its side, the beaker next to it. The beer mug, a glassy lump now, is coated with the ashes from the fired chair, and has rolled almost to Martel's feet.

The landlady follows his glances, sees the melted mug, connects it with the ashes of the chair and the hole in the roof, and gasps.

"Called himself Gil Nash. Swam out of the water and asked if he could have a beer. Didn't see any harm in it. He seemed nice enough."

"And that goes to show you, Mr. Martel, what happens on Aurore when strange people arrive from the sea. Like as not he was a ruined demigod trying to escape his just punishment. Lucky as not you're an innocent. Knowing mortals who help the wicked uns, the gods have no mercy on them."

Martel shakes his head slowly. No innocent, just fast enough with an energy screen . . . and yet . . . how long was he unconscious? Certainly long enough for anyone disposed to do him in to do so.

What had Nash said? Tempting him to strike out?

He shakes his head again, more violently. No striking out, period!

"Luck, I guess," he answers the waiting woman. "I'll pay, as soon as I can, for the damage. Not on purpose, but, as you said, I should have known better."

"No, Mr. Martel. How would you know, being new and all? It's not that I'm short on funds. You are, and I should have warned you. Just be a mite bit more careful what strangers you strike up with. Time comes and you'll sense the queer ones."

"I will. Certainly will."

He sweeps the ashes into a bag, where he deposits the lump of glass that had been a mug, and carries the bag out to the recycling pickup next to the coast road below Mrs. Alderson's house. By the time he climbs back up the long steps, she has rearranged the porch furniture and placed another chair next to the table. Except for the hole in the roof and a darker shade of decking where Nash's chair had been, the setting is again as it had been.

Most people, reflects Martel, wouldn't see the difference unless they looked up. And who makes a habit of looking up?

"Thank you again, Mrs. Alderson." The words feel awkward, but he doesn't know what else to say.

"No problem, Mr. Martel. We all have to get used to new places, now, don't we?"

He nods, trying to repress a smile. Some individuals, like Mrs. Alderson, like Rathe Firien, have a down-to-earth friendliness that puts everything in perspective.

Rathe . . . He purses his lips.

"Do you have a directory? For Sybernal?"

"Aye, and so do you. Second drawer, under the vid." She picks up her broom and with quick steps is halfway down the porch steps before he can speak.

"Thank you again. I appreciate, I really do, your understanding."

She smiles.

"Without that, wouldn't be much, would I? But you do be careful, Mr. Martel." She turns, like a sprightly terrier, and marches back down to the main house.

He shakes his head. *Of course, she's right, Martel.*

He does not know if it is his thought or another's. It doesn't matter.

The directory is in the second drawer under the vidfax, and he does find the listing: Firien, R., NW of Sybernal.

His fingers tap out the codes.

There is no answer as the beeps pulse and pulse and pulse.

"Not even an answer slot?" he mumbles.

A check of the instructions reminds him that autoscreens are not available on Aurore.

He tries again, but she is still not there.

Next, he surveys the drawers in the small kitchen, mentally inventorying each utensil.

He taps out the number again, and there is no answer.

He reads the autochef manual, cover to cover, beginning with the installation date stamped inside the front fold and ending with the recipe for time-roasted scampig.

Rather than try her number again, he looks for some cobwebs to dust, but his memory reminds him that Aurore has no spiders, and therefore no cobwebs. He keys Rathe's codes into the limited memory of his faxer, then jerks his hands off the access plate.

Should he have let her go?

No.

Was he going to let her go?

No.

Thinking about it, he smiles. Listening to the soft chittering of birds through the open windows, the muted swash of the sea beyond the hill, and, feeling the sharp edge of the salt air, he smiles.

X

▼

The receive channel on the relay ship opens for nanounits.

The monitor blinks green, signifying that the relay has been completed.

The Brother at the controls touches one plate, a stud, begins the quick sequence to take the ship into underspace to wait for the next transmission.

Once the small ship is underspace, he stabilizes the controls, touches the replay stud, and waits for the equipment to return the message to real time.

The image on the screen is that of Brother Geidren, current domni of the Council.

"By order of the Council, all Brothers and Sisters of the Order are hereby requested to give their full prayers to the Congregation of the Fallen One, in accordance with the Writ of Perception.

"Though all will not be accomplished that might, though the hours of the very stars are numbered, still we persevere until each is weighed and numbered."

The screen blanks.

The Brother frowns.

Like all Brotherhood quicksends, it has a double message, and for the first time in many years, he does not understand the logic behind the second message.

In effect, the Brotherhood is being disbanded, being told to join and fully support the Church of the Fallen God while continuing the basic goals of the Brotherhood.

The relay pilot pinches his fat lips together.

The command releases the ship to him, for whatever purpose, and the same effect apparently will take place throughout the Brotherhood.

He rechecks the authentications, and taps a query into the

sender. The whole idea of the message is absurd. There will always be a Brotherhood, Empire or no Empire.

To go underground even more thoroughly has been expected since the ejection from the Empire, but to join such an offbeat group of lunatics as the Church of the Fallen One?

He readies his ship for the real-space transfer to send his query.

xi

▼

CASTCENTER—a simple bronzed plaque over the portal.

Martel steps through.

The foyer on the inside is small. Indirect yellowed lighting combines with the brown plasteel to convey a clean dinginess. The entry console is vacant, as are the two armless chairs across from it.

Martel sits down, lets his perceptions range through the small building.

There are, from what he can tell with a quick scan, three studios, several smaller rooms, four or five offices, a larger screening room, plus fresher facilities, editing rooms, and the reception area.

He picks up three people in the entire circular building. One engineer, one caster, and one administrator. A man and two women.

The administrator, female, is walking down the corridor toward Martel.

Martel stands up.

"You must be Martel. Certainly took your time in getting here."

He frowns. He is reporting eight weeks earlier than he has to.

"Does everyone report early?"

"I forgot." The woman smirks. "You had adjustment problems." She has sandy hair, cropped straight at chin level, and bangs that are trimmed squarely above her eyebrows. The washed-out gray of her eyes matches the gray tunic and trousers she wears.

Martel wonders about her obnoxiousness, but answers evenly. "That's right. I had adjustment problems. But I'm here and ready to work."

She slouches into the lounger behind the console.

"Aren't you the chiever-beaver. Just like that."

Martel waits.

"Sit down. Sit down. Farell's on the board, will be for the next two stans. Few comments from KarNews on the in-feed. That's about it. That's all it ever is, except for the specs and the logos, the gossip pieces, the once-in-a-god-year storm warning. Feed the touries their home-planet news. We handle Karnak."

Karnak? The one fax outlet on Aurore handling Karnak, and that's where the Brotherhood has placed him? He files the point for reference, and turns his attention to the woman.

Her eyes are bright. Too bright. Cernadine. Do the demigods allow addiction?

Why not? So long as it doesn't impair performance or hurt anyone else. Cernadine is safe and available. And explains the washed-out look in her eyes.

"Fine. Farell's on the board. You are . . . ?"

"Hollie Devero, at your service, Masterfaxer Martel." Her mouth quirks upward even farther, then twitches into a thin line before she continues. "And how did a Regent's Scholar with a masterfax rating end up on Aurore, the punkhead of faxing?"

"You seem to know all the answers. Since I'm not sure, you tell me."

"You're right. I do know full feed on you, Marty Martel. How you actually put a little love into a greeter's life, and how you really like to take long walks alone on the sands, and how you avoid people. And how the first things you bought were black tunics and trousers. And you had to special-order them!" She laughs and the sound is brittle.

Martel bites his lip. No one should be greeted like this! No one!

"Then you know why I'm here."

Her voice loses its edge. "No. I don't. First new faxer in ten standard years, first one not even a Guild prentice, and the Guild approves you . . . and no record marks."

Martel probes at the fringes of her thoughts, gently, uncertain how cernadine affects her sensitivity, unsure how sensitive she is.

. . . say that? . . . Did I . . . what . . . Martel . . . the one . . .

Her curiosity is building against the damping waves of the cernadine, but Martel senses she does not know what she has just said. How? Why?

Someone else is walking down the corridor from control area—the engineer.

Danger. Danger! *Danger!* DANGER!

Martel strikes, lets his mind go in a blast of energy, lashing at the man in a way he only half believes.

"Gods! *No!* . . ." The scream from inside and outside Hollie Devero catches at the edge of his attack, and he holds back the darkness . . . finds himself staring from a slumped position against Hollie's console at a man lying facedown, antique slug-thrower gripped in his hand.

Martel knows the man is dying or dead. Maybe.

"You . . . you killed him . . ." Tears, real tears, tears not from the cernadine, well from the corners of her eyes.

Even from under the blanket of the drug, he feels the grief, her ties to the dying man.

Can he do anything? Has he done too much?

Martel sends his perceptions out, touches the heart, adds strength to the beat, oxygen, repairs a torn artery, a stripped vein, and, standing back in his mind and watching himself do the miraculous, finishes by rebuilding a damaged nerve chain.

His knees wobble as he staggers up and over toward the now-unconscious man. His vision blurs momentarily as he bends to pick the slugger from a flaccid hand. He removes the shells and drops the empty weapon on the console.

"You . . . owe . . . me . . . one . . . Hollie."

He sits down heavily, concentrating on breathing for himself. Half watches the woman as she kneels beside her lover.

"I thought you'd killed him."

"No." *I did, but I undid it, and flamed if I know how.*

"Why?"

"Why, yourself? Why did"—and he picks the name out of her thoughts—"Gates want to kill me? Given the demi-gods, maybe you owe me two."

Her eyes widen. Her face crumples, gray to match her washed-out eyes. "Why? Why? Why?"

Martel echoes her thoughts silently, blocking them as well.

Gates Devero had been primed to explode as soon as one Martel, faxcaster, student, Brother, showed up at the Cast-Center. But the attempt had been direct. Too direct.

Gates was supposed to fail. That meant Martel had been set up to kill the engineer, which meant . . . Martel shivered.

He remembers something Rathe said.

"The gods are jealous, Martel. Jealous."

"Jealous" seems an understatement.

Martel finally answers the question Hollie asked. "Because he was supposed to fail, Hollie, because he was supposed to fail."

"Oh, gods, no! Why us?"

"Not you. Me. Don't worry. You're safe. So's Gates. A second time would be too obvious." *For now.*

"Second time?"

"Forget it. Just tell Gates he tripped."

Martel lurches to his feet, knees solid at last, picks the weapon off the console, and drops it into a pocket.

"Tripped?"

"Got any better ideas, smart lady?" His voice burns, and the anger in it turns the gray-faced administrator grayer.

"But the gods . . ."

Martel swallows, hard. Only the thoughts count.

"Gates tripped, Hollie. That's all that happened."

And with that his thoughts follow, changing the pictures in her mind, then in Gates'. Both would remember that Gates tripped.

Martel is sure that the gods will know that the memories are false, should they check, but what really happened is erased, gone, except in his own mind.

"In answer to your other question," he goes on as if nothing has occurred, "I'm here—"

"I don't need to know. I don't want to know."

"—because I was Queried by the Emperor and the Grand Duke of Kirsten."

Hollie turns her head from side to side, slowly, still on her knees by Gates.

"And the only ambition I have is to get paid for being a faxer while I sort things out."

He looks at the time readout. Almost a full stan has passed since he walked into the CastCenter.

One stan? One whole stan?

He tightens his lips. Apparently his mental excursion into the physiology of one Gates Devero has taken longer than he has realized.

"You'd better help Gates up," he suggests mildly as he lets the engineer wake and groan. "By the way, am I expected to follow Farell?"

"No. She'll brief you, give you a handful of procedures, and walk you through. Double duty for her. Double pay. Doesn't happen enough. So she won't mind."

Martel can tell her thoughts are on Gates, her genuine

worry about the fall he has taken. Martel heads down the corridor toward the control center.

He scans Farell from outside the control room.

She is dark-haired, from her own mental image relaxed, and, so far as he can tell, untrapped.

He waits until she finishes the locals and is into the KarNews feed before opening the portal.

"Martin Martel," he announces quietly.

"Swear I'd locked that."

He looks vacant.

"Guess not." She gives him a half-smile, accented by naturally red lips. "You're Giles' replacement. Our new wunderkind from Karnak."

"Green from Karnak," he admits, "and so far as faxing goes, green as gold. Lots of ratings, a few degrees, and no more than the minimum uncontrolled airtime."

"No illusions, at least." She gives a fuller smile.

Her arm sweeps the circular room. "This is it. All older than you or me. Just a reader-feeder op, with enough of us in it to assure the touries that they're seeing real, live people before they get the latest from home."

The control center is clean, and from his mental runover Martel knows that the equipment all works, everything except a disassembled line feed on the end of the counter where the portable faxers are lined up.

"By the time, I'm Marta Farell. You ready to start, or is this just social?"

"Ready to start. But let me get a few things straight before we start on technicals."

Martel gestures at the old but clean equipment around them.

"From what you just said, there's no local base to the operation. No, if you will, native support. Who foots the bill?"

Marta pushes a loose strand of hair off her forehead, carefully pats it back into place.

"Not much of a bill, really. We don't have any of the extras here. No image enhancers, no multijection feeds, no strictly outside faxers. We all do the outside work. Not really news usually, but the froth." She shrugs. "Learn a lot about the basics here. That's all we've got."

"So it's a small bill. But who pays it?" Martel resists the urge to snap. Like everyone else Marta Farell seems to avoid straight answers.

"You do. Partly. The rest is from fees and donations."

"Me? Fees?"

"Wait . . ."

Farell eases into the focal seat, uses the finger-touch controls, and settles herself into a position as the holo scanners focus on her.

"That's the stan update from Karnak. I'm Marta Farell with CastCenter . . . official fax outlet for KarNews on Aurore. At the chime, stan time will be fourteen-thirty, Aurore Standard, Imperial Central, Karnak Regent.

"Next we'll be taking you with Gates Devero on a tour of the eastern beaches, and a look at a few out-of-the-way spots you may have missed."

Martel admires the way she slips into the local feed. He wonders if the Devero slot is a repeat.

"Repeat?"

"Right. Geared on the Karnak tourie. Run it twice a bloc month. Once you get the feel of things you'll be out there as well. Interests?"

"Not using my full name," slips out before he thinks. *Flame! Why did you say that?*

Marta Farell only nods. "You a drinker, adventurer, a shopper, anything like that? Rockgrubber or sailor?"

"Loner, I guess. Would a slot on places to really escape fly, really fly?"

"Martel, we got more stans to fill than you dream, and you're only the fifth faxer for a round-the-clock operation. Even an extra half-stan slot a week would help."

"And who pays the bills . . ."

"If you're that persistent about faxing, half my problems will be solved. All right. There's a standard ten percent deduction from all pay on Aurore. To pay for services. And we're a service. About one-tenth of one tiny percent goes to the four faxcenters. Mostly for power costs. The fees are from docuslots. The one that's running now was picked up by both KarNews and the MatNet on Halston.

"One of mine ran prime on Tinhorn. You never know. We back-feed regularly, and sometimes they catch. You get two percent commission on the back-feed sales."

"What's the rate?" Martel doesn't have the faintest idea of what the majors would pay for a backwater documentary.

"Average is maybe a hundred thousand credits a quarter-stan."

Martel figures. The faxer would get two thousand Imperial credits for each quarter-stan, or four thousand for a standard half-stan bloc. Two full blocs equaled his annual contract. There had to be a catch.

"How many have you had picked up?"

"In the past ten years, I've averaged three full blocs a year. That's the problem." Farell turns in the seat, waiting as if to see whether he can solve the puzzle.

He spreads his hands, admitting his bewilderment.

"Really good faxcaster can buy out his contract in five years, with enough left for first-class passage anywhere. But you've got to be good, because we can't doctor the tape. Edit, yes, but no image enhancement, viewpoint real-terations, threshold emotionals, none of the fancy techniques they taught you at the Institute."

"Why not?" *Stupid question, Martel!*

Farell looks around the studio.

"With what? We've got two portaunits that are up, and one that sometimes works." She catches her breath and plunges into the next sentence, again unconsciously patting a stray hair back into place. "The reason why we don't have the latest equipment is that the Empire doesn't send it. We buy second-, third-hand. Besides, I doubt that propafax is wanted on Aurore. You'll notice that our relay doesn't carry the emotional bands."

Martel wants to ask why, but Marta Farell doesn't pause.

"Don't ask. Just say it's not wanted."

"Stet." It isn't all right, but what can he say? "Why don't the majors send their own teams?"

"Expensive. Fuel costs once you break sub are twice any other planet in the Empire. Second, let's just say that outside fax teams aren't exactly welcome."

"Sort of like Imperial agents aren't welcome?" Martel asks with a grin.

"Yes. Not something I'd advise smiling about."

Martel frowns, turns toward the monitor, rubs his forehead with the middle three fingers on his right hand. He senses the hostility his last remark has triggered.

Why? Awfully sensitive. Just take over the shift and let her go. Right? Wrong. You don't even know the feed parameters.

"Is there a center manual and a set of engineering specs I could study?" he offers.

The woman does not answer, walks over to the console, and pulls out two discs.

"Here. Why don't you use the vidfax in the lounge, second port on the right as you leave. Ought to be able to go through those in a stan or two. Then I'll check you out on the system."

Martel feels her relief, but does not go into her thoughts to double-check.

The control lock snicks into place as he steps out.

There! Her thought is as clear as if she had spoken.

Martel smiles. The lock had been engaged when he entered.

Gates Devero, recumbent in a recliner, nods at Martel as he enters the blue-paneled lounge.

"Martel . . . sorry I was so clumsy when you came in. Don't know what came over me. Really upset Hollie."

The younger man scans the room.

Gates picks up the inquiring glance and answers. "She's left. Be back later. Getting me a coldpak for this flamed bruise."

The cheek below Devero's right eye shows the beginning of a dark blotch.

"I hope it wasn't my fault, being later than you expected."

"No. Need another faxer. Understand your problem. You also carry a second-tech cert?"

"Right."

"Good. We're only a Beta Class. Means you can handle swings by yourself, long as I'm on call. Better for everyone."

"Fine with me, once I know what's where." Martel lifts the discs thrust on him by Marta Farell. "Where's the console?"

"Corner."

Martel spots it before the engineer finishes his directions.

"Not much," Gates adds. "Dates from the First Republic."

Martel's mouth drops open. That would make the unit more than an antique. More like a museum piece.

"Not really." Gates smiles. "Just what it feels like. Older than anything else in the station. About a century old, if you don't count all the replacements. And don't believe everything I say . . ."

Martel shakes his head, not fully listening to the engineer's patter, trying to remind himself to doubt things, not to be so flamed accepting.

". . . more than one way to do a story, make it good without all the fancy gear those Imperial automatons deck themselves with. Hades! Done better stories myself. So's Hollie. We can't hold a pinlight to Farell or Boster. Probably not to you, if what the record says is true. Even half true."

"Don't believe all the records, either." Martel forces a laugh. "I've had all the courses, but no experience."

"You'll get that quick here. Another thing those big flames on Karnak don't understand. Go there and hold faxers' disc-cases five years before you get a three-clip slot on your own. Farell'll have you out doing half-stan slots in days. 'Course, she won't use it all. Rip you pretty good. But you'll learn."

Another voice, Hollie Devero's, breaks in.

"She already has you out of the control center?" Her tone is pleasant.

Martel automatically lets his perceptions check her over, but her pleasantness is genuine, as if her "forgetfullness" has taken fully. He hopes so.

"Not exactly. She suggested that I learn the rules, procedures, and schematics."

"Funny, she is," Gates comments. "Good editor, good teacher. Has to be, to get a dumb engineer like me to run sub. But sure doesn't want anyone in with her when it's hot. In the other studio, the one she uses to train, another story." He shrugs. "All got problems. What's yours, Martel?"

Martel returns the shrug. "I suppose my biggest problem is that the Regent and the Grand Duke Kirsten don't like me."

Gates claps his hands. "Bravo! A step ahead. Don't like most of us till *after* we get here. Why? Offend the Imperial pride? Student prank?"

Martel fingers his chin before answering. "It has something to do with the Grand Duke's daughter."

"The goddesses will love you!" roars Gates Devero, breaking the laugh off sharply to touch his bruised cheek.

"I didn't know he had a daughter. I'm sure he doesn't. Not one old enough, or young enough, for Martel." Hollie's voice conveys absolute certainty.

"But I went to the Institute with her," protests Martel. "And why would the Duke . . . and why all the body-guards . . ."

Hollie shakes her head once. "I know what I know. There was no sign of a daughter ten years ago."

"But the Duke wouldn't chase me, Query me, and the

Brotherhood wouldn't—" Martel breaks off, realizing his gaffe in referring to the Brotherhood, but neither seems to care, and the reference only succeeds in increasing Hollie's confusion.

"Maybe he had her hidden away. Maybe . . . well, the Duchess wasn't much for children."

"She went to school in New Augusta. Didn't come back until my second year at the Institute. That's when I met her."

"How long ago?" asks the woman.

"About five years, I'd guess. You see, I only saw her in the corridors at first. I wondered who had the bodyguard with the matching colors. But it wasn't until the middle of my third year that we had a class together or I ever talked to her. Dr. Dorlan warned me about her father, but I never really did much except talk to her."

I'll bet! The thought from Gates takes Martel off guard.

"But she seemed to like you?" asks Hollie.

"I thought so."

Gates shakes his head. "That's more than enough, Martel. The Dukes don't like Regent's Scholars until *after* they're rich or powerful. In this Empire, you don't marry into money."

"Especially with a mother like the Duchess," adds Hollie. *Especially her!* The thought has a trace of bitterness, and a touch of nostalgia, but the deepest feeling is repugnance.

Martel closes his eyes, trying to sort things out. Hollie was convinced that there is no Kryn, no daughter of the Grand Duke, and the strength of her feelings and even her surface thoughts show she knows something she is not telling and does not want to tell about the Duke. The depth of those feelings, which his perceptions can only sense generally, also tells Martel that she has buried those memories from herself, and especially from Gates.

"Kryn didn't seem to care much for her mother," Martel temporizes.

"That must be it. Still . . . well, the Duke would act like that if he cared enough." *Which he didn't always.* She waits a moment, then lifts her head. "Before you start studying all those discs from Marta, I have some forms for you to authorize. We need to report that you've started work."

Martel nods. The less he says the better.

Hollie Devero marches out through the portal, expecting Martel to follow.

Gates gives a half-wave, and Martel returns the gesture before hurrying after Hollie. As far as he can tell, their false memories have stuck.

Now all he has to do is learn how to be a decent faxer, if he can avoid being distracted by all the contradictions that keep popping up.

xii

▼

Despite the multiplicity of the theories regarding the "seeding" of the known Galaxy with so-called *Homo sapiens,* no satisfactory explanation exists which can adequately describe why so many human and humanoid cultures apparently began at the same absolute point in time, or why a number of humanoid remnants have been discovered on habitable planets with no evolutionary train which would have led to such beings.

With centuries of concentrated archeology behind us, we have yet to discover any real traces, besides the so-called fleet anomalies, of a star-spanning civilization which predates our own. Yet the odds of two separately evolved humanoid races possessing genetic compatibility, let alone the hundreds with absolute interlockability, and the other handful which are

close enough for sterile crossbreeding, are prohibitive. . . .
One might as well leave it to the "will of God" as attempt any
rational scientific explanation at this time. . . .

—*Essays*
Fr. Adis SterHillion
New Augusta, 2976

xiii

▼

Martel watches the monitor of the direct feed from Karnak.
The feed is a wasteout, and is displayed on the aux screen,
because it features a ballad singer. A redisc of Gates Devero
is the actual on-air program.

Martel has seen Gates' tape twice, and three times would
be too much. So he watches the unused feed from Karnak.

Unusual as it is for him, he is tired, with another five stans
left on his shift.

The singer, a young man with kinky black hair, pointed
mustache, and a fluorescent green bodysuit, warbles the
words in a false tenor, thin but true. The song was old, Martel knew, a variant on words that predated the First Republic, which had predated the Empire by a good millennium.

> . . . *and where have all the poor men gone,*
>   *Gone to slavers, every one.*
> *Ah, where will they ever turn, where will they ever*
>   *turn?*

Good Question. Where have all the poor men gone?

On Karnak, the answer was simple enough. Gone to the
sewers, the Brotherhood, before it was driven underground
and off-Empire, or gone to the wellhouses.

The Fuards make their poor cannon fodder. Who knows about the Matriarchy?

Martel leans forward in the swivel to check the remaining run time against I.D. schedule. He wants to have everything ready, because he will have to give the I.D., with a cube scene of the ocean, voiced over, before switching to the upcoming news feed from Karnak.

"The poor ye shall always have."

Wasn't that the antique quote? What about the poor on Aurore? Couldn't be as many, not with the nearly mandatory work ethic Rathe had pointed out.

He smiles.

Strong-willed lady.

She knows more than he does. Even so, he has to discount all the hints that he is much more than a bright faxer with a bit of esp. More than that . . . absurd.

Is it? Really? He pushes away the nagging question, decides to think about the poor.

But he doesn't have the time, yet. With the units flicking off the downcount, he touches the feedmesh and begins to fade over the scene-cube.

"CastCenter of Aurore. Path station from Sybernal. Gate Seven."

He drops his vocal an octave, easy enough for those with the right relaxation techniques, and begins the scene logo fade to prep the newsline.

"Straight from Karnak, Imperial Regency News Central, comes the latest update. From Gate Seven, here's Fax Central."

As he completes his last word he switches to the outstation signal, an eight-frame of the Fax Central logo, and from that to the mainline cut, featuring the slim figure of Werl K'rio, silver-voiced and silver-clad.

"Brief power failure at the Regent's Palace . . . described as not serious. Concerns that the Grand Duchess is failing . . . and a dedication."

Martel takes himself fully off-line, but continues to watch the story on the power outage at the Regent's Palace. No one could explain the failure of both the main and backup systems, and the outage lasted nearly a full stan. No details were forthcoming. A Regency spokesman dismissed the occurrence as "a freak happening." Rumors of a strange appearance coincident with the blackout were dismissed by the Major Door-keeper as "absurd."

Have to wonder what was behind a power outage in the palace. What ambitious officer suffered an unfortunate accident? Or "perished" in protecting the Prince Regent?

Someday, the mere tradition of the Prince Regent wouldn't be enough. Someday, someone like the Grand Duke would succeed.

Wonder what that will do to the Empire? And Karnak? And Kryn?

He shies away from the thought of her, grasps at the earlier questions, the one of the poor on Aurore.

Had he ever seen any?

He concentrates, trying to drag up memories of shabby clothes, a beggar on a corner, unshaven faces outside a crowd of touries or happy norms.

Martel squints, looking through his console, but cannot drag up that kind of image.

But there have to be poor on Aurore. Have to be!

Where else would they be? Where would they be hidden away? Or is Aurore so prosperous or so conditioned that none are in need?

Ding! The warning chime interrupts his mental search, reminding him that he has to go local.

First, the I.D. and the logo. He'd dragged an old one from the cube library, featuring a woman who could have passed for a goddess—golden hair and golden eyes, and a voice that could have sold freezers on the poles of Tinhorn. The phrasing wasn't current, but complied with the stat requirements. The date on the cube made it over forty stans since it had been used last, but Martel's tests showed it was technically acceptable. Besides, it would be a nice change from the scenery that Marta Farell used.

She'd said he could use whatever he wanted from the library, provided it wasn't sealed. Not that anyone would notice, not on his shift.

Despite the eternal daylight of Aurore, most of the norms and all of the tourists stayed with standard Karnak time, which meant that Martel's shift ran through their "night." Most faxviewers were touries, with a few norms.

Martel wonders if he is a norm or a native. No one had ever described the difference, except Hollie Devero.

"Natives understand Aurore, live with it. Norms don't. That makes Gates a native, and me a norm." That was what she'd said, and it was all anyone had said to Martel, including Rathe.

He refocused on the board in front of him, matching the frame counts, then precisely plugging in the I.D. cube.

"The CastCenter of Aurore. Gate Seven. From Sybernal and for your information and your pleasure."

Even after forty standard years of storage, the cube fires a bolt, and then some.

Martel wonders who she was, whether she will see the cube and not recognize the woman she once was. But his fingers are busy. As he feels the gut-level impact of the face and voice, he is already triggering the next program.

Again he matches the frame count to perfection as he brings the title logo of the holodrama on line.

A "romantic and escapist" plot, the summary had indicated, called *Yesterday, the Stars,* the drama featured a junior cruiser commander in the Imperial Fleet forced to choose between his career, which he loves, and a young Duchess, the woman he loves.

The cube was on the list Marta had suggested as suitable for his time slot. For now, he was relying heavily on her guidance. Sooner or later, he'd have to strike out on his own, he supposed.

Martel sets the warning chime and eases himself out of the control chair to head for the index for the station cube files. He hopes to find some more interesting I.D. spots, or some standard dramas that hadn't been faxed to gray oblivion.

Buzz!

The incoming fax line was lit, for the first time since he'd been doing night shifts.

He leans over the console and taps the accept stud.

"CastCenter."

The screen remains black, only the green light beneath blinking to indicate the caller remains on the circuit.

"May I help you?" he tries again.

"Do not show HER again. This time it is ignorance. Next time will indeed be blasphemy." The low voice sounds feminine.

"What?"

The red light blinks that the connection has been broken.

Martel touches the stud, frowning.

Strange. Most strange.

Buzz!

Two in the same night? Incredible, when for months no one has faxed at all.

He accepts the second call more tentatively.

The caller is Marta Farell, disheveled hair pushed back off her forehead, a robe thrown around her shoulders, and close up to the screen, as if to block off the view into the rest of the room.

Is there a faint golden glow visible over her shoulder? Martel wonders why anyone would need artificial light.

He keeps his smile to himself. At least in private Marta is human, and in the hurriedly thrown-on robe, she even looks desirable.

"That I.D., Martel? Has anyone faxed?"

How did she know?

"Uh . . . yes. Blind. Said if I ran it again, it would be—"

"Blasphemy," she finishes.

"Right."

"That one's not sealed. Gates ran the other one like it once a couple of years ago, and the same thing happened. I didn't know we had another. Don't run it again. Or any other one that has Her on it.

"Her?"

"I think it was the Goddess in one of Her lighter moods. She probably wouldn't mind, but Her followers certainly do. I'll talk to you about it tomorrow."

As she reaches down to sign off, her eyes flicker to the side, and the robe parts slightly, enough to show that she had indeed thrown it on hurriedly.

Strange. Why would Marta interrupt what she was obviously enjoying to warn you? The Goddess? What goddess? Ridiculous.

"You're saying words like that too much." His words echo in the empty control room.

Obviously, some people take the god and goddess business seriously. Very seriously.

He looks down at the small vidfax unit, but the amber light stays amber. No more calls.

The poor? What about the poor? Do we always have them? And what does that have to do with "Her"?

Just as he thinks he is learning something, another series of questions pops up.

He pushes the poor out of his mind, and turns back to the index to see what else features the golden woman and to find another I.D., hopefully one that won't be classified as blasphemy by one cult or another.

xiv

▼

The sand is warm, even without the directness of sunlight, and Martel turns over onto his stomach.

Rathe lies facedown, her head on a small towel, her toes pointed at the thin line of foam where the wavelets break on the golden sands of the beach. She is relaxed, nearly asleep.

Martel frowns, unable to forget the incident with the logo cube.

Something about the goddess is familiar, but he cannot put his finger on it.

Should you tell Rathe?

He shakes his head and stretches, letting his weight sink farther into the clinging sand. He places his right arm across the middle of Rathe's back, just below her shoulder blades, and squeezes her gently.

She turns her head on the towel and looks at him from sleepy eyes.

"You had the late shift, and I'm sleepy. How come?"

He shrugs, then grins as he realizes how meaningless the gesture is from someone lying on his stomach and half buried in sand.

"Don't know. Guess I'm still trying to get used to this place."

He squeezes her again, and she squirms the few centimeters necessary toward him until their bare legs touch.

"It's so peaceful here."

"Thanks to you," he answers. "If you hadn't found the cottage . . ."

"But you chose it."

He does not answer, but squeezes her again, then closes his eyes, trying to let himself relax.

When he wakes, Rathe is sitting cross-legged and spreading food from the basket she has brought.

"You finally hungry, sleepyhead?"

"Sleepyhead? You fell asleep first."

He props his chin up with both hands and grins at her.

Rathe uses her left hand to tousle his short and curly black hair. Then she smooths the cloth on which she sits and gestures to the space across from her, palm upward.

"Would you care to join me?"

"I'd be honored."

First, he stands and brushes the clinging sand from his legs and arms. He sits across from her, his legs to one side, for he has never been comfortable in trying to sit cross-legged, and takes her left hand and touches his lips to it.

"You're so gallant." She pauses. "However, I am—"

"Hungry," he finishes.

Not only is there Springfire, for him, but an assortment of cheeses, genuine wheat crackers, and two corm-apples.

Martel strokes her calf, finishes by squeezing her knee gently, and then picks up the beaker of Springfire.

"You have excellent taste."

"For you, anything."

She is so warm, so unlike . . . Kryn . . . the golden goddess. . . . Why does the goddess bother you, Martel?

Martel holds back his frown and takes another sip of the Springfire as Rathe picks up one of the corm-apples and begins to cut it into slices.

Before too long he will have to leave for the CastCenter, but he pushes the thought away.

XV

▼

"And now, straight from Karnak, the day's wrap-up with Lorel Littul."

Snap. Tap. Tap. *Ease the pressure up, and fade out.* Martel's fingers dance across the board as the in-feed from Karnak blankets Aurore, letting the touries and the norms know how little had really happened with the Regency the day before.

Outside the control room someone waits. Farell.

Martel touches the stud that breaks the lock circuit, although as the fax manager and senior faxer, Marta Farell certainly could override the circuits at any time.

"Greetings," he offers.

"Same to you, Martel. Have you thought about a cube project?"

She sits on one of the low ledges beneath the storage lockers.

"Hmm. I've thought about several. I guess I'm not too thrilled about any of the ideas. Every travelogue I could think of has been done, except maybe something on all of the out-of-the-way beaches—the unique ones—like the hidden sands under the White Cliffs, that sort of thing."

"Sands under the White Cliffs? I didn't know there were any." She laughs, easily, and for an instant the tightness that usually surrounds her is gone. "That might be interesting. What else?"

"People stories are always interesting. But outside of the gods, what people do here has so much less intrigue, so much less danger or strangeness, than on Karnak, or Tinhorn. People sail the seas, but the winds are so even that it's tame. We have no safaris, no treks across sandy deserts . . . are there even any deserts?" He waits, trying to provoke a reaction.

Marta Farell stays within the tight shell of her professionalism, within the barriers that say "Do not touch!" to Martel, even without his mental probing.

The quiet hum of the tie receiver is the only sound in the control center.

Martel scans the monitors, the feed time remaining, before shifting his eyes back to Farell.

"The unknown-beaches bit is a good long-term subject. The settings have to be perfect," she comments, as if no time had passed since his last question.

Martel nods, understanding what she is driving at. Off-worlders are treated to exotic fax scenes every day. So his beach story will have to be not only spectacular, but artistic as well, as artistry takes time. If it works, the royalties will be substantial, and deserved.

"You're right about the human-interest angle, too," adds Farell, "but you've sealed the problem."

"Of course," Martel slips in, "there are always the gods."

"Not if you value your continued existence. And whether you do or not, remember that the gods may just decide to wipe out anyone who approves or contributes to a slot they didn't like. So forget it. Now."

Martel ignores the edge in Farell's voice, at the same time wondering.

Jumpy about the gods. Why? What has she done? Another hidden story like Rathe's?

He debates a gentle probe, then backs off. *What right do you have to dig into people's thoughts? No better than these so-called gods if you do.*

"What about something the gods favor?" he pushes.

"Anything concerned with the gods is dangerous!"

"No. There have to be things they like."

"Name one."

"What about the postulant communities? Not on candidates or demigods or priests or priestesses," he adds hurriedly, "but just on the community life, habits, what have you."

"I don't know, Martel."

"There's nothing in any of the back indexes on them, and there's nothing remotely resembling the subject on any of the closed lists."

"Look. You don't really know what you're talking about. Hasn't your lady friend, or someone, convinced you that meddling with the gods is dangerous? Especially dangerous for someone like you."

Here we go again. Someone like you.

"Would you care to explain that?" Two black glittermotes pop into view above his left shoulder as he stands abruptly.

Farell does not change position, but seems to withdraw against the storage lockers. Shrinks further into herself, and does not speak.

"Everyone seems to think I'm different. And every time I question something, people back away. But they still don't answer. Except to tell me not to question, not to challenge. So answer that, Farell. If I'm more than the simple esper I think I am, what makes me so? Why does everyone think so? And what difference does it make? If the so-called gods are so flamed powerful and if I'm such a threat . . . Flame! It doesn't make sense. If I'm a threat, then they're not really that powerful. And if they're so almighty, then I'm no real threat. So answer that, Farell!"

Martel can feel the thin edge within him, the one that separates him from the darkness beneath, blurring as the now-familiar tide of inner darkness rises.

Suddenly he can see the two women that Marta Farell is. The first is a small, frightened girl, protected by a shell of professional competence. The second, not nearly so clear in focus, might better be called . . . but Martel can find no words, no concepts. For the hidden Farell has a trace of wantonness, a trace of tomboyishness, an abiding warmth . . .

. . . and in the confusion, the dark side of his own self ebbs, and he wonders why he is standing and shouting, and why Marta Farell is merely waiting. And he laughs.

"For an instant, I really got carried away. I'm sorry." He

takes one step toward her, stops as he sees her shrink away. Instead, he turns and reseats himself in the console chair.

"Guess I got a little overwrought, a little carried away. Don't really understand why."

She shifts her weight, finally faces him head on.

"Because you don't understand Them, and you won't really face what you are. And no one else can afford to help you out. The costs could be far too high. I know. I know. That's why I agreed you could work here. But even I didn't—" her voice breaks off, but Martel catches the last words as unspoken thoughts, *expect this.*

Martel shakes his head. Every answer creates more questions. He decides to return to the original discussion.

"What about a slot on the postulant communities?"

"Do you really understand how dangerous it is?" Her quiet voice has a touch of resignation, desperation.

"No. But I'd like to try."

"That's obvious. If it goes right, you gain nothing. And if it goes wrong, a lot of people will suffer besides you."

Farell flips her thin legs and hips off the low ledge and alights lightly in front of the console. "But I doubt that will stop you. And, at this point, I'm not going to try to save you from yourself any longer." Her voice drops. "Martel, please be careful."

She is out the port before he can answer.

He rechecks the feed time, sets himself for the break and the return to local control.

What was that all about? Careful about what?

He shakes his head again.

A story on the postulant communities can give him a better insight into the gods, into how much real control they have, into their powers, and into the fears that everyone seems to have buried within.

We'll see, he promises.

That's right, the answer comes, but Martel cannot say whether the second thought is his or another's.

xvi

▼

Martel peers through the peephole, although he does not need to. Gates is busy with the equipment in the off-line studio. Marta Farell is on the board in the prime studio. While the prime studio portal is locked and that peephole closed, the mental static announces her presence.

Martel shakes his head and tramps back down the narrow corridor to the lounge. He wants to run through some of the older I.D.'s, either to get some idea for new ones or to see if any appeal to him for his own programs.

"You could use the fax console in the lounge." His words are not addressed to anyone, since Hollie is busy in the front area, and the other two faxers, Dlores and Morgan, are out working on their own documentary projects.

The lounge console is serviceable, but without projecting the images full-length into the room, he will not be able to determine the technical quality of the cubes he wants to review.

Still . . . what choice is there?

His decision made, he pulls the index cube and places it in the console. He can use the screen for the first part, at least.

About half the cubes are listed as technically deficient. Four have been deleted from the records, and only a faint hesitation marks their former existence. Since the index is merely a record, he wonders why all reference to those four was removed.

From the entire cube, only six seem interesting from the three-line descriptions. Martel notes the key numbers in the console memory and returns the index to storage.

"You work too hard. It won't do a bit of good."

Hollie Devero stands inside the portal, wearing a mint-green one-piece coverall. She is too thin to carry off an out-

fit that severe, and the brightness of her eyes, reflecting all
too obviously her cernadine habit, accentuates her angular-
ity and the plainness of the coverall.

"Just trying to get a handle on what I'm supposed to be
doing."

"You're not due in until the late swing, and it's barely
twelve hundred."

Martel flicks off the screen. This is the first time Hollie
has seemed friendly, and making an approach of sorts, yet.
He swivels in the chair to face her, gestures to the vacant seat
across from him.

"Thank you."

Wonder what she is thinking.

He touches the edge of her thoughts, recoils at the turmoil.

Is that the cernadine?

"Why do you take so much cernadine?" he blurts out, off
his guard from the mental confusion he has touched.

"If you're going . . . Flame! Try to be civil, Martel! Flame
you anyway!"

She has not seated herself. Rather, she draws back and
puts both hands on the top of the chair. She leans forward.
Martel smells the sour spice of the drug on her breath.

He tilts back, trying not to seem too obvious.

"Sorry. I'm not diplomatic. I don't know what came over
me."

"You're right. You're not diplomatic. Flame! Everyone else
knows. Why should you be any different? I take too much.
Didn't use to. But that's my problem. It's not why I came in
to see you, anyway."

She comes around the chair and plops herself into it, right
across from him, oblivious to the strand of hair dangling in
front of her right eye.

"Marta's afraid of you. I'm not sure why, but you're the
only one she's ever been scared of. That's in the ten years
since we've been stuck here. Why?"

Scared of me? Why?

Martel shrugs, trying to think of an answer.

"Is she? I thought she was very professional."

Hollie leans forward. "Believe me. She's scared of you. So am I, sort of. Except I don't matter."

. . . don't matter to anyone . . . Gates? Martel cannot ignore the stray thought fragment.

He decides to change the subject.

"You've been here ten years. Isn't that a little unusual?"

"Not necessarily. Terms range up to forty-fifty years. Some people like it here." *But not me . . . not here . . . flamed cernadine . . .*

"I didn't realize there were that many long-termers, particularly with such generous contracts. How did you get here, if I could ask . . ."

He would ask! Busybody.

Hollie crosses her arms, sits up squarely.

"That's no secret. Gates supported the Popular Front on Nalia. Did so publicly, and the Regency felt embarrassed and suggested to MatNews that Gates shouldn't be welcome. The Matriarchy agreed. So . . . I came with him." *. . . to this exotic stinkhole.*

The picture is clearer. Gates had somehow gotten tangled with Regency/Matriarchy politics, and Hollie had followed him. Now Hollie is hooked on cernadine, expensive as it is. That means that despite the lucrative possibilities for a first-class faxer on Aurore they'd never be able to leave. Not unless Hollie could kick her habit. Few do, because the addiction feeds on a poor self-image, not only physically but psychologically as well. In a word, cernadine makes the world seem more interesting and imparts an artificial sense of self-esteem to the user.

A clink from down the hallway signals the opening of a studio portal.

"You both from Nalia?"

"No. Herdian."

"But how did you get involved with Nalia?"

"MatNews covers the entire Matriarchy and reports on outsystem news."

" 'Covers' is a good word," interjects Gates from the entryway. "Like a nice warm blanket."

"I'm confused. What did your coverage on Herdian have to do with Nalia?"

"Call it a matter of politics," says Gates dryly.

"Politics?" Martel asks lamely, knowing he should see the pattern Hollie and Gates are weaving.

"You should know," Gates returns with a smile. "From what I hear, you've had a bit of a brush with politics. One of the crew, I gather."

"Well . . . the Grand Duke didn't care much for me, but it wasn't for any great public display of courage." Martel shifts his weight in the chair.

Gates has moved across the lounge to the counter, onto which he levers his blocky body, equidistant from Hollie and Martel.

"Not sure my stand on the Nalian Popular Front reflected courage. Not sure I would have said what I said if I'd realized the consequences. Always easier to be brave when you're dumb."

Hollie disagrees with the tiniest of headshakes.

"Or young," adds Martel. "But why would a comment by a faxer on Herdian upset the Regency enough for the Regent to pressure the Matriarch of Halston to have you removed? Isn't that a bit farfetched?"

"I thought so at first. Of course, Herdian is the closest Matriarchy system to Nalia. Didn't think anyone would mind my comments all that much, though. Who listens to fax comments, anyway? But it turned out that the Matriarchy was behind the Popular Front, and all of a sudden that nearness became more important."

Martel shakes his head. "Wait a stan! Your government had you canned because you publicly endorsed what they were privately supporting?"

"Right. Win some, lose some."

"I still don't understand," protests Martel, half afraid that he does.

"Let's put it another way. The Matriarchy wanted to destabilize the LandRight government, which was backed by the Regency. If they came out directly in support, then the Regency would have had a pretext to act directly against Halston. At that time, and even now, who wants to take on the Empire over a fifth-rate system?"

"I understand the military aspect, but how did that affect you?"

"If the Empire could prove the Matriarchy really was behind the Popular Front, then the Empire would have had the excuse to annex the entire Nalian system as a threat to its security. If they hadn't canned me once the Empire protested, then the Matriarch would be admitting she supported the Popular Front."

Martel shakes his head. Gates is talking about webs within webs as if they were real.

"Still don't understand, do you?" rumbles Gates. "Look. Think of it this way. People never react to what's real. They react to what they want to believe. To what they believe they see or to what they want to see. What's real doesn't matter unless it coincides with their beliefs."

"So the Matriarchy kicked you out because of what they believed, rather than for what you'd done?"

"More complicated than that, but that's basically it."

Martel frowns.

"But why—"

"Martel, do you work at being dense?" snaps Hollie. *Nobody can be that stupid . . . what's he playing at? Why? . . . Questions about the cernadine . . . after what . . . deep agent . . . godpawn?*

Martel spreads his hands helplessly. He has trouble following the flitting shifts in her thoughts, perhaps a result of the cernadine.

"No, he's not," says Gates. "We keep forgetting this is his first job, and right out of the Institute. And his exile was scarcely political." *Good green faxer . . . but is that all?*

"It's all new. Frankly, I've been trying to figure out the gods more than the politics." Martel tries to reinforce Gates' point.

Why do they both suspect you, Martel?

Gates trying to warn me?

Hollie's thought adds to Martel's concerns.

"You want the off-line studio?" asks Gates.

"I did have some prep I was working on."

"Fine. We're off." Gates smiles, but the smile is perfunctory. He slides off the counter, and his boots hit the flooring with a muffled thud.

"But—"

"No problem. No problem," interrupts the older man. "One thing, though. You might consider that everyone plays politics, even gods. You can't escape it." *Wish we could.*

Hollie jerks herself from the chair and follows Gates. Martel gets up from his own seat as the other two exit.

How much you need to learn, Martel. And those who know don't tell.

Martel belatedly realizes that his shields are down, that he still has not learned to keep his mental blocks in place automatically. How long have his thoughts been open to the world?

He shrugs.

Gates is right, you know . . . don't you?

Gates is right. He deserves better than Aurore . . . if he wants it.

Martel sits down again, lets himself go limp, and extends his perceptions.

Hollie and Gates are still in the front entryway. Hollie is shifting the console to full automatic, with the direct in-line straight to the live studio.

Martel power-slips under her conscious thoughts, probes

for the subtle weaknesses that must exist. They do. He inserts an idea, a prohibition, a small compulsion, and what others might call an optimistic feed loop, for want of a better term. The adjustments complete, he withdraws.

Unless he has miscalculated, Hollie Devero will discover over the days and years ahead that she needs less and less cernadine, if any. Hopefully, the gradual nature of the change will let her believe that the change is hers, not his.

He takes a deep breath and climbs back to his feet.

Each time, such extensions of his abilities take less and less effort. Each time, he has a better idea of what to do and how.

Some things, Martel, some things you are learning.

He picks up the cubes he needs and heads for the vacant studio, absently noting that Gates and Hollie have left the CastCenter.

xvii

▼

According to the datacenter, three main religious orders maintain communities and worship centers in the hills above Pamyra—the Apollonites, the Ethenes, and the Taurists. The fourth major order, the Thoradians, has a small mission at Pamyra, but lists no main community anywhere.

Martel frowns.

Even before getting into the fieldwork, he is digging up as many questions as answers. And more questions are bound to follow.

He tabs the numbers into his console, switches the fax from the datalink into the commlink, and begins his contacts.

Father Sanders G'Iobo of the Apollonites says yes, provided Martel faxes only the postulants themselves and the lay community, not the Brothers or sacred aspects.

Sister Artemis Dian agrees, if no facial close-ups or religious scenes are faxed.

Head Taurist Theseus politely explains that no internal faxshots of the community are permitted.

The Thoradian Chief Missionary grants Martel permission to fax anything he can except the interior of the Smithhall, the place of worship.

So when do you start? He blocks his own questions but nods to himself. *Now . . . before it's too late.*

Martel stands, leans over the console, and logs out. Theoretically, today is his "break" day, which gives him the time he will need before he is due back on the board.

Tonight Gates will take his shift, and Hollie will probably use the time in the spare studio to edit her slot on crafts.

Crafts? Who knows? Who knows if anyone will care about a bunch of worshipers and their offbeat gods?

Martel represses a shiver. *Maybe they'll care too much.* He recalls the warning about the logo slot by the goddess.

He pushes the uneasiness to the back of his mind and lifts the portafax unit. It will take several trips to load the flitter.

Pamyra is two stans' flight time by the CastCenter flitter, and another half-stan beyond is his first stop, the Apollonite community.

From the air the sunburst pattern is clear—radial lanes, yellow-paved, linked at the center where the temple stands, fan outward and cross regularly spaced and circular ways. The temple rises from the absolute center of the community to a pointed beacon fifty meters above-ground which pulses with a golden glow.

The last circular lane marks the perimeter between the community buildings and the supporting lands, and on it is a row of low structures, some with pens attached.

Martel circles the entire community twice, taking his

wide-angle and pan shots, and ends them with a close-focused zoom in on the temple.

He drops the flitter on the pad midway between the agricultural buildings and the temple.

Father G'Iobo, clean-shaven, tanned, silver hairs streaking his golden curls, and flowing pale yellow robes not quite covering his sandals, meets Martel as he begins to unload the portafax from the flitter.

A sunburst, radiating a gentle light, hangs from a golden chain around the good Father's neck.

"Greetings, in the name of Apollo," offers G'Iobo.

Martel holds back a smile. Without probing, he can sense the priest's disapproval of his black tunic, trousers, and boots.

"Greetings to you, Father, and my thanks, both for me and for those who will have a chance to glimpse the kind of life you offer the faithful and those who would join your Order." Martel inclines his head in a gesture of respect.

"What exactly do you have in mind, my son?"

Martel finishes loading the next cube into the unit and adjusts the harness, ready to shoulder it.

"Fairly standard approach, Father. Pan shots of the community; then a mixture of shots of the secular activities . . . what people do in the way of support activities—I understand that the postulants do some crafts for the tourie trade—and perhaps a back shot or two over the shoulders of the novices of the other . . . Apollonites? Is that what those who are accepted are called?"

G'Iobo nods.

"Like a shot of them, not their faces, but from behind, as they enter the temple, with perhaps an uptake into the beacon."

"Flame," corrects the priest.

"Would any of that be a problem?" asks Martel, still balancing the fax unit on his knee, his right foot resting on the landing strut of the flitter.

"If that's all, it shouldn't be." The older man pauses, then asks, "What do you expect to get from this? What's the real purpose of your visit?"

Martel reflects. The question seems hostile, but Father G'Iobo radiates no hostility, though he wears a mindshield. Shields do not block emotions, just thoughts. Martel calculates whether he should attempt to break through the shield, decides against it.

"Twofold, I guess. First, no one has ever done a story on the religious communities. Not in any of the records. That makes it a possibility for a good story, and I need one. Second, I'm new. And I hope to learn something in the process."

G'Iobo relaxes fractionally, though his professional smile has not varied an iota.

"That seems reasonable. Please do not point your unit at any of the Brothers, the Apollonites wearing sunbursts like mine. If you feel it necessary to have some faces, a picture of a postulant or two, the ones in the plain yellow robes, would not be out of place."

Martel catches sight of a taller, more massively built Apollonite approaching.

G'Iobo turns toward the newcomer, his smile a shade broader. "Administrative duties call me, but Brother Hercles will be your guide and adviser."

Martel again inclines his head and looks up at the giant, who towers a full two meters plus.

"Brother Hercles," says G'Iobo, "this is Faxer Martel from the CastCenter at Sybernal. He knows the guidelines, and I am sure he will do his best to follow them."

"Greetings," Martel says quietly.

"A pleasure to meet you. I've seen you on the fax." Hercles' voice rumbles like a bass organ.

"I will return to see you off," adds Father G'Iobo as he steps away toward the temple.

"Where do you wish to start?" asks the giant.

Martel hefts the fax unit into the shoulder harness.

Be nice to have his muscles to carry this, he thinks.

"I sort of thought we'd start with the outbuildings and work in, ending up with what shots I can take of the temple."

Before he finishes, Martel is talking to empty air and hurrying to catch up.

The first place where the massive Apollonite halts is in the center of a narrow barn, filled with empty stalls.

"This is the sunram barn."

Martel does a quick once-over, then focuses on a single immaculate stall.

"The sunrams?"

"Out in the fields. Not far. Do you want to see them?"

Actually, while a shot of the animals might round out the slot, Martel really wants faxtime of people. He nods.

"Not far" turns out to be across two hills. Two yellow-robed novices and another Apollonite are watching the small flock. The animals, from their black hooves to their curling golden horns and thick yellow fleece, are spotless.

As he moves closer to the sunrams Martel realizes the animals do not smell like normal sheep, but almost like flowers.

He sniffs. Sniffs again. A clean smell.

"Heather," supplies Hercles. "A good smell."

The closer sunrams raise their heads at Martel's approach. He zooms in on the head of the nearest, narrowing in on the eyes. The eye itself contains a star-shaped pupil within the golden iris.

He shifts focus from that ram to another, eating the golden grass. Neither, Martel realizes, tears at the roots the way many sheep and goats do.

The way they chew isn't your subject, he reminds himself.

Martel looks at his guide.

"Some cube on the novices?"

"I beg your pardon?" rumbles the giant.

"According to father G'Iobo, I cannot fax Apollonites, only the postulants and lay members of the community."

The herder Apollonite frowns as Martel speaks, but moves to one side before the guide gestures.

Both novices are beardless. One is fresh from academics; the other shows gray in his brown hair, laugh lines radiating from his eyes. The golden wide-link chains around their necks are plain, without the sunburst.

"Do you comb the sunrams every day?" asks Martel of the older novice at the same time as he splits the focus between the animal and the man.

The novice's eyes run to the animal, back to the faxer, and Martel catches it all on the cube.

The man shakes his head in agreement.

"Are they easy to work with?"

A more vigorous headshake.

Martel angles in on the younger. "Do you like working with sunrams?"

An almost shy smile and a headshake answer the question.

The faxer fades from the man's face to a wide pan of the flock to the nearby hilltop, as yet uncropped, where the tall grass waves against the sky.

"Thank you," he tells the shepherd Apollonite.

A fourth nod, curt, is the only response.

Martel looks to his guide.

"Vows of silence?"

"No. Nothing to say. Chatter to mortals seems unnecessary when one has beheld the grandeur of God."

"How about the furniture operation?" *Time to change the subject,* Martel thinks.

"The basket shop is closer."

"Fine. Then the furniture shop."

Once again, Martel finds himself trailing the fast-moving Apollonite.

The double time march leads to another low building. Once inside, Martel sees why the term "basket shop" is inappropriate.

On the left side of the building, nearly one hundred meters from one end to the other, stretch built-in bins, each filled with stacked and dried reeds, wickers, palms, and grasses.

Across from the nearest set of bins are three rows of short tables. Perhaps twenty are occupied. Two Apollonites rove the aisles, offering advice, assistance.

Martel concentrates his unit on the raw materials first, then on the building, and finally on the novices. Two young girls also silently weave wicker into larger baskets, but do not wear the pale yellow robes of the novices.

"Lay members of the community?" Martel half points with his free hand.

"Wards. Each community supports and aids and educates some who have no other resources, and who are too young or too disabled through no fault of their own to make their own way."

The answer raises another series of questions, which Martel chooses not to pursue, but files mentally as he focuses close-ups on the postulants. He follows the fax-ins of the younger men with shots of the girls, first of the redhead, then of the brunette.

Neither is a beauty, but each has good features, a clear complexion, and a deftness in her hands. The redhead smiles broadly as she recognizes she is the object of the fax unit.

Martel lingers on her smile before stopping.

He unshoulders the unit to check the settings. Even the girls do not look at him.

After a long moment, Martel reshoulders the fax unit.

"Furniture shop?"

This time the tall Apollonite waits for Martel to take a step before starting off with his ground-devouring strides.

The furniture shop is housed in another low building like the basket-making facility, but instead of the smell of grass, and the smells of autumn, is filled with the scents of oil and wood. Again, along the left side of the interior are bin after bin of stacked woods stretching from one end to the other.

A finished marwood chest gleams just inside the entrance. The black surfaces are so smoothly finished that even without wax, lacquer, or glaze, the wood reflects Martel and the Apollonite guide.

Martel lets out a low whistle as he admires it and plays the faxer over it from every possible angle.

"Fit for a king," he murmurs.

"Scheduled for the Matriarch of Halston," says Hercles with a laugh.

Among the workers are more Apollonites, heavy leather aprons over shortened yellow robes, than in the basket shop, and the novices all seem older.

Martel faxes a simple inlaid game table, which, for all its simplicity, could have adorned any palace, any Duke's salon.

Along with the close-ups of the novices, he adds several shots over the shoulders of the Apollonite craftsmen, careful not to appear too obvious about his intentions.

From the carpentry and cabinet making, Martel is escorted to the weavers, where the golden wool is carded, stretched, treated, woven, and tailored; to the tannery; to the clinic, which is empty except for a young man who is having his left hand treated for a gash suffered in an orchard accident; to the recreation center; to one of the living quarters; to the empty dining hall being readied for the midday meal; and finally to the administration building.

The total time on the cube reads out at close to three stans.

That ought to be enough, Martel thinks, keeping the thought to himself as he follows Hercles back to his flitter.

Father G'Iobo, having torn himself away from his administrative duties, is waiting.

"We're sorry you could not spend more time with us, Faxer Martel."

Martel doesn't believe a word of it, and the good Father's emotions show no sign of the regret he is expressing.

"And so am I," he responds in kind, "but it's been most interesting. I hope you enjoy the program once it's aired in final fax form."

"We'll be looking forward to that," says G'Iobo.

Martel can sense the unease behind the statement, even though the priest's face carries the same warm and friendly smile.

Martel racks the one used fax cube in the storage locker, reloads the unit, thumbs the locker shut, and sets the fax unit in place for the next series of aerial shots.

As he settles behind the controls he looks up to see Father G'Iobo and Hercles standing back by the admin building, apparently waiting for his departure.

Father G'Iobo had been waiting much closer when Martel had arrived, much closer.

How about another kind of checklist? Martel asks himself, thoughts fully shielded.

He lets his perceptions range through the start circuits, mentally tracking, searching . . . and comes up with the "wrong" feeling. A small cartridge of something above the turbine blades, liquid.

Concentrating, he extends his energies, lets his thoughts remove the liquid to a small space in the bottom of the flitter.

With a touch of a stud he starts up, waves to the waiting Apollonites, and begins the short checklist.

Shortly he lifts off, heading toward the Ethene community.

Once in flight, he tries to analyze the captive liquid mentally, some sort of acid. Obviously placed to weaken the turbine blades, the acid would have loosened several blades at once, certainly exploding the engine, and possibly the whole flitter.

Martel lets the liquid eat through the bottomplate and bleed away into the open air.

What surprises will I get from the ladies?

From the air, the Ethene community shows more of a grid system, with its lanes converging in a fan toward the temple on the hillside south of everything else. The simple white stone structure, half set into the hill, lies open in the center.

Martel sees the sacred white flame from the air, takes the liberty of faxing it along with his other pan shots.

Sister Artemis Dian, the very name a position title, waits by the landing pad. She wears a white metal circlet and a veil, seemingly thin, but totally concealing. From the golden hue of her hair and the curve of her calves, which show below the three-quarter length of her off-white robes, Martel guesses she is beyond first youth, but not too far. Either that or thoroughly rejuved.

"Faxer Martel?" Well modulated, with a hint of throatiness, her voice does nothing to discourage his first impression.

"The same. Greetings, Lady."

"Sister will do, and greetings to you."

"Greetings, Sister," Martel corrects himself. "Anything I should know before we start?"

"The Goddess watches over everything, and in her wisdom will correct all that goes amiss."

Translated loosely, Martel, if you blow it, you'll get fired on the spot with celestial fury.

"I think I understand, Sister, and will follow your instructions to the letter." *Not to the spirit, however.*

The Ethene community, while laid out in a different physical pattern, bears remarkable similarity to the Apollonite village in the activities, the cleanliness, the sense of purpose and quiet. There is no furniture shop, but instead, a ceramic facility, and in place of the basket shop there is, surprisingly, the winery that produces the Springfire of which Martel has become so fond.

Sister Artemis Dian is his guide through the entire tour, even to the front steps of the temple.

"No farther," she says in her controlled contralto.

"Mind if I pan up the steps and to the mountain behind?"

"That would be acceptable."

The stroll back to the flitter is absolutely quiet, and the stillness seems to accentuate the weight of the fax unit on Martel's shoulders. Only the pad of feet and the swish of robes intrude. The Sister, like Father G'Iobo, is mind-shielded.

Her apparent young age, her young step, bother Martel, do not fit. She seems totally at ease with him, but as if he is really not present.

As he stows the used fax cube and reloads, as he resets the unit for aerial shots, she waits, far closer than the Apollonites had. Martel uses his extended perceptions to scan the flitter even before starting to climb back in.

An aura of danger clings to the power cells. But why?

Martel scans superficially, then deeply, before realizing that both original sets have been replaced with a new set, blocked somehow.

If you touch the starter, all that power will turn on itself, fuse the cells . . . and boom. *No more flitter, no more Martel, and no more Sister Artemis Dian.*

Ergo . . . Sister Artemis Dian wasn't. Rather some poor flunky mind-washed into being a victim. Or . . .

Martel doesn't like the second possibility. The "Sister" might be the goddess herself, able to shield herself from the fiery blast and point the finger at someone. Or claim that Martel had tried to defile the community.

Martel was either a victim or a pawn. He didn't like the possibilities, and adjusted another strap, stalling and trying to think his way out of the situation.

If he announced the problem, it would reveal abilities he really hadn't had the chance to develop fully and might open him to more scrutiny.

Slowly, carefully, he lets his thoughts disconnect the leads to the power cells, and allows the power to bleed off into the field through a "channel" he opens, until the cells are totally inert.

He finishes adjusting his harness, shifts his weight, and closes the canopy. Then, and only then, Martel touches the starter stud, and watches the "Sister" for a reaction. There is none, none that he can detect, either physically or mentally, as the flitter rises into the sky.

He shivers, partly from the effort in supplying the current needed for the start through mental ability, and partly from the strain of the undercurrents he does not understand.

He shakes his head. If everyone is so secretive about their religious communities, why haven't they all taken the stance of the Taurists and merely refused him permission to visit? He might have complained or even woven it into a faxcast, but nothing would have changed.

The Thoradian mission would be the last stop, but before landing there, he wants to complete as much of his aerial flyby and faxshot pass as he can of the Taurist community.

Every sense would have to be alert, with his mental perceptions spread as far as possible. If those who had welcomed him are trying to destroy him, what can he expect from those who declared themselves off limits from the beginning?

Nothing.

Where the Apollonite community was circular, and the Ethene a fan-shaped grid, the Taurist is rectangular, with black buildings, black-paved roads, and a central black square, in the center of which burns a strange black flame. No temple.

And no interference.

Martel rechecks the fax unit as he swings the flitter back toward the Thoradian mission.

Where the other three communities had appeared regular from the air, and orderly, the Thoradians built wherever they pleased. Some of the buildings appear to have fallen roofs, and the outlying streets are grass-choked.

No one waits at the landing stage.

Martel dons the unit, seals the flitter, not that such a precaution has been helpful before, and starts out.

Sunrams they have, unkempt and grazing around the outbuildings, but with normal, unstarburst pupils.

The scent of fire and hot metal draw him to a plain, unpainted wooden building, in good trim, but obviously old, and weathered planking that has been replaced over the years, lending the walls a patchwork impression.

Inside, two burly men, sweat pouring from foreheads into full red beards, beat out blades on the wide black anvils, totally oblivious to Martel and his fax unit.

Neither wears robes, but rather a short kiltlike battle skirt, with alternating leather and metal strips. Their upper bodies, outside of a reddish tan, leather aprons, and copper armbands and wristbands, are bare.

Martel focuses in on their concentration, then onto the compact and unvarying flame over which they labor.

He departs, apparently unnoticed.

More shots of abandoned structures follow.

Across the red stone lane from the log temple, distinguished from the other buildings by the symbol of the crossed graystone hammers, Martel finds a tall figure waiting for him.

Like the others, the man is burly, muscular, tall, and dressed in battle kilt. In addition, a wolfskin cloak is thrown back over his shoulders, and hair curls from under a metal helmet decorated with twin ramhorns. From the leather loop circling his right wrist hangs the heavy graystone hammer.

"So you're the one! Upstart they all question."

"Your pardon?" asks Martel.

"Say they question. Fear what you may become. Nonsense. All of it. Thor fears none of it. Nor you. Nor what you become. Do you challenge the hammer and might?"

Martel steps back.

Thor? The so-called god himself? This barbarian rumbling gutturals?

The hammer swings and is released skyward.

A blaze of lightning follows, slashes into the suddenly dark sky.

"Doubt not Thor! Unbeliever!" The voice bellows like thunder.

Martel steps back another step, still faxing the entire incredible scene.

"That'll do. Teach them all," rumbles the old warrior, and Martel can sense the age in the god, even though the figure and the voice are those of a man in his prime.

The hammer screams back to the upraised arm, and yet another lightning bolt flares.

Martel retreats another step, aware his hands are damp, but still recording.

He stumbles, looks down to keep from letting the unit overbalance him, and when he looks up, Thor is gone. The red rock lanes are again deserted.

Martel brings the fax unit to bear on the temple, zooms in the focus, and discovers that the doors which were open are now barred.

No one stops him on his way back to the flitter, which is as he left it. Untouched.

Martel is still shaking his head as he pilots the light craft back toward Sybernal, toward the CastCenter, hoping the scenes with the thunder-god are indeed in the cube.

A small part of his mind hopes they are not, for if they are, he will use them. Must use them.

xviii

▼

Martel tenses.

The quartered image stands out in front of the single flat wall of the CastCenter lounge—four separate scenes, and each with its own message.

On the upper left graze a flock of sunrams, their fleeces glittering with lights of their own. On the upper right stretch long rows of golden vines, leaves half covering the ripening grapes. On the lower left extends a grass-choked pavement. Finally, on the lower right, an aerial shot of a black-walled, black-laned community.

The music wells up, subsides. A selection from *Winds of Summer.*

"The postulant communities of Aurore, as they present themselves to visitors, and to the universe . . . postulants to gods who are real, and who demonstrate their powers on an everyday basis.

"Now . . . a first-time-ever look at the worshipers of the living gods of Aurore . . ."

The four images fade into one—the sunspire of the temple of Apollo, which fades into the white marble of the Ethene temple, which fades into an aerial shot of the black flame in the black square of the Taurist community, and then to the closed and hammer-barred front view of the Thoradian mission under sullen clouds.

"Not a bad intro, Martel," says Marta Farell.

Gates Devero nods in agreement, while Hollie makes no statement or gesture.

Martel realizes his palms are damp, rubs them on his trousers as the cube continues running through the apparently innocuous activities of the Apollonite community, and then through a similar routine in the Ethene community.

"Good shot of his expression . . . really wrapped up in what he's doing."

What's he playing for? Martel picks up the thought from Marta.

"Oohhh . . . the eyes on that sunram . . ."

"Lot of contentment showing . . ."

". . . nice view of the reflection off the marwood chest . . ."

Martel swallows, waiting for the transition from the light of the Ethenes to the aerial shots of the Thoradian mission.

Apollo!

". . . so deserted . . . old . . ."

The cut from the desolation focuses down a grass-choked lane and into the blacksmith shop, with the bearded barbarians pounding, pounding out blades, the metal glowing, the heat welling out.

". . . looks like a Darian view of Hades . . ."

Don't like where this is going. That thought came from Marta Farell.

From the focus on the blades the view shifts to the blank, concentrating faces of the smiths, oblivious to the watchers, robotic in their duties, and then cuts back away to the grassy pavement and what Martel had seen as he had walked through the nearly deserted community, ending up before the temple, its rough doors gaping.

The god Thor looms in the center of the scene, as if he had appeared from nowhere.

"Doubt not Thor!"

The fifth time through, Martel still marvels a bit at the swing of the magnificent graystone hammer, and the lightnings that follow, the clouds that roil in on cue from the thunder-god.

". . . don't believe it . . ."

". . . how . . . how did you do it?"

Fry Martel, fry us all, if this screens.

From the lightnings the fax zeroes back in on the empty

square, then on the barred and closed temple, with its crossed graystone hammers.

"The Taurist community, unlike the other three," Martel's narrative rolls onward, "is closed to outsiders."

With only the low thunder of the *March of the Directorate* by Pavenne as accompaniment, the aerial view of the Taurist community unrolls, concluding with the square of the black flame.

"The postulant communities of the living gods, from light—"

The fax shows the Apollonite sunram, golden spire in the backdrop, cuts to the golden iris of the ram's eye with the dark starburst pupil. That dark star grows and grows until the entire screen is black.

"—to light—"

The scene mists from black through gray to the open Ethene square and the steps leading up to the white marble temple of the goddess.

"No farther." The words of Sister Artemis Dian roll up over the track music, and the view pans up the temple and to the dark-shadowed point of the sacred mountain. Again . . . the darkness expands to encompass the entire holo image.

"—to light—"

With a quick slash view of the thunder-god's face, his lips caught twisted, the scene follows not the hammer but the lightning, on the upward stroke and the downward return. As the last lightning flash fades, the image fills with the dark clouds, which gray out and thin.

"—to dark."

From the thinning gray of the clouds the view switches to the aerial vista of the Taurist community, laid out in black, the blackness of the lanes, the blackness of the buildings, emphasized by the filters Martel has overlaid. Steadily the focus narrows until the only identifiable object is the black flame, within its black square and centered in the middle of the holo.

The last measures of the *March of the Directorate* die away as the image blanks to black.

"Flame!" mutters Marta Farell.

"You trying a fancy form of suicide, Martel?" That from Gates.

Hollie Devero shakes her head, slowly. *Knew he was crazy.*

"But do you like it?" Martel asks, knowing the question is expected. He gets out of the narrow chair and stretches.

Silence.

"You know," says Hollie quietly, "faxers have lost their minds for less than that."

"For what? Showing a few scenes of the communities?"

"You're missing the point on purpose, Martel!" snaps Marta Farell. "Without a single negative word, without a single disparaging musical note, without a single scene of a suffering human being, you've painted the four prime gods of Aurore as petty and almost evil. And I don't want any part of it."

"How good is it?" counters Martel.

"Good enough to have the entire CastCenter leveled if we run it," retorts Hollie.

"What if you credit me with exclusive production?"

"Not good enough."

"All right. I'll can it."

"No."

Marta stretches. In her hand is a stunner.

"Unload that cube. Now. Put it on the counter."

Martel steps toward the holojector, one step at a time, narrowing his thoughts, concentrating as he does.

Hollie and Gates back away, trying to get to the side, as far from the line of fire as possible.

Martel's thoughts touch Farell's, catch the low block there, and vault into her mind.

. . . got to stop him . . . say so . . . so glorious . . . do what HE wants . . .

Martel reaches the nexus he needs, touches the nerves. Marta Farell's knees crumple. Her eyes roll up and close, and she collapses in a heap.

Martel lets himself go in the same way, unaffected as he is. His thoughts reach out to seize Hollie and Gates Devero.

Once all three are safely unconscious, Martel climbs to his feet, fingers the bruise on his forearm where it had collided with the leg of the lounger. He unloads the cube from the holojector and carries it into the control center, where a full-stan documentary on the wind dolphins of Faldarin is concluding.

Martel keys the back-feed for Karnak, bringing the tie transmitter up full and alerting the Regency network that a new outprogram would be coming. He'd already done the attributions, foreseeing the reaction he has gotten.

As soon as the documentary finishes and the I.D. spot plugs through, he will run *Postulants of Aurore* straight through.

With the off-planet net, once the title line alone has run there is no way that Apollo and crew will dare to stop his cube. Not before the fact.

Martel has his perceptions fully spread, but detects nothing out of the ordinary. He is banking on the fact that even the so-called gods of Aurore can handle only so many things at once, and that they do not expect him to take matters into his own hands so quickly.

Just in case anyone thinks about mechanical niceties, he wipes the cube clean of fingerprints, as well as the feeding equipment. He makes most of the adjustments by thought alone.

Once the cube runs through, without further instructions the console will pick up the KarNews feed.

The details taken care of, once the cube begins he returns to the recording studio, drains the power from Marta's stunner and from the laser knife she also carries, and resumes the position the others had seen him fall into.

He blocks off his conscious physical control and waits.

Waits until he feels someone shake him, slap him across the face. Hard. Flamed hard.

Marta, of course.

"Damn you! Damn, damn! *Damn!*"

"Wha . . . stop . . . you . . . why . . . stun me . . ." He lets the words stumble out.

"Because I want to live. Because I want to get off this planet. Because you and your cutesy idea have ruined everything. *Everything!*"

Martel snakes his head, realizes he is swallowing something. His blood. Marta's slap has apparently caused him to bite his cheek.

He looks around. Gates, white-faced, is leaning over the counter. Hollie, leaning forward in her chair, is holding her head in her hands.

"What happened? I went to get you the cube, just like you asked. Hollie and Gates saw me. You saw me. And you stunned me, even before I got there. Now you're slapping me, and screaming that it's all my fault. You're the one who's crazy! Flamed crazy!"

"I didn't stun you. Someone else did, and they ran the cube. Ran it right out to all Aurore and back-fed to Karnak. There'll be flame to pay. And it's all on your head."

"You're crazy! You said I could try the idea. I did. You said no. I agreed, and now it's on my head. Why me? I didn't do anything."

"You made the damned cube. You made a mockery out of the Taurists, and their unnamed god can't be pleased. If he doesn't get you, then Thor will, unless the others get to you first."

"But why? It isn't our fault somebody ran the cube."

Gates says nothing, but glares at Martel, and staggers out of the studio lounge, dragging Hollie by the arm.

Marta Farell's eyes smoke. "You just might be right. And you might not. But I won't risk anyone else's life because of your stupidity. For the sake of everyone else, Martel, when you're on duty here, no one else is going to be here. Ever! You're perm night shift. Until you pack up and quit. Or until your brains, or whatever passes for brains, rot."

Martel lets a puzzled expression cross his face, as if he can't understand her hysteria. In fact, he has difficulty, although he can sense the emotional desperation welling from her.

"That's starting right now! And while you're off duty, I'll do my best to see that no one comes close to you, especially no one from any faxcast center. But don't worry. You'll get full credit for this one. Every last credit from that docuslot is yours. Even the station's cut. It should make you wealthy. If you live to enjoy it."

Martel stands there.

Marta marches toward the portal, then half turns.

"You've got about a quarter-stan before we go local. Program's on the up sheet. If I ever talk to you again, other than by fax, and that's only when necessary, count yourself flamed lucky."

Marta is gone. From the lack of mental echoes, he can tell the entire CastCenter is deserted.

"Some reaction . . ." he mutters.

He had expected concern, but not the violent paranoia they'd all displayed.

He shrugs, heals the cut inside his mouth, and heads for the on-line control center.

He leaves his mental shields up. If half of what Marta has screamed is correct, he will need them.

xix

▼

Dull rumbles echo, bounce, skip like flat stones over the leaden surface. Green-golden water heaves itself at the rocky fingertip of land that seems to dive into the waves.

The wind whips spray around the man standing atop the one boulder, black, that protrudes from the flat and bare rock.

The atmosphere itself shrouds the dark clouds, sulfurs the honesty of rain with the false promise of the sunlight that never has been.

Raindrops shatter as they strike the sea, fragment on crystal rocks, dissolve into the flanking beaches, nourish the high grasses on top of the cliffs above.

The difference in the fate of each raindrop is not in the rain.

Martel watches the sea, looks out across the surf that breaks below his feet and foams around his boulder perch.

A golden streak of lightning flashes, flares, flashes down at an unbroken wave climbing above its sisters.

Steam hisses, the sound audible to Martel though the crest is fully three kilos out.

Standing on the wave, appearing from nowhere, is a figure dripping cobalt water, despite the greenness of the water above which he towers, bearing a trident. He strikes the water on which he stands, and from the strike rises blue lightning toward the clouds.

Another golden bolt spears down. Hisses and steams. Haloes the sea-god.

And another.

In return comes a fainter blue upward strike.

The trident whirls, and close upon the whirling rises a waterspout, not black-green, but brilliant blue, that hurls itself toward the low-hanging clouds.

The clouds lift. The waterspout follows, howling.

Another golden bolt strikes downward, then a shower, attacking the tower of water like the arrows of a besieging army.

The tower quivers, wavers, and tilts. Drops in an instant waterfall into the sea.

Within moments, the tattered fragments of the clouds are gone, and the waves subside, the air fresh with the memory of rain.

In the distance, beyond the vision of most but clear to Martel, a pair of nymphs skates the breaksides of the remaining waves, their laughter chiming like the bells of holidays past.

The empty quarter, the empty half, the empty outside of a full beaker . . . why are these the things he looks for?

Really, it is a most unusual occurrence when analyzed—a storm to set the scene, followed by a short battle between Apollo the sun-god and the sea-god, completed with a musical finale of two nymphs with laughter. Now, hasn't that been your typical evening on your everyday deserted beach?

Oh, yes, and add to the foregoing that evening isn't evening, but everlasting day, and that most beaches away from Sybernal, Pamyra, and Alesia are usually deserted, O expert on beaches.

All quite understandable, since Sybernal had twenty kilos of perfect beach, and Pamyra another ten. The normal tourist is rich and sedentary or poor and transportationless.

The twinge in his left leg reminds Martel that he has lost track of time. Again.

The wetness of the quick rain has begun to fade with the return of full daylight, and the scent of spring fades into the perpetual golden haze that lies across the sky.

The regular beat of waves against the stone point resumes.

Martel frowns, concentrates, and a short cloak of darkness flows from his shoulders. With quick steps he crosses the flat green-gray stone, his feet leaving no trace on the damp rock.

From the back of the small peninsula rises a cliff, the gray rock cleft in the middle. The cleft is filled with broken stone. Each boulder is roughly as wide as the armspan of an average man. None is smaller than a small table, and no sand cushions the space between the rectangular blocks. The sides of the cleft are smooth, and the gray-striped stone is scarred with black lines.

Martel jumps from the top of the bottommost stone to the next one, zigzagging his way up the jumble toward the grassy plateau.

By the time he reaches the short golden grass, the flitter he senses in the distance, coming south from Sybernal, should arrive. Piloted by Rathe Firien.

Martel drops his shadow cloak even before his first step out onto the grass. Black enough for Rathe as he stands. Black trousers, tunic, belt, and boots.

The old words rise into his thoughts and to his lips.

Tell me now, if you can,
What is human, what is man . . .

He shakes his head, half aware that Rathe sees the gesture as she brings the flitter down, knowing also that she will not misinterpret, that she understands how he argues with himself.

Crooked in her left arm as she swings from the flitter is a wicker basket, the kind made by the Apollonite postulants for the tourist trade, and which would be called old-fashioned almost anywhere else in the Empire of Man.

"Flitter?" he asks, still in full stride toward her.

"Clinic's. Slow time now, and it has been for weeks. Maybe the Fuardian-Halston thing. Who knows?"

Rathe's red-silk hair is longer these days, covers her ears. With the length has come a slight wave, and a certain softness to her features.

She sets the basket on the grass. From the top she brings

forth a thin cloth, which she shakes out and spreads on the ground. The basket then goes in the middle.

Rathe seats herself cross-legged and motions.

"I know you're restless, but since I've brought you the picnic dinner I don't deserve, at least sit down and enjoy it with me."

"You don't deserve?" He sits down, not cross-legged but half lying on his left side. He props his head with his left hand and looks across the top of the basket at her freckled face.

"To have dinner with one of Aurore's top faxcasters? Of course I don't deserve. And if all the rich norm ladies knew where you hid when you're not at the CastCenter, I'd never see you."

"Marta's blacked me."

"Oh, that. As long as He hasn't, I wouldn't worry."

Martel caught the anxiety beneath the bantering tone, the darkness behind the forced smile.

"You caught the special on the postulants?"

"No. But everyone's talking about it. Talking about how none of the other faxers are supposed to talk to you. I don't think it set well. Father H'Lerry is supposed to speak on it next service."

Rathe pursed her lips, returned her attention to the basket, from which she pulled a bottle of Springfire and two tulip glasses.

"I hope he's generous," Martel answers, forcing a chuckle that sounds hollow even to himself. He extends his arm for a glass. "Farell said it was on my head. Marta Farell, my dear supervisor." *How literally had Farell meant it?* He blocks the thought automatically.

Rathe licks her lips, twice catches her lower lip with her upper teeth, worries it, stares down at her half-filled tulip glass.

Martel takes a small sip of the Springfire and waits.

Rathe stares at the picnic basket.

"You're worried."

She nods, without looking up.

He can read exactly what she is thinking.

. . . not kind to the gods . . . shows them spoiled . . .
Thor . . . who am I to say . . . Martel . . .

"You're thinking that I was foolish to fax it?"

"Brave. And foolish. That's why I love you. For as long
as I can."

From inside the basket she pulls a small package and
thrusts it at him.

"What?"

"Open it. Please."

He sets his glass on a level spot in the short grass and
avoids reading her thoughts so that the gift will be the surprise she intends.

The belt, for that is what it is, uncoils from the wrappings,
with the softness and jet-black of natural wehrleather. The
buckle is pure silver, a simple triangle, yet hard.

Martel frowns. The buckle alone, with its monalloyed silver, represents an enormous free credit balance. Neither is
wehrleather native to Aurore or easy to come by.

He gets up and kneels on both knees to don the belt, looking down at it, admiring the way it feels and fits, and the
shine of the buckle, neither muted nor too bright.

"You look so good!"

"Thanks to you." He grins, looking back down at the belt,
then across to her. "Rathe . . ."

His fingertips brush hers, link, and grasp her hand, draw
her across the cloth to him, against him.

Lips linger. A touch of salt, a warmth radiating from lip
to cheek to . . .

Yes . . . no . . . not now . . . later . . . he liked it.

Martel cradles her face in both hands as he releases her,
runs his fingertips down the side of her face.

"You didn't need to."

"I know, but I wanted to." Her eyes glisten even in the

pervasive indirect light, and that alone tells him that she is pleased.

"I'm hungry," he announces, not only to change the subject but because the sudden growl of his gut has reminded him that he is.

"Ha! Your stomach spoke first."

"I admit it. So what else is in the basket?"

"Sea duck and kelip."

"Then serve, wench."

"Yes, Masterfaxer. At once, sir."

Rathe does not notice the dark cloud in the distance, toward the sacred mountain behind Pamyra. Martel sees the cloud, notes it, and concentrates on the sea duck.

"Napkin?"

"At once, sir! Here you go."

"More Springfire!"

Rathe arcs the bottle across the cloth at him, but he catches it without spilling a drop. Inhales deeply of the aroma, lets it mingle with the scent of Rathe and the pinsting of the sea below.

> *The days of wine and youth*
> *Are days of love and truth . . .*

Martel listens to the song, to the feelings behind the words, and to the hidden harmony that Rathe does not know she brings to the short song.

"Martel."

She stares at him.

He starts, realizing his cheeks are wet.

"Must have gotten something in my eyes."

Martel, crying . . . see that?

The wonder in her thoughts leeches the emotion cleanly from him.

He picks up the tulip glass from the grass and takes a swig, a long pull to empty it.

The distant cloud is no closer, but darker. Suddenly it disappears, and a chill breeze swirls the picnic cloth and is gone, and with it goes the sense of summer.

"We'd better go."

Rathe nods.

He folds the cloth while she puts the bottle and glasses away. Only crumbs from the sea duck and kelip remain, left for the shy dories, who will flutter down to feast once the flitter and the man and the woman have left.

XX

▼

The myth of the "thousand ships" persists even in nontechnic cultures. . . . As a practical matter, less than seven hundred possible instances of space colonization fall within the parameters outlined by Corenth. . . . The implications of a power which could scatter a fleet of one thousand warships of advanced design obviously render the whole question moot and leave unanswered the source of an unverifiable panhumanoid myth. . . .

—*In Search of the Thousand Ships*
Pier V. RonTaur
Alphene, II, 3123 A.A.T.

xxi

▼

The white-tipped peak juts through the white carpet of clouds like an imperfect obelisk, evenly lit and evenly shadowed at the same time.

On the empty air, close enough to reach out and touch the impossibly knife-pointed tip of the mountain, sits a man clothed in a pale sunbeam-yellow tunic, leather sandals with the straps circling his crossed and perfect legs and ankles up to his knees, and wearing a crown of light that blurs his features.

Across the peak from him stands a dark and cloudy figure, combining both the blockiness of a Minotaur and the indistinctness of a thunderstorm.

At the third vertex of the imaginary triangle appears another figure, slender, tall, feminine, and ghostly, clad in white with long golden-blond hair flowing down her back.

Martel puts another foot forward, takes another step upward through the cotton clouds, through the indistinctness, knowing the three figures above await him.

Step, step, step.

The fog swirls around him, parts in front of him, closes behind him. But it has no scent, no smell of salt and fish like sea fog, no smell of pine and rock like mountain fog, no sting of ice needles like arctic fog.

His head breaks through, and he steps clear of the fog, standing on nothing at all, to face the trio.

"Slow, Martel," observes Apollo.

The bull-god says nothing.

The golden goddess turns her head toward Apollo. Martel cannot see her eyes.

"Still . . . a slow demigod is better than no demigod."

Martel does nothing. Knows he should do something. Knows he does not know what he should do.

He clenches his hands at his sides.

"If I knew . . . if I only knew . . ."

"But you don't, Martel. And you never will, not unless you accept that you are a god. Then you'll understand. Then you'll be just like us."

"Never! *Never!*"

Martel throws himself at the brilliance of the sun-god.

"Martel! No!"

The scene dissolves around him. The white clouds flare red, fade into a backdrop of dark wood.

He is half lying, half sitting on his bed, sweat dripping off his forehead. His left hand is falling away from Rathe's forearm.

"You started talking in your sleep again, and you grabbed me. Hard. Screamed something about knowing, and never, never . . ." Her voice is filled with pain, as are her thoughts.

Martel sees the dampness on her cheeks and looks down at the arm she cradles, strangely crooked, resting below her bare and full breasts. The quilt is wound around her waist and legs still.

Her arm is broken.

Control, Martel. When are you going to get control over yourself?

"Let me see." He runs his fingers over her skin, letting his awareness build, realizing the damage is worse than Rathe knows—both bones, blood vessels, ripped muscles.

With a sudden jab at her thoughts, he takes them over, lets himself flow into her, trying to put her to sleep for what he has to do. Unlike the case with Gates Devero, this time he cares, and will spare Rathe the pain, if he can.

In slow motion, as she loses consciousness, the pictures and words float past him.

Item: "Fierce" and "gentle," coupled with a black lamb frolicking across an unfenced clearing. The lamb jumps and does not land. In its

place glares a black mountain ram, black
lightning for horns.

Item: A man dressed in black, standing silhouetted
against the sea, wearing a cloak. The cloak
whips around him, but there is no wind.

Item: Two bodies moving as one upon a bed.

Item: A man lying in a hospital bed, asleep, face
contorted, one hand bending the metal
railing that rings the bed.

Item . . . item . . . item . . . item . . .

Martel breaks out of Rathe's thoughts, stares down at the
freckles on the tear-streaked face, at the closed eyes still
tight-tensed, at the smooth skin, the light nipples, the short
red-silk hair.

His own cheeks are damp, he knows. He wipes the right
side of his face with his upper right arm, still holding his
unconscious lover, his unconscious greeter, and perhaps his
unconscious conscience.

Gently he moves, stretches her out on the bed, concentrates on the arm, straightens it, using his perceptions, and
gets the bone ends aligned. Now, kneeling beside the bed, he
thinks, his thoughts reaching out to repair the damage he has
wrought, trying to mend nerves, to touch the right cells in the
right way to heal what has brought the pain and the tears.

Time stands silent as he works.

He is done.

And done, he lets go, feels himself sink toward the hard
floor, exhausted.

"Martel . . ."

A cool hand touches his face. Rathe's.

"The arm? How are you?" The words burst forth even as
he tries to uncurl from the stiff heap he has become.

"Sore, but just a little."

He heaves himself upward and sits on the edge of the bed
next to her.

Rathe pulls the quilt over her breasts, leaving her shoulders bare, and turns to face him.

"Kiss me."

Warm lips, salty, and her eyelashes flutter against his closed eyes like butterflies.

Butterflies, but Aurore has no butterflies, and the glittermotes are no substitutes.

The quilt drops away as two bodies meet, hold . . . and hold.

Rathe sobs, buries her head against his shoulder, sobs once more, then again. Harder and quicker, the sad shudders mount.

Martel finds himself aroused, hard against her softness, her sadness. Finds himself angry at his arousal.

He takes her face, takes her lips, kisses her once, long, evenly, trying to add heat to the salty chill, draws her to him more tightly still.

After a time, her shudders subside, and another motion begins, which he joins. And joins. And joins again.

After the joinings comes sleep.

He wakes first, leaves his arm around her, studies her body, from her full thighs through narrow waist to light-nippled and full breasts . . . smooth skin, creamy with the ubiquitous freckles of a true redhead. His eyes trace her features, the nose sharp enough for character but straight, the green eyes hidden under sleeping lids, the light eyebrows, the narrow lips that kiss so fully.

She smiles, sleeping, and the happiness lifts a corner of the darkness from him.

He thinks, finally reaches into her thoughts as narrowly as he can, makes a change, an adjustment.

After a time, she wakes. She smiles again, then frowns. Starts to pull the dark green quilt over her, then lets it drop.

"You like seeing me? You always have. Will you remember?"

"Remember?"

"Martel. Please. Be gentle. I'm not meant to sleep with gods. Not once we both know. I kept hoping you were just crazy, not divine. But you're not. It hurts too much to love you, and They'll just use me to hurt you. It's too hard . . ."

"I know."

He could feel the tears well up in his eyes again.

Why? Cried more in the last day than in my whole life . . . going to pieces?

"I know you know. But that won't stop you. It can't. But it doesn't matter."

"What will you do?"

"Now that I don't have to be a greeter?"

He nods.

"I don't know. Maybe I won't change. Maybe I will. It's nice to have the choice."

He lies back, watches as she stands, still naked. Drinks in each movement as she dresses. Against the dark panels of the bedroom her skin lends her the air of a classical statue.

Her pale green tunic all in place, she comes over to the bed and sits down next to him.

"In your own way, Rathe, dear, you're a goddess."

"Remember me that way. And don't fix my memories. Broken arms need to be fixed, but I am what I remember."

He turns his face toward her, arms reaching to enfold her.

She plants a quick kiss on his forehead and ducks away under his arms.

"Wouldn't be the same now."

She is gone through the portal.

Martel lies propped on the bed for a time. Then he arises and heads to the ultrashower.

He is scheduled for his usual night shift at the CastCenter, and lots of time for thought.

xxii

▼

The sky outside the cottage grumbles. The room within is dark, dimmed by clouds, which are natural, and therefore rare. No artificial light, also rare on Aurore, or glittermotes, which are not, intrude. Though the corner where the vidfax is mounted gathers shadows, the man does not need light to see.

He touches the address studs, and his fingers run through the combination with the effortlessness of habit. For he knows the pattern by heart.

By *heart,* he affirms.

His hand hovers near the contact plate, ready to break the connection when she does not answer.

"Greetings," she says automatically, her eyes widening as she recognizes the caller on the screen. "Persistent, aren't you?"

"Yes," he admits, drinking in her green eyes and warm face. " 'Persistent,' I suppose, is as good a word as any."

He realizes her hair is longer now, as it could be after a standard year.

"Foolish, and blind, too," she says and he can sense the bitterness.

He waits.

"I hope this doesn't seal my death, dear one," she continues conversationally, "but you're still acting human and refusing to face what you are. Still appearing on the nightly faxcast, as if it were common for a god to broadbeam the evening trivia. Still trying to persuade a very human woman that you are, too."

"Your death?" His words sound lame.

"My death. Possibly. Possibly yours as well, although I doubt that for reasons I couldn't possibly explain." She sighs. Loudly. "Don't you understand? They want you as a god. If you won't because of me, then They'll do away with me . . . or take all my memories. Do you want to take back everything you've given me? Do you want to become just like Them?"

By now the tears are streaming down her face.

"Let me have my memories, at least. Something. Go on and be what you are! You have all I can give. I can't be some god's plaything. And I won't! If I come back to you, then that's all I'll be. Don't you understand? Don't you?"

He waits, again.

"You could come and twist my thoughts, change me into a willing tool. But you don't. Does that make you good? Or just stubborn? Or waiting until later?

"For my sake, if not for both of us, leave me alone. If you love me, if you ever loved me, please, please, let me be. If you care at all, let me alone. Let me have a memory. Before it's too late . . . already there's so little. I was stupid to fall in love with you, and you were stupid to give me back myself . . . and that's enough stupidity . . ."

"All right . . ." His words sound unsteady to himself.

He cannot speak more. Nods, reaches toward the contact plate, looks once again, only to see her looking down, and not at the screen. He presses the plate, and the screen blanks.

His room is dark, though not so dark as previously. The storm clouds are dispersing.

He walks out onto the covered porch, then down onto the hillside, where he stares into the distance toward a peak others cannot see. A peak called Jsalm. The sacred mountain.

He shakes his head. Once. Violently.

He turns, slowly, until he faces the small cottage. With deliberate and heavy steps he mounts the three risers to the porch, crosses it, and reenters the dwelling.

A black glittermote circles the space where he had faced the distant peak before vanishing.

The dorles, tentatively, hop to the outer branches of the quince. The largest half-spreads her wings, then chitters a long note that echoes, that hangs on the hillside.

xxiii

▼

The two figures could be meeting on a mountaintop, or on a sea bottom, or in a cloud of glittermotes that would drive a man mad, or in the pitch darkness of the caves deep beneath Pamyra.

Instead, they stand on a ledge over the White Cliffs.

You've bet too much on this one.

Not yet. Oaks take longer to grow.

So do the bristlepines, but they don't challenge. Just endure.

He's young.

So you doubt already?

Sometimes, but not about the potential.

A vision of black thunderbolts passes from the lighter to the darker.

Strong enough to take us on? Never.

Two words to avoid—"always" and "never."

If you fear, why encourage?

I don't. Just watch. The lighter one laughs, a laugh that breaks like glass against the hard rock at his back. Before the shards can reach the breakers below, he shimmers like the sun Aurore never sees and launches himself like a sunbeam into an afternoon that is not and has never seen one.

The darker one picks up a laugh crystal, studies it, ponders.

In time, he, too, departs after his own way.

Neither has noticed the white bird perched in the nearby tree, a white bird with golden eyes and dark pupils that reach back farther than any bird's should, windows into more than soul.

In turn, the bird flutters off the bristlepine branch, lands lightly next to the laugh crystal that has begun to evaporate, cocks her head as if to catch something within the frozen sound as it vaporizes.

Beneath the White Cliffs, a thousand meters below, the golden-green breakers crash, foam against sheer quartz, crash and foam, crash and foam, in even rhythm.

The white bird, larger than a dove, for there are no doves on Aurore, and smaller than a raven, takes wing, and with effortless strokes clears the cliff edge, merges with a vagrant mist that has no business so high above the waves, and disappears.

xxiv

▼

Martel leaves his own screen blank, but taps out the code for hers.

He sighs, knowing there will be no answer. There never is, hasn't been for months.

Instead, this time, a message flashes across the screen.

FAXEE UNKNOWN. NO FORWARDING CODE.

Martel disconnects, taps out the numbers again. He must have used the wrong code.

How likely is that, Martel?

He does not answer his own question, but looks across the room at the open window, and through it sees the light breeze fluff the hillside grass.

Rathe moved? Impossible!

Besides, changing location wouldn't change the code. Permanent residents kept their codes, unless they decided to delist. If she had delisted, the screen would have told him that and indicated that her personal code was unavailable.

FAXEE UNKNOWN. NO FORWARDING CODE. The same message scripted out.

"Two options," he mutters under his breath, not liking either. Rathe has either emigrated off-planet, which is unlikely but possible, or she is dead.

How long has it been?

Martel breaks the connection and stares at the closer stretch chair, the creme one. The farther one, the black one, is where he usually sits.

Black, that's your color, not that there's much black on Aurore.

Martel picks up the faint hum of an electrobike on the coast highway, with the underlying whine that indicates it is climbing the gentle hill toward Mrs. Alderson's on its way into Sybernal.

So what do you do now? You waited too long, Martel.

He has two choices, either to see if he can track Rathe down or to finish cutting the strings right now.

Three, you can also track her down and then cut the strings.

Martel half smiles to himself.

That makes the choice.

He walks into the bedroom and sits on the end of the bed closest to the wardrobe. Off come the sandals and on go the black formboots.

He stands up and checks his tunic and trousers. Clean enough. Four stans before he is scheduled on duty at the CastCenter, certainly enough time to get to where Rathe lives—used to live—and find out what he can.

Is it really? he asks himself. *If you walk, it will take nearly a stan to get there. More. She lives/lived north of Sybernal.*

"So what are you telling yourself? That you don't have time?"

If you walk, he answers mentally.

"So don't, is that it?"

Instead of leaving through the front portal, he walks out the back way and marches over to the quince.

The resident dorle chirps once and quiets as he approaches.

You're crazy, Martel.

"Absolutely, absolutely. But you knew that before I got here, didn't you? Doesn't everyone?"

He is not certain whether he is answering himself or an intruder, but it does not matter.

Concentrating on the blackness that is somehow related to the field and yet not a part of it, he thinks of flying, of wings, and of ravens, symbols of night, symbols of that darkness.

The darkness enfolds him, washes over him, and where he stood hops a raven.

His takeoff is awkward, but with each wingbeat his flight is steadier, and he remembers to climb into the wind as he circles upward.

The southern rim of Sybernal stretches under his wings. He glides toward it, straight for an imaginary point directly over the CastCenter.

Sybernal, roughly clam-shaped, arcs around the natural harbor, which is used mainly by pleasure craft and the few fishing vessels that challenge the gold-green seas. The ring closest to the sea is the constant-width beach, from which protrude several points, including the North and South Piers. Behind the beach is the Petrified Boardwalk, and then the town houses of the permanent touries, interspersed with a sprinkling of restaurants and shops.

Behind the narrow district of red and gold awnings and roofs that sparkle even without the direct lighting of a sun runs the Greenbelt, and through the middle of the Greenbelt the coastal highway marches.

The trade district and the residences of most natives and norms are inland of the Greenbelt, and the most affluent of those who call Aurore home have their houses on the higher grounds west and north of the town.

The poorest live closest to the trade district, where the light breezes seldom penetrate.

Martel lifts his right wing, turns more toward the west in

order to cross the CastCenter directly. From above the Cast-Center, the five-unit complex where Rathe lives is north-west. He had located it after she left the last time, although he'd never been invited inside.

How can you be someone's lover and never see where she lives?

The question is just another he cannot answer.

His perceptions fan outward, to sense the thermals, to soak up the feeling of being airborne, and sense a turbulence. Darkness that is not darkness looms before him, building as he flies toward the five-sided communal dwelling.

Martel simultaneously leaves his perceptions extended and builds his shields, walls of darkness, his own darkness, behind them.

While he can sense dorles, sparrows, grimmets, and other birds flying well below him, the air at his altitude is clear.

Reserved for the gods?

Martel starts to shake his head, but stops as he realizes he has lifted his left wing and lost ten meters nearly instantly.

BEAR OFF, SMALL BIRD!

Martel blinks at the power of the command, surveys the sky, and extends his perceptions further.

Directly ahead, and several hundred meters higher, circles an enormous eagle, a golden eagle, whose feathers glitter with the light of a sun.

Martel draws upon his own depths, and the raven he is enlarges, with wingtips that would cover a small flitter. He climbs, wings beating, upon a thermal he has created, until he is level with the golden bird.

So intent is he upon his efforts that he does not see the departure of the golden eagle. But when he reaches the point where the eagle had circled, the heavens are vacant, the skies absent any trace of the giant bird.

Probing the air around him, Martel finds nothing.

He circles, slowly losing altitude, extending his mental search until his probes touch the buildings below.

. . . such an enormous black bird . . .

. . . the black vulture of the gods . . .

"Did you see that? The big black one drove off the sun eagle."

. . . has to be an omen . . . god of darkness . . .

Among the jumble of thoughts he can find no trace of the warm and friendly thoughts he seeks, no sign of the woman he has known.

His shape retreats to the classical raven as he drops to the buildings below, where he alights in a fir next to the complex where Rathe lived.

Her rooms are empty. That he can tell from a quick probe.

Martel the raven launches himself from the branch toward the windowsill. He skids on the sill's smooth stone, flaps wildly for a moment to catch himself, and falls against the plastipane.

"You see that clumsy bird, Armal?"

What do you expect? Martel questions mentally, blocking the thought from any transmission. *Perfection from an instant raven?*

He peers through the clear pane. Bare is the main room. Nothing remains, not even the floor covering. The ceramic floor tiles shimmer with the cleanliness of recent scrubbing.

He casts his thoughts into the rooms, but the sterility blocks any attempt at linking anything in the four rooms to Rathe Firien. Martel casts farther. The man called Armal is the landowner and the landlord.

Martel touches his mind, feels the strangeness, and enters his thoughts. Part of Armal's memories are gone. Martel can feel the void. There are no memories of the tenant in number four. None whatsoever.

The raven who is a man withdraws his probe and tries the woman who lives with Armal. A blowsy, wire-haired brunette originally from Tinhorn, she has no memories of Rathe either.

Neither do the tenants in the other units, nor is there even a trace of such a memory in the scattered mental impressions of the guardhound.

Martel turns his bird frame on the narrow ledge, forgetting he now possesses a tail. The long feathers brush the pane, and the thrust overbalances him into the thin air of the courtyard.

"Skwawk!" *Flame!*

He instinctively spreads his wings and beats his way out of the confined space.

"Clumsiest bird I ever saw, Armal. Biggest, too. Except for that golden eagle the other day."

Martel knows the golden eagle, but short of tackling Apollo head on or sifting the minds of all Aurore one by one, what can he do?

You waited too long, Martel . . . too long if you really cared.

He does not answer himself, but flaps toward the trees in the Greenbelt. From there he can emerge as a man and walk to the CastCenter.

XXV

▼

To whom do the beaches belong?
They are the sea's, the sands', and the land's.
They belong to the summer, the spring, and the fall,
To winter, to joy, to heartbreak, and no one at all.

The flitter, golden, with a rainbow sprayed across the lower fuselage, hovers over the beach grass at the edge of the sand, but the air from the ducts still swirls sand around the five who tumble out.

First comes a tall man in khaki shorts and blouse, wearing

a leather belt hung with all the implements of the overt and professional bodyguard. Next comes a woman, wrapped in a robe that billows around her, who keeps her balance despite the interference of the robe and the softness of the sand into which she jumps.

An older woman, sharp-featured, with golden hair, and another man, younger, golden-skinned and blond, who also wears a beach robe, follow.

Last is a heavyset man who floats to the sand rather than drops.

Once the last has stepped away from the flitter, the aircraft rises and circles to set down on the plateau above the secluded beach and wait for the return trip to Sybernal.

Secluded the beach may be, but not deserted, not as empty as the golden sands seem.

Near the base of the cliff, south of where the beach party disembarked, crouches a bristlepine. On the clear limb that offers a view of the sands where the five set up their keeper, chairs, and umbrellas waits Martel.

Today he is a raven. Tomorrow, or yesterday, a man. But today, he has decided to watch the private party of Cordin D'Alamay, well-known wealthy businessman from Percoln, and rumored esper. Only rumored, for the gods of Aurore do not permit known espers to visit without preventive quarantine.

Martel is not the only watcher. That he can tell from the number of glittermotes that flicker in and out over the surf and around a certain ledge even closer to the bathers than the bristlepine.

D'Alamay gestures at one of the folded chairs, all of which are golden. The one on which his attention is riveted is the sole chair with the rainbow across the back. The sought-after chair rises from the pile, unfolds, and deposits itself on the sand facing the low surf.

The heavy man wipes his sweating forehead with the back

of his black-haired and tanned arm before dropping his bulk into the chair.

"Very impressive." The older woman, who shares the same eagle nose, narrow face, and approximate age, places her chair next to her brother's. "I didn't know you could handle objects that heavy."

"It's easier here." He beckons to the other woman, who has stripped off the concealing beach robe to display a figure, barely covered, that would bring top prices at the Pleasure Mart of Solipsis. Not surprisingly, since that is where Cordin D'Alamay purchased her three-year contract. "Honey! You and Cort set up here."

Honey nods, and favors D'Alamay with professional smile number two—slight promise.

Cort, the male counterpart of Honey, sets up his beach chair next to the older woman and Honey's next to D'Alamay.

The bodyguard, impassive, surveys the surf, the cliffs, the sands, the skies, one right after the other.

Atop the cliff, the flitter pilot also surveys the flat seas and the line of beach that stretches near level in both directions.

D'Alamay takes another deep breath from deep within his chair. He looks at the sand in front of him. A small hill begins to grow. Soon the rough outlines of a classical-period castle appear, along with the return of perspiration to D'Alamay's forehead.

Cort, sitting on the edge of his beach lounger, feet dug into the sand, purses his lips.

"Whew!" he whistles. "Just like Castle D'Alamay."

The slumping of the sand into rougher outlines signals D'Alamay's shift of concentration.

The heavy man's eyes settle on Honey, who views the sea from beside her lounger. His appraisal travels the length of her tanned body. Honey wears a minimal two-piece bathing suit, unlike the more conservative suit of Arabel, D'Alamay's sister. While most women of any age would be pleased with Arabel's figure and skin tone, Arabel chooses not to flaunt hers.

Cort finds his job somewhat easier because Arabel is physically attractive. No matter that the figure and the skin tone represent the best from New Augusta's medical profession.

A tenseness drops onto the beach, like an unseen dark cloud.

The raven jerks his head from side to side, but can detect no new physical arrivals.

More glittermotes flicker around the boulder behind the D'Alamay party and above the point where the waves begin to crest before they break.

Honey. Come here!

The mental command from D'Alamay is faint but clear.

Honey's cold gray eyes glaze over momentarily, but she shakes her head, and the compulsion.

Come here!

"Whatever you're doing, Cordin, stop it!" Her cold eyes again glaze over.

"Remember who owns your contract." D'Alamay smiles, showing too much tooth.

Come here. Take off your suit.

"No," Honey says to the unspoken command. Her voice shakes. "I won't."

Perspiration beads on D'Alamay's forehead.

Come here . . . take off your suit.

Honey turns, takes one step toward D'Alamay, almost within his arm's reach.

"No!"

Yes! Now!

"No . . ."

Yes. Now, take it off . . . that's it . . . like that . . .

Slowly, slowly, Honey's right hand reaches to the knot at the back of her neck. Jerkily her hand tugs at it. The cords loosen, and she lets the halter fall away into the breeze. Both arms drop to her sides.

Now the bottom . . .

. . . no . . . someone, please help me . . . please . . . no . . .

Her hands go to the tops of her bikini briefs.

CRACK!

A single bolt of golden light strikes at the damp sand between D'Alamay and Honey, throwing D'Alamay out of his chair and tossing the bare-breasted woman several meters down the beach, almost to where the waves lap against the sand.

"My god!" gasps Honey.

"Damn!" That from Cort.

But neither Cordin D'Alamay nor his sister says anything to the figure in the pale golden tunic, dark leather sandals, and sunburst crown. The god-figure stands where the light had struck.

Ten meters away, the bodyguard clutches for his stunner. He is too late.

The golden god points.

Another flash of lightning, and the bodyguard is gone, only a glassy place on the sand and the offending stunner remaining to mark his presence.

"Who are you?" snaps D'Alamay, now on his feet, but taking a step backward.

The golden figure says nothing, just stares at D'Alamay, who pales.

If you are mortal, you may not impose your mind upon others. If you seek godhood, you impose on mortals only at your own risk, challenging any god who may dispute you. Are you mortal? Or do you seek to be a god?

"Nobody makes me choose! Stettin! Stettin! Flame him!"

A narrow laser beam flares from the guard atop the cliff, but it bends away from its target.

Again the golden man gestures. Again there is a brilliant flash of light, and this time nothing remains of the cliff guard or the flitter.

D'Alamay's eyes dart from the golden crown of Apollo to

the cliff and back. By the time his eyes have completed the traverse, the god is no longer there, but, instead, a whirlwind, a swirling maelstrom of dark gold and glittermotes twice the height of Cordin D'Alamay.

"Scare tactics . . . scare tactics," stammers the heavy man.

Honey's eyes widen and widen, until they close, and she slumps to the sand.

Arabel shrinks away from both her brother and the whirlwind while rooting herself deeper into her lounger.

Cort stands and edges away, quickly backing down the beach toward the bristlepine, his eyes glancing from the whirlwind to D'Alamay and back again.

"Cordin D'Alamay! You must choose what you will be!" The voice of the whirlwind sounds with the power of a grand orchestra and the focused intensity of a single note.

D'Alamay shivers, shakes off the power of the whirlwind like a wet dog shaking off water, but takes a backward step.

Is that a sea-goddess that the raven alone sees beneath the face of the breakers? Just beneath a cloud of glittermotes?

Cort catches sight of something, someone, under those glittermotes and turns to face them.

Honey stretches as if she is a child waking from a long sleep and looks at her outstretched legs for a time before getting up.

Arabel sits silently.

"Choose!" demands the whirlwind.

D'Alamay shakes his head from side to side, violently. *Never!*

"No one makes Cortin D'Alamay choose." But he backs farther away from the golden swirl that had been a god and may still be.

"You could run to the ends of Aurore and never escape your choice, and never escape the wind."

The man clenches his jaw and backpedals two more steps.

"Can you outrun the wind?" rumbles the whirlwind.

D'Alamay does not answer, retreats another step up the beach, his face whiter than before.

His sister Arabel shudders in her chair, which, surprisingly, still sits where she placed it. The umbrella, unnecessary as it was, under which she sat lies a good hundred meters down the beach, even beyond the bristlepine whence watches the raven. The umbrella's fabric and struts twist and tangle among themselves.

The woman called Honey stands above the high-water line of the sand and stares vacantly at the sea, a childlike look on her face.

Cort, on the other hand, stares at a vision no one else can see and takes a step into the gently lapping water.

"Can you outrun the wind?" whistles the whirlwind, its gold-and-black shape now less than twice the height of D'Alamay. "Are you a god? Or are you mortal?"

D'Alamay backs away, almost falling in the soft golden sand.

Cort takes another step into the water.

Arabel shudders.

Honey stares.

The raven watches.

D'Alamay keeps backing away from the pursuing cyclone, backing, stumbling, until his back is to the rock, the flat side of a cottage-sized boulder.

Arabel will not look, but hunches, shivering, in her chair.

Cort is now neck-deep in the water, still pushing toward a vision, his eyes bright, his progress steady.

Honey is curled up on the sand, asleep, tears drying on her face.

Three bell-like notes sound from the depths of the dark and gold twisting wind.

Bong! Bong! Bong!

"Choose what you are, what you will be!"

"No! No, no, no . . ."

"That is a choice," roars the wind, and further words, if there are any, are lost in the shrieking whine as the whirlwind rises from the sand and into the golden-hazed sky.

Silence holds, except for the ragged breathing of D'Alamay, the lapping of the sea on sand, the dry sobs of Arabel, and the sleep sounds of a grown-up child once called Honey.

D'Alamay gulps a deep breath, and another. He concentrates on a small stone at his feet. Frowns, then scowls. His face reddens, moisture popping out on his forehead, but the stone does not move.

"Gone . . ."

The heavyset man, who suddenly wears his skin like a loose cloak, looks up and across the beach.

His steps thud as he wallows toward the sobbing heap that is his sister.

Arabel does not look up as her brother stands over her, does not hear as he concentrates on her and finally mutters, "Gone, too . . ."

The only other human figure on the beach is the sleeping figure of Honey, curled into a half-circle on the dry sand above the high-water line.

D'Alamay's study turns toward the glassy patch of sand where his bodyguard had stood. The stunner lies where the guard dropped it.

D'Alamay waddles toward the weapon, staggers once, stumbles twice, and drops down on his knees to cradle the stunner in both hands.

His hands twitch, but he manages to lever the intensity setting up to lethal, and he looks squarely at the tip of the stunner before his thumbs press the firing stud.

The raven yet observes, for he knows that more will occur.

In time, less than a standard Imperial hour, two flitters set down on the hard wet sand by the sea.

The first bears the green cross of the Universal Aid Society. A man and a woman from the UAS flitter place Arabel upon a stretcher, and the body of the man D'Alamay upon a second, and the stretchers within the aircraft. As they do so, a second man polices the beach and stacks all the chairs, the foodkeeper, and the tangled umbrella, plus the scattered clothes, in the cargo bin.

The green-cross flitter lifts off toward Sybernal.

The second flitter bears the sunburst of Apollo. The two Apollonites wake the woman/child Honey and gently escort her into their conveyance. It, too, lifts off, but heads southward toward Pamyra.

The light dims on the narrow beach. Sudden thunderheads build offshore and above the beach.

Rain, driving into the sand, pools, puddles, and runs back into the sea.

Surf foams, pounds, rises, scours the upper beach, and subsides.

The raven shakes himself, waits.

Eventually, in less than a stan, the clouds break; the rain disperses; the surf lapses into a gentle lapping at the clean beach; and the eternal day returns to the again-pristine sands, which show no signs of footprints or human presence.

The raven fluffs his wings, shakes himself again, spreads his wings, and departs.

xxvi

▼

According to the universal time, Aurore Standard, it is 0600. Not that the clock matters on Aurore, but heredity and biology are stubborn. Martel knows that, knows they are the reasons why most businesses, except for entertainment, credit, and others catering to basic needs, are closed or part-staffed.

He strides through the portal out of the CastCenter and down the glowstone steps two at a time onto the Petrified Boardwalk. Imported slab by slab, legend has it, it was carted all the way from Old Earth to appease an early demigod, Avihiro.

Martel makes a two-hand vault up and sits on the low parapet, letting his feet dangle in midair above the sand, watching the ever-parallel waves hit the surf-break, climb, and crash down onto the straight lines of the beach. The waves are higher than normal tonight, if one can call very early morning night on the planet of eternal day.

He takes a deep breath, lets it go with a long hiss which is lost, a hiss less than a transitory footnote against the text of sand, sea, and surf.

A single figure retreats farther northward along the North Promenade of the boardwalk.

Like Kryn? No . . . step's all wrong . . . why . . . why do you keep thinking about Kryn?

He takes his eyes from the distant woman and looks down at the sand under his boots.

Why? . . . You'll never see her again . . . remember, Martel, she didn't protest when the Grand Duke had you Queried . . . sorry, Martel, and what will you do?

He looks up at the surf.

Your unattainable bitch goddess . . . that's Kryn . . . that's why you lost Rathe . . . wouldn't give up your impossible image.

Martel shakes his head.

How could you ever believe you meant anything to her?

Does it matter?

Does it matter?

The tight beam from Karnak has only opened the old doubts, the old questions. And the carefully phrased statements from New Augusta had only stirred the old confusions.

"The Regent is dead. Long live the Emperor!"

"Grand Duke Kirsten sits tonight at the foot of the Amber Throne, faithful to the Emperor, and faithful to the Regency, awaiting the decision of Emperor N'Troya."

That was what he, Martel the faxcaster, had announced to the tourists who wanted the news. The natives never watched faxnews. They didn't care that much about the rest of the Galaxy, and the gods knew it all before it happened. Or so it seems.

Martel still doesn't understand the Regent's "accidental" death. Was it suicide? Was Duke Kirsten, or the Duchess, that power-hungry? What of Kryn? Who attacked Karnak? How? Why? . . . And what of Kryn?

He frowns, for he has no answers.

Something has happened in Karnak. Something like a black nuke cloud has appeared next to the Tree of the Regent at the daily Moment of Silence. The Guard Force attacked, and most of the park has been wiped out. An enormous crater remains.

The dislocation destroyed the majority of the convenient power grids, and the weather system collapsed. A storm followed, the father of all storms, and the crater is now a lake.

Fine enough, Martel reflects, if such an unforeseen catastrophe can be called fine . . . but who would dare? Has the Brotherhood reacted at last to the Edict of Exile? Has some Brother smuggled in a mininuke? Is the whole thing an enormous hoax?

Martel shakes his head again.

No one on Aurore seems to care. Not a single call back to the CastCenter. The whole report sinking into the pond of public unawareness like a stone cast that created no ripples.

An accident with a hunting laser? Why would the Prince Regent suicide? Especially when the old Emperor is nearing the end.

The Regency Fleets are on full alert, but no unknown ships have been detected in the entire Karnak system.

No radiation has been detected in or around the lake that was the Regent's Park. Early reports mentioned a scorched faxtape recovered from the debris, but once it was turned over to the Grand Duke, all mention of it has been omitted.

And on Aurore, no one seems to care.

"No one cares," mutters Martel, knowing the words, all too self-pitying, will become one with the sound of the all-too-regular surf. "The Regent suicides. The park is destroyed, and the reports drop into Aurore like a stone into the sea."

A faint sound of bells tinkles in the back of his mind.

Martel jerks his head up, scanning both sides of the Petrified Boardwalk. He sees no one.

The off-duty newsie lets his senses slide away from his body, extends his perceptions. Nothing, except the faint feeling of bells. Silver bells. Tiny bells. Just the feeling of bells, and no sound of bells.

He shakes his head.

Ten standard hours the news has come in, and every stan since the first, it is the same pap. The Imperial Marine Twentieth has arrived in Karnak. All's well. The Fifth, Twelfth, and Eighth Fleets patrol the system. All's well. The Grand Duke assumes the duties as acting Regent. All's well. Power is restored. All's well. Sunrise occurs without incident east of Karnak the morning following the explosion. All's well. The Emperor confirms the Grand Duke as acting Regent. The Fleets return to standby alert. All's well.

Martel frowns. Like flame all is well.

He'd been suspicious years ago when the Regent's Palace had denied reports of a confirmed power failure. The two events should be connected, and Martel gropes for the time and the details . . . not that it matters. Or does it? A corner of his mind says that it is important.

"A brooding philosopher, is that it?" With the words is the same feeling of bells, though her voice is low.

He yanks his head away from the ocean view to the woman who stands by his shoulder.

She is taller than he is, and her shoulder-length golden hair, eyes to match, and the intensity she conceals all remind him of Kryn. Yet Kryn's hair is black, he remembers. The woman is familiar . . . where has he seen her?

"I take it that Kryn is your long- and forever-lost ladylove, Martel?"

Who is she? How does she know? How had he missed her approach?

"Who are you?"

"I could be mysterious, but I won't. Call me Emily. It's not my name, but it will do for now."

"How do you know my name?" Martel feels the bells more strongly now, almost warning him. He pushes the feeling away. He needs to know more.

"Who doesn't?"

"And who is Kryn?" he bluffs.

"Martel, I know everything about you. Including the fact that you're powerful and powerless, and friend to all and friend of none."

"Fancy words . . ."

". . . and you're appealing."

Despite the sincerity in her voice, Martel senses the mockery beneath, some of which is not directed at him. He acknowledges the unstated sarcasm, ignores it, and vaults down off the wall, even though he could appear more graceful with a mental push. He still dislikes using his powers for purely physical aids; three decades have not changed that.

"Where to?" he asks.

"Wherever. Until we sleep and wake again, I'm yours. Until then, I'm yours."

There is no mockery in that statement, no warning bells to accompany it.

"All mine? Without reservations?"

"All yours. Perhaps a reservation or two, though not likely to be the ones you'd normally get to."

Martel stops in midstride, looks the golden-haired woman straight in the eyes. She meets his glance without blinking, the black depths of her pupils seeming a thousand kilos deep and a thousand years old.

"Who are you?"

"I'm Emily. Tonight. Tomorrow . . . who knows?" She laughs, and the laugh carries the sound of bells and hunting horns.

"Emily . . . or Diana?"

"There's a saying about gift horses . . ."

"Flame . . ." Martel turns and walks northward, vaguely conscious that the woman is matching him stride for stride. Her legs are longer than his, her steps effortless.

At the North Pier he stops, wipes the sweat from his forehead. She stands there, smiling, cool, golden, as crisp as she appeared four kilos back down the Petrified Boardwalk.

Martel chuckles.

"You weren't offering a choice, were you?" He pauses. "All right, I'll take you up on it. Let's drink, and be merry. At the top of the North Pier tower there's a small restaurant . . . open all the time, and quiet . . . not that you don't know that already."

They are the only ones there, besides the host, who seats them at the table on the seapoint of the Star Balcony. The chairs are dark leather that matches the old wood of the circular brassbound table. Both the railing and the overhanging beams lower the light level of perpetual day to that of twilight on another planet.

The damper chill of the air is a relief to Martel, who refuses to use his powers to alter his metabolism, and who wonders how Emily remains so cool, unless she is indeed tapping the field. If she is, her action is at such a low level as to be unnoticeable. Martel pushes away the thought that brings.

He tries to push away the other thoughts as well, but they do not stay pushed. No one can sneak up on him. No one! But she has. No one can keep up with him for four kilos. But she has, and without breaking a sweat. Diana, not Emily, has to be the right name.

And she is familiar, but he doesn't remember how, where, and he doesn't want to think about that now, either.

"What's happening on Karnak, lady who knows everything?" As he finishes the question, he lifts the glass, just delivered by the unsmiling and dark-skinned host, swallows, and lets the cold Springfire ease down the back of his throat. He would prefer it from a jasolite beaker, but jasolite beakers and old Anglish decor apparently do not go together.

"You're right. They don't," responds Emily/Diana/????, "but then the old Anglish never would have created an open and paneled balcony above the sea, either."

"Karnak?" prompts Martel, consciously shielding his thoughts and taking another sip of the Springfire.

"You can take the student out of Karnak, but not Karnak out of the student. Isn't that how the saying goes? Karnak the soul of the Empire of Man . . . Karnak the Magnificent." Her lips twist slightly as she finishes.

Martel nods, looks away from the woman, all too conscious of the tanned body beneath the thin white chiton, of the fine-sculptured neck under the antique copper choker.

The regular beat of the surf drops a level. Martel knows it will maintain the lower waves for several standard hours, unless a sudden storm comes up, or a flurry of so-called god waves.

"Can you get there by candlelight?" he murmurs.

"Yes, and back again."

He twitches.

"I've studied you, Martel. Turned from your great ladylove Kryn, you did, to the words, to the dusty tapes of antiquity."

He pushes back his chair, puts both hands on the wide armrests.

Emily raises a hand, and he feels a gentle force pushing him back into his seat.

"You really are the bitch goddess. You really are."

"Did I say I wasn't?" She smiles.

Martel likes the smile, drinks it in, and doesn't trust it.

The candle on the table, dark green, square, winks out.

Martel relights it with a thought, lets it burn, lets the flame flare, and squeezes it into a narrow column that flickers level with Emily's golden eyes, and turns the flame black. He relaxes his hold, and the golden-green flame returns to normal.

"Very impressive for a nongod."

"Flame tricks, dear bitch goddess. What's happening on Karnak?"

"You're the newsie. Tell me."

"You're the goddess. Tell me what's behind the news."

"Either an old, old god or a new god, and the gods themselves don't know."

"So the gods are only gods. Is that it?"

Martel again turns the candle flame black, this time to stay . . . at least until snuffed and relit.

"Why do you fight everything, Martel? You could be a god, and you fight that. You could have light, and you fight that. You could have me, and you fight that. Some things are meant to be."

He looks up at Emily. Even though she returns the study, her eyes open, they are hooded. But her words ring true, like gold coins dropped on a stone table.

Martel stands, walks around the table, and eases back the heavy chair for her.

"Some things I don't fight. Not forever. Shall we go?"

He reaches for her hand.

The fires crackle, black flames licking from his arms and white from hers, twining in the space and instants before their fingers touch.

A plain gold flitter crouches at the end of the pier, empty. They enter.

The hillside villa is small, five rooms in all, with limited access. The cliffs to the back are impassable to any casual visitor, and the lawns and gardens to the front stretch into what seems an endless forest, though he can spot a trail several kilos beneath the villa.

The master chamber opens to the south and to a vista including Sybernal. Martel takes another look at the sweeping emerald lawns that drop toward the distant town, toward the pine forests that seem to guard the grounds.

Emily, or Diana, reappears at his elbow, still wearing the thin white chiton and antique necklace. She is barefoot, without the white leather sandals.

"You're determined to waste all the time you have, aren't you?"

"Me?"

"You."

"Why did you find me?"

"Why not? Opposites attract."

"Oh. I'm mortal, and you're a goddess? I wear black, and you wear white?"

"Nothing that simple. You could be a god, but refuse. You could wear any color, but chose black, which is all colors or none. You could have any woman, but spurn them all."

"You make it sound so simple," growls Martel, refusing to look at her, knowing that the minute he does he will want her. "Nothing's simple."

"You, Martel, assume that everything is linked. I'm not asking for the future. I want the now."

Her hand touches the back of his wrist. He can feel the electricity build in him, holds it to himself, holds back from looking away from the view of Sybernal.

"You find me unattractive? Or are you afraid?"

The oldest ploys in the universe.

Of course she's attractive. And of course you're afraid. You're afraid of your own shadow, Martel, he thinks, not realizing that he has projected his doubts.

Emily says nothing. Stands next to him, her fingers touching his hand, letting the breeze from the open vista wash over them.

Goddesses don't need sashes or sills, do they, the half-thought strikes him, strikes him as he feels his body responding to the desire Emily projects. Not projects, just plain has.

She wants him.

Does he want her? Really want her? Does it matter? What about Rathe? Or Kryn?

". . . Then love the one you're with," he murmurs, and turns toward Emily, golden Emily, gilded Diana, whose arms come around his neck, and whose lips meet his.

Kryn, Rathe, Kryn . . . he buries the names before they emerge as his hands tighten on the bitch goddess he holds, as he drops into the depths and the eternities she represents.

He should feel sleepy, but doesn't, as they lie next to each other, hands touching, arms touching, legs touching.

"What was she like, Martel?" Emily's voice is softer than he'd imagined it could be.

"Who?"

"Your lady Kryn."

"Bitch." His voice is flat.

"If you don't want to talk, you don't have to. Were you making love to me or to her?"

"Suppose I say both and neither? Suppose I say her?"

"Suppose you did. You still wanted me."

"Yes."

"Then that's enough for now. Now is all you have, Martel. Unless you stop fighting it, and become a god. Or recognize that you are."

"Do you want me just because I'm stubborn?"

She laughs, and the silver bells ring in her voice and in his mind. "Touché."

The pines outside the marble pillars sigh with the breeze.

Her hand leaves his, touches his bare shoulder, caresses the back of his neck.

"Martel?"

"Umm?"

"Don't waste any more time."

He rolls on his side to face her, lets his eyes run over her slender body, over the high breasts of the huntress goddess, over the even golden skin . . .

The second time is gentler.

He awakes alone in the bed, scrambles to his feet.

The villa is empty, except for the master chamber closet, where three identical white chitons hang, with three sets of identical white sandals beneath. In the bathing chamber, a heated bath steams as he opens the portal. A thick black towel is laid out. His tunic and trousers, immaculately clean, are hung next to the towel, with his boots beneath.

Next to his clothes hangs also a black cloak, with an attached collar pin, a black thunderbolt that glistens.

He uses his perceptions to probe the cloak and pin, but they are what they are, merely a cloak and a pin.

He steps into the bath.

Later, clad in his own clothes and the cloak he knows is a present from Emily, he walks out to the landing stage where the golden flitter waits, empty and door ajar.

Now . . . he remembers where he has seen Emily.

On the I.D. cube at the CastCenter, on that single cube that had brought the call of blasphemy and knocked poor Marta Farell right out of bed.

Of course. The goddess in one of her playful moments.

That is not quite right, he knows, but he shivers, and glances back at the white villa for a last look before he enters the flitter.

xxvii

▼

A raven—consider the bird.

Bulky, black-feathered, wings stubby for the size of its body, raw-voiced and scratchy-toned, if you will, a scavenger, an overgrown crow. And yet a raven is more than the sum of the description.

Consider the raven, who stands for the darkness and destruction, who embodies all the forebodings of those who cannot fly, and who brings the night to day.

Is then the eagle, who is also scavenger and predator, feathered and screeching in broad daylight, whose sole superiority over the raven is size, the better bird, the more magnificent symbol?

Which would be the mightier were their sizes reversed?

Could we accept all that the raven is . . . and grant him the wingspan of an eagle?

Or is it that we who eat carrion do not like to be reminded of that and revere the predator who tears bloody meat from just-killed corpses?

On planets where the sun kills and the night revives, which would be the better power symbol—eagle or raven?

—*Comparative Symbols*
Edwy Dirlieth
Argo, A.D. 2356

xxviii

▼

Taking the last steps two at a time, Martel reaches the top of the walk that leads to his cottage.

Mrs. Alderson is asleep. That he can tell from the sense of quiet around the bigger house.

The quince by the front portal of the cottage has finally decided to bloom, one of the few times since he arrived on Aurore.

As he approaches the low stone slab that serves as porch, front stoop, and delivery area, he stops. Tucked into the portal is a white oblong.

He leans forward and picks it up. The old-fashioned white paper envelope contains an equally antique handwritten letter.

The name on the envelope is his and also handwritten, but he does not recognize the hand, though it does not belong to any of his ladies. Of that he is certain.

He casts his thoughts around the cottage, but finds no one, no sense of lingering. That means the letter within the envelope was left or delivered while he was still at the Cast-Center beaming forth his cubes of reassurance on behalf of Gate Seven.

Martel frowns. He sniffs the envelope. The scent, faint indeed, and overlaid with the acridity of ship ozone, is feminine.

Willing the portal to open rather than using his thumb, he steps inside.

After debating whether to open the envelope immediately, he compromises and fills a beaker half full with Springfire before retreating to the rear porch to open and read the letter.

Eridian/Halston

Martel—

I don't know whether you heard. Gates and I bought out our contracts and settled here. We never knew what you heard after Marta's "Edict." For reasons you can understand, we were afraid to risk contacting you while we were still on Aurore.

So this is sort of an apology, and a long-delayed thank-you. Long-delayed because I realized my dreams were true. They weren't dreams at all.

Gates had an accident last year. He was hit by a malfunctioning flitter and almost didn't make it. The doctor made a real fuss. They insisted Gates was fifty standard years younger than he is. His heart and arteries especially. The phrase that sticks in my mind is "almost as if his heart and aorta were rebuilt."

That's where the dreams come in. One dream I've had ever since you showed up at the CastCenter. Gates is pointing a needler at you. Stupid, I suppose, since Gates has never owned one. But you were throwing a black thunderbolt at him. Next thing, he's lying on the ground, and you are keeping him from dying. Don't ask me how.

The neurotechs tell me that they aren't dreams. I either saw it or I believe I saw it. It doesn't make any difference which. For whatever reason, you saved Gates twice, in effect.

I also wonder why I gave up cernadine. Your influence?

As always, the questions are unanswered, and I don't expect a reply.

You are what you are, and for that I am grateful now. I hope you stay that way. Your road is long, I know, and Gates and I, despite your gifts, will be dust long before you scale your heights.

Hollie

P.S. You're also the best faxer left on Aurore, whatever else you may be.

Martel leans back in the chair, places the letter on the table, and picks up the beaker to take another sip of Springfire.

A single chirp from the dorle in the back quince breaks the morning quiet.

So your road is long, Martel. How long?

He pushes his own question away and puts down the beaker without taking another sip.

As he stands the breeze from his abruptness swirls the paper letter to the floor, half under the table. Martel leaves it there and paces to the window to look up the hill at the farthest pair of quince trees.

"Even when you erase the footprints and change the memories . . . just like the song." The words slip out before he thinks.

He does not sing, but, instead, the words hang in the air next to him, glowing.

I saw your footprints on the sand, Yesterday;
I saw your smile so close at hand, Yesterday.

Yet twenty years have come and gone, Since then;
My hair has silvered from our dawn, Since then.

And all my days have passed away,
All my nights are yesterday.

Martel does not look at the golden words he has wrought. Slowly they dim, and after a time the last *yesterday* fades. Only a single black glittermote circles his left shoulder.

He remembers the letter and retrieves it from under the table, looks at it as if it represents a puzzle he cannot solve. Finally, he places it on the shelf next to the book of poems by Ferlinol. The thin white sheets of paper, with their message from Eridian and the past, fold in upon each other, glow briefly, darken, and stretch into a single black rose.

Martel wipes his forehead and looks away from the flower that will outlast the cottage, and, perhaps, Martel himself.

Always harder, isn't it, when you start to care again?

He picks up the beaker from the table and downs the rest of the Springfire with a single gulp, ignoring the line of fire that sears his palate and flames down his throat.

The dorle chirps once again from the quince.

xxix

▼

Some stores are open at all hours, and when Martel leaves the CastCenter, his steps bear him toward the southern edge of the merchants' district, toward Ibrahim's.

He needs Springfire, perhaps some scampig, if Ibrahim has any today, and a few other, more common, items.

Good thing you've got an autochef, Martel.

Without it, the culinary monotony would have been un-relieved.

The air is quiet on this morning of eternal day and becomes even more motionless as he enters the white-gray paved lanes that indicate the area where the natives, and Martel, shop.

Aldus the bootmaker, oblivious to anyone, is letting down his awning as Martel approaches, scowling and wrestling with the heavy black iron crank.

Martel waves.

Aldus wipes the scowl from his face and, smiling a faint smile, waves back.

Across the land and three shops down from the boot-maker's is the next open doorway. As he nears it Martel can already smell the aroma of liftea and freshly baked ceron rolls.

The bakery must be new, since he does not recall it. Outside the fresh white walls and polished door he pauses, then decides to go inside.

Entering, from the corner of his eye he sees an older woman, her brown hair shot with gray, disappear through a side door into another room, leaving only her son, a boy of perhaps eleven standard years, behind the counter where the just-baked ceron rolls are laid out.

The liftea has been brewed in an enormous samovar that stands alone on the counter next to the baked goods. Neatly racked beside the tea machine is a tray of blue porcelain mugs, each facedown on a white linen napkin.

"Good day, young man," offers Martel.

"Good day, sir. What would you like, sir?"

The youngster smiles easily, and Martel smiles back.

"Are the rolls as good as they smell?"

"I like them, but we also have the plain ones on the other tray."

"If you like them," says Martel with a laugh, "I'll have to try one, and a mug of the liftea."

He hands the boy his credit disc.

"Oh, sir. I couldn't." The boy looks away.

"Why not?"

"I . . . I . . . just . . . well . . . ah . . ." His eyes are still fixed on the floor tiles.

Flame! Flame! Flame!

"My credit's good, young man, and I would rather be charged for it."

The boy finally recovers. "It would be our pleasure, sir."

"I'm afraid I'll have to insist. If people like me eat and don't pay, how would you and your family stay in business?"

The boy's mouth drops open, only for an instant, but he takes the proffered disc and sets it in the reader, which transfers the small credit balance to the bakery.

"Thank you, sir. I hope you like the ceron. It really is my favorite, except maybe for the spice sticks, and we don't have any of those this morning."

"Ceron it is."

He picks up one of the sticky rolls and takes a bite. The orange-and-spice taste is as good as the smell, and he finishes the roll in three quick bites. He wipes his fingers on one of the small square napkins laid out on the counter next to the mugs.

The pungent liftea clears the slightly cloying aftertaste of the ceron from his mouth.

Martel looks up from the mug to see a man half enter the bakery, then abruptly back out into the lane.

Martel downs the last of the liftea and places the mug on the empty tray where, he presumes, it should go.

"As good as you said," he tells the boy, who is still alone in the room with him.

"Thank you, sir. Have a good day."

"I suppose I will. You too."

Martel leaves the shop with a smile on his face.

Ought to do that more often, Martel. You stay too much to yourself these days.

He glances toward the bootmaker's shop, but the awning is fully down and extended, and Aldus has gone back inside.

Should get another pair of boots one of these days, I suppose.

The lane is deserted, except for two girls playing in the emerald grass next to the linen shop across from the bakery.

The proprietor of the linen shop half steps out of her door, then darts back inside, as if she has forgotten something.

Martel shrugs and resumes his walk toward Ibrahim's.

A muted clanging becomes increasingly more insistent, and by the time he reaches the middle of the next row of small businesses, each with a low-fenced and trimmed side yard, the sound resembles an off-tune gong.

Behind the grassy lawn that circles a single cormapple, a double door to a metalworking shed stands open, and through the open doors Martel can see two men wrestling with what seems to be a metal tank.

For several units he stands and watches the two as they struggle to straighten the crumpled end of the tank. After the bent metal is smoothed, however, they apply the patch plate quickly, and the two lift the tank onto a small delivery wagon.

Martel looks away from the shed to discover he is being studied by a small, wide-eyed girl who hangs over the half-story railed balcony.

He looks back at her, directly.

She continues her study.

He smiles.

Her dark brown eyes widen farther, if possible.

". . . oh . . ."

The sound comes from behind him, from the metalworking shed, and he glances toward it.

Standing frozen in the double doorway is one of the two men who had been working on the tank. The sleeveless tunic emphasizes his burliness and the bronzed nature of his skin. The man is black-haired, clean-shaven, and his mouth hangs open as he stares at Martel.

For a long instant, the three of them stand locked in that triangle, unmoving.

Martel breaks the pattern by grinning at the girl, who could not possibly stand taller than his waist.

"Have a good day, young lady."

He waves and turns to continue his steps toward the food shop.

"Bye-bye." The girl's response drifts back.

There is also the sound of air being exhaled, a deep breath, as if the metalworker had forgotten to breathe.

Martel sees no one else in the two blocks before he reaches the food store.

Ibrahim's shop is empty, except for the proprietor, who is seated, as he always is, in his dark brown tunic and trousers, on the high stool behind the counter.

"Who's there?"

"Martel. I need two bottles of Springfire, a few other things."

"Heard your beach story again the other day. I wish I could have seen it."

"Thank you."

Martel picks the Springfire out of the racks and sets both bottles on the counter, then checks the meat cooler for the scampig. He is in luck; several small fillets are available. He wraps them in the transparency and places the package next to the bottles. Taking a pear from the fruit section, he adds a scoop of rice which he bags, a box of noodles, and a scattering of vegetables, all of which he has wrapped into a single package.

At last, he stands before the counter.

"What's this?" asks the shopkeeper as his fingers flicker over the package of combined and mixed fresh vegetables.

"Mixed-up vegetables. Just charge me for whatever's the most expensive. That would be the garnet beans."

"The whole thing is thirty-five credits, sir."

"That's fine, Ibrahim. Run it through."

"Yes, sir."

The entire order will fit in the collapsible pack Martel unrolls from his belt pouch. He packs the items as Ibrahim feeds his credit disc into the reader and transfer system.

As Martel lifts the pack to his back he sees a young woman, blond, green-eyed, heavyset, and wearing a burgundy overtunic, peer in the doorway and immediately back away.

"Have a good day," Martel says as he leaves the counter, placing the credit disc back in his pouch.

"You, too. I'll be listening tonight."

Not that the poor bastard could do otherwise, Martel, not both blinded and blessed for his sins.

"You're probably one of the few natives who do listen, Ibrahim, one of the very few. Take care."

Not that he has much choice there, either.

"Thank you, sir."

Martel pauses in the entranceway and looks back up the lane. As far as he can see, no one has set foot on the stones of the pavement, no one at all.

Should you remove Ibrahim's blindness? You could, you know.

Martel looks down at the white-gray stones underfoot, then back up the deserted lane. Finally he shakes his head.

Apollo would just reblind him, and, besides, where would you shop then, without everyone running away?

He sets his steps toward the south, toward the isolated house and cottage beyond Sybernal. His paces are not light, but they are quick, and eat away the distance.

XXX

▼

The man—who wonders whether he is—sits under the covered porch.

He glances up at the wooden planks over his head, lets his eyes trace out the old, old wood from the newer old wood. To the eye, the difference is not great, though he can sense the lack of harmony that the best carpentry cannot fully disguise.

Smoothing the sundered patterns would be easy enough. Like melding into the flowing day-to-day existence of Aurore. Like forgetting dark-haired girls with golden eyes, or fire-haired women with green eyes, or demigods cast back into the sea.

"Except—" The words break as he stands, stretches.

"Except what, Martel?" he snaps at himself.

Except you're a lousy forgetter.

Shaking his head, he picks up the cup from the low table and gulps down the last of the yasmin tea.

He wears only a pair of black shorts, and is barefoot and clean-shaven. His heavy steps thud as he crosses the porch.

The cup floats from his hands and stacks itself in the cleaner.

He continues on into his sleeping quarters.

In the wardrobe are three dusty pale yellow tunics, with matching trousers, kept to remind him, and three sets of matching black tunics and their trousers.

Martel pulls on the nearest set of black pants, then the black tunic and the black belt. He sits in midair and pulls on the heavy black boots.

At one end of the closet is the black cloak. He has not worn it since it was given to him, but it repels the dust and is as fine as the day Emily left it in her villa for him.

He looks at the belt, with the triangular silver buckle that is his only ornamentation.

You wear the belt but not the cloak. Rathe, not Emily. What does that mean?

He frowns, gathers a hint of darkness around him, and, his dressing done, strides from the sleeping room back into the main room of the cottage.

The darkness, and the power it represents, both are things apart from the golden energy field of Aurore.

Just as you're a thing apart? Come off it, Martel.

He shakes his head again. Harder.

On Aurore, how can you tell what you believe from what is real? Or from what some god would have you believe is real?

He stretches out his left arm, palm open and upward, and inhales, leaving his senses to take in the faint tang of the ocean beyond the hillcrest, to take in the subdued chitter of the dorles in the quince trees.

In his open palm shimmers a black oval, a miniature door-way to . . . where? Martel is not sure, releases his mental grasp on the cold depths, and lets the blackness vanish.

Is it real? Or illusion?

Real, he decides. For the hundredth time or so.

There is a feel to power, and an absolute feel to absolute power. Call it certainty, reflects Martel.

He gestures toward the inside wall, the blank one, letting his fingers trace a figure. From his hand flows the stuff of darkness, outlining a crude figure, something not seen in the indirect and omnipresent lighting of Aurore.

Shadow, shadow, on the wall,
Who casts the longest shade of all?
Is it death; or yet desire?
Is it night, tamed by fire?

Who's the man who lights the lamp
And calls the storm that brings the damp?
Which the god who blocks the sun
And fills the rivers in their run?

Call the hammer, call the lightning . . .

He closes his mouth. The old words have power still, lift-ing him into the role, letting him imagine he is a god.

Not now. Not yet. Not ever.

And yet . . .

Who can say "ever" or "never" and know? Really know?

Martel shrugs.

The shadow vanishes from the wall, the only remnant the small cloud of black glittermotes that hovers above Martel before winking out.

One touches down on Martel's left shoulder, clings.

Letting his perceptions slide around the corner from where he stands, he checks the timer above the autochef.

Time to leave for the CastCenter.

Walking will give him the time to think over the puzzles.

Don't you just like to walk? Admit it, Martel. Do you really think then?

He leans to touch the light panel on his way out, cannot quite reach it, and turns it off with a mental tap.

Another black glittermote appears and settles on his right shoulder, paired nearly invisibly on the black of his tunic opposite the other mote.

As he heads down the steps to the coast highway, a dorle chitters once. He knows not why, but Rathe comes to mind.

Rathe?

Why do you keep thinking about her? She left. You didn't search, not really.

Short strides, quick strides, untiring strides bear him toward Sybernal, toward the CastCenter.

She called you a god, and you let her go.

A quick glance toward the flat surface of the ocean tells him that the waves, long and sleek in their golden greenness, are flatter than usual.

Why are you so hung up on this esper crew that calls themselves gods? Talented, yes. Gods, no. Right?

The air seems a shade more golden, along with the calm, and the highway is deserted.

Like when Rathe found you the cottage?

Stop it!

Do you love her? Honestly?

No.

Like her? Respect her?

Yes.

POWER! LIGHT!

His dialogue with his unseen devil or conscience is brought to a halt with his perception of the sheer raw energy ahead.

His legs keep pumping as he quick-steps up the paved highway and over the gentle hilltop.

Just over the crest sits the doctor/god Apollo in an insubstantial chair. The four legs of the chair are yellow snakes. The back is composed of two fanned dragon wings.

Beneath his golden ringlets Apollo's face is expressionless.

At his right foot lies the body of a man . . . young, dark-haired, facedown. Dead.

By his left quivers a redheaded woman, sobbing silently, dryly. Rathe.

Rathe.

"Balance, Martel. You do not understand the need for balance. Power must be balanced with the understanding of its impact on mere mortals. Belief is more powerful than power."

Apollo tells the truth as he sees it, Martel knows; his words ring like a flat carillon.

Martel gathers his darkness around him, bemused as the clouds of black glittermotes appear from nowhere.

"Before you try to employ that energy, Martel, be so kind as to observe."

Martel nods, reaching out a thin thread of thought to re-assure Rathe.

Apollo outlines a golden square in the air. Colors swirl and resolve into a picture.

Martel watches, a corner of his mind still occupied with the huddled figure that is Rathe Firien, as the small drama comes to an end.

Rathe is helping another of Apollo's would-be demigods become accustomed to Aurore. Except . . . except this time she does not offer her body and soul.

Does not. Does not humble herself.

The man, pursuing, strikes out with all his mental force . . . and the force misses Rathe and rebounds upon him. Partly, Martel surmises, because Rathe is wearing the same shielding as when she first met him, partly because the man is a lower-level esper, and partly because . . .

Martel wonders if along with his physical gifts he had given her some shields of her own.

In the picture conjured by Apollo, the last scene shows Rathe looking down at a body, the same body that lies at Apollo's feet.

"You see, Martel, what you have done."

I? Come off it, you pious fraud!

Martel twists raw hunks of power, not from the energy field of Aurore, from his own depths, and marshals it within.

You cannot harm me, Martel.

"No! . . . No . . ." murmurs a small voice.

Martel looks at his former lover and holds his energies.

"Why not?" he temporizes.

"Because—"

Her statement is never completed, for Apollo touches her, and she is gone. A flash of flame, and she is gone.

. . . you'll be like him. Those were her last thoughts, and they fade into the golden haze.

Martel hesitates. Looks at Apollo, standing yellow-bright, smirking, daring Martel to strike.

Martel gathers his darkness even tighter into himself . . . and walks around the chair with the flickering legs, around the smirking god, and begins to trot toward Sybernal.

Step, step, step, step . . . and wipe your cheek. Step, step, step. Wipe. Step, step, step . . .

She asked you not to.

But Rathe is gone.

For what?

Gone in flame because of a mad god. And he, Martel, had not seen it coming. Had not seen the total disregard, the snuffing out of a vital woman, snap. Had not believed power so cavalierly used.

But she asked you not to.

Rathe had not asked for help, had not begged for anything . . . just for Martel not to attack Apollo. And not because she feared Martel would be hurt.

"Because you'll be like him." That was what she'd said.

Martel shudders even as he keeps trotting.

Are all gods like that?

Isn't everyone with power?

Kryn. Lovely Kryn, having her guards fire on a lonely Martin Martel just because he'd been discovered to have esper potential.

The Grand Duke, who ruled high in Karnak, throwing the Imperial Marines after a solitary student who had displeased his daughter.

Emily, the carnal goddess, taking what she wanted and leaving. No good-bye. Just the power to arouse and take and discard. And leave a black cloak as a thank-you.

Is that what becoming a god of Aurore means?

Does it have to mean that?

Step, step, step.

He lets his pace slow to a quick walk as he crosses the "official" southern boundary of Sybernal, where the Petrified Boardwalk begins.

The refrain from the "Heroes' Song" echoes in his thoughts:

> *Tell me now, and if you must,*
> *That a man's much more than dust.*

If Aurore is light, if Apollo is the sun-god . . . no god will I be. Not by choice, nor by accident. Not now, not ever.

Stuffing the swirling energies, the black fires, deep inside himself, Martel touches the CastCenter entry plate.

"Martel, evening shift."

That's right. Evening, evening in youth. Evening in full light. Why not? Light is a lie, promising everything and signifying nothing.

xxxi

▼

A small, dark-haired girl stands on a half-story balcony and looks to the south. She inclines her head slightly, as if bowing to an unseen presence, then lifts it and stares into the southern distances.

"Derissa?"

She ignores the call and continues to watch the southern heavens, and their eternal gold.

"Derissa!"

The girl makes the sign of the inverted and looped cross and walks back into her bedroom to obey her mother's call.

. . . Up the lane, behind closed doors of a workroom, the bootmaker Aldus labors over a pair of black formboots.

He checks the seams of the left upper, squinting as he draws the black leather next to his eye.

He nods and puts it down, begins to check over the right upper.

The door opens behind him.

"How are you doing, dear?"

"So far, so good."

"Your supper's ready."

"I'll be there in a moment, as soon as I check this one over."

"You've checked, and checked, and checked."

"It has to be perfect."

"Would He know the difference?"

"No, probably not, but you never know. And I would. Unlike some of Them, He pays, and pays what they're worth. Almost, anyway."

The bootmaker does not lift his eyes from the black leather.

After a time, the woman looks away, shakes her head silently, and retreats to the kitchen.

. . . On a golden sand beach, across the Middle Sea, a boy, playing on the sheltered beach under the cliff on which his parents' house rests, scoops up a handful of sand for his castle.

The dark glitter catches his eye. In among the golden and silver grains of sand are black ones, sands so black that each grain seems to absorb the light, but glistens all the same.

He begins to separate the black grains from the silver and gold ones, until at last he has a small handheld heap of mostly black and glittering sand.

"Mom! See what I found!"

His mother wades in from the low surf to meet him in the ankle-deep water.

"See! See how shiny it is!"

"Pierre, put that sand down. The black ones are dangerous."

"But why?"

"Put it down. All of it."

"I want to know why."

"When you're older, I'll tell you. Put it down."

"But why?"

"I told you it was dangerous. When you are older, I will tell you why. Now . . . put . . . it . . . down!"

"All right." He throws the black glimmerings into the water lapping around his ankles. "All right, but you'd better tell me. You promised. You promised."

"I will. I will. Now . . . let's see if you can still float on your back."

. . . In the secret hollowed-out space beneath the old stone house, they begin to gather.

By ones, by twos, the figures drift in and take their places in the small chapel, until the requisite score has assembled.

The man in the brown robe finally approaches the cube, black on all sides, on which stands a single black candle.

He does not light it.

"Oh, hear our prayers, undeclared God of Night. God of Darkness, deliver us from Light."

"Hear our prayers."

"Oh, hear our songs, God of the Evening, God of Blackness."

In time, up wells the familiar refrain:

> . . . And the Hammer of Darkness will fall from the
>   sky;
> The old gods must fly, and the summer will die . . .

The black candle remains unlit on the black stone cube.

"Deliver us from Light; deliver us from the flame of our oppression, from eternal day that lets us rest not, nor slumber. Hear us, and deliver us, thy servants, from the bondage of eternal brilliance . . ."

xxxii

▼

For the third day running, the waves break over the top of the golden sand beach, and the biting spray reaches over the hillcrest and down to the porch where Martel sits.

As all mortals do, his landlady, Mrs. Alderson, had succumbed to time, even though her life had been prolonged a great deal more than she had expected. For reasons unknown to Martel, who remains uninterested in the finer details of cellular biology, his attempts to rejuvenate the gray-haired woman failed, though she was unaware of his efforts.

Surprisingly, her testament, last declared less than a standard year after he had come to live in the small cottage, had offered him the right to buy either the cottage or the house, or both.

With the continuing royalties from his reruns—both *Forgotten Beaches of Aurore* and *Postulant Communities of Aurore* are a steady source of income—he purchased both and rented the house out, preferring to stay in the cottage.

The present occupants of the house are a middle-aged couple on sabbatical from the University of Karnak. Most of Martel's renters have been outsider norms. Those who decide to stay move elsewhere.

Martel shakes his head. The mannerism is unnecessary, he knows, but he enjoys hanging on to some of his useless habits.

Martel sniffs the air, and the salt tang reminds him of the waves whose muffled crashes he can hear from the other side of the hill.

The continuing waves are unnatural, even on Aurore. After three days, they are not likely to disappear, not until they achieve their purpose.

Another challenge? Or annoyance?

He rises, his face clear, eyes hooded, dark. A stocky man, modest in height, black-haired, lightly tanned, apparently in the health of first maturity.

His steps are heavy, but they have been heavy since youth, as he descends the three steps from the porch to the hillside. He walks up the grassy slope to the top of the hill that overlooks the small bay.

At the crest he pauses.

The spray flings itself upward in misty patches, glistening in the indirect light that gives the breakers themselves a threatening yellow look.

From his vantage point he can see the outward path of at least one riptide.

He shrugs as he starts down the hillside, the shadows gathering around his black-clad form.

A dorle chitters at him, but wings over and glides across the hilltop to perch in one of the quinces and to wait.

Any close observer would note that Martel's feet do not quite touch the grass over which he marches and that there is no direct light to cast the shadows that trail him.

From the grass that does not bend under his tread to the sand that does not receive his footprints he heads straight toward the waters, and they part around him.

He walks through gold-green breakers as if they are not there, and the waters crash over the places where he has been without touching him.

Overhead, a white bird with deep golden eyes and black pupils circles, then vanishes.

His head beneath the water's surface, he follows the line of the sloping beach at least a kilo outward. By now the waves are nearly a hundred meters over his head, yet his hair is still in place, and he moves, bone-dry, over the seabed sands.

At the edge of the rocky shelf he stops, knowing that beneath his feet is the beginning of a slope that will drop nearly a kilo in several hundred meters.

By rights, that for which he searches should be near.

Out into the nearby waters he casts his thoughts, and on the first cast snares nothing.

Nor on the second. Nor on the third.

Some little patience has evolved in his years of avoiding what others regard as inevitable, and he changes his cast, refocuses his thoughts, and tries again. And again.

At last, a glimmer, a slight tug.

That is enough, and he turns his steps southward, paralleling the dropoff, striding quickly, as if the water were not surrounding him.

Above the sea the white bird, golden-eyed, circles, following his general track.

A giant sea eagle, spotting the smaller avian, stoops to kill, and is brushed aside with a sudden gust of wind. The eagle tries again and is again brushed aside, and circles in confusion before deciding on the easier prey of a flying ray. In midskim from wavetop to wavetop the ray twists. But the intended evasion is too late, and the eagle flaps heavily toward his cliff eyrie with his meal.

Circling still, the white bird follows Martel.

As Martel proceeds toward his objective the clear water becomes less clear, and then even less so, until eyesight becomes useless. Martel is untroubled and unaffected and disappears into the cloud of sediment and suspended sand.

A few hundred strides farther on, he halts.

The suspended material whirls from an ever-expanding pit. Although Martel cannot see, he knows that at the center of the pit is a restrained and chained demigod. One suffering the punishment of a major god, and perhaps, placed in such a way as to infuriate the not-quite-major goddess who rules the shallows.

Should he free the chained demigod, the one creating the turbulence in his twin efforts to escape the eternal chains and to fight off the minions of Thetis?

If he frees the unknown demigod, both may turn on him. The former because only by subduing Martel can he return to the good graces of those who chained him. By now Martel has discovered that the demigod is male and that his principal tool is the fire of lava.

In turn, Thetis may attack because Martel will have intruded and robbed her of her due. She would have all thrown to her serve her, for at least a time.

Martel steps forward and descends through the swirls of boiling water and glass rain, down until the only light is the heat that surrounds the captive, light that is dimmed a fraction of a meter from its source.

For though the eternal chains are metal, no heat will melt them, no superhuman strength rend the unseamed black links which, no matter how deep the chained one melts away the rock, stretch yet deeper into the depths.

Do not free me unless you will pay the price.

Martel snorts at the contradiction. Any being who can free the demigod must have power superior to his.

Martel smiles, faintly, knowing the other cannot sense his humor, gathers further his own darkness, his own chill depths, and touches one link, then the other chain.

The metal draws back from his touch, glistens more blackly, if possible, then fades and is gone.

Martel gestures, and the water is crystal-clear again. Of the eternal chains there is no sign.

The onetime captive, dressed in skintight red, reaches forth across the water he has warmed to grasp the man in black. As he does his arms lengthen impossibly. Those arms burn, and the water vaporizes away from them.

Fool!

Instead of turning away, Martel glides forward into the heat, into the grasp of Hades, lets the would-be god of fire enfold him.

No!

For now Martel holds the other's arms, more tightly than the eternal chains, for yet a moment before he releases the one in red.

He steps away and points. With the shadow he dispatches through the water goes the one in red, wrapped for delivery to the Sacred Peak.

Was that wise, Martel?

Still in the depths hollowed by the demigod of fire, Martel looks up the green-glass side of the submarine amphitheater to the one who addressed him.

Thetis?

Who else?

Your pardon, but the unnaturalness of the waves beckoned.

He walks up the glass-smooth slope that would be impassable for most, as if walking up a sheer glass incline a hundred meters undersea and remaining totally dry were not at all unusual.

Thetis, at home, in her ocean, is not dry. Rather, the water enfolds her, and her clear green hair flows over her naked shoulders, front and back, like a cloak. In her right hand is a small trident. Her left is open, empty, as Martel approaches.

The unnaturalness was meant to call you. So I waited. To see what you would do.

And?

Why did you not destroy him? He would have done that to you.

And give them a reason?

Your refusal to accept godhood on their terms is reason enough.

Martel shrugs, smiles a small smile. *But I would not give them reason were I in their place. That is what is important.*

She lifts her trident halfway.

Do not, dear Thetis. For I love the sea, and I would grieve.

You mock me. You mock the gods.

No.

The energy gathers around the green goddess.

Martel gathers his darkness, the black from the depths out and beyond the field, out and beyond Aurore. The cold and the fire and the remoteness invest him. No longer a mere human figure, no longer merely immortal, he stands apart.

The water draws farther back from him, as if in fear. The sand under his feet shrinks from the soles of the black boots.

His eyes are the depths of the places where there are no stars, the distances from whence stars cannot be seen, and his eyes . . . they burn. They burn black, with a light that casts shadow across the entire seabed. A light where there should be no light, and a shadow where none should be.

Still is the sea, and awful.

The trident drops, and with it the bare knee, followed by the inclined head.

For all this, Thetis, for all this, dear lady, no more am I god than this water, or that boulder.

She shivers, though she is not cold.

God of darkness, god of night, that you endure where light reigns, that you are, that you triumph, means there are no gods. Not as you would call them.

Martel nods, releases his hold on the darks and on the depths.

That may be. I am no god. Only a man who knows more than many, and a little more than some.

No. Her thought bears sadness. *Not just man. Thinking so will bring sorrow to you, to all who surround you. More sorrow than you have experienced. Already you ignore the tears. Is it not so?*

He does not answer, except with a short furrow of his brows.

Thetis belts the small trident, blows Martel a kiss, one that crosses the water between them and caresses his forehead.

If not god, accept what you are, Martel.

He salutes the departing sea-goddess with an upraised hand, and, in turn, directs his steps toward the shoreline.

The sea is flat, motionless yet as he emerges, and as his black boots touch the sand. The air is quiet, and hawks, the dorles, and the golden sea eagles all perch where perches each, waiting.

When his last step clears the water, when he turns and again salutes the mistress of the sea, only then do the gentle waves resume, the sea breezes flow, and the sea birds fly.

Martel realizes his cheeks are wet, not from the water, for no water has touched him.

In response, he presses lips to fingertips and breathes the kiss back across to the sea, back to Thetis.

xxxiii

▼

Help!

Martel stumbles, trying to pinpoint the direction of the thought, looking around, glancing up toward the shore and the Petrified Boardwalk.

A scattered handful of people—mostly natives—make their way through the fully lit and evening streets of Sybernal. Not a one of the three within ten meters of Martel has even flinched.

Despite the faintness of the thought, the aura of the plea is familiar. He cocks his head, trying to remember, to make a comparison. Not poor lost Rathe, for even the desperation of the thought holds a hardness that Rathe would never possess.

Why dig that up? She's gone. Gone.

Martel trots to the next corner, peering around it. No one notices him in the Street of Traders, not even the old man whose boot store is yet open with its green awning overhanging the public way.

Martel darts into the narrow lane around the corner from the bootery, gathers his shadows about him, and rises into the light. He does not notice the looped sign the bootmaker traces in the air as the black raven circles up from the lane, nor the averted glance of the young girl whose balcony he passes as he flaps awkwardly northward, from where he thinks the plea for help has come.

Martel! God of the Darkness! Save me!

Martel's wings miss a beat, and he loses altitude, then converts his drop into a dive, wings folded. For the desperate prayer has indeed come from the CastCenter.

The locked portals open at his touch.

Already the center feels empty, devoid of life. Martel's

thoughts precede his body through the corridors toward the main control center. An aura of power is fading, an aura that Martel recognizes, from the control room, where Martel knows he will find what he does not want to see.

In the center, in the open space before the console, which is slaved to remote and broadcasting an opera from Karnak, on that open floor are three objects.

The first is a sheet of golden parchment, scrolled, on which a name appears. The name is *Martel.*

The second is a pile of heavy gray ashes, greasy in appearance, spilling across a golden starburst that has been etched into the permaplast flooring. A starburst, Martel knows, that had not been there the day previous.

The third item, collapsed in and around the ashes, is a pale golden one-piece coverall.

There may be other small objects, such as a sunburst pin, a thin golden chain, mixed in the ashes as well, but Martel does not touch anything. Except for the sheet of parchment, which he stoops to pocket.

Martel gestures. The darkness swirls over the control room, and the floor is as it was, unmarked. Ashes, coverall, objects, all are gone, taken into the darkness.

From darkness she came, and unto darkness will she go, now and forever.

The cold knot inside Martel does not dissolve, but reaches to chill his fingers, numb his thoughts.

"Flame!"

Darkness has fire, also, and that will I claim, for those who are mine, and those who claim me.

Martel stands, letting time swirl around him, then clamps himself back into reality.

He leaves without touching anything, departs as he came, and even young Alsitar, who is rushing through the main portal in response to the automatic alarm and who passes the one who was called God of Darkness as He steps outside the portal, even Alsitar does not see what he sees. For Martel wills it otherwise.

Believing in a god who will not accept divinity is obviously a dangerous business, reflects Martel. He shivers as his feet carry him along the Petrified Boardwalk.

He strides down the boardwalk until it becomes a patch along the back of the beachline, until Sybernal is behind him, until the roofs are less than smudges on the southern horizon.

Then he takes out the golden parchment scroll with the sunburst in the upper right corner.

Until what is proper is done,
    the followers of those who challenge shall suffer,
    for an undeclared god is no god,
    and blasphemy is death.

Martel shakes his head. Rathe he could understand. But Marta Farell?

Does Apollo really think this would force him to take them all on?

Won't it?

Yes, but not yet, not now.

Ever?

He touches the parchment with shadow, and it is no more.

For a time he regards the ocean in the perpetual light that could be morning or evening, and is both and neither.

At last he turns back to the south. Where his feet touch the sand, each quick step leaves a black print, each grain of once-golden sand now the color of the space between galaxies.

The line of jet footprints on the shimmering golden sands points toward a distant cottage that has become emptier by the absence of one who never lived there, and never would have.

Soon a storm will rise and scatter the dark grains. After that storm, or the next, or the following, some child will look at a black grain and wonder. For all know that the sands of Aurore are golden, and there is no black sand.

xxxiv

▼

Rathe?

Should he re-create her? The odds are good that he can duplicate her essence.

Are they?

He twirls the beaker that contains the last of the second bottle of Springfire he has consumed since he began the debate with himself.

Would she be Rathe? Even if I caught everything? Remembered it all?

He looks from his chair on the porch up the hillside. The topmost quince is dying, he can tell.

Why don't you rejuve the quince? Re-create it?

Plants don't rejuve.

Then re-create it.

It wouldn't be the same quince. Might as well plant another.

He sips what should be the next-to-last sip from the beaker. Through two bottles the questions have not changed. Neither have the answers.

And Rathe? Would your creation be the same? Could you bear not to make changes? Even if you didn't, would she be the same?

He does not answer the questions. Instead, his sip becomes a gulp as he downs the last drops of the Springfire from the jasolite beaker.

"Flame! Flame! Flame!"

Even as he stands and gathers the darkness to him, even as he hurls the beaker into the flooring with enough force to shatter it and embed the crystal shards into the wood, he knows the answer.

Rathe is dead.

Dead is dead.

No miraculous re-creation will restore the woman who loved him.

All you'll have is a duplicate doomed to repeat the mistakes of the real Rathe. A pale copy without the fire of the original. A living doll without the soul of the only Rathe who lived.

"A pale copy? Sure. Just a pale copy! And what are you, Martel? A pale protoplasmic copy of distant ancestors who screwed around!"

Say what you will . . . dead is dead.

"Easy enough to say. Easy enough to think. But you're alive."

Exactly.

"You can throw your thunderbolts. You can summon the eternal darkness. You can heal the sick. You can walk on air and on water. So why can't you create a new Rathe?"

You can. You just can't bring back the old.

"So why don't you?"

The darkness freezes with the question, and even outside the cottage the breeze stills and the dorles quiet.

Because she's not strong enough. Because you'd destroy her again.

"Me? You wonderful subconscious, tell me again I destroyed her."

Didn't you force her to leave and not protect her?

Martel does not answer himself in the quiet and dark that wait for his decision.

Do you want to spend every moment guarding her from Apollo? Can you make her a goddess? And if you could, would she be Rathe?

"Flame!"

His breath comes out in a long hiss, and the silence is broken. Outside, the two dorles in the nearest quince chitter. The low waves in the bay across the hill swish once more, and the breeze ruffles his short hair. The darkness ebbs beneath the moment.

At last, he looks down and wills away the crystal shards in and on the floor. The polished wood returns to an unblemished state as the scratches erase themselves.

Although there is another bottle of Springfire in the cooler, he will not need it. Not today, not tonight, though they are one and the same on Aurore.

Even gods, even you, have limits, Martel.

He would cry, but cannot, as he looks to the hillcrest and the twilight that will be centuries in coming. Instead, he stares at the dying quince.

XXXV

▼

Time, like a loose-flowing river, does not, will not, flow the same for all individuals, neither mortals nor immortals.

That thought flits through his mind as he takes quick step upon quick step along the narrow pathway that leads toward a white villa.

Technically, the answer is simple. Technically, the answer is not an answer, but chance. Chance alone seems to determine who lives and who dies. Some mortals become gods, and no scientist can determine why. An increasing number of mortals, even within the Empire, do not age, or age far less quickly than others.

"Miracles?" he mutters as the path begins to rise. Any demigod on Aurore can return youth to a mortal, at least in body. But whether the youth remains so for more than a few years depends again on the individual.

"My individual?" he asks the trail, both recalling and trying to forget the lady upon whom he had bestowed the gift, recalling also how he had hoped she would remain beautiful in her own way beyond her time.

Beyond her time? That time was so short.

Had he only made the effort . . . had he made the effort he had not, for the reasons he can understand but not accept.

Will you ever accept them? Will you ever fight the gods for one individual?

You can't fight them all.

Won't you have to, sooner or later?

Perhaps. But not for one individual.

Then for what? For what, for whom, will you fight, Martel?

He turns himself away from the question, lets the day enfold him, lets himself be one with the trees, the golden grass, the scrub thistles, and the meadow flowers . . . with the dorles, with the white birds that dip their beaks into the clear brooks beyond his sight.

The key is mind over matter, but not the mind of thought. Rather the mind of the mind.

He frowns. Is he rationalizing, once again, his feeling of desertion toward Rathe?

Mind over matter, indeed.

He concentrates on his pace. Quick step, quick step, and the trail unrolls before him, stretching into the low hills, beckoning him away from Sybernal.

Most of the pines, wide-trunked and long-needled, whisper in the afternoon day, murmur in the perpetual breeze that cools these hills to the north of Sybernal, and hint at the power that naps in the scattered villas that nestle on the few cleared hillsides.

Martel wipes his forehead on his short black sleeve, halts where the path forks, and casts his thoughts down both hard-packed trails.

Why are they hard-packed? No sign anyone uses them.

The right-hand path dips down toward a brook, perhaps a hundred meters beyond what he can see directly with his eyes, and leads another kilo before ending in a small park-like clearing. Although his perceptions relay no structure to him, the impression is of a small freehold left to the elements, but tidied occasionally by a passing demigod.

He casts his thoughts out along the left path, resuming his rapid pace before evaluating what he perceives.

Others may be monitoring him. That he assumes from the feather-light tendrils of power that flicker in and out of his awareness, particularly when the breeze dies to a mere ghost.

Not that you mind, Martel.

He stops and studies the hillside to his left, the abrupt clearing that slants down the slope the length of three tall pines before the old trees close in.

Old trees . . . not many young ones, nor any dead ones . . . and what does that tell you, Martel?

How old are the pines? Or the few deciduous trees that mingle with them?

Martel shakes his head, once, quickly.

The faint scent of the pines and the swish of their boughs as the breeze picks up are saying something, trying to tell him something important. What, he cannot decide.

He kicks a rock, scarcely more than a pebble. He watches as it skids down the trail before bouncing sideways and disappearing into the golden grass that he thinks of as native. This high in the hills the emerald grass of Sybernal has not penetrated, except within some estates. Yet the trees are Arthtype.

Another tendril of power, stronger, flickers over him, dismisses him, and moves on.

Martel leaves his shields fully in place and smiles as the thin probe withdraws. The prober lies a long way from the path upon which he stands and does not recognize that Martel's shields conceal his darkness. But then, sentry duty is boring for most sentries in most times and places.

Martel gives the clearing beside the trail a last look before he continues onward. The scene is not quite idyllic. From between the golden grasses peer crimson flowers, while a few scattered scrub thistles ring the far edge just inside the pines.

Order . . . very definitely ordered, Martel.

The pines are all healthy. Massive. Tall. Mature, but not old, though their size lends that impression. No gnarled branches or fallen or rotten trunks detract from the evidence of strength.

He cannot recall any such evidence of decay during his entire hike from the outskirts of Sybernal.

"The trees militant," he says with a low laugh, and picks up his pace as the trail narrows and begins to turn back on itself. He cannot explain, but in their own way the pines remind him of soldiers.

The chitter of a lone dorle rises over the swish of the pine branches. Otherwise the trail is silent, as it has been all along.

"Wild chase, after something that . . ." He does not finish the sentence, for his perceptions catch the power somehow trapped on the far side of the particular hill his trail circles.

Power . . . always power . . . nowhere on Aurore it doesn't show up, sooner or later.

No . . . you draw power like a lightning rod.

Is the thought his?

It does not matter, and he proceeds along the trail until it straightens at the other side of the hill.

A stone wall, the first thing he has seen that shows lack of attention, appears on the right-hand side of the trail, which has widened into a grass-covered path.

The path meanders along the flat between two low hills. On the left continues the hill Martel has been circling, pine-covered and silent.

On the right is what he seeks. While he cannot see directly beyond the stone wall, even though several stones have toppled out of the top row and down next to the wall, he knows that behind the remaining stones are tree gardens. Behind the gardens are emerald-green lawns that rise to formal gardens and to a white villa.

Both the grounds and the villa broadcast an air of desertion, and emptiness that stretches impossibly far back in time. Since Martel has visited that villa, he knows the impression is false, strong as it is, overpowering as it threatens to become with each step he takes toward the shambling graystone wall.

To the sense of desertion, underneath it, nearly lost in the mental patina of age that the wall and the estate behind it radiate, clings a sense of danger, and of power.

Tend to be synonymous on Aurore . . . danger and power do.

Martel ignores the estate, for he has found it, found it deserted. He is not disappointed.

Rather . . . relieved.

And why might that be?

"I don't have to answer that," he mumbles to himself.

The clear path beckons, and with it his apprehensions.

Brushing them aside, he marches down the grassy trail that soon becomes a wider lane next to the tumbled stone wall. With each step the unseen tension tightens, although he sees nothing in front of him. His vision is limited because both lane and wall curve gently to the right.

After another quarter-stan, three separate chitters form a dorle on the far side of the wall, and after another two kilos, he sees the fountain.

As he nears the circular basin the feeling of danger mounts. Strangely, the fountain operates, for all the desertion, for all the apparent lack of life. The water does not spray from the single stone figure on the square pedestal in the middle of the deep basin, but from jets around the young man, lending the statue a curtain of mist. Likewise, all the mist falls within the basin, whose black depths stretch toward the center of Aurore.

Though the statue is that of a young man, handsome, in a simple tunic and trousers, much like Martel's, his face is contorted in agony.

Martel stands at the edge of the fountain, understanding all too well both the agony and the danger.

He probes, lets his thoughts enfold the statue, and draws from the darkness that he knows will always be near him.

Raising his left hand, he gestures. For an instant, a shadow passes over the statue. When it has fled, the curtain of mist remains, but the figure is gone.

Martel nods.

While he hopes the other will be wise enough not to return, or not to repeat his folly in another way, the irony is all too striking.

Saved him from what might have happened to you . . . right, Martel?

He takes a last look at the fountain, at the jets of mist and water concealing nothing, then at the wall, and finally behind the stones at the unkempt emerald grass, the straggling gardens, and at the empty rooms and columns.

He stares at his feet.

After a time, he turns to retrace his steps back toward Sybernal, back along a trail he has already trod once without understanding why.

This time, occasionally, he whistles.

xxxvi

▼

Should be evening. Or twilight.

Beneath his feet the golden sands stretch down to the waters of the circular bay. The golden green of the water touches the sand with a gentle swish-swash, swish-swash.

It is always twilight beneath the waters, Martel. The answering thought is faint but clear.

He looks around the bay, but no one else is present. When he first moved into the cottage, picnickers and others from Sybernal often swam in the clear waters. Over the years, its popularity has declined, and now no one comes. No one comes, except Martel, although the waters are as clear as ever, and the sands are as warm and golden as always.

With a shrug, he walks into the waters, which part around him, flowing, encircling, but not touching him.

Thetis joins him as he reaches the underwater shelf where the depths begin. The green gown flows around her like water, like liquid flame, and she bears no trident. Not this time. Her hands are open and empty.

Have you come to walk with me?

Seemed like a good idea. Don't ask me why.

Her fingertips reach out to touch his, and the warmth sends a jolt through him.

She laughs.

I'm not cold-blooded, Martel. Even my mermaids are warm and loving, for all their tails and scales.

He shakes his head, mentally contrasting the goddess beside him to Rathe . . . both full-bodied, but one he pictures, holds in his mind, as red, and Thetis is green, cool and green, goddess of the sea.

. . . and capable of storms and cruelty . . . like the sea?

He feels her stiffen at his unguarded thought, but her fingertips remain with his.

Aren't we all?

He nods, not looking at her, but aware that she is one of the few goddesses he overtops, one of the few he can physically look down at.

Ahead, rising out of the silver sands, sands unmarked by any marine growth, stands a rock cube, each pink face smooth stone, polished and glistening.

Not exactly natural.

No. This is my park, if you will.

Hand in hand, they climb on steps of nothing until they stand on the flat top of the cube.

Martel looks up. The surface of the ocean is at least fifty meters above, and it is indeed twilight where he stands.

Twilight, and it will come in turn for Aurore.

Thetis shivers, and disengages her hand from Martel's, turns to face him.

You could be more terrible than Apollo.

Me? Me? *Good old Martel the wishy-washy? Who has yet to really lift a hand?*

She takes both his hands in hers.

Apollo does not know what suffering is. You suffer, and do not know how to grieve. And when you have suffered enough, all Aurore will grieve.

Martel shakes his head again, strongly enough to fluff his hair out, but he does not remove his hands from hers.

Thetis drops her eyes to the pale pink of the rock underfoot.

You will be so powerful that nothing can touch you, nor your heart, except as you wish. You will have everything, and nothing.

And you?

Thetis does not look up, but shivers again.

And you? Martel presses.

When you are done, I will have only what you leave me, and a leaden shield, gray in color. Unlike some that I know. And for all his strength . . .

Thetis is sobbing silently, refusing to look up to Martel. He frowns.

None of what she has said makes any sense, any sense at all.

. . . a leaden shield, gray in color? . . . Whose strength? . . .

Her arms drop from his hands, and she steps back and

stares squarely into his eyes, her own gray eyes clear, while the tears stream down her face.

They stand there silently, both dry, yet deep in the shallows of the sea.

They stand there, neither moving.

Let us suffer together, Martel, for I see what lies before us both. Even with a companion, no one will bear what you must. And I must lose all. So let us join before we separate, for you must give me what is demanded, and I must leave you to the far future.

She steps to him, and her arms draw him down, and the green water flames that have covered her are no more, and her mouth is warm on his in the twilight that cannot elsewhere be found on Aurore.

His arms encircle her, and he tries to forget, for a moment, the ones in red, and the ones in white and blue, and to feel the cool warmth of the green goddess and the heat of her sadness, though he understands not the reasons. He will, he knows.

. . . for the son will be carried on the shield of the past, and the father on the shield of the future . . .

His fingers dig into the warm skin of her shoulders as he tries, as he succeeds in blocking away the certainty of her visions, for he knows, whatever she has seen, it will be. And he does not want to know. Not now.

And the green flame and the black flame twine in the twilight of the shallow depths of the green-golden sea, and the fires within both hold back the past and the future.

For now.

xxxvii

▼

From his small table overlooking the Great East Beach of Sybernal, Martel can sense a wave of energy approaching the establishment.

Should you make it harder for him?

Why not? he answers his own question.

With that, he wraps the darkness around him tightly enough that only the closest observer would see him, or sense his presence.

He waits, cradling the untouched beaker of Springfire.

Steps, on the wooden entryway leading to the bar, tap lightly, are misleading, for the man who strides in with a slight wobble to his step is tall, a full head taller than the man who sits shrouded in black.

You expected something of the sort, Martel. But from a mere demigod?

He shakes his head.

The newcomer sits on a high stool at the bar and orders.

"Cherry Flare." He does not look around the room, but Martel can feel his energies probing.

Martel lets the tendrils of power slide over him, nonreacting, and waits. He takes a small sip from his beaker.

Outside, the regular waves crest, break, foam, and subside, one wave after the other. Crest, break, foam, and subside, and each time the golden-green water slips back under the crisp foam of the incoming breaker like black ice under lace.

The man at the bar, the one wearing peach trousers and tunic offset with a crimson sash, the one with the tight-curled blond hair, taps his glass on the counter.

"Another Cherry Flare. 'Nother Cherry Flare."

Martel takes another sip from his beaker. The liqueur warms the back of his throat as he swallows.

"'Nother Cherry Flare!"

Martel says nothing as the lady keep refills the younger man's glass.

"You! You in the corner! What do you think?"

Martel raises his eyebrows and says nothing.

"I asked you what you thought!"

"I wasn't thinking, friend. I was listening and looking at the waves."

"Asked you what you thought!"

Martel sets his beaker on the table.

"So tell me what you think!" demands the man in peach.

"I'd like to hear what you think, friend." The word "friend" is clearly a courtesy.

"Think you sit there. Sit there like one of those useless gods. Dare me to say what I think."

Martel shrugs. "I'm no god. Think what you want." He looks down at the beaker.

"No difference. Gods or no gods. Too many gods. Too many demigods. Never know where they are. Never know where they are." He gulps the remainder of the second Cherry Flare as if the liquor were water.

Thud!

He slams the heavy glass on the bar. "Cherry Flare! Let's have another, lady!"

This time the woman replaces his glass with a full one almost before he has completed his demand.

"You!" he shouts at Martel. "Think I'm crazy. So do the gods."

Martel takes another sip from his beaker.

How will he play this out?

"The gods. Too many gods. Too careless. Careless, and care less about us." He laughs at his pun. "Treat us like dirt. Dirt!"

The heavy glass, still nearly full, comes down on the bar, but the speaker is oblivious to the liquor that slops onto the wood.

The keep hesitates, leans toward a concealed button, her blue eyes narrowing.

"Let him talk, Sylvia," suggests Martel.

"Very good. Let me talk. Talk about every rich norm that comes to be a god. Throws creds like light. And what we get? Nothing. Nothing but bowing and scraping, and having our brains scrambled every time we think wrong."

Not much finesse here, Martel.

Does Apollo need finesse? he responds to his own question.

Martel gestures for the other to continue.

"Even the Regent, bitch she is, doesn't follow you in and out of bed, day on day, waiting, hounding till you think wrong."

"Neither do the gods," snaps Sylvia.

"Worse!" The peach-dressed man hops off the stool, well balanced despite the slur in his speech, and wheels toward Martel. His right hand blurs as it slashes down through the heavy wood seat of the adjoining barstool.

For an instant the two halves of the barstool balance, teetering in midair. Then both sides crash to the floor.

"Ha!" The man vaults more than a meter into the air and onto the flat surface of the bar itself. "Behold the remains of Lendl the Terrible! Bar tricks! Once I could do that to any man. But here . . . here . . . one can do nothing. Nothing!"

Sylvia retreats to the far corner of the bar, away from the splash of light that sweeps out from the peach-clothed man who bestrides her bar.

"Magnificent show," comments Martel dryly, "Lendl, or whatever your real name is. Apollo at his cruelest has a sense of restraint and drama. You're merely burlesquing the whole business."

Martel finally stands, and as he speaks the darkness rises from the wood surrounding him, draws in from the corners of the room to confer a solidity upon him that leaves Lendl a tinsel shape.

"You mock me. Therefore, you mock the gods." Stars corruscate from the ends of Lendl's peach-lacquered fingertips.

"I mock no one. I merely state what is obvious. Those who consider truth mockery only mock themselves."

"Meet your end, unbeliever!" The tinsel stars at his fingertips turn brighter before they arc toward Martel.

Another one sent for an ordeal . . . or to test you, Martel.

Martel smiles, and, seeing that smile, Sylvia makes a sign, that of the looped and inverted cross, and shudders in her corner.

Lendl, lost in his madness, straightens his right arm and flings a blaze of fire at the shadowed figure that is Martel.

The missile, though brighter than the smaller stars that die in the darkness around Martel, slows, dims, and flickers out long before it crosses the short distance to Martel.

A second, even brighter, starbolt flares toward Martel, and, in turn, extinguishes itself. Lendl drags forth another from the field of Aurore.

In turn, Martel reaches for a certain energy, turns it to twist and isolate Lendl from his energies. He steps toward the star-thrower.

"Do you believe in darkness, Lendl the Terrible? Have you seen sunset in a shadow?"

The darkness crashes like a wave, like a falling cliff, over the demigod. As it flows back to the place from which it rose, it carries the paralyzed demigod, lacquered fingers and starbolts included, back with it, back into the depths of time and space.

Releasing his hold on that corner of the universal darkness, Martel sits back down at his table and studies the flattened waves as they break up on the Great East Beach. He sips the last of the Springfire.

As an afterthought, he touches Sylvia's thoughts and removes the memory of a peach-and-crimson-clad demigod. That loss of memory will protect her and confound Apollo.

For it has to be Apollo or the Smoke Bull who sends such emissaries.

He lifts the empty jasolite beaker, knowing Sylvia will re-fill it, waiting for the warmth of the Springfire to drown the memories that the demigod has raised . . . again.

So easy to strike out . . . but you don't combat fire with fire . . . not unless you want to burn both out.

Still, you remember, don't you, Martel?

He nods to his own thoughts and takes a sip from the lat-est beaker Sylvia has placed before him.

The images flash across the dark screen within his mind.

Kryn, who was spark, and Rathe, who was fire, and The-tis, who is sea, and Emily, who is deceit, and more, and Apollo, who is the cruelty of desert sun, and . . . and . . .

He sips the Springfire, and lets the darkness curl around him, settle deeper within.

xxxviii

▼

As he walks to the exit portal Martel can sense the morning shift, engineer and faxer, at the other entrance, the land-side one, waiting for the clearance that he has left.

"For all they see, I'm a myth, a creation of the nightly fax show. Martel the mysterious, featured on Path Seven and seen occasionally in Sybernal, if the rumors can be be-lieved."

The words sound hollow, and he blocks away the memo-ries that accompany them . . . along with one name.

Farell . . . Marta Farell.

Someday you'll have to repay that one.

Someday—but not till the time comes.

He touches the plate and steps out into the eternal day of

Aurore, though the standard clock indicates it is not quite dawn on Aurore or Karnak Imperial. He pauses.

Someone else is waiting.

"Emily . . . what a pleasant surprise." Martel almost laughs as he discovers his voice has involuntarily blunted the sarcasm he meant.

"I thought I would let you recover on your own. You do insist on doing things your way."

"And you are so different?"

She smiles, and the expression is warm. "We are alike in some ways."

He nods. "But to what do I owe this unexpected courtesy?"

Goddess or not, as a woman she had approached, and it is to that approach he intends to respond.

"That's what I'd hoped for," she replies to his unthought words. The sound and thought of silver bells tinkle in his head. He pushes them away, knowing he does not want to, and takes her arm, tanned lightly, as always.

"The North Pier restaurant again?"

"Not this time." She points to a flitter landing a hundred meters up the Petrified Boardwalk. "Not unless you miss the high cuisine terribly."

Martel reflects. If he is condemned, he might as well enjoy it. For some reason, the image of Marta Farell flickers through his mind.

"Your fault, but not totally," agrees Emily.

Martel reinforces his blocks, not only frustrated at her knowing his every thought, but also angry at his own carelessness.

"Not exactly friendly."

"Neither is snooping."

She squeezes his hand. "I wasn't snooping. You were broadcasting, and there is a difference."

He lets the outer barriers drop. What difference will it make?

The flitter looks the same, even after, what—fifty standard years? Just like Emily.

"And just like you, Martel. The world changes around you, and yet you really don't notice it. You decry the gods, and the number of demigods that Apollo and the Smoke Bull are raising, but you're the most visible god of all."

He thinks about protesting the charge, but lets it drop.

"That's part of what makes you fascinating. Why do you think the royalties on your shows are so high? Not that they're not good, you understand, but how many gods in the universe are faxers?

"And why do you think Apollo is so ambivalent about you? At the same time you oppose him, you're supporting the whole idea of the gods by your own actions."

She smiles and gestures toward the open door of the flitter.

He returns the gesture. "After you, lovely lady."

She inclines her head, hesitates, then steps inside.

Martel slides in next to her.

The door swings shut behind him, and the flitter, with neither at the controls, lifts.

"Why is there no one who will enter the CastCenter while you're there? Don't tell me it's because of a generation-old edict of a defunct center chief. That provides the excuse. Working with, or loving, gods is dangerous, Martel. You know it, and so do they."

"So why am I with you?"

"Because . . . but that's beside the point. I won't answer that question until you're willing to. Until you're honest with yourself, totally honest, no one else can afford to be. In the meantime, I will take what we can both afford."

Her left hand touches his right, squeezes it, and her right reaches for his left shoulder, draws him toward her, across the golden upholstery.

Martel holds back momentarily, then lets himself slide into her, lips meeting, his arms encircling her.

The flitter shivers, shaking them. Martel lets his lips break free.

"I can't seem to concentrate on two things at once." As she struggles from half under him her laugh chimes with the bells he has heard before only in thought. Or has he?

He dredges his memories for . . . what? . . . as she concentrates on her mental control of the aircraft.

Presently he recognizes the villa. While the surrounding trees may be taller, little else has changed.

"It shouldn't have. Except for caretaking, I haven't been here since you were last here."

The words ring true, and that truth disturbs him. Why?

How could a goddess be interested in a mere mortal? One who shies away from even considering a trip toward godhood?

Emily frowns, but says nothing as the flitter descends toward touchdown.

"This time, the dinner choice, and it will be dinner, is mine. I'm sure you'll enjoy it."

As she finishes the last word, as if on cue the flitter settles onto the landing stage, and the door swings open.

No footman, no liveried functionary, waits as she alights. Yet the white marble columns hold the aura of expectation, as if an Imperial ball is about to occur.

Through the atrium, where not a speck of dust clings to the polished floors or to the classical columns, and through the center courtyard where the light-fountain plays in the circular basin surrounded by white flowers, she leads Martel. Only the swish of her sandals, the pad of his boots, and the splash of the fountain break the silence.

On the open portico is a table, linened, in gold and crystal and set for two.

He bows to her.

She acknowledges the bow with a faint smile. "If you will be seated . . ."

"But how can I be seated and seat you, as is proper?"

"You can't. I intend to serve you, and serve you I will."

He sits, again disturbed, unable to put his finger on the reasons for his unease.

Were Emily out to destroy him, she would not have proceeded so. His reasoning is flawed, he knows, but true all the same. Emily does not intend him harm. Far from it. Not tonight.

First is the salad, of greens sprinkled with crushed nuts. The greens are the end shoots from the yanar tree, of which there are only a handful growing at the mist line, so it is said, on less than a dozen peaks of Aurore.

The nut he does not recognize, though it brings out every spice-mint nuance of the yanar tips.

"A local variety of an old Home nut."

Martel nods. He can expect no less. Still . . . something about the dinner nags at him.

"Why did you invite me to dinner?"

"Always direct, dear Martel." She laughs, and the sound warms him. He fights the sensation. "But if I told you, it would destroy the effect."

"And you're as evasive as ever."

"There's an old saying, 'Ask me no questions, and I'll tell you no lies.'"

Martel studies her, realizes that her gown is cut lower than he remembers, that she wears nothing beneath.

Before he can speculate further, she is up.

"The main course." She disappears, to return moments later with two gossamer-thin plates, one of which she places before Martel.

The porcelain catches Mattel's attention even more than the golden fish that is reputed to taste more delicate than the Emperor's cultured game trout. The porcelain is A'Mingtera, of which no complete set is known to exist.

Beside the golden fish is a thin slice of something in a light brown sauce, which Martel samples. Slightly bitter, but with a bubbling tang.

"Try the fish first."

He does, and understands the use of the thin brown mushroom, which amplifies the delicacy and sensation of the golden fish.

Even so far, goddess or not, the meal is extreme, and carries a meaning beyond seduction, though that will come, he knows, and as he knows he wants her.

Desirable as she is, sitting across from her . . . Martel blocks the thought before it surfaces.

"You're upset?"

"Confused."

She finishes a last bite and wipes her lips with the silken napkin.

"Confused about you, about me," he goes on. "Any god on Aurore would be flattered by all this, all that you could offer. Why me?"

From the glint in her eyes he realizes he has not been the only one.

"No," she confirms. "What choice do I have when you turn away from me and from what you are?" Her voice is soft, with the touch of bells in it, and totally at odds with the hint of anger he has seen buried within her.

"Let's pretend I don't know anything about you, which I don't," says Martel, in an effort to retrack the conversation. "Where did you grow up and when did you discover—"

"That I was what I was? At least, you didn't ask how old I am." She pauses. "Let's just say I grew up very young long enough ago for me to be uncertain about the details."

She takes a sip of the wine, neither white nor rosé, but some of both and better than the best of either.

Martel lifts his glass to her, sips silently.

How little we know.

How little we need to know comes her answering thought.

The portico is off the bedroom Martel has been in once before.

He slips to his feet and she to hers, and they move around

the linen and gold and crystal, and the white fire from her and the black from him touch and join. And join. And join.

A black shadow, more like smoke, in the upper branches of the nearby bristlepine thins and fades.

A yellow eagle hawk in the sky above circles, circles, and is gone.

This time, Martel wakes first, or Emily has let him wake first. He looks over her body, tanned, smooth as if in the first flush of young womanhood, with the high breasts, narrow waist, fine features, and high cheeks under closed eyes.

Though her hair is all golden blond, and her genes would show the same, he knows, now, that she was born with black hair like Kryn. He imagines that, changes a feature in his mind . . . and cold like ice cascades down his spine.

He shakes his head violently.

Kryn is on Karnak, the Viceroy after long positioning to succeed the Grand Duke, while Emily has been on Aurore for too long.

He also realizes another thing. Emily has never been young. Not in eons, perhaps longer. While she plays at youth, she does not love as if she were ever young, as if she had ever been fully human. And that is why he misses Rathe, why he misses Kryn, though Kryn, he knows full well, stands at the beginnings of power, at the base of ambition that will grow. Somewhere within her, he hopes with a certain sadness, she will remember being young and in love. Perhaps.

If she ever really was.

The cold thought is his own.

Emily is awake and studying him, in turn.

"And perhaps you're right. Again," she says, but her hands draw him back to her, and he does not resist. Nor is he young, either, as the fires fight and join.

xxxix

▼

Martel's long strides carry him up the coastal highway. The dorles chitter from the quinces and from the zebrun trees that line the empty highway.

Though he cannot hear it yet, he knows an electrobike approaches from the south, purring behind him toward the common destination of Sybernal.

Likewise, he can sense the group of young natives, perhaps five or so, who are gathered on the lane that leads to the CastCenter.

The sky is clear, as clear as it ever is under the omnipresent golden haze of the field, and the faint scent of trilia is carried from the hills on the light breeze.

Martel frowns. His stride breaks momentarily.

The youngsters are waiting for him. From his present distance he can sense no malice, no negative feelings, except a faint fear, combined with curiosity.

But waiting for you, Martel?

He shrugs and picks up his stride, letting the frown fade away.

Martel could avoid the group that awaits him, but then he would not have a clear picture of why they are interested in him, interested enough to wait, and knowledgeable enough to know where to wait.

From a distance he can only touch the clearest of surface thoughts, and certainly not what is behind such thoughts. Besides, their actions will tell as much as their thoughts. More, if the gods are involved.

As his steps take him into Sybernal, into the long, narrow Greenbelt that surrounds the highway, he reaches out again to the young natives, but the picture is no clearer.

Again he shrugs.

Finally he tops the little hill that leads down to the lane which, in turn, leads back up to the CastCenter.

That's HIM!

Three of the male students wear the gold-and-white-striped tunics of the Sybernal Academy. One, the youngest and shortest, steps forward to block Martel's path.

Martel stops, waits.

The stillness draws out.

Martel smiles faintly, but says nothing, remains motionless.

"Honored Sir, are . . . are You . . . the One?"

"The one what?" answers Martel.

"The One . . . One . . ." stammers the boy. The top of his red hair is level with Martel's shoulder.

The Dark One . . . God of Night . . . God of Shadows . . . GOD, why me? Why . . .

Martel looks at the others.

The five, three adolescent boys and two girls, fidget, wanting to move close enough to hear his answer, but wanting to back off at the same time.

Martel does not answer, and instead takes his time to run his eyes over the entire group, one by one, letting himself pick up thoughts from each.

. . . he's strange . . . expected the question . . . Elson not forceful enough . . . little coward . . .

Dark, and the black . . . like a shadow . . . why did we listen? What if He is?

Thought it was a joke, but . . . so dark . . . moves like a shadow . . .

Silly . . . boys . . . all that way. Just has to look mysterious, and they shiver . . .

Doesn't look old. Darfid says the records don't tell . . . centuries . . . years . . . all the same . . .

Martel lets his eyes flick back over the six again. No

mental sign of who, or which god, has put them up to their question.

How do you answer them, Martel? You're no god . . . why give Apollo the satisfaction? Either way?

He frowns.

They draw back, even Elson, the questioner who has blocked his path.

"A name is only what others want you to believe." He pauses, hoping that the pause will let the meaning sink in. "I am what I am, not what others would have you believe."

Martel smiles.

"And a pleasant evening to you all."

Now let Apollo figure that out!

He steps around Elson and breaks into his quick stride toward the CastCenter at the end of the lane.

Evening? What did he mean by that?

"But there isn't any evening here," protests one of the Academy students.

"So . . . you have to have evening before night. Before it gets dark," snaps the older girl, a rail-thin brunette.

"You didn't get an answer, Elson! You failed!"

"No! He gave you an answer. He really did. Don't! Don't hit me!"

Martel lifts a corner of darkness from beneath the light and flicks it toward the youngsters.

"What's that?"

"He's gone!"

"Where? He was just walking away."

"That couldn't have been a shadow . . . could it?"

"Look! Up there!"

An enormous raven/night eagle circles overhead, low, glittering black, dripping shadows, dives away, and disappears behind the low hill on which the CastCenter sits.

"See!" answers Elson. "If that isn't an answer, then what is?"

. . . what is . . . The thought echoes in eight minds, and Martel senses that one is not his or the youngsters'.

He emerges from behind an ancient pine, certain that no one has seen his descent, and enters the empty CastCenter. On time. Again.

xl

▼

The hillcrest is bare. Bare except for the grass, and for the view of the lands leading northward to Sybernal and south toward the sacred peak. Bare except for the man in black who stands looking southward down at the bay.

The time is midnight, Aurore, and midnight, Karnak Standard, but irrelevant, since the eternal light varies only with the weather. Tonight there are no clouds, only the normal sea breeze.

So now she's the Viceroy?

The Grand Duke, the acting Viceroy, is dead, and the Regent's Guard has hailed the Lady Kryn as Viceroy. Not as acting Viceroy, but Viceroy.

The Third, Fifth, and Seventh Fleets have also acclaimed her. New Augusta has accepted the inevitable and confirmed her position.

Martel draws a dark square in the air, concentrates, and is rewarded with an image of the black-haired woman, dressed in the blue and gold he has remembered for so long.

Shaking his head, he releases the picture, and it dissolves into a swirl of black glittermotes.

Emily?

This time his headshake is more violent.

Her soul is cold.

So . . . are not the souls of all gods cold?

You could become a god.

With that thought, his eyes lift toward the peak Jsalm. Though it lies beyond the reach of unaided vision, he can see its dark bulk and ice-tipped summit, can see the figures in the air above its needled tip.

So . . . Martel . . . you cannot have Kryn, for she has obtained what she has sought and will not relinquish the power and the glory that is Karnak. And you cannot have Rathe, for she is dead. Dead because of your carelessness. Or your unwillingness to make any commitment to anything. Have it either way. And you do not want Emily, or to be a god.

He turns his eyes from Jsalm toward the grass at his feet, then back to the gentle waves in the bay below the hillside. The nip of the salt air reminds him of Thetis.

Thetis?

He laughs.

No. Though a lady she certainly is.

Then what do you want?

Kryn . . . and to be me.

He turns to face the other way, down the hillside at the cottage, and at the quinces.

What are you, Martel? What are you that makes you want what you cannot have and turn from what you are?

The thought is not his, but echoes as if from a great distance.

He frowns, wondering who had been monitoring his private soliloquy, and as his eyebrows furrow, the breeze dies, and the air stills.

I am what I am, and I will have what I want!

How, pray tell?

He laughs, and the laugh echoes across the hillside, down toward the cottage on one side and toward the bay on the other. In the bay, the sound freezes the waves, holds the pair of dorles in midflight, and ripples the beach like an earthquake.

Darkness wells, and spreads, and for kilos around, night falls. At last, Martel speaks aloud, and the words rumble like thunder as they roll outward over the lands from his mouth.

"Time! Time is mine, and so is the night. Day will end, must end. And at that time comes night. Enjoy your days in the sun you cannot see, for though centuries pass, though the sons of those centuries pass, I will wait, and remember. Remember till the day when night will fall, and so will you!"

This time, this one time, Martel does not release his darkness to let it disperse. Instead, he lets it break, in waves, away from him, and in breaking that dark washes around Aurore so that all on Aurore behold a moment of night.

That darkness flies across Sybernal, across Jsalm, across Pamyra, on across the White Cliffs, across a certain white villa, across beaches, and across vacant golden waters.

That instant of night wings over the lands and waters like a night eagle whose shadowed pinions cover but briefly the ground beneath.

In certain streets of Sybernal, men crouch. Some make an obscure sign dating from the depths of history; others gape. Still others fail to notice, and others observe the strange darkness and dismiss its significance. Such it is. So has it always been.

Some notice. Some do not.

Some are pleased. Some are not.

By the time the light returns to the empty hilltop, Martel has returned to his cottage. Returned smiling, though that smile would chill most and leave their souls frozen hulks.

Outside, it is still night, despite the light of eternal day, although the clocks state it is night.

On Karnak, the Viceroy sleeps.

part two

THE COMING
of the HAMMER

xli

▼

The Lady dreams. For now, to call her Lady is sufficient. She is that, and more.

In her dream, she falls down a long, black tunnel, shot with streaks of white. As she drops she passes point rainbows of light, all the colors she can see, and colors besides those. Colors she once could see, but knows she can no longer distinguish.

She reaches out to touch the sides of the tunnel, but they retreat from her clutching fingers.

The Lady wants to cry, but knows she must not, knows she should remember why, but cannot.

She wakes . . . alone . . . in a dimly lit room. To call her chamber a small hall would be more precise.

Shuddering at the all-too-familiar dream, she sits up.

"It's been a while," she murmurs, checking the time, "a long while since the last time."

"Dreams of the tunnel?" inquires her diary from the bed-side table. "Yes, it has been. Nine years, eleven standard months, roughly."

"I wonder what crisis is coming," she says softly.

The diary does not answer.

The Lady resettles herself on her pillows and pulls the silksheen cover up over her shoulders, though she is not cold.

She avoids thinking about the two questions the dream has returned to her thoughts, and after some time passes into a hot and dreamless sleep.

xlii

▼

Tap, tap.

The sound raises Martel from his study of the small beaker, which is empty, and the bottle of Springfire, which is full.

Tap, tap.

He sighs, replaces the bottle on the keeper shelf, and closes the appliance. Martel decides not to probe, hoping the intruder will leave. While the visitor does, he leaves a package.

By the time Martel reaches the front portal and opens it, no one is there. An electrobike is purring back toward Sybernal.

An envelope lies squarely on the top step.

Martel purses his lips. When was the last time he saw an honest envelope? From Hollie? Sometime in the days of the old Empire of Man? Before the fall of the Prince Regent? Before his former ladylove who wasn't seized the reins of power . . . he shunts that thought away, regards the envelope.

Finally he bends and picks it up. A large envelope, to say the least, so white that the paper, parchment really, nearly blinds. His name in flowing script assures him that he is the recipient.

Martel, it reads, and across from the name, in the same black ink, is a thunderbolt, stylized, but a thunderbolt nonetheless.

He probes the inside with his perceptions, but only inert material rests there.

Closing the portal, he returns to the main room, and to the table with the beaker.

Can it be from his latest tenants?

Unlikely, for neither could write in such a flowing hand. He knows this, though he has seen neither write.

From the chief at the CastCenter, the latest of the more than several dozen for whom he has theoretically worked the "night" shift over the centuries?

Also unlikely.

He sniffs, holds the envelope up, trying to see if some perfume clings to it. For the hand proclaims that a woman wrote his name.

Emily?

He shakes his head. He cannot imagine the writing of a goddess, or the reasons why she would take the time to write. He holds the envelope, hesitates, puts it down on the table, and stands there.

Why are you afraid? You, the dark shadow of Aurore?

Not denying his fear, he walks around the table, stares out the window at the nearest quince tree, the latest of the generations he has planted, and down at the main house, rebuilt last year for the fiftieth time since he purchased it from Mrs. Alderson's estate.

After all the years, why now?

He knows the answer. He has felt it on the wind, and in his probes of what lies beyond the energy field that is Aurore.

"There is a season . . ." And after the season of light comes the season of change. Has he not said so himself?

He replaces the beaker on its shelf and walks back to his sleeping room, toward the wardrobe and the black tunics and trousers. He dons tunic, then trousers, and for the first time in many years, instead of the plain black belt, puts on the one with the triangular silver buckle. The black boots follow.

Fully dressed, he walks back to the table, regards the envelope.

After a time, he picks it up and touches the flap, which unseals at his touch, as he knew it would.

Three holos tumble out on the table, all landing face up.

Rathe Firien, snub-nosed, red-haired, full-breasted under the clinging tunic, and friendly, the warmth obvious, as if the holo had been canned the day before.

Marta Farell, not the stern-faced CastCenter chief, but smiling as if to welcome her lover, and wearing a golden gown.

And . . . at the end, Kryn Kirsten, daughter of the Grand Duke, golden-eyed and black-haired, in tunic and trousers of blue shot with threads of gold. Slim like a bitch goddess, and bitchlike in her own way.

A narrow slip of parchment remains in the envelope.

Martel leaves it there as he studies the pictures.

Two dead women, one who loved him, and one who hadn't. Both dead because of him. And a third, possibly the most powerful person in the Empire of Light, immortal and yet not a goddess, and not on Aurore. The enigma he has not seen in more than a millennium, her holo in with that of two dead women.

An obvious conclusion to be drawn, one meant to be drawn. But why now? And by whom?

Underlying all was the assumption that he would care, that he had to care, that he could care.

The three-dimensional images looking up from the table asked a question, too. Two of them, at least, and Martel dislikes the question.

Is he going to let someone else die, as he has the other two, because he will not listen?

Or is someone using the question to force you to act?

Does it matter?

He shrugs, not sure that it does.

Who knows him well enough to ask the question in such a knifing way?

Emily. She is the only answer.

She is the goddess Dian, but Emily will do. Has always done between them.

He takes the narrow slip from the envelope, reads it.

The No-Name. 2200. My love.

Her love?

He tosses that question into his mental file with all the other unanswered questions he has ignored over the centuries, knowing that it cannot stay ignored, not this time.

He looks down at the images of the three women, all beautiful in their own way, all intelligent, and, in their own way, all dead to him.

If you believe that, Martel, you're crazier than Thor.

He wonders who expressed the thought, then realizes it is his own, not letting him lie to himself this time.

The stars have changed, and his time has come round at last, rough beast, and it may be time to slouch forward . . . he does not finish the thought, but, instead, fingers the slip and lets it burst into flame.

The ashes are light and drift from his fingertips into the still air of the room and slowly toward the floor.

Martel locks the rear portal onto the porch, as well as the front as he leaves, for the first time since he originally entered the cottage with Rathe Firien. He will not be back soon.

The three holos gaze adoringly at the wooden beams of the ceiling above the table, and the black thunderbolt on the envelope protects them.

A man who is no longer just a man, clad in two black cloaks, one fabric, one shadow, strides along the coast path toward Sybernal, and those who see him do not. But they shiver as he passes, not knowing why.

xliii

▼

In the strictest sense of the word, the old Empire of Man "fell" with the death of the Regent and the succession of the Grand Duke of Kirsten. Practically speaking, however, the impact was the permanent division of the Empire. Both the "eastern" Empire, ruled from New Augusta by the Emperor, and the "western" Empire, ruled from Karnak by the Viceroy, claimed to be only parts of the new Empire of Light.

In a strange way, the claims were true. In the millennium that the Empire of Light existed, never did either ruler contest a prior claim of the other, nor was there a recorded instance of the fleets of one firing upon the fleets of the other.

To the Viceroy, of course, most credit should be given. Never before or since in human history has a ruler endured, not only relatively sane, but apparently young and healthy, for a millennium. During the same period, there were twenty-four Emperors, five palace revolts, and three lineal changes associated with the Emperors of New Augusta. . . .

—Basic Hist-Tape
Hsein-Fer
Karnak 4413

xliv

▼

The golden goddess glitters.

Glitters as she walks, glitters as she never glittered before, and the words she has not spoken dance across the dull air to shimmer from the darker corners created by her very presence in Sybernal. Seldom has she donned her aspect so blatantly in the city of gold sand beaches and eternal sunlight that comes from no sun and turns the seas golden-green at all hours. Seldom has she been seen in recent centuries, not since she was rumored to have consorted with the god who is and never was.

Yet she is, and she glitters as she walks from the Petrified Boardwalk down a narrow lane toward a narrower staircase. The women turn away without looking, and the men look and turn away, wishing they dared to look longer, but knowing that she has chosen the dark god, the one no one dares mention, and been rejected.

Inside the No-Name, a man dressed in black sits alone at a table. The row of tables nearest his is vacant, and the bar is slowly emptying. No one wears black in Sybernal, no one of Aurore, not without tempting the gods or the dark one, and the man in black does both.

A rumormonger who has seen better times mutters, "The Emperor kills the truth," before collapsing on the hardwood counter, and, yes, it is real hardwood, genuine steelbark from Sylvanium, that counter of the nameless bar where the media downers congregate, where they ignore the one called Martel who sits among them, where they tempt fate and gods by remaining in his presence.

Martel knows the collapsed one could not have been a good newsie, not after spouting such garbage. The news itself kills truth, for the news media can never encompass all that happens and, by omission, present only a scattering of accurate facts sufficient to kill the truth. Rulers, among them Emperors and Viceroys, merely use the media's reported facts to ensure that the truth remains dead and buried.

In waiting, Martel has drunk too much Springfire, more than anyone should drink, he knows, and particularly more than he should drink. Still, he hesitates to change his metabolism to burn it off . . . yet.

"Martel . . ." The voice has a golden sound, but its fullness cannot quite hide the trace of silver bells beneath.

He turns and looks through the glitter. Even without the coruscating auras, the veil of glittermotes, and the projected sensuality, she is still impossibly impressive. Her natural, but genetically back-altered, golden hair streams over her shoulders like a cloak. The golden ruby of her lips and the clean lines of her still- and forever-young face combine with her tan and slenderness to strike a silence deeper than that at the bottom of the well of souls.

Martel, wishing again he could have remained merely a newsie, but knowing she had indeed sent him the three holos, ignores the temptation to see her as she wishes and concentrates on her as she is. Physically, of course, there is no difference, but, without all the attributes, she stands before him as a collection of clashing traits—the face of a girl with eyes that have seen Hell, the figure of a virgin with the body posture of experience, a complexion that demands dark hair with golden.

"Emily, Queen of Harlots and Whore of Gods, nice of you to pay your respects."

"Martel, your words have been nicer. Not to mention your actions."

The two newsies closest to the arched doorway scuttle through it and up the stairway into the light. Another crouches in the corner of his solitary booth.

Martel readjusts his metabolism, holds back the churning in his stomach, and wipes the instant sweat boils off his forehead as his system burns off the poisons he has so recently drunk from the jasolite beaker.

"That was then. When I was young and did not know you weren't, and when I had not learned the price. Not that I have yet paid it, but I will. Oh, I will."

"Not that one, I hope." She turns.

Martel watches, not quite ready to follow, not quite rid of the Springfire toxins.

The golden girl turns up her glitter, spraying the room with the hope that kills. The single woman, a caster from

Path Five, sees that false hope and hates. Hates instantly, and dies nearly as instantly.

Martel reaches out with a twist of thought and readjusts her thoughts before her death is final, before she knows she has died. But he leaves the hatred. That is a personal matter.

Wiping off the last of the sweat-poison boils with a towel flown from across the bar, he stands away from his table and strides through the sparkling motes left by the golden girl, letting them cloak his black tunic and trousers for the instants before they understand what he is and expire.

Like a knife of night he cuts through the residues of the worthless hope left by Emily as he tracks her from the No-Name.

On the long beach called Beginning he finds her. On Aurore any beach can be a beginning, for it is on the beach that most who would be gods find their calling.

There are no shadows on the beach.

He ignores his thought and lets his steps take him to Emily, who watches the waves break, who holds her cloak of glittermotes to call attention and repel it.

His own shield of darkness wraps around him tighter than swirls his black hair into patterns no re probe, but he ignores it.

l Martel," observes Emily, releasing back into the field.

her shallow/deep gold eyes. Why did cepted godhood have eyes, eyes that stand nothing?

wer, he thinks.

"A thousand years, and you still think about eyes and philosophy?"

"How many thousand and you still don't?" he counters. Shielded or unshielded makes no difference. Her powers have not grown.

Martel stands fractionally above the soft sand that would climb into his boots, given half a chance. The nouveaux riches of the Empire flock to Aurore to lie on the beaches, to tan, and to let the sand drift over and about them, hoping the god field would select them. And Martel stands above the sand, well above the salt.

"Philosophy is a substitute for power, or a rationale for not using it."

"Did you intrigue me out here just to insult me?" Martel knows he should have waited until Emily made her offer, whatever it is. But the time has passed, long passed, for him to take matters on her terms.

You think so?

Martel does not answer.

Emily gathers back her light cloak and draws upon the field. She expands until she is half again Martel's height, until she has a fistful of small lightnings within her right hand, until dark clouds swirl over the beach called Beginning.

Martel ignores the temptation and watches the always regular breakers coasting in to foam up on the square-lined beach that stretches kilos north and south.

The lightnings flash, and Martel accepts them, one by one, without flinching, without injury, and without expression.

From the depths of the field building around Emily comes the roaring whistle of tormented air emerging onto the sands into a sandspout that bears down on Martel. The winds die as they strike Martel, and the sands slough away.

Emily makes no other moves and says nothing. Martel is determined not to speak again.

Locking his time sense into a trance, he waits, personal defense screens alerted, only half conscious of his immediate surroundings as he feels the planet turn, if Aurore indeed is a planet, a fact contested by approximately 49.49567 percent of the physical scientists in the Empire to have studied Aurore.

Alone in his time-slowed thoughts, Martel again senses the wrongness of the beach, that wrongness he has glimpsed so many times before in passing, whether gathering background cubes for the CastCenter, or cloud-diving, or just in walking the Petrified Boardwalk.

Waiting for Emily, he ponders.

Pondering, he waits.

Multiple drains on the field around him prick his alert screens, and Martel flashes directly into double-speed awareness, without shifting a single muscle.

Item: Five full foci surround him.

Item: Emily hovers outside the pentagonal force lines.

Item: Sixteen standard hours have elapsed.

Item: All five of the foci circling him are asexual.

Never has Martel experienced an asexual focus. Theoretically, the user is either ancient or alien, but while alien gods are possible in theory, Martel has never run across one. Therefore, either the foci are ancient human-derived gods or artificial.

As a practical matter, neither is likely to be a danger, and Martel returns to normal awareness, increasing his circulation level to lessen the possibility of physical stiffness.

He blinks.

While he can sense the five foci, he can see none, only Emily hovering at an angle, her eyes shielded by her customary veil of glitter, emotions cloaked in a jangle of discordant projections.

Lust rolls in so strongly the beach air reeks of rancid trilia blossoms, so pungent that Emily would have cast a double shadow on any other planet.

Martel does not move.

"You still believe in all that ethical restraint," Emily notes as she touches down several body lengths in front of him.

"No. Or not exactly. I don't like being pushed into making decisions."

"Apollo wagered that you would break the elementals."

"And you bet I wouldn't?"

Emily makes a curious gesture in the air, and the five foci are reabsorbed into the field.

"You know, you do believe in ethical restraint. One woman, one god, one set of beliefs, and that's what They're fearing."

Martel looks away, back at the thin edge of foam that coasts into the beach ahead of the waves.

Finally he speaks.

"Why now?"

"You've given Them a millennium. Isn't that enough?"

Since Emily never quite tells the whole truth, Martel makes the necessary translation. Apollo has finally decided that Martel is no danger and is moving against him. Either that, or Emily has decided that Apollo is no danger to Martel and is pressing Martel.

"Not necessarily."

Emily takes a step sideways, toward the water.

Martel casts around, but, outside of a few norms farther up the beach, they are alone. No gods or demigods are standing by.

"Why don't you go to Karnak, Martel?" suggests Emily.

"Why Karnak?"

Why indeed Karnak? Is she playing to your curiosity, Martel? Or trying to get you off Aurore, and away from the field?

Before he has finished the thought, the girl who glitters has bent the field and is half Aurore away, or playing with the dolphins in midocean, or reporting to Apollo.

He can go to Karnak or he can stay on Aurore.

That is not the question, but then, it never has been.

xlv

▼

"Shuttle from the *Grand Duke Kirsten* now arriving at port ten. Passengers from Tinhorn, Accord, and Sahara. *Grand Duke Kirsten* at port ten."

One would have thought that the Viceroy would have retired the *Grand Duke* before having the former pride of the transport liners relegated to backwater runs. One might have thought, unless one knew the Viceroy. Even so, before long the *Grand Duke* would be scrap or an outsystem tramp with a new name.

Eventually, another *Grand Duke Kirsten* of the Imperial Western Flag Fleet would be built and christened—the fifth of the same name—and the cycle would repeat.

In the meantime, the fourth *Grand Duke* carries passengers on the Karnak-Tinhorn-Sahara-Accord quadrangle, and often carries far less than a full complement, for the schedule is more important than the profit, the regularity a quietly impressive reinforcement of Viceregal power cheaper than corresponding calls by appropriate fleets. Not that the fleets do not call . . . just that they call less frequently, but just as impressively as ever.

The first shuttle's passengers file down the sloping corridor toward the clearance officers and their fully instrumented cubicles.

One customs inspector fingers his power spray syringe, reviewing the small holo of a black-haired man with a young face and deep eyes, a face that seems to cast a shadow even through the holo cube. His partner should steer the man toward his station. Then it will be his job to complete the operation.

The killer, for that is an accurate description of his profession, paid as he is by the Assassins' Guild of Karnak, relaxes as he sees the man approach, mentally measures the distance between the unsuspecting traveler and his inspection console, and flexes his arm to ensure the proper function of the syringe hidden within his sleeve.

The victim wears black except for a silver triangle mounted on the plain black metal buckle of his black belt. He carries no luggage, not even a small carrying case or the effects pouch of a postulant.

The false inspector feels a twinge of unease, but stifles it with a cheerful call.

"This way, honored sir."

The traveler in black turns his gaze on the assassin, and the look alone sends a chill down the professional killer's spine, for the look is simply an acknowledgement of what is.

Nearly convulsively the assassin triggers the syringe.

For the first time in years, if ever, an assassin's weapon fails, but the Guild insists on backup plans, and the man's hands flick to the clearance lights: green for clear, red for danger—smuggling, weapons, or attack.

Even while his hands are triggering the switch that will bring a red light while alerting the guards in the overhead blisters, he reaches for his own stunner, a special model designed to burn out enough nerves to render the question of survival academic.

The clearance light turns green, and the traveler turns to move through the opening portal to the open shuttle terminal, to Karnak itself.

Frantically the assassin jerks the stunner from inside the hidden pouch, levels it, and squeezes the firing stud. No energy flows from the circular tubes pointed at the back of the departing man in black, but the jolt to the killer's arm is enough to slam his fingers apart and let the fused hand weapon clatter on the hard flooring.

Though his arm looks intact, he cannot feel anything below the elbow.

The sound of the dropped stunner echoes through the rest of the receiving tunnel.

Three red lights blink on in the consoles above, one in each guard blister. The energy-concentration detectors focus on the heat of the discarded stunner, but the guards zero in on the figure standing above the weapon.

The assassin bites hard on a back tooth, one designed in a special way, but before the nerve poison can take full effect he collapses under three separate stun beams, one from each overhead blister.

The remaining travelers gingerly step around the twitching body, avoid looking down, and make their declarations to the other two customs officials.

The man in black does not look back.

After a time, the assassin's body is still, and, shortly, is removed. Three disposal units roll from a recess in the tunnel wall. The body is lifted into the first. The second sterilizes the floor and surrounding area. The third does nothing.

The last of the passengers from the *Grand Duke* steps around the three metallic units and presents her declaration to the sole customs officer left. By the time the clearance light has flashed green, the tunnel is empty, and the guards in their blisters have punched the standby studs, to wait for the next arrivals.

xlvi

▼

May the wind rise in dusty rooms, rooms for sex and sensuality, and let us not call either a sin, for sinning is a term implying an absolute morality, and the gods of the Empire, the gods of Aurore, accept no morality and know no absolutes.

While they know no absolutes, they know well the power of belief in absolutes, and revel in that power.

While the winds of sex and not-sinning spin in quiet circles, rise and die, rise and die in polished sheets and damp skin, in eternal light and in eternal darkness, and in the grubby universe in between, the gods of Aurore gather upon the holy peak Jsalm.

Some glitter, like Emily, and some, like the Smoke Bull, wrap misty darkness around themselves like a cloak. Each has an individual aspect and an energy presence, but what these gods that are, beings that were, do with their appearance with the light and power they draw from the field matters little.

That they have all met on the sacred peak in person is what matters, for it was in the time of the immortal Viceroy's grandfather before the Empire of Man became the Empire of Light that they last gathered. Two have often met, perhaps three, even five, but never have all met since that time.

Apollo flares and bends the light around him, and the Smoke Bull snorts and casts little rings of darkness at the feet of those who manifest them.

"Martel has left," announces Apollo.

"Karnak," verifies the winged siren Direne, and the gods who are close enough to their maleness bend toward the lure of her voice.

Another goddess closes her eyes, thinks of her son, and wonders how soon before she will behold a leaden shield.

"I must think," thunders the hammer-thrower.

"Think . . . think while you can, old throwback to antiquity," murmurs the Goat, his red eyes laughing at the prospect of chaos.

"Remember," adds Apollo, "he is still the undeclared god, and the hope of the hopeless, and all that implies."

. . . *and all that implies* . . . The thought hangs over Jsalm long after the congregation has departed, long after they have turned their thoughts to the future, all but two, whose thoughts are on the past, and what it means.

xlvii

▼

Martel wanders down the long parade of Emperors, past the glittering lights of the Everlight Palaces, past the modest coolights of the Longlife Homes, past even the Mausoleums of Remembrance, as the promenade narrows to a boulevard to an avenue to a street to a lane and to less than an alley among the hulks of empty walls.

One fully intact structure still stands, but the steps to the temple are barred by a laser screen. Organized religion has been banned on Karnak since the Great Upheaval, the greatness of that catastrophe attested to by the fact that not even the Empire dares to raze the temple of the Black One, only spend gigawatts of hard-earned power to shield the black marble columns with a robe of death-light.

The teletales of the sweepers flicker, throwing amber flashes on the tumbled walls outside the laser beams.

"Do I dare to touch the strings of time . . . to taste the tartness of the lime . . . to think no thoughts in rhyme." Martel stops. The words are in a tongue too old for even the databanks of the sweepers, and besides, the wench is not dead, but the ruler of the sweepers.

He studies the walls of fire before the temple and sighs.

"'Tis hardest to refrain, and therein lies the paradox . . . just a chatty old man you are, Martel, obsessed with your words, and knowing words are enough, and yet not enough."

He stares at the temple another long moment, then ignores the bones that crunch beneath his feet as he approaches the light knives that have claimed so many over the past millennium.

"Just a gesture, for old times' sake," he says, knowing that the banks of recorders will relay it all to the Viceroy of Karnak.

Wrapping the darkness tighter about him, he bends and picks up a jawbone, several teeth still intact, and thrusts it through the weaving net of lasers. The bone and teeth vanish in an acrid puff of smoke. Martel withdraws his untouched arm and black sleeve.

As the flashing of the teletales begins to build, the one who calls himself Martel strides into the shadows dripping from the shattered walls of the ancient dwellings that surround the Black One's temple. He is gone, gone even from the wide-angle, time-perfected spyeyes of the teletales.

xlviii

▼

The Viceroy watches the scene from the third teletale disc, and although the angle differs, the picture is the same. The stocky figure in black, white bone in the left hand, thrusts through the laser screens with a puff of smoke. The bone is gone, but he withdraws his untouched hand and arm and disappears into the shadows. None of the teletales have been able to catch the man's face.

"Tell me what you saw, Forde," commands the actual and titular ruler of Karnak, planet of long life and capital of the Western Reaches of the Empire of Light.

"I saw what you saw, Lady," answers the man in red, who has begun to resign himself to a drastic reduction in his life expectations.

She purses her lips, then laughs.

"Forde, you please me. That is one answer which I might accept."

Forde bows. Tall as he is, overtopping the slender figure worn by the Viceroy, he is all too aware of how appearances deceive, all too aware his continuation rests on a patience that can be as short-lived as a laugh.

"You may go."

Forde bows again, and strides for the portal.

The Viceroy lifts her finger, then lowers it. Forde's second in command would have tried to answer the question. Better a clever schemer who knows his limits than an ambitious power-grabber who recognizes neither limits nor gods.

The man in black seemed familiar, whether she could see his face or not, and that bothers the Viceroy. The color black has unpleasant associations, reminding her of matters better left forgotten.

She represses a shudder. Perhaps she can again forget. Perhaps.

She touches the arm of the high chair that is not quite a throne.

"Query?" The well-modulated voice of the databanks forms in the empty space in front of her. She could use her screen faster than the vocal mode, but she isn't in the mood. Or she could link directly with the system, but that is not called for at the moment, she feels. Besides, she wants to be alone with her thoughts, and with the direct link she certainly does not feel alone.

"Linkage probabilities between the man in black at the temple of the Black One and the code file 'Interest Black'?"

The Throne Room is silent.

"Linkage between the recently observed man in black and the Black One variable, depending on validity of Kyre-Brackell hypothesis and associated Auroran phenomena. Range from thirty percent to eighty percent.

"Linkage between man in black and code file 'Interest Black' approaches unity.

"Linkage between the Black One and code file cannot be calculated.

"Further query?"

The Viceroy purses her lips once more.

Why would there be any linkage between the man in black and the Black One? But why would her sources on Aurore merely have suggested her agents assassinate the man in black? How had he managed the failure? For that alone he deserved to live, at least until she could discover if he had a certain method for beating the Guild. That she could use.

She frowns.

Why was his bearing familiar?

At last, she shakes her head. Maybe the familiarity was only an illusion, a similarity to someone else.

xlix

▼

Rydal and Commoron drift across the Lake of Dreams in a swanboat, a common swanboat with second-degree time-stretching and pleasure-lifting intensifiers. They thus prolong each instant into hours, trying to grasp the feeling of eternal life and youth.

The swanboats on the Lake of Dreams are all the two will know of long life or of centuries as frequent as sunrises. Rydal and Commoron are poor, limited to extensive wardrobes, limited in travel to the grand city of Karnak, limited to one "now," waiting for a death that will arrive long before the Viceroy has skimmed another millennium down the timetrack.

"I saw a streak of black along the far shore."

"No one walks that shore, Commoron. That's from the ruins of death."

"That's why I noticed it."

"You shouldn't be noticing such things now."

"Why doesn't the Viceroy," persists Commoron, "just

level the Black One's temple?" She finishes with the symbol of the looped cross.

"Because," answers her lover, the poor Rydal, "the Black One remains trapped within the temple, like you're trapped within my boat."

Rydal ignores the fact that the swanboat is not his, as youths have done in all times and in all cultures.

"No one wears black on Karnak," Commoron muses.

"Then you didn't see a streak of black," he responds, before kissing her hand and drawing her to him.

The swanboats, including the one containing Rydal and Commoron, circle the Lake of Dreams on their preprogrammed patterns, twining their intricate paths for poor lovers clutching a moment out of time.

And yet . . . do those poor lovers know something in their blindness?

They do not. It only seems so, particularly to gods who are searching for humanity in a race that has never really had it.

Martel knows about the swanboats and favors them with a glance as he walks the ruinshore side of the Lake of Dreams, the side he had never walked as a student. He inhales the too-strong scent of trilia and novamella that crosses the water from the pleasure groves on the opposite side, beyond the dreaming couples in the swanboats.

Too much of a scent, like too much power, often has the wrong effect.

He smiles at the thought, but the smile is not a pleasant one, for his eyes are cold.

The Viceroy's Palace is at the far end of the lake, where the dark water lightens into the brilliant blue bay and where the sun always shines, even when it has set.

The swanboats do not go nearly that far, milling around as they do near the end of the Avenue of Emperors, not nearly far enough from a small square and a jet-black temple that has resisted a millennium and more of the Empire's best weapons.

The temple is guarded only because it could not be destroyed, not without taking most of the city with it, and neither the Regent nor the Grand Duke had wished that, not when the Park of Summer had already been destroyed by the Dark One and the Tree of Darkness.

The Dark One has not been seen since, excepting reports that He has reappeared on Aurore and will return to His true believers. Or reports that he has appeared on Tinhorn, or Mardreis, or Sileom, or any one of a hundred worlds outside the mainstream of the Empire.

In the interim, neither age nor weapons have changed the temple, and the faithful still worship, though no litany exists, nor any true priests.

Martel knows these facts and quickens his pace. The Viceroy is waiting.

The Viceroy has a name, not that anyone has dared to use it since the Great Upheaval. She is addressed as "Lady" and other honorifics by those who must answer to her, and in other terms by those who do not.

She bites her lower lip as she gazes from her window at the morning light playing upon the blue waters of the great Lake of Dreams.

The fallen one, the man in black who is more than he seems, will arrive shortly. Of that she is certain.

Turning from the wide unglassed and open window, through which nothing but light and clean air can pass, she takes a deep breath. This day, the palace has given the air the delicate scent of sand fir.

She returns to pondering the matter of the man in black.

What remains most uncertain is the purpose for which he has left Aurore and come to Karnak. His modesty also bodes ill, for the gods of Aurore, who have seldom returned to the Empire, are not known for their modesty.

The last time a god came to the people, rather than the other way around, led to the revivals that led to the Great Upheaval and the downfall of the Prince Regent. The Viceroy's edict banning organized religion still stands, although the temples, shrines, and churches are open to all—except for the one black marble temple. Anyone can worship any god, or none, but there are no priests and no services.

The precautions have worked for a thousand years.

Still . . . she shivers.

Why would anyone want to leave being a god to come back to risk death, or destruction, at the hands of the Empire?

She has no doubts that the full firepower of an Imperial battle cruiser will turn the strange man in black to ashes and vapor—at least away from Aurore.

So why does he court death?

Or does he?

Is that flicker of black along the far side of the lake the man-god she expects? So soon?

She speaks to the empty air.

"A man in black will arrive shortly. I will see him as soon as he arrives."

"Yes, Lady."

The Viceroy taps a series of studs on the wide gold belt she wears, and she is enveloped in a coruscation of auras, each a defense against some form of attack. She is merely testing the system; the triggers are automatic.

The room she enters and paces is not the largest in the Viceroy's Palace. Only a pinnace could be safely hangared within, and the weapons that the unseen guard operators can bring to bear on any intruder would destroy any such pinnace as well.

Comforting herself with that thought, the cold-eyed Viceroy looks from the lake vista on the far wall to the creme-golden hangings of the room and the gentle arch of the high ceiling.

Should she take her seat upon the raised dais, or should she greet the fallen one in midroom?

She decides on informality, sacrificing some of the defenses contained within the dais.

She hopes the man in black will come soon. One way or another she can dispose of the issue, perhaps of the man, and clear her mind for the everyday schemes necessary to keep Karnak supplying the bodies for the Fleet, the souls for the arts, and the young aristocrats for amusement.

Waiting, the Viceroy ponders.

Aurore, planet of eternal dawn, home of the gods, and refuge for independent newsies—pondering these, Kryn does not know which aspect of Aurore she likes least. Rulers distrust dawns, gods, and independent information media, and Aurore hosts all three.

The Lady who holds an Empire shivers and waits, knowing she is wasting time, afraid she will recognize the man-god in black, and afraid she will not.

"The gentleman in black has arrived and is ascending. I asked his name, but he only said he was expected."

"Thank you. Put all internal defense systems on full alert."

"It is done, Lady."

That alone would set the firevine burning with gossip, she reflects. She had not ordered full internal defenses since the previous State visit of the Prince a century earlier. Internal defenses against a man whose only attribute is sleight of hand while wearing black clothing?

Is he really the fallen one, the undeclared one, that even the gods of Aurore are rumored to oppose? The one who escaped the Assassins' Guild and her own sweepers' scans? Can she be sure? The port records missed that one's face also.

Too many questions—for that reason alone the Viceroy must see the man in black. As a Lady she is also curious. A good millennium has passed since a man has refused her his name. The last had not fared well. She smiles at the recollection, and her eyes glitter ice-bright.

She half turns at the internal warning of his approach.

The man is stocky, but not big, nor overweight, and the top of his head reaches only to the shoulders of the guardsmen who flank him into the room.

The guards halt at the arched entrance. Martel walks straight ahead to meet the Viceroy.

"Lady, a pleasure to see you again after all these years."

She smiles, even with the icy stab of fear that penetrates her. She remembers not his face, but knows she should. She cannot recall the last time she forgot an important face.

"I confess I do not recall our last meeting," she returns with a smile that includes her eyes but not her heart.

"That is not surprising, Lady. It has been some time."

He bends to touch his lips to the back of her extended hand.

"Will you continue the mystery or enlighten me before we proceed?"

"I notice you still have the lasers around the old temple," he comments.

"Yes. I see no reason to remove them. They do serve a useful purpose in attracting those who believe in death." She realizes the man will not give his name until he is ready.

"You admit that your subjects still respect death?"

"There will always be those who reject life."

"Life and death are one and the same, Lady. After more than a millennium, you certainly should recognize that."

Something about his words bothers her, rings the faint chimes of a distant memory, a cold and faraway recollection of a time before . . .

She inclines her head to the side, noncommittally.

Martel sees her struggling with the memories she has

suppressed. All souls have their price. All power is bought with the stuff of the soul and paid in pain. Martel had not wanted oblivion, only occasional forgetfulness, bought with a jasolite beaker and the routine of a practicing newsie/faxer.

Never has he been more conscious, never has he realized . . .

. . . how much Kryn and Emily are alike . . . almost as if . . .

He thrusts the thought aside. That price he cannot pay, not now.

Martel also knows Kryn will not accept him, readies himself, drawing his cloak of darkness from the closet of time around the corner from now, preparing to use it at the proper instant.

"The Empire would not have survived without you and without Aurore and its gods, Lady and Viceroy. But the time has come for the people to accept both death and life and to create their own idols and their own rules.

"Have we not had time enough to accept that, Kryn Kirsten?" He almost added the words "my love," for she has been once, when the Lake of Dreams was the Park of Summer, and the Prince Regent had ruled Karnak.

"Strike!"

Pale skin blanching, she triggers her own shields and the palace's full internal defense/attack systems. As she begins to glow in her cocoon of energy, before the lasers flash and the disruptors scream, the hall is filled with blackness.

"Martin Martel, my god." But her words are lost in the fury that fills the blackness.

By the shore of the Lake of Dreams, Martel studies the Viceroy's Palace.

The faint green corona shifts fractionally toward the blue as the internal defense systems continue squandering millions of energons trying to destroy a man who isn't even inside the palace.

Martel begins his stroll back toward the black temple, this

time along the populated and fashionable side of the lake, his feet not touching the silver sands, his black cloak flapping in the breeze like ravens' wings.

As the golden dust inside the Receiving Hall of the Viceroy's Palace finished settling into a golden carpet, as the massive heat exchangers lower the temperature to where an unmodified mortal can exist unshielded, and as the various devices within the walls begin to re-create the golden hangings and the furniture that had been turned to dust, the Viceroy releases her shields.

"I take it Martel escaped," she notes to no one in particular or to the empty air.

"No person was in the room besides yourself at the instant the disruptors focused."

She turns to the lake vista again, neither frowning nor smiling, to see if she can discern a flicker of black.

"Martel . . ."

The word dies softly in the empty hall.

li

▼

"He has retraced the steps of the Fallen One," observes the Goat, shedding light as a proof sheds water.

"Is *he* the Fallen One?" questions a demigod at the edge of the circle that hovers above the sacred mountain.

"How?" snorts the Smoke Bull. "When the Fallen One toppled the Regency, Martel was an apprentice newsie who had just fled the Grand Duke."

"But the holos?"

"Holos be flamed! And you, too!" With that the god who has chosen the Bull (or perhaps it is the opposite, for on Aurore those things which are lies elsewhere may be true) makes an unnecessary gesture and trusses the outspoken demigod in ropes of dark smoke that drag the impertinent to the golden-green depths of the ocean. He will emerge a decade or so hence, reflects the Smoke Bull, chastened, strengthened, and more aware of his position.

Apollo releases his hold on the rays of dawn, channels them, and stands, basked in their glow, at the center of the circle.

Cooperatively the Smoke Bull places a wreath of darkness in the air at Apollo's feet, and the brilliance of the scene creates a contrast only a grand master could fully appreciate, or convey. But there are no mortals present, and the talents of the gods do not run to mere depictions of their realities. This scene, like so many behind history, will go unpainted, unholoed, unrecorded.

"I am not concerned with what has happened, but with what may happen," begins Apollo, his musical baritone cascading down and out from the mountain.

By the time his voice reaches the resort town of Pamyra, with its homes clustered around the cove fifteen thousand meters below, all that remains is a series of carillon notes, a gentle melody that the locals have called the organ of the gods.

Apollo knows this, has cultivated his voice, and is not displeased.

"For I have monitored the field, and Martel is not drawing on it, though he maintains his link. Yet large mounts of energy are being expended in Karnak, and they center on Martel."

"Certain?" questions Emily, as curt among the gods as seductive among mortals. Deadly in both places.

"You are welcome to check yourselves. I merely call it to your attention."

"Let me summon my chariot and my hammer and end this nonsense," growls the bearded hammer-thrower, and his voice rumbles down the mountainside.

"As you please," murmurs Apollo. He sweeps his arm to encompass the group. "Should we send Thor after Martel, the hammer-thrower after the hammer?"

"Chaos!" exclaims the Goat, and his hidden red eyes dance. His meaning is not understood, or ignored. Or ignored.

"A hunt," whispers the other Huntress, savoring the blood that has not been shed . . . yet.

The handful of demigods, recalling the example of outspokenness that preceded the discussion, either nod in agreement or make no gesture.

"I will wait," mutters the Smoke Bull, and the storm clouds spin from his words.

"Then it is decided?" asks Apollo, though his tone is rhetorical.

"Decided!" claims Emily.

"Decided," adds the Huntress.

"Decided," agrees the Goat. "Decided in chaos."

The others say nothing, either through their voices or their powers. A demigod wrestles in the bottom of the sea with chains of darkness, and a tidal wave smashes the first line of houses on the beach at Pamyra, the ones reserved for the rich tourists.

"Agreed," rumbles the god of the thunder, summoning his chariot with a bolt of lightning.

"Agreed."

Decided and agreed. The thought echoes from the darkness beyond Aurore, splinters the light corona around Apollo, and vibrates in the minds of the gods and demigods.

. . . decided and agreed . . .

Emily looks at Apollo, who turns to the Smoke Bull. Their eyes meet, but not their thoughts.

Thor ignores the thought and the three and vaults into his chariot for the trip to Karnak. The goats paw at empty air, and the battle cart is gone.

lii

▼

CLING!

The off-key alarm note of the system jolts her awake instantly. Catlike, she stretches and keys into the full command network even before pulling her lean body into the golden singlesuit.

"Report!"

"Discontinuity. Class four. Vector Aurore to Karnak. Nondrive." The disembodied voice goes directly into her nervous system through the command implant, but she prefers to believe she has "heard" it.

"Ship class?" she snaps, though a subvocalization would have been sufficient.

"Nondrive. No characteristics of known ships."

"Defenses on full alert. Response only. Response only, I repeat.

"From Aurore?" she mutters, forgetting to downgrade the commlink.

"From Aurore, Lady."

The Viceroy downplays the link and finishes drawing on the singlesuit. The full defense belt follows, then boots.

After splashing cool water over her face, patting it dry with the old-fashioned towel, she runs the styler over her hair, adjusts her complexion, and steps from her sleeping rooms into the lift shaft to the command center beneath the palace.

While she plummets, her hands recheck her defense field, and her fingers tap the belt studs one by one, touching the smooth-gritty controls with the force of ingrained habit, hardly noticing the conflicting tactile sensations produced by the smaller field that surrounds the belt itself.

The energy barrier barring the entrance to Karnak's defense center flickers green as she passes through. With the same flicker, it could annihilate anything short of a full battle cruiser not attuned to the screen.

"Lady, the center is ready," offers Forde.

"What is it?"

"The source of the discontinuity, you mean?" Forde frowns and lowers a shoulder toward the Marshal for Strategy, who stands a half-pace behind him.

"Ah . . . yes . . . Lady and Viceroy . . . the discontinuity. Could be caused by several phenomena—a new type of ship, a natural occurrence unobserved before, a generator malfunction in an existing ship . . ." His voice drags to a halt in the face of the Viceroy's glare.

"Exactly how likely are any of those ridiculous possibilities?"

"Almost nil," admits Forde, smoothing a wrinkle in the front of his rumpled red tunic.

"Something to do with the gods of Aurore?" suggests the Viceroy, twitching her nose in a frown.

Forde backs off a pace, realizing his fear-drenched sweat may have reached her. He wipes his forehead with the back of his left hand, his right hand resting on the controls of his own shields—futilely, should the Viceroy have decided to terminate his position or him.

"A possibility, admittedly," offers the Marshal. "The measured field strength might be possible, although, as you know, we have been unable to obtain any accurate readings on the powers of the so-called gods of Aurore, and, so far as we know, none has ever left Aurore."

"If this is one, Marshal, he or she will be the third," snaps the Lady.

The Marshal darts a look at Forde. Forde wipes his forehead again.

The Viceroy ignores both, steps around the two, and takes a quick dozen steps into the master control consoles and screens.

Is Martin Martel really the newsie/demigod/god named

Martel? Or is Martel the god toying with her? Has he come to repay debts, old debts?

She shivers. Forde has followed her quickly enough to catch the gesture, but draws back again, wiping his sweat-streaming face. The control center air is cool, scented with lemon-orange.

Forde wipes his forehead again as the Viceroy's fingers run over the power displays.

The Marshal steps toward the board, theoretically his to command physically under the direction of the Viceroy.

Forde's long arm comes up with a snap to stop the military officer's second step. The Marshal opens his mouth, looks at Forde, then at the stiff back of the woman controlling the center, and shuts his mouth without uttering a word.

"Very sensible, Forde. Very sensible. You gentlemen may sit on the wing consoles, or leave, as you please."

Forde eases into the left wing observer's chair, the Marshal into the right.

The screen is centered on the airspace above the temple of the Fallen One, ten kilos east of the palace.

"Nothing yet to see," comments the Viceroy. "According to the energy board, some minor but nonsystemic sources are building."

"Götterdämmerung," mutters the Marshal, dredging the reference from he knows not where.

"Not exactly. More like . . ." The Viceroy halts. She wants to say Armageddon, but that is not it either. She sniffs. The faintly musky odor is not Forde. Rather Lady Kryn. She is afraid, and she withholds the shiver the thought could bring.

Why?

The questions leap into her head again. One she lets stay. After all, Martel had worn black. Why does she fear men in black? Why poor Martin Martel?

Except—is he still poor Martin Martel, penniless Regent's Scholar? Or does that Martin even exist? Or was he dust a millennium ago? Who is the real Martel? Does she really want to know?

A locator arrow flicks to the bottom of the screen before her, identifying a new and building energy concentration. Her eyes dart toward the red arrow, and the black dot it identifies.

"Magnification," she says quietly, heart pounding none-theless.

She centers the screen on the dot she recognizes as Martel even before the picture is fully focused.

"The same one," whispers Forde to the Marshal.

The Marshal frowns, then raises his line-thin black eyebrows in a question, as if to ask which one.

Another locator arrow flares, and the Viceroy splits the main screen into two views. The right-hand view holds Mar-tel in dead center, standing inside the laser screens of the temple of the Fallen One on the steps. The left-hand vision refocuses on an object sweeping out of the dawn sun.

"Goats," mumbles Forde.

"A god of Aurore, apparently," observes the Viceroy, her voice but a fraction tighter than normal, the tension unno-ticed by either subordinate.

Both Forde and the Marshal stare, wide-eyed, at the ap-parition that fills the left screen.

Two goats, each the size of a bison, red-eyed and yoked to a four-wheeled bronze cart, paw their way through the cloudless morning skies. A red-haired, red-bearded man, ar-mored and complete with pointed and horned helmet, leans forward in the cart and brandishes a graystone hammer in his right hand. In his left are the red leather reins.

The Regent's hands suddenly begin to play across the power controls.

CLANG! CLANG! RED ALERT! RED ALERT! FULL DEFENSE SCREENS! FULL DEFENSE SCREENS!

Another call goes to the Fifth and Seventh Fleets, not that they could accomplish anything in the space above the Vice-regal city itself, but Kryn knows they will be of help after the clash between the two gods. And their records may be of great assistance in documenting the power of the gods of Aurore.

The lights in the control center flicker.

"All power sources outside the palace screens have been diverted," reports the power center.

"Diverted? Where?" As she speaks she realizes the stupidity of the question. Martel would be grabbing power from wherever he can find it, and that may not be enough if Thor, assuming he is a god from Aurore, can draw on the entire field from that distance.

Half the controls before her are dead. Nothing outside the palace shields is operative.

She watches, merges the two screen visions into one as the goat cart swings down out of the rising sun toward a black marble temple and a man in black. Watches, fists clenched at her sides, not knowing what outcome she wants, not knowing if either outcome is what she wants.

liii

▼

THE HAMMER OF DARKNESS
Though the wind joy-sings, it's a long way from here.
Though the boughs whisper, they whisper of fear.
Though the leaves linger, they lean to the wind,
And the wind, it is colder for those who have sinned.
The wind it is colder; the wind it is cold;
The wind it is colder for those who have sinned.

The ravens are winging; their wings are so black.
The lightnings are singing; the sun is turned back.
The storm clouds are drawing; the sun grows so dim;
And the dark god is coming; I know it is Him!

The dark god is coming; the dark god is coming;
The dark god is coming; I know it is Him!

Up on the hillside, where the grasses are gold,
The blossoms will fold to the touch of the cold.
The grasses love sunshine; the trees love the shade;
But neither will stand to the cold He has made.
But neither will stand to; neither will stand;
But neither will stand to the cold He has made.

The sunshine we've prayed for, but here comes the
  night.
The darkness is gathering to blot out the light.
The hammer of darkness will fall from the sky;
The old gods must fly, and the summer will die.
The old gods must fly; the old gods must fly;
The old gods must fly, and the summer will die.

Though the wind joy-sings, it's a long way from here.
Though the boughs whisper, they whisper of fear.
Though the leaves linger, they lean to the wind.
And the wind, it is colder for those who have sinned.
The wind it is colder; the wind it is cold;
The wind it is colder for those who have sinned.

—Hymn, Church of the Fallen One
Composer unknown

liv

▼

Martel waits. Stands on the temple steps. On the steps of the
temple where he slept through the night, slept knowing the
hammer-thrower has been dispatched after him, carrying
the mandate of the gods, particularly of Apollo and Emily.

He does not question how he knows what transpired above Jsalm. Knowing is enough. The time to question will be later, if there is a later. As he feels the instrument of vengeance draw near, he prepares to accept the blows of the hammer-thrower.

One does not fight the blows of a single old god, not when the field of Aurore is massed behind that tottering old god. One fights all the gods.

The goat chariot clatters out of the sun, a black point in the white-gold circle of light, wheels spinning backward, and hums battle chants from a warriors' tongue forgotten longer than the languages of the obscure poets Martel has made a practice of quoting.

Thrummm! Thrummm, da-dum, da-dumm.

Martel hears the rhythm. Smiles. Husbands the energy he had drawn from his confrontation with the Lady Kryn, readies his shunts from the Viceroy's power system, and holds his darkness for the assault.

Thrumm! Thrumm, da-dumm, da-dummm.

The sound is nearer, and it rattles the looser shutters of the battered gray villas that border the black temple.

Thrummm! Thrummm, da-dum, da-dummm.

The sun darkens, though no clouds mar the blue-green of the morning sky. The Viceroy has activated the city's defense screens.

"Hsssst! Hssst!"

The breathing of the battle goats falls like rain across the pavements of the city of the Viceroy, each fragment carrying a sparkle of light that breaks as it strikes the ground or hard surface.

The sun flickers again as the goat chariot and its master hurdle through the defense screens, haloed in the energy that bathes them momentarily.

A violet pencil of light leaps from a hidden emplacement, stabs at the bearded god, touches the cart, its bronze bosses, its time-darkened wood.

The god, for it is Thor, and his graystone hammer is mighty, lifts that hammer, points it, but does not trouble himself to release it. Along the path he has pointed, back along the searing violet, strikes a bolt of lightning.

The violet light knife is no more, and above the blackened hole a small thunderstorm gathers, raining metal among the boiling water that it drops.

"Behold! Behold!" thunders Thor, his eyes burning red, his beard flaming. "Oppose not the gods!"

His words crash across the city. Two dozen men, five women, and three children die instantly from the sonic concussion. Another 231 will be permanently deaf unless major auditory surgery is performed.

"I oppose," says Martel, standing on the steps of the small black temple, and his words, scarcely more than a whisper, reverberate through Karnak, even into the sealed chambers of the Viceroy, even through the triple screens of the core-tap power stations, even into the brains of those who cannot hear, and into the awareness of those who cannot reason.

The thunderstorms, the fire vortex, and the glitter rain of the battle goats dissolve into mist at the words of the man in black.

"OPPOSE NOT THE GODS! NOR THE HAMMER OF THOR!" thunders the hammer-thrower. The chariot of the ages and its hiss-breathing goats veer leftward as they rumble down toward the temple.

Another group of unfortunates, somewhat larger now that the thunder-god is near atop the city, perish.

"I oppose."

And again, the quiet words soothe the injured, damp the thunderstorms, and enrage the hammer-thrower of Aurore.

"THEN PERISH! FALLEN ONE! RETURN WHENCE YOU CAME! *BEGONE!*"

Thor does not gesture this time. He throws his hammer, that mighty graystone hammer, and he hurls it full at the stocky man in black, who stands upon black marble steps, at that man who would seem slight beside the burliness of the ancient god. In that moment, the sun flickers, and brightens.

The hammer falls. Falls like thunder, falls like the point of massive lightning. Falls like death.

The city shakes, as if wrenched by the grasp of a wounded earth giant. Roofs crack, split asunder. Waves on the Lake of Dreams swamp the empty swanboats, spend their force in inundating the gardens bordering the lake.

The ancient oaks, brought light-years to serve no purpose but the whim of a departed Prince, bend. Bend more, then, as one, snap in two like dry sticks across a kindler's knee.

The yellow light flowers lining the paths from the lake to the palace flare, then crumble into black dust.

The lights of the city fail. Fail, reeling from the stroke of the graystone hammer. Reeling from the power of an ancient god. And darkness pounces, from house to hovel to villa to palace.

Across the void, behind a golden field, on a planet that is not a planet, the cast of the graystone hammer is felt by those gathered in the air above a sacred mountain. Two gods, a goddess, and a scattering of demigods nod. A certain shore trembles with the turning of a chained being in the depths below.

In the last nanoseconds before the hammer reaches Martel, the villas around the black temple, their walls already flattened and scattered, are pulverized into particles, and the gray dust rises. Rises to block the receptor screens, to shield the view of the teletales, those few that are self-powered and still functioning.

Before her screens, a woman finds her view blanked by the swirled dust. The Viceroy finds tears upon her cheeks, tears unsummoned. Tears unknown since before the fall of the Prince Regent, tears unknown in a millennium.

Somewhere, a red-haired child sobs.

The man in red smashes a balled fist into his left palm,

shaking his head, unaware of the shower of sweat that flies from him.

The chariot, battle goats pawing, circles the cloud of gray dust, passes over the miles of rubble and fallen towers. Thor leans over, his eyes trying to pierce the gloom where his senses cannot penetrate. His right hand is empty, though his left grasps the red leather of the reins more tightly.

He gestures with his empty right hand, calls for his hammer.

The chariot circles, a vulture above the ruins of the Vice-regal city.

The Viceroy waits, not understanding, hoping.

The man in red leans forward as the dust settles.

The sun dims, then flares even brighter, and as the dust cloud parts, the black temple emerges. Stands. Stands untouched.

"I oppose."

On the temple steps remains the man in black—not smaller, not larger, not darker, not brighter. He does not smile, nor does he frown.

In his left hand is a graystone hammer.

Martel lifts the hammer, lifts it high above his head.

"I oppose the ways of the gods, and I will break you as I will break your hammer. Behold, agent of the gods, and god no more. Behold. This hammer is your life and your strength, and it is no more."

Martel squeezes the haft, and as he does the wood cracks and the stone shatters, and the shards crumble into dust.

Thor shakes his fist at Martel, turns his battle goats and the chariot into a dive toward the man in black.

"I am of the Fallen One," admits Martel conversationally, and yet his words carry through the ruins of the city. "And the Fallen One will not be denied. Nor will He be mocked. Your hammer is gone, Thor, and you have no power over me."

The chariot is almost upon Martel, and the hiss of the battle goats is rain in his ears.

"Guess we have to make it formal, old thunder-god."

He raises his left hand again and cracks his voice like lightning across the morning.

"Begone! Forever!"

With the words flows a tidal wave of blackness. When the darkness subsides, moments later, the sky is empty.

The steps of the black temple, the only fully intact structure in the city of the Viceroy, are vacant, and the sirens begin to wail as the power returns.

lv

▼

Martel appears in the cart, his feet planted shoulder-width apart.

The battle goats do not seem to mind, but continue their hissing breath as they paw meaninglessly at the blackness beneath their hooves.

Martel glances around the square wooden cart. In the corner floor bracket beneath his right shoulder is a built-in quiver, originally bronze, but dulled with a green patina. The horn bow is stringless and would doubtless break if strung, since Thor had never liked archery before he became god of thunder, let alone after.

If he could smell in the undertime, Martel knows, the goat cart would reek of age, and dust. Not of goat urine, for the battle goats are not goats at all, but focal elementals, harnessed through the field of Aurore.

He sighs, more of a mental reaction than a physical one, because purely physical actions really do not take place in the subwarp/subtime/subspace corridor that the gods have drilled for Thor's transit and return. With his own methods,

Martel could already have been on Aurore. But then, he could not have returned as Thor.

His hair goes from black to red and lengthens. A full red beard appears. His stockiness becomes burliness, and were he to speak, his voice would rumble.

Martel is Thor.

Presently the chariot emerges above the sacred mountain, begins a circling descent.

Martel remembers one last detail, conjures up a graystone hammer, and brandishes it, much as Thor would have done.

On the peak, or rather hovering above it, in an unnecessary expenditure of energy, reflects Martel/Thor, are Apollo, the Smoke Bull, and Emily. Assorted demigods wait beyond them.

All for the conquering hero. He blocks the thought. Thor would have thought it only his just due.

"The traitor is no more!" rumbles the returning thunder-god. "He fell under the Hammer of the Gods!"

Thor vaults across the railing of the goat cart, dispatches it to an outer circle to wait, and takes three giant steps across the cloud tops toward the triad.

"Welcome back, Thor," murmurs the Smoke Bull, the darkness falling from his mouth with the words.

"Welcome," adds Apollo. And his voice chimes down the mountainside to ring through the towns below.

Emily nods. Curtly.

"No welcome from you?" growls the returned warrior. "Ah," he chortles, "but you were once fond of him."

He turns toward Apollo.

"Martel was a danger. But he didn't gloat about destruction." The words of the goddess ring in the stillness.

Thor turns back.

"Bitch goddess. Talk not to me of gloating. Talk not to me when more blood has flowed from your hands and your names than mine. Thor am I. Thor am I! Hammer and lightning, like the thunderstorms."

"Rather eloquent, Thor," adds Apollo. "Didn't know you had it in you."

"Thor?" asks Emily. "Answer one question. Did you actually see the hammer strike Martel?"

"He was there. The hammer struck, and he was not. Same as always. No draw on the field since."

"What about Karnak?"

"Flattened," admits Thor, shrugging. "You knew that would happen."

Emily frowns, and Apollo, seeing her expression, clears his throat. Even the half-cough is somehow musical.

"Is it possible, barely possible, Thor, honored hammerthrower, that Martel ducked your blow?"

"I say he was under the hammer, and he was gone. Never has anyone escaped the graystone hammer! *Never!* NEVER!"

The three gods wince as the thunderclouds roll in at his voice, and a small tornado touches the edge of Pamyra, destroying an unoccupied cottage.

"Then it is possible," observes the Smoke Bull. "Else Thor would not be so angry."

"You old fraud!" screeches Emily. "You had him, and you missed him. Destroyed a beautiful city for nothing! Made a fool out of the gods, and left the Viceroy ready to declare war on the entire Aurore system."

"YOU LIE!" rumbles Thor, and he lifts the hammer.

"Wait!" commands Apollo, and both Emily and Thor turn to the chimes of his speech.

"Thor *may* have destroyed Martel, and he may not have. But one thing is clear. If Martel escaped and did not again confront Thor, then he does fear the hammer. Since the hammer is but one attribute of the gods, Martel may be a difficulty, but one we can handle should he reappear."

"I destroyed him," insists Thor.

"You did not," returns Emily.

"It does not matter," observes the Smoke Bull. "Apollo is right. Whether Thor destroyed Martel, or whether Martel escaped at the last instant, the result is that Thor was the stronger. Thor, by himself."

Emily almost snickers, understanding the implication behind the Smoke Bull's words.

Thor raises his hammer again.

"Put down your toy, Thor. *I* do not fear your hammer, though Martel may."

Thor glares at the Smoke Bull, raises his left hand to recall the chariot, then faces Emily.

"Bitch, best you fear the hammer of Thor!"

"Is that a challenge, old blusterer?"

Thor vaults into the chariot without answering, brandishes his hammer, and the battle goats careen across the heavenfield of Aurore, away from the sacred peak Jsalm.

"I'm not sure that sending Thor was the best idea, after all," muses Apollo.

"How soon before we can confirm what he said?" asks the god of black smoke and guile.

"You don't believe him?"

"Only that he flattened the city. No communications from Karnak."

"Why doesn't one of you go to Karnak and see?" snaps Emily.

Apollo shakes his head.

"If Thor is telling the truth, there's no need. If he isn't, then we can't afford to leave Aurore to find out."

"I'll take care of that," says Emily, "with Thor."

"Can you?" asks Apollo.

But Emily is gone, and only the glitter at the end of the rainbow remains, fading moments after she has left.

"One way or the other, you win, Apollo."

"Not if Thor wins."

"No. We both lose then. A pity about Martel. Could have

been a real help, if he'd only thought more about it. Too tied up in the worldly things."

"I wonder. I wonder."

"A little late for that, now."

The two depart, each in his own fashion, and, following them, so do the demigods.

The clouds above the sacred peak are empty, and without the gods to shield, they dissipate to allow the faithful below to worship.

From Pamyra, the conical peak glows green above the shadowed slopes, for the one thing that differentiates the sacred mountain, besides its sacredness, is that its upper slopes are cloaked in shadow, unlike any other peaks on Aurore.

Thor is not hard to find, Emily discovers.

Hammer resting on his knees, the thunder-god stares down at the waves crashing against the sheer quartz cliffs that stretch kilos east and west from his vantage point. His location, across the Midland Sea from the Sacred Mountain, is scarcely hidden, though neither Apollo nor the Smoke Bull has ever cared for the White Cliffs. The Goat can sometimes be found nearby.

"It was a challenge, Thor."

The hammer-god does not acknowledge her presence, nor even the concentration of energy that the golden goddess, mistress of the rainbow, gathers about her.

"A challenge, Thor," she snaps.

"No, bitch." He lets the hammer fall as he stands, and it vanishes. "No challenge. You followed the behest of Apollo and the Minotaur to carry out the execution of another of their enemies. You, who could rule an Empire, cannot rule yourself."

"Flame, Thor. Apollo and the Bull rule Aurore. No one stands against them. Not Martel, not me, not you."

Thor smiles, and the smile does not suit him.

"None so blind as will not see, bitch goddess. None so deaf as will not hear."

"Quoting Martel won't help either, old blusterer."

Thor shrugs, unfastens the great bronze clasps that hold his bearskin cloak, and lets the skin drop. A gust from the sea wind carries it high over the waves.

A gesture from the hammer-thrower, and the cloak bunches, becomes a dark bird that spreads its wings and glides toward the calmer water out beyond the ridge of black rock over which the solid gold-green waves are breaking.

Emily laughs. The harsh notes knife the harmony of the surf noises. As she draws the colors to her the brilliance of the rainbow glitters, iridesces, mounts to eye-sear, a small nova at the top of the White Cliffs.

Two hundred fifty kilometers across the Midland Sea, the priests at the temple in Pamyra note the strange light and genuflect.

The rock under the feet of the golden goddess puddles, and she stands in a pool of molten stone.

"Very pretty, bitch, but is one supposed to be impressed?"

You talk too much, Thor!

The thought lances at Martel with the power of an Imperial battle cruiser.

You have forgotten nothing and learned nothing, Emily, and for that you shall pay. Pay with your memories, pay with service, and pay for the love that has left your soul.

Strong thoughts . . . And her sending falters.

Where is my hammer, Emily? Where is my lightning? And yet bind you will I in darkness, and in time, and away from all you hold dear.

A small sunburst crashes against Thor's shoulders. He does not even bend, but darkness rises from the White Cliffs beneath his feet and through his hand toward the miniature sun that is a goddess. As the blackness flows toward her the pool of molten rock traps her feet as it freezes, holds her like a fly in amber.

Thor takes one step toward the sun that has dwindled to a rainbow, then another.

Who are you? Who . . . what . . .

The clifftop is empty. No sign remains of the two, except three black footprints in the white rock leading toward a perfectly white and perfectly circular depression melted into the stone.

A single raven, not native to Aurore, circles, then flaps over the waves inland toward the lowlands.

Ivi

▼

The woman wakes, shaking, from a nightmare. The details fade even as she tries to recall them.

Her hair is long and black, her waist narrow, breasts high but adequate, certainly not small, nor large enough to merit the term voluptuous.

All her physical characteristics, from golden eyes to lightly tanned skin, from black hair to oval face, are irrelevant to her at this particular moment.

She does not know who she is, where she is, or why.

In the starlight, she looks at her hands. The nails are neatly trimmed, short, unadorned. The hands are uncallused, but not soft.

She looks down at her body, discovers she is wearing a light blue one-piece coverall of a luxurious material, but without underwear, she can sense, and formfitting boots a shade or two darker than the singlesuit.

She wonders how she knows the colors in the dim light.

The gentle *terwhit* of a bird in the tree above her startles her, and she studies her location.

First, it is night. That she had realized earlier. Second, she is sitting on the ground. The grass is trimmed short, and there is no undergrowth. To her right, as she looks through the darkness, is a luminous glow, against which she can see the regular outlines of other trees and of a line of bushes, presumably bordering a walk or path that leads . . . where?

She wants to bury her face in her arms and cry, but she should not. She is too important for that, she knows. She knows not why, but she feels it nonetheless.

One moment she is alone.

The next she is not.

"It's time for me to take you to your home," says the man. A figure in black, he is no taller than she is, but well muscled, despite the swirling black cloak.

How can she tell what she cannot see? She does not know, but accepts it all the same, as she accepts the kindness in the stranger's voice. Perhaps, perhaps he is not a stranger.

She stands.

He offers his arm, and they head down the path, which turns out to have a dim light of its own and leads in a sinuous fashion toward the glow she had noticed earlier.

"Terwhit!"

She jumps, knowing she should not.

"The tercels are the only nightbirds the Regent permits in the Park of Summer."

"Why?"

"One would have to ask the Regent, I suppose."

The path winds up a gentle incline. The glow in the sky ahead increases, and the girl can see that the path is a pale yellow and that the border shrubs have small yellow flowers with white centers and are evenly spaced.

She knows that the man in black will be gone before long, and even as she trusts him she fears him. Even as she fears him she knows only he can answer the questions she has and cannot ask.

"Who . . . ?" she stutters as they approach the top of the hill.

"Am I?" he asks. He chuckles, as if he finds it amusing, but she hears the bitterness behind the sound. "Who am I?

I could tell you who I really am, but that wouldn't mean anything. If I gave you a name you'd recognize, then I would have to take that, too."

She shivers, starts to pull away.

His grip is like iron, and she finds her feet marching in step with his.

"Let us say, Lady-to-be, that I am your penance and hope to be your reward, and you mine. But that lies a long time from here and now . . . if either of us survives. And you will not remember this in any case."

The path widens as they come down the hill. The two take a narrower offshoot that leads to a small gate. The main path continues toward a series of towers outlined in ghostly, pervading light. She cannot turn her head toward the towers of light, but understands they are there.

At the smaller gate stands a sentry in dark blue. His eyes are blank as the man in black leads his charge past.

"You are Lady Kryn Kirsten, the only daughter and child of the Duke of Kirsten, first loyalist behind the Prince Regent. You have suffered an accident in your return to Karnak."

The dark man smiles at her, then wipes his expression blank.

"You will find it has all happened this way, though some has yet to happen that already has. Remember, Lady-to-be, do not marry."

She stands in the courtyard, sinking to her knees, head swimming as the alarms explode around her, clutching at the memories of the man in black that fade as her thoughts lose their hold on them, finding herself left with memories of a long black tunnel and with new memories, recollections of a tall man, a forbidding woman, and towers.

The last words, words someone else has spoken, remain.

"Do not marry."

lvii

▼

From within the tunnel he has wrapped around himself, Martel can sense a spark, a familiar flame separated from him by the thinnest of margins. He knows what the spark represents, and wills his course away from it. Too close to that spark, and the energy he controls will short-circuit across more than a millennium. Without the focus he embodies . . . he pushes away the thoughts, locks his mind on the place and the time where he is heading, and the tunnel of energy trails him.

Martel pushes himself away from the spark, thoughts lashing against time, most of his energy devoted merely to keeping his links with his starting point open.

"Can't go where you haven't been, is that it?" he mutters, though he neither speaks nor is heard in the nontime nexus where he finds himself suspended, but his thoughts form as though he had spoken.

He lets himself drift forward with the tide, though that motion is an illusion, because there is no tide to time, and casts his thoughts into the real time outside his energy tunnel for an anchor.

If Kryn had been born when the Duke thought she had, when she thought she had, now she would be away at Lady Persis' School on Albion. Chronologically, in real fact, the Duke does not yet have his daughter, though she has been placed already.

Martel shakes his head.

If you can only keep track until all the pieces are in place . . .

As Martel sets foot on the golden tiles, the pathway to the back gate of the Duke's holding, the one on the park, is still shrouded in mist.

"Halt!" The stun rifle is centered on Martel's midsection.

"Halted I am, my friend."

"Your business?"

"To bring a report to the Duke on his daughter Kryn."

"Daughter Kryn? The Duke has no daughters—"

Martel reaches out, holds the man's mind frozen as he supplies vague recollections of a slender, dark-haired girl . . . seen from a distance practicing with a light saber, rushing by the gate on the way out to the park, smiling with a new sunkite, sulking . . . and finally leaving by the main gate with four trunks and three guards.

Martel finds his vision blurring with the effort, realizes how much energy he is using merely to hold himself in this place and time.

"Oh, her . . . gone away to school."

"I know. I know. The Duke asked me to report. Here are my credentials."

Martel might have been able to alter the man's memories from a distance, but no feedback would have been possible. With Kryn's life the question, he had to do as well as he could.

The guard looks at Martel's empty hands, and nods.

"Lord Kirsten won't be receiving yet."

"Realized that after I'd left the port. Anywhere I could wait?"

Lowering the blue-barreled weapon, the sentry wrinkles his forehead, chews at his lower lip with sharp upper canines.

"Don't know. Let me ask the Captain."

"You don't have to wake him. I'll wait out here." Martel eases himself onto the bench across from the guard box and ignores the stunner.

Didn't realize it would be this much of a drain . . .

"He's up. Already been round once."

Martel senses the Guard Captain before the man steps from the nearer wing. Senses him and inserts the memories of Kryn, subtly different, before the security chief sees him.

"Captain Herlieu, this gent needs a place to wait 'fore he makes his report to the Duke."

Martel stands and bows.

"Averil Seine, Captain. From Albion with a report for His Grace."

Herlieu frowns.

"About?"

"His daughter."

"Would have thought Her Grace would be the one to get that."

Martel shrugs. Even with a bogus set of memories, Herlieu was rationalizing to fit the situation. Obviously, the Duchess had a great deal of power.

"Ah, yes . . . perhaps it should be. My commission was signed by the Duke, and . . . alas, not knowing the ways, I assumed . . ."

Herlieu laughs, his voice booming in the narrow space by the gate, the echoes bouncing back from the high and totally unnecessary bluestone battlements above.

"Of course you wouldn't know. The Duke, bless his soul, signs all the documents, sits on the Regent's Council, and fine advice he gives there. But her Ladyship runs Southwich here. Still . . . he's the Duke."

Martel bows again. "I understand. Thank you for setting straight the record and for keeping me from a mispresumption."

"Sure she'll see you. Early riser she is. Now, what was your name?"

"Averil Seine. From Albion."

"Just sit here on the bench, and I'll tell her myself."

Martel sits, letting his mind follow the Guard Captain, touching the Imperial Marine's thoughts.

Funny-looking fellow . . . why would they want to know about Lady Kryn? Lots kept quiet on her . . . him not knowing about the Duke, either . . .

Martel searches for the Duchess, not that it is hard. Her

thoughts are clear. Crystal-clear and strong. He recoils, but not before easing in a thought or two about the Duchess' daughter.

He waits on the bench.

"You're to follow me, Master Seine."

Martel bows again and follows Captain Herlieu up the slidechutes to the tower room that views both the park and the palace.

"You may leave us, Captain."

"Yes, Your Ladyship."

The slidedoor closes.

"You're a fraud, and soon to be a dead one, Master Seine or whatever your real name is, unless you can tell me what your game is. Then you might have a shot at a permanent lower-level apartment."

Martel probes at her mind. Strong enough, talented enough, that she would be a goddess if she sought Aurore— and he is limited indeed by the need to hold his links to the future from which he has come. Does he dare to tap power sources of a local nature? Will they break down the insulation between him and the present?

"It's simple," he temporizes. "You have no heirs. I offer you a daughter who will become Regent and Viceroy, who will become second only to the Emperor in power."

NO!

"An interesting idea," she says aloud. "But why should I believe it? Much less from an unknown from nowhere?"

A lurid thought surfaces in her mind, an image of Martel ripping off her clothes, followed by an image of her ordering him tortured.

"I think you misunderstand, Madame. The young woman already exists. She will honestly believe that she is Kryn Kirsten. She resembles you, and, to some degree, the Duke, and she will be accepted as your daughter."

Martel surveys the room. The Duchess has set aside her breakfast, and, silver hair pulled back into a tidy knot, peers down from the meter-plus bed platform at him. The marble platform is a single slab, partly draped in blue, the fabric shot through with a gold thread glittering with a light of its own.

Martel senses she is ready to push the red button. He reroutes the energy, but does not absorb it.

"Go ahead. I'm standing in the fire zone. But it won't work. Neither will the guard call."

She jabs the button.

A weak red light pulses over Martel and dies.

"What do you really want?"

"A good home for a girl who deserves it."

"You expect me to believe that?"

"No. But you will."

He throws his mind at her, as much of it as he dares, while still holding the links foretime. Unlike the Guard Captain, the sentry, there will be no insinuating memories, not quiet manipulation.

OUT! GET OUT! SCUM! Her mental screams pound at Martel.

Martel reels, knees bending with the effort of holding the circuits diverted, the energies from future and present separate, and pressing convictions and memories upon the Duchess Marthe at the same time, without destroying her in the process.

He forces an image of Kryn at her.

Your daughter . . . your hope for the future . . .

Mental pictures of Kryn, smiling, romping in the courtyard of Southwich, pictures of Marthe holding her arms out to her daughter, pictures of a small face looking up wide-eyed.

NO! I'M THE LITTLE GIRL.

Martel feels the sweat beading on his forehead.

Should have been sneaky . . . stupid . . . never figured on this kind of strength.

The energy link back to Karnak future dwindles. He doesn't want to have to live the same millennium twice.

He staggers, still beaming images at the Duchess.

She throws them back.

NO! CHILDREN ARE PIGS. EVERYONE WOULD KNOW. NOT FOR ME TO BE DEGRADED. WON'T BE A SOW. WON'T LET THEM THINK THAT!

The temperature in the bedchamber, expansive as it is, has to have risen twenty degrees.

Martel shifts his probes toward the Duchess' nerve centers.

DIE! DIE!

His shifts and the lack of images give her the room to counterattack.

Martel feels his body crumpling, and in a desperate effort seizes the power directly from the palace sources, ignoring the emotional impact the sudden blackness creates for the staff in all the scattered and endless rooms.

With the surge of renewed energy he slams aside her defenses and feels her go unconscious.

That done, he switches his concentration to the fraying edge between his own links to the blackness of the future.

DANGER! TWO CANNOT BE ONE, NOT NOW, NOT EVER.

He wrenches the two energy lines apart, somehow welds them separate, before the blackness closes in on him.

Thud! Thud!

Martel opens his eyes. His is sprawled on the pale yellow heatstones of the Duchess' receiving room/bedchamber.

Thud! Thud!

He wobbles as he climbs to his feet.

His forehead is wet, and he wipes it away with the back of his left hand. His sleeve comes away with a mixture of blood and sweat. Knees rubbery, he peers up at the bed block.

Head aching, he probes.

The Duchess Marthe is unconscious, but breathing.

His eyes water with the pain, but he keeps probing.

Stroke—the mental strain of his last probes has apparently triggered it.

Should he leave well enough alone?

He shakes his head, regretting the motion as it drives needles into his thoughts.

Kryn will need a strong protector, and the Duchess is as strong as they come. Besides, the Duchess, for all her bias against motherhood, also deserves better.

Thud! Thud!

Conscious of the attempts to break through the massive door, he returns his attention to the woman, repairing the damage and insinuating the necessary memories at the same time. In some ways he is lucky. The Duchess is the type of woman who will keep precious few keepsakes of her "daughter." Those few he can supply.

He completes his work with a mental report on Kryn's progress at Lady Persis' School, awakens the Duchess, and lets himself collapse again.

"What's this?" demands the Lady Marthe as she keys open the door.

Three guards and the Captain stumble through.

"You didn't answer, Milady. Even the emergency call. We were concerned."

"You had right for your concern, I suppose, Captain, but not for me. Master Seine had some sort of seizure, and I was simply distracted. My controls malfunctioned, and I couldn't seem to reach you. At the same time, I certainly wasn't going to leave Master Seine."

Martel groans.

"Help the poor man up. And get someone up here to clean up the mess he made. Immediately!"

"Yes, Milady."

"Get him some attention. Put him in the Red Room. When he recovers, he should see the Duke."

That is fine with Martel. So far the Duchess is reacting as he has planned . . . after his setbacks. Martel needs the rest and a quiet place from which he can influence more of the staff and get to the Duke.

He lets himself be carried while mentally reaching out toward the Duke's sleeping quarters.

The Duke of Kirsten is still asleep. The woman with him is not, but pretends to be, bored as she is.

Martel ignores her and first plants the memory chains of Kryn in the Duke's mind, then plants a more limited set and a few vagrant thoughts in the woman's mind.

She calls herself Alicia, and officially she is the Duchess' first maid. What that means to Martel is that the Duchess chooses the Duke's mistresses, and carefully.

Alicia is cunning, but the shrewdness is realistic.

Old bloat, she thinks, *some lover. Sort of kind, but the Duchess pushes him around. Still, a good thing for me. And when he's satisfied, she lets me alone.*

Martel pushes an image of Kryn at her.

Never could figure out how they got together long enough for even one. She's sharp, sharp like the Duchess. Little nicer, maybe, but when they're young you never know.

Martel relaxes, lets himself go limp as the two guards ease him into the oversized stratobed, drifts his thoughts back from the palatial sleeping room where the Duke snores and Alicia, the bored and blond young maid, pretends with closed eyes.

"The medtech should be here in a couple of units."

"Gerson," orders the Captain, "you wait."

"Yes, sir."

Once the door has irised shut, Martel opens his eyes.

The title Red Room is appropriate. Fabric walls, red with gold threads, twinkling like the ones in the fabric hangings of the Duchess' bedchamber. Red coverlet on the square stratobed. Red heatstone tiles on the floor. The arched ceiling overhead is red, as are the silksheen sheets that show at the upper edge of the bed.

Martel wonders at the picture—a religious figure from the ancient times before the Empire—then realizes it has been chosen because the man is dressed in red robes . . . merely for the color.

Gerson, the guard, sits in a red slouch chair, facing the door.

"Oh," moans Martel, "my head."

Gerson says nothing.

Martel eases up into a sitting position, looking around the room.

"What happened? Where am I?"

"You had a fall. Duchess had us bring you here. Red Room," supplies Gerson.

"I remember telling her about her daughter, Kryn." As he spoke Martel supplied a set of memories for Gerson as well, tinted to match the guard's underlying prejudices and experiences.

This is getting too complicated, Martel. The more people you meet, the more memories that seem necessary . . . could spend months at this.

Martel squints, thinking about all the records involved, the possible travel to Albion to make sure that records exist at Lady Persis' School and in the minds of the necessary teachers, as well as a few "classmates." Plus the Prince Regent's court and the society media.

He groans again, not entirely acting.

Will the result be worth it?

Do you have any choice?

He shakes his head, wincing at the jab of pain, leaning back and letting his thoughts set about the tasks of self-repair.

You don't have to do it all today, you know. You've got a few years . . . maybe.

He tests his energy link foretime. So far, the use of present-time energies hasn't damaged the linkage. But he can sense the limits to his control and to the total energy he can command here in the backtime. He cannot handle as many focal points, nor with as much precision.

Does it have to do with his location, the development of Aurore later on, or with the energy shunts backtime?

He shakes his head again. This time the ache is gone, but the questions remain.

Life had been much simpler as a simple newsie, playing at a minor god in the wings, coming up for breath every few decades, and avoiding any real commitment or involvement.

Now there is the question of Emily. He has taken care of her immediate future, but he still knows nothing of her past.

Does it matter?

He dozes, pushing aside the questions that hammer at him.

"Master Seine?"

He jerks to alertness.

"Medtech Nerril. Let's take a look at that business on your forehead."

Martel sits and lets the medtech clean the scrape. He could have healed the superficial damage, but what would have been his excuse for staying? Besides, a look at the Regency society from inside, even from the semiservant's position he has created, might be helpful and interesting. Might make his next efforts easier.

Might be stalling, too. Martel pushes away his own doubts, knowing the mental reservations will return, and return.

As Nerril cleans the cut with the sonic spray, Martel injects a series of memories of Kryn. He also plants the compulsion for the medtech to update Kryn's medical records. Nerril will actually be creating the records, while thinking that he is merely adding to them.

Martel catalogues all he must do . . . at a bare minimum.

The Hall of Records must be visited for the official record of Kryn's birth to be created, plus the peerage registry and the social lists. A few references would slip by, but Kryn would have years to mend the gaps by her physical presence, and who would deny her existence, when she was so obviously present and the records showed her birth? Particularly with such a powerful mother and respected and doting father?

"I said . . . that's all, Master Seine."

"Oh . . . sorry . . . daydreaming."

"Are you sure you're all right?"

"Fine. Fine."

Nerril packs up his equipment, collapsing it into the ubiquitous green bag.

Gerson stands by the door, twiddling his thumbs.

"Why don't you report back to Captain Herlieu that I'm fine?"

"Orders. Wait for him."

"All right."

Gerson leans back against the wall, eyes running from Martel to the picture on the wall and back again.

"Where are you from originally?" asks Martel.

"Newhebb. Isle of Narrows. Joined the Impies. When my term was up, followed the Captain here. There he was a Force Leader. One of the best. Should have seen him at New Reimer. Something, it was. Took the entire crivet, himself. Well . . . him and two others. Got the Marshal's Cross for it."

Herlieu didn't look that old. That meant part of his contract with the Duke was the cost of rejuv treatments. Probably worth it to the Duchess, since Herlieu ran a tight operation.

Gerson was saved from the need for further conversation by the arrival of a young woman. Blond, dressed in the blue-and-gold tunic and trousers, in the colors of Kirsten, she was narrow-waisted, slim-hipped, and large-breasted.

After an instant Martel realizes he is seeing Alicia, maid to the Duchess and bed partner to the Duke.

"Master Seine?"

Martel inclines his head.

"The Duke would like to see you, sir. In his study."

Martel puts his feet on the floor, gingerly. The floor stays firmly underfoot. Running a quick check on himself, he decides he is in surprisingly good shape for all the energy he has expended.

Alicia leads the way.

The hallway, windowless, is lit with a uniform glow from the high ceiling and from the pale yellow heatstone flooring.

The fabric-covered walls display a pale cream-and-blue pattern of intertwined lilies and swords.

The Duke's study is in the tower opposite the Duchess' morning receiving room. Unlike the other rooms through which Martel has passed, the walls are of dark wood, or wooden bookshelves, though each shelf is permaglassed over and sealed.

The Duke, standing behind a massive and all-wooden desk of a design centuries old, wears a dark green dressing robe and white silksheen shirt, open at the neck.

"How's Kryn, Master Seine?" The Duke's voice booms as he extends his hand down toward Martel from his near-two-meter height.

Alicia, notes Martel, does not leave, but seats herself in a window seat in the far corner of the book-lined room. She will report to the Duchess.

Martel reaches out, taking in the man's thoughts, and freezes time for them both for an instant.

Do I really have a daughter? My own daughter? All seems so vague. . . . And Seine . . . why . . . who is he? What report? Why can't I remember more? Damned rejuv. Takes the good memories with the bad.

Duke Kirsten will be good to Kryn. Perhaps too good, but the Duchess' hardheaded approach will provide balance.

Martel supplies more memories . . . image after image . . . thought after thought . . . Kryn as a dark-haired, serious-faced infant; Kryn taking a first step, holding on to the

Duke's hand; Kryn drawing a squiggly tower meant to be Southwich; Kryn stamping her foot in the courtyard; Kryn . . . Kryn . . . Kryn . . .

. . . and the Duke's mind laps them up, image after image.

Martel stretches his reach further and time-freezes Alicia as well. Then he walks to the desk, places a small album on the corner. The cover is plain blue, bordered in gold, with the Duke's seal in the center.

Inside are copies of holos he remembers from the Kryn of so long ago and some he has done just for this purpose. The Duke would have had such an album, since he lives in the past as much as the present. The Duchess would not. She believes she has had a daughter for her husband, most reluctantly, and while she will ensure that Kryn meets her standards, meaning excellence in everything, the Duchess lives in the present and future. No sentimental holos for her!

Martel retreats to where he had stood and unlooses the moment he has held in check.

"She's fine, Your Lordship. Just fine. Adapting well, and doing excellently. Frankly, I don't see why you were so concerned, or why you hired me for a personal report. I'm certain Lady Persis is giving you much the same information, or will. She's an outstanding young woman and could go far if she chooses."

"Like her mother," muses the Duke. He looks down at the album quizzically, opens it, sees the first holo, smiles fondly, and shuts the cover.

"Her studies?"

"She excels, particularly in languages and in science. Very strong-minded."

"Don't know if I should have sent her away, Master Seine. I don't know, but I probably spoil the girl too much. She needs a wider perspective, and I know the Duchess feels that way."

"Are you asking me for a recommendation, sir?"

"No . . . but what would you do?"

"I cannot recommend, sir. Lady Persis runs a fine school. No school is home. But then, private tutors cannot teach the interplay of other fine minds, nor the relations between one's peers."

"Good points."

Martel waits.

The Duke looks across at Alicia, as if to mark her presence, then looks back down at the album, which he picks up, fingers, and sets down again before continuing.

"All damned confusing . . ." he muses.

His face clears, and he looks straight at Martel.

"Would you join us for dinner, the main meal of midday here?"

"Your offer is most generous, and I would enjoy that."

"Fine, just fine."

Martel coughs, gently.

"Your Lordship . . . I did not anticipate such an invitation, and, alas, can wear only what I have on."

"We're not that formal. Wear what you have on. Black's appropriate most places, anyway . . . except the Regent doesn't seem to like it. Doesn't bother me, though."

The Duke looks at Alicia.

"Alicia, will you escort Master Seine back to his quarters . . . but first get him a bite to eat, and then give him a tour of the place. I'll be late getting back."

The Duke returns his eyes to Martel. "Sorry I can't chat longer, but due at the Regent's Council meeting. Sure you understand."

"Most assuredly, Your Lordship. Most assuredly."

Alicia rises to her feet and departs, letting Martel follow as he will.

Kryn? What about me if she comes back? I'm for his pleasure and her convenience. He lives for Kryn. Was it always this way? Don't remember it like this . . . Black scares me. Master Seine . . . master of what? They all accept him . . . from nowhere . . . why?

Martel understands her questions and her fears. He tries to disarm some of them with another question he places in her thoughts.

What woman could show Kryn love?

Alicia frowns.

Love? Who knows love? Not hen not the Duke . . . for his daughter . . . maybe . . . for me? Just lust.

Martel decides to make a few more arrangements. He touches the Duke's mind, even as the Grand Duke Kirsten is entering the flitter to take him to the palace. Alicia will be safe . . . and loved.

Next . . . a quick touch to the Duchess' thoughts, giving her relief that the Duke loves the maid she has so conveniently provided.

How do you know, Martel, he asks himself, *that your thoughts haven't been rearranged the same way?*

He drives the cold chill into his own deeps and pushes the thought away.

By the time they reach the kitchen, Alicia has thawed and Martel is ready for the warmed rolls and juice that are shoved at him in the back pantry.

From the kitchen the tour begins, and Alicia is thorough.

For that Martel is thankful, though his feet hurt long before they finish, because virtually everyone at Southwich has a memory of Kryn. And if some of the staff wonder at the bemused look on Master Seine's face, so be it.

Once he leaves the environs of Kirsten, he will have to cover the palace, as well as some nobles and key staff in the Houses of Gatwick, Ngaio, and Sulifer. After that will come all the peerage records, and the records of Lady Persis' School.

Along the way he will plant as many memories as he can with the general populace, the gossip columnists, and the opinion leaders. Not that total coverage is necessary, particularly when the subject is the daughter of a Duke renowned for his privacy in a Regency court society that revolves around the Prince Regent and his latest boyfriend.

Dinner is served promptly at 1300 hours in the family dining room to exactly five people—the Duke, the Duchess,
Captain Herlieu, Madame Herlieu, and Master Seine.

"How was the Council meeting this morning?" That is the
Duchess, uninterested, but trying to break the silence.

"Same. Interesting problem, you know." The Duke pauses
to slurp his red-turtle soup. "Prince Edwin asked the Council to suggest ways to increase revenues while reducing taxes.
Little difficult, would you say, Master Seine?"

"I'm not an expert in high finance, Your Lordship. It does
seem rather paradoxical."

"Polite way of saying it's confusing. Those ninnies sat
there and hee-hawed. Perhaps this . . . perhaps that." The
Duke frowns, puts down his soup spoon.

The Duchess takes another delicate sip of her soup, almost
a consommé, lays her spoon on the Blackshire china, and
surveys the table. The softness of the glow lights and the
dimness of the exterior light, blocked as it is by the heavy
draperies, reduce the sharpness of her nose, display her face
as ten years younger or more, hinting at the beauty she once
had been. Her silver hair, maintained by cosmetology, adds
to the regal impression.

"Did the Council make any decision?" Martel asks.

"Of course! They made a decision to study the request.
That's what happens most of the time."

"How did you vote?" asks the Duchess.

"Last," rumbles the Duke, "and for it—the study, that is.
Stupid study, but stupid to oppose it now. Right, Milady?"

The Duchess nods.

"Don't they see the danger?" That comes from Herlieu.

"Which danger?" questions the Duchess. Her soft voice
carries, silken with the feel of iron behind it. "The danger
from within or the danger from without?"

"I'm a simple fighting man," answers Herlieu, "and I worry
about the dangers from outside. Once they're taken care of,
you always have a chance to set your own house in order."

"But doesn't a weak or disorderly house invite attack, and a strong one discourage it?"

"Makes my point, Your Ladyship. You have to be ready to fight in either case. If your house is disorderly or if it isn't."

Martel adds nothing. The last time around, he hadn't cared to try understanding the intricacies of Regency infighting, and he still doesn't. The Duke admits voting for something that is worthless with a total stranger present, and the Duchess agrees.

Martel lets his mind soak up the loose thoughts.

Few escape from the Duchess . . . a loose mélange from Herlieu . . . and a surprisingly ordered progression from the Duke. Martel zeroes in on the big man.

Edwin . . . not half the man his father the Emperor is . . . queer . . . doesn't understand economics or military power . . . amused by politics . . . way to favor is to amuse him, and they all do . . . from Mersham to Stelstrobel . . . the Fuards pour credit after credit into R&D, ships, men . . . and Edwin asks about financing his annual carnival . . . Karnak, guard of the Empire's Marches, does nothing. You, admit it, Kirsten, you do nothing either . . . too many jackals . . . all ready to pull you down . . . amusing, they'd find it . . . and they're younger . . . maybe Kryn . . . if it's right . . . haven't thought that . . .

"Does Councilor Mersham feel more committed to internal or external problems?" ventures Martel.

"Councilor Mersham is gravely concerned about all problems, as they all are."

"And the reaction to the Fuards?"

"Ha! We all are deeply concerned . . . deeply concerned . . . but also we are deeply concerned about the unrest caused by the latest tax levy which went to expand the Regent's Palace and for a ten percent increase in the basic dole."

"Did the increase make people happier?" asks Martel, remembering full well how his mother had snorted.

He is rewarded by a sniff from Madame Herlieu, a thin-faced redhead, a snort from the good Captain, and a raised eyebrow from the Duchess.

"I can see why you sent your daughter away."

"Not sure I agree now," mumbles the Duke. "Seemed good at the time. Now I wonder."

"Experience in other milieus might give her a broader outlook," comments the red-haired woman.

The Duchess nods again, and Martel reaches for the thoughts behind the nod.

Needs a lot more experience . . . maybe trip to New Augusta itself when she gets back. Then a cadet tour. Not many women do, but she can. Kryn will handle it.

For not having had a daughter until that morning, the Duchess is certainly busy plotting the path Kryn will take, Martel thinks to himself, a bit sadly.

"Why so downcast, Master Seine?" booms the Duke.

"Thinking about your daughter, I just wondered. My children," he lies, having none, "won't have to worry about high finance and privy councils, and sometimes I think they'll be the happier for it. Lady Kryn will become our outstanding Duchess, maybe more, but I wonder if she'll be happy."

"Are any of us ever really happy?" replies the Guard Captain.

"Maybe not. Maybe we delude ourselves into thinking so. Is happiness everything? And can anyone stay happy if someone isn't out guarding, and someone else ruling?"

What's he want?

The Duchess is sharp, too sharp, and Martel keeps forgetting it. The sooner he leaves the better, and the less he says the better.

The main course is scampig, roasted and lightly basted with Taxan brandy. Martel enjoys it and says little.

". . . 'course the Prince got the next bird with that needle rifle. Not at all sporting. Single-action, but never have to reload. Real sport would do it with an old-style shotgun. . . . You hunt, Master Seine?"

"Not my province. Travel too much. Can't do something well, usually don't care to do it."

I'll bet there are some exceptions your wife knows. The unexpectedly salacious thought from Madame Herlieu catches Martel off guard, and he barely keeps from flushing.

The Duke doesn't notice.

". . . and the time he decided to use a bow against the dualhorn. Sounds fair, but he used an explosive arrowhead. What's the difference between that damned electronic contraption he called a bow and a full-bored laser? Oh, so he could say he got the beast with a bow and arrow . . ."

Martel takes it all in, notes the names, and listens.

The dinner drags into the early afternoon, and later, and later.

It is close to 1600 before Martel walks out through the park gate, down the slight hill toward the Regent's Palace, and into nowhere.

He has several days, weeks, of hard work ahead. But this time, damned if *anyone* is going to see him!

lviii

▼

What the hammer? What the forge?
What the bellows? From what gorge
Came the fire, came the light,
Came the beasts that sowed the night?

Martel knows that the gods on high, specifically on Aurore, do not know he is backtime. Knows, also, that they do not believe travel backtime is possible.

In his wrapping of time energy, he debates his next move.

Which player next? Or players? The Fallen Ones, the Brotherhood, the Prince Regent? All the pieces need to be moved quickly, before the disappearance/destruction of the hammer-thrower can be verified.

The Brotherhood is the choice.

Brother Geidren. The image of the brown-robed "brother" slips into his mind as clearly as if it had been yesterday when he confronted her across the shield wall in the underground headquarters of that secretive and now-exiled group.

None of his experiences on Aurore have shed much more light on his knowledge of the Brotherhood, and the questions have only grown with their banishment and disappearance.

Are the Fallen Ones an adjunct to the Brethren? Allies? Antagonists with mutual goals? All three rumors have persisted for a millennium . . . without answers.

Martel knows only when and where Brother Geidren had been once, and the single logical possibility is to relocate that position and follow with an appearance—once the Martel he had been has left for Aurore.

First, the underground and shielded quarters of the Brotherhood. That is simple.

More difficult is locating Geidren after Martin Martel has left for Aurore. Meeting himself would be catastrophic, in more ways than one. The energy release would render the entire point of the search moot, but not in any way in which Martel would be around to appreciate.

Are you ready for this?

Do you have any choice?

The answer to both questions is no.

From the requisite undertime distance, he tracks the departure of one young and stunned Martin Martel, and thence hastens back to the bunker of the Brethren, emerging in a silent corridor, wrapped in darkness, cloaked in his energies, and invisible to all but the most talented of espers.

Geidren is not alone, rather unsurprisingly, but with two

others in a room which could only be described as a communications and command center.

Martel observes from a corner, bemused that the three, all espers, are so wrapped in their own dynamics and so trusting of their mechanical detectors and guard technicians that his presence goes unnoticed.

As an afterthought, he reaches out and puts the three guards who scan the command center into a deep sleep.

Kirsten? Main threat? Overthrow the Regent? Those thoughts come from the thin-faced blond and bearded man. Call him Aquinas.

More than meets the eye. Foreboding . . . doom on the horizon. Aurore? From the older man. Call him Mystic.

The Master Game Player? Or God? One choice or the other. Or your fears? Doesn't matter. We're outlawed. Queried Scholar pretext. How do we fight? Raise the Brethren? Underground? Passive resistance over time? Religion? Gerri Geidren's thoughts ring with a soft chime.

Martel is impressed. Aquinas and Mystic are definitely second-raters next to the woman.

Religion . . . the great crusade, offers Aquinas.

Put the Unknowable against the Empire? Pervert the sacrament of Faith?

Would it work? asks Geidren.

Yes.

No.

NO! Martel lets himself become visible, half shading his face in a shadow of his own, and offers an observation.

"The problem with relying on religion is that you give the temporal authorities the power to ban it. Banned religions are effective only in limited circumstances—like when the god involved is willing to use force on behalf of his or her followers or when the oppression of the regime approaches terrorism."

His last half-sentence is lost in the blaze of the lasers concentrated on the corner where Martel stands.

He absorbs what he can, diverts the rest into his personal undertime/underspace reservoir that grows with each appearance and reduces his need to tap his own foretime reserves.

The way things are going, Martel, you're going to have your own fields back- and foretime, that is, if everyone keeps throwing energy at you.

Geidren stops the waste of energy with her own mental override of the controls she had activated. Mystic and Aquinas blanch as they see Martel still stands untouched.

"Trite, but who are you?"

"It doesn't matter. I'd like to offer some observations. One: The Prince Regent will fall, but the Regency will remain, more powerful than before. Two: Despite whatever you do, and it may be a great deal, the power of the House of Kirsten will wax, not wane. Three: There is a Master Game Player. Three at least, as a matter of fact. Four: You will not even attempt any injury to Martin Martel. It might make him angry, and it will definitely make me angry."

Him? Master Game Player?

Can't be!

Three of them?

Martel decides to emphasize his points, and amplifies his next message to the split point.

THERE IS A FALLEN ONE. CALL HIM THE MASTER GAME PLAYER I REPRESENT. CALL THE TWO OTHERS APOLLO AND THE SMOKE BULL, IF YOU WILL.

Mystic and Aquinas crumple, both twitching heaps. Geidren leans heavily against the commset.

Don't overplay . . . your . . . hand.

Martel smiles, points at the commset, lets the energy flow from his fingertips, and waits until the equipment is a molten heap of slag.

At the first blast, Gerri Geidren has staggered back, staring as if to penetrate the shadow that surrounds Martel's face.

No esper . . . that power.

"As I said," Martel resumes conversationally, ignoring the

twitches of the two on the floor, "the Brotherhood will have to live with reality."

What would you do?

Oppose the Empire.

"But," she breaks out verbally, "you said that wouldn't do any good!"

"That is not what I said. I said the Regency would fall, but that Kirsten's power would not. In opposing the Regency and what follows, the Brethren can do a great deal of good by placing some checks on tyranny. The times will demand raw power. An organization based on promoting the best development of each individual's abilities is restricted by its very ideals from exerting the kind of power necessary. And if you give up your ideals, you lose the power you have. So . . . don't."

Damned philosopher.

Few would call me that.

"Two facets work better than one," he continues aloud. "You might call the churchly half the Church of Man, and in turn the Regency will come to regard its priests as the servants of the Fallen One, who has not really fallen yet. That should not frighten you, because the Fallen One is of and for the people, which should indeed frighten them."

He is distracted by the shuddering gasp of Aquinas, who stops breathing. Martel turns his attention to the man, makes a few adjustments, and lets Aquinas slip into a deep sleep. He repeats the pattern with Mystic, and makes similar changes in the metabolism and body of Geidren.

You merely represent a Master Game Player?

"In a manner of speaking."

Merely represent?

No man is a god, no matter how powerful!

Martel lets his thoughts check the area again, scanning the monitors that guard the control center. Still under the control of his earlier meddling, they show nothing amiss, and the guard technicians sleep peacefully.

"The other half," he plods on, "the Brethren, could act as the temporal government in exile, doing what it can to remind the Empire and the Regency of the human rights of their people. Remember, neither will last forever, and some organized group should be there to guide the way when they fall."

They? They fall? Why should we do what you suggest? They? Only one Empire . . .

Martel smiles.

"You can do whatever you want. But remember that your strength lies in your ideals."

Still the damned philosopher-god.

No god, no philosopher, and a damned prophet, corrects Martel in the instant before he vanishes.

The next step is forty years forward in time and to the palace of the aging Prince Regent.

lix

▼

3. And it came to pass in those days, when the son of the King of Kings sat upon the gilded throne of Karnak and ruled, and saw naught, that upon that night that was declared the servants brought food to the great table. When it was served, the lamps flickered. Flicker did the lamps twice, and after the third flicker were they extinguished, though no man had laid hands upon them.

4. Light! Let there be light! commanded the Prince, who was mighty and beholden in all the universe only to his Father, the King of Kings, the Emperor of Man. But the darkness remained, and the ser-

vants fell to their knees, and the courtiers were struck speechless.

5. Let there be light! demanded the Prince, and he stamped his boots, and the echo filled the halls, but there was no light.

6. In the midst of the darkness then appeared a light, and in that light was a demon in the likeness of a man, and he wore the black of a prophet.

7. What mean you, miserable creature, to deny a Prince of Princes light in his own hall? So saying, the Prince cast a thunderbolt at the demon. But the demon raised his hand, and the thunderbolt returned to the Prince and struck him dumb.

8. Mark well what I say, responded the demon, and low was his voice, yet all in the great halls of Karnak that was heard it, from the kitchens to the dungeons and even unto the towers that speared the heavens and called unto the stars.

9. Mark what I say, for thy days are numbered, even as the hour after the opening of the seventh seal. You shall be extinguished even as I have extinguished the lights of your hall and your mightiness. And none shall mourn you. No, none shall mourn you.

10. Before this shall come to pass, I will raise a temple, which cannot be cast down, though you and your legions will try. The mightiest tree of the world shall be uprooted, and the heavens will open, and a woman shall save thy people. And she will lead them.

11. Your people will be saved, but not you. For none shall mourn you and your passing, not even the King of Kings. For though I am vested in dark, I will bring light, and though you claim light, you are a judgment of darkness.

12. Dumbstruck stood the Prince of Princes until the demon had vanished and the lamps had rekindled themselves.

13. What heard you? asked the son of the King of Kings. What heard you?

14. But of those who heard the black demon none would look to their ruler, nor would they speak.

Ix

▼

Martel holds the nexus point, hangs in the gray of not-time, thoughts seeking the true timeline to the Karnak he had known as a student, to the time when he and Kryn had strolled the ways of the great Park of Summer, Park of the Regent.

Is the true path the reedy gray line twisting into the dark that becomes black, or the pulsing red one?

The colors he perceives are all in his mind, for the gray chaos where he waits has no color, but color is how he sees them. The solid black path, almost a road arrow of time, leads back to Aurore. That aura leaves no doubts.

A green line is the one he wants, and Martel wills himself back against the current until the feel of the reality outside the undertime river matches his images. Physics says there is no flow to time, that the flow is only in the mind of man; but Martel is used to fighting his own mind, if indeed that is where the flow of time exists.

He emerges from the undertime next to a towering red-barked tree, just outside the silver glitter fence that surrounds the giant. So high is the mutated sequoia that its noon shadow covers acres.

Martel's black cloak droops over him in the windless quiet.

Cling! Cling! Cling!

The chimes from the carillon announce the beginning of the Moments of Thankfulness. Thankfulness for the generosity of the Prince Regent. A time when all stand silent. A time when the blue-uniformed proctors ensure that silence.

Martel throws his cloak over his shoulders, casts his senses out across the acres, knows he will do what he now knows he did, and draws an aura of blackness around himself.

He strides across the shadowed grass with a light step—jaunty, daring the blue proctors and their blue helmets and their blue blast rifles to incinerate him.

Fifty-one paces later—not that Martel has counted them, he knows—the first proctor has Martel in his sights. Martel pities the man, raises his hand, and points.

The blast rifle melts.

The proctor drops it, suffers a burn as a splash of molten metal splats on his lower forearm, eats through his gauntlet.

Proctors travel in pairs. His companion, seeing the damage, turns, sights, and fires.

He explodes in a column of flame as the blast bends, impossibly, and returns to him.

Martel leaves the shadow of the mighty Tree of the Regent and casts his own acres-long shadow as he marches toward the golden towers of the palace.

In their dark blue singleskits, a second set of proctors races toward the black interloper. They race from the blue cupola that stands at the corner of the ten-kilometer-square park closest to the palace.

Any military authority would deem the singleskits, armed as they are with disruptors, stunners, tanglers, and full riot-control equipment, more than a match for a single black-shadowed man who marches upon the palace.

Deeming is not sufficient.

Martel waits to see if the bluesuits are determined to destroy him merely for moving at the time appointed as sacred to the Prince Regent.

They are.

First, they focus the longer-range disruptors, for they are well over a kilo from Martel. The disruptors refuse to operate. As the two proctors scream closer the shock waves bend the ornamental shrubs that line the carved stone walks, rustle the leaves of the trees the singleskits barely clear, and bowl over the few children who are in the park at noon.

Martel gestures, and the proctors and their vehicles are gone. Not destroyed, although that would have been easier. Gone. Thrust through the tunnels in the around time and place to the Star Room of the Marshal of Proctors. The Marshal is not present, but the defense systems are always alert, and there will be enough wreckage to confound the Prince Regent and the Marshal.

The flow of energy from another set of disruptors bouncing from his screens draws Martel from his thoughts back into the park.

Martel admires efficiency, and the kill instinct of the blue-suits is efficient.

Less than units in the Park of the Regent and six proctors have attempted to destroy him for being so inconsiderate as to ignore the ritual silence and stillness devoted to the Prince. The last two are squandering energy on yet another attempt.

Martel's cloak flaps in the energy currents swirling around him, drips bits of shadow toward the burnt grass beneath his feet as he channels the energy into the reservoir from which he draws, and walks toward the remaining two singleskits, walks through the curtain of fire, through the disruptor beams and accompanying harmonics.

Cling! Cling! Cling!

The carillon chimes the end to the five units of stillness devoted to the greatness and beneficence of the Prince Regent whose minions continue their efforts to annihilate the Fallen One, for who but a Fallen One would dare profane the sacred stillness?

Freed from the bondage of immobility, heads in the park turn to view the pillar of flame, to see the growing pool of blackness around the figure of a single man, to hear the crusty sound of energy weapons.

From the farthest corner of the great park, screeching in on another wave of wind, comes yet one more pair of singleskits, disruptors and blasters flaring.

Martel bends the energy, forces it skyward into a grotesque parody of the Tree of the Regent, into a tree of flame casting its own shadow of dark, a flame tree visible from the towers of the palace, and from far beyond. A tree visible to the sensors of the Fleet in orbit, a tree building brightness with each instant till heads that turned toward it turn away, eyes stinging from unaccustomed tears, hands shaking.

And still the proctors fire, pouring the reserves from their singleskits, drawing from the power beams of the city.

Around the Old City of Karnak, most distant from the palace, lights fail. Next the lift/drop shafts in the towers fail and draw on their emergency reserves just to shut down and to put their emergency catch nets in place.

The Pleasures Pyramid that floats over the Lake of Hopes on the outskirts of the Old City loses lift, drifting inexorably downward, its lower floors first resting on the perfumed and green water, then crumpling as more and more of the inverted structure brings its weight to bear on the smaller lower stories.

A man, wearing nothing and one of the few who can see what is happening, dives from an upper window when the restraining fields fail. The green water is less than a meter deep.

A woman, holding up an impossibly long skirt, decked in copper fronds and blueglass jewels belonging to some vanished history that never really happened, climbs from a terrace once protected by an energy screen and struggles through thigh-deep water. She has waited too long. Her scream is drowned in hundreds of others as the entire Pleasures Pyramid collapses outward and down, on her, on the water, on the floating body of the dead diver.

Martel feels the deaths, feels part after part of the city die.

The flame tree darkens, soul-sucking, energy-seeking, cold, bending light away from it. But it grows, fueled by the energy Martel funnels into it, overtopping the Regent's Tree, overtopping the highest spires of the Prince's palace.

Finally, the growth halts. The black tree stands. Untouched. Silent. Silent while the singleskits pour flame at Martel, silent while the palace's long-range disruptors and lasers add their weight to the attack. Silent while the ground beneath Martel and his tree is consumed. Silent while the innocents in the park die and the city fractures.

Silent while Martel's soul screams and tallies each death with a black weight in his mind.

The tree of the black flame vanishes. So does Martel. So do the four singleskits. So does the Park of the Regent, the Park of Summer, and so does the once-mighty Tree of the Regent.

The tree? Martel bends space and time again and sends the tree back into antiquity, back to a planet long since forgotten. And that is as it should be.

The singleskits and bluesuits are sent journeying, too, to another place, where their spirits may mingle with those of their victims.

Martel hovers undertime, drawing the thunderstorms, the clouds, the rain, overriding the climate satellites, fusing their circuits.

He is done. The rains pound Old Karnak, filling the glass-lined hole that was once the Park of Summer, filling that hole that will become the Lake of Dreams, chilling the citizens who have never felt day rain, and leaving the Prince shivering in his powerless palace.

Martel twists his place in space, fractionally, and appears in a narrow street. His cloak is wrapped around him. No one notices, for attention is focused on the coal-black clouds above, on the lack of power, on the portals that will not open, on those trapped inside and out.

A small boy is squeezed between the iris edges of a portal door. His mother is begging passersby for help, but in this district, at this time, no one will stop.

Martel gestures, and the door collapses in powder. The child falls and skins his knee, falls silently, for he can barely breathe. The mother looks sideways at Martel, then darts toward her son, scoops him up, holding him to her shoulder and brushing the sticky gray powder off him. He should be dying, squeezed between industrial doors of such power, but Martel has taken care of that as well, and the child sleeps on his mother's shoulder.

In the rain, the cloak droops behind Martel. He looks nearly and merely human, a black rat looking for the darkest corner of Old Karnak.

"Mister . . . can't wear black. Bluesuits burn you spot."

Martel smiles at the urchin, dressed in faded red and yellow, his green eyes peering from under a red thatch, with a green sandal on one foot, a red one on the other.

"Death cannot burn, young man. And life is death," he replies, pleased with himself for remembering the Litany at this point.

"Maybe no. Dead you no feel."

"Which way to Old Center? Polony's mansion?"

"That wreck?"

Martel nods, lets a little blackness seep from his soul, well out around him.

"Trick neat. You magician, something?"

"Something like that. Polony's house?"

"Turn left next alley, three streets on right, and take another left . . . real narrow. Watch Gert. Hangs there with viber."

Martel reaches out with his thoughts, checks the boy, changes a few minor metabolic matters, and ambles on toward his destination.

Three streets on down, he turns right into a narrower way, barely broad enough for three men elbow to elbow.

Gert is there, removing his viber from the inert form of an unwarned man.

Time for a demonstration.

Martel bends time, again adjusts a few metabolic details. The figure on the plastistone pavement retches, groans, and sits up.

Gert is not impressed, kicks the man away, and advances on Martel. The stench of stale ale and of sweat on sweat precedes him, a weapon in itself.

Gorillalike, brown hair streaming down over his shoulders, Gert grabs for Martel, who does not move, embraces the man in black with his right arm, which is as thick as a small oak, and carves with his left, viber on full power.

Martel should collapse into a heap from either the force of the grasp or from the impact of the weapon. He does not. Neither does the viber make any impression on him or his garments.

Gert is still not impressed, and locks both hands together and brings them down in a mighty swing on Martel's head.

There is a sharp crack through the narrow passage.

"Aeiiii!"

Gert's hands break each in a half-dozen places. Martel stands unmoved.

The man who had been the victim has regained his feet, uncertain whether he can profit by picking on Gert or on the strange figure in black, uncertain whether he should run. He temporizes by darting behind a wastebloc.

Gert stares at his hands.

Martel feels some pity, but not much. He gestures, and behind the gesture makes a few adjustments to Gert and to his hands and arms.

"You sought to give death. That is not yours to give. I have returned life. But as my reminder . . . your hands will never heal."

Gert's former victim looks at the slash in his tunic, at the man in black, and slinks quietly down the alley.

Martel steps around Gert and proceeds.

At the end of the narrow way, in a small square by itself, surrounded on all sides by another street wide enough only for a handful of people to pass shoulder to shoulder, stands a ruined dwelling. Wide steps of ancient green marble encircle the structure, modeled as it was after another ancient building on a long-forgotten planet. The columns are intact, but the roof has tumbled in.

Martel surveys the wreck. No life, except the rodents, the insects, and two tarrants who, weasellike, prey on the rodents. Drawing on the enormous field of energy poured at him by the proctors, he channels a portion into Polony's house, rebuilding, restoring, turning it to the function of the building from which it was copied.

At the center, in the hall of worship, he creates a black altar, a solid black cube with each side measuring exactly his own height. At another touch, he infuses the marble walls and columns with a slight glow, while changing the stone entirely to jet-black, streaked with a few isolated shots of silver. Finally he sets up the self-sustaining energy fields that will enable it to withstand the Empire's weapons for the centuries to come. His defenses will last. Time has proven that.

A quick tour of his handiwork convinces him of the faithfulness of his artistry and of his memory. He walks down the front steps, though "front" is not exactly correct, since the central hall may be approached through the columns from any side.

A small crowd is gathered by this time: several urchins, including the one in red and yellow; the shambling figure of Gert; a woman in a privacy cloak with the hard and painted eyes of a harlot; and, of course, the habitual representative of the Thieves' Guild, standing near the front, ready to demand tribute, and backed by several others in the shadows, who are armed with old projectile weapons and one stolen blaster.

Martel ignores the thief as he leaves the steps and stops to heal the skin ulcers of one of the urchins, a job that could have been done by any corner autodoc, though not so quickly.

"Don't you have something for me, stranger?" asks the thief.

"Life and death are one. You have life, and life is death. Without death there is no meaning to life. Without life there is no death. Be content with what you have."

Martel makes the sign of the looped and inverted cross, the one he has remembered from his student days, bestowing it as a benediction, and continues up the narrow street.

The thief throws his first knife. It hits the swirls of the black cloak and drops to the pavement with a thud.

A child in stained maroon overalls scrabbles for the blade, but drops it as if it burned. It might, reflects Martel, since it is now solid rock.

The thief ignores the byplay and throws his second knife, which suffers the same fate, though none of the crowd attempts to retrieve the weapon.

The bystanders, increased by another cloaked harlot, an older unveiled woman with braided silver hair, and a bent old man with a cane who is neither bent nor old, but an Imperial agent, draw back.

The thief draws his projectile gun and sights it dramatically at Martel's back.

Martel freezes the man, turns, reverses the benediction he had made moments before, and addresses the man, whose eyes dart from side to side as he sees Martel approach.

"I withdraw my blessing, given though you had evil in your heart. Twice have you struck, and twice have you been warned. You have not turned from your wickedness, and your heart is like stone. So be it! Life and death are one, and life is death."

The man makes no outcry, not surprisingly, for he, too, has been transmuted into black stone.

The urchin in yellow and red touches the stone tunic of the thief.

"Stone! The priest of death turned him stone!"

The Imperial agent scuttles away down another alley, hurrying as he can within the limits of his cover to make a report to the palace.

Martel turns, following the route he has pursued for the Viceroy a millennium later, not sure that anyone will pick up the parallel, but leaving the clue if anyone should choose to understand.

Every block or so he pauses, either rewarding or punishing as he sees fit. From the original crowd gathered at the temple steps, only the red-haired child has followed.

At last, on the outskirts of Old Karnak, he stops and climbs atop a stone bench on the edge of a neglected park.

All the pieces are in place from the past, and the puzzle is almost complete, except for the last pieces, and for those he must return to whence he came.

He raises his left hand.

"From the Fallen One I come, and to Him I go!"

A curtain of darkness drops across the long grass and cracked stones of the park, and when it lifts, the stone bench is bare.

The red-haired boy kneels and makes the sign of the looped and inverted cross.

lxi

▼

The Viceroy makes no move to wipe the dusty streaks from her cheeks, but centers her screens on the row of burned-out yellow glowbushes that lies both beneath her tower apartments and nearly a kilo above her head.

A walk in darkness, with bushes like those glowing yellow, and a mist over the lawn . . . she had been afraid. Like a distant song, she remembers.

Afraid . . . you, the Viceroy, afraid? When?

And there had been a voice . . . "if I told you my name, I'd have to take that, too."

Where have you heard that voice?

She does not want to know.

"Forde! Marshal Reitre!"

"Yes, Lady," the two chorus from the observers' positions flanking her.

"It is time to do something about the interference from the so-called gods of Aurore. Assemble the Grand Fleet, with a great deal of fanfare."

"But . . . my Lady . . . is that wise?" That is the Marshal.

"My Lady?" That is Forde.

"No, it is not wise. Wisdom would do nothing." She looks at Forde. "Operation Suntunnel."

Reitre blanches. Forde's face remains blank.

"You disapprove?"

"Against the power I saw on your screens, my Lady," Forde draws his words out slowly, "I question the chances of success. There were only two, and well away from their base of power."

"That is why we must remove their base of power. Without Aurore, and its sun, their power will dissipate."

"Without the Fleet, so will the Regency's." Forde's face whitens another shade as his words spill out.

"That is a chance, but unless we react to those who have smashed Karnak, the Empire will fall." She gestures at the screen, which now shows the city as it appears from the palace tower. "Out there, at this moment, thousands are flocking to the temple of the Fallen One. The Brethren are emerging, and doubtless both the Fuards and the Matriarchy are mobilizing."

As if to echo her words, the screen focuses on the small

black temple, its steps packed, and the streets and lanes leading to it thronged with supplicants.

"The power of an Empire is nothing to the power of a living god." She pauses and smiles a cold smile, one that Forde has not seen, ever, and one that bears a trace of god-like aloofness. "But if the Empire should destroy such a god . . ."

Forde bows.

She turns and leaves the control center to the two men and a score of technicians.

Instead of returning to her apartments, she takes the lift all the way to the top of the Regent's Tower, the highest point of the palace.

She studies the city, spending time at each battlement of the four-sided tower. Even from her height, it is apparent that the damage is nearly as bad as the time when the Fallen One destroyed the Park of Summer. Perhaps worse.

The shock waves of the graystone hammer amounted to the impact of a low nuclear airburst, whereas the energy and the crater created by the Fallen One had more the characteristics of a surface burst. In neither case had there been radiation, which made the situation more puzzling.

She tightens her lips. Maybe there had been no Fallen One, but who had created the black temple? If the Brotherhood had had the power to protect the temple, certainly they could have stood up to her father.

She frowns. The reports about the Fallen One had been all too clear. The temple had been restored and protected overnight, and the damage of the park had been inconsistent with any known weapon, not to mention the total destruction of the tree.

Before that, years before, there had been the power failure that had turned the Prince Regent into a blabbering idiot, swearing that a black demon had appeared in his private dining room, foretelling his fall.

According to the sealed records of the palace, the ones her

father had kept, one tape of the appearance of the Fallen One in the park had been recovered and screened privately by the Prince, the Grand Duke, and the High Marshal. After the screening, the Prince had destroyed the tape and retired. His bodyguards found his body the next morning.

Shortly thereafter, the High Marshal had suffered a seizure and had been relieved of command by the Grand Duke, acting as Viceroy for the Emperor.

The Lady stares out at her city, the city that has been hers and hers alone for more than a millennium, while others have aged and passed away, while others have plotted and failed, while others have feared and died. She recalls what she knows, knowing again that she knows not everything, that answers to what she does not know or to the questions she asks are locked behind the sealed portal in her mind that does not let her remember growing up or the days before she returned to Karnak from her schooling.

The wind brings her the acrid scent of fused insulation and ozone, and she half shrugs. A millennium since has given her enough memories.

Then why are they so empty, Lady?

She triggers the screens and turns in time to see the energies wash over the man in black who had called himself Martel. Sees the energies dispel themselves without touching him.

"Why are you so concerned with my memories?"

"One hopes, Kryn. One hopes."

Except for the distant wail of sirens, the tower top is silent.

At last, he speaks again.

"Why are you attempting to destroy Aurore? Both the Fleet and the Suntunnel will fail, you know."

"I don't know." She looks at him levelly. "As Viceroy, I have little choice. Karnak has been attacked."

"Neither of us has any choice. Not now. And I'm not sure we ever did." He smiles faintly, a smile that barely turns the corner of his mouth. "You'll lose. In losing, both the people and you will win, and in winning, the gods will lose."

"What sort of double-talk is that?" she snaps.

"Just ask yourself three questions, Kryn. Why can't you remember growing up? Why don't you grow older? And why do you fear black?"

She triggers the screens again, futilely, she knows, as tears stream again from eyes she had thought never cried.

Martel is gone. She knows he is Martel, and that is more frightening than the thought that she will lose her Fleet.

She shudders, waits until her eyes clear, and walks toward the lift shaft back down to the command center.

First, the beginning of reconstruction. Then the attack on Aurore.

Martel will see. Flamehell, he'll see.

lxii

▼

Again, around the sacred peak Jsalm gather the gods of Aurore. They assemble themselves for the second time in less than a standard year, the frequency in itself a remarkable occurrence.

The Regency gathers all its Fleet against Aurore.

Laughter suffuses the group.

Where are Thor and Dian? For surely Thor should stand in the forefront to defend us against the Empire, since he has caused this expedition of vengeance. And Dian should stand for Martel, who is no more.

Laughter again rains upon the assembled gods.

Apollo and the Smoke Bull cross glances, if Apollo's glance at the insubstantial substance and infinite depths of the Minotaur can be considered a crossing of glances.

Still, the meaning is plain, for each suspects the other.

No one answers the anonymous question. No one knows.

First, Martel has gone. Then Thor and Dian/Emily.

The unseen danger may be more threat than the Empire, offers Thetis, green and wet.

The Smoke Bull nods.

After a time, Apollo agrees.

But first Karnak must be smashed, taught a lesson to end all lessons. Then we will seek out the unseen danger.

The gods and demigods find Apollo's summation to their liking, and they repair to where they individually repair and begin their preparations for the Grand Fleet of the Empire.

A sleeping woman turns over in silksheen sheets, where she has dreamed what has transpired, and sobs, but wakes not, and will remember nothing of what she has dreamed.

A man in black watches from a distance, and smiles a grim smile, and begins his preparations.

The Fleet Commander touches a switch, and the Grand Fleet swings to point toward a relatively ordinary star which is circled by an extraordinary planet.

The twenty-third Emperor of the Empire of Light shakes his head as a shadow passes before his eyes, but continues his play with his latest mistress.

A man in red addresses silent prayers to an undeclared god, while the Marshal of Strategy makes sure his laser is fully charged.

A goddess watches a demigod exercise with shield and sword, trying to hold back a vision of a leaden shield wreathed in black. She shudders and turns away.

lxiii

▼

For the importance of the mission, the ship is termed a cruiser, but, in reality, is nothing more than a corvette with a cruiser's drives and screens. The Captain, uniformed in Imperial blue, is a recently promoted full Captain looking toward a complete and distinguished career.

"Range?" he barks.

"Point five, closing at point two per stan, sir."

The Captain settles himself back into his padded command seat. Another two stans must pass before he can start the deployment. In the meantime, the main Fleet should be arriving near outsystem Aurore.

"Not for a while yet, I suspect," a strange voice intrudes.

The Captain bolts upright, grabs for his sidearm, and points the laser at the man in black who has appeared beside him.

"My name's Martel, Captain Ellerton. You can use that if you want, but I can assure you it won't work."

The Captain, his belief in visible technology supreme, thumbs the firing stud. Nothing happens.

"Now that we've gotten that out of the way—"

"Marines! Imperial Marines to the bridge!"

Martel smiles.

The Captain looks at the rest of the bridge crew, who proceed with their routine as if nothing out of the ordinary were occurring.

For them, nothing is.

. . . mad, going mad . . . mad . . .

"No, you're quite sane, Captain. Quite."

Martel waits again, waits until the Captain is ready to accept his presence. Then he lays a hand upon the man's shoulder to emphasize his physical reality.

"What do you want?"

"Your understanding and your cooperation."

"Maybe the first, but never the second!" blusters the officer.

"Both, I think," Martel contradicts, "once you understand. You see, very shortly, in about one stan, I imagine, I'm going to appear out in empty space on your screens, and as you release the components of the Suntunnel, I'm going to blast them and their boosters out of existence. Now, without a record of that, Captain, you are going to be in very deep trouble. Even with such a record, you'll probably face a court-martial. So I would suggest two things. First, that you use the next stan to arrange to get a permanent record of what will in fact appear on your screens. Second, that you do your absolute and total best to destroy me."

"Sounds like that's what you want. Why should I?"

"Look at it this way. If I'm just a figment of your imagination, you'll have a perfect recording of your successful deployment. If not, you're covered. And if I do destroy all your hardware, and you don't make an all-out effort to destroy me, where does that leave you?"

The Captain wipes his suddenly damp brow.

"All right," the skipper concedes, "but tell me what's in it for you."

"That's simple, Captain. It just might save me the difficulty of having to destroy three or four successors to you."

The Imperial Captain looks away. "I don't understand. Who are you?"

"I'm Martel. I told you that. I don't like destroying ships, and I'd just as soon not. If the Viceroy keeps sending ships with devices to destabilize Aurore's sun, I'll eventually have to do something drastic, and I'd rather give advance warning. Then I won't feel quite so guilty."

The Captain realizes he is still holding down the firing stud on his laser, and he releases it. The ache in his thumb reminds him how long he has pressed the stud. He looks up at Martel to find the space next to himself empty. The man in black is gone.

As a believer in visible technology, he checks the charge meter on the butt of the sidearm. Empty. He knows it had been fully charged when he took the bridge, and he has only used it once . . . without effect. He tries to persuade himself that he has seen nothing and talked to no one, but after a few units he touches the commweb.

"Communications? Captain Ellerton here. Send Commander Sirien to the bridge."

Whoever, whatever, Martel is, his logic, flame it all, is unassailable.

lxiv

▼

GERMIC: Ah, what's the bigger mystery?
           That man ever was,
           Or that he'll always be?
JORIS: Some say one night a thousand ships
           Fell across a thousand skies,
           Like hope, which always flies.
GERMIC: Dear lady, from whence we came,
           Either from the thousand ships and skies,
           Or from a single orb of fame,
           Matters not when each man dies.
                    —Excerpt from Act II, *Home Divided*
                    Yves N. Dorben

lxv

▼

Martel paces across the porch, one quick step after another.

Both the problem of arrogant gods, himself among them, and an arrogant Viceroy, whom he has created, remain.

The real Empire is the Regency, not New Augusta, and its power lies in the Viceroy. The time of the Brotherhood has come, but unless both the Empire and the gods are vanquished, one will re-create the other.

"Götterdämmerung," he whispers, and it is a promise.

Not only to himself, but to his followers, for he can no longer escape them. Declared or not, gods of human societies are created in part by their worshipers, which is what Apollo has known and feared for a millennium.

Martel pictures the thousands who thronged a small black temple on Karnak, and all of the small shrines on Aurore where shadows are cast.

"Perhaps the forbidden fruit is best," he says to no one, for no one is with him, now or ever. He looks down at the silver triangle upon his black belt, then touches the glistening black thunderbolt pin that holds his cloak. Both are appropriate.

Can he do what he plans?

He does not know, for no one has ever tried. At least, it is nowhere recorded.

Colossal arrogance, Martel . . . colossal arrogance . . .

He agrees with his thought, gathers the darkness around himself, and removes himself to a point in space where he can watch the planet which is not a planet, but which is called Aurore, as if the name were the answer to everything.

First . . . to remove the base of power of the gods.

Second . . . to scatter the gods.

Third . . . to destroy the Fleet as the basis of power for the Viceroy.

Fourth . . . the Viceroy.

To begin, he looks upon Aurore, looks upon the planet that should not be, in a way that none of the gods before him has. He understands why the forty-nine percent of the human scientists who have studied Aurore and who insist it is not a planet are correct.

Or, rather, why Aurore is more than just a planet.

He imposes, for to impose is the only way to describe what he does, the imprint of darkness across the upper reaches of the golden-hazed energy field that is, that surrounds, Aurore.

ANGER!

A ray of golden haze gathers itself from the field and arrows out from Aurore toward the point of blackness, within the wider darkness, that is Martel.

Four demigods hovering around a certain sacred peak feel their powers abruptly waning and move themselves to solid ground, their faces nearly as white as the snow that caps the peak they had soared above.

The E.W. officer of the Viceroy's lead scout gulps as his power registers, focused on Aurore, peg off the scale. He hesitates, then jabs the commweb with one hand while defocusing his receivers with the other. He is not fast enough, and the power amplifiers for the last intake screen sag into molten plastics, ceramics, and metal.

Martel calls shadows from beneath the here and now, from beneath the past, and from a future that may never be, drawing as he never has, knowing that without all that he can focus, he will not be able to deflect the raw force that the field which is Aurore has directed at him.

The cold of black fires shimmers around him, both blinding and swallowing light, one and the same. And the black fires build, and build to an intensity that will befuddle astronomers across the galaxies for so long as the energies carry.

"Flamehell! See what I see?" asks the Scout Captain, who is but a subcommander.

"I think so." That is his navigator, who sees it all through unpowered screens, the forces are so great.

Both know that what they see has long since transpired, and that lends to the wrenching at their guts.

In a series of flashes, one after another, bolts of brilliant yellow flare from the "nightside" of Aurore, each one some-how brighter than the last, until each rivals momentarily the brilliance of the sun unseen by Aurore's inhabitants. Each energy bolt, millennia into the future, will confuse and confound astronomers, those few who are looking as the light recording the phenomena slips through their system, throughout the Galaxy.

Each bolt strikes the black dot, englobed in black fire, which stands in space. Each fails to splash or to penetrate, but disappears. Disappears, and with each disappearance the blackness grows, becomes more deeply luminescent.

With the energy he has summoned, and with that he has gathered, Martel does two things.

The first is a gentle nudge, enough to shake a few build-ings, to raise foot-high waves on the stillest ponds, to the ce-lestial body called Aurore.

The second is a cast of darkness around the planet that has not known it in millennia, perhaps in eons, since it was created by the energy field that has made Aurore what it is.

Apollo stands upon the portico of a vacant pale golden and marble villa west of Sybernal, where he seeks some sign. As he stands the sky dims, and dims further, until the gloom resembles twilight.

Martel, he thinks, though he knows not why, except that the darkness itself calls to mind the one whom Thor had thought vanquished, and who, Apollo knows with cold certainty, is not vanquished. Who may be triumphant. Who will triumph, the sun-god fears.

STOP!

Apollo reels under the force of the projection.

The transmission is not a word, but a massive concept rolling outward from Aurore and bouncing back from the wall of darkness which Martel has drawn around the golden sphere that has been called Aurore.

STOP!

Martel knows what he must do, if he can, and girds himself.

Apollo watches from the villa as the golden haze above the sky thins, flows in ebbing sheets eastward until it coalesces into a golden ball, a dim second sun.

The western sky is black and starless, and the sungod who was shivers.

The new-formed golden-haze sun contracts, brightens, and elongates into a wedge, pointed against the darkness, finally launching itself toward that darkness.

The sky of Aurore is jet-black where the sun-god stands, and for the first time since man has been on Aurore, darkness falls. Falls like thunder, but with no flash of lightning to break the black depths that are the sky.

Martel smiles as he views the energy field that was Aurore, that created Aurore, flee the planet it built. He parts the darkness to let the golden and white glittermotes flee their planet and the energy-sucking darkness that he has fastened upon it.

From his dark heights, he tosses darkness at the golden wedge, black lightning thrust after lightning thrust. Then, as he chevies the ancient ones on their way, he opens a tunnel, a tunnel in time, back to when a certain FO star was younger, and without a planet.

The circle is complete. What is, is.

The field, the glittermotes, will remember, and when they

do, they will build the planet they remember, the one human astronomers will claim is impossible.

Which it is, but that's beside the point.

Without the field, the place that is now just a planet called Aurore will not be habitable. For that reason, Martel has already nudged Aurore toward its ultimate destination. In the meantime, the cloak of darkness, which will thin over time, will protect it and its cargo until the planet reaches that stable orbit which Martel has planned for it and for the delicate organisms that inhabit its surface.

Martel, drawing on his powers of darkness again, twists time, so that what will be done is done. He withdraws the curtain of protection.

And Apollo beholds the first sunrise on Aurore and weeps. That is, before the shadow of the Raven catches him and before he is swirled back through another tunnel of time to a back-distant place where he will be worshiped.

The Smoke Bull, standing upon the heights on the far side of the Middle Sea, observes the approaching sunset and anticipates the darkness that will fall. Before this occurs, another darkness descends upon him and carries him back to the time when he will see sunrises above a wine-dark sea and bring his own darkness to those who will cause his name to remain a symbol of fear for well beyond the years he has left without the energy field upon which he once relied.

In turn, the shadow of the Raven falls across the fallen gods and demigods of Aurore, and they are dispatched to generate the legends from which they sprang. All but two.

One is Martel, the Raven, the undeclared god.

The second he will deal with later, for now he must meet the third challenge. The Grand Fleet, discounting the reports of the scoutship, draws near, intent upon reducing Aurore to a cinder.

Martel, in his cloud of darkness, sighs, and rises once again into the night.

He ignores the genuflections that accompany his departure.

lxvi

▼

Martel debates but a moment before drifting through time and space to meet the Grand Fleet before it nears the new orbit of Aurore, which is now merely a planet, albeit a technically impossible one with a slightly tilted axis and a too-circular orbit.

Should I have given it a greater axial angle than a mere seven and a half degrees?

He shrugs. For all the powers he has mastered, he has never learned orbital mechanics, nor the mathematics necessary. As for the distance from the sun that should be planetless . . . that was merely the matching of energy flows. The "year" will be longer, much longer, and the architecture will have to change with the introduction of nights, cold winds, seasons, and chill.

Aurore will lose much of its attraction as the resort of endless day and home of the gods and source of gods and demigods. Two called gods remain, and Martel knows he is not a god, but merely an immortal with godlike powers in some limited areas.

Gods are omniscient and omnipresent, and Martel is neither. That is why he must crush the Grand Fleet before it splits, and before either the Marshal or the Viceroy realizes he is the last defender of Aurore.

Space fleets are not awe-inspiring. The longest line of battle cruisers, cruisers, corvettes, and scouts, even with all screens flaring, flooding the emptiness of the night sky beyond Aurore with squandered energy, is less than a needle in that sky.

All the energy contained in the metal and composite hulls of the Grand Fleet is less than a small percentage of that represented by the smallest sun, and the combined life spans of

the captains and commanders and subcommanders and officers and crews are but a fraction of the life span of the
briefest star. And all the energy marshaled by one immortal
called a god is insignificant against the total energy of even
a small corner of a small galaxy.

*Nonetheless, large enough to render a certain large fleet
less significant,* thinks Martel, guarding his thoughts while
recognizing that few are left with the power to monitor them,
and none with the power to stop him.

Old habits die hard.

Martel waits in darkness beyond the new orbit of the
still-impossible planet of Aurore, waits and watches, perceptions extended, as the Grand Fleet emerges from its subspace tunnel and wedges toward the FO star that is the ships'
destination.

*A thousand ships, fifty thousand men and women, and all
because you play games with the Viceroy you created.*

Martel acknowledges the debt, wondering how he can
avoid the slaughter that looms before him.

The obvious strikes him.

What's good for gods . . .

He waits . . . waits as the Grand Fleet regroups.

Two basic formations, those are the options the Marshal
for Strategy must consider: the Force Wedge or the Flying V
to a Point.

Both formations have advantages. The wedge concentrates defense screens and firepower at a relatively localized
point in space, while the Flying V brings all the Fleet elements together at the last possible moment for such concentration, and thus requires any enemy to spread his defensive
forces.

Since the number of gods on Aurore must be finite, reflects the Marshal, and since the power he had already seen
can be terribly concentrated, he advises the Fleet Commander of his recommendation, the Flying V to a Point,
and his reason.

CONCUR, prints the screen from the command bridge, and the decision has been made, and the Grand Fleet spreads from its subspace breakpoint.

Marshal Reitre feels a chill wind at his back, dismisses it as imaginary, but rechecks his laser sidearm all the same.

The lead scouts sprint toward the growing image of the star, toward the star and its single planet, where waits a god of darkness in darkness.

Here's where the myth came from!

The far lead scout sees the blackness, the darkness deeper than that through which it travels, and attempts to reverse its momentum.

"Captain! No indications ahead!"

"Full reverse!" commands the Lieutenant, but as he does the stars in the scout's screens wink out.

A black-shaded rainbow coruscates across the controls and is gone.

The stars, rather another set of stars, reappear on the screens.

Buzz!

"Navigation null!"

The Lieutenant scratches the back of his head. The star on which they are closing is not the FO type on which the *Bassett* had been centered instants before.

The navigation banks contain enough data to reconstruct virtually any locale within ten thousand lights of Karnak and have come up blank.

The Lieutenant wipes his forehead.

"Proceed," he creaks out, hoping they can discover where they are, somehow.

Back in another time, Martel refocuses the tunnel that he has willed into existence and picks off the rest of the lead scouts.

Leaves 985 to go.

On the command bridge far out from the FO star in question, the screen makes the reports, one after the other, sometimes separated by moments, sometimes by close to half a standard hour.

LOCALIZATION AT 10.0. ABNORMAL ENERGY CONCENTRATION OBSERVED AT TARGET.

PROCEEDING. RATE 1.5 AND CONSTANT.

PROCEEDING. TARGET AT 9.5 RATE 1.5 AND CONSTANT.

SPATIAL DISCONTINUITY, CLASS 8. INBOUND RADIAN 0.

Marshal Reitre raises his bushy eyebrows. Class-eight discontinuities were only theoretical. Six is the greatest ever observed outside an actual nova. Reitre wonders whether the Fleet Commander understands what he is getting into.

The second advance line consists of three spread chevrons of corvettes, 120 in all, and Martel prepares to spray them all into the past after the scouts.

TARGET AT 8.5.

SPATIAL DISCONTINUITY. CLASS 9.

SQUADRON 7. REPORT.

SQUADRON 7 DOES NOT REGISTER ON MASS DETECTORS. RADIATION NIL. DRIVE DISCONTINUITIES NIL.

REGROUP AND CLOSE LINE.

REGROUPING COMPLETE.

PROCEEDING. TARGET AT 7.0 RATE 1.5 AND CONSTANT.

SQUADRON 5 DOES NOT REGISTER ON MASS DETECTORS. RADIATION NIL. DRIVE DISCONTINUITIES NIL.

PROCEEDING. TARGET AT 6.0.

SQUADRON 4 DOES NOT REGISTER ON MASS DETECTORS . . .

Marshal Reitre's hand reaches for the commweb.

ABORT MISSION, he signals, knowing the Regent will have his position and possibly his head for the override of the Fleet Commander. But the transmission from the command bridge screen tells him what he does not want to see.

NEGATIVE. CLOSING AND CONTINUING, the signal returns.

Reitre sighs, wonders if he should use the sidearm on himself, hopes against hope that something, somehow, somewhere will save the Grand Fleet, for the squadrons are disappearing faster than the screen can script, and of the Fleet the Viceroy has dispatched to Aurore nothing will return to Karnak. Of that the Marshal is absolutely certain. He returns his eyes to the screen to watch what he fears will happen.

The remaining flanks of the Grand Fleet are beginning to curl away from Aurore, and for that reason Martel concentrates his attention on the right flank, the heavy cruisers commanded by the Duke of Trinan, who certainly would not have minded being the next Viceroy.

You can be Viceroy wherever you are. No one will be there to tell you no.

Martel does not count, only continues his tunnels to the past until a single ship remains, waits until the light cruiser *Eltiran* turns and reenters its subspace tunnel back to Karnak.

The critics were right. A thousand ships didn't fall across the skies of the past. Only 999, and none of them before the time of the first flight from old Home. That would not have been fair.

Martel pauses.

Though who's to say what's fair?

He has one other task, perhaps the hardest, yet to do.

Martel hangs in the darkness, suspends himself, juggles his thoughts and the long-buried feelings he knows churn beneath.

He turns toward Aurore. His planet. His impossible planet and the home of his impossible dreams.

lxvii

▼

Midnight cloaks the Petrified Boardwalk . . . true midnight, moonless, for Aurore has never had a moon, with the stars only for light. For who had ever thought to provide outside lights for a planet that had never seen darkness?

The polished stone walks are deserted, and Martel can sense the fear. For darkness was accepted only when it was rare and isolated, but now that night has fallen, truly fallen, not a few of his worshipers are having second thoughts.

Let them.

He shrugs and surveys the low waves that still break across the night-silver sand.

Tonight there is no Emily to rescue you.

Nor Rathe.

Nor even a Marta Farrel to recall.

Hollie and Gates Devero shipped back to Halston, what— nine standard centuries ago? They're doubtless dust, or buried in some family vault.

On Karnak waits Kryn. Or Emily, if you wish to open that issue. You're an Immortal, perhaps the last who can claim godhood, or what passes for it. Now that the field of Aurore, flickering glittermotes and all, is gone, who is left?

Emily, the answer comes. Or Kryn, for they are one and the same, and both are older than Martel. Far older.

"Are they, really?" he asks the breakers in a low voice.

The waters mumble back the answer, which he cannot hear because he has lifted his eyes to the brightest star in the east.

Martel does not address a question to the star, instead drops his head and looks across the dark jumbles that are homes and shops and taverns where darkness and fear are being rediscovered again, and yet again.

A stone rattles, displaced by a cat.

Odd, a cat that has not known darkness. Does she see as well?

Martel tries to follow the small beast with his thoughts, but he is too late, and cannot locate that particular feline.

Do we seem that indistinguishable to whatever gods there are?

He smiles a hard smile as he asks himself the question,

then lets his cloak flutter in the night breeze. The sea wind bears a saltier tang than it used to.

Martel takes three steps northward, recalling another night when it was night only by the clock, and perpetual day by the light. With another step, he recalls the second night like the first.

The images mix, and on top of them comes another, a young woman, dark-haired and dressed in blue leathers. And all three are the same.

Truly a goddess you are, Dian. Or Emily. Or Kryn.

He snorts, a rough bark that causes three cats and a dorle to jump from their respective perches. The third cat pounces on the dorle, but before she can dispatch the hapless songbird, Martel throws a handful of darkness at the pair and separates them.

Do you dare to hope, Martel? Or are you still refusing to act? Turn the universe upside down on principle, but don't make the last move?

He shakes his head and observes the northward hills, his eyes centering on a space where he knows a building of white marble stands. Has stood a good millennium or longer.

Silence drops like a second darkness on the Petrified Boardwalk.

Shortly, a large raven flaps toward a white villa, dark, unlit, and deserted now for some time, though visited once by a recently created ancient god.

Martel roams from room to room, from chamber to chamber, from porch to portico, as he waits for the dawn.

Even you, last god, bringer of darkness, cannot bring the dawn quicker.

The rose color of the eastern horizon is only the first of a handful of dawns since the re-creation of Aurore. Martel sits on the columned wall above the ravine, dangling his black-booted feet over the edge.

The dampness of the dew lends a sharpness to the corel blooms that cascade from the overgrown garden and across the far end of the same stone wall on which Martel sits.

Corel . . . Emily's villa, and Kryn's scent. Can you separate them?

He reflects upon his twists in time, letting his feet drum against the stone.

Can you put them back together again? Should you?

A dorle chitters with the first ray from the rising sun.

So much smaller than on Karnak the sun was, and yet the heat was the same. Should be, since he'd planned it that way, but the visual sense was different, a touch of strangeness, with the high sky a greener shade, holding a hint of green, green seas.

In the early-morning light, the villa is still vacant, emptier now than when the white marble had stood gray in the predawn darkness.

Martel gathers his own blackness and casts it, extending himself throughout the villa and the grounds, letting time flow around him as he becomes one with the deserted structure.

As he touches the stone, reinforces it, repairs it, he rejects time itself. As he changes half the marble from white to black. As he wills the gardens back into their formal states, and the emerald grass back into the lawns, and the rose trees back into their guards. As he adds black roses among the white. As he hopes . . .

If not, someone will be most amazed.

His last effort is to bind a corner of time around what he has wrought, letting the villa sleep immaculate and untouched, until he returns. If he returns.

Once more, the raven spreads wing and departs, this time to cross the Middle Sea toward the White Cliffs.

Atop the White Cliffs the raven alights, still a black bird that perches above a smooth circular pool of whitestone. Three black footprints, inked into the white rock, yet lead to the circular stone depression that resembles nothing so much as a petrified pool.

A pair of dorles chitter. The lone sea gull has been gone for some time.

The raven stares unblinking at the white stone pool, at the black footprints.

The bird disappears, and a man stands atop the boulder.

For a space he stands. Then he walks down through empty air to the precipice, from where he looks over the edge, as if to reassure himself that the waves still crash in against the sheer stone face far below.

They do, and the water foams golden green, as it did before and will again.

Martel steps out into the emptiness. He gathers his cloak about him and is gone, replaced instantly by the wide-winged raven he also is.

The two youths who have climbed the gentle slope from the upland meadows drop their jaws open as they watch the transformation. The taller one, red-haired, recovers first and sprints for the edge, peers over, and sees nothing.

He looks up and sees the raven beating into the distance.

The shorter, brown-haired boy has found the stone pool and the black prints.

The two look at each other. The shorter makes the sign of the inverted and looped cross. They shake their heads and hurry back to tell their parents, who have not slept well in previous nights, and who will sleep even less well in nights to come.

Martel notes this as he flaps off, but does not hesitate.

His destination is a small cottage behind a larger home, south of the city called Sybernal, a cottage he once thought of as home, or the closest thing to it.

Someone has kept the quince pruned, even planted a younger tree close by the oldest, as if to ensure there will always be the same number of quinces.

Which means there will not be.

The cottage is as he left it days, or has it been years, ago. Except that a black velvet rope is looped to bar access from either the porch or the front entry. A small black looped and inverted cross is mounted upon a black marble pedestal beside the pathway leading to the cottage. The cross is not new, though its location is.

Martel extends his perceptions and finds that the cottage is empty, although recently it has been cleaned.

Seeing the black velvet ropes, he does not enter, though he knows that two sets of black tunics and trousers hang in the closet in his sleeping chamber, as do three preserved sets of pale yellow tunics and matching trousers.

Instead, he crosses the hillside and stretches his steps toward the crest from where he can see both sides, the cottage and the sheltered bay. The heavy grass on the hilltop is longer now, and thicker, as if it relished the nights and grew in response.

Is that true of men and women as well?

There is no answer, not that he expected any.

The bay is calm, and only the smallest of waves lap at the golden sands.

The times when the waves roiled and beckoned he remembers, and when he walked the sea, and the seabed.

Thetis? Gone. You, too, and that demigod you tried to protect. And how many others have I banished? Yes, how many, Martel?

But she has gone where he has sent her, and there is no answer.

He recalls the last image from Thetis—a leaden shield, circled in black—cast at him as he left her and her charge next to a wine-dark sea.

Should you regret what is done? Should you undo it?

Those are not the questions. They never were, Martel knows as he gazes down at the green waters.

The time for gods, for an ever-growing pantheon of powerful beings with little restraint and less morality, has gone.

Morality now, Martel? How high and mighty you sound. Morality from you? How moral was it to force the Prince to use his hunting laser? How moral was it for you to block Emily's memory to create your own dreams? To send Thor back to the barbarians? To scatter nearly a thousand ships across desolate planets? To do nothing when Apollo snuffed out Rathe?

Morality aside, what he has done is right.

You hope.

Martel turns from the sea to the cottage, its lines as firm as when Mrs. Alderson first owned it. The dorles chitter in the quinces. The grass grows, and now there is sunlight, and a natural shadow down the slope of the lawn.

Sunlight . . . and shadow.

What more is life . . . than sunlight and shadow?

He turns back to the other side of the hill to watch the waves. They have picked up, and gnaw at the beach, already beginning to change, ever so slowly, the countours of the sand, to change what was so long unchanged.

> *. . . Tell me now, and if you must,*
> *Is a man much more than dust?*

His words are low, hardly louder than the dorles, or the swish of the water against the sand. But the birds cease their twittering, as if to hear the next line of the ancient song. The waves pause. The air is still. The shadow of the cottage shortens, darkens, as the distant sun rises.

The hillcrest is empty, and not even a raven crosses the heavens.

lxviii

▼

"Where did you get it?" the Matriarch asks as she freezes the holo that fills the end of the hall.

More than three battle lasers are focused on the figure of a man, dressed in black and hanging in the void. Although he wears only a cloak to guard him against the chill of deep space, the power sheets around him, haloing him.

"Where did you get it?" This time her tone is sharper.

"From M-7a. The molecular patterns match those of the Viceregal forces. So do the focal lengths and energy levels."

The Matriarch takes a last look at the figure, tries to identify the face shrouded in shadow, but finally touches the control on her throne. The holo vanishes.

"Do you believe what's on the cube?"

Her Admiral turns his eyes to the floor without answering.

"Do any of you believe what you see?"

Still there is no answer.

"Then why did you bring it to me?"

"Because we dared not to do otherwise. . . ."

"What are the associated probabilities?"

"According to Stats, the probability is nearly unity that he destroyed the Grand Fleet of Karnak. We ran the series twice, with a complete systems check in between."

The Matriarch smiles, a cold smile, one that would make the poles of Tinhorn seem warm by comparison.

"There's one other thing, Matriarch. . . ." The tall woman who wears the winged stars of a Commodore waits.

"Yes?"

"Aurore has been moved."

"Impossible, I'd say. At least if the conventional wisdom is correct."

"According to conventional wisdom, Matriarch, that holo

is impossible as well, but every test we can devise bears out its truth. And Stats computes that the destruction of the Grand Fleet and the removal of Aurore to its present distance from its primary are linked. Probability eighty-five percent. And Aurore was moved *before* the Grand Fleet broke subspace."

"Before? Are you positive?"

"Absolutely."

"Command the Fifth Fleet to avoid the entire Karnak system. Otherwise proceed on plan. And make it a standing order that *no* armed Matriarchy ship is to approach Aurore. *Ever.*"

"Yes, Matriarch. . . ." The quiet stretched out.

"You question my orders, or the wisdom behind them?" The Matriarch barked a sound that might have been a laugh. "Remember that the Grand Fleet of the Viceroy was ten times the size of our Fifth Fleet, and even the Grand Fleet couldn't move planets. If we're fortunate, the Fuards won't understand that in time, but I doubt they are that dense."

"Matriarch . . . I don't understand," confessed the tall Commodore.

"You will, one day. Just because some gods are men doesn't lessen their powers. Check the name Martel under the Apollo files. You might also note why he fled to Aurore."

The Matriarch gestures, and both the Admiral and the Commodore step back, bow, and depart to carry out their orders.

lxix

▼

Except for Forde, the Viceroy knows, the palace is vacant.

The screens will hold against small arms for a century, if necessary, although the mob has not yet formed.

The four towers strike into the morning, blunted spears

glittering as they have for more than nine centuries, ever since she completed the rebuilding from the ruins of the Prince's Palace.

The gold-shot blue of the synthestone walls stands unmarred, stands on the hill above the rubble that is the city that has fallen to the vagaries of two gods.

Kryn had hoped that her city of Karnak would have stood longer than the city of the Prince Regent which it replaced, much longer. Instead, she stands on the East Tower, overlooking the tumbled chaos that had been order such a short time before.

By shifts, Forde has instructed the entire retinue, even the Generals and Marshals who have protested their undying loyalty, to depart.

In few cases, few indeed, was force required.

The reconstruction, directed from the fringes of the city by the Marshal of Strategy, the man named Reitre, is under way. Reitre has enough fear to be wise, and enough caution to deal with whoever follows the Viceroy.

A gold-winged bluetail alights on the corner of the battlement. Useless as they are, her father had liked battlements. Not that he had really been her father. The gene patterns hadn't matched, but what else could she have called him? And how else could she have been named Viceroy out of the Times of Trouble?

Her thoughts are broken by the sound of footsteps.

"All gone, my Lady."

"Thank you, Forde."

Forde, in red trousers, tunic, and boots, stands like the obsolete column he is, ready yet to support a ruler who knows her time has passed.

"Forde, you are the last. Reitre will need you, and you him. Serve him, and through him, my people."

"My Lady . . ."

His protest is formal. They both know it.

". . . do you think . . . ?"

"Yes. Shortly. And that will be between Us."

The way she says the word "Us" sends shivers down Forde's spine, and he bows.

"As you wish, Lady and Viceroy."

"Lady will do, Forde."

She inclines her head to dismiss him.

The footsteps echo as he heads for the drop shaft.

The people grieve now, she knows. They grieve and dig their own from the rubble left by two gods. When their grief is buried with their dead, then they will decide why they should blame their Ruler. Who did not protect them.

Who could not, she thinks.

The gold-winged bluetail preens, spreads his wings, and leaves the battlement.

A pair of sirens howl, and another overloaded skitter makes another emergency flight to another overcrowded health center. Shortly there will be more deaths as rejuve treatments lapse for all but the most powerful and secure, and that means those with private armies and independent power sources.

The people do not know that the Grand Fleet has failed. Or that Karnak lies defenseless. Or that the Twenty-third Emperor of New Augusta has been poisoned by his second wife. Or that the Fuardian First Fleet is on its way to declare Karnak a protectorate. As is the Fifth Fleet of the Matriarchy of Halston.

Occasionally, through the pall of smoke over the city, she can see a brown-robed figure surveying the defense lines of the palace. A scent of that smoke reaches her, and the bitterness waters her eyes momentarily.

The teletale at her belt indicates that Forde is outside the screens, that he has left the defenses intact.

Not altruism, nor loyalty, but realism is represented in that action. While an intact palace, with all its shielded weapons, should not fall into the hands of the first armed adventurer, neither should the palace, the symbol of the Viceroy, fall, or fall too easily. For then the mob will require more destruction to avenge the betrayal they will feel.

After a millennium of protection under the hand of the Viceroy, they will feel betrayed, and there are more than enough who will use that sense of betrayal as the rein to power.

"So why don't you do something?" she asks herself.

Instead, she crosses the tower top slowly until she can see the Lake of Dreams.

"I can just remember when it was the Park of Summer," she tells the redbird that chirps from the empty jackstaff.

She stretches forth a hand to the songster, but the bird takes flight.

"You should have been a blackbird," says the Viceroy. "But you couldn't be. Not here."

She turns back to the bench and sits, waiting, wondering if she should descend to the vacant strategy center to await the coming of the Fleets, to do her best to protect her people. Or would the few screens she could throw up now merely make the eventual situation worse?

The teletale chimes.

Forde, for some reason, is returning. Alone.

Reitre would need Forde. Therefore, Reitre is no more. No ships have arrived except two medical relief freighters.

Who? It can only be the Brotherhood, and they must have heavy weapons, for nothing less could have taken Reitre, even away from the shields of the palace.

She can only wait now.

Presently, Forde arrives on the parapet.

"Lady, do you have some way to depart? Unknown?"

"Is it the Brotherhood?" she asks, a faint quirk to her lips. After all, the brown-clad monks had started the whole thing, in one sense, by helping Martin to escape. Or had Martin maneuvered them into helping him? Or . . . she shrugged.

For all she knows, the man she knew as Martin Martel is more than that and has been all along. If he had been, had been that experienced, why would he have been interested in a mere slip of a woman, and one without much memory of her past at that?

Unless he knew she would be Viceroy. Unless he planned she would succeed the Prince. If he had known, had planned for those eventualities, why has he destroyed her Fleet, her capital, and left her alone in the wreckage of the Grand Millennium?

"My Lady?" Forde's voice breaks through her reverie.

"Yes, Forde. Is it the Brotherhood?"

"So they say." He pauses, then asks again, "Escape routes?"

"No, Forde. No escape routes for me. Not yet. Take the courier in the west tunnel from the strategy center."

"But you? How will you leave?"

"There is another, if I need it. I need to stay to see the curtain fall. To see if it will fall."

The man in red moves not.

"Go!" Her voice lashes around him and causes the wind to halt momentarily.

"Yes, my Lady. The Brotherhood has captured three armories and is turning the battle lasers against the palace."

"Let them. It will take more than that. Now go."

Her hands drop to her belt, and he turns, scurrying across the glowstones back toward the drop shaft. He reminds her of a lizard scuttling under a rock, but her laugh is mirthless.

She waits until the courier winks out overhead before returning to the battlement. A faint haze has built at the palace defense lines, and her teletales show that less than ten percent of the screens' capacity has been taxed.

A strange pair, she thinks. *The blue Viceroy and the black god. Is the only thing more deadly than a woman scorned a man still in love with the woman who scorned him?*

Purple light flares to the east.

A pulsed battle laser deflected by the shields. Her teletale shows that single pulse claimed, only momentarily, thirty percent of the screens' capacity.

Another flare follows, then another.

"The Brotherhood doesn't waste much time, does it?"

His voice carries an edge she does not remember.

There is a great deal you don't remember.

She turns to face him, not wanting to, but realizing she has little choice.

Martel stands no taller, no stockier, and his face is still unlined. And so is hers, she knows.

The blackness of his eyes is darker than deep space, and she tears her glance away, blinks with the next laser flare against the palace shields.

"You don't have to accept me, Kryn. And you don't have to accept you. That's your choice."

With his left hand he takes the black thunderbolt pin from his cloak, lays it in his right hand, and stretches his hand forth. The jet-blackness of the pin glitters.

Without looking at his face, Kryn studies the pin. She has never seen it. Yet the miniature thunderbolt is familiar.

"It is nine centuries old, Emily, and it was yours before it was mine, and if you so desire, it can be yours again."

She wants to shiver, though the laser blasts warm the air circulating across the top of the tower. She will not.

"Emily?"

"Emily. You are Kryn, but before Kryn you were Emily, and long before that you were called Dian. I knew you first as Kryn, then as Emily, and never as Dian. They think I am old, with my darkness and shadows, but your first youth lies long before the thousand ships fell, long before I scattered those hulls across the stars. No one but you knows how far back stretches your ageless youth. All you have to do is look."

Look!

Kryn feels the black wall in her mind, the one behind which who knows what is locked, splintering.

"No!" Her cry is involuntary.

He smiles, faintly, bends his head, almost as if in homage to her, but does not step forward.

The curtain has fallen away from the darkness, and the images leap at her, one after another, falling into her lap like the ships Martel has strewn across the stars.

She staggers. With an effort she is unaware of making, she catches her balance and sinks onto the glowstones, dark hair catching the purple highlights from the laser pulses, and shakes, the dry sobs racking her frame.

He sits down, not cross-legged, for his muscles have always been too tight for that, across from her and waits, helping her catch each memory as it tumbles forth.

. . . She stands before the four square limestone blocks that are the altar, obsidian knife in hand, and looks down at the young face. She does not hesitate, and with a clean downward stroke . . .

. . . The hunter stands across the clearing from her, arrow nocked, his blond eyebrows invisible in the gloom, but raised in puzzlement. She draws the moonlight to her and watches as he gently lets the tension off the bow, as he slowly goes down on bended knee while the light around her pulses. Then, and only then, does she gesture. She remains the only human figure in the clearing, and the harshness of her laugh chases the blond stag into the woods. The dogs begin to bay . . .

. . . Though the sedge has withered, and the wind's bitterness has stripped most of the leaves from the oaks, she stands on the hillside, barefoot and in a clinging shift. On her left arm rests the handle of a wicker basket as she waits for the horseman who picks his path up the hillside. His armor, though scarred, glitters in the late-afternoon light. Although his surcoat is ripped, the green and gold are still bright. Her black hair flows back over her shoulders as she waits for the knight to place her before him on his horse . . .

. . . She stares at the two vials, finally picking the one on the right and tucking it into the hidden space in her lace cuff. The Duke will be on her left, and he will down at least three full goblets of wine . . .

. . . She crouches next to the transmitter, waiting for the red light to blink on, eyes darting toward the berm a hundred meters away, over which she can see the top of the hangar. Inside, a young man waits for the same red light, and when it blinks will dash for his cockpit. She knows the pilot, every line of his body. The light blinks, red, and she touches the switch, does not look back as the hangar explodes in flame . . .

. . . She slides onto the bridge, wearing only a clinging white singlesuit, not even her pilot's rings. The watch officer looks up from his console, touches the standby stud, and rises to greet her. Lips meet, and his freeze as the jolt from her wrist stunner hits his spine. She lowers the unconscious form to the plastic of the sleepship's deck and seats herself at the console. Next comes the course tape, the one that will take the sleepship beyond the Federation's borders . . .

. . . She waits by the stone wall, idly studying the grain of the petrified walk. The one she seeks is sitting on a low stone wall, and she can sense the immense darkness of the energies he does not yet know he carries. He looks out over the water, oblivious to anything but his concerns about the troubles on Karnak.

"A brooding philosopher, is that it?"

He jerks his head to look at her . . .

. . . She stands in midair, hovers above a certain snow-tipped sacred peak, across from a bull figure in carved smoke, across from a hammer-bearing barbarian, across from a sun-wreathed god in pale yellow.

"Decided!" she declares . . .

. . . The breeze darts into the courtyard, ruffles her hair. The black-haired student stares at her, his eyes widening, as her hands touch the studs on her belt.

"I wish you hadn't, Kryn. Wish you hadn't," he says as he walks through the stunner beam that should have dropped him in his tracks. He leaves her and her guard without looking back . . .

The top of the tower is darker now, surrounded with a twilight brightened intermittently with muted purple light pulses.

After a time, she lifts her eyes.

The defenses? Yours now? The Brotherhood? Her thoughts are clear again, ring with the unheard sound of silver bells.

Down. Mine for now. Yes.

Martel stands, stretches, then extends his left hand.

She takes it, though she does not need the assistance, and gets to her feet.

With her free hand, her left, she extends a black thunderbolt pin.

I meant it then. And now.

He bends his head slightly, and she can see the wetness in the corners of his eyes.

She takes two steps, until she is close enough to pin the thunderbolt back on his cloak. She does.

He waits until she finishes before placing both her hands in his.

The East Tower of the Viceroy's Palace is abruptly empty, and with that emptiness the afternoon sunlight returns, and the ravening purple glare of the Brotherhood's newly acquired battle lasers.

Shortly the tower is gone, following the rest of the palace, and the powder-fine blue dust, gold-speckled, begins to settle on what remains of the city and the parks, and their fallen trees.

From the depths of the ruins emerge the citizens, hurrying toward one of the few intact structures, a small black temple in the old section, where preside a handful of brown-clad Brothers.

None wear black, for it is sacred.

lxx

▼

The trees are old and exude a feeling older than their height and massive trunks would indicate.

Behind the last line of trees runs a wall of unmortared rectangular stone blocks. The barrier stretches into the distance on each side and looms half again as tall as stood the tallest of the long-defunct Imperial Marines. No gates break the expanse of stone, but thin white marble columns are embodied in the blackness at regular intervals.

The small but hot noon sun has fatigued the traveler, and he sits on one of the white marble benches beneath the trees and wipes his damp forehead.

His boots are dusty, but even so clash with the faded brown tunic and trousers he wears. He wipes his forehead again, replaces the cloth in his belt pouch, and pushes a strand of gray hair back over his ear.

He stares at the wall.

Is that all?

A black-and-white stone wall? Even on a miracle planet?

He could climb the wall. After all, it is only twice as tall as he is. Despite the aches in his joints and the years in his bones, the climb would not be difficult.

The grass grows right up to the stone, but not into or be-tween it. Nor do any of the vines that curl up some of the mossy trunks actually touch the stone.

The path he has taken, the one on which he stands, paral-lels the wall ahead for perhaps half a kilo before winding back into the forest.

He looks at the wall, ignoring the heavy footsteps behind him on the hard-packed earth.

"I wouldn't, if I were you."

The voice belongs to a short and heavyset man, clad in an off-white monk's robe.

The traveler looks up but does not otherwise acknowledge the statement.

"It's not called the Wall of Forgetfulness for nothing, pil-grim. You touch it, and you may forget why you wanted to. You try to climb it, and you forget Martel-near everything.

"Every couple of years, some young scientist from the Matriarchy or the Fuardian Empire shows up with a bunch of high-energy weapons to prove there's nothing unusual about it."

"And?" asks the man with the red boots sardonically.

"The Governor, whoever it is, tries to discourage them. Shows the scientist the old cubes. Sometimes that works. Mostly, it doesn't. The last one I remember. She smuggled in one of the old Imperial battle lasers. The beam just bent back off the wall. You could see it twist into the looped cross. Just came back and destroyed the laser. Her, too."

The traveler turns away. Always the superstitions. On every planet where he had searched for Her.

"Have it your way." The monk smiles and continues his patrol.

The older man eases himself to his feet and edges toward the wall. At the base of the stone is a clear line where the grass stops growing, knife-sharp.

He stretches his hand to touch the stones . . .

. . . and finds himself lying facedown in the grass. His nose is scraped. He sits up, realizing that the small, hot sun is lower in the blue-green sky.

Small dark splotches stain the front of the dusty tunic, where blood has somehow found its way.

"Nonsense," he mutters.

But he does not reach out toward the wall again as he lurches to his feet. His eyes range over the crispness of the stones, then lift to the treetops he can see above the wall.

"Nonsense," he grumbles.

His eyes travel down the pathway toward a flicker of white that may represent the monk who had warned him.

With a last look at the gateless wall, he turns and sets his steps back along the way he had already come. The hard-packed pathway will lead him back to the coast and to the extension of the Petrified Boardwalk north of Sybernal. His stride lengthens.

The shuttleport south of the old planetary capital is more than a few units away, and he wants to make the midlight lift.

"Can't believe anything anymore. Not anything. But I'll find Her someday, somewhere. Find Him, too. The bastard!"

He looks back over his shoulder at the crisp lines of the black-and-white stone wall, unmortared, that has resisted lasers and time, then shakes his head.

"Can't believe anything."

Forde's fingers stray toward the hidden shoulder holster where rests the aged but fully charged Imperial Marine blaster.

"Somehow . . ." He sighs, putting one foot in front of the other. "Somehow . . ."

lxxi

▼

The man and the woman sit on the portico, savoring the short twilight.

Down the hillside and into the trees stretch the gardens and the emerald-green lawn. Beyond the forest is a simple black-and-white stone wall, and beyond that the rest of the universe.

A dorle twitters from the branches of the newest quince tree, the one the man planted a decade ago.

As one, the man and woman stand and drift to the low marble railing of the portico, arms touching.

Poor Forde. Her thoughts chime gently.

He has what he wants. If he found you, then . . . he'd have nothing.

But how many years?

Close to two hundred. Hatred and longing keep him going.

Longing . . . you know about that.

Without turning from the distant vision of an old and red-booted man, he knows she has smiled.

Don't forget the hatred . . . some of that, too . . .

She touches his fingertips with hers. In turn, his eyes refocus on the quince tree before he looks at her.

He has his vision, she adds.

Don't we all?

Some men look, and others create . . .

. . . and still others think they are gods. He turns to her, their eyes nearly level. *Even for me, the temptation is great.*

The time is coming when you will have to surrender to it. Our time must come round again.

He shakes his head, for he knows it is true. She is right.

While the past few centuries have been quiet, the times are again changing, and new gods and new empires are building. Gods without understanding, who will have to be cast down, and empires without humanity, which will have forgotten their origin and their purpose.

He sighs, quietly, and looks back at the quince, which is beginning to lose its leaves as the fruit ripens.

She picks the thread of the old song from his thoughts.

> *Tell me now, and if you can,*
> *What is human, what is man.*
> *Tell me now, and if you must,*
> *Where's the god that men can trust?*

He laughs, and his laugh echoes alone above the emerald grass. The pieces fracture and float like mist above the turf, finally dissolving into the sod.

He laughs, and the haunting notes still even the crickets.

He laughs, and the twilight becomes night.

She laughs, gently, in return. Silver bells in the evening wrap themselves around the haunted notes of his rejoicing.

The two laughs mingle, build, rustle the forest leaves and needles as they carry the wind across the black-and-white stone wall, where the monks hear the sacred bells and bend their heads in worship.

On the portico of a white-and-black marble villa, a man and a woman hold hands, just like any other man and woman.

A red-booted old man boards a shuttlecraft.

Three monks in white lift their heads and finish sweeping the nave before replacing the tapers.

The evening star glitters in the eastern sky, and the man and the woman hold that brightness in their hands, and the blackness from his hands and the light from hers twine around it, the one following the other, black and white, black and white.